CTHULHU 2000

CTHULHU 2000
A LOVECRAFTIAN ANTHOLOGY

Edited by Jim Turner

The Ballantine Publishing Group • *New York*

A Del Rey ® Book
Published by The Ballantine Publishing Group

Compilation copyright © 1995 by Arkham House Publishers, Inc.

τέλος δεδωκώς, Χθύλου, σοὶ χάριν φέρω.

—Θεόδωρος Φιλήτας*

*(Marginal gloss entered by scholiast Theodorus Philetas after translating *Al Azif* from the Arabic.)

Contents

Cthulhu 2000

1.

In a career as editor of Arkham House that has lasted now for twenty years, I have received a certain type of letter—over and over and over again—arriving from all parts of the world. The correspondent is usually, though not invariably, a young man, but the message is always the same: I have just encountered H.P. Lovecraft, and golly! what a writer. Here is a fairly recent example from a student in Greece, and please recall that what follows is the unemended transcript of someone using English as a foreign language:

> In the early 80's a Hellenic publishing house . . . released a book that consisted of stories of various authors. One of them was meant to become an everlasting influence and inspiration for my humble self. His initials were H.P.L. Since then fiction, imaginary landscapes, supernatural and cosmic horror entertain my lonely hours. . . .

Why is it, one wonders, that a reclusive writer of weird-fantasy stories, who during his lifetime couldn't even earn a decent living, now possesses the power to inspire, and even to affect the lives of, readers around the globe?

Over the past half century, Lovecraft has emerged as a classic exponent of the weird-fantasy narrative, and as a general principle, there is only one acceptable type of such a story: a great one. Either a weird tale overwhelms the reader with what Lovecraft termed "the strange reality of the unreal" (in which case weaknesses are irrelevant), or it doesn't (in which case strengths are irrelevant). To reiterate Lovecraft's weaknesses at this point would be gratuitous, for his technical shortcomings are apparent to even the most insensitive reader; one may as well complain that the Venus de Milo has no arms. What then are

Lovecraft's positive qualities to account for his sorcerous hold upon readers the world over?

In his 1932 essay "Notes on Writing Weird Fiction," Lovecraft establishes at the outset the creative criteria for his craft: "My reason for writing stories is to give myself the satisfaction of visualising more clearly and detailedly and stably the vague, elusive, fragmentary impressions of wonder, beauty, and adventurous expectancy which are conveyed to me by certain sights, ideas, occurrences, and images. . . ." But wait, you ask, what's all this about wonder and beauty and adventurous expectancy; isn't Lovecraft supposed to be a preeminent American *horror* writer? Well, yes, he is, and further along in his opening paragraph Lovecraft allows that his stories "frequently emphasise the element of horror because . . . it is hard to create a convincing picture of shattered natural law or cosmic alienage or 'outsideness' without laying stress on the emotion of fear."

Never during the final decade of his life—a period coinciding more or less with the Cthulhu Mythos fiction—did Lovecraft expressly consider himself to be a horror writer. He rather, as a cosmic fantasist, endeavored "to weave gossamer ladders of escape from the galling tyranny of time, space, and natural law." Lovecraft further explains that "In relation to the central wonder, the characters [in weird fiction] should shew the same overwhelming emotion [i.e. fear] which similar characters would shew toward such a wonder in real life"; the horror element, in other words, is an ineluctable concomitant to his aesthetic theories, not an end in itself. Only decades after Lovecraft's death, when he was rediscovered by a shell-shocked postwar generation who had endured a cataclysmic global holocaust, followed by the omnipresent specters of Cold War paranoia and atomic annihilation—only then was Lovecraft adjudged a "horror writer" by a generation of readers who had forgotten the meaning of cosmic wonder. Thus the reclusive Providence dreamer was invoked as orchestrator of the major uncertainties of our century, his Cthulhu deities the mythopoeic presentiment of everything from societal collapse to nuclear devastation.

The reason the mature Lovecraft was never a writer of conventional horror fiction is that horror presupposes an actively malicious universe, both within and without the individual, whereas Lovecraft all his life was a scientific materialist for whom the concept of "evil" conveyed no absolute meaning. "Only another collection of molecules" was his characterization of an unfortunate encounter with a fellow human being, while in his relation to the cosmos-at-large, Lovecraft described himself as an "indifferentist": "The interplay of forces which govern climate, behaviour, biological growth and decay, and so on, is too purely universal, cosmic, and eternal a phenomenon to have any relationship to the immediate wishing-phenomena of one minute organic species on our transient and insignificant planet."

The Judeo-Christian theological tradition, on the other hand, posited a great cosmic drama of sin and redemption in which man, perched precariously between heaven and hell, was at the very center of Creation. But beginning in the fifteenth century, the Copernican revolution displaced the Earth as the center of the universe, and today our third-from-the-Sun planetary habitat is simply an inconsequential aqueous orb amid a whirl of other planets in a tiny outpost of the Milky Way galaxy, itself but one of billions of other galaxies in the visible universe; the divinely Edenic origin of our species likewise has given way to a creeping carbon-based creature struggling to emigrate from a primordial planetary pool. American physicist Steven Weinberg concluded his 1977 book *The First Three Minutes* with the chilling phrase "the more the universe seems comprehensible, the more it also seems pointless." Four decades earlier, in a 1935 letter to one of his correspondents, Lovecraft had written presciently of "the blind, indifferent cosmos, and the fortuitous, deterministically motivated automata who form a sort of momentary insect part on the surface of one of the least important of its temporary grains of dust."

If the scientifically minded Lovecraft had no belief in conventional notions of good versus evil, there remains to account for the extraordinary fascination he continues to exert over a worldwide readership. In a 1930 letter to James F. Morton, Lovecraft extols "the quality of mystic adventurous expectancy itself—the indefiniteness which permits me to foster the momentary illusion that almost any vista of wonder and beauty might open up, or almost any law of time or space or matter or energy be marvellously defeated or reversed or modified or transcended. That is the central keynote of my character and personality. . . ." Despite Lovecraft's obdurate lifelong atheism, his fervently expressed feelings of "mystic adventurous expectancy" are similar to what some would term a religious—or at the very least, an unabashedly ecstatic—experience; they are mystical and transcendent feelings, albeit engendered from dispassionate contemplation of a marvelous natural order.

A few years after the Lovecraft letter cited above, Albert Einstein wrote of the cosmos that "The most beautiful experience we can have is the mysterious. It is the fundamental emotion which stands at the cradle of true art and true science. Whoever does not know it and can no longer wonder, no longer marvel, is as good as dead. . . . A knowledge of something we cannot penetrate [i.e., the infinite universe], our perceptions of the profoundest reason and the most radiant beauty . . . it is this knowledge and this emotion that constitute true religiosity."

And here, in comparison, is Lovecraft's definition of the "true function of fantasy": ". . . to give the imagination a ground for limitless expansion, and to satisfy aesthetically the sincere and burning curiosity and sense of awe which a sensitive minority of mankind feel toward the alluring and provocative abysses of unplumbed space. . . ."

The "rapturous ecstasy of the unknown," shall we call it? Lovecraft's implacable aesthetic revolt against the temporal and the corporeal cannot be easily articulated, but exists as an unmistakable philosophic underpinning to his entire adult fictional oeuvre, from the early Dunsanian stories to the mature Mythos masterworks. And this intensely obsessive tension between a finite mind grappling with infinite reality will serve to ensure Lovecraft's reputation among future generations. In his 1994 essay "The Creatures Of Hyperspace," astronomer Alan Dressler argues that within a few hundred years, science is likely to reach its limit regarding a fundamental model of the universe. At that point, all continuing cosmological conundrums— what happened before the Big Bang? what lies beyond the visible universe? and so forth—will remain inaccessible to the human race, probably forever. And then the incomparable Lovecraft will be recalled: "We live on a placid island of ignorance in the midst of black seas of infinity, and it was not meant that we should voyage far."

Yes, H.P.L., that's what you told us all along, wasn't it?

2.

There remains to account for the eighteen stories assembled herein as a sort of Lovecraftian festschrift.

The late Leo Margulies, who during his long lifetime published as much popular fiction as anyone, once observed that "storytellers are born and not made." And the same might be said for cosmic fantasists: the steps of the Hall of Dagon are littered with the bones of would-be pasticheurs who tried to write a Lovecraftian story but, lacking the Silver Key, failed utterly to attain the incantatory awe of their intended prototype. In a 1930 letter to Clark Ashton Smith, Lovecraft himself commented on the relative rarity of this cosmic sensibility among his acquaintances: "I have taken some pains to sound various persons as to their capacity to feel profoundly regarding the cosmos and the disturbing and fascinating quality of the extraterrestrial and perpetually unknown; and my results reveal a surprisingly small quota."

And yet the cosmic element is *there*, compulsively present in Lovecraft's own fiction: In "The Other Gods," Barzai the Wise climbs to the summit of Hatheg-Kla in order to confront the gods of earth and encounters instead "the *other* gods . . . of the outer hells . . . !" In "The Music of Erich Zann," a garret room in a tottering house on the Rue d'Auseil opens onto "the blackness of space illimitable . . . having no semblance of anything on earth." And in "The Shadow Out of Time," a college professor confirms on the final page that his "present body [had] been the vehicle of a frightful alien consciousness from palae-ogean gulfs of time."

Three stories, from three different areas of Lovecraft's creative work—Dunsany, Poesque/Gothic, and Mythos—yet all incorporate the author's characteristic cosmic epiphany, his hallucinatory ecstasy of the unknown. Truth to tell, there is more in common between an early (1921) Dunsanian fable such as "The Other Gods" and a mature (1934) Mythos tale like "The Shadow Out of Time," than there is between "The Shadow Out of Time" and a contemporary Mythos imitation written by someone other that Lovecraft. An inimitable cosmic vision shines throughout Lovecraft's work like a beacon; the latter-day Mythos pastiche will simply be a banal modern horror story, preceded by the inevitable *Necronomicon* epigraph and indiscriminately inter-spersed with sesquipedalian deities, ichor-oozing tentacles, sundry eldritch abominations, and then the whole sorry mess rounded off with a cachinnating chorus of "Iä! Iä!"–chanting frogs. Literary cosmi-cists, to paraphrase Leo Margulies, are born and not made.

If only H.P. Lovecraft could write an Azathoth-approved Love-craftian story, it follows that the works collected in the present volume are not great Lovecraft stories; they rather are great stories in some way inspired by Lovecraft. Each reader is invited to determine for himself the Lovecraftian influences in the pages that follow; some-times these will be immediately apparent, at other times quite subtle. For this introduction I'll specifically consider only the concluding work, Roger Zelazny's Hugo Award–winning novella "24 Views of Mt. Fuji, by Hokusai."

Zelazny presents a Japanese death odyssey in which a dying woman seeks to destroy her former husband, who in turn has survived his physical body to become an increasingly aberrant presence on the "data-net," a sort of cosmic cyberspace. At the ninth "station" in this woman's pilgrimage, Zelazny interjects an ostensible narrative divaga-tion: his protagonist tells of an ancient religious shrine near the sea, "far older" than the indigenous Shinto faith, and whose monks display "a certain thickening and extension of the skin between their fingers and toes. . . ." The monks, we learn, are acolytes of the infamous Old Ones, preserving their abominable rituals in anticipation of a beatific return to the lost city of sea-sunken R'lyeh.

Zelazny teases us with these playful references to the Cthulhu Mythos, and then the allusion is abandoned for many subsequent pages. Only near the very conclusion, when his protagonist realizes that she has been followed by two strange monks, does she notice "the heavy ridge of callous along the edge of [the monk's] hand," the monks themselves being affiliated with a mysterious unmarked temple. Inferentially throughout this extended narrative, the woman has been stalked by demonic emissaries from the unhallowed R'lyeh cult.

Now Roger Zelazny, in such classic novels as *This Immortal* and *Lord of Light*, has demonstrated a masterful command of world mythology; why in "24 Views" would he decide to incorporate (admittedly secondary) elements from Lovecraft's imaginary cosmogony? It's my guess that the author felt the need to employ a pseudomythology of sufficient grandeur to accommodate his culminating concept: "It will mean that everyone on Earth is in far greater peril than I had assumed," his protagonist warns us; "for I am not dealing only with *things*, but of something closer to the time-honored Powers and Principalities. . . ." Given the corrosive menace, the transcendent maleficence, of his adversary, Zelazny could only summon the cosmic realm of H.P. Lovecraft for a mythopoeic underpinning of appropriate magnificence and awe.

Thus if Lovecraft, on the one hand, will be remembered by future generations for the sheer intensity of his cosmic vision, Roger Zelazny's novella suggests a second intimation of immortality. Kadath and Cthulhu, Arkham and Ulthar, *Necronomicon* and Nyarlathotep—the incomparable dreamworld conceived by this strange Rhode Island recluse has become, in the decades since his death, a permanent contribution to our popular culture. And as the portals of the twenty-first century swing open, a man-eating frog named Cthulhu joins Shelley's Frankenstein, Stoker's Dracula, and Tolkien's hobbits among the perdurable icons of world literature.

Jim Turner

CTHULHU 2000

The Barrens

F. PAUL WILSON

1. IN SEARCH OF A DEVIL

I shot my answering machine today. Took out the old twelve gauge my father left me, and blew it to pieces. A silly, futile gesture, I know, but it illustrates my present state of mind, I think.

And it felt good. If not for an answering machine, my life would be completely different now. I would have missed Jonathan Creighton's call. I'd be less wise but far, far happier. And I'd still have some semblance of order and meaning in my life.

He left an innocent enough message:

"The office of Kathleen McKelston and Associates! Sounds like big business! How's it going, Mac? This is Jon Creighton calling. I'm going to be in the area later this week and I'd like to see you. Lunch or dinner—whatever's better. Give me a buzz." And he left a number with a 212 area code.

So simple, so forthright, giving no hint of where it would lead.

You work your way through life day by day, learning how to play the game, carving out your niche, making a place for yourself. You have some good luck, some bad luck, sometimes you make your own luck, and along the way you begin to think that you've figured out some of the answers—not all of them, of course, but enough to make you feel that you've learned something, that you've got a handle on life and just might be able to get a decent ride out of it. You start to think you're in control. Then along comes someone like Jonathan Creighton and he smashes everything. Not just your plans, your hopes, your dreams, but *everything*, up to and including your sense of what is real and what is not.

I'd heard nothing from or about him since college, and had thought of him only occasionally until that day in early August when he called my office. Intrigued, I returned his call and set a date for lunch.

That was my first mistake. If I'd had the slightest inkling of where that simple lunch with an old college lover would lead, I'd have slammed down the phone and fled to Europe, or the Orient, anywhere where Jonathan Creighton wasn't.

We'd met at a freshmen mixer at Rutgers University back in the sixties. Maybe we each picked up subliminal cues—we called them "vibes" in those days—that told us we shared a rural upbringing. We didn't dress like it, act like it, or feel like it, but we were a couple of Jersey hicks. I came from the Pemberton area, Jon came from another rural zone, but in North Jersey, near a place called Gilead. Despite that link we were polar opposites in most other ways. I'm still amazed we hit it off. I was career-oriented while Jon was . . . well, he was a flake. He earned the name Crazy Creighton, and he lived up to it every day. He never stayed with one thing long enough to allow anyone to pin him down. Always on to the Next New Thing before the crowd had tuned into it, *always* into the exotic and esoteric. Looking for the Truth, he'd say.

And as so often happens with people who are incompatible in so many ways, we found each other irresistible and fell madly in love.

Sophomore year we found an apartment off campus and moved in together. It was my first affair, and not at all a tranquil one. I read the strange books he'd find and I kept up with his strange hours, but I put my foot down when it came to the Pickman prints. There was something deeply disturbing about those paintings that went beyond their gruesome subject matter. Jon didn't fight me on it. He just smiled sadly in his condescending way, as if disappointed that I had missed the point, and rolled them up and put them away.

The thing that kept us together—at least for the year we were together—was our devotion to personal autonomy. We spent weeks of nights talking about how we had to take complete control of our own lives, and brainstorming how we were going to go about it. It seems silly now, but that was the sixties, and we really discussed those sorts of things back then.

We lasted sophomore year and then we fell apart. It might have gone on longer if Creighton hadn't got in with the druggies. That was the path toward loss of *all* autonomy as far as I was concerned, but Creighton said you can't be free until you know what's real. And if drugs might reveal the Truth, he had to try them. Which was hippie bullshit as far as I was concerned. After that, we rarely ran into each other. He wound up living alone off campus in his senior year. Somehow he managed to graduate, with a degree in anthropology, and that was the last I'd heard of him.

But that doesn't mean he hadn't left his mark.

I suppose I'm what you might call a feminist. I don't belong to

NOW and I don't march in the streets, but I don't let anyone leave footprints on my back simply because I'm a woman. I believe in myself, and I guess I owe some of that to Jonathan Creighton. He always treated me as an equal. He never made an issue of it—it was simply implicit in his attitude that I was intelligent, competent, worthy of respect, able to stand on my own. It helped shape me. And I'll always revere him for that.

Lunch. I chose Rosario's on the Point Pleasant Beach side of the Manasquan Inlet, not so much for its food as for the view. Creighton was late and that didn't terribly surprise me. I didn't mind. I sipped a chablis spritzer and watched the party boats roll in from their half-day runs of bottom fishing. Then a voice with echoes of familiarity broke through my thoughts.

"Well, Mac, I see you haven't changed much."

I turned and was shocked at what I saw. I barely recognized Creighton. He'd always been thin to the point of emaciation. Could the plump, bearded, almost cherubic figure standing before me now be—?

"Jon? Is that you?"

"The one and only," he said and spread his arms.

We embraced briefly, then took our seats in a booth by the window. As he squeezed into the far side of the table, he called the waitress over and pointed to my glass.

"Two Lites for me and another of those for her."

At first glance I'd thought that Creighton's extra poundage made him look healthy for the first time in his life. His hair was still thick and dark brown, but despite his round, rosy cheeks, his eyes were sunken and too bright. He seemed jovial, but I sensed a grim undertone. I wondered if he was still into drugs.

"Almost a quarter century since we were together," he said. "Hard to believe it's been that long. The years look as if they've been kind to you."

As far as looks go, I suppose that's true. I don't dye my hair, so there's a little gray tucked in with the red. But I've always had a young face. I don't wear makeup—with my high coloring and freckles, I don't need it."

"And you."

Which wasn't actually true. His open shirt collar was frayed and looked as if this might be the third time he'd worn it since it was last washed. His tweed sport coat was worn at the elbows and a good two sizes too small for him.

We spent the drinks, appetizers, and most of the entrées catching up on each other's lives. I told him about my small accounting firm, my marriage, my recent divorce.

"No children?"

I shook my head. The marriage had gone sour, the divorce had been a nightmare. I wanted off the subject.

"But enough about me," I said. "What have you been up to?"

"Would you believe clinical psychology?"

"No," I said, too shocked to lie. "I wouldn't."

The Jonathan Creighton I'd known had been so eccentric, so out of step, so self-absorbed, I couldn't imagine him as a psychotherapist. Jonathan Creighton helping other people get their lives together—it was almost laughable.

He was the one laughing, however—good-naturedly, too.

"Yeah. It *is* hard to believe, but I went on to get a Master's, and then a Ph.D. Actually went into practice."

His voice trailed off.

"You're using the past tense," I said.

"Right. It didn't work out. The practice never got off the ground. But the problem was really within myself. I was using a form of reality therapy, but it never worked as it should. And finally I realized why: I don't know—really *know*—what reality is. Nobody does."

This had an all-too-familiar ring to it. I tried to lighten things up before they got too heavy.

"Didn't someone once say that reality is what trips you up whenever you walk around with your eyes closed?"

Creighton's smile showed a touch of the old condescension that so infuriated some people.

"Yes, I suppose someone would say something like that. Anyway, I decided to go off and see if I could find out what reality really was. Did a lot of traveling. Wound up in a place called Miskatonic University. Ever heard of it?"

"In Massachusetts, isn't it ?"

"That's the one. In a small town called Arkham. I hooked up with the anthropology department there—that was my undergraduate major, after all. But now I've left academe to write a book."

"A book?"

This was beginning to sound like a pretty disjointed life. But that shouldn't have surprised me.

"What a deal!" he said, his eyes sparkling. "I've got grants from Rutgers, Princeton, the American Folklore Society, the New Jersey Historical Society, and half a dozen others, just to write a book!"

"What's it about?"

"The origins of folktales. I'm going to select a few and trace them back to their roots. That's where you come in."

"Oh?"

"I'm going to devote a significant chapter to the Jersey Devil."

"There've been whole books written about the Jersey Devil. Why don't you—"

"I want real sources for this, Mac. Primary all the way. Nothing secondhand. This is going to be definitive."

"What can I do for you?"

"You're a Piney, aren't you?"

Resentment flashed through me. Even though people nowadays described themselves as "Piney" with a certain amount of pride, and I'd even seen bumper stickers touting "Piney Power," some of us still couldn't help bristling when an outsider said it. When I was a kid it was always used as a pejorative. Like "clam-digger" here on the coast. Fighting words. Officially it referred to the multigenerational natives of the great Pine Barrens that ran south from Route 70 all the way down to the lower end of the state. I've always hated the term. To me it was the equivalent of calling someone a redneck.

Which, to be honest, wasn't so far from the truth. The true Pineys are poor rural folk, often working truck farms and doing menial labor in the berry fields and cranberry bogs—a lot of them do indeed have red necks. Many are uneducated, or at best undereducated. Those who can afford wheels drive the prototypical pickup with the gun rack in the rear window. They even speak with an accent that sounds southern. They're Jersey hillbillies. Country bumpkins in the very heart of the industrial Northeast. Anachronisms.

Pineys.

"Who told you that?" I said as levelly as I could.

"You did. Back in school."

"Did I?"

It shook me to see how far I'd traveled from my roots. As a scared, naive, self-deprecating frosh at Rutgers I probably had indeed referred to myself as a Piney. Now I never mentioned the word, not in reference to myself or anyone else. I was a college-educated woman; I was a respected professional who spoke with a colorless Northeast accent. No one in his right mind would consider me a Piney.

"Well, that was just a gag," I said. "My family roots are back in the Pine Barrens, but I am by no stretch of the imagination a Piney. So I doubt I can help you."

"Oh, but you can! The McKelston name is big in the Barrens. Everybody knows it. You've got plenty of relatives there."

"Really? How do you know?"

Suddenly he looked sheepish.

"Because I've been into the Barrens a few times now. No one will open up to me. I'm an outsider. They don't trust me. Instead of answering my questions, they play games with me. They say they don't know what I'm talking about but they know someone who might, then they send me driving in circles. I was lost out there for two solid days last month. And believe me, I was getting scared. I thought I'd never find my way out."

"You wouldn't be the first. Plenty of people, many of them experienced hunters, have gone into the Barrens and never been seen again. You'd better stay out."

His hand darted across the table and clutched mine.

"You've got to help me, Kathy. My whole future hinges on this."

I was shocked. He'd always called me "Mac." Even in bed back in our college days he'd never called me "Kathy." Gently, I pulled my hand free, saying, "Come on, Jon—"

He leaned back and stared out the window at the circling gulls.

"If I do this right, do something really definitive, it may get me back into Miskatonic where I can finish my doctoral thesis."

I was immediately suspicious.

"I thought you said you 'left' Miskatonic, Jon. Why can't you get back in without it?"

" 'Irregularities,' " he said, still not looking at me. "The old farts in the antiquities department didn't like where my research was leading me."

"This 'reality' business."

"Yes."

"They told you that?"

Now he looked at me.

"Not in so many words, but I could tell." He leaned forward. His eyes were brighter than ever. "They've got books and manuscripts locked in huge safes there, one-of-a-kind volumes from times most scholars think of as prehistory. I managed to get a pass, a forgery, that got me into the vaults. It's incredible what they have there, Mac. *Incredible!* I've got to get back there. Will you help me?"

His intensity was startling. And tantalizing.

"What would I have to do?"

"Just accompany me into the Pine Barrens. Just for a few trips. If I can use you as a reference, I know they'll talk to me about the Jersey Devil. After that, I can take it on my own. All I need is some straight answers from these people and I'll have my primary sources. I may be able to track a folk myth to its very roots! I'll give you credit in the book, I'll pay you, anything, Mac, just don't leave me twisting in the wind!"

He was positively frantic by the time he finished speaking.

"Easy, Jon. Easy. Let me think."

Tax season was over and I had a loose schedule for the summer. And even if I was looking ahead to a tight schedule, so what? Frankly, the job wasn't anywhere near as satisfying as it once had been. The challenge of overcoming the business community's prejudice and doubts about a woman accountant, the thrill of building a string of clients, that was all over. Everything was mostly routine now. Plus, I no longer had a husband. No children to usher toward adulthood. I had to admit that my life was pretty empty at that moment. And so was I. Why not take a little time to inspect my roots and help Crazy Creighton put his life on track, if such a thing was possible? In the bargain maybe I could gain a little perspective on my own life.

"All right, Jon," I said. "I'll do it."

Creighton's eyes lit with true pleasure, a glow distinct from the feverish intensity since he'd sat down. He thrust both his hands toward me.

"I could kiss you, Mac! I can't tell you how much this means to me! You have no idea how important this is!"

He was right about that. No idea at all.

2. THE PINE BARRENS

Two days later we were ready to make out first foray into the woods.

Creighton was wearing a safari jacket when he picked me up in a slightly battered four-wheel-drive Jeep Wrangler.

"This isn't Africa we're headed for," I told him.

"I know, I like the pockets. They hold all sorts of things."

I glanced in the rear compartment. He was surprisingly well equipped. I noticed a water cooler, a food chest, backpacks, and what looked like sleeping bags. I hoped he wasn't harboring any romantic ideas. I'd just split from one man and I wasn't looking for another, especially not Jonathan Creighton.

"I promised to help you look around. I didn't say anything about camping out."

He laughed. "I'm with you. Holiday Inn is my idea of roughing it. I was never a Boy Scout, but I do believe in being prepared. I've already been lost once in there."

"And we can do without that happening again. Got a compass?"

He nodded. "And maps. Even have a sextant."

"You actually know how to use one?"

"I learned."

I dimly remember being bothered then by his having a sextant, and not being quite sure why. Before I could say anything else, he tossed me the keys.

"You're the Piney. You drive."

"Still Mr. Macho, I see."

He laughed. I drove.

It's easy to get into the Pine Barrens from northern Ocean County. You just get on Route 70 and head west. About halfway between the Atlantic Ocean and Philadelphia, say, near a place known as Ongs Hat, you turn left. And wave bye-bye to the twentieth century, and civilization as you know it.

How do I describe the Pine Barrens to someone who's never been there? First of all, it's big. You have to fly over it in a small plane to appreciate just how big. The Barrens runs through seven counties, takes up one-fourth of the state, but since Jersey's not a big state, that doesn't tell the story. How does two thousand square miles sound? Or a million acres? Almost the size of Yosemite National Park. Does that give you an idea of its vastness?

How do I describe what a wilderness this is? Maps will give you a clue. Look at a road map of New Jersey. If you don't happen to have one handy, imagine an oblong platter of spaghetti; now imagine what it looks like after someone's devoured most of the spaghetti out of the middle of the lower half, leaving only a few strands crossing the exposed plate. Same thing with a population density map—a big gaping hole in the southern half where the Pine Barrens sits. New Jersey is the most densely populated state in the U.S., averaging a thousand bodies per square mile. But the New York City suburbs in north Jersey teem with forty thousand per square mile. After you account for the crowds along the coast and in the cities and towns along the western interstate corridor, there aren't too many people left over when you get to the Pine Barrens. I've heard of an area of over a hundred thousand acres—that's in the neighborhood of 160 square miles—in the south-central Barrens with twenty-one known inhabitants. *Twenty-one.* One human being per eight square miles in an area that lies on the route through Boston, New York, Philadelphia, Baltimore, and D.C.

Even when you take a turn off one of the state or federal roads that cut through the Barrens, you feel the isolation almost immediately. The forty-foot scrub pines close in behind you and quietly but oh so effectively cut you off from the rest of the world. I'll bet there are people who've lived to ripe old ages in the Barrens who have never seen a paved road. Conversely, there are no complete topographical maps of the Barrens because there are vast areas that no human eyes have ever seen.

Are you getting the picture?

"Where do we start?" Creighton asked as we crawled past the retirement villages along Route 70. This had been an empty stretch of road when I was a kid. Now it was Wrinkle City.

"We start at the capital."

"Trenton? I don't want to go to Trenton."

"Not the state capital. The capital of the pines. Used to be called Shamong Station. Now it's known as Chatsworth."

He pulled out his map and squinted through the index.

"Oh, right. I see it. Right smack in the middle of the Barrens. How big is it?"

"A veritable Piney megalopolis, my friend. Three hundred souls."

Creighton smiled, and for a second or two he seemed almost . . . innocent.

"Think we can get there before rush hour?"

3. JASPER MULLINER

I stuck to the main roads, taking 70 to 72 to 563, and we were there in no time.

"You'll see something here you won't see in any place else in the Barrens," I said as I drove down Chatsworth's main street.

"Electricity?" Creighton said.

He didn't look up from the clutter of maps on his lap. He'd been following our progress on paper, mile by mile.

"No. Lawns. Years ago a number of families decided they wanted grass in their front yards. There's no topsoil to speak of out here; the ground's mostly sand. So they trucked in loads of topsoil and seeded themselves some lawns. Now they've got to cut them."

I drove past the general store and its three gas pumps out on the sidewalk.

"*Esso,*" Creighton said, staring at the sign over the pumps. "That says it all, doesn't it."

"That it do."

We continued on until we came to a sandy lot occupied by a single trailer. No lawn here.

"Who's this?" Creighton said, folding up his maps as I hopped out of the Wrangler.

"An old friend of the family."

This was Jasper Mulliner's place. He was some sort of an uncle—on my mother's side, I think. But distant blood relationships are nothing special in the Barrens. An awful lot of people are related in one way or another. Some said he was a descendant of the notorious bandit of the pines, Joseph Mulliner. Jasper had never confirmed that, but he'd never denied it, either.

I knocked on the door, wondering who would answer. I wasn't even sure Jasper was still alive. But when the door opened, I immediately recognized the grizzled old head that poked through the opening.

"You're not sellin' anything, are you?" he said.

"Nothing, Mr. Mulliner," I said. "I'm Kathleen McKelston. I don't know if you remember me, but—"

His eyes lit as his face broke into a toothless grin.

"Danny's girl? The one who got the college scholarship? Sure I remember you! Come on in!"

Jasper was wearing khaki shorts, a sleeveless orange T-shirt, and duck boots—no socks. His white hair was neatly combed and he was freshly shaved. He'd been a salt hay farmer in his younger days, and his hands were still calloused from it. He'd moved on to overseeing a cranberry bog in his later years. His skin was a weathered brown and looked tougher than saddle leather. The inside of the trailer reminded me more of a low-ceilinged freight car than a home, but it was clean. The presence of the television set told me he had electricity, but I saw no phone nor any sign of running water.

I introduced him to Creighton, and we settled onto a three-legged stool and a pair of ladder-back chairs as I spent the better part of half an hour telling him about my life since leaving the Barrens and answering questions about my mother and how she was doing since my father died. Then he went into a soliloquy about what a great man my father was. I let him run on, pretending to be listening, but turning my mind to other things. Not because I disagreed with him, but because it had been barely a year since Dad had dropped dead and I was still hurting.

Dad had not been your typical Piney. Although he loved the Barrens as much as anyone else who grew up here, he'd known there was a bigger though not necessarily better life beyond them. That bigger world didn't interest him in the least, but just because he was content with where he was didn't mean that I'd be. He wanted to allow his only child a choice. He knew I'd need a decent education if that choice was to be meaningful. And to provide that education for me, he did what few Pineys like to do: he took a steady job.

That's not to say that Pineys are afraid of hard work. Far from it. They'll break their backs at any job they're doing. It's simply that they don't like to be tied down to the same job day after day, month after month. Most of them have grown up flowing with the cycle of the Barrens. Spring is for gathering sphagnum moss to sell to the florists and nurseries. In June and July they work the blueberry and huckleberry fields. In the fall they move into the bogs for the cranberry harvest. And in the cold of winter they cut cordwood, or cut holly and mistletoe, or go "pineballing"—collecting pinecones to sell. None of this is easy work. But it's not the same work. And that's what matters.

The Piney attitude toward jobs is the most laid-back you'll ever encounter. That's because they're in such close harmony with their surroundings. They know that with all the pure water around them and flowing beneath their feet, they'll never go thirsty. With all the wild vegetation around them, they'll never lack for fruit and vegetables. And whenever the meat supply gets low, they pick up a rifle and head into the brush for squirrel, rabbit, or venison, whatever the season.

When I neared fourteen, my father bit the bullet and moved us close to Pemberton, where he took a job with a well-drilling crew. It was steady work, with benefits, and I got to go to Pemberton High. He pushed me to take my schoolwork seriously, and I did. My high grades coupled with my gender and low socioeconomic status earned me a full ride—room, board, and tuition—at Rutgers. As soon as that was settled, he was ready to move back into the Barrens. But my mother had become used to the conveniences and amenities of town living. She wanted to stay in Pemberton. So they stayed.

I still can't help but wonder whether Dad might have lived longer if he'd moved back into the woods. I've never mentioned that to my mother, of course.

When Jasper paused, I jumped in: "My friend Jon's doing a book, and he's devoting a chapter to the Jersey Devil."

"Is that so?" Jasper said. "And you brought him to me, did you?"

"Well, Dad always told me there weren't many folks in the Pines you didn't know, and not much that went on that you didn't know about."

The old man beamed and did what many Pineys do: he repeated a phrase three times.

"Did he now? Did he now? Did he really now? Ain't that somethin'! I do believe that calls for a little jack."

As Jasper turned and reached into his cupboard, Creighton threw me a questioning look.

"Applejack," I told him.

He smiled. "Ah. Jersey lightning."

Jasper turned back with three glasses and a brown quart jug. With a practiced hand he poured two fingers' worth into each and handed them to us. The tumblers were smudged and maybe a little crusty, but I wasn't worried about germs. There's never been a germ that could stand up to straight jack from Jasper Mulliner's still. I remember siphoning some from my father's jug and sneaking off into the brush at night to meet a couple of my girlfriends from high school, and we'd sit around and sing and get plastered.

I could tell by the way the vapor singed my nasal membranes that this was from a potent batch. I neglected to tell Creighton to go slow. As I took a respectful sip, he tossed his off. I watched him wince as he swallowed, saw his face grow red and his eyes begin to water.

"Whoa!" he said hoarsely. "You could etch glass with that stuff!"

He caught Jasper looking at him sideways and held out his glass. "But delicious! Could I have just a drop more?"

"Help yourself," Jasper said, pouring him another couple of fingers. "Plenty more where this came from. But down it slow. This here's sippin' whiskey. You go puttin' too much of it down like that and you'll get apple palsy. Slow and leisurely does it when you're drinking Gus Sooy's best."

"This isn't yours?"

"Naw! I stopped that long time ago. Too much trouble and gettin' too civilized 'round here. Besides, Gus's jack is as good as mine ever was. Maybe better."

He set the jug on the floor between us.

"About that Jersey Devil," I said, prompting him before he got off on another tangent.

"Right. The ol' Devil. He used to be known as the Leeds' Devil. I'm sure you've heard various versions of the story, but I'll tell you the real one. That ol' devil's been around a spell, better'n two and a half centuries. All started back around 1730 or so. That was when Mrs. Leeds of Estellville found herself in the family way for the thirteenth time. Now she was so fed up and angry about this that she cried out, 'I hope this time it's the Devil!' Well now, someone must've been listenin' that night, because she got her wish. When that thirteenth baby was born, it was an ugly-faced thing, born with teeth like no one'd ever seen before, and it had a curly, sharp-pointed tail, and leathery wings like a bat. It bit its mother and flew out through the window. It grew up out in the pine wilds, stealing and eating chickens and small piglets at first, then graduating to cows, children, even growed men. All they ever found of its victims was their bones, and they was chipped and nicked by powerful sharp teeth. Some say it's dead now, some say it'll never die. Every so often someone says he shot and killed it, but most folks think it can't be killed. It gets blamed for every missing chicken and every pig or cow that wanders off, and so after a while you think it's just an ol' Piney folktale. But it's out there. It's out there. It's surely out there."

"Have you ever seen it?" Creighton asked. He was sipping his jack with respect this time around.

"Saw its shadow. It was up on Apple Pie Hill, up at the top, in the days before they put up the firetower. Before you was born, Kathleen. I'd been out doing some summer hunting, tracking a big ol' stag. You know what a climb Apple Pie is, don'tcha?"

I nodded. "Sure do."

It didn't look like much of a hill. No cliffs or precipices, just a slow incline that seemed to go on forever. You didn't have to do much more than walk to get to the top, but you were bushed when you finally reached it.

"Anyways, I was about three-quarters the way up when it got too dark to do any more tracking. Well, I was tired and it was a warm summer night, so's I just settled down on the pine needles and decided I'd spend the night. I had some jerky and some pone and my jug." He pointed to the floor. "Just like that one. You two be sure to help your-selves, hear me?"

"I'm fine," I said.

I saw Creighton reach for the jug. He could always handle a lot. I was already feeling my two sips. It was getting warmer in here by the minute.

"Anyways," Jasper went on, "I was sitting there chewing and sip-ping when I saw some pine lights."

Creighton started in midpour and spilled some applejack over his hand. He was suddenly very alert, almost tense.

"Pine lights?" he said. "You saw pine lights? Where were they?"

"So you've heard of the pine lights, have you?"

"I sure have. I've been doing my homework. Where did you see them? Were they moving?"

"They were streaming across the crest of Apple Pie Hill, just skirting the tops of the trees."

Creighton put his tumbler down and began fumbling with his map.

"Apple Pie Hill . . . I remember seeing that somewhere. Here it is." He jabbed his finger down on the map as if he were driving a spike into the hill. "Okay. So you were on Apple Pie Hill when you saw the pine lights. How many were there?"

"A whole town's worth of them, maybe a hunnert, more that I've ever seen before or since."

"How fast were they going?"

"Different speeds. Different sizes. Some gliding peacefully, some zipping along, moving past the slower ones. Looked like the turnpike on a summer weekend."

Creighton leaned forward, his eyes brighter than ever.

"Tell me about it."

Something about Creighton's intensity disturbed me. All of a sudden he'd become an avid listener. He'd been listening politely to Jasper's retelling of the Jersey Devil story, but he'd seemed more inter-ested in the applejack than in the tale. He hadn't bothered to check the location of Apple Pie Hill when Jasper had said he'd seen the Jersey Devil there, but he'd been in a rush to find it at the first mention of the pine lights.

The pine lights. I'd heard of them, but I'd never seen one. People tended to catch sight of them on summer nights, mostly toward the end of the season. Some said it was ball lightning or some form of Saint Elmo's fire, some called it swamp gas, and some said it was the souls of dead Pineys coming back for periodic visits. Why was Creighton so interested?

"Well," Jasper said, "I spotted one or two moving along the crest of the hill and didn't think too much of it. I spot a couple just about every summer. Then I saw a few more. And then a few more. I got a little excited and decided to get up to the top of Apple Pie and see what was going on. I was breathing hard by the time I got there. I stopped and looked up and there they was, flowing along the treetops forty feet above me, pale yellow, some Ping-Pong sized and some big as beach balls, all moving in the same direction."

"What direction?" Creighton said. If he leaned forward any farther, he was going to fall off his stool. "Which way were they going?"

"I'm getting to that, son," Jasper said. "Just hold your horses. So as I was saying, I was standing there watching them flow against the clear night sky, and I was feeling this strange tightness in my chest, like I was witnessing something I shouldn't. But I couldn't tear my eyes away. And then they thinned out and was gone. They'd all passed. So I did something crazy. I climbed a tree to see where they was going. Something in my gut told me not to, but I was filled with this wonder, almost like holy rapture. So I climbed as far as I could, until the tree started to bend with my weight and the branches got too thin to hold me. And I watched them go. They was strung out in a long trail, dipping down when the land dipped down, and moving up when the land rose, moving just above the tops of the pines, like they was being pulled along strings." He looked at Creighton. "And they were heading southwest."

"You're sure of that?"

Jasper looked insulted. "Course I'm sure of that. Bear Swamp Hill was behind my left shoulder, and everybody knows Bear Swamp is east of Apple Pie. Those lights was on their way southwest."

"And this was the summer?"

"Nigh on to Labor Day, if I 'member correct."

"And you were on the crest of Apple Pie Hill?"

"The tippy top."

"Great!" He began folding his map.

"I thought you wanted to hear about the Jersey Devil."

"I do, I do."

"Then how come you're asking me all these questions about the lights and not asking me about my meeting with the Devil?"

I hid a smile. Jasper was as sharp as ever.

Creighton looked confused for a moment. An expression darted across his face. It was only there for a second, but I caught it. Furtiveness. Then he leaned forward and spoke to Jasper in a confidential tone.

"Don't tell anybody this, but I think they're connected. The pine lights and the Jersey Devil. Connected."

Jasper leaned back. "You know, you might have something there. 'Cause it was while I was up that tree that I spotted the ol' Devil himself. Or at least his shadow. I was watching the lights flow out of sight when I heard this noise in the brush. It had a slithery sound to it. I looked down, and there was this dark shape moving below. And you know what? It was heading in the same direction as the lights. What do you think of that?"

Creighton's voice oozed sincerity.

"I think that's damn interesting, Jasper."

I thought they both were shoveling it, but I couldn't decide who was carrying the bigger load.

"But don't you go getting too interested in those pine lights, son. Gus Sooy says they're bad medicine."

"The guy who made this jack?" I said, holding up my empty tumbler.

"The very same. Gus says there's lots of pine light activity in his neighborhood every summer. Told me I was a fool for climbing that tree. Says he wouldn't get near one of those lights for all the tea in China."

I noticed that Creighton was tense again.

"Where's this Gus Sooy's neighborhood?" he said. "Does he live in Chatsworth?"

Jasper burst out laughing.

"Gus live in Chatsworth? That's a good 'un! Gus Sooy's an old Hessian who lives way out in the wildest part of the pines. Never catch him *near* a city like this!"

City! I didn't challenge him on that.

"Where do we find him then?" Creighton said, his expression like a kid who's been told there's a cache of M&M's hidden somewhere nearby.

"Not easy," Jasper said. "Gus done a good job of getting himself well away from everybody. He's well away. Yes, he's well away. But if you go down to Apple Pie Hill and head along the road there that runs along its south flank, and you follow that about two mile and turn south onto the sand road by Applegate's cranberry bog, then follow that for about ten–twelve mile till you come to the fork where you bear left, then go right again at the cripple beyond it, then it's a good ten mile down that road till you get to the big red cedar—"

Creighton was scribbling furiously.

"I'm not sure I know what a red cedar looks like," I said.

"You'll know it," Jasper said. "Its kind don't grow naturally around here. Gus planted it there a good many year ago so people could find their way to him. The *right* people," he said, eyeing Creighton. "People who want to buy his wares, if you get my meaning."

I nodded. I got his meaning: Gus made his living off his still.

"Anyways, you turn right at the red cedar and go to the end of the road. Then you've got to get out and walk about a third of the way up the hill. That's where you'll find Gus Sooy."

I tried to drive the route across a mental map in my head. I couldn't get there. My map was blank where he was sending us. But I was amazed at how far I did get. As a Piney, even a girl, you've got to develop a good sense of where you are, got to have a store of maps in your head that you can picture by reflex, otherwise you'll spend most of your time being lost. Even with a good library of mental maps, you'll still get lost occasionally. I could still travel my old maps. The skill must be like the proverbial bicycle—once you've learned, you never forget.

I had a sense that Gus Sooy's place was somewhere far down in Burlington County, near Atlantic County. But county lines don't mean much in the Pinelands.

"That's *really* in the middle of nowhere!" I said.

"That it is, Kathy, that it is. That it surely is. It's on the slope of Razorback Hill."

Creighton shuffled through his maps again.

"Razorback . . . Razorback . . . there's no Razorback Hill here."

"That's because it ain't much of a hill. But it's there all right. Just 'cause it ain't on your diddly map don't mean it ain't there. Lots of things ain't on that map."

Creighton rose to his feet.

"Maybe we can run out there now and buy some of this applejack from him. What do you say, Mac?"

"We've got time."

I had a feeling he truly did want to buy some of Sooy's jack, but I was sure some questions about the pine lights would come up during the transaction.

"Better bring your own jugs if you're goin'," Jasper said. "Gus don't carry no spares. You can buy some from the Buzbys at the general store."

"Will do," I said.

I thanked him and promised I'd say hello to my mom for him, then I joined Creighton out at the Wrangler. He had one of his maps unfolded on the hood and was drawing a line southwest from Apple Pie Hill through the emptiest part of the Barrens.

"What's that for?" I asked.

"I don't know just yet. We'll see if it comes to mean anything."
It would. Sooner than either of us realized.

4. THE HESSIAN

I bought a gallon-sized brown jug at the Chatsworth general store;
Creighton bought two.

"I want this Sooy fellow to be *real* glad to see me!"

I drove us down 563, then off to Apple Pie Hill. We got south of it
and began following Jasper's directions. Creighton read while I drove.

"What the hell's a cripple?" he said.

"That's a spong with no cedars."

"Ah! That clears up everything!"

"A spong is a low wet spot; if it's got cedars growing around it, it's a
cripple. What could be clearer?"

"I'm not sure, but I know I'll think of something. By the way, why's
this Sooy fellow called a Hessian? Mulliner doesn't really think
he's—?"

"Of course not. Sooy's an old German name around the Pine Barrens. Comes from the Hessians who deserted the British Army and fled
into the woods after the battle of Trenton."

"The Revolution?"

"Sure. This sand road we're riding on now was here three-hundred-
odd years ago as a wagon trail. It probably hasn't changed any since.
Might even have been used by the smugglers who used to unload
freight in the marshes and move it overland through the Pines to avoid
port taxes in New York and Philly. A lot of them settled in here. So did
a good number of Tories and Loyalists who were chased from their
land after the Revolution. Some of them probably arrived dressed in tar
and feathers and little else. The Lenape Indians settled in here, too, so
did Quakers who were kicked out of their churches for taking up arms
during the Revolution."

Creighton laughed. "Sounds like Australia! Didn't anyone besides
outcasts settle here?"

"Sure. Bog iron was a major industry. This was the center of the
colonial iron production. Most of the cannon balls fired against the
British in the Revolution and the War of 1812 were forged right here in
the Pine Barrens."

"Where'd everybody go?"

"A place called Pittsburgh. There was more iron there and it was
cheaper to produce. The furnaces here tried to shift over to glass production, but they were running out of wood to keep them going. Each
furnace consumed something like a thousand acres of pine a year.

With the charcoal industry, the lumber industry, even the cedar shake industry all adding to the daily toll on the tree population, the Barrens couldn't keep up with the demand. The whole economy collapsed after the Civil War. Which probably saved the area from becoming a desert."

I noticed the underbrush between the ruts getting higher, slapping against the front bumper as we passed, a sure sign that not many people came this way. Then I spotted the red cedar. Jasper had been right—it didn't look like it belonged here. We turned right and drove until we came to a cul-de-sac at the base of a hill. Three rusting cars hugged the bushes along the perimeter.

"This must be the place," I said.

"This is not a place. This is *no*where."

We grabbed our jugs and walked up the path. About a third of the way up the slope we broke into a clearing with a slant-roofed shack in the far left corner. It looked maybe twenty feet on a side, and was covered with tarpaper that was peeling away in spots, exposing the plywood beneath. Somewhere behind the shack a dog had begun to bark.

Creighton said, "Finally!" and started forward.

I laid a hand on his arm.

"Call out first," I told him. "Otherwise we may be ducking buckshot."

He thought I was joking at first, then saw that I meant it.

"You're serious?"

"We're dressed like city folk. We could be revenuers. He'll shoot first and ask questions later."

"Hello in the house!" Creighton cried. "Jasper Mulliner sent us! Can we come up?"

A wizened figure appeared on the front step, a twelve gauge cradled in his arms.

"How'd he send you?"

"By way of the red cedar, Mr. Sooy!" I replied.

"C'mon up then!"

Where Jasper had been neat, Gus Sooy was slovenly. His white hair looked like a deranged bird had tried to nest in it; for a shirt he wore the stained top from a set of long johns and had canvas pants secured around his waist with coarse rope. His lower face was obscured by a huge white beard, stained around the mouth. An Appalachian Santa Claus, going to seed in the off-season.

We followed him into the single room of his home. The floor was covered with a mismatched assortment of throw rugs and carpet remnants. A bed sat in the far left corner, a kerosene stove was immediately to our right. Set about the room were a number of Aladdin lamps with the tall flues. Dominating the scene was a heavy-legged kitchen table with an enamel top.

We introduced ourselves, and Gus said he'd met my father years ago.

"So what brings you two kids out here to see Gus Sooy?"

I had to smile, not just at the way he managed to ignore the jugs we were carrying, but at being referred to as a "kid." A long time since anyone had called me that. I wouldn't let anyone call me a "girl" these days, but somehow I didn't mind "kid."

"Today we tasted some of the best applejack in the world," Creighton said with convincing sincerity, "and Jasper told us you were the source." He slammed his two jugs on the table. "Fill 'em up!"

I placed my own jug next to Creighton's.

"I gotta warn you," Gus said. "It's five dollars a quart."

"Five dollars!" Creighton said.

"Yeah," Gus added quickly, "but seein' as you're buying so much at once—"

"Don't get me wrong, Mr. Sooy. I wasn't saying the price is too high. I was just shocked that you'd be selling such high-grade sipping whiskey for such a low price."

"You were?" The old man beamed with delight. "It is awful good, isn't it?"

"That it is, sir. That it is. That it surely is."

I almost burst out laughing. I didn't know how Creighton managed to keep a straight face.

Gus held up a finger. "You kids stay right here. I'll dip into my stock and be back in a jiffy."

We both broke down into helpless laughter as soon as he was gone.

"You're laying it on awful thick," I said when I caught my breath.

"I know, but he's lapping up every bit."

Gus returned in a few minutes with two gallon jugs of his own.

"Hadn't we ought to test this first before you begin filling our jugs?" Creighton said.

"Not a bad idea. No, sir, not a bad idea. Not a bad idea at all."

Creighton produced some paper cups from one of the pockets in his safari jacket and placed them on the table. Gus poured. We all sipped.

"This is even smoother than what Jasper served us. How do you do it, Mr. Sooy?"

"That's a secret," he said with a wink as he brought out a funnel and began decanting from his jugs into ours.

I brought up Jon's book, and Gus launched into a slightly different version of the Jersey Devil story, saying it was born in Leeds, which is at the opposite end of the Pine Barrens from Estellville. Otherwise the tales were almost identical.

"Jasper says he saw the Devil once," Creighton said as Gus topped off the last of our jugs.

"If he says he did, then he did. That'll be sixty dollar."

Creighton gave him three twenties.

"And now I'd like to buy you a drink, Mr. Sooy."

"Call me Gus. And I don't mind if I do."

Creighton was overly generous, I thought, with the way he filled the three paper cups. I didn't want any more, but I felt I had to keep up appearances. I sipped while the men quaffed.

"Jasper told us about the time he saw the Jersey Devil. He mentioned seeing pine lights at the same time."

I sensed rather than saw Gus stiffen.

"Is that so?"

"Yeah. He said you see pine lights around here all the time. Is that true?"

"You interested in pine lights or the Jersey Devil, boy?"

"Both. I'm interested in all the folktales of the Pines."

"Well, don't get too interested in the pine lights."

"Why not?"

"Just don't."

I watched Creighton tip his jug and refill Gus's cup.

"A toast!" Creighton said, lifting his cup. "To the Pine Barrens!"

"I'll drink to that!" Gus said, and drained his cup.

Creighton followed suit, causing his eyes to fill with tears. I sipped while he poured another round.

"To the Jersey Devil!" Creighton cried, hoisting his cup again.

And again they both tossed off their drinks. And then another round.

"To the pine lights!"

Gus wouldn't drink to that one. I was glad. I don't think either of them would have remained standing if he had.

"Have you seen any pine lights lately, Gus," Creighton said.

"You don't give up, do you, boy," the old man said.

"It's an affliction."

"So it is. All right. Sure. I see 'em all the time. Saw some last night."

"Really? Where?"

"None of your business."

"Why not?"

"Because you'll probably try to do something stupid like catch one, and then I'll be responsible for what happens to you and this young lady here. Not on my conscience, no thank you."

"I wouldn't dream of trying to catch one of those things!"

"Well, if you did you wouldn't be the first. Peggy Clevenger was the first." Gus lifted his head and looked at me. "You heard of Peggy Clevenger, ain't you, Miss McKelston?"

I nodded. "Sure. The Witch of the Pines. In the old days people used to put salt over their doors to keep her away."

Creighton began scribbling.

"No kidding? This is great! What about her and the pine lights?"

"Peggy was a Hessian, like me. Lived over in Pasadena. Not the California Pasadena, the Pines Pasadena. A few miles east of Mount Misery. The town's gone now, like it never been. But she lived thereabouts by herself in a small cabin, and people said she had all sorts of strange powers, like she could change her shape and become a rabbit or a snake. I don't know about that stuff, but I heard from someone who should know that she was powerful interested in the pine lights. She told this fella one day that she had caught one of the pine lights, put a spell on it, and brought it down."

Creighton had stopped writing. He was staring at Gus.

"How could she . . . ?"

"Don't know," Gus said, draining his cup and shaking his head. "But that very night her cabin burned to the ground. They found her blackened and burned body among the ashes the next morning. So I tell you, kids, it ain't a good idea to get too interested in the pine lights."

"I don't want to capture one," Creighton said. "I don't even want to see one. I just want to know where other people have seen them. How can that be dangerous?"

Gus thought about that. And while he was thinking, Creighton poured him another cupful.

"Don't s'pose it would do any harm to show you where they was," he said after a long slow sip.

"Then it's settled. Let's go."

We gathered up the jugs and headed out into the late afternoon sunshine. The fresh air was like a tonic. It perked me up but didn't dissipate the effects of all the jack I'd consumed.

When we reached the Wrangler, Creighton pulled out his sextant and compass.

"Before we go, there's something I've got to do."

Gus and I watched in silence as he took his sightings and scribbled in his notebook. Then he spread his map out on the hood again.

"What's up?" I said.

"I'm putting Razorback Hill on the map," he said.

He jotted his readings on the map and drew a circle. Before he folded everything up, I glanced over his shoulder and noticed that the line he had drawn from Apple Pie Hill ran right by the circle that was Razorback Hill.

"You through dawdlin'?" Gus said.

"Sure am. You want to ride in front?"

"No thanks," Gus said, heading for the rusty DeSoto. "I'll drive myself and you kids follow."

I said, "Won't it be easier if we all go together?"

"Hell no! You kids have been drinkin'!"

When we stopped laughing, we pulled ourselves into the Wrangler and followed the old Hessian back up his private sand road.

5. THE FIRING PLACE

"I used to make charcoal here when I was young," Gus said.

We were standing in a small clearing surrounded by pines. Before us was a shallow sandy depression, choked with weeds.

"This used to be my firing place. It was deeper then. I made some fine charcoal here before the big companies started selling their bags of 'brick-*ettes*.' " He fairly spat the word. "Ain't no way any one of those smelly little things was ever part of a tree, I'll tell you that."

"Is this where you saw the lights, Gus?" Creighton said. "Were they moving?"

Gus said, "You got a one-track mind, don't you, boy?" He glanced around. "Yeah, this is where I saw them. Saw them here last night and I saw them here fifty years ago, and I seen them near about every summer in between. Lots of memories here. I remember how while I was letting my charcoal burn I'd use the time to hunt up box turtles."

"And sell them as snail hunters?" I said.

I'd heard of box turtle hunting—another Pinelands mini-industry—but I'd never met anyone who'd actually done it.

"Sure. Folks in Philadelphia'd buy all I could find. They liked to let them loose in their cellars to keep snails and slugs under control."

"The lights, Gus," Creighton said. "Which way were they going?"

"They was goin' the same way they always went when I seen them here. That way."

He was pointing southeast.

"Are you sure?"

"Sure as shit, boy." Gus's tone was getting testy, but he quickly turned to me. "'Scuse me, miss," then back to Creighton. "I was standing back there right where my car is when about a half dozen of them swooped in low right overhead—not a hunting swoop, but a floaty sort of swoop—and traveled away over that pitch pine there with the split top."

"Good!" said Creighton, eyeing the sky.

A thick sheet of cloud was pulling up from the west, encroaching on the sinking sun. Out came the sextant and compass. Creighton took his readings, wrote his numbers, then took a bearing on the tree Gus had pointed out. A slow, satisfied smile crept over his face as he drew the latest line on his map. He folded it up before I had a chance to see where that line went. I didn't have to see. His next question told me.

"Say, Gus," he said offhandedly. "What's on the far side of Razorback Hill?"

Gus turned on Creighton like an angry bear.

"Nothing! There's nothing there! So don't you even think about going over there!"

Creighton's smile was amused. "I was only asking. No harm in a little question, is there?"

"There is. There is. Yes, there surely is! Especially when those questions is the wrong ones. And you've been asking a whole lot of wrong questions, boy. Questions that's gonna get you in a whole mess of bad trouble if you don't get smart and learn that certain things is best left alone. You hear me?"

He sounded like a character from one of those old Frankenstein movies.

"I hear you," Creighton said, "and I appreciate your concern. But can you tell me the best way to get to the other side of that hill?"

Gus threw up his hands with an angry growl.

"That's it! I'm havin' no more to do with the two of you! I've already told you too much as it is." He turned to me, his eyes blazing. "And you, Miss McKelston, you get yourself away from this boy. He's headed straight to hell!"

With that he turned and headed for his car. He jumped in, slammed the door, and roared away with a spray of sand.

"I don't think he likes me," Creighton said.

"He seemed genuinely frightened," I told him.

Creighton shrugged and began packing away his sextant.

"Maybe he really believes in the Jersey Devil," he said. "Maybe he thinks it lives on the other side of Razorback Hill."

"I don't know about that. I got the impression he thinks the Jersey Devil is something to tell tall tales about while sitting around the stove and sipping jack. But those pine lights . . . he's scared of them."

"Just swamp gas, I'm sure," Creighton said.

Suddenly I was furious. Maybe it was all the jack I'd consumed, or maybe it was his attitude, but I think at that particular moment it was mostly his line of bull.

"Cut it, Jon!" I said. "If you really believe they're swamp gas, why are you tracking them on your map? You got me to guide you out here, so let's have it straight. What's going on?"

"I don't know what's going on, Mac. If I did, I wouldn't be here. Isn't that obvious? These pine lights mean something. Whether or not they're connected to the Jersey Devil, I don't know. Maybe they have a hallucinatory effect on people—after they pass overhead, people think they see things. I'm trying to establish a pattern."

"And after you've established this pattern, what do you think you'll find?"

"Maybe Truth," he said. "Reality. Who knows? Maybe the meaning— or meaninglessness—of life."

He looked at me with eyes so intense, so full of longing, that my anger evaporated.

"Jon . . . ?"

His expression abruptly shifted back to neutral, and he laughed.

"Don't worry, Mac. It's only me, Crazy Creighton, putting you on again. Let's have another snort of Gus Sooy's best and head for civilization. Okay?"

"I've had enough for the day. The *week*!"

"You don't mind if I partake, do you?"

"Help yourself."

I didn't know how he could hold so much.

While Creighton uncorked his jug, I strolled about the firing place to clear my fuzzy head. The sky was fully overcast now, and the temperature was dropping to a more comfortable level.

He had everything packed away by the time I completed the circle.

"Want me to drive?" he said, tossing his paper cup onto the sand.

Normally I would have picked it up—there was something sacrilegious about leaving a Dixie cup among the pines—but I was afraid to bend over that far, afraid I'd keep on going headfirst into the sand and become litter myself.

"I'm okay," I said. "You'll get us lost."

We had traveled no more than a hundred feet or so when I realized that I didn't know this road. But I kept driving. I hadn't been paying close attention while following Gus here, but I was pretty sure it wouldn't be long before I'd come to a fork or a cripple or a bog that I recognized, and then we'd be home free.

It didn't quite work out that way. I drove for maybe five miles or so, winding this way and that with the roads, making my best guess when we came to a fork—and we came to plenty of those—and generally trying to keep us heading in the same general direction. I thought I was doing a pretty good job until we drove through an area of young pines that looked familiar. I stopped the Wrangler.

"Jon," I said. "Isn't this—?"

"Damn right it is!" he said, pointing to the sand beside the road. "We're back at Gus's firing place! There's my Dixie cup!"

I turned the Jeep around and headed back the way I came.

"What are you doing?" Creighton said.

"Making sure I don't make the same mistake twice!" I told him.

I didn't know how I could have driven in a circle. I usually had an excellent sense of direction. I blamed it on too much Jersey lightning and on the thickly overcast sky. Without the sun as a marker, I'd been unable to keep us on course. But that would change here and now. I'd get us out of here this time around.

Wrong.

After a good forty-five minutes of driving, I was so embarrassed when I recognized the firing place again that I actually accelerated as we passed through, hoping Creighton wouldn't recognize the spot in the thickening dusk. But I wasn't quick enough.

"Hold it!" he cried. "Hold it just a damn minute! There's my cup again! We're right back where we started!"

"Jon," I said. "I don't understand it. Something's wrong."

"You're stewed, that's what's wrong!"

"I'm not!"

I truly believed I wasn't. I'd been feeling the effects of the jack before, true, but my head was clear now. I was sure I'd been heading due east, or at least pretty close to it. How I'd come full circle again was beyond me.

Creighton jumped out of his seat and came around the front of the Wrangler.

"Over you go, Mac. It's my turn."

I started to protest, then thought better of it. I'd blown it twice already. Maybe my sense of direction had fallen prey to the "apple palsy," as it was known. I lifted myself over the stick shift and dropped into the passenger seat.

"Be my guest."

Creighton drove like a maniac, seemingly choosing forks at random.

"Yeah, Mac," he said. "I'm going whichever way you *didn't*! I think."

As darkness closed in and he turned on the headlights, I noticed that the trees were thinning out and the underbrush was closing in, rising to eight feet or better on either side of us. Creighton pulled off to the side at a widening of the road.

"You should stay on the road," I told him.

"I'm lost," he said. "We've got to think."

"Fine. But it's not as if somebody's going to be coming along and want to get by."

He laughed. "That's a fact!" He got out and looked up at the sky. "Damn! If it weren't for the clouds we could figure out where we are. Or least know where north is."

I looked around. We were surrounded by bushes. It was the Pine

Barrens's equivalent of an English hedge maze. There wasn't a tree in sight. A tree can be almost as good as a compass—its moss faces north and its longest branches face south. Bushes are worse than useless for that, and the high ones only add to your confusion.

And we were confused.

"I thought Pineys never get lost," Creighton said.

"Everybody gets lost sooner or later out here."

"Well, what do Pineys do when they get lost?"

"They don't exhaust themselves or waste their gas by running around in circles. They hunker down and wait for morning."

"To hell with that!" Creighton said.

He threw the Wrangler into first and gunned it toward the road. But the vehicle didn't reach the road. It lurched forward and rocked back. He tried again and I heard the wheels spinning.

"Sugar!" I said.

Creighton looked at me and grinned.

"Stronger language is allowed and even encouraged in this sort of situation."

"I was referring to the sand."

"Don't worry. I've got four-wheel drive."

"Right. And all four wheels are spinning. We're in a patch of what's known as 'sugar sand.' "

He got out and pushed and rocked while I worked the gears and throttle, but I knew it was no use. We weren't going to get out of this superfine sand until we found some wood and piled it under the tires to give them some traction.

And we weren't going to be able to hunt up that kind of wood until morning.

I told Creighton that we'd only waste what gas we had left and that our best bet was to call it a night and pull out the sleeping bags. He seemed reluctant at first, worrying about deer ticks and catching Lyme disease, but he finally agreed.

He had no choice.

6. THE PINE LIGHTS

"I owe you one, Jon," I said.

"How was I to know we'd get lost?" he said defensively. "I don't like this any more than you!"

"No. You don't understand. I meant that in the good sense. I'm glad you talked me into coming with you."

I'd found us a small clearing not too far from the jeep. It surrounded the gnarled trunk of an old lone pine that towered above the dominant brush. We'd eaten the last of the sandwiches, and now we sat on our respective bedrolls facing each other across the Coleman lamp sitting between us on the sand. Creighton was back to sipping his applejack. I would have killed, or at least maimed, for a cup of coffee.

I watched his face in the lamplight. His expression was puzzled.

"You must still be feeling the effects of that Jersey lightning you had this afternoon," he said.

"No. I'm perfectly sober. I've been sitting here realizing that I'm glad to be back. I've had a feeling for years that something's been missing from my life. Never had an inkling as to what it was until now. But this is it. I'm . . ." My throat constricted around the word. "I'm home."

It wasn't the jack talking, it was my heart. I'd learned something today. I'd learned that I loved the Pine Barrens. And I loved its people. So rich in history, so steeped in its own lore, somehow surviving untainted in the heart of twentieth-century urban madness. I'd turned my back on it. Why? Too proud? Too good for it now? Maybe I'd thought I'd pulled myself up by my bootstraps and gone on to bigger and better things. I could see that I hadn't. I'd taken the girl out of the Pinelands, but I hadn't taken the Pinelands out of the girl.

I promised myself to come back here again. Often. I was going to look up my many relatives, renew old ties. I wasn't ready to move back here, and perhaps I never would, but I'd never turn my back on the Pinelands again.

Creighton raised his cup to me.

"I envy anyone who's found the missing piece. I'm still looking for mine."

"You'll find it," I said, crawling into my bedroll. "You've just got to keep your eyes open. Sometimes it's right under your nose."

"Go to sleep, Mac. You're starting to sound like Dorothy from *The Wizard of Oz*."

I smiled at that. For a moment there he was very much like the Jonathan Creighton I'd fallen in love with. As I closed my eyes, I saw him pull out a pair of binoculars and begin scanning the cloud-choked sky. I knew what he was looking for, and I was fairly confident he'd never find them.

It must have been a while later when I awoke, because the sky had cleared and the stars were out when Creighton's shouts yanked me to a sitting position.

"They're coming! Look at them, Mac! My God, they're coming!"

Creighton was standing on the far side of the lamp, pointing off to my left. I followed the line of his arm and saw nothing.

"What are you talking about?"

"Stand up, damn it! They're coming! There must be a dozen of them!"

I struggled to my feet and froze.

The starlit underbrush stretched away in a gentle rise for maybe a mile or two in the direction he was pointing, broken only occasionally by the angular shadows of the few scattered trees. And coming our way over that broad expanse, skimming along at treetop level, was an oblong cluster of faintly glowing lights. *Lights.* That's what they were. Not glowing spheres. Not UFOs or any of that nonsense. They had no discernible substance. They were just light. Globules of light.

I felt my hackles rise at the sight of them. Perhaps because I'd never seen light behave that way before—it didn't seem right or natural for light to concentrate itself in a ball. Or perhaps it was the way they moved, gliding through the night with such purpose, cutting through the dark, weaving from tree to tree, floating by the topmost branches, and then forging a path toward the next. Almost as if the trees were signposts. Or perhaps it was the silence. The awful silence. The Pine Barrens are quiet as far as civilized sounds are concerned, but there's always the noise of the living things, the hoots and cries and rustlings of the animals, the incessant insect susurration. That was all gone now. There wasn't even a breeze to rustle the bushes. Silence. More than a mere absence of noise. A holding of breath.

"Do you see them, Mac? Tell me I'm not hallucinating! Do you see them?"

"I see them, Jon."

My voice sounded funny. I realized my mouth was dry. And not just from sleep.

Creighton turned around in a quick circle, his arms spread.

"I don't have a camera! I need a picture of this!"

"You didn't bring a camera?" I said. "My God, you brought everything else!"

"I know, but I never dreamed—"

Suddenly he was running for the tree at the center of our clearing.

"Jon! You're not really—"

"They're coming this way! If I can get close to them—!"

I was suddenly afraid for him. Something about those lights was warning me away. Why wasn't it warning Creighton? Or was he simply not listening?

I followed him at a reluctant lope.

"Don't be an idiot, Jon! You don't know what they are!"

"Exactly! It's about time somebody found out!"

He started climbing. It was a big old pitch pine with no branches to speak of for the first dozen feet or so of its trunk but its bark was knobby and rough enough for Creighton's rubber-soled boots to find purchase. He slipped off twice, but he was determined. Finally he made it to the lowest branch, and from there on it looked easy.

I can't explain the crawling sensation in my gut as I watched Jonathan Creighton climbing toward a rendezvous with the approaching pine lights. He was three-quarters of the way to the top when the trunk began to shake and sway with his weight. Then a branch broke under his foot and he almost fell. When I saw that he'd regained safe footing I sighed with relief. The branches above him were too frail to hold him. He couldn't go any higher. He'd be safe from the lights.

And the lights were here, a good dozen of them, from baseball to basketball size, gliding across our clearing in an irregular cylindrical cluster perhaps ten feet across and twenty feet long, heading straight for Creighton's tree.

And the closer they got, the faster my insides crawled. They may have been made up of light but it was not a clean light, not the golden healthy light of day. This was a wan, sickly, anemic glow, tainted with the vaguest hint of green. But thankfully it was a glow out of Creighton's reach as the lights brushed the tree's topmost needles.

I watched their glow limn Creighton's upturned face as his body strained upward, and I wondered at his recklessness, at this obsession with finding "reality." Was he flailing and floundering about in his search, or was he actually on the trail of something? And were the pine lights part of it?

As the first light passed directly above him, not five feet beyond his outstretched hand, I heard him cry out.

"They're humming, Mac! High-pitched! Can you hear it? It's almost musical! And the air up here tingles, almost as if it's charged! This is fantastic!"

I didn't hear any music or feel any tingling. All I could hear was my heart thudding in my chest, all I could feel was the cold sweat that had broken out all over my body.

Creighton spoke again, he was practically shouting now, but in a language that was not English and not like any other language I'd ever heard. He made clicks and wheezes, and the few noises that sounded like words did not seem to fit comfortably on the human tongue.

"Jon, what are you doing up there?" I cried.

He ignored me and kept up the alien gibberish, but the lights, in turn, ignored him and sailed by above him as if he didn't exist.

The cluster was almost past now, yet still I couldn't shake the dread, the dark feeling that something awful was going to happen.

And then it did.

The last light in the cluster was basketball-sized. It seemed as if it was going to trail away above Creighton just like the others, but as it approached the tree, it slowed and began to drop toward Creighton's perch.

I was panicked now.

"Jon, look out! It's coming right for you!"

"I see it!"

As the other lights flowed off toward the next treetop, this last one hung back and circled Creighton's tree at a height level with his waist.

"Get down from there!" I called.

"Are you kidding? This is more that I'd ever hoped for!"

The light suddenly stopped moving and hovered a foot or so in front of Creighton's chest.

"It's cold," he said in a more subdued tone. "Cold light."

He reached his hand toward it and I wanted to shout for him not to, but my throat was locked. The tip of his index finger touched the outer edge of the glow.

"*Really* cold."

I saw his finger sink into the light to perhaps the depth of the finger-nail, and then suddenly the light moved. It more than moved, it *leapt* onto Creighton's hand, engulfing it.

That's when Creighton began to scream. His words were barely intelligible, but I picked out the words "cold" and "burning" again and again. I ran to the base of the tree, expecting him to lose his balance, hoping I could do something to break his fall. I saw the ball of light stretch out and slide up the length of his arm, engulfing it.

Then it disappeared.

For an instant I thought it might be over. But when Creighton clutched his chest and cried out in greater agony, I realized to my horror that the light wasn't gone—it was inside him!

And then I saw the back of his shirt begin to glow. I watched the light ooze out of him and re-form itself into a globe. Then it rose and glided off to follow the other lights into the night, leaving Creighton alone in the tree, sobbing and retching.

I called up to him. "Jon! Are you all right? Do you need help?"

When he didn't answer, I grabbed hold of the tree trunk. But before I could attempt to climb, he stopped me.

"Stay there, Mac." His voice was weak, shaky. "I'm coming down."

It took him twice as long to climb down as it had to go up. His movements were slow, unsteady, and three times he had to stop to rest. Finally, he reached the lowest branch, hung from it by one hand, and made the final drop. I grabbed him immediately to keep him from collapsing into a heap, and helped him back toward the lamp and the bedrolls.

"My God, Jon! Your arm!"

In the light from the lamp his flesh seemed to be smoking. The skin on his left hand and forearm was red, almost scalded-looking. Tiny blisters were already starting to form.

"It looks worse than it feels."

"We've got to get you to a doctor."

He dropped to his knees on his bedroll and hugged his injured arm against his chest with his good one.

"I'm all right. It only hurts a little now."

"It's going to get infected. Come on. I'll see if I can get us to civilization."

"Forget it," he said, and I sensed some of the strength returning to his voice. "Even if we get the jeep free, we're still lost. We couldn't find our way out of here when it was daylight. What makes you think we'll do any better in the dark?"

He was right. But I felt I had to do something.

"Where's your first-aid kit?"

"I don't have one."

I blew up then.

"Jesus Christ, Jon! You're crazy, you know that? You could have fallen out of that tree and been killed! And if you don't wind up with gangrene in that arm it'll be a miracle! What on God's earth made you do something so stupid?"

He grinned. "I knew it! You still love me!"

I was not amused.

"This is serious, Jon. You risked your life up there! For what?"

"I have to know, Mac."

" 'Know'? What do you have to 'know'? Will you stop giving me this bullshit?"

"I can't. I can't stop because it's true. I have to know what's real and what's not."

"Spare me—"

"I mean it. You're sure you know what's real and so you're content and complacent with that. You can't imagine what it's like not to know. To sense there's a veil across everything, a barrier that keeps you from seeing what's really there. You don't know what it's like to spend your life searching for the edge of that veil so you can lift it and peek—just peek—at what's behind it. I know it's out there, and I can't reach it. You don't know what that's like, Mac. It makes you crazy."

"Well, that's one thing we can agree on."

He laughed—it sounded strained—and reached for his jug of apple-jack with his good hand.

"Haven't you had enough of that tonight?"

I hated myself for sounding like an old biddy, but what I had just seen had shaken me to the core. I was still trembling.

"No, Mac. The problem is I haven't had enough. Not nearly enough."

Feeling helpless and angry, I sat down on my own bedroll and watched him take a long pull from the jug.

"What happened up there, Jon?"

"I don't know. But I don't ever want it to happen again."

"And what were you saying? It almost sounded as if you were calling to them."

He looked up sharply and stared at me.

"Did you hear what I said?"

"Not exactly. It didn't even sound like speech."

"That's because it wasn't," he said, and I was sure I detected relief in his voice. "I was trying to attract their attention."

"Well, you sure did that."

Across the top of the Coleman lamp, I thought I saw him smile.

"Yeah. I did, didn't I?"

In the night around us, I noticed that the insects were becoming vocal again.

7. THE SHUNNED PLACE

I'd planned to stay awake the rest of the night, but somewhere along the way I must have faded into sleep. The next thing I knew there was sunlight in my eyes. I leaped up, disoriented for a moment, then I remembered where I was.

But where was Creighton? His bedroll lay stretched out on the sand, his compass, sextant, and maps upon it, but he was nowhere in sight. I called his name a couple of times. He called back from somewhere off to my left. I followed the sound of his voice through the brush and emerged on the edge of a small pond rimmed with white cedars.

Creighton was kneeling at the edge, cupping some water in his right hand.

"How'd you find this?"

"Simple." He gestured toward a group of drakes and mallards floating on the still surface. "I followed the quacking."

"You're becoming a regular Mark Trail. How's the water?"

"Polluted." He pointed to a brownish blue slick on the water. "Look at that color. Looks like tea."

"That's not polluted," I told him. "That's the start of some bog iron floating over there. And this is cedar water. It gets brown from the iron deposits and from the cedars, but it's as pure as it comes."

I scooped up a double handful and took a long swallow.

"Almost sweet," I said. "Sea captains used to come into these parts to fill their water casks with cedar water before long voyages. They said it stayed fresher longer."

"Then I guess it's okay to bathe this in it," he said, twisting and showing me his left arm.

I gasped. I couldn't help it. I'd half convinced myself that last night's incident with the pine light had been a nightmare. But the reddened, crusted, blistered skin on Creighton's arm said otherwise.

"We've got to get you to a doctor," I said.

"It's all right, Mac. Doesn't really hurt. Just feels hot."

He sank it past his elbow into the cool cedar water.

"Now *that* feels good!"

I looked around. The sun shone from a cloudless sky. We'd have no trouble finding our way out of here this morning. I stared out over the pond. Water. The sandy floor of the Pine Barrens was like a giant sponge that absorbed a high percentage of the rain that fell on it. It was the largest untapped aquifer in the Northeast. No rivers flowed into the Pinelands, only out. The water here was glacial in its purity. I'd read somewhere that the Barrens held an amount of water equivalent to a lake with a surface area of a thousand square miles and an average depth of seventy-five feet.

This little piece of wetness here was less that fifty yards across. I watched the ducks. They were quacking peacefully, tooling around, dipping their heads. Then one of them made a different sound, more like a squawk. It flapped its wings once and was gone. It happened in the blink of an eye. One second a floating duck, next second some floating bubbles.

"Did you see that?" Creighton said.

"Yeah, I did."

"What happened to that duck?" I could see the excitement starting to glow in his eyes. "What's it mean?"

"It means a snapping turtle. A big one. Fifty pounds or better, I'm sure."

Creighton pulled his arm from the pond.

"I do believe I've soaked this enough for now."

He dipped a towel in the water and wrapped it around his scorched arm.

We walked back to the bedrolls, packed up our gear, and made our way through the brush to the Wrangler.

The jeep was occupied.

There were people inside, and people sitting on the hood and standing on the bumpers as well. A good half-dozen in all.

Only they weren't like any people I'd ever seen.

They were dressed like typical Pineys, but dirty, raggedy. The four men in jeans or canvas pants, collared shirts of various fabrics and colors or plain white T-shirts; the two women wore cotton jumpers. But they were all deformed. Their heads were odd shapes and sizes, some way too small, others large and lopsided with bulbous protrusions. The eyes on a couple weren't lined up on the level. Everyone seemed to have one arm or leg longer than the other. Their teeth, at least in the ones who still had any, seemed to have come in at random angles.

When they spotted us, they began jabbering and pointing our way. They left the Wrangler and surrounded us. It was an intimidating group.

"Is that your car?" a young man with a lopsided head said to me.

"No." I pointed to Creighton. "It's his."

"Is that your car?" he said to Creighton.

I guessed he didn't believe me.

"It's a jeep," Creighton said.

"Jeep! Jeep!" He laughed and kept repeating the word. The others around him took it up and chorused along.

I looked at Creighton and shrugged. We'd apparently come upon an enclave of the type of folks who'd helped turn "Piney" into a term of derision shortly before World War I. That was when Elizabeth Kite published a report titled *The Pineys* that was sensationalized by the press and led to the view that the Pinelands was a bed of alcoholism, illiteracy, degeneracy, incest, and resultant "feeblemindedness."

Unfair and untrue. But not entirely false. There has always been illiteracy and alcoholism deep in the Pinelands. Schooling here tended to be rudimentary if at all. And as for drinking? The first "drive-thru" service originated before the Revolution in the Piney jug taverns, allowing customers to ride up to a window, get their jugs topped off with applejack, pay, and move on without ever dismounting. But after the economy of the Pine Barrens faltered, and most of the workers moved on to greener pastures, much of the social structure collapsed. Those who stayed on grew a little lax as to the whys, hows, and to-whoms of marriage. The results were inevitable.

All that had supposedly changed in modern times, except in the most isolated area of the Pines. We had stumbled upon one of those areas. Except that the deformities here were extraordinary. I'd seen a few of the inbreds in my youth. There'd been something subtly odd about them, but nothing that terribly startling. These folk would stop you in your tracks.

"Let's head for the jeep while they're yucking it up," I said out of the corner of my mouth.

"No. Wait. This is fascinating. Besides, we need their help."

He spoke to the group as a whole and asked their aid in freeing the jeep.

Somebody said, "Sugar sand," and this was repeated all around. But they willingly set their shoulders against the Wrangler and we were on hard ground again in minutes.

"Where do you live?" Creighton said to anyone who was listening.

Someone said, "Town," and as one they all pointed east, toward the sun. It was also the direction the lights had been headed last night.

"Will you show me?"

They nodded and jabbered and tugged on our sleeves, anxious to show us.

"Really, Jon," I said. "We should get you to—"

"My arm can wait. This won't take long."

We followed the group in a generally uphill direction along a circuitous footpath unnavigable by any vehicle other than a motorcycle. The trees thickened, and soon we were in shade. And then those trees opened up and we were in their "town."

A haze of blue woodsmoke hung over a ramshackle collection of shanties made of scrap lumber and sheet metal. Garbage everywhere, and everyone coming out to look at the strangers. I'd never seen such squalor.

The fellow with the lopsided head who'd asked about the jeep pulled Creighton toward one of the shacks.

"Hey, mister, you know about machines. How come this don't work?"

He had on old TV set inside his one-room hut. He turned the knobs back and forth.

"Don't work. No pictures."

"You need electricity," Creighton told him.

"Got it. Got it. Got it."

He led us around to the back to show us the length of wire he had strung from a tree to the roof of the shack.

Creighton turned to me with stricken eyes.

"This is awful. No one should have to live like this. Can we do anything for them?"

His compassion surprised me. I'd never thought there was room for anyone else's concerns in his self-absorbed life. But then, Jonathan Creighton had always been a mother lode of surprises.

"Not much. They all look pretty content to me. Seem to have their own little community. If you bring them to the government's attention, they'll be split up and most of them will probably be placed in institutions or group homes. I guess the best you can do is give them whatever you can think of to make the living easier here."

Creighton nodded, still staring around him.

"Speaking of 'here,' " he said, unshouldering his knapsack, "let's find out where we are."

The misshapen locals stared in frank awe and admiration as he took his readings. Someone asked him, "What is that thing?" a hundred times. At least. Another asked, "What happened to your arm?" an equal number of times. Creighton was heroically patient with everyone. He knelt on the ground to transfer his readings to the map, then looked up at me.

"Know where we are?"

"The other side of Razorback Hill, I'd say."

"You got it."

He stood up and gathered the locals around him.

"I'm looking for a special place around here," he said.

Most of them nodded eagerly. Someone said, "We know every place there is around here, I reckon."

"Good. I'm looking for a place where nothing grows. Do you know a place like that?"

It was as if all these people had a common plug and Creighton had just pulled it. The lights went out, the shades came down, the "Open" signs flipped to "Closed." They began to turn away.

"What'd I say?" he said, turning his anxious, bewildered eyes on me. "What'd I *say*?"

"You're starting to sound like Ray Charles," I told him. "Obviously they want nothing to do with this 'place where nothing grows' you're talking about. What's this all about, Jon?"

He ignored my question and laid his good hand on the shoulder of one of the small-headed men.

"Won't you take me there if you know where it is?"

"We know where it is," the fellow said in a squeaky voice. "But we never go there so we can't take you there. How can we take you there if we never go there?"

"You *never* go there? Why not?"

The others had stopped and were listening to the exchange. The small-headed fellow looked around at his neighbors and gave them a look that asked how stupid could anyone be? Then he turned back to Creighton.

"We don't go there 'cause nobody goes there."

"What's your name?" Creighton said.

"Fred."

"Fred, my name is Jon, and I'll give you. . . ." He patted his pockets, then tore the watch off his wrist. "I'll give you this beautiful watch that you don't have to wind—see how the numbers change with every second?—if you'll take me to a place where you *do* go and point out the place where nothing grows. How's that sound?"

Fred took the watch and held it up close to his right eye, then smiled.

"Come on! I'll show you!"

Creighton took off after Fred, and I took off after Creighton.

Again we were led along a circuitous path, this one even narrower than before, becoming less well defined as we went along. I noticed the trees becoming fewer in number and more stunted and gnarled, and the underbrush thinning out, the leaves curled on their edges. We followed Fred until he halted as abruptly as if he had run into an invisible wall. I saw why: the footpath we'd been following stopped here. He pointed ahead through what was left of the trees and underbrush.

"The bald spot's over yonder atop that there rise."

He turned and hurried back along the path.

Bald spot?

Creighton looked at me, then shrugged.

"Got your machete handy, Mac?"

"No, Bwana."

"Too bad. I guess we'll just have to bull our way through."

He rewrapped his burned arm and pushed ahead. It wasn't such rough going. The underbrush thinned out quickly, and so we had an easier time of it than I'd anticipated. Soon we broke into a small field lined with scrappy weeds and occupied by the scattered, painfully gnarled trunks of dead trees. And in the center of the field was a patch of bare sand.

. . . a place where nothing grows . . .

Creighton hurried ahead. I held back, restrained by a sense of foreboding. The same something deep within me that had feared the pine lights feared this place as well. Something was wrong here, as if Nature had been careless, had made a mistake in this place and had never quite been able to rectify it. As if . . .

What was I thinking? It was an empty field. No eerie lights buzzing through the sky. No birds, either, for that matter. So what? The sun was up, a breeze was blowing—or at least it had been a moment ago.

Overruling my instincts, I followed Creighton. I touched the tortured trunk of one of the dead trees as I passed. It was hard and cold, like stone. A petrified tree. In the Pinelands.

I hurried ahead and caught up to Creighton at the edge of the "bald spot." He was staring at it as if in a trance. The spot was a rough oval, maybe thirty feet across. Nothing grew in that oval. Nothing.

"Look at that pristine sand," he said in a whisper. "Birds don't fly over it, insects and animals don't walk on it. Only the wind touches and shapes it. That's the way sand looked at the beginning of time."

It had always been my impression that sand wasn't yet sand at the beginning of time, but I didn't argue with him. He was on a roll. I remembered from college: you don't stop Crazy Creighton when he's on a roll.

I saw what he meant, though. The sand was rippled like water, like sand must look in areas of the Sahara far off the trade routes. I saw animal tracks leading up to it and then turning aside. Creighton was right: nothing trod this soil.

Except Creighton.

Without warning he stepped across the invisible line and walked to the center of the bald spot. He spread his arms, looked up at the sky, and whirled in dizzying circles. His eyes were aglow, his expression rapturous. He looked stoned out of his mind.

"This is it! I've found it! This is the place!"

"*What* place, Jon?"

I stood at the edge of the spot, unwilling to cross over, talking in the flat tone you might use to coax a druggie back from a bad trip, or a jumper down from a ledge.

"Where it all comes together and all comes apart! Where the Truth is revealed!"

"What the hell are you talking about, Jon?"

I was tired and uneasy and I wanted to go home. I'd had enough, and I guessed my voice showed it. The rapture faded. Abruptly, he was sober.

"Nothing, Mac. Nothing. Just let me take a few readings and we're out of here."

"That's the best news I've heard this morning."

He shot me a quick glance. I didn't know if it conveyed annoyance or disappointment. And I didn't care.

8. SPREADING INFECTION

I got us back to a paved road without too much difficulty. We spoke little on the way home. He dropped me off at my house and promised to see a doctor before the day was out.

"What's next for you?" I said as I closed the passenger door and looked at him through the open window.

I hoped he wouldn't ask me to guide him back into the Pines again. I was sure he hadn't been straight with me about his research. I didn't know what he was after, but I knew it wasn't the Jersey Devil. A part of me said it was better not to know, that this man was a juggernaut on a date with disaster.

"I'm not sure. I may go back and see those people, the ones on the far side of Razorback Hill. Maybe bring them some clothing, some food."

Against my will, I was touched.

"That would be nice. Just don't bring them toaster cakes or micro-wave dinners."

He laughed. "I won't."

"Where are you staying?"

He hesitated, looking uncertain.

"A place called the Laurelton Circle Motor Inn."

"I know it."

A tiny place. Sporting the name of a traffic circle that no longer existed.

"I'm staying in room five if you need to get hold of me but . . . can you do me a favor? If anybody comes looking for me, don't tell them where I am. Don't tell them you've even seen me."

"Are you in some sort of trouble."

"A misunderstanding, that's all."

"You wouldn't want to elaborate on that, would you?"

His expression was bleak.

"The less you know, Mac, the better."

"Like everything else these past two days, right?"

He shrugged. "Sorry."

"Me, too. Look. Stop by before you head back to Razorback. I may have a few old things I can donate to those folks."

He waved with his burnt hand, and then he was off.

Creighton stopped by a few days later on his way back to Razorback Hill. His left arm was heavily bandaged in gauze.

"You were right," he said. "It got infected."

I gave him some old sweaters and shirts and a couple of pairs of jeans that no longer fit the way they should.

A few days later I bumped into him in the housewares aisle at Pathmark. He'd picked up some canned goods and was buying a couple of can openers for the Razorback folks. His left arm was bandaged as before, but I was concerned to see that there was gauze on his right hand now.

"The infection spread a little, but the doctor says it's okay. He's got me on this new antibiotic. Sure to kill it off."

Looking more closely now in the supermarket's fluorescent glare, I saw that he was pale and sweaty. He seemed to have lost weight.

"Who's your doctor?"

"Guy up in Neptune. A specialist."

"In pine light burns?"

His laugh was a bit too loud, a tad too long.

"No! Infections."

I wondered. But Jon Creighton was a big boy now. I couldn't be his mother.

I picked out some canned goods myself, checked out behind Creighton, and gave the bagful to him.

"Give them my best," I told him.

He smiled wanly and hurried off.

At the very tail end of August I was driving down Brick Boulevard when I spotted his Wrangler idling at the Burger King drive-thru window. I pulled into the lot and walked over.

"Jon!" I said through the window and saw him jump.

"Oh, Mac. Don't ever do that!"

He looked relieved, but he didn't look terribly glad to see me. His face seemed thinner, but maybe that was because of the beard he had started to grow. A fugitive's beard.

"Sorry," I said. "I was wondering if you wanted to get together for some *real* lunch."

"Oh. Well. Thanks, but I've got a lot of errands to run. Maybe some other time."

Despite the heat, he was wearing corduroy pants and a long-sleeved flannel shirt. I noticed that both his hands were still wrapped in gauze. An alarm went off inside me.

"Isn't that infection cleared up yet?"

"It's coming along slowly, but it's coming."

I glanced down at his feet and noticed that his ankles looked thick. His sneakers were unlaced, their tongues lolling out as the sides stretched out to accommodate his swollen feet.

"What happened to your feet?"

"A little edema. Side effect of the medicine. Look, Mac, I've got to run." He threw the Wrangler into gear. "I'll call you soon."

It was a couple of weeks after Labor Day, and I'd been thinking about Creighton a lot. I was worried about him, and was realizing that I still harbored deeper feelings for him than I cared to admit.

Then the state trooper showed up at my office. He was big and intimidating behind his dark glasses; his haircut came within a millimeter of complete baldness. He held out a grainy photo of Jon Creighton.

"Do you know this man?" he said in a deep voice.

My mouth was dry as I wondered if he was going to ask me if I was involved in whatever Creighton had done; or worse: if I'd care to come down and identify the body.

"Sure. We went to college together."

"Have you seen him in the past month."

I didn't hesitate. I did the stand-up thing.

"Nope. Not since graduation."

"We have reason to believe he's in the area. If you see him, contact the State Police or your local police immediately."

"What's he done, Officer?"

He turned and started toward the door without deigning to answer. That brand of arrogance never failed to set something off in me.

"I asked you a question, *Officer*. I expect the courtesy of a reply."

He turned and looked at me, then shrugged. Some of the Dirty Harry facade slipped away with the shrug.

"Why not?" he said. "He's wanted for grand theft."

Oh, great.

"What did he steal?"

"A book."

"A *book*?"

"Yeah. Would you believe it? We've got rapes and murders and armed robberies, but this book is given a priority. I don't care how valuable it is or how much some university in Massachusetts wants it, it's only a book. But the Massachusetts people are really hot to get it back. Their governor got to our governor and . . . well, you know how it goes. We found his car abandoned out near Lakehurst a while back, so we know he's been through here."

"You think he's on foot?"

"Maybe. Or maybe he rented or stole another car. We're running it down now."

"If he shows up, I'll let you know."

"Do that. I get the impression that if he gives the book back in one piece, all will be forgiven."

"I'll tell him that if I get the chance."

As soon as he was gone, I got on the phone to Creighton's motel. His voice was thick when he said hello.

"Jon! The state cops were just here looking for you!"

He mumbled a few words I didn't understand. Something was wrong. I hung up and headed for my car.

There are only about twenty rooms in that particular motel. I spotted the Wrangler backed into a space at the far end of the tiny parking lot. Number five was on a corner of the first floor. A DO NOT DISTURB sign hung from the knob. I knocked on the door twice and got no answer. I tried the knob. It turned.

It was dark inside except for the daylight I'd let in. And that light revealed a disaster area. The room looked like the inside of a Dumpster behind a block of fast-food stores. Smelled like one, too. There were pizza boxes, hamburger wrappers, submarine sleeves, Chinese food cartons, a sampling from every place in the area that delivered. And it was hot. Either the air conditioner had quit, or it hadn't been turned on.

"Jon?" I flipped on the light. "Jon, are you here?"

He was in a chair in a corner on the far side of the bed, huddled under a pile of blankets. Papers and maps were stacked on the night table beside him. His face, where visible above his matted beard, was pale and drawn. He looked as if he'd lost thirty pounds. I slammed the door closed and stood there, stunned.

"My God, Jon, what's wrong?"

"Nothing. I'm fine." His hoarse, thick voice said otherwise. "What are you doing here, Mac?"

"I came to tell you that the State Police are cruising around with photos of you, but I can see that's the least of your problems! You're really sick!" I reached for the phone. "I'm calling an ambulance."

"*No!* Mac, please *don't!*"

The terror and soul-wrenching anguish in his voice stopped me. I stared at him but still kept a grip on the receiver.

"Why not?"

"Because I'm begging you not to!"

"But you're sick, you could be dying, you're out of your head!"

"No. That's one thing I'm not. Trust me when I say that no hospital in the world can help me—because I'm not dying. And if you ever loved me, if you ever had any regard for who I am and what I want from my life, then you'll put down that phone and walk out that door."

I stood there in the hot, humid squalor of that tiny room, receiver in hand, smelling the garbage, detecting the hint of another odor, a subtle sour foulness that underlay the others, and felt myself being torn apart by the choice that faced me.

"Please, Mac," he said. "You're the only person in the world who'll understand. Don't hand me over to strangers." He sobbed once. "I can't fight you. I can only beg you. Please. Put down the phone and leave."

It was the sob that did it. I slammed the receiver onto its cradle.

"Damn you!"

"Two days, Mac. In two days I'll be better. You wait and see."

"You're damn right I'll see—I'm staying here with you!"

"No! You can't! You have no right to intrude! This is *my* life! You've got to let me take it where I must! Now leave, Mac. Please."

He was right, of course. This was what we'd been all about when we'd been together. I had to back off. And it was killing me.

"All right," I said around the lump in my throat. "You win. See you in two days."

Without waiting for a reply, I opened the door and stepped out into the bright September sunlight.

"Thanks, Mac," he said. "I love you."

I didn't want to hear that. I took one last look back as I pulled the door closed. He was still swaddled from his neck to the floor in the blankets, but in the last instant before the door shut him from view, I thought I saw something white and pointed, about the circumference of a garden hose, snake out on the carpet from under the blankets and then quickly pull back under cover.

A rush of nausea slammed me against the outer wall of the motel as the door clicked closed. I leaned there, sick and dizzy, trying to catch my breath.

A trick of the light. That was what I told myself as the vertigo faded. I'd been squinting in the brightness and the light had played a trick.

Of course, I didn't have to settle for merely telling myself. I could simply open the door and check it out. I actually reached for the knob, but couldn't bring myself to turn it.

Two days. Creighton had said two days. I'd find out then.

But I didn't last two days. I was unable to concentrate the following morning and wound up canceling all my appointments. I spent the entire day pacing my office or my living room; and when I wasn't pacing, I was on the phone. I called the American Folklore Society and the New Jersey Historical Society. Not only had they not given Creighton the grants he'd told me about, they'd never heard of him.

By nightfall I'd taken all I could. I began calling Creighton's room. I got no answer. I tried a few more times, but when he still hadn't picked up by eleven o'clock, I headed for the motel.

I was almost relieved to see the Wrangler gone from the parking lot. Room five was still unlocked and still a garbage dump, which meant he was still renting it—or hadn't been gone too long.

What was he up to?

I began to search the room. I found the book under the bed. It was huge, heavy, wrapped in plastic with a scrawled note taped to the front:

Please return to Miskatonic U. archives

I slipped it out of the plastic. It was leather-bound and handwritten in Latin. I could barely decipher the title—something like *Liben Damnatus*. But inside the front cover were Creighton's maps and a sheaf of notes in his back-slanted scrawl. The notes were in disarray and probably would have been disjointed even if arranged in proper order. But certain words and phrases kept recurring: *nexus point* and *equinox* and *the lumens* and *the veil*.

It took me a while, but eventually I got the drift of the jottings. Apparently a section of the book Creighton had stolen concerned "nexus points" around the globe where twice a year at the vernal and autumnal equinoxes "the veil" that obscures reality becomes detached for a short while, allowing an intrepid soul to peek under the hem and see the true nature of the world around us, the world we are not "allowed" to see. These "nexus points" are few and widely scattered. Of the four known, there's one near each pole, one in Tibet, and one near the east coast of North America.

I sighed. Crazy Creighton had really started living up to his name. It was sad. This was so unlike him. He'd been the ultimate cynic, and now he was risking his health and his freedom pursuing this mystical garbage.

And what was even sadder was how he had lied to me. Obviously he hadn't been searching for tales of the Jersey Devil—he'd been searching for one of these "nexus points." And he was probably convinced he'd found one behind Razorback Hill.

I pitied him. But I read on.

According to the notes, these "nexus points" can be located by following "the lumens" to a place shunned equally by man, beast, and vegetation.

Suddenly I was uneasy. "The lumens." Could that refer to the pine lights? And the "bald spot" that Fred had showed us—that was certainly a place shunned by man, beast, and vegetation.

I found a whole sheet filled with notes about the Razorback folk. The last paragraph was especially upsetting:

> The folks behind Razorback Hill aren't deformed from inbreeding, although I'm sure that's contributed its share. I believe they're misshapen as a result of living near the nexus point for generations. The semi-annual lifting of the veil must have caused genetic damage over the years.

I pulled out Creighton's maps and unfolded them on the bed. I followed the lines he had drawn from Apple Pie Hill, from Gus's firing place, and from our campsite. All three lines represented paths of pine lights, and all three intersected at a spot near the circle he had drawn and labeled as Razorback Hill. And right near the intersection of the pine lights paths, almost on top of it, he had drawn another circle, a tiny one, penciled in the latitude and longitude, and labeled it Nexus!

I was worried now. Even my own skepticism was beginning to waver. Everything was fitting too neatly. I looked at my watch. Eleven thirty-two. The date read "21." September 21. When was the equinox? I grabbed the phone and called an old clam-digger who'd been a client since I'd opened my office. He knew the answer right off: "The autumnal equinox. That's September twenty-second. 'Bout a half hour from now."

I dropped the phone and ran for my car. I knew exactly where to find Jon Creighton.

9. THE HEM OF THE VEIL

I raced down the Parkway to the Bass River exit and tried to find my way back to Gus Sooy's place. What had been a difficult trip in the day proved to be several orders of magnitude more difficult in the dark. But I managed to find Gus's red cedar. It was my plan to convince him to show me a short way to the far side of Razorback Hill, figuring the fact that Creighton was already there might make him more tractable. But when I rushed up to Gus Sooy's clearing, I discovered that he wasn't alone.

The Razorback folk were there. All of them, from the looks of the crowd.

"What do you want?"

Before I could answer, the Razorback folks recognized me and a small horde of them crowded around.

"Why are they all here?" I asked Gus.

"Just visiting," he said casually, but did not look me in the eye.

"It wouldn't have anything to do with what's happening at the bald spot on the other side of Razorback Hill, would it?"

"Damn you! You've been snoopin' around, haven't you? You and your friend. They told me he was coming around, askin' all sorts of questions. Where's he now? Hidin' in the bushes?"

"He's over there," I said, pointing to the top of Razorback Hill. "And if my guess is correct, he's standing right in the middle of the bald spot."

Gus dropped his jug. It shattered on the boards of his front step.

"Do you know what'll happen to him?"

"No," I said. "Do you?" I looked around at the Razorback folk. "Do they?"

"I don't think anyone knows, leastmost them. But they're scared. They come here twice a year, when that bald spot starts acting up."

"Have you ever seen what happens there?"

"Once. Never want to see it again."

"Why haven't you ever told anyone?"

"What? And bring all sorts of pointyheads here to look and gawk and build and ruin the place. We'd all rather put up with the bald spot craziness twice a year than pointyhead craziness every day all year long."

I didn't have time to get into Creighton's theory that the bald spot was genetically damaging the Razorback folks. I had to find Creighton.

"How do I get there? What's the fastest way?"

"You can't—"

"*They* got here!" I pointed to the Razorback folks.

"All right!" he said with open hostility. "Suit yourself. There's a trail behind my cabin here. Follow it over the left flank of the hill."

"And then?"

"And then you won't need any directions. You'll know where to go."

His words had an ominous ring, but I couldn't press him. I was being propelled by a sense of enormous urgency. Time was running out. Quickly. I already had my flashlight, so I hurried to the rear of his shanty and followed the trail.

Gus was right. As I crossed the flank of the hill I saw flashes through the trees ahead, like lightning, as if a very tiny and very violent electrical storm had been brought to ground and anchored there. I increased my pace, running when the terrain would allow. The wind picked up as I neared the storm area, growing from a fitful breeze to a full-scale gale by the time I broke through the brush and stumbled into the clearing that surrounded the bald spot.

Chaos. That's the only way I can describe it. A nightmare of cascading lights and roaring wind. The pine lights—or *lumens*—were there, hundreds of them, all sizes, unaffected by the rushing vortex of air as they swirled about in wild arcs, each flaring brilliantly as it looped through the space above the bald spot. And the bald spot itself—it glowed with a faint purplish light that reached thirty or forty feet into the air before fading into the night.

The stolen book, Creighton's notes—they weren't mystical madness. Something cataclysmic was happening here, something that defied all the laws of nature—if indeed those laws had any real meaning. Whether this was one of the nexus points he had described, a fleeting rent in the reality that surrounded us, only Creighton could say for sure right now.

For I could see someone in the bald spot. I couldn't make out his features from where I was, but I knew it was Jonathan Creighton.

I dashed forward until I reached the edge but slowed to a halt in the sand before actually crossing into the glow. Creighton was there, on his knees, his hands and feet buried in the sand. He was staring about him, his expression an uneasy mix of fear and wonder. I shouted his name, but he didn't hear me above the roar of the wind. Twice he looked directly at me, but despite my frantic shouting and waving, did not see me.

I saw no other choice. I had to step onto the bald spot . . . the nexus point. It wasn't easy. Every instinct I possessed screamed at me to run in the other direction, but I couldn't leave him there like that. He looked helpless, trapped like an insect on flypaper. I had to help him.

Taking a deep breath, I closed my eyes and stepped across—and began to stumble forward. Up and down seemed to have a slightly different orientation here. I opened my eyes and dropped to my knees, nearly landing on Creighton. I looked around and froze.

The Pine Barrens were gone. *Night* was gone. It seemed to be predawn or dusk here, but the wind still howled about us and the pine lights flashed around us, appearing and disappearing above as though passing through invisible walls. We were someplace . . . *else:* on a huge misty plain that seemed to stretch on forever, interrupted only by clumps of vegetation and huge fog banks, one of which was nearby on my left and seemed to go on and up forever. Off in the immeasurable distance, mountains the size of the moon reached up and disappeared into the haze of the purple sky. The horizon—or what I imagined to be the horizon—didn't curve as it should. This place seemed so much *bigger* than the world—our world—that waited just a few feet away.

"My God, Jon, where are we!"

He started and turned his head. His hands and feet remained buried in the sand. His eyes went wide with shock at the sight of me.

"No! You shouldn't be here!"

His voice was thicker and more distorted than yesterday. Oddly enough, his pale skin looked almost healthy in the mauve light.

"Neither should you!"

I heard something then. Above the shriek of the wind came another sound. A rumble like an avalanche. It came from somewhere within the fog bank to our left. There was something massive, something immense, moving about in there, and the fog seemed to be drifting this way.

"We've got to get out of here, Jon!"

"No! I'm staying!"

"No way! Come on!"

He was racked with infection and obviously deranged. I didn't care what he said, I wasn't going to let him risk his life in this place. I'd get him out of here and let him think about it for six months. *Then* if he still wanted to try this, it would be his choice. But he wasn't competent now.

I looped my arms around his chest and tried to pull him to his feet.

"Mac, please! Don't!"

His hands remained fixed in the sand. He must have been holding on to something. I grabbed his right elbow and yanked. He screamed as his hand pulled free of the sand. Then I screamed, too, and let him go and threw myself back on the sand away from him.

Because his hand wasn't a hand anymore.

It was big and white and had these long, ropey, tapered, rootlike projections, something like an eye on a potato when it sprouts after being left under the sink too long, only these things were moving, twisting and writhing like a handful of albino snakes.

"Go, Mac!" he said in that distorted voice, and I could tell from his face and eyes that he hadn't wanted me to see him like this. "You don't belong here!"

"And you do?"

"*Now* I do!"

I couldn't bring myself to touch his hand, so I reached forward and grabbed some of his shirt. I pulled.

"We can find doctors! They can fix you! You can—"

"*NO!*"

It was a shout and it was something else. Something long and white and hard as flexed muscle, much like the things protruding from his shirtsleeve, darted out of his mouth and slammed against my chest, bruising my breasts as it thrust me away. Then it whipped back into his mouth.

I snapped then. I scrambled to my feet and blindly lurched away in the direction I'd come. Suddenly I was back in the Pine Barrens, in the cool night with the lights swirling madly above my head. I stumbled for the bushes, away from the nexus point, away from Jonathan Creighton.

At the edge of the clearing, I forced myself to stop and look back. I saw Creighton. His awful transformed hand was raised. I knew he couldn't see me, but it was almost as if he was waving good-bye. Then he lowered his hand and worked the tendrils back into the sand.

The last thing I remember of that night is vomiting.

10. AFTERMATH

I awoke among the Razorback folk who'd found me the next morning and watched over me until I was conscious and lucid again. They offered me food, but I couldn't eat. I walked back up to the clearing, to the bald spot.

It looked exactly as it had when Creighton and I had first seen it in August. No lights, no wind, no purple glow. Just bare sand.

And no Jonathan Creighton.

I could have convinced myself that last night had never happened if not for the swollen, tender, violet bruise on my chest. Would that I had. But as much as my mind shrank from it, I could not deny the truth. I'd seen the other side of the veil, and my life would never be the same.

I looked around and knew that everything I saw was a sham, an elaborate illusion. Why? Why was the veil there? To protect us from harm? Or to shield us from madness? The truth had brought me no peace. Who could find comfort in the knowledge that huge immeasurable forces beyond our comprehension were out there, moving about us, beyond the reach of our senses?

I wanted to run . . . but where?

I ran home. I've been home for months now. Housebound. Moving beyond my door only for groceries. My accounting clients have all left me. I'm living on my savings, learning Latin, translating Jon's stolen book. Was what I saw the true reality of our existence, or another dimension, or what? I don't know. Creighton was right: knowing that you don't know is maddening. It consumes you.

So I'm waiting for spring. Waiting for the vernal equinox. Maybe I'll leave the house before then and hunt up some pine lights—or *lumens*, as the book calls them. Maybe I'll touch one, maybe I won't. Maybe when the equinox comes, I'll return to Razorback Hill, to the bald spot. Maybe I'll look for Jon. He may be there, he may not. I may cross into the bald spot, I may not. And if I do, I may not come back. Or I may.

I don't know what I'll do. I don't know anything anymore. I've come to the point now where I'm sure of only one thing: nothing is sure anymore.

At least on this side of the veil.

Pickman's Modem

LAWRENCE WATT-EVANS

I hadn't seen Pickman on-line for some time; I thought he'd given up on the computer nets. You can waste hours every day reading and posting messages, if you aren't careful, and the damn things are addictive; they can take up your entire life if you aren't careful. The nets will eat you alive if you let them.

Some people just go cold turkey when they realize what's happening, and I thought that was what had happened to Henry Pickman, so I was pleased and surprised when I saw the heading scroll across my monitor screen, stating that the next post had originated from his machine. Henry Pickman was no Einstein or Shakespeare, but his comments were usually entertaining, in an oafish sort of way. I had rather missed them during his absence.

"From the depths I return and greet you all," I read. "My sincerest apologies for any inconvenience that my withdrawal might have occasioned."

That didn't sound at *all* like the Henry Pickman I knew; surprised, I read on, through three screens describing, with flawless spelling and mordant wit, the trials and tribulations of the breakdown of his old modem, and the acquisition of a new one. Lack of funds had driven him to desperate measures, but at last, by judicious haggling and trading, he had made himself the proud owner of a rather battered, but functional, 2400-baud external modem. The case proclaimed it to be a product of Miskatonic Data Systems, of Arkham, Massachusetts, and Pickman inquired innocently whether anyone in the net was familiar with that particular manufacturer.

I posted a brief congratulatory reply, denying any such knowledge, and read on.

When I browsed the message base the next day I found three messages from Pickman, each a small gem of sardonic commentary. I marveled at the improvement in Pickman's writing—in fact, I wondered whether it was really Henry Pickman at all, and not someone else using his account.

It was the day after that, the third day, that the flamewar began.

For those unfamiliar with computer networks, let me explain that in on-line conversation, the normal social restraints on conversation don't always work; as a result, minor disagreements can flare up into towering great arguments, with thousands of words of invective hurled back and forth along the phone lines. Emotions can run very high indeed. The delay in the system means that a retraction or an apology often arrives too late to stop the war of words from raging out of control.

These little debates are known as "flamewars."

And Pickman's introductory message had triggered one. Some reader in Kansas City had taken offense at a supposed slur on the Midwest, and launched a flaming missive in Pickman's direction.

By the time I logged on and saw it, Pickman had already replied, some fifty messages or so down the bitstream, and had replied with blistering sarcasm and a vituperative tone quite unlike the rather laid-back Pickman I remembered. His English had improved, but his temper clearly had not.

I decided to stay out of this particular feud. I merely watched as, day after day, the messages flew back and forth, growing ever more bitter and vile. Pickman's entries, in particular, were remarkable in their viciousness and in the incredible imagination displayed in his descriptions of his opponents. I wondered, more than ever, how this person could be little Henry Pickman, he of the sloppy grin and sloppier typing.

Within four or five days, both sides were accusing the other of deliberate misquotation, and I began to wonder if perhaps something even stranger than a borrowed account might not be happening.

I decided that drastic action was called for; I would drop in on Henry Pickman in person, uninvited, and talk matters over with him—*talk*, with our mouths, rather than type. Not at a net party, or a convention, but simply at his home. Accordingly, that Saturday afternoon found me on his doorstep, my finger on the bell.

"Yeah?" he said, opening the door. "Who is it?" He blinked up at me through thick glasses.

"Hi, Henry," I said. "It's me, George Polushkin—we met at the net party at Schoonercon."

"Oh, yeah!" he said, enlightenment dawning visibly on his face.

"May I come in?" I asked.

Fifteen minutes later, after a few uncomfortable silences and various mumbled pleasantries, we were both sitting in his living room, open cans of beer at hand, and he asked, "So, why'd you come, George? I mean, I wasn't, y'know, *expecting* you."

"Well," I said, "it was good to see you back on the net, Henry. . . ." I hesitated, unsure how to continue.

"You're pissed about the flamewar, huh?" He grinned apologetically.

"Well, yes," I admitted.

"Me, too," he said, to my surprise. "I don't understand what those guys are doing. I mean, they're *lying* about me, George, saying I said stuff that I didn't."

"You said that on-line," I said, "but I hadn't noticed any mis-quotations."

His mouth fell open and he stared at me, goggle-eyed. "But, George," he said, "*look* at it!"

"I *have* looked, Henry," I said. "I didn't see any. They were using quoting software; they'd have to retype it to change what you wrote. Why would anyone bother to do that? Why should they change what you said?"

"I *don't know*, George, but they *did*!" He read the disbelief in my face, and said, "Come on, I'll show you! I logged everything!"

I followed him to his computer room—a spare bedroom upstairs held a battered IBM PC/AT and an assortment of other equipment, occupying a secondhand desk and several shelves. Printouts and soft-ware manuals were stacked knee-deep on all sides. A black box, red lights glowering ominously from its front panel, was perched atop his monitor screen.

I stood nearby, peering over his shoulder, as he booted up his com-puter and loaded a log file into his text editor. Familiar messages appeared on the screen.

"Look at this," Henry said. "I got this one yesterday."

I had read this note previously; it consisted of a long quoted passage that suggested, in elaborate and revolting detail, unnatural acts that the recipient should perform, with explanations of why, given the recipient's ancestry and demonstrated proclivities, each was appro-priate. The anatomical descriptions were thoroughly stomach-turning, but probably, so far as I could tell, accurate—no obvious impossibili-ties were involved.

The amount of fluid seemed a bit excessive, perhaps.

To this quoted passage, the sender had appended only the comment, "I can't believe you said that, Pickman."

"So?" I said.

"So, I *didn't* say that," Pickman said. "Of course I didn't!"

"But I read it. . . ," I began.

"Not from *me*, you didn't!"

I frowned, and pointed out, "That quote has a date on it—I mean, when you supposedly sent it. And it was addressed to Pete Gifford. You didn't send him that message?"

"I posted a message to him that day, yeah, but it wasn't anything like *that*!"

"Do you have it logged?"

"Sure."

He called up a window showing another file, scrolled through it, and showed me.

"PETE," the message read, "WHY DO'NT YUO GO F*CK YUORSELF THREE WAYS ANYWAY."

I read that, then looked at the other message, still on the main screen.

Three ways. One, two, three. In graphic detail.

I pointed this out.

"Yeah," Pickman said, "I guess that's where they got the idea, but I think it's pretty disgusting, writing something that gross and then blaming me for it."

"You really didn't write it?" I stared at the screen.

The message in the window was much more the old Henry Pickman style, but the other, longer one was what I remembered reading on my own machine.

"Let's look at some others," I suggested.

So we looked.

We found that very first message, which I had read as beginning, "From the depths I return and greet you all. My sincerest apologies for any inconvenience that my withdrawal might have occasioned."

Pickman's log showed that he had posted, "BAck from the pits—hi, Guys! Sorry I wuz gone, didja miss Me?"

"Someone," I said, "has been rewriting every word you've sent out since you got your new modem."

"That's silly," he said. I nodded.

"Silly," I said, "but true."

"How *could* anyone do that?" he asked, baffled.

I shrugged. "Someone is."

"Or something." He eyed the black box atop the monitor speculatively. "Maybe it's the modem," he said. "Maybe it's doing something weird."

I looked at the device; it was an oblong of black plastic, featureless save for the two red lights that shone balefully from the front and the small metal plate bolted to one side where incised letters spelled out MISKATONIC DATA SYSTEMS, ARKHAM MA, SERIAL #RILYEH.

"I never heard of Miskatonic Data Systems," I said. "Is there a customer-support number?"

He shrugged. "I got it secondhand," he said. "No documentation."

I considered the modem for several seconds and had the uneasy feeling it was staring back at me. It was those two red lights, I suppose. There was something seriously strange about that gadget, certainly. It buzzed; modems aren't supposed to buzz. Theories about miniature AI rambled through the back corridors of my brain; lower down were other theories I tried to ignore, theories about forces far more sinister. The brand name nagged at something, deep in my memory.

"It probably is the modem that's causing the trouble," I said. "Maybe you should get rid of it."

"But I can't *afford* another one!" he wailed.

I looked at him, then at the screen, where the two messages still glowed side by side in orange phosphor. I shrugged.

"Well, it's up to you," I said.

"It isn't really *dangerous*, anyway," he said, trying to convince himself. "It just rewrites my stuff, makes it better. More powerful, y'know."

"I suppose," I said dubiously.

"I just need to be more careful about what I say," he said, wheedling.

"You don't need to convince *me*," I said. "It's *your* decision."

We were both staring thoughtfully at the screen now.

"I've always wanted to write like that," he said. "But I just couldn't, you know, get the *hang* of it. All those rules and stuff, the spelling, and getting the words to sound good."

I nodded.

"You know," he said slowly, "I've heard that some magazines and stuff will take submissions by E-mail now."

"I've heard that," I agreed.

"You ready for another beer?"

And with that, the subject was closed; when I refused the offer of more beer, the visit, too, was at an end.

I never saw Pickman in the flesh again, but his messages were all over the nets in the subsequent weeks—messages that grew steadily stranger and more lurid. He spoke of submitting articles and stories, at first to the major markets, and then to others, ever more esoteric and bizarre. He posted long diatribes of stupendous fury and venom whenever a piece was rejected—the usual reason given was apparently that his new style was too florid and archaic.

Sometimes I worried about what he might be letting out into the net, but it wasn't really any of my business.

And then, after the last of April, though old messages continued to circulate for weeks, new ones no longer appeared. Henry Pickman was never heard from on the nets again, except once.

That once was netmail, a private message to me, sent at midnight on April 30.

"Goerge," it began—Henry never could spell—"I boroed another modem to log on, I could'nt trust it any more, but I think its angry with me now. Its watching me, I sware it is. I unplugged it, but its watching me any way. And I think its calling someone, I can hear it dieling.#$"

And then a burst of line noise; the rest of the message was garbage.

Line noise? Oh, that's when there's interference on the phone line, and the modem tries to interpret it as if it were a real signal. Except instead of words, you get nonsense. The rest of Henry's message was all stuff like "Iä! FThAGN!Iä!CTHulHu!"

I didn't hear anything from Henry after that. I didn't try to call him or anything; I figured it might all be a gag, and if it wasn't—well, if it wasn't, I didn't want to get involved.

So when I went past his place a couple of weeks later, I was just in the neighborhood by coincidence, you understand, I wasn't checking up on him. Anyway, his house was all boarded up, and it looked like there'd been a bad fire there.

I figured maybe the wiring in that cheap modem had been bad. I hoped no one had been hurt.

Yeah—bad wiring. That was probably it. Very bad.

After that, I sort of tapered off. Telecommunicating made me a bit uneasy; sometimes I almost thought my modem was watching me. So I don't use the nets anymore. Ever.

After all, as I've always said, the nets will eat you alive if you let them.

Shaft Number 247

BASIL COPPER

> The process of delving into the black abyss is to me the keenest
> form of fascination.
>
> —H. P. LOVECRAFT

Driscoll looked at the dial reflectively. The Control Room was silent
except for the distant thumping of the dynamos. The dim lights
gleamed reassuringly on the familiar faces of the instruments and on
the curved metal of the roof, its massive nuts and bolts and girders
holding back the tremendous weight of the earth above their heads.
The green luminous digits of the triangular clock on the bulkhead
pointed to midnight.

It was the quietest part of the Watch. Driscoll shifted to a more
comfortable position in his padded swivel armchair. He was a big man,
whose hair was going a little white at the edges, but his features were
still hard and firm, unblurred by time, though he must have been past
fifty.

He glanced across at Wainewright on the other side; he had the
earphones clamped over his head and was turning one of his cali-
brating instruments anxiously. Driscoll smiled inwardly. But then
Wainewright always had been the worrying type. He could not have
been more than twenty-nine, yet he looked older than Driscoll with
his lean, strained features, his straggly moustache, and the hair that
was already thinning and receding.

Driscoll's gaze rested just a fraction on his colleague, drifted on to
bring into focus a bank of instruments with large easy-read dials on the
far bulkhead, and finally came to rest on the red-painted lettering of the
alarm board situated to his front and in a commanding position. The
repeater screen below contained forty-five flickering blue images, which
showed the state of the alarm boards in the farthest corners of the complex for which Driscoll, as Captain of the Watch, was responsible.

All was normal. But then it always was. Driscoll shrugged and turned his attention to the desk in front of him. He filled in the log with a luminous radionic pencil. Still two hours to go. But he had to admit that he liked the night duty better than the day. The word *enjoy* was frowned on nowadays, but the word was appropriate to Driscoll's state; he actually enjoyed this Watch. It was quiet, almost private, and that was a decreasing quality in life.

His musings were interrupted by a sharp, sibilant exclamation from Wainewright.

"Some activity in Shaft 639!" he reported, swivelling to look at the Captain of the Watch with watery blue eyes.

Driscoll shook his head, a thin smile on his lips.

"It's nothing. Some water in the shaft, probably."

Wainewright tightened his mouth.

"Perhaps . . . Even so, it ought to be reported."

Driscoll stiffened on the seat and looked at the thin man; the other was the first to drop his eyes.

"You have reported it," he said gently. "And I say it is water in the shaft."

He snapped on the log entries, read them off the illuminated repeater on the bulkhead.

"There have been seventeen similar reports in the past year. Water each time."

Wainewright hunched over his instruments; his shoulders heaved as though he had difficulty in repressing his emotions. Driscoll looked at him sharply. It might be time to make a report on Wainewright. He would wait a little longer. No sense in being too precipitant.

"Shaft clear," Wainewright mumbled presently.

He went on making a play of checking instruments, throwing switches, examining dials, avoiding Driscoll's eye.

Driscoll sat back in his chair again. He looked at the domed metal roof spreading its protective shell over them; its rivets and studs winking and throwing back the lights from the instrument dials and the shaded lamps. He mentally reviewed Wainewright's case, sifting and evaluating the facts as he knew them.

The man was beginning to show signs of psychotic disturbance. Driscoll could well understand this. They did not know what was out there, that was the trouble. He had over forty miles of galleries and communicating tunnels alone in the section under his own command, for example. But still, that did not excuse him. They had to proceed on empirical methods. He yawned slightly, looked again at the time.

He thought of his relief without either expectation or regret; he was quite without emotion, unlike Wainewright. Unlike Wainewright again, well suited to his exacting task. He would not be Captain of the

Watch otherwise. Even when he was relieved he would not seek his bunk. He would descend to the canteen for coffee and food before joining Karlson for a brief session of chess.

He frowned. He had just thought of Deems again. He thrust the image of Deems from his mind. It flickered momentarily, then disappeared. It was no good; it had been two years now, but it still came back occasionally. He remembered, too, that he had been Wainewright's particular friend; that probably explained his jumpiness lately. Nevertheless, he would need watching.

He pursed his lips and bent forward, watching the bright green pencil of tracery on the tube in front of him. He pressed the voice button, and Hort's cavernous voice filled the Control Room.

"Condition Normal, I hope!"

There was a jovial edge to his query; the pronouncement was intended to be a joke, and Driscoll permitted himself a smile of about three millimeters in width. That would satisfy Hort, who was not really a humorous man. There was no point in knocking himself out for someone so devoid of the absurd in his makeup.

"Nothing to report," he called back in the same voice.

Hort nodded. Driscoll could see his multi-imaged form flickering greenly at the corner of his vision, but he did not look directly at it. He knew that annoyed Hort, and it pleased him to make these small gestures of independence.

"I'd like to see you when you come off Watch," Hort went on.

He had a slightly sardonic look on his thin face now.

Driscoll nodded.

"I'll be there," he said laconically.

He waved a perfunctory hand, and the vision on the tube wavered and died, a tiny rain of green sparks remaining against the blackness before dying out.

He was aware of Wainewright's troubled eyes seeking his own; he ignored the other man and concentrated instead on a printout which was coming through. It was a routine check, he soon saw, and he leaned back, his sharp eyes sweeping across the serried ranks of instruments, his ears alert for even the slightest aberration in the smooth chatter of the machinery.

He wondered idly what Hort might want with him. Probably nothing of real importance, but it was best to be prepared; he pressed the repeater valve on the desk in front of him, instantly memorising the latest data that was being constantly fed in by a wide stream of instruments. There were only three sets of numbers of any importance; he scratched these onto his pad and kept it ready at his elbow.

There would be nothing else of note in the Watch now, short of an unforeseen emergency. He momentarily closed his eyes, leaning back in the chair, lightly resting his fingertips on the smooth polished metal of the desk. He savoured the moment, which lasted only for a few seconds. Then he opened his eyes again, refreshed and wide-awake. A faint humming vibration filled all the galleries and corridors adjacent to the Control Room. The vents were open for the moment; all was as it should be.

The rest of the Watch passed almost too quickly; Wainewright was already being relieved by Krampf, Driscoll noted. The bulkhead clock indicated nine minutes to the hour. But then Krampf always was more zealous than most of the personnel here. Driscoll really knew little about him. He glanced incuriously at the man now, dapper and self-confident, his dark hair bent over the panel opposite, listening to Wainewright's handing-over report. Then he had adjusted the headphones and was sliding into the padded seat.

Wainewright waited almost helplessly for a moment, and then went hurriedly down the metal staircase. Krampf's eyes rested on Driscoll and his lips curved in a smile; he gave the Captain of the Watch a jaunty thumbs-up signal. Driscoll felt vaguely irritated.

There was something about Krampf he did not quite understand. He had none of the anxiety to please that Wainewright displayed; indeed he exuded a disconcerting air of suppressed energy and egotistical drive.

Still, it was none of his business; he only saw Krampf for a very few minutes when they were changing over Watches. Three or four minutes in a week, perhaps, for sometimes their duties failed to overlap. His own relief was at his elbow now and Driscoll got up, almost reluctant to vacate the seat. He handed over with a few smooth phrases and went down the staircase in the wake of Wainewright.

There was no one in the canteen but Karlson. A plump, balding man, he nodded shyly as Driscoll came up. He rose and made room for him on the smooth plastic bench. Soft music was drifting from louvers in the ceiling. Karlson had already set up the board and had made his opening move. It was his turn to start. Driscoll glanced briefly at the problem and then crossed over to study the menu on the screen.

He put his token in the tray and drew out the hot coffee and the thin wheaten biscuits with honey that he liked so well. He did not eat very much when he came off Watch at this time, as it impaired his digestion and interfered with his sleep. He went back to the table in the corner where he and Karlson always sat and sipped the hot, strong coffee slowly, his eyes seemingly inattentive but all the time studying the board and Karlson's concentrated face.

But it was obvious that his attention was waning. He fidgeted for a moment and then turned away from the board, his eyes fixed on the table before him. Karlson looked at him quickly, a sympathetic smile already flowering at the corners of his mouth.

"Tired?"

Driscoll shook his head.

"No more than usual. It is not that, no."

He folded firm, capable hands round the rim of his beaker and stared into the steaming black surface of his coffee as though the answer to his unspoken question lay there.

"Then it is something which happened on Watch?"

Karlson's eyes were alert, questioning now. Driscoll knew he had to be very careful in his choice of words. Karlson was a particular friend, but the system had to come first, whatever else happened. He sipped the coffee slowly, playing for time. Karlson watched him without impatience, a sort of majestic contentment on his outwardly placid face. Yet there was a wary and unusual brain beneath the banal exterior. Driscoll had ample evidence of that.

Then Karlson's face relaxed. He smiled slowly.

"Not Wainewright again. And his shaft noises?"

Driscoll's surprise showed on his face.

"So you know about it?"

Karlson nodded.

"It's no secret. We have our eye on things. He was on Watch with Collins three weeks ago, when you were indisposed."

Driscoll cast his mind back, failed to remember anything of significance. He avoided Karlson's eye, looked instead at the gleaming metal dome of the roof that stretched above them. Wherever one went in the miles of corridors, there was nothing but the smooth unbroken monotony.

"Your loyalty does you credit," Karlson said drily. "But it is not really necessary in this case. Wainewright's nerve was never strong. And he has certainly not been the same since Deems went to. . . ."

He broke off suddenly and leaned forward at the table. His sharp, attentive attitude made him look almost as if he were listening for something. Something beyond the roof. Which was absurd, under the circumstances. Driscoll allowed himself a thin smile at the thought. He took up Karlson as though his friend had not hesitated.

"Out There," he finished bluntly.

Karlson looked momentarily startled; his bland facade abruptly cracked. He drummed with thick spatulate fingers on the table. He looked almost angry, Driscoll thought.

But his voice was calm and measured when he spoke.

"We do not mention that," he said gently. "But since you have seen fit to raise it—yes."

Driscoll picked up one of his special biscuits and took a fastidi-ous bite.

"I have kept a close watch on Wainewright," he said, more stiffly than he had intended. "If there had been the slightest doubt in my mind. . . ."

His companion interrupted him by laying a hand on his arm.

"There was no criticism intended," he said gently. "As I said, we are all aware of Wainewright's problems. They are being monitored at a higher level. Long before any danger point we shall take him out."

Karlson focused his gaze back on the game before them.

"It does not seem as though we shall get any further tonight. With your permission . . ."

Driscoll nodded. Karlson animated the lever. Board and men sank back into the surface of the table with a barely audible whine. Karlson folded his hands on the spot where the board had stood.

"Wainewright reported five occurrences in the one Watch," he said bluntly. "In various shafts."

Driscoll licked his lips. He said nothing, merely bending his head politely as he waited for Karlson to go on.

"It was unprecedented," Karlson continued. "It could not be over-looked. So Collins reported it to me direct. Wainewright has been under close surveillance ever since."

He looked at Driscoll reproachfully.

"You have not reported anything yourself."

Driscoll flushed. He bit his lip.

"Is that why Hort wants to see me?"

Karlson spread his hands wide in a gesture of apology.

"I do not know," he said simply. "Perhaps. Perhaps not. But it would be wise to go carefully."

He smiled then. A full-mouthed, sincere smile.

"Thank you," Driscoll said. "There is nothing, really. Wainewright is fidgety, it is true. And he was dubious about Shaft Number 639 tonight. That is all."

Karlson let his breath out in a sigh of relief.

"That is good. Nevertheless, I should let Hort know."

He got up suddenly, as though summoned by an inaudible alarm bell. He looked down at Driscoll thoughtfully.

"Don't worry about it," he said. "But let Hort know."

He went out quietly and unhurriedly, leaving Driscoll to his coffee and biscuits and the insect humming of the hidden machinery.

Hort was a tall, thin, ascetic man with a bald head and hooded grey eyes. He wore a blue tunic zipped up to the neck and the scarlet badge denoting his rank of Gallery Master. He was in his early sixties, but despite his years there was a dynamic athleticism in his wiry frame that many people found unnerving. Driscoll did not find it so, but there was a faint core of wariness within him as he came up the spiral glass staircase leading to Hort's office.

He could see Hort through the armoured glass wall that separated his quarters from the other administration units. Driscoll slid the door back and went in. Hort sat down at his semicircular desk with its battery of winking lights and motioned Driscoll to take a seat on the divan in front of him. Driscoll sank down cautiously, as though afraid the cushions would not bear his weight. Hort's eyes looked slightly amused as he stared for a moment without speaking. Then he made a pretence of examining his fingernails and came to the point.

"I expect you've guessed why I've asked you to come here?"

Driscoll nodded curtly.

"Wainewright?"

Despite himself he thought his voice had a defensive quality in it which he had not intended.

"Exactly."

Hort sat back in his padded chair and went through the nail-examining charade again.

"I won't conceal from you, Driscoll, that we're worried. Especially after the other business."

His eyes had grown serious, and he looked searchingly at the Captain of the Watch.

"Deems?" Driscoll said.

Hort nodded.

"Exactly. We have to be so careful. You understand almost better than I the implications of such a situation. We must avoid any leakage. . . ."

He broke off, avoided Driscoll's eyes, and focused his own gaze on his fingernails again.

"It is difficult to put delicately, Driscoll. But we have to avoid also the arousing of any uneasiness among the personnel. . . ."

Driscoll put on his blank-faced look.

"I'm afraid I don't quite follow you. Wainewright has reported certain disturbances in several of the main shafts. There have been a number of such incidents over the past year or so. I fail to see why that should be considered anything abnormal."

Encouraged by Hort's silence and his relaxed manner as he sat staring at his nails, he went on.

"Obviously, Wainewright is disturbed. But I have been keeping him under close observation. And I understand the Captains of other Watches have done the same when the circumstances arose."

Hort wagged his head gravely, as though in agreement with every word Driscoll had spoken.

"I am glad to hear it," he said mildly. "But there is something more than that. There must be no repetition—"

He broke off, the points of his fingers trembling on the desk. Driscoll realised that he had been applying pressure to the desktop all the while he had been speaking. Hort turned his head to Driscoll with an effort.

"There must be no repetition," he said with calm finality. "That is all, unless you have anything further to add."

The matter was perfectly clear in Driscoll's mind; he did not like Hort and the other man knew it, but he respected his abilities. He would not have held his present position if he had not been immensely able. And it was one of his duties to prevent problems arising. Driscoll realised for the first time what a shock Deems must have given the Administration.

He got up slowly, expecting dismissal. But Hort's mind had apparently gone on to other things. He chatted amiably of various trivialities before the interview came to an end.

Driscoll turned back when he reached the staircase. Hort was still standing by the desk as he had left him, as though lost in thought. Then, aware that Driscoll could see him through the armoured glass wall, he sat down again at his desk.

Driscoll walked back down the stairs; he gained the sloping metal corridor that led to his own quarters. Long after he sought his bunk his mind was absorbed with unaccustomed thoughts. He heard the soft burring of the alarm bell for the next Watch before sleep found him.

Driscoll slid back the door of Central Records and went over the shining parquet to the main desk. He was off Watch today and he often spent some time here, researching his particular projects. Today he went to the Historical Section and scratched his notation on a pad in front of the request screen. It was quiet in the library; only about two dozen people were spread out at the metal desks beyond the transparent screen. Light shimmered evenly on their bowed heads, and the faint humming of the machinery filled the air.

A soft breeze was coming through the vents; the scent was jasmine today, Driscoll noted. Driscoll liked Jasmine Day above all others. It was a pity it only came around about once every two months. The speaker was quietly braying into his ear.

"Your request has been programmed. Desk number sixty-four."

The door slid back automatically as Driscoll walked over; it was warmer in the Historical Section, and he unbuttoned the top layers of his clothing. He went down the aisles to where the number sixty-four glowed on the identification tag and sank into the padded chair. He had asked for the records of the entire year. It would not do to be too specific. And somehow he felt it might be dangerous. He did not quite know why.

He looked listlessly as the image of the first page of the log appeared, greatly enlarged, on the brightly lit screen in front of him. He pressed the button, displacing the entry, working quietly through, pretending to take notes. He spent more than an hour on this stage. He felt his palms slightly sweating as he neared the relevant dates.

He selected an entry that came in the middle of the period that interested him, as though at random. He immediately knew there was something wrong. The familiar bleeping noise began and the crimson light commenced winking. The screen went blank and the recorded voice bleated: "The information you require is in the Restricted Section. To consult the entry you require verified permission of Authority."

Driscoll sighed. He pressed the neutral button, and the screen came up with the bland entries of the log for the last date before the restricted period. Driscoll did not try any further dates. He knew the response would be the same. If he tried three successive entries in the Restricted Section, it would bring the curator to the desk in person to inquire about his interest in the information. He could not risk that.

He sat back at the desk and consulted the notes on his pad. There was only one other thing to do. He would have to talk to Wainewright. Even then there might be difficulties. Driscoll had become interested in the problem. When he was interested in something he never let go. If Hort had not asked to see him; if there had not been some subtle expression on Karlson's face; if Wainewright's own features had not borne some furtive evidence of secret shock. . . .

Driscoll drummed with his capable fingers on the desk surface in the glutinous silence while the muted background hum that was almost inaudible to its hearers lapped the library in its almost apian susurrus.

He was irritated with himself; something had occurred to cause ripples on the smooth and placidly ordered surface of his life. He did not like that. He sat there frowningly for another ten minutes or so, silently wrestling with the problem. Then he rose and abruptly quitted the Historical Section. The long armoured glass doors slid to quietly behind him, leaving the earnest questers after knowledge to their hermetic silence.

Driscoll waited until after lunch. There was no difficulty. There was nothing against his visiting Wainewright. It was unusual, perhaps. Driscoll knew that television cameras scanned all public places and main thoroughfares. There was really no reason for secrecy, but he pre-ferred to be more discreet. So he walked out as though for the exercise and caught a car on an obscure junction where it was unlikely he would be seen.

He had to change twice, but he felt justified in the procedure. Wainewright lived in Gallery 4,034, and Driscoll was not quite sure of the exact location of his apartment. In the event it took him more than an hour, and during that time Driscoll evolved his story. He did not quite know how to approach Wainewright; that there was something about Deems's death which had profoundly shocked him was obvious. To one of Driscoll's fibre such things were a little unusual, but nothing to upset the stolid norm of everyday living.

Yet Deems's departure had evidently upset the authorities more than they had cared to admit; Karlson's guarded attitude had not really deceived Driscoll. He had half suspected that Hort had asked him to make inquiries, and his own interview with Hort had crystallised his suspicions. Driscoll's mind was still full of half-formulated impulses when he slid back the folding door of the car at Station 68 and walked up the tiled concourse in the direction of Gallery 4,034.

He soon located Wainewright's apartment and ascended to the third stage, where it was situated. Wainewright's lean, strained features revealed their frank astonishment as he slid back the door to answer Driscoll's summons. His watery blue eyes looked up at Driscoll half-defiantly, half-defensively.

"I am sorry," said Driscoll almost hesitantly. "If it is not convenient. . . ."

"No, of course not," Wainewright stammered.

He drew back, his left hand making an expressive gesture.

"Come in, come in, please. I am quite alone."

Driscoll stepped past his host and stood lost in thought in the radi-ance of the dim overhead light. He waited until Wainewright had closed the door.

"Forgive my apparent confusion," Wainewright went on, leading the way into the circular living room where soft music oozed from hidden louvers. He went over to the switch and killed the recital. He waved Driscoll to a divan opposite him and sank into a steel-backed chair facing his guest.

"You see," Wainewright went on, "your visit is most unusual so that I was naturally surprised. I hope there is nothing wrong. . . ."

Driscoll shook his head; he spoke some anodyne words, allaying the other's fears.

"It is nothing, really, yet I felt I would like to come for an hour. If you can spare the time. . . ."

"Certainly, certainly."

Wainewright had recovered his poise now.

"May I offer you some refreshment? I am partial to tea."

Driscoll smiled thinly; there was something a little old-maidish about Wainewright. He supposed it came from living alone as he did.

"Only if you are making something. It is nothing of real importance that I wished to discuss. It will keep."

Wainewright got up, obviously relieved. While he busied himself making the tea, Driscoll sat with his heavy hands folded in his lap, quite at ease, his lids drooping over his eyes as though half-asleep. But he missed nothing that went on in the small world in which he found himself. It was not easy to shake off the habits of a lifetime.

Wainewright reappeared at last, with mumbled apologies. Driscoll was silent until after he had poured the tea. He sat watching the liquid descend in a steaming amber arc into the burnished metal cup. He made polite small talk until the ceremony was over. His host sat back on the chair opposite and regarded him warily. Caution and confusion struggled somewhere in the depths of his eyes.

"I was surprised at your visit," he said. "I will not conceal it. I wondered if there was something wrong at Control. My records are quite in order. . . ."

He broke off for a second. Then, reassured by Driscoll's expression, he continued.

"Of course, I know there have been complaints. It was perhaps inevitable. But I have not been sleeping at all well lately."

"It was about that I wanted to talk to you," said Driscoll quickly, feeling his way clear. "It is obvious there was something on your mind. It is the private sector, you understand. This has nothing to do with Control."

He waited to see what effect his words were having on Wainewright. The thin man sat in an immobile posture, his watery blue eyes blinking rapidly. Only the restless clenching and unclenching of his hands revealed his inner tension; it was almost as though his naked nerve-ends were exposed to Driscoll's probing gaze. The visitor knew his man. He abruptly changed the subject.

"Excellent tea," he said cheerfully, extending his cup for a refill. "Where do you get such quality these days?"

Wainewright's apprehensive face flushed with pleasure.

"I blend it myself," he answered. "It is something of a lost art."

Driscoll agreed, making a mental note regarding his inmost thoughts on Wainewright. His sleepy eyes went on probing the apartment.

"It was your reports of movements in the shafts," he went on gently. "The subject interests me. And after what happened . . ."

He broke off abruptly, leaving the sentence hanging awkwardly in the air. For a moment he thought he had overplayed his hand. Wainewright bit his lip. His fingers shook perceptibly, so much so that he set down his teacup on the tray. He put both hands together in front of him, as though to control their shaking.

"Did Hort ask you to come?" Wainewright said heavily.

There was a sort of sullen defiance on his rather weak face. The blue eyes looked baffled and defeated. Driscoll felt a sudden flash of pity for him. He shook his head.

"I was speaking the truth," he said simply. "This is entirely private. I wanted to help if I could. . . ."

Again he broke off the sentence, let it hang in the air. The echoes of his voice seemed to go on reverberating round the apartment long after their natural resonance should have died away. There was an odd, dead silence between the two.

Wainewright sat, his body awkwardly constricted, his hands together in his lap, slightly leaning forward as though listening for something that could not be heard by anyone else. Driscoll had often noted it when they were on night Watch together. They still kept Earth Time, even though there was nothing but artificial light now. They had long adapted to it.

Driscoll had noted that Wainewright seemed more apprehensive on night duties. Curious that it should be so. He gave his host a reassuring smile, moved on the divan slightly, and then picked up his teacup again. Normality seemed to flow back into the room.

"There is much I could say," Wainewright said heavily. "You see, after Deems went. . . ."

He swallowed and broke off. To Driscoll it seemed as though there were some sort of mute appeal in his eyes.

"It was Deems I really wanted to speak about," Driscoll prompted him. "And whatever you imagine is in the shafts."

A shudder seemed to pass through Wainewright's thin form. His attitude was more than ever one of someone listening intently for something to happen. The notion was absurd, but Driscoll could not dismiss it from his mind.

"In the shafts?" Wainewright repeated dully.

Driscoll nodded encouragingly.

"Out There."

Wainewright stirred on the chair with a visible effort. Then he made a convulsive movement and raised his cup to his lips. He drank as though he were thirsty, taking great gulps, his eyes tightly closed as if to erase the memory of something from his sight. Though Driscoll might have mistaken his motives, it might merely have been the effect of the hot steam against his eyelids.

"Deems was a very good friend of yours, wasn't he?" Driscoll said gently.

The eyelids had opened. The watery blue eyes regarded him intently.

"The best. There is no one now."

His voice was so low the words were almost inaudible. Driscoll was more sure of his ground. He leaned forward across the tea things.

"I tried to check on the log entries regarding Deems this afternoon. They were not available in Central Records."

Wainewright's face had gone white. He visibly trembled. He shook his head.

"That was extremely unwise. Though I am surprised that you are so interested."

His face changed as he was speaking. Some of the tension drained out of it. He looked at Driscoll steadily.

"Does this mean that you understand? That you might even believe me?"

Driscoll knew all was well now. He leaned back easily on the divan.

"Let us just say I have an open mind. And I shall be extremely discreet."

Driscoll smiled at Wainewright. He had a frank, open face, and the confidence he exuded seemed to extend to his companion. Wainewright's features seemed more relaxed, and the haunting tightness round the eyes and temples was momentarily eased. He looked steadily at Driscoll.

"You want to know about Deems?"

Driscoll nodded.

"If it will help me to an understanding of what troubles you, yes."

He knew at once he had said the right thing; Wainewright seemed visibly moved. He half got up, as though he would come over to his guest's side, then he sank back into his seat again.

"You may not understand," he said.

"I do not understand now," Driscoll said. "When I have learned what troubles you, I surely cannot know less."

Wainewright nodded slowly. Sitting there stiffly, blinking his eyes, he seemed to Driscoll like something left over from an earlier age; an age when gentleness and learned pursuits had value, and when purifying winds blew across the surface of the earth. But there was no indication of his thoughts as he sat with his steady gaze surveying Wainewright calmly. The latter restlessly knotted and unknotted his fingers.

"Deems was my friend," he said. "My only real friend. His going was a dreadful shock."

"I can understand that," Driscoll said gently. "I want to help."

Wainewright shifted on his seat. His eyes looked vague and half-frightened.

"If only I could believe that. . . ."

Driscoll showed a faint flicker of impatience. He cupped his big hands round his right kneecap and rocked himself to and fro.

"You have ample proof of it," he pointed out. "My very presence here. You know we are not supposed to meet off Watch."

The point struck home; Wainewright narrowed his eyes and flinched back slightly, as though his companion had struck him. He made up his mind. He started to talk, breathing heavily between sentences, as though he were running.

"Deems knew," he said. "He was always telling about it. On Watch as well as off. He knew there was something."

"Out There?" Driscoll prompted.

Wainewright nodded. He swallowed once or twice but realised he had to go on; he had committed himself, and it was too late to turn back.

"It started with Shaft Number 247. You didn't know that, did you?"

Driscoll stared at him. He shook his head. Wainewright smiled thinly.

"It was a well-kept secret. It's right on the edge of our section. It's a strange place. No one wants to say anything about it. The lighting system is always going there, so that the tunnels are often in semidarkness. There have been odd noises and movements in the shafts. Water has come through in one or two places, and some of the valves are rusting."

Driscoll looked at Wainewright incredulously. He licked his lips, but there was the stamp of sincerity in the look he returned.

"It's perfectly true," he said. "Only none of the official reports refer to it. Special teams attend to it, and no formal records are kept."

Driscoll stared at his companion in silence for a long moment.

"I take it you know what you're saying?"

Wainewright nodded. He kept his watery eyes fixed on the other.

"This thing has been with me for a long time. I know exactly what I'm saying. And I am choosing my words with care."

Driscoll kept his bleak gaze fully ahead of him, not seeing Wainewright for the moment. His brain was heavy with dark thoughts.

"Go on."

Wainewright made a pathetic little flourishing movement with his hands.

"Did you know, for instance, that there have been breaks in the tunnel? Water in the shafts and, as I said, rust on the valves?"

"I find that difficult to believe."

His voice sounded a little unsteady, even to himself. Wainewright permitted himself a shy, hesitant smile. He stirred uneasily, his eyes searching Driscoll's face.

"You will not find it in the records. But he knew."

Driscoll's senses must have been a little dulled this afternoon. He looked blankly at Wainewright, the bland, smooth lighting of the room beating down on them, turning their figures to a pale butter yellow.

"Deems, of course," Wainewright went on, as though a flood of emotion had been released in him. "He was determined to know. He confided in me. The thing had been on his mind for some time. He was convinced there was something in the shafts. And Shaft Number 247 was the obvious. . . ."

"Why obvious?" Driscoll interrupted.

Wainewright passed a bluish tongue across dry lips.

"Surely you must know that. It is the largest. It was the inspection tunnel years ago. When people went Out There to check on conditions."

Driscoll was slightly irritated with himself; he put his hands round his kneecap again and rocked to and fro. Of course, he remembered now. He smiled confidently at his companion.

"The shaft with the inspection capsule? Is it still there?"

Wainewright shook his head.

"The authorities had it taken out. But the chamber still exists. And it would be no great thing to undo the bolts of the hatch."

Driscoll was startled; he sat, his strong face immobile as he stared at Wainewright.

"Why would anyone want to do that?"

Wainewright shrugged.

"Why would Deems want to go there? To find out. To increase the sum of human knowledge, of course. The movement in the shafts . . ."

Despite himself, a slight chill had spread over Driscoll. He looked at the indicator on the bulkhead near where he sat, wondering if the temperature of the chamber had been altered. But it was quite normal. His tone of voice was absolutely level when he spoke.

"What do you think is there, Wainewright?"

The watery blue eyes had a strange filmy expression in them.

"There is something . . . animate, shall we say. Something that wants to get in touch with us. Why should Shaft Number 247 leak, for example? The situation is almost unprecedented."

Driscoll leaned forward, his eyes intent on the other's face.

"Why does Shaft Number 247 leak?"

Wainewright licked his lips again, and his eyes were dark and haunted as he stared back.

"Because something is turning the bolts from the other side," he said simply.

* * *

"I think you had better tell me how Deems died," said Driscoll quietly.

There was a sulphurous silence in the room now. Wainewright's eyes were like pale blue holes in the blankness of his face. He gestured toward the teapot. Driscoll declined with a brief shake of his head. He had to hold his impatience in check.

"Deems?"

Wainewright passed his tongue over his lips again.

"He knew about Shaft 247, you see. He had found how to open it. There was a temporary fault on the circuits in that section. He went there unknown to the authorities. The place had a fascination for him."

He paused again and looked at Driscoll. There was an imploring look on his face as though he were asking his companion for help he knew the latter was unable to give.

"How do you know this?"

"Deems was my best friend. It emerged over a long period. He had made up his mind, you see."

Wainewright's eyes were closed now as though he could no longer bear to look at Driscoll.

"You mean to go Out There?"

Driscoll's voice was unsteady. Wainewright opened his eyes. For once they were sharp and unwavering. He nodded.

"He found life intolerable here. He could not adjust. And he had to discover what lay Outside. He made his plans carefully. But even I did not entirely realise his determination."

Driscoll sat on in heavy silence. He was aware that it was dangerous to listen to Wainewright; that he had now become his confidant. That would be knowledge difficult to live with. He was becoming confused, which was a completely unknown quantity with him hitherto. Yet he had to find out more about Deems.

None of this showed on his face, which expressed only polite interest as he waited for his companion to continue. But Wainewright seemed to have become aware of the enormity of his conduct. For one did not talk like this, especially to persons of Driscoll's rank and calibre. Yet Wainewright was encouraged by the other's silence; by the calm, intent look on his face. He stirred on the chair opposite and then went on without hesitation, as though he had finally made up his mind.

"Deems came to see me before he went Out," he said. "He was more than usually agitated that night. He called here just as you have called today, which was an equally extraordinary circumstance."

"Did he tell you what he was going to do?"

Wainewright shook his head.

"Hints only. But he was tremendously disturbed. More than I had ever seen him before. He had studied the phenomena, you see. And it was my conviction that he knew what was moving in the shafts Out There."

Wainewright cleared his throat nervously.

"He talked about wanting to be free. He was convinced contact was being made for some purpose. That there was a benevolence . . . a peace. . . ."

He fell silent for long moments. Driscoll felt the whole weight of the roof covering the miles of tunnels and galleries on his shoulders, pressing him downward into the black bowels of the earth. It was a feeling completely alien to him and he did not like it.

"What happened that night? When the alarm bells rang?"

"I relieved Deems," Wainewright went on. "He appeared quite normal. We exchanged no formal word. We just looked at one another. I did not remember that look until afterward. Then he went off, to seek his bunk, I thought. The alarm bells rang about half an hour later. Collins was in charge that night. He did not give me formal permission to leave, but he must have noticed something in my expression, for he nodded as I got up.

"I ran down the corridors. I knew exactly where to go. There was no lighting in the section housing Shaft Number 247. And I knew it would take the emergency squad more than twenty minutes to reach the area. I had no fear. But I think also I knew what I would find."

He swallowed, a thin glaze of sweat on his face; then, as Driscoll ventured no comment, he hurried on.

"I had a torch with me. There was a lot of water in the tunnel. The cover of the shaft was open. Or rather it was unlatched. I shone the light in the inspection chamber. There was a note at the bottom, addressed to me. And a grey viscous material that had been crushed in the edge of the metal doors. It looked like primitive embryonic fingers."

Wainewright stopped and shuddered. He seemed to fight for breath and then turned and gulped mouthfuls of hot strong tea. Driscoll sat immobile, but his big hands were locked together; his knuckles showed white.

"What was in the note?"

" 'This is the first. There will be many others. Come Outside. There is a shining peace, a brightness, a freedom. . . .'

"The writing was spidery, as though it had been cut off suddenly."

Wainewright looked pale, his eyes haunted by forbidden knowledge.

"It was then that I knew Deems had not written it."

* * *

Driscoll slept badly that night. Wainewright's words and the image of his tense, strained form kept coming back to him. Finally Driscoll got up, put on the lights, and sat staring at the full-scale chart of the gallery system covered by his section. He could not recall such a night, which was disturbing in itself. He decided to tell no one of his interview with Wainewright; it could do no good, and he knew Wainewright himself would say nothing.

The authorities must have realised that Wainewright had been at the shaft. Driscoll knew, though he had not specifically asked, that Wainewright must have disposed of the note and the material in the inspection chamber, but even so there would have been suspicion. Which was no doubt why Hort and Karlson were so interested; and why there was an embargo on the official reports of the incident.

The cameras would have noted in which direction Wainewright was hurrying, even if the area surrounding the shaft had been in darkness; and in any case Collins would immediately have switched to infrared. No, there must be some other reason why no action had been taken over Wainewright. But it had been decidedly dangerous, Driscoll's visit to his apartment; he would have to be especially careful, particularly if he went there again.

Driscoll was surprising himself by the convolution of his thoughts this evening; he wondered what reports Collins himself had made of Wainewright's absence from Control on that occasion, and what log entries related to it. He would carry out his own check, though he had no doubt that Hort would have skillfully covered up the situation.

He stared at the blueprint of the tunnels, noting exactly what junctions would make the best approach. His heart was beating slightly faster than normal as he returned the document to its case. He went back to bed and this time slept better.

But his doubts returned on the following day. He had an earlier Watch that evening and had no opportunity of seeing Collins. In any case it would be unwise to make verbal inquiries. And it was certain that he would again draw a blank if he returned to Central Records.

Driscoll thought long about his interview with Wainewright and particularly his last few words; the implications were distinctly disturbing. He liked neither the message nor the somewhat imprecise description of what Wainewright had seen in the inspection chamber. If he had read Wainewright aright, the material had disappeared— "dissolved" was Wainewright's term—before the emergency squad had arrived. And though he had not told Driscoll so, he had doubtless removed the note.

So that the official records, whatever they were, would not tell the complete story as Driscoll had it from Wainewright. But the authorities were undoubtedly right to have their suspicions of Wainewright; Driscoll himself would have to be careful, extremely careful.

The Captain of the Watch looked round the crowded restaurant. He was having lunch and had studiously avoided the glances of recognition from various acquaintances in the big room with its subdued lighting.

However, as he was about to leave he suddenly noticed Karlson near the entrance. He had evidently finished his meal and was on his way out. He gave Driscoll an enigmatic look, and the latter could not be sure that he had seen and recognised him. Yet something vague and disquieting remained in his mind. There was another man with Karlson.

Driscoll only glimpsed his back before the sliding doors cut him off, but it looked extraordinarily like Hort. Supposing that the Gallery Master and Karlson had been discussing him? Or, worse still, spying on him? Driscoll almost laughed aloud. Yet the supposition was not so fanciful as it might appear on the surface. Driscoll's smile died on his lips. He wore a thoughtful expression as he went to prepare for his Watch.

Normally Driscoll enjoyed his periods of duty; he was like all those who were able to wield power and accept responsibility and yet find it sit lightly on their shoulders. For all the shining instruments, the humming machinery, the routine purpose in the mechanics, and the meticulous attention to detail of those on Watch, there was yet an awesome responsibility for one who sat in Driscoll's chair.

One momentary lapse of attention, and the result could be chaos within the streamlined galleries, the miles of tunnels, and the sleeping city beyond. Driscoll had not faltered through long years, and yet on this occasion he found his well-ordered mind wandering; his thoughts troubled as he mused again on Wainewright and the indiscreet revelations he had made.

But the training and self-discipline that had brought him to this pitch of well-ordered perfection carried on mechanically, and for four hours, as he noted and evaluated, coordinated the routines of personnel miles apart along the galleries, scanned the dials and vision tubes, and smoothly manipulated the switches and levers that motivated the electronics of this subterranean complexity, a residue of his mind was still engaged in sombre and deep-seated self-searching.

It was near the end of the Watch when it happened; indeed, Driscoll had already handed over to his relief and was standing engaged in small talk on the details, when the alarm bells began to bleep and a flurry of activity animated the Control Room. He already knew before a glance confirmed it that the abnormality emanated from Shaft Number 247, and he had slipped silently out of Control before those bent over the desks and instrument panels were aware that he had gone.

He ran down the gallery as unobtrusively as possible, though he realised that his image was being transmitted through the mounted cameras in each gallery and corridor back to Central Control. Ostensibly, he was making for his own quarters, but he diverged at right angles to bring himself into line with the section that interested him. He knew that if he hurried he would be first on the scene.

He hardly understood why he was running at such speed; the situation was abnormal, of course, but there was some inner compulsion beyond that; something within himself that impelled him onward, despite the cautious core of reserve that advised against. Incredibly, Wainewright had been correct: the illumination of the approach tunnel was out.

Driscoll ran quickly back to his cabin, returned with a pocket-torch, and retraced his steps. Whether or not he could still be seen by the cameras he did not know; neither, at this precise moment in time, did he care. He only knew that the overpowering curiosity over Shaft Number 247 which Wainewright had aroused in him had to be satisfied. He was in darkness now, the beam of the torch dancing luminescent and elongated across the shining metal surface and massive studs of the gallery.

The burring of the alarm went on; Driscoll knew that it would continue until the trouble had been put right. That was an invariable rule with the repeater system. He could imagine Hort's figure hunched over the screen as he manipulated switches to give his orders. Driscoll pounded forward, grimly aware that he would have only ten minutes in which to satisfy himself of the accuracy of Wainewright's statements. But ten minutes should be enough.

He paused at a right-angle junction in the gallery, gained his bearings. He was astonished to hear a slopping noise as he ran down toward the main shafts. He played his torch on the floor of the tunnel, saw the beam reflected back from the creeping tide of water. He was running through the thin trickle now, heedless of the splashing. The gallery had an acrid salt smell, like that of the tang of the sea as Driscoll had smelled it when screened in ancient actuality material.

But he had no time for analysis. He noticed that the cameras in the roof of the tunnel here were all out of action; the dim glow of the red emergency lights made his hands and the torch beam look like blood. There was only a hundred yards to go now. Driscoll knew that he would be first. No one else could possibly catch up with him, and there was no sign of anyone following behind.

Not that anyone would come on foot; and the rubber-tyred trolleys of the emergency squad made only a faint whispering sound. But he would be able to hear their sirens from a long way off. Almost there now. Driscoll shone the torch onto the roof fittings; strange that the lighting had failed here and only here. It could not be due to the water. The pumps were working normally, which made it doubly strange.

There must be seepage from one of the shafts. Even as he ran forward the last few yards, Driscoll knew in his inmost soul that the leakage was almost certainly from Shaft Number 247. Not only Wainewright's story but all his inquiries had prepared him for that. There was a strange stench in his nostrils now; one that was vaguely repellent but at the same time familiar.

Driscoll stumbled on something slimy and almost fell. He swore and recovered himself, but he was badly shaken just the same. The torch beam trembled as he waved it wildly across the floor. Dark rivulets of water flowed across the tiling; curiously, there were many dry patches, which told Driscoll immediately that there were a number of shafts involved.

He was almost there now. His footsteps echoed monstrously back from the ceiling. He was no longer conscious of the water slopping over his feet. Driscoll was only vaguely aware of why he had come here. But there was a strong compulsion at the back of his mind; he had to come. And he knew it had something to do with Wainewright.

He stumbled again and almost fell. He put out his hand to the shafting and supported himself. He saw without surprise the black-painted letters as his torch danced across them: SHAFT NO. 247.

There was a strange odour now; something that he had not smelled before. He could not place it and paused hesitantly, the torch in his suddenly nervous hand trembling across the arched metal ceiling of the tunnel. There was dampness, of course; that was something to be expected with the water underfoot. But there was something else, something almost obscene. An animal smell, pungent and rotting to the nostrils; reptilian, if you like.

Driscoll had once visited the zoological gardens long ago, where the few remaining specimens were kept. The aquarium had particularly fascinated him. There was something of that now. The great saurians, some almost a hundred years old, sleeping caked in their beds of mud; glazed green eyes immobile for hours on end. The torch wavered again, and Driscoll sharply snapped his mind back to the present.

He moved cautiously, deliberately blocking out the heavy miasma as he splashed the last yard to the shaft. It was enormous; he couldn't quite remember its original purpose, though it was primarily to do with inspection. Wainewright had been correct about one thing. There was rust on the casing and the bolts. He touched the cold metal with a tentative forefinger, saw it come away red in the light of the torch.

The inspection-chamber hatch was ajar. Driscoll soon saw why.

There was something protruding from it. Something grey and rubbery from which the stench emanated. Driscoll did not like to touch it. Instead, he worked the hatch pivot with his torch. The thing that was jammed in the gap moved as the aperture grew. It looked like an embryonic hand with tiny fingers. Driscoll was startled; his hand slipped on the torch, the metal slid back with a harsh rumble, disturbing in the gloom of the tunnel, and the mass fell with a slopping splash into the water, where it was presumably carried away. Driscoll felt relieved.

The inspection chamber was empty, as he had hoped. The door that connected with the Outside was firmly closed and latched. Driscoll bent his head and listened intently. He could hear nothing but the sound of running water. It was absurd really. He did not know what he expected to hear.

But there was another odour; something like a musky perfume that made his head swim. Driscoll knew what had fascinated Wainewright and his friend Deems before him. The heady odour had something in it that reached back deep into his roots. He saw green fields; a blue sky; corn waving in the breeze. This was not something on the vision tube, but an atavistic memory of reality.

Driscoll staggered and reached out a hand to save himself; he saw the message pad then, lying in the bottom of the chamber. He knew before he picked it up that it was Wainewright's. It bore his own name, he saw without surprise. It merely repeated in block capitals: FREEDOM! And underneath, in smaller letters: UNTIL WE MEET OUT- SIDE. A scribbled *W* ended the message. Driscoll stood and an overwhelming sadness enveloped him; a sadness that was dispelled only by the faint wail of the emergency-squad siren. He took the message pad with him as he went splashing back up the tunnel.

Driscoll was suspended, of course. Someone must have seen him before he regained his quarters, or perhaps the cameras had been working before the lights came on. Hort did not ask to see him; there was merely the dreaded green chit with the official stamp slipped beneath his door as he slept. There would be an official hearing in a week's time.

Driscoll did not wait for the hearing. Something had happened to him. He was hardly conscious of it himself. Nothing seemed to have changed, yet everything had subtly altered. There were no more chess games with Karlson. Nothing was said, but Karlson was never in evidence when Driscoll took his meals. Strangely enough, Krampf, the only person in Central Control who secretly irritated Driscoll, seemed sympathetic at this time of crisis.

Twice Driscoll had met him in the corridors, and it seemed to him that there was a strange secret compassion in his eyes. But he dare not speak to Driscoll; no one dare while he was awaiting the hearing. Similarly, he was no longer welcome in Records, and Driscoll felt he would be under surveillance if he went out. He was no longer trusted; that was the brutal truth. And a person who was no longer trusted here was a nonperson.

He kept his cabin; he could use the restaurant facilities and watch the vision tube. In effect he was limited to eating, sleeping, and passing his time as best he might. No messages came for him; there was no communication from above apart from the green chit; and Hort certainly had no wish to see him. That might prejudice the proceedings.

Driscoll thought about it for three days and three nights; then he made up his mind. It was night as time was measured here, and there would be few people on duty. Driscoll packed a few things; he carried with him a hammer, a wrench, and heavy-duty wire cutters with insulated handles, together with a food supply for three weeks. At the intersection of the first corridor he smashed the camera lens there. He went purposefully down the passages, smashing every installation he could find. Within a minute the alarm was reverberating along the corridors. Driscoll did not care. He was running strongly now, every sense alert.

He was smashing light fixtures too; he was surprised how easily they broke. No one had ever done this before. It was absurdly easy. At the time he hoped that the tunnel section was not guarded; there could be no turning back now. He found his way with difficulty. He must have fused something at the last light installation he smashed, for all these corridors were plunged into darkness.

The small cone of his torch wavered ahead, steadying on the smooth metal surface of the tunnel walls, the heavy bolts and rivets overhead. Here was the place; there was no one about. Water dripped somewhere up ahead as Driscoll splashed unhesitatingly through the puddles. The strange nostalgic stench was in his nostrils. He adjusted the pack on his back and set off at a staggering run over the last quarter of a mile. His heart was beating a little more unsteadily than he would have liked. Still there was no siren of the emergency squad.

The shafting was in front of him. Driscoll could almost taste the stench in his nostrils. It was not oppressive. On the contrary. He breathed deeply. It brought back things he had forgotten ever existed. Sunlight; waving corn; clouds moving across a blue sky; a woman's smile; a child tottering toward an old woman in a white dress.

He stood before Shaft Number 247, noting its massive strength and immense size. Quite without surprise he saw that the hatch of the inspection chamber was half-open. It slid easily beneath his touch. Dance music was reverberating from somewhere; a girl in a bathing suit plunged into blue water, droplets of spray raining downward; there were flowers and with them the fragrant perfume that had been lost for so many decades.

The girl was smiling again. A grave grey-eyed girl, with tawny-gold hair. Driscoll stepped into the inspection chamber. It was cold, and he instinctively shrank at the dampness which settled on his face and clothing. A hurdy-gurdy was playing, and he could smell roast chestnuts. A child bounded past on a scooter, his feet making a click-clacking noise on the setts of the paving. There was the distinctive impact of a cricket bat connecting with a ball on a summer afternoon. Driscoll nodded at the ripple of applause.

He could see the point now. Everything down here was negative. He had to know. He thought of Krampf, Deems, and Wainewright; of Hort and Karlson. He had no real friends; hitherto, the only reality was the tunnels burrowing beneath the earth and the remorselessly efficient humming of the machinery.

It did not seem to be enough. Driscoll set his teeth. Perspiration was streaming down his face as he reached out to the interior hatch of the inspection chamber of Shaft Number 247. A child lifted her head and put her arms round Driscoll's neck. He was smiling as he began to turn the bolts.

His Mouth Will Taste of Wormwood

POPPY Z. BRITE

"To the treasures and the pleasures of the grave," said my friend Louis, and raised his goblet of absinthe to me in drunken benediction.

"To the funeral lilies," I replied, "and to the calm pale bones." I drank deeply from my own glass. The absinthe cauterized my throat with its flavor, part pepper, part licorice, part rot. It had been one of our greatest finds: more than fifty bottles of the now-outlawed liqueur, sealed up in a New Orleans family tomb. Transporting them was a nuisance, but once we had learned to enjoy the taste of wormwood, our continued drunkenness was ensured for a long, long time. We had taken the skull of the crypt's patriarch, too, and it now resided in a velvet-lined enclave in our museum.

Louis and I, you see, were dreamers of a dark and restless sort. We met in our second year of college and quickly found that we shared one vital trait: both of us were dissatisfied with everything. We drank straight whiskey and declared it too weak. We took strange drugs, but the visions they brought us were of emptiness, mindlessness, slow decay. The books we read were dull; the artists who sold their colorful drawings on the street were mere hacks in our eyes; the music we heard was never loud enough, never harsh enough, to stir us. We were truly jaded, we told one another. For all the impression the world made upon us, our eyes might have been dead black holes in our heads.

For a time we thought our salvation lay in the sorcery wrought by music. We studied recordings of weird nameless dissonances, attended performances of obscure bands at ill-lit filthy clubs. But music did not save us. For a time we distracted ourselves with carnality. We explored the damp alien territory between the legs of any girl who would have us, sometimes separately, sometimes both of us in bed together with one girl or more. We bound their wrists and ankles with black lace, we lubricated and penetrated their every orifice, we shamed them with their own pleasures. I recall a mauve-haired beauty, Felicia, who was brought to wild sobbing orgasm by the rough tongue of a stray dog we trapped. We watched her from across the room, drug-dazed and unstirred.

When we had exhausted the possibilities of women we sought those of our own sex, craving the androgynous curve of a boy's cheekbone, the molten flood of ejaculation invading our mouths. Eventually we turned to one another, seeking the thresholds of pain and ecstasy no one else had been able to help us attain. Louis asked me to grow my nails long and file them into needle-sharp points. When I raked them down his back, tiny beads of blood welled up in the angry tracks they left. He loved to lie still, pretending to submit to me, as I licked the salty blood away. Afterward he would push me down and attack me with his mouth, his tongue seeming to sear a trail of liquid fire into my skin.

But sex did not save us either. We shut ourselves in our room and saw no one for days on end. At last we withdrew to the seclusion of Louis's ancestral home near Baton Rouge. Both his parents were dead—a suicide pact, Louis hinted, or perhaps a suicide and a murder. Louis, the only child, retained the family home and fortune. Built on the edge of a vast swamp, the plantation house loomed sepulchrally out of the gloom that surrounded it always, even in the middle of a summer afternoon. Oaks of primordial hugeness grew in a canopy over the house, their branches like black arms fraught with Spanish moss. The moss was everywhere, reminding me of brittle gray hair, stirring wraithlike in the dank breeze from the swamp. I had the impression that, left too long unchecked, the moss might begin to grow from the ornate window frames and fluted columns of the house itself.

The place was deserted save for us. The air was heady with the luminous scent of magnolias and the fetor of swamp gas. At night we sat on the veranda and sipped bottles of wine from the family cellar, gazing through an increasingly alcoholic mist at the will-o'-the-wisps that beckoned far off in the swamp. Obsessively we talked of new thrills and how we might get them. Louis's wit sparkled liveliest when he was bored, and on the night he first mentioned grave robbing, I laughed. I could not imagine that he was serious.

"What would we do with a bunch of dried-up old remains? Grind them to make a voodoo potion? I preferred your idea of increasing our tolerance to various poisons."

Louis's sharp face snapped toward me. His eyes were painfully sensitive to light, so that even in this gloaming he wore tinted glasses and it was impossible to see his expression. He kept his fair hair clipped very short, so that it stood up in crazy tufts when he raked a nervous hand through it. "No, Howard. Think of it: our own collection of death. A catalogue of pain, of human frailty—all for us. Set against a backdrop of tranquil loveliness. Think what it would be to walk through such a place, meditating, reflecting upon your own ephemeral essence. Think of making love in a charnel house! We have only to assemble the parts—they will create a whole into which we may fall."

(Louis enjoyed speaking in cryptic puns; anagrams and palindromes, too, and any sort of puzzle appealed to him. I wonder whether that was not the root of his determination to look into the fathomless eye of death and master it. Perhaps he saw the mortality of the flesh as a gigantic jigsaw or crossword that, if he fitted all the parts into place, he might solve and thus defeat. Louis would have loved to live forever, though he would never have known what to do with all his time.)

He soon produced his hashish pipe to sweeten the taste of the wine, and we spoke no more of grave robbing that night. But the thought preyed upon me in the languorous weeks to come. The smell of a freshly opened grave, I thought, must in its way be as intoxicating as the perfume of the swamp or a girl's most intimate sweat. Could we truly assemble a collection of the grave's treasures that would be lovely to look upon, that would soothe our fevered souls?

The caresses of Louis's tongue grew languid. Sometimes, instead of nestling with me between the black satin sheets of our bed, he would sleep on a torn blanket in one of the underground rooms. These had originally been built for indeterminate but always intriguing purposes—abolitionist meetings had taken place there, Louis told me, and a weekend of free love, and an earnest but wildly incompetent Black Mass replete with a vestal virgin and phallic candles.

These rooms were where our museum would be set up. At last I came to agree with Louis that only the plundering of graves might cure us of the most stifling ennui we had yet suffered. I could not bear to watch his tormented sleep, the pallor of his hollow cheeks, the delicate bruiselike darkening of the skin beneath his flickering eyes. Besides, the notion of grave robbing had begun to entice me. In ultimate corruption, might we not find the path to ultimate salvation?

Our first grisly prize was the head of Louis's mother, rotten as a pumpkin forgotten on the vine, half shattered by two bullets from an antique Civil War revolver. We took it from the family crypt by the light of a full moon. The will-o'-the-wisps glowed weakly, like dying beacons on some unattainable shore, as we crept back to the manse. I dragged pick and shovel behind me; Louis carried the putrescent trophy tucked beneath his arm. After we had descended into the museum, I lit three candles scented with the russet spices of autumn (the season when Louis's parents had died) while Louis placed the head in the alcove we had prepared for it. I thought I detected a certain tenderness in his manner. "May she give us the family blessing," he murmured, absently wiping on the lapel of his jacket a few shreds of pulpy flesh that had adhered to his fingers.

We spent a happy time refurbishing the museum, polishing the inlaid precious metals of the wall fixtures, brushing away the dust that frosted the velvet designs of the wallpaper, alternately burning incense and charring bits of cloth we had saturated with our blood, in order to give the rooms the odor we desired—a charnel perfume strong enough to drive us to frenzy. We traveled far in our collections, but always we returned home with crates full of things no man had ever been meant to possess. We heard of a girl with violet eyes who had died in some distant town; not seven days later we had those eyes in an ornate cut-glass jar, pickled in formaldehyde. We scraped bone dust and nitre from the bottoms of ancient coffins; we stole the barely withered heads and hands of children fresh in their graves, with their soft little fingers and their lips like flower petals. We had baubles and precious heirlooms, vermiculated prayer books and shrouds encrusted with mould. I had not taken seriously Louis's talk of making love in a charnel house—but neither had I reckoned on the pleasure he could inflict with a femur dipped in rose-scented oil.

Upon the night I speak of—the night we drank our toast to the grave and its riches—we had just acquired our finest prize yet. Later in the evening we planned a celebratory debauch at a nightclub in the city. We had returned from our most recent travels not with the usual assortment of sacks and crates, but with only one small box carefully wrapped and tucked into Louis's breast pocket. The box contained an object whose existence we had only speculated upon previously. From certain half-articulate mutterings of an old blind man plied with cheap liquor in a French Quarter bar, we traced rumors of a certain fetish or charm to a Negro graveyard in the southern bayou country. The fetish was said to be a thing of eerie beauty, capable of luring any lover to one's bed, hexing any enemy to a sick and painful death, and (this, I think, was what intrigued Louis the most) turning back tenfold on anyone who used it with less than the touch of a master.

A heavy mist hung low over the graveyard when we arrived there, lapping at our ankles, pooling around the markers of wood and stone, abruptly melting away in patches to reveal a gnarled root or a patch of blackened grass, then closing back in. By the light of a waning moon we made our way along a path overgrown with rioting weeds. The graves were decorated with elaborate mosaics of broken glass, coins, bottle caps, oyster shells lacquered silver and gold. Some mounds were outlined by empty bottles shoved neck-downward into the earth. I saw a lone plaster saint whose features had been worn away by years of wind and rain. I kicked half-buried rusty cans that had once held flowers; now they held only bare brittle stems and pestilent rainwater, or nothing at all. Only the scent of wild spider lilies pervaded the night.

The earth in one corner of the graveyard seemed blacker than the rest. The grave we sought was marked only by a crude cross of charred and twisted wood. We were skilled at the art of violating the dead; soon we had the coffin uncovered. The boards were warped by years of burial in wet, foul earth. Louis pried up the lid with his spade, and by the moon's meager and watery light, we gazed upon what lay within.

Of the inhabitant we knew almost nothing. Some said a hideously disfigured old conjure woman lay buried here. Some said she was a young girl with a face as lovely and cold as moonlight on water, and a soul crueler than Fate itself. Some claimed the body was not a woman's at all, but that of a white voodoo priest who had ruled the bayou. He had features of a cool, unearthly beauty, they said, and a stock of fetishes and potions that he would hand out with the kindest blessing . . . or the direst curse. This was the story Louis and I liked best; the sorcerer's capriciousness appealed to us, and the fact that he was beautiful.

No trace of beauty remained to the thing in the coffin—at least not the sort of beauty that a healthy eye might cherish. Louis and I loved the translucent parchment skin stretched tight over long bones that seemed to have been carved from ivory. The delicate brittle hands folded across the sunken chest, the soft black caverns of the eyes, the colorless strands of hair that still clung to the fine white dome of the skull—to us these things were the poetry of death.

Louis played his flashlight over the withered cords of the neck. There, on a silver chain gone black with age, was the object we had come seeking. No crude wax doll or bit of dried root was this. Louis and I gazed at each other, moved by the beauty of the thing; then, as if in a dream, he reached to grasp it. This was our rightful night's prize, our plunder from a sorcerer's grave.

"How does it look?" Louis asked as we were dressing.

I never had to think about my clothes. On an evening such as this, when we were dressing to go out, I would choose the same garments I might wear for a night's digging in the graveyard—black, unornamented black, with only the whiteness of my face and hands showing against the backdrop of night. On a particularly festive occasion, such as this, I might smudge a bit of kohl round my eyes. The absence of color made me nearly invisible: if I walked with my shoulders hunched and my chin tucked down, no one except Louis would see me.

"Don't slouch so, Howard," said Louis irritably as I ducked past the mirror. "Turn around and look at me. Aren't I fine in my sorcerer's jewelry?"

Even when Louis wore black, he did it to be noticed. Tonight he was resplendent in narrow-legged trousers of purple paisley silk and a silvery jacket that seemed to turn all light iridescent. He had taken our prize out of its box and fastened it around his throat. As I came closer to look at it, I caught Louis's scent: rich and rather meaty, like blood kept too long in a stoppered bottle.

Against the sculpted hollow of Louis's throat, the thing on its chain seemed more strangely beautiful than ever. Have I neglected to describe that magical object, the voodoo fetish from the churned earth of the grave? I will never forget it. A polished sliver of bone (or a tooth, but what fang could have been so long, so sleekly honed, and still have somehow retained the look of a *human tooth*?) bound by a strip of copper. Set into the metal, a single ruby sparkled like a drop of gore against the verdigris. Etched in exquisite miniature upon the sliver of bone, and darkened by the rubbing in of some black-red substance, was an elaborate *vévé*—one of the symbols used by voodooists to invoke their pantheon of terrible gods. Whoever was buried in that lonely bayou grave, he had been no mere dabbler in swamp magic. Every cross and swirl of the *vévé* was reproduced to perfection. I thought the thing still retained a trace of the grave's scent—a dark odor like potatoes long spoiled. Each grave has its own peculiar scent, just as each living body does.

"Are you certain you should wear it?" I asked.

"It will go into the museum tomorrow," he said, "with a scarlet candle burning eternally before it. Tonight its powers are mine."

The nightclub was in a part of the city that looked as if it had been gutted from the inside out by a righteous tongue of fire. The street was lit only by occasional scribbles of neon high overhead, advertisements for cheap hotels and all-night bars. Dark eyes stared at us from the crevices and pathways between buildings, disappearing only when Louis's hand crept toward the inner pocket of his jacket. He carried a small stiletto there, and knew how to use it for more than pleasure.

We slipped through a door at the end of an alley and descended the narrow staircase into the club. The lurid glow of a blue bulb flooded the stairs, making Louis's face look sunken and dead behind his tinted glasses. Feedback blasted us as we came in, and above it, a screaming battle of guitars. The inside of the club was a patchwork of flickering light and darkness. Graffiti covered the walls and the ceiling like a tangle of barbed wire come alive. I saw bands' insignia and jeering death's-heads, crucifixes bejeweled with broken glass and black obscenities writhing in the stroboscopic light.

Louis brought me a drink from the bar. I sipped it slowly, still drunk on absinthe. Since the music was too loud for conversation, I studied the clubgoers around us. A quiet bunch, they were, staring fixedly at the stage as if they had been drugged (and no doubt many of them had—I remembered visiting a club one night on a dose of hallucino-genic mushrooms, watching in fascination as the guitar strings seemed to drip soft viscera onto the stage). Younger than Louis and myself, most of them were, and queerly beautiful in their thrift-shop rags, their leather and fishnet and cheap costume jewelry, their pale faces and painted hair. Perhaps we would take one of them home with us tonight. We had done so before. "The delicious guttersnipes," Louis called them. A particularly beautiful face, starkly boned and androgy-nous, flickered at the edge of my vision. When I looked, it was gone.

I went into the restroom. A pair of boys stood at a single urinal, talking animatedly. I paused at the sink rinsing my hands, watching the boys in the mirror and trying to overhear their conversation. A hairline fracture in the glass seemed to pull the taller boy's eyes askew. "Caspar and Alyssa found her tonight," he said. "In some old ware-house by the river. I heard her skin was *gray*, man. And sort of with-ered, like something had sucked out most of the meat."

"Far out," said the other boy. His black-rimmed lips barely moved.

"She was only fifteen, you know?" said the tall boy as he zipped his ragged trousers.

"She was a cunt anyway."

They turned away from the urinal and started talking about the band—Ritual Sacrifice, I gathered, whose name was scrawled on the walls of the club. As they went out, the boys glanced at the mirror and the tall one's eyes met mine for an instant. Nose like a haughty Indian chief's, eyelids smudged with black and silver. Louis would approve, I thought—but the night was young, and there were many drinks left to be had.

When the band took a break we visited the bar again. Louis edged in beside a thin dark-haired boy who was bare-chested except for a piece of torn lace tied about his throat. When he turned, I knew his was the androgynous and striking face I had glimpsed before. His beauty was almost feral, but overlaid with a cool elegance like a veneer of sanity hiding madness. His ivory skin stretched over cheekbones like razors; his eyes were hectic pools of darkness.

"I like your amulet," he said to Louis. "It's very unusual."

"I have another one like it at home," Louis told him.

"Really? I'd like to see them both together." The boy paused to let Louis order our vodka gimlets, then said, "I thought there was only one."

Louis's back straightened like a string of beads being pulled taut. Behind his glasses, I knew, his pupils would have shrunk to pinpoints: the light pained him more when he was nervous. But no tremor in his voice betrayed him when he said, "What do you know about it?"

The boy shrugged. On his bony shoulders, the movement was insouciant and drop-dread graceful. "It's voodoo," he said. "I know what voodoo is. Do you?"

The implication stung, but Louis only bared his teeth the slightest bit; it might have been a smile. "I am *conversant* in all types of magic," he said, "at least."

The boy moved closer to Louis, so that their hips were almost touching, and lifted the amulet between thumb and forefinger. I thought I saw one long nail brush Louis's throat, but I could not be sure. "I could tell you the meaning of this *vévé*," he said, "if you were certain you wished to know."

"It symbolizes power," Louis said. "All the power of my soul." His voice was cold, but I saw his tongue dart out to moisten his lips. He was beginning to dislike this boy, and also to desire him.

"No," said the boy so softly that I barely caught his words. He sounded almost sad. "This cross in the center is inverted, you see, and the line encircling it represents a serpent. A thing like this can trap your soul. Instead of being rewarded with eternal life . . . you might be doomed to it."

"Doomed to eternal life?" Louis permitted himself a small cold smile. "Whatever do you mean?"

"The band is starting again. Find me after the show and I'll tell you. We can have a drink . . . and you can tell me all you know about voodoo." The boy threw back his head and laughed. Only then did I notice that one of his upper canine teeth was missing.

The next part of the evening remains a blur of moonlight and neon, ice cubes and blue swirling smoke and sweet drunkenness. The boy drank glass after glass of absinthe with us, seeming to relish the bitter taste. None of our other guests had liked the liqueur. "Where did you get it?" he asked. Louis was silent for a long moment before he said, "It was sent over from France." Except for its single black gap, the boy's smile would have been as perfect as the sharp-edged crescent moon.

"Another drink?" said Louis, refilling both our glasses.

When I next came to clarity, I was in the boy's arms. I could not make out the words he was whispering; they might have been an incantation, if magic may be sung to pleasure's music. A pair of hands cupped my face, guiding my lips over the boy's pale parchment skin. They might have been Louis's hands. I knew nothing except this boy, the fragile movement of the bones beneath the skin, the taste of his spit bitter with wormwood.

I do not remember when he finally turned away from me and began lavishing his love upon Louis. I wish I could have watched, could have seen the lust bleeding into Louis's eyes, the pleasure racking his body. For, as it turned out, the boy loved Louis so much more thoroughly than ever he loved me.

When I awoke, the bass thump of my pulse echoing through my skull blotted out all other sensations. Gradually, though, I became aware of tangled silk sheets, of hot sunlight on my face. Not until I came fully awake did I see the thing I had cradled like a lover all through the night.

For an instant two realities shifted in uneasy juxtaposition and almost merged. I was in Louis's bed; I recognized the feel of the sheets, their odor of silk and sweat. But this thing I held—this was surely one of the fragile mummies we had dragged out of their graves, the things we dissected for our museum. It took me only a moment, though, to recognize the familiar ruined features—the sharp chin, the high elegant brow. Something had desiccated Louis, had drained him of every drop of his moisture, his vitality. His skin crackled and flaked away beneath my fingers. His hair stuck to my lips, dry and colorless. The amulet, which had still been around his throat in bed last night, was gone.

The boy had left no trace—or so I thought until I saw a nearly transparent thing at the foot of the bed. It was like a quantity of spiderweb, or a damp and insubstantial veil. I picked it up and shook it out, but could not see its features until I held it up to the window. The thing was vaguely human-shaped, with empty limbs trailing off into nearly invisible tatters. As the thing wafted and billowed, I saw part of a face in it—the sharp curve left by a cheekbone, the hole where an eye had been—as if a face were imprinted upon gauze.

I carried Louis's brittle shell of a corpse down into the museum. Laying him before his mother's niche, I left a stick of incense burning in his folded hands and a pillow of black silk cradling the papery dry bulb of his skull. He would have wished it thus.

The boy has not come to me again, though I leave the window open every night. I have been back to the club, where I stand sipping vodka and watching the crowd. I have seen many beauties, many strange wasted faces, but not the one I seek. I think I know where I will find him. Perhaps he still desires me—I must know.

I will go again to the lonely graveyard in the bayou. Once more—alone, this time—I will find the unmarked grave and plant my spade in its black earth. When I open the coffin—I know it, I am sure of it!—I will find not the mouldering thing we beheld before, but the calm beauty of replenished youth. The youth he drank from Louis. His face will be a scrimshaw mask of tranquility. The amulet—I know it; I am sure of it—will be around his neck.

Dying: the final shock of pain or nothingness that is the price we pay for everything. Could it not be the sweetest thrill, the only salvation we can attain ... the only true moment of self-knowledge? The dark pools of his eyes will open, still and deep enough to drown in. He will hold out his arms to me, inviting me to lie down with him in his rich wormy bed.

With the first kiss his mouth will taste of wormwood. After that it will taste only of me—of my blood, my life, siphoning out of my body and into his. I will feel the sensations Louis felt: the shriveling of my tissues, the drying-up of all my vital juices. I care not. The treasures and the pleasures of the grave? They are his hands, his lips, his tongue.

The Adder

FRED CHAPPELL

My Uncle Alvin reminds the startled stranger of a large, happy bunny. He is pleasantly rotund, and with silver-blond hair that makes him look a full decade younger than his sixty years. His skin has a scrubbed pink shine that the pale complexions of English curates sometimes acquire, and he has a way of wrinkling his nose that one irresistibly associates with—well, I've already mentioned rabbits. He is a kindly, humorous, and often mildly mischievous fellow.

My admiration of Uncle Alvin has had a large measure of influence upon my life. His easygoing manner has seemed to me a sensible way to get along in the world. And his occupation is interesting and leisurely, though it's unlikely he'll ever gain great wealth by it. I can support this latter supposition by my own experience: I followed my uncle into the antiquarian book trade, and I am not—please let me assure you—a rich man.

We don't compete with one another, however. Uncle Alvin lives in Columbia, South Carolina, and runs his mail-order business from his home. The bulk of my trade is also mail order, but I run it from a shopfront in Durham, North Carolina. My shop sells used paperbacks, mostly to Duke University students; in the back I package and mail out rare and curious books of history, the occult, and fantasy, along with some occasional odd science fiction. Uncle Alvin specializes in Civil War history, which in South Carolina almost guarantees a living income, however modest.

But anyone in the trade is likely to happen upon any sort of book, whether it belongs to his specialty or not. When Uncle Alvin called one Saturday morning to say that he had come into possession of a volume that he wanted me to see, I surmised that it was more in my line than his, and that he thought I might be interested in making a purchase.

"What sort of book is it?" I asked.

"Very rare indeed—if it's genuine. And still rather valuable if it's only a forgery."

"What's the title?"

"Oh, I can't tell you that on the telephone," he said.

"You can't tell me the title? It must be something extraordinary."

"Caution never hurts. Anyway, you can see it for yourself. I'll be by your place with it on Monday morning. If that's all right with you."

"Say, that's grand," I said. "You'll stay overnight, of course. Helen will be thrilled to see you."

"No," he said. "I'm driving through to Washington. I'll stop off on the way. Because I don't want to keep this book in the car any longer than I have to."

"We'll have lunch, at least," I said. "Do you still crave lasagne?"

"Day and night," he replied.

"Then it's settled," I said, and we chatted a little longer before ringing off.

Monday morning he entered my shop—called Alternate Histories—carrying a battered metal cashbox, and I knew the book was inside it. We sounded the usual pleasantries that friendly kinfolk make with one another, though ours may have been more genuinely felt than many. But he was anxious to get to the business he had in mind. He set the cashbox on top of a stack of used magazines on the counter and said, "Well, this is it."

"All right," I said. "I'm ready. Open her up."

"First, let me tell you a little bit about what I think we have here," he said. "Because when you see it, you're going to be disappointed. Its appearance is not prepossessing."

"All right."

"In the first place, it's in Arabic. It's handwritten in a little diary in ordinary badly faded ink and it's incomplete. Since I don't read Arabic, I don't know what's missing. I only know that it's too short to be the full version. This copy came to me from the widow of a classics professor at the University of South Carolina, an Egyptologist who disappeared on a field excursion some thirty years ago. His wife kept his library all this time, hoping for his return. Then, last year, she offered up the whole lot. That's how I happen to be in possession of this copy of *Al Azif*."

"I never heard of it," I said, trying not to show the minor disappointment I felt.

"It's the work of a medieval poet thought to have been insane," Uncle Alvin said, "but there is debate as to how crazy he actually was. His name was Abdul Alhazred and he lived in Yemen. Shortly after composing *Al Azif* he met a violent and grisly death—which is all we know about it because even the eyewitnesses dispute the manner of his dying."

"Abdul Alhazred. Isn't that—?"

"Yes indeed," he said. "The work is more recognizable under the title of its Greek translation, *The Necronomicon*. And the most widely known text—if any of them can really be said to be widely known—is the thirteenth-century Latin translation of Olaus Wormius. It has always been surmised that the original Arabic text perished long ago, since every powerful government and respected religious organization has tried to destroy the work in all its forms. And they have largely succeeded in doing so."

"But how do you know what it is, if you don't read Arabic?"

"I have a friend," he said proudly. "Dr. Abu-Saba. I asked him to look at it and to give me a general idea of the contents. When I handed it to him and he translated the title, I stopped him short. Better not to go on with *that*. You know the reputation of *The Necronomicon*."

"I do indeed," I said, "and I don't care to know what's in it in any detail. In fact, I'm not really overjoyed at finding myself in such close company."

"Oh, we should be safe enough. As long as we keep our mouths closed so that certain unsavory groups of cultists don't hear that we've got it."

"If you're offering it to me for sale—" I began.

"No, no," he said hastily. "I'm trying to arrange to deposit it in the Library of Congress. That's why I'm going to Washington. I wouldn't put my favorite nephew in jeopardy—or not for long, anyway. All I would like is for you to keep it for a week while I'm negotiating. I'm asking as a personal favor."

I considered. "I'll be happy to keep it for you," I said. "To tell the truth, I'm more concerned about the security of the book than about my own safety. I can take care of myself. But the book is a dangerous article, and an extremely valuable one."

"Like an atomic weapon," Uncle Alvin said. "Too dangerous to keep and too dangerous to dispose of. But the Library of Congress will know what to do. This can't be the first time they've encountered this problem."

"You think they already have a *Necronomicon*?"

"I'd bet money," he said cheerfully, "except that I wouldn't know how to collect. You don't expect them to list it in the catalogue, do you?"

"They'd deny possession, of course."

"But there's a good chance they won't have an Arabic version. Only one is known to have reached America, and it was thought to have been destroyed in San Francisco around the turn of the century. This volume is probably a copy of that version."

"So what do I do with it?" I asked.

"Put it in a safe place. In your lockbox at the bank."

"I don't have one of those," I said. "I have a little old dinky safe in my office in back, but if anyone came to find it, that's the first place they'd look."

"Do you have a cellar in this shop?"

"Not that I'd trust the book to. Why don't we take a hint from Edgar Allan Poe?"

He frowned a moment, then brightened. "A purloined letter, you mean?"

"Sure. I've got all sorts of books scattered about in cardboard boxes. I haven't sorted them yet to shelve. It would take weeks for someone to hunt it out even if he knew it was here."

"It might work," Uncle Alvin said, wrinkling his nose and rubbing his pink ear with a brisk forefinger. "But there's a problem."

"What's that?"

"You may wish to disregard it because of its legendary nature. I wouldn't. In the case of *Al Azif*, it's best to take every precaution."

"All right," I said. "What's the legend?"

"Among certain bookmen, *The Necronomicon* is sometimes known as *The Adder*. Because first it poisons, then it devours."

I gave him a look that I intended to mean: not another one of your little jokes, Uncle Alvin. "You don't really expect me to believe that we've got a book here that eats people."

"Oh no." He shook his head. "It only eats its own kind."

"I don't understand."

"Just make sure," he said, "that when you place it in a box with other books, none of them is important."

"I get it," I said. "Damaged cheap editions. To draw attention away from its true value."

He gave me a long, mild stare, then nodded placidly. "Something like that," he replied at last.

"Okay," I agreed, "I'll do exactly that. Now let's have a look at this ominous rarity. I've heard about *The Necronomicon* ever since I became interested in books. I'm all aflutter."

"I'm afraid you're going to be disappointed," Uncle Alvin said. "Some copies of this forbidden text are quite remarkable, but this one—" He twitched his nose again and rubbed it with the palm of his hand.

"Now don't be a naughty tease, Uncle Alvin," I said.

He unlocked the metal box and took out a small parcel wrapped in brown paper. He peeled away the paper to reveal a rather thin octavo diary with a worn morocco cover that had faded from what would have been a striking red to a pale brick color, almost pinkish. Noticing the expression on my face, he said, "See? I told you it would be a disappointment."

"No, not at all," I said, but my tone was so obviously subdued that he handed it to me to examine without my asking.

There was little to see. The pinkish worn binding felt smooth. The spine was hubbed and stamped *Diary* in gold, but the gold, too, had almost worn away. I opened it at random and looked at incomprehensible Arabic script so badly faded that it was impossible to say what color the ink had been. Black or purple or maybe even dark green—but now all the colors had become a pale uniform gray. I leafed through almost to the end but found nothing in the least remarkable.

"Well, I do hope this is the genuine article," I said. "Are you sure your friend, Dr. Hoodoo—"

"Abu-Saba," said Uncle Alvin primly. "Dr. Fuad Abu-Saba. His knowledge of his native tongue is impeccable, his integrity unassailable."

"Okay, if you say so," I said. "But what we have here doesn't look like much."

"I'm not trying to sell it. Its nondescript appearance is in our favor. The more undistinguished it looks, the safer we are."

"That makes sense," I admitted, handing it back to him.

He glanced at me shrewdly as he returned it to the cashbox, obviously thinking that I was merely humoring him—as to a certain extent I was. "Robert," he said sternly, "you're my favorite nephew, one of my most favorite persons. I want you to follow my instructions seriously. I want you to take the strongest precautions and keep on your guard. This is a dangerous passage for both of us."

I sobered. "All right, Uncle Alvin. You know best."

He wrapped the volume in the brown paper and restored it to the scarred box and carried it with him as we repaired to Tony's Ristorante Venezia to indulge copiously in lasagne and a full-bodied Chianti. After lunch he dropped me back at Alternate Histories and, taking *Al Azif* out of the metal box, gave it over to my safekeeping with a single word of admonition. "Remember," he said.

"Don't worry," I said. "I remember."

In the shop I examined the book in a more leisurely and comprehensive fashion. But it hadn't changed; it was only one more dusty, faded, stained diary like thousands of others, and its sole distinction to the unlearned eye was that it was in handwritten Arabic script. A mysterious gang of sinister thieves would have to know a great deal about it merely in order to know for what to search.

I decided not to trust it to a jumble of books in a maze of cardboard boxes. I took it into my little backroom office, shoved some valueless books out of the way, and laid it flat on a lower shelf of a ramshackle bookcase there that was cluttered with every sort of pamphlet, odd periodical, and assorted volume from broken sets of Maupassant, Balzac, and William McFee. I turned it so that the gilt edge faced outward and the word *Diary* was hidden. Then I deliberated for a minute or two about what to stack on top of it.

I thought of Uncle Alvin's warning that no important books were to be placed with *Al Azif*, and I determined to heed it. What's the point in having a favorite uncle, wise and experienced in his trade, if you don't listen to him? And besides that, the dark reputation of the book was an urgent warning in itself.

I picked up an ordinary and utterly undistinguished copy of Milton's poems—Herndon House, New York, 1924. No introduction and a few sketchy notes by an anonymous editor, notes no doubt reduced from a solid scholarly edition. It was a warped copy and showed significant water damage. I opened to the beginning of *Paradise Lost* and read the first twenty-six lines, then searched to find my favorite Miltonic sonnet, number XIX, "On His Blindness."

> When I consider how my light is spent
> Ere half my days, in this dark world and wide,
> And that one Talent which is death to hide,
> Lodg'd with me useless, though my Soul more bent
> To serve therewith my Maker, and present
> My true account, lest He returning chide . . .

Well, you know how it goes.

It's a poem of which I never tire, one of those poems that has faithfully befriended me in periods happy and unhappy since the years of my majority. Milton's customary stately music is there, and a heartfelt personal outcry not often to be found in his work. Then there comes the sternly contented resolution of the final lines. Milton requires, of course, no recommendation from me, and his sonnet no encomium. I only desire to make it clear that this poet is important to me and the sonnet on his blindness particularly dear.

But not every copy, or every edition, of Milton is important. I have personal copies of fully annotated and beautifully illustrated editions. The one I held in my hand was only a cheap mass edition, designed in all probability to be sold at railway bookstalls. I placed it on top of the Arabic treasure and then piled over both books a stack of papers from my desk, which is always overflowing with such papers: catalogues, book lists, sale announcements, and invoices. Of this latter item especially there is an eternal surplus.

Then I forgot about it.

No, I didn't.

I didn't in the least forget that I almost certainly had in my possession *Al Azif*, one of the rarest documents in bibliographic annals, one of the enduring titles of history and legend—and one of the deadliest. We don't need to rehearse the discomfiting and unsanitary demises alleged of so many former owners of the book. They all came to bad ends, and messy ones. Uncle Alvin had the right idea, getting the volume into the hands of those prepared to care for it. My mission was merely a holding action—to keep it safe for a week. That being so, I resolved not to go near it, not even to look at it until my uncle returned the following Saturday.

And I was able to keep to my resolution until Tuesday, the day after I'd made it.

The manuscript in its diary format had changed when I looked. I noticed right away that the morocco covers had lost their pinkish cast and taken on a bright red. The stamped word *Diary* shone more brightly, too, and when I opened the volume and leafed through it, I saw that the pages had whitened, losing most of the signs of age, and that the inked script stood forth more boldly. It was now possible to discern, in fact, that the writing actually was clothed in different colors of ink: black, emerald green, royal purple, Persian rose.

The Necronomicon, in whatever version, is a remarkable book. All the world knows something of its reputation, and I might have been more surprised if my encounter with it had been uneventful than if something unusual transpired. Its history is too long, and a knowledgeable scholar does not respond to mysterious happenings in the presence of the book by smiting his breast and exclaiming, "Can such things be?"

But a change in the physical makeup of the book itself was something I had not expected and for which I could not account. Not knowing yet what to think, I replaced it just as it had been, beneath the random papers and the copy of Milton, and went on with my ordinary tasks.

There was, however, no denying the fact of the changes. My senses did not belie me. Each time I examined it on Tuesday and Wednesday— I must have picked it up a dozen times all told—our *Al Azif* had grown stronger.

Stronger: as silly as that word seems in this context, it is still accurate. The script was becoming more vivid, the pages gleamed like fresh snowbanks, the staunch morocco covers glowed bloodred.

It took me too long to understand that this manuscript had found something to feed upon. It had discovered a form of nourishment that caused it to thrive and grow stout. And I am embarrassed to admit that more hours elapsed before I guessed the source of the volume's food—which had to be the copy of Milton's poems I had placed on top of it.

Quickly then I snatched up the Milton and began to examine it for changes. At first I could discover no anomalies. The print seemed perhaps a little grayer, but it had already been rather faded. Perhaps, too, the pages were more brittle and musty than I'd thought—but, after all, it was a cheap book some sixty-odd years old. When I turned to the opening of *Paradise Lost*, all seemed well enough; the great organ tones were as resonant as ever:

> Of Man's First Disobedience, and the Fruit
> Of that Forbidden Tree, whose mortal taste—
> Brought Death into the World, and all our woe . . .

And I thought, Well, I needn't have worried. This poetry is immune to the ravages of time and of all circumstance.

So it was in anticipation of a fleeting pleasure that I turned idly to glance at sonnet XIX:

> When I consider how my loot is spent
> On Happy Daze, a fifth of darling wine . . .

But the familiar opening of the sonnet had lost much of its savor; I was missing something of that intimate stateliness to which I was accustomed. I set down my pallid reaction to tiredness and excited nerves. Anxiety about Uncle Alvin's treasure was beginning to tell on me, I thought.

I shook my head as if to clear it, closed my eyes and rubbed them with both hands, then looked once more into the volume of Milton open on the counter, sonnet XIX:

> When I consider how my lute is bent
> On harpy fates in this dork woolly-wold,
> And that dung-yellow witches' breath doth glide,
> Lobster and toothless . . .

No use—I was too confused to make sense of the lines at all. It's only nerves, I thought again, and thought, too, how glad I would be for my uncle's return on Sunday.

I laid the copy of *Al Azif* down and determined to put the puzzle out of my mind.

I couldn't do that, of course. The idea had occurred that our particular copy of Abdul Alhazred's forbidden work was changing the nature of Milton's lines. What was it Uncle Alvin had compared it to? An adder, was it? First it poisons, he'd said, then it devours. Was it indeed poisoning the lines of the great seventeenth-century poet? I took up the Milton again and opened to the beginning of his immortal religious epic:

> Of Man's First Dish of Beetles, and the Fat
> Of that Forboding Fay, whom Myrtle Trent
> Brought fresh into the World, and Hollywood . . .

The words made no sense to me, none at all—but I couldn't remember them any differently than how they appeared on the page. I couldn't tell whether the fault lay in the book or in myself.

A sudden thought inspired me to go to my poetry shelves and find another edition of Milton's poems so that I could cross-check the strange-seeming verses. If *Al Azif* truly was changing the words in the other, then a book untouched by the diary would render up only the purest Milton. I went round to the front and took down three copies of Milton's poems in different editions and used my favorite sonnet as touchstone. The first one I examined was Sir Hubert Portingale's Oxbridge edition of 1957. It gave me these lines:

> When I consider to whom my Spode is lent,
> Ear-halves and jays on this dark girlie slide . . .

It seemed incorrect somehow. I looked at the poem in Professor Y. Y. Miranda's Big Apple State University Press volume of 1974:

"Winnie's Corn Cider, how my lust is burnt!"

That line was wrong, I felt it in my bones. I turned to the more informal edition edited by the contemporary poet Richmond Burford:

> When I consider how a lighter splint
> Veered off my dice in this dour curled end-word
> And that wan Talent . . .

I shook my head. Was that correct? Was it anywhere near correct?

The trouble was that I couldn't remember how the lines were supposed to read. I had the vague feeling that none of these versions was the right one. Obviously, they couldn't all be right. But why couldn't I remember my favorite poem, more familiar to me than my Social Security number?

Uncle Alvin's warning had been "First it poisons, then it devours."

Now I began to interpret his words in a different way. Perhaps *The Necronomicon* didn't poison only the book it was in physical contact with, perhaps it poisoned the actual content of the work itself, so that in whatever edition it appeared, in whatever book, magazine, published lecture, scholarly essay, commonplace book, personal diary—in whatever written form—a polluted text showed up.

It was an altogether terrifying thought. Uncle Alvin had not warned against placing it with an important *edition*; his warning concerned an important *book*. I had placed it with Milton and had infected the great poems wherever they now might appear.

Could that be right? It seemed a little far-fetched. Well no, it seemed as silly as picturing Milton, the poet himself, in a Shriner's hat. It seemed just dog-dumb.

But I determined to test my wild hypothesis, nevertheless. I got to the telephone and called my old friend and faithful customer in Knoxville, Tennessee, the poet Ned Clark. When he said hello, I was almost rude: "Please don't ask me a lot of questions, Ned. This is urgent. Do you have a copy of Milton's poems handy?"

He paused. Then: "Robert, is that you?"

"Yes it is. But I'm in an awful hurry. Do you have the poems?"

"In my study."

"Can you get the book, please?"

"Hold on," he said. "I have an extension. I'll pick up in there." I waited as patiently as I was able until he said, "Here we are. What's the big deal?"

"Sonnet XIX," I said. "Would you please read it to me?"

"Right now? Over the phone?"

"Yes. Unless you can shout very loud."

"Hey, man," he said. "Chill out, why don't you?"

"I'm sorry, Ned," I said, "but I think I may have made a big mistake. I mean, a heavy *bad* mistake, old son. So I'm trying to check up on something. Could you read the poems to me?"

"Sure, that's cool," he replied, and I heard him leafing through his book. "Okay, Robert. Are you ready? Here goes: 'When icons in a house mild lights suspend, Or half my ties in this stark world have died. . . .' "

I interrupted. "Okay, Ned. Thanks. That's all I need to hear right now."

"That's all? You called long distance to hear me say two lines of your favorite poem?"

"Yes I did. How did they sound to you?"

"As good as Milton gets."

"Did they sound correct? Are those the words as you've known them all your life?"

"I haven't known them all my life," he said. "You're the wild-haired Milton fan. He's too monumental for my taste, you know? I mean, massive."

"Okay, but you've read the poem, at least."

"Yes indeedy. It's a big-time famous poem. I read all those babies, you know that."

"And these lines are the ones you've always known?"

Another pause. "Well, maybe not exactly," he admitted. "I think the punctuation might be a little different in this book from what I'm used to. But it mainly sounds right. Do you want publication information?"

"Not now," I said, "but I may call back later for it." I thanked my friend and hung up.

It seemed that my surmise was correct. All the texts were now envenomed. But I wanted to make certain of the fact and spent the next four hours telephoning friends and acquaintances scattered throughout America, comparing the lines. Not every one answered, of course, and some of my friends in the western states were groggy with sleep, but I got a large enough sample of first lines to satisfy me.

Walt Pavlich in California: "One-Eye can so draw, my late sow's pen. . ."

Paul Ruffin in Texas: "Wind I consider now my life has bent . . ."

Robert Shapard in Hawaii: "Wound a clean liver and the lights go out . . ."

Vanessa Haley in Virginia: "Wind a gone slider and collide a bunt . . ."

Valerie Colander in West Virginia: "Watch a corned beef sandwich bow and bend . . ."

These were enough and more for me to understand the enormity of my mistake. All the texts of Milton that existed were now disfigured beyond recognition. And I had noted a further consequence of my error. Even the texts as they resided in memory were changed; not one of my friends could remember how the lines of sonnet XIX were *supposed* to read. Nor could I, and I must have been for a decade and a half one of the more constant companions of the poem.

The copy of *Al Azif* was flourishing. I didn't need even to pick it up to see that. The gilt edge shone like a gold bar fresh from Fort Knox and the morocco binding had turned ruby red and pulsed with light like a live coal. I was curious how the inks would glitter, so now I did pick up the volume—which seemed as alive in my hands as a small animal—and opened it at random.

I was right. The different colors of the inks were as vivid and muscular as kudzu and looked as if they were bitten into the thick creamy pages like etching. However disquieting these changes, they had resulted in a truly beautiful manuscript, a masterpiece of its kind. And though I knew it to be a modern handwritten copy, it also seemed to be regaining some of its medieval characteristics. Most of the pages were no longer totally in Arabic; they had become macaronic. Toward the end pages a few English words were sprinkled into the Eastern script.

Oh no.

As long as *Al Azif* was in Arabic it was relatively harmless. Most people would be unable to read the spells and incantations and the knowledge to be found there that is—well, the traditional epithet is *unspeakable*, and it is accurately descriptive. I certainly would not speak of the contents, even if I was able to read them.

I flipped to the front. The first lines I found in the first page were these:

Wisely did Ibn Mushacah say, that happy is the tomb where no wizard hath lain, and happy the town at night whose wizards are all ashes. For the spirit of the devil-indentured hastes not from his charnel clay, but feeds and instructs the very worm that gnaws. Then an awful life from corruption springs and feeds again the appointed scavengers upon the earth. Great holes are dug hidden where are the open pores of the earth, and things have learned to walk that ought to crawl.

I snapped the cover shut. Those phrases had the true stink of *The Necronomicon.* You don't have to be an expert upon the verses of Alhazred to recognize his style and subject matter.

I had read all of these pages that I ever wanted to read, but even so I opened the volume again, to the middle, to confirm my hypothesis. I was right: *Al Azif* was translating itself into English, little by little. There was only a sprinkling of English in the latter pages; the early pages were English from head to foot; the middle pages half Arabic, half English. I could read phrases and sentences, but not whole passages. I could make out clearly, "they dwell in the inmost adyta"; then would follow lovely Arabic calligraphy. Some of the passages I comprehended were these:

Yog-Sothoth knows the gate; in the Gulf the worlds themselves are made of sounds; the dim horrors of Earth; Iä Iä Iä, Shub-Niggurath!

Nothing surprising, and nothing I wanted to deal with.

But I did understand what had happened. When I had so carelessly allowed this copy of *Al Azif* to batten upon Milton's poetry, it took the opportunity to employ Milton's language in the task of translating itself. With a single thoughtless act, I had given *The Necronomicon*— call it accursed or unspeakable or maddening, call it whatever minatory adjective you choose—both life and speech, and I saw the potential for harm that I had set in place.

I flung the volume into my flimsy little safe, clanged shut the door, and spun the dial. I put up the CLOSED sign on my shop door, called my wife, Helen, to tell her I wouldn't be home, and stood guard like a military sentinel. I would not leave my post, I decided, until Uncle Alvin returned to rescue me and all the rest of the world from a slender little book written centuries ago by a poet who ought to have known better.

Nor did my determination falter.

As soon as Uncle Alvin laid eyes on me Sunday morning, he knew what had gone wrong. "It has escaped, hasn't it?" he said, looking into my face. "*Al Azif* has learned English."

"Come in," I said. When he entered, I glanced up and down the empty street, then shut the door firmly and guided my uncle by his arm into my office.

He looked at the desk, at the crumpled brown paper bags that held my meals and at the dozens of empty Styrofoam cups. He nodded. "You set up a watch post. That's a good idea. Where is the volume now?"

"In the safe," I said.

"What's in there with it?"

"Nothing. I took everything out."

"There's no cash in the safe?"

"Only that book you brought upon me."

"That's good," he said. "Do you know what would happen if this copy was brought into contact with cash money?"

"It would probably poison the whole economy of the nation," I said.

"That's right. All U.S. currency everywhere would turn counterfeit."

"I thought of that," I said. "You have to give me some credit. In fact, this never would have happened if you had given me a clearer warning."

"You're right, Robert, I'm sure. But I feared you'd think I was only pulling your leg. And then I thought maybe you'd experiment with it just to see what would happen."

"Not me," I said. "I'm a responsible citizen. *The Necronomicon* is too powerful to joke around with."

"Let's have a look," he said.

I opened the safe and took the volume out. Its outward appearance was unchanged, so far as I could tell. The ruby morocco was rich as a leopard pelt, and the gilt edge and gold stamping gleamed like fairy-tale treasure.

When I handed it to Uncle Alvin, he didn't bother to glance at the exterior of the book, but turned immediately to the latter pages. He raised his eyebrows in surprise, then began reading aloud: " 'The affair that shambleth about in the night, the evil that defieth the Elder Sign, the Herd that stand watch at the secret portal each tomb is known to have and that thrive on that which groweth out of the tenants thereof: All these Blacknesses are lesser than He Who guardeth the Gateway—' "

"Stop, Uncle Alvin," I cried. "You know better than to read that stuff aloud." It seemed to me that it had grown darker in my little office and that a certain chill had come into the room.

He closed the book and looked at it with a puzzled expression. "My word," he said, "that is an exotic and obsolescent diction. What has *Al Azif* been feeding on?"

"Milton," I answered.

"Ah, Milton," he said, and nodded again. "I should have recognized that vocabulary."

"It has poisoned all of Milton's works," I said.

"Indeed? Let's see."

I picked up one of the copies on the desk and handed it to him.

He opened it and, without showing any expression, asked, "How do you know this book is Milton?"

"I brought all my copies in here and stacked them on the desk. I've been afraid to look at them for two days, but I know that you're holding a fairly expensive edition of John Milton's poetic works."

He turned the open book toward me. The pages were blank. "Too late."

"It's eaten all the words," I said. My heart sank. I tried to remember a line of Milton, even a phrase or a characteristic word. Nothing came to mind.

"Well, maybe not *eaten*," Uncle Alvin said. "Used up, let's say. *Absorbed* might be an accurate term."

"No more Milton in the world . . . How am I going to live my life, knowing I'm responsible for the disappearance of Milton's works?"

"Maybe you won't have to," he replied. "Not if we get busy and bring them back."

"How can we do that? *Al Azif* has—swallowed them," I said.

"So we must get the accursed thing to restore the poems, to spit them up for us, the way the whale spat Jonah whole and sound."

"I don't understand."

"We must cause this manuscript to retract its powers," he said. "If we can reduce it to its former state of weakness, the way it was when I first met it in Columbia, the works of John Milton will reappear on the pages—and in the minds of men."

"How do you know?"

"You don't think this is happening for the first time, do you? It has been such a recurring event that restoration procedures have been designed and are followed in a traditional—almost ritualistic—manner."

"You mean other authors have been lost to it and then recovered?"

"Certainly."

"Who?"

"Well, for instance, the works of all the Cthulhu Mythos writers have been lost to the powers of the evil gods that they describe. Stories and poems and novels by Derleth, Long, Price, and Smith have all had to be recovered. The works of Lovecraft have been taken into the domain of *Al Azif* at least a dozen times. That's why his work is so powerfully pervaded by that eldritch and sinister atmosphere. It has taken on some of the shadow of its subject."

"I never thought of that, but it makes sense. So what are the restoration procedures?"

"They're simple enough," he said. "You keep watch here while I go to my car."

He gave me the book and I set it on the edge of the desk, well away from any other written matter. I couldn't help thinking that if Uncle Alvin succeeded in defeating the powers of *Al Azif* and rescuing the hostage works of Milton, these moments represented my last opportunity to read in the great bibliographic rarity. And simply as a physical object it was inviting: The lush red glow of the binding offered a tactile pleasure almost like a woman's skin, and I knew already how the inks shone on the white velvety pages. *The Necronomicon* seemed to breathe a small breath where it lay on the desk, as if it were peacefully dozing like a cat.

I couldn't resist. I picked it up and opened it to a middle page. The seductive Persian rose ink seemed to wreathe a perfume around the couplet that began the fragment of text: "That is not dead which can eternal lie, And with strange aeons even death may die." A large green fly had settled on the bright initial that stood at the beginning of the next sentence, rubbing its legs together and feasting on the ink that shone as fresh and bright as dripping blood. I brushed at it absentmindedly, and it circled lazily toward the ceiling.

"That is not dead . . ."

The lines sang hypnotically in my ear, in my head, and I began to think how I secretly longed to possess this volume for myself, how indeed I had burned to possess it for a long time, and how my ridiculous rabbit-faced Uncle Alvin was the only obstacle in my way to—

"No, no, Robert," Uncle Alvin said from the doorway. "Close the book and put it down. We're here to break the power of the book, not to give in to its spells."

I snapped it shut in a flash and flung it onto the desk. "Wow," I said. "Wow."

"It's an infernal piece of work, isn't it?" he said complacently. "But we'll have a hammerlock on it shortly."

He set down the metal cashbox he had formerly carried the book in and opened it up. He then laid *The Necronomicon* inside and produced from a brown paper bag under his arm a small book bound in black cloth and placed this second book on top of the other and closed the metal box and locked it with a key on his ring. I noticed that the black book sported no title on cover or spine.

"What are we doing now?" I asked.

"The inescapable nature of this book is to cannibalize other writings," he said. "To feed upon them in order to sustain its ghoulish purposes. If it is in contact with another work, then it *must* try to feed; it cannot stop itself. The method of defeating it is to place it with a book so adamantine in nature, so resistant to evil change, to the inimical powers of darkness, that *The Necronomicon* wastes all its forces upon this object and in exhausting itself renders up again those works it had consumed earlier. It simply wears itself out, and that which formerly had disappeared now reappears."

"Are you certain?" I asked. "That seems a little too simple."

"It is not simple at all," he said. "But it is effective. If you'll open up one of your copies of Milton there, we ought to be able to watch the printed words return to the pages."

"All right," I said, and opened one of the blank-paged books to a place toward the front.

"The process is utterly silent," he said, "but that is deceptive. Inside this box, a terrific struggle is taking place."

"What is the unconquerable book that you put in with it?"

"I have never read it," he said, "because I am not worthy. Not yet. It is a great holy book written by a saint. Yet the man who wrote it did not know he was a saint and did not think of himself as writing a book. It is filled with celestial wisdom and supernal light, but to read it requires many years of spiritual discipline and ritual cleansing. To read such a holy book one must first become holy himself."

"What is the title?"

"Someday soon, when I have accomplished more of the necessary stages of discipline, I will be allowed to say the title aloud," he told me. "Till then I must not."

"I am glad to know there is such a book in the world," I said.

"Yes," he said. "And you should look now to see if Milton is being restored to us."

"Yes he is," I said happily. "Words are beginning to reappear. Wait a second while I find our control poem." I leafed through rapidly to find sonnet XIX and read aloud:

> "When I consider how my light is spent
> Ere half my days—"

"Why are you stopping?" he asked.

"It's that damned pesky green fly again." I brushed at the page. "Shoo!" I said.

The fly shooed, lifting from the book in a languorous circle, buzzing around the office for a moment, and then departing the premises through the open window there beside a broken bookshelf.

"You need to put in a screen," Uncle Alvin said. He wrinkled his nose, pawed at his ear.

"I need to do a lot of things to this old shop," I replied. "Let's see now, where were we?" I found my place on the page and began again:

> "When I consider how my light is spent
> Ere half my days, in this dark world and weird—"

"Wait a minute," my uncle said. "What was that last word?"

I looked. "*Weird*," I said.

He shook his head. "That's not right."

"No, it's not," I said. "At first I didn't see it was wrong because the fly covered it, the same old fly that was gobbling up the ink in *The Necronomicon*."

"A carrier," he said slowly. "It's carrying the poison that it contracted from the ink."

We looked at each other, and as the knowledge came clear to me, I cried out: "*The fly!*" Then, just as if we had rehearsed to perform the single action together, we rushed to the window.

But out there in the sleepy southern Sunday morning would be countless indistinguishable green flies, feeding, excreting, and mating.

Fat Face

MICHAEL SHEA

*They were infamous, nightmare sculptures even when telling
of age-old, bygone things; for shoggoths and their work ought
not to be seen by human beings or portrayed by any beings. . . .*
— AT THE MOUNTAINS OF MADNESS,
HOWARD PHILLIPS LOVECRAFT

When Patti came back to working the lobby of the Parnassus Hotel, it
was clear she was liked from the way the other girls teased her and
unobtrusively took it easy on her for the first few weeks while she got
to feel steadier. She was deeply relieved to be back.

Before she had to go up to State Hospital, she had been doing four
nights a week at a massage parlor called The Encounter, of which her
pimp was part owner. He insisted the parlor beat was like a vacation to
her, because it was strictly a hand-job operation and the physical
demands on her were lighter than regular hotel whoring. Patti would
certainly have agreed that the work was lighter—if it hadn't been for
the robberies and killings. The last of these had been the cause of her
breakdown, and though she never admitted this to Pete, her pimp, he
had no doubt sensed the truth, for he had let her go back to the Parnassus and told her she could pay him half rate for the next few weeks,
till she was feeling steady again.

In her first weeks at the massage parlor, she had known with all but
certainty of two clients—not hers—who had taken one-way drives
from The Encounter up into the Hollywood Hills. These incidents still
wore a thin, merciful veil of doubt. It was the third one that passed too
nearly for her to face away from it.

From the moment of his coming in, unwillingly she felt spring up in
her the conviction that the customer was a perfect victim; physically
soft, small, fatly walleted, more than half drunk, out-of-state. She
learned his name when her man studied his wallet thoroughly on the

109

pretext of checking his credit cards, and the man's permitting of this liberty revealed how fuddled he was. She walked ahead swinging her bottom, and as he stumbled after, down the hall to a massage room, she could almost feel in her own head the ugly calculations clicking in Pete's.

The massage room was tiny. It had a not-infrequently-puked-on carpet, and a table. As she stood there, pounding firmly on him through the towel, trying to concentrate on her rhythm, she beheld an obese black cockroach running boldly across the carpet. Afterward she was willing to believe she had hallucinated, so strange was the thing she remembered. The bug, half as big as her hand, had stopped at midfloor and *stared* at her, and she in that instant had seen clearly and looked deep into the inhuman little black-bead eyes, and had known that the man she was just then firing off into the towel was going to die later that night. There would be a grim, half-slurred conversation in some gully under the stars, there would be perhaps a long signing of traveler's checks payable to the fictitious name on a certain set of false I.D. cards, and then the top of the plump man's head would be blown off.

Patti was a lazy girl who lazily wanted things to be nice, but was very good at adjusting to things that were not nice at all, if somebody strong really insisted on them. Part of it was that Patti was indecisive by nature. Left alone, she was made miserable by the lonely struggle of deciding what to do. Pete was expensive, but at least he kept Patti's time fully planned out for her. With him to supervise, Patti's life fit her snugly, with no room for confusing doubts.

But this plump man's head, all pale in moonlight, blown wide open—the image wouldn't leave her; it festered in her imagination. The body was found in three days and got two paragraphs, but the few lines included corroboration of her fantasy, in the words "gunshot wounds to the head."

By the time she read these paragraphs, Patti was already half sick with alcohol and insomnia, and that night she took some pills that she was lucky enough to have pumped out of her an hour or so later.

But now, with the hospital's Xanax just fading from her system and a little of her appetite and her energy coming back, Patti decided that if there was any best therapy for her kind of nightmare, it was this, hooking again out of the lobby of the Parnassus. Some of the bittersweet years of her apprenticeship had been served here. The fat, shabby red furniture still had a voluptuous feel to her. The big, dowdy Parnassus, uptown in the forties, now stood in the porno heartland of Hollywood. It was a district of neon and snarled traffic on narrow overparked streets engineered before the Great Depression. And Patti loved to watch it all, the glitter and glossy vehicles, through the plate-glass window of the lobby, taking it easy, only getting up and ambling out to the sidewalk now and then when there was eye-contact from a shopping john driving past. This was the way hooking should be.

Before this whole massage parlor thing, she was working harder, maybe half her time in the lobby, and half walking. But now she felt still queasy, thin-skinned after all those drugs and the hospital. She thought of walking, and it made her remember her painful amateur years, the beatings, the cheats who humped and dumped her, the quick, sticky douches taken with a shook-up bottle of Coke while squatting between trash bins in an alley. Yes, here in the lobby was the best kind of hooking. The old desk-guys took a little gate on one or two rooms, but very few tricks actually went down here. This lobby was a natural showcase. The nearby Bridgeport or Aztec Arms was where 90 percent of the bedwork went on.

This suited Patti. She was small-town born, central California, and had a certain sunny sentimentalism, an impulse for community and camaraderie, that had led her to be called "Hometown" by some of the other girls, most of them liking her for it while they laughed at her. She laughed along, but stubbornly she cherished a sense of neighborhood on these noisy carnival streets. She cultivated acquaintances. She infallibly greeted the man at the drugstore with cordial remarks on the traffic or the smog. The man, bald and thin-moustached, never did more than grin at her with timid greed and scorn. The douches, deodorizers, and fragrances she bought so steadily had prejudiced him, and guaranteed his misreading of her folksy genialities.

Or she would josh the various pimply employees at the Dunk-O-Rama in a similar spirit, saying things like, "They sure got you working, don't they?" or, of the tax, "The old Governor's got to have his bite, don't he?" When asked how she wanted her coffee, she always answered with neighborly amplitude: "Well, let's see—I guess I'm in the mood for cream today." These things, coming from a vamp-eyed brunette in her twenties, wearing a halter top, short-shorts, and Grecian sandals, disposed the adolescent counter-hops more to sullen leers than to answering warmth. Yet she persisted in her fantasies. She even greeted Arnold, the smudged, moronic vendor at the corner newsstand, by name—this in spite of an all-too-lively and gurgling responsiveness on his part.

Now, in her recuperation, Patti took an added comfort from this vein of sentiment. This gave her sisterhood much to rally her about in their generally affectionate recognition that she was much shaken and needed some feedback and some steadying.

A particular source of hilarity for them was Patti's revival of interest in Fat Face, whom she always insisted was their friendliest "neighbor" in their "local community."

An old ten-story office building stood on the corner across the street from the Parnassus. As is not uncommon in L.A., the simple box-shaped structure bore ornate cement frieze work on its facade, and all along the pseudo-architraves capping the pseudo-pillars of the building's sides. Such friezes always have exotic clichés as their theme—they are an echo of DeMille's Hollywood. The one across from the Parnassus had a Mesopotamian theme—ziggurat-shaped finials crowning the pseudo-pillars, and murals of wrenched profiles, curly-bearded figures with bulging calves.

A different observer from Patti would have judged the building schlock, but effective for all that, striking the viewer with a subtle sense of alien portent. Patti seldom looked higher than its fourth floor, where the usually open window of Fat Face's office was.

Fat Face's businesses—he ran two—appeared to be the only active concerns in the whole capacious structure. The gaudy unlikelihood of both of these "businesses" was the cause of endless hilarity among the Parnassus girls. The two enterprises lettered on the building's dusty directory were: HYDROTHERAPY CLINIC and PET REFUGE.

What made the comedy irresistible was that sometimes the clients of the two services arrived together. The hydrotherapy patients were a waddling pachydermous lot, gimping on bulky orthopedic boots, their wobbly bulks rippling in roomy jumpsuits or bib overalls. And, as if these hulks required an added touch, they sometimes came with cats and dogs in tow. These beasts' wails and struggles against their leashes or carrying cages made it plain that they were strays, not pets. The misshapen captors' fleshy, stolid faces, as if oblivious to the thrashings of the beasts, added that last note of slapstick to the spectacle.

Fat Face himself—they had no other name for him—was often at his high window, a dear, ruddy bald countenance beaming avuncularly down on the hookers in the lobby across the street. His bubble baldness was the object of much lewd humor among the girls and the pimps. Fat Face was much waved-at in sarcasm, whereas he always smiled a crinkly smile that seemed to understand and not to mind. Patti, when she sometimes waved, did so with pretty sincerity.

Because though you had to laugh at Fat Face, the man had some substance to him. He had several collection vans with the Pet Refuge logo—apparently his hydrotherapy patients also volunteered as drivers for these vans. The leaflet they passed out was really touching:

> Help us Help!
> Let our aid reach these
> unfortunate creatures.
> Nourished, spayed, medicated,
> They may have a better chance
> for health and life!

This generosity of feeling in Fat Face did not prevent his being talked about in the lobby of the Parnassus, where great goiter-rubbing, water-splashing orgies were raucously hypothesized, with Fat Face flourishing whips and baby oil, while cries of "rub my blubber!" filled the air. At such times Patti was impelled to leave the lobby, because it felt like betrayal to be laughing so hard at the goodly man.

Indeed, in her convalescent mellowness, much augmented by Valium, she had started to fantasize going up to his office, pulling the blinds, and ravishing him at his desk. She imagined him lonely and horny. Perhaps he had nursed his wife through a long illness and she at last expired gently. . . . He would be so grateful!

But forward though Patti could be, she found in herself an odd shyness about this. It would be easy enough to cross the street, go up to his clinic, knock on his door. . . . But she didn't. A week, seven nice long convalescent days, rolled by, and she did nothing about this sentimental little urge of hers.

Then late one afternoon, Sheri, her best friend among the girls, took her to a bar a few blocks down the street. Patti drank, got happy and goofy. The two girls sat trading yo-mammas and boasts and dares, and then it just popped naturally out of Patti's mouth: "So why don't you go up and give old Fat Face a lube?"

"Jesus, girl, if all of him's fat as his face is, it'd be like lubing a hill!"

But there was the exploit on the table between them, and they both felt too jolly and rowdy to back down. "So whatta you saying, you trick only superstars? So what if he's fat? Think how *nice* it'd be for him!"

"I bet he'd blush till his whole head looked like an eggplant. Then, if there was just a slit in the top, like Melanie was saying—" Sheri had to break off and hold herself as she laughed. She had already done some drinking earlier in the afternoon. Patti called for another double and exerted herself to catch up, and meanwhile she harped on her theme to Sheri and tried to get her serious attention:

"I mean I've been working out of the Parnassus—what? Maybe three years now? No, four! Four years. I'm part of these people's community—the druggist, Arnold, Fat Face—and yet we never do anything to show it. There's no getting together. We're just faces. I mean like Fat Face—I couldn't even *call* him that!"

"So let's *both* go up—there's enough there for two!"

Patti was about to answer when, behind the bar, she saw a big roach scamper across a rubber mat and disappear under the baseboard. She remembered the plump body in the towel, and remembered—as a thing actually seen—the slug-fragmented skull.

Sheri sensed a chill. She ordered two more doubles and began making bawdy suppositions about the outcome of their visit. The pair of them marched out laughing a quarter hour later, out into the late afternoon streets. The gold-drenched sidewalks swarmed, the pavements were jammed with rumbling motors. Jaunty and loud, the girls sauntered back to their intersection and crossed over to the old building. Its heavy oak-and-glass doors were pneumatically stiff and cost them a stagger to force open. But when they swung shut, it was swiftly, with a deep click, and they sealed out the street sound with amazing, abrupt completeness. The glass was dirty and put a sulphurous glaze on the already surreal copper of the declining sun's light outside. Suddenly it might be Mars or Jupiter beyond those doors, and the girls themselves stood within a great dim stillness that might have matched the feeling of a real Mesopotamian ruin, out on some starlit desert. The images were alien to Patti's thought—startling intrusions in a mental voice not precisely her own. Sheri gave a comic shiver but otherwise made no acknowledgment of similar feelings.

They found the elevator had an out-of-order sign fixed to the switch plate by yellowed Scotch tape. The stairway's ancient carpet was blackish-green, with a venerable rubber corridor mat up its center. Out on the street the booze in Patti's system had felt just right; in this silent, dusty stairwell it made her slightly woozy. The corridor mat, so cracked with age, put her in mind of supple reptilian skin. Sheri climbed ahead of her, still joking, cackling, but her voice seemed small, seemed to struggle like a drowner in the heavy silence. It amazed Patti, how utterly her sense of gaiety had fled her. It had been clicked off, abrupt as a light switch, when those heavy street doors had closed behind them.

At the first two landings they peeked down the halls at similar vistas: green-carpeted corridors of frosted-glass doors with rich brass knobs. Bulbs burned miserly few, and in those corridors Patti sensed, with piercing vividness, the feeling of *kept* silence. It was not a void silence, but a full one, made by presences not stirring.

And as they climbed her sense of strangeness condensed in her, became something that gripped her by the spine. She was afraid! My God, what *of*? It was ridiculous, but when Sheri led them into the fourth-floor corridor, performing a comic bow, Patti's legs felt cold and leaden, and carried her unwillingly.

"Come *on*!" Sheri mocked. There was something too much, something feverish about the hilarity in her eyes.

Patti balked. "It's a bad idea. You win, I'm chicken—let's get outta here."

"Ha! And you call yourself a working girl! Well, just a minute here." She took out the little pad she carried for phone numbers and addresses, and hurried down the hall with a parody butt-swinging hooker's prowl. The doors nearest Patti said HYDROTHERAPY CLINIC with an arrow—she watched Sheri pass other doors, sashaying all the way to the corridor's far end. Patti stood waiting. Did she hear, ever so faintly, a kind of echo from behind these closed doors? Sooo faint, but the echoes of something resonating in a vast cavernous space? And there . . . ever so soft . . . it was almost like the piping of a flute. . . .

Sheri stood by the last door, scribbling on the pad. She ripped off the sheet and slipped it under the door. Then she came running back like a kid who's played a prank. Patti willingly caught her mood—they rushed giggling back down the stairs like larking twelve-year-olds. Patti wondered if Sheri too was giggling from sheer relief to be out of this building.

"What'd you write him, fool?!" Patti was elated to be back on the street, out in its noise and its colors; she felt like someone who has just escaped drowning. "You trying to steal my date?" Sheri had once tampered with a note that Patti had passed at a party, so that the trick would show up at Sheri's house instead of Patti's.

Sheri mimed outrage. "What you take me for? Come on for a beer, on me!"

As they walked, every outdoor breath reassured Patti. "Hey, Sher— did you hear any, like, music up there?" Even out here in the traffic noise she could call up clearly the weird piping tune, not so much a tune, really, as an eerie melodic ramble. What bothered her as much as the strange feeling of the music was the way in which she had received it. It seemed to her that she had not *heard* it, but rather *remembered* it—suddenly and vividly—though she hadn't the trace of an idea now where she might have heard it before. Sheri's answer confirmed her thought:

"Music? Baby, there wasn't a sound up there! Wasn't it kind of spooky?" Sheri's mood stayed giddy and Patti gladly fell in with it. They went to another bar they liked and drank for an hour or so— slowly, keeping a gloss on things, feeling humorous and excited like schoolgirls on a trip together. At length they decided to go to the Parnassus, find somebody with a car, and scare up a cruising party.

As they crossed to the hotel, Sheri surprised Patti by throwing a look at the old office building and giving a shrug that may have been half shudder. "Jesus. It was like being under the ocean or something in there, wasn't it, Patti?"

This echo of her own dread made Patti look again at her friend. Then Arnold, the vendor, stepped out from the newsstand and blocked their way.

The uncharacteristic aggressiveness gave Patti a nasty twinge. Arnold was unlovely. There was a babyish fatness and redness about every part of him. His scanty red hair alternately suggested infancy or feeble age, and his one eyeless socket, with its weepy red folds of baggy lid, made his whole face look as if screwed to cry. Over all his red, ambling softness there was a bright blackish glaze of inveterate filth. And moronic though his manner was most of the time, Patti felt a cunning about him, something sly and corrupt. The cretinous wet-mouthed face he now thrust close to the girls seemed, somehow, to be that of a grease-painted con man, not an imbecile. As if it were a sour fog that surrounded the newsman, fear entered Patti's nostrils and dampened the skin of her arms. Arnold raised his hand. Pinched between his smudgy thumb and knuckle were an envelope and a fifty-dollar bill.

"A man said to read this, Patti!" Arnold's childish intonation now struck Patti as an affectation, like his dirtiness, part of a chosen disguise.

"He said the money was to pay you to read it. It's a trick! He gave me twenty dollars!" Arnold giggled. The sense of cold-blooded deception in the man made Patti's voice shake when she questioned him about the man who'd given him the commission. He remembered nothing, an arm and a voice in a dark car that pulled up and sped off.

"Well, how is she supposed to read it?" Sheri prodded. "Should she be by a window? Should she wear anything special?"

But Arnold had no more to tell them, and Patti willingly gave up on him to escape the revulsion he so unexpectedly roused in her.

They went into the lobby with the letter, but such was its strangeness—so engrossingly lurid were the fleeting images that came clear for them—that they ended taking it back to the bar, getting a booth, and working over it with the aids of beers and lively surroundings.

The document was in the form of an unsigned letter that covered two pages in a lucid, cursive script of bizarre elegance, and that ran thus:

Dear Girls:
How does a Shoggoth Lord go wooing? You do not even guess enough to ask! Then let it be asked and answered for you. As it is written: "The Shoggoth Lord stumbleth unto his belusted, lo, he cometh heavily unto her, upon alien feet. From the sunless sea, from under the mountains of ice, cometh the mighty Shoggoth Lord unto her." Dear, dear girls! Where is this place the Shoggothoi come from? In your tender, sensual ignorance you might well lack the power to be astonished by the prodigious gulfs of Space and Time this question probes. But let it once more be asked and answered for you. Thus has the answer been written:

Shun the gulf beneath the peaks
The caverned ocean black as night,
Where star-spawned gods made their retreat
From the slowly freezing world of light.

For even star-spawn may grow weak,
While what has been its slave gains strength;
Even star-spawn's will may break,
While slaves feed on their lords at length.

Sweet harlots! Darling, heedless trollops! You cannot imagine the Shoggoth Lord's mastery of shapes! His race has bred smaller since modern man last met with it. Oh, but the Shoggoth Lords are limber now! Supremest polymorphs—though what they are beneath all else, is Horror itself. But how is it they press their loving suit? What do they murmur to her they hotly crave? You must know that the Shoggoth craves her fat with panic—full of the psychic juices of despair. Therefore he taunts her with their ineluctable union; therefore he pipes and flutes to her his bold, seductive lyric, while he vows with a burning glare in his myriad eyes that she'll be his. Thus he sings:

Your veil shall be the wash of blood
That dims and drowns your dying eyes.
You'll have for bridesmaids Pain and Dread,
For vows, you'll jabber blasphemies.
My scalding flesh will be your gown,
And Agony your bridal song.
You shall both be my bread
And, senses reeling, watch me fed.

O maids, prepare her swiftly!
Speedily her loins unlace!
Her tender paps anoint,
And bare unto my seething face!

Thus, dear girls, he ballads and rondelets his belusted, thus he waltzes her spirit through dark, empty halls of expectation, of always-hearkening Horror, until the dance has reached that last, closed room of consummation!

As many times as the girls flung these pages onto the table, they picked them up again after short hesitation. Both Sheri and Patti were very marginal readers, but the flashes of coherent imagery in the letter kept them coming back to the cryptic parts, trying to pick the lock of their meaning. They held menace even in their very calligraphy, whose baroque, barbed elegance seemed sardonic and alien. The mere sonority of some of the obscure passages evoked vivid images, a sense of murky submersion in benthic pressures of fearful expectation, while unseen giants abided nearby in the dark.

The document's cumulative effect on Patti was more of melancholy than fear. The john who wrote it was a hurt-freak, sure, but the letter-writing types blew it off that way and never came to dealing harm. The girls had done some blow from Sheri's vial to clear their heads from the beers, and Patti's body was liking it; she was feeling stronger than she had for days. The letter-writer's words were strange, yes, this incredible gloominess hung over them—but then, bottom line, this was a very easy fifty bucks.

Sheri, on the other hand, got a little freaked about it. She'd started drinking much earlier in the day, she'd had a lot more blow than Patti, and her nerves now were wearing down. She was still laughing at things, but the humor was very thin. "I'll tell you what, girl, these are weird vibes I'm getting today. You know what? I *did* kinda hear like, music. Behind the door . . . ? Now we get this shit!" and she swept her hands at the pages but not touching them, as a woman might try to shoo off a spider. "You know what let's do? Let's have a sleep-over at your place, I'll come sleep over, just like slumber parties."

"That'd be fun! But you sleep in my bed, no kicking, OK?"

Sheri cawed with relieved laughter—her sleep-kicking a joke with them. Sensing Sheri's fear—her desperation not to be alone tonight—scared Patti in turn.

They walked the sidewalks through the almost-night, headlights blazing everywhere, both of them so glad of each other's company it almost embarrassed them.

At the all-night Safeway they got provisions: sloe gin, vodka, bags of ice, 7-UP, bags of chips and puffs and cookies and candy bars. They repaired with their purchases to Patti's place.

She had a small cottage in a four-cottage court, with very old people living in the other three units. The girls shoved the bed into the corner so they could drop pillows against all the walls to lean back on. They turned on the radio and the TV, then got out the phone book and started making joke calls to people with funny names while eating, drinking, smoking, watching, listening, and bantering with each other.

Their consciousness outlasted their provisions, but not by long. Soon, back to back, they slept; bathed and laved by the gently burbling soundwash and the ash-grey light of pulsing images.

They woke to a day that was sunny, windy, and smogless. They rose at high, glorious noon and walked to a coffee shop for breakfast. The breeze was combing buttery light into the waxen fronds of the palms, while the Hollywood Hills seemed most opulently brocaded—under the sky's flawless blue—with the silver-green of sagebrush and sumac.

As they ravened breakfast, they plotted borrowing a car and taking a drive. Then Sheri's pimp walked in. She waved him over brightly, but Patti was sure she was as disappointed as herself. Rudy took a chair long enough to inform Sheri how lucky she was he'd run into her, since he had something important for her that afternoon. Contemptuously he snatched up the bill and paid for both girls. Sheri left in tow, and gave Patti a rueful wave from the door.

Patti's appetite left her. She dawdled over coffee and stepped at last, unwillingly, out into the day's polychrome splendor. Its very clarity took on a sinister quality of remorselessness. Behold, the whole world and all its children moved under the glaring sun's brutal, endless revelation. Nothing could hide. Not in this world . . . though of course there were other worlds, where beings lie hidden immemorially. . . .

She shivered as if something had crawled across her. The thoughts had passed through Patti, but were not hers. She sat on a bus-stop bench and tightly crossed her arms as if to get a literal hold on herself. The strange thoughts, by their feeling, she knew instinctively to be echoes raised somehow by what they had read last night. Away with them, then! The creep had had more than his money's worth of reading from her already, and now she would forget those unclean pages. As for her depression, it was a freakish sadness caused by the spoiling of her holiday with Sheri, and it was silly to give in to it.

Thus she rallied herself and got to her feet. She walked a few blocks without aim, somewhat stiff and resolute. At length the sunlight and her natural health of body had healed her mood, and she fell into a pleasant, veering ramble down miles of Hollywood residential streets, relishing the cheap cuteness of the houses and the lushness of their long-planted trees and gardens.

Almost she left the entire city. A happy, rushing sense of her freedom grew upon her, and she suddenly pointed out to herself that she had nearly four hundred dollars in her purse. She came within an ace of swaggering into a Greyhound station with two quickly packed suitcases and buying a ticket to either San Diego or Santa Barbara, whichever had the earlier departure time. With brave suddenness to simplify her life and remove it, at a stroke, from the evil that had seemed to haunt it recently. . . .

In the end, it was Patti's laziness that made her veer from this decision. The packing, the bus ride, the looking for a new apartment, the searching for a job . . . so many details and hours of tedium! And as she meditated on the toilsomeness of it all, she found that these familiar old Hollywood residential streets were taking on a new allure.

And, really, how *could* she leave? After what had it been? Four?

Five years? After so long, Hollywood was basically her hometown. These shady little streets with their root-buckled sidewalks—they were so well known to her, yet so full of interest.

She had turned onto a still, green block, gorgeously scented and overhung by huge old peppertrees. She was some few dozen yards into the block before she realized that the freeway had cut it off at the far end. But at that end a black-on-yellow arrow indicated a narrow egress, so she kept walking. Then, several houses ahead, a very large man in overalls appeared, dragging a huge German shepherd across the lawn.

Patti saw a new brown van parked by the curb, and recognized it and the man at once. The vehicle was one of two belonging to Fat Face's stray refuge, and the man was one of his two full-time collectors.

He had the struggling brute by the neck with a noosed stick. He stopped and looked at Patti with some intensity as she approached. The vine-drowned cottage whose lawn he stood on was dark, tight-shut, and seemed deserted—as did the entire block—and it struck Patti that the man could have spotted the dog by chance and might now be thinking it hers. She smiled and shook her head as she came up.

"He's not mine! I don't even *live* around here!"

Something in the way her words echoed down the stillness of the street gave Patti a pang. She was sure they had made the collector's eyes narrow. He was tall, round, and smooth, with a face of his employer's type, though not as jovial. He was severely clubfooted and bloat-legged on the left, as well as being inordinately bellied, all things to which the coveralls lent a merciful vagueness. The green baseball cap he wore somehow completed the look of ill-balance and slow wit that the man wore.

But as she got nearer, already wanting to turn and run the other way, she received a shocking impression of strength in the uncouth figure. The man had paused in a half turn and was partly crouched—not a position of firm leverage. The dog, whose paws and muzzle showed some Bernard, surely weighed well over a hundred and fifty pounds, and it fought with all its might, but its struggles sent not even a tremor through its captor's massive arm; the animal was as immovably moored as to a tree. Patti edged to one side of the walk, pretending a wariness of the dog, which its helplessness made droll, and moved to pass. The collector's hand, as if absently, pressed down on the noose. The beast's head seemed to swell, its struggles grew more galvanic and constricted by extreme distress. And while thus smoothly he began throttling the beast, the collector cast a glance up and down the block and stepped into Patti's path, effortlessly dragging the animal with him.

They stood face-to-face, very near. The ugly mathematics of peril swiftly clicked in her brain; the mass, the force, the time—all were sufficient. The next couple of moments could finish her. With a jerk he could kill the dog, drop it, seize her, and thrust her into the van. Indeed, the dog was at the very point of death. The collector began to smile nastily, and his breath came—foul and oddly cold—gusting against her face. Then something began to happen to his eyes. They were rolling up, like a man's when he's coming, but they didn't roll white; they were rolling up a jet-black—two glossy obsidian globes eclipsing from below the watery blue ones. Her lungs began to gather air to scream. A taxicab swung onto the street.

The collector's grip eased on the half-unconscious dog. He stood blinking furiously, and it seemed he could not unwind his bulky body from the menacing tension it had taken on. He stood, still frozen on the very threshold of assault, and the cold foulness still gusted from him with the labor of his breathing. In another instant Patti's reflexes fired and she was released with a leap from the curb out into the street, but there was time enough for her to have the thought she *knew* that stench the blinking gargoyle breathed.

And then she was in the cab. The driver sullenly informed her then of her luck in catching him on his special shortcut to a freeway on-ramp. She looked at him as if he'd spoken in a foreign tongue. More gently he asked her destination, and without thought she answered, "The Greyhound station."

Flight. With sweet, simple motion to cancel Hollywood, and its walking ghosts of murder, and its lurking plunderers of the body, and its nasty, nameless scribblers of letters whose pleasure it was to defile the mind with nightmares. But of course, she must pack. She rerouted the driver to her apartment.

This involved a doubling back that took them across the street of her encounter. The van was still parked by the curb, but neither collector nor dog was in sight. Oddly, the van seemed to be moving slightly, rocking as if with interior movement of fitful vigor. Her look was brief, from a half-block distance, but in the shady stillness the subtle tremoring made a vivid impression.

Then she remembered Fat Face. Of course! She could report the driver to him. His majestic face, his bland avuncular smile—the comforting aura of him flooded soothingly over her fear. What, after all, had happened? A creepy disabled guy with an eye infection had been dangerously tempted to rape her. Fat Face would talk to him. Fat Face would vigorously protect her from any further danger. And meanwhile, in the telling of the story . . . Patti smiled, planning her pretty embarrassment at the intimate topic; she would express her girlish gratitude so warmly. It would lead smoothly to the tender seduction of her fantasy.

She rerouted the taxi yet again, not without first giving the driver a ten-dollar tip in advance. She had him drop her on the Boulevard. She would cop a little blow and get some donuts before going back to the Parnassus, and across the street to Fat Face.

But instead she spent the rest of the afternoon on the Boulevard. Having kindly Fat Face close on hand to fix things neutralized the terror of the near-rape. Patti believed in finding effective antidotes to her problems. Fat Face, the remedy, was on hand, so there was no rush about it. She did a couple healthy knuckles full of flake in the ladies' room of Dunkin' Donuts, and then went out and enjoyed two chocolate frosted Old-Fashioneds with thickly creamed coffee. She mused that while there was relief in Fat Face's presence, there was a creepiness about his entire enterprise that was a real obstacle to visiting him, and that she might as well put it off till tomorrow morning and just relax today. It was cruel, of course, to see deformity as creepy—that had to be what was freaking her in Fat Face's building yesterday, and it was unfair, even that huge creep—strangling the dog one-handed, his eyes fixed on her, rolling black—even he deserved sympathy for his deformity. That was what was so great about Fat Face, he was so humanitarian, but the flip side was that his humanitarianism associated him with all these creeps.

She went to a double bill, and then went to another one a block away. She nursed a flat of Peppermint Schnapps and honked discrete knuckles of flake, all snug up in her corner balcony seat, mind-surfing through the bright, delirious tumult of car chases and exploding spacecraft and skull-spraying gunfights and screaming falls from the peaks of skyscrapers. This was relaxation! Her favorite way to spend an afternoon.

But her mood began to falter as the movies ground on. She kept thinking of her almost-attacker. It was not his grotesque image that nagged her so much as it was a fugitively familiar aura he had about him. The more she worked to shake this thought, the more its persistence frightened her and the more vivid grew the haunting sensations. A cold malignance gusted off the man like a breath of some alien world's atmosphere, yet it was an air somehow obscurely known to her. What dream of her own, now lost to her, had shown her that world of dread and wonder and colossal age that now she caught—and knew—the scent of, in this man? The thought was easy to shake off as a freak of mood, but it was insistent in its return, like a fly that kept landing on her. After the movies, when she stepped out onto the sidewalk, the noise and the blaze of neon and headlights in the dusk made her edgy. She felt cold. It may have been the flake still revving in her system, but her legs seemed to feel a hollow *thrumming*, a big uneasy emptiness somewhere beneath her foot soles. She walked for a while, picking up a new flat of Schnapps. Finally she stepped into a booth and called Sheri.

Her friend had just got home, exhausted from a multiple trick, and wearing a few bruises from a talk afterward with Rudy.

"Why don't I come over, Sher? Hey?"

"No, Patti. I'm wrung out, girl. You feel OK?"

"Sure. So get to sleep, then."

"Naw, hey now—you come over if you want to, Patti, I'm just gonna be dead to the world, is all."

"Whaddya mean? If you're tired, you're tired, and I'll catch you later. So long." She could hear, but not change, the anger and disappointment in her own voice. It told her, when she'd hung up but remained staring at the phone, how close to the territory of Fear she stood. Full night had surrounded her glass booth. Against the fresh purple dark, all the street's scribbly neon squirmed and swam, like sea-things of blue and rose and gold, bannering and twisting cryptically over the drowned pavements.

And, almost as though she expected a watery death, Patti could not, for a moment, step from the booth out onto those pavements. Their lethal cold strangeness lay, if not undersea, then surely in an alien poisonous atmosphere that would scorch her lungs. For a ridiculous instant, her body defied her will.

Then she set her sights on a bar half a block distant. She plunged from the booth and grimly made for that haven.

Some three hours later, no longer cold, Patti was walking to Sheri's. It was a weeknight, and the stillness of the residential streets was not unpleasant. The tree-crowded streetlamps shed a light that was lovely with its whiskey gloss. The street names on their little banners of blue metal had a comic flavor to her tongue, and she called out each as it came into view.

Sheri, after all, had said to come over. The petty cruelty of waking her seemed, to Patti, under the genial excuse of the alcohol, merely prankish. So she sauntered through sleeping Hollywood, knowing the nightwalker's exhilaration of being awake in a dormant world.

Sheri lived in a stucco cottage that was a bit tackier than Patti's, though larger, each cottage possessing a little driveway and a garage in back. And though there was a light on in the living room, it was up the driveway that Patti went, deciding, with sudden impishness, to spook her friend. She crept around the rear corner and stole up to the screened window of Sheri's bedroom, meaning to make noises through a crack if one had been left open.

The window was in fact fully raised, though a blind was drawn within. Even as Patti leaned close, she heard movement inside the darkened room. In the next instant a gust of breeze came up and pushed back the blind within.

Sheri *was* on her back in the bed and somebody was on top of her, so that all Patti could see of her was her arms and her face, which stared round-eyed at the ceiling as she was rocked again and again on the bed. Patti viewed that surging, grappling labor for two instants, no more, and retreated, almost staggering, in a primitive reflex of shame more deep-lying in her than any of the sophistications of her adult professional life.

Shame and a weird childish glee. She hurried out to the sidewalk. Her head rang, and she felt giggly and frightened to a degree that managed to astonish her even through her liquor. What was with her? She'd been paid to watch far grosser things than a simple coupling. On the other hand, there had been a foul smell in the bedroom and nagging hint of music, too, she thought, a faint, unpleasant, twisty tune coming from somewhere indefinite. . . .

Those vague feelings quickly yielded to the humorous side of the accident. She walked to the nearest main street and found a bar. In it, she killed half an hour with two further doubles and then, reckoning enough time had passed, walked back to Sheri's.

The living room light was still on. Patti rang the bell and heard it inside, a rattly probe of noise that raised no stir of response. All at once she felt a light rush of suspicion, like some long-legged insect scuttling daintily up her spine. She felt that, as once before in the last few days, the silence she was hearing concealed a presence, not an absence. But why should this make her begin, ever so slightly, to sweat? It could be Sheri playing possum. Trying by abruptness to throw off her fear, Patti seized the knob. The door opened and she rushed in, calling:

"Ready or not, one, two, three."

Before she was fully in the room, her knees buckled under her, for a fiendish stench filled it. It was a carrion smell, a fierce, damp rankness that bit and pierced her nose. It was so palpable an assault it seemed to crawl all over her—to wriggle through her scalp and stain her flesh as if with brimstone and graveslime.

Clinging still to the doorknob she looked woozily about the room, whose sloppy normality, coming to her as it did through that surreal fetor, struck her almost eerily. Here was the litter of wrappers, magazines, and dishes—thickest around the couch—so familiar to her. The TV, on low, was crowned with ashtrays and beer cans, while on the couch that it faced lay a freshly opened bag of Fritos.

But it was from the bedroom door, partly ajar, that the nearly visible miasma welled most thickly, as from its source. And it would be in the bedroom that Sheri would lie. She would be lying dead in its darkness.

For, past experience and description though it was, the stench proclaimed that meaning grim and clear: death. Patti turned behind her to take a last clean breath, and stumbled toward the bedroom.

Every girl ran the risk of rough trade. It was an ugly and lonely way to die. With the dark, instinctive knowledge of their sisterhood, Patti knew that it was only laying out and covering up that her friend needed of her now. She shoved inward on the bedroom door, throwing a broken rhomb of light upon the bed.

It and the room were empty—empty save the near-physical mass of the stench. It was upon the bed that the reek fumed and writhed most nastily. The blankets and sheets were drenched with some vile fluid, and pressed into sodden seams and folds. The coupling she had glimpsed and snickered at—what unspeakable species of intercourse had it been? And Sheri's face staring up from under the shadowed form's lascivious rocking—had there been more to read in her expression that the slack-faced shock of sex? Then Patti moaned:

"Oh, Jesus God!"

Sheri was in the room. She lay on the floor, mostly under the bed, only her head and shoulders protruding, her face to the ceiling. There was no misreading its now-frozen look. It was a face wherein the recognition of Absolute Pain and Fear had dawned, even as death arrived. Dead she surely was. Living muscles did not achieve utter fixity. Tears jumped up in Patti's eyes. She staggered into the living room, fell on the couch, and wept. "Oh, Jesus God," she said again; softly, now.

She went to the kitchenette and got a dish towel, tied it around her nose and mouth, and returned to the bedroom. Sheri would not, at least, lie half thrust from sight like a broken toy. Her much-used body would have a shred of dignity that her life had never granted it. She bent, and hooked her hands under those dear, bare shoulders. She pulled and, with her pull's excess force, fell backward to the floor; for that which she fell hugging to her breasts needed no such force to move its lightness. It was not Sheri, but a dreadful upper fragment of her, that Patti hugged: Sheri's head and shoulders, one of her arms . . . gone were her fat, funny feet they used to laugh at; for she ended now in a charred stump of rib cage. As a little girl might clutch some unspeakable doll, Patti lay embracing tightly that which made her scream, and scream again.

Valium. Compazine. Mellaril. Stelazine. Gorgeous technicolored tabs and capsules. Bright-hued pillars holding up the Temple of Rest. Long afternoons of Tuinal and TV; night sweats and quiet, groggy mornings. Patti was in County for more than a week.

She had found all there was to be found of her friend. Dismemberment by acid was a new wrinkle, and Sheri got some press, but in a world of trashbag murders and mass graves uncovered in quiet backyards, even a death like Sheri's could hope for only so much coverage. Patti's bafflement made her call the detectives assigned to the case at least once a day. With gruff tact they heard through her futile rummagings among the things she knew of Sheri's life and background, but soon knew she was helpless to come up with anything material.

Much as Patti craved the medicated rest the hospital thrust on her, a lingering dread marred her days of drug-buoyed ease. For she could be waked, even from the glassiest daze, by a sudden sense that the number of people surrounding her was dwindling—that everywhere they were stealing off, or vanishing, and that the hospital, and even the city, was growing empty around her.

She put it down to the hospital itself—its constant shifts of bodies, its wheelings in and out on silent gurneys. She obtained a generous scrip for Valium and had herself discharged, hungry for the closer comfort of her friends. A helpful doctor was leaving the building as she did, and gave her a ride. With freakish embarrassment about her trade and her world, Patti had him drop her at a coffee shop some blocks from the Parnassus. When he had driven off, she started walking. The dusk was just fading. It was Saturday night, but it was also the middle of a three-day weekend (as she had learned with surprise from the doctor) and the traffic on both pavement and asphalt was remarkably light.

Somehow it had a small-town-on-Sunday feel, and alarm woke in her and struggled in its heavy Valium shackles, for this was as if the confirmation of her frightened hallucinations. Her fear mounted as she walked. She pictured the Parnassus with an empty lobby and imagined that she saw the traffic beginning everywhere to turn off the street she walked on, so that in a few moments it might stretch deserted for a mile either way.

But then she saw the many lively figures through the beloved plate-glass windows. She half ran ahead, and as she waited with happy excitement for the light, she saw Fat Face up in his window. He spotted her just when she did him, and beamed and winked. Patti waved and smiled and heaved a deep sigh of relief that nearly brought tears. This was true medicine, not pills, but friendly faces in your home community! Warm feelings and simple neighborliness! She ran forward at the WALK signal.

There was a snag before she reached the lobby, for Arnold from his wooden cave threw at her a leer of wet intensity that scared her even as she recognized that some kind of frightened greeting was intended by the grimace. There was such . . . *speculation* in his look. But then she had pushed through the glass doors, and was in the warm ebullience of shouts and hugs and jokes and droll nudges.

It was sweet to bathe in that bright, raucous communion. She had called the deskman that she was coming out, and for a couple of hours various friends whom the word had reached strolled in to greet her. She luxuriated in her pitied celebrity, received little gifts, and gave back emotional kisses of thanks.

It ought to have lasted longer, but the night was an odd one. Not much was happening in town, and everybody seemed to have action lined up in Oxnard or Encino or some other bizarre place. A few stayed to work the home grounds, but they caught a subdued air from the place's emptiness at a still-young hour. Patti took a couple more Valium and tried to seem like she was peacefully resting in a lobby chair. To fight her stirrings of unease, she took up the paperback that was among the gifts given her—she hadn't even noticed by whom. It had a horrible face on the cover and was entitled *At the Mountains of Madness*.

If she had not felt the need for some potent distraction, some weighty ballast for her listing spirit, she would never have pieced out the ciceronian rhythms of the narrative's style. But when, with frightened tenacity, she had waded several pages into the tale, the riverine prose, suddenly limpid, snatched her and bore her upon its flowing clarity. The Valium seemed to perfect her uncanny concentration, and where her vocabulary failed her, she made smooth leaps of inference and always landed square on the necessary meaning.

And so for hours in the slowly emptying lobby that looked out upon the slowly emptying intersection, she wound through the icy territories of the impossible and down into the gelid nethermost cellars of all World and Time, where stupendous aeons lay in pictured shards, and massive sentient forms still stirred, and fed, and mocked the light.

Strangely, she began to find underlinings about two-thirds of the way through. All the marked passages involved references to *shoggoths*. It was a word whose mere sound made Patti's flesh stir. She searched the flyleaf and inner covers for explanatory inscriptions, but found nothing.

When she laid the book down in the small hours, she sat amid a near-total desertion that she scarcely noticed. Something tugged powerfully at memory, something that memory dreaded to admit. She realized that in reading the tale, she had taken on an obscure, terrible weight. She felt as if impregnated by an injection of tainted knowledge whose grim fruit, an almost physical mass of cryptic threat, lay a-ripening in her now.

She took a third-floor room in the Parnassus for the night, for the simplest effort, like calling a cab, lay under a pall of futility and sourceless menace. She lay back, and her exhausted mind plunged instantly through the rotten flooring of consciousness, straight down into the abyss of dreams.

She dreamed of a city like Hollywood, but the city's walls and pavements were half alive, and they could feel premonitions of something that was drawing near them. All the walls and streets of the city waited in a cold-sweat fear under a blackly overcast sky. She herself, Patti grasped, was the heart and mind of the city. She lay in its midst, and its vast, cold fear was hers. She lay, and somehow she knew the things that were drawing near her giant body. She knew their provenance in huge, blind voids where stood walls older than the present face of Earth; she knew their long cunning toil to reach her own cringing frontiers. Giant worms they were, or jellyfish, or merely huge clots of boiling substance. They entered her deserted streets, gliding convergingly. She lay like carrion that lives and knows the maggots' assault on it. She lay in her central citadel, herself the morsel they sped toward, piping their lust from foul, corrosive jaws.

She woke late Sunday afternoon, drained and dead of heart. She sat in bed watching a big green fly patiently hammer itself against the windowpane where the gold light flooded in. Endlessly it fought the impossible, battering with its frail bejeweled head. With swift fury and pain, Patti jumped out of bed and snatched up her blouse. She ran to the window and, with her linen bludgeon, killed the fly.

Across the street, in a window just one story higher than her own, sat Fat Face. She stood looking back for a moment, embarrassed by her little savagery, but warmed by the way the doctor's smile was filled with gentle understanding, as if he read the anguish the act was born of. She suddenly realized she was wearing only her bra.

His smile grew a shade merrier at her little jolt of awareness, and she knew he understood this too, that this was inadvertence, and not a hooker's come-on.

And so, with a swift excitement, she turned it into coquetry and applied her blouse daintily to her breasts. This was the natural moment—she had been right to wait because now her tender fantasy would bloom with perfect spontaneity. She pointed to herself with a smile, and then to Fat Face with inquiry. How he beamed then! Did she even see his eyes and lips water? He nodded energetically. With thumb and forefinger she signaled a short interval. As she left the window she noted the arrival, down the sidewalk, of a gaggle of hydrotherapy patients, several with leashed strays in tow.

It chilled her somewhat. And would the patients' arrival interfere with the intimate interview she imagined? Her preparations slowed. She stepped down to the lobby some ten minutes later and walked slowly to stand by the front doors. The lobby was empty and so were the sidewalks. All lay in a sunny Sunday desolation. It was dreamlike, beautiful in a way, but it caused her a delicate shudder, too. She stepped outside and looked around her—and felt suddenly the craziness of kinky sexual charities such as she intended. Maybe she should forget it, just go party somewhere. And right then, as she stood there, a car full of her friends pulled up to the curb in front of her. In a chorus they invited her to join them. They were off to cruise, maybe crash out of town, had some parties they knew about.

Almost, Patti went. But then she noted that Sheri's kid sister Penny was in the car. She shuddered at so near a reminder and waved them off with a laugh. She began to move down the sidewalk, weighing how strong her urge to visit Fat Face still was, not looking up toward him because maybe she would just walk on down to the bar. . . . And then Arnold lurched from his booth and made a grab for her arm.

She was edgy and quick, and jumped away. He seemed to fear leaving the booth's proximity and came no nearer, but pleaded with her from where he stood:

"Please, Patti! Come here and listen."

Like a thunderbolt, the elusive memory of last night now struck Patti. "Shoggoth" was eerie, and that whole story familiar, because they were precisely what that letter had been all about! She was stunned that she could so utterly banish from her mind that lurid document. It had spooked Patti badly the night before her friend died. It had come from Arnold—and so had that book! That was the meaning of his look. The red moronic face glared at her urgently.

"Please, Patti. I've had knowledge. Come here—" He darted forward to catch her arm and she sprang back, again the quicker, with a yelp. Arnold, thus drawn from the screening of his booth, froze fearfully. Patti looked up, and thrilled to find Fat Face looking down— not in amity, but in wrath upon Arnold. The newsman gaped and mumbled apologetically, as if to the sidewalk: "No. I said nothing. I only *hinted*. . . ." Joyfully, Patti sprang across the street and in moments was flying up those green-carpeted stairs she had climbed once before with such reluctance.

The oppression she had first found in these muted corridors was not gone from them—the quality of dread in some manner belonged there—but she outran it. She moved too quickly in her sunny fantasy to be overtaken by that heaviness. She ran down the fourth-floor hall and, at the door where Sheri had knelt giggling and she had balked, seized the knob and knocked simultaneously while pushing her way in, so impetuous was her rush toward benign sanity. There Fat Face sat at a big desk by the window she'd always known him through. He was even grosser-legged and more bloat-bellied than his patients. It gave her a funny shock that did not changer her amorous designs.

He wore a commodious doctor's smock and slacks. His shoes were bulky, black, and orthopedically braced. Such a body less enkindled by spirit might have repelled. His, surmounted by the kindly beacon of his smile, seemed only grandfatherly, afflicted—dear. From somewhere there came, echoing as in a large enclosed space, a noise of agitated water and of animals—strangely conjoined. But Fat Face was speaking:

"My dear," he said, not yet rising, "you make an old, old fellow very, very happy!" His voice was a marvel that sent half-lustful gooseflesh down her spine. It was an uncanny voice, reedy and wavering and shot with flutelike notes of silver purity, sinfully melodious. That voice knew seductions, quite possibly, that Patti had never dreamed of. She was speechless, and spread her arms in tender self-preservation.

He sprang to his feet, and the surging pep with which his great bulk moved sent a new thrill down the lightning rod of her nerves. On pachydermous legs he leapt spry as a cat to a door behind his desk, and bowed her through. The noise of animals and churning water gusted fresher from the doorway. Perplexed, she entered.

The room contained only a huge bowl-shaped hydrotherapy tub. Its walls were blank cement, save one, which was a bank of shuttered windows through which the drenched clamor was pouring. She finally conquered disbelief and realized a fact she had been struggling with all along: those dozens of canine garglings and cat shrieks were sounds of agony and distress. Not hospital sounds. Torture chamber sounds. The door boomed shut with a strikingly ponderous rumble, followed by a sharp click. Fat Face, energetically unbuttoning his smock, said, "Go ahead and peek out, sweet heedless trollop! Oh yes, oh yes, oh yes— soon we'll *all* dine on lovely flesh—men and women, not paltry vermin!"

Patti gaped at the lurid musicality of his speech, struggling to receive its meaning. The doctor was shucking his trousers. It appeared that he wore a complex rubber suit, heavily strapped and buckled, under his clothes. Dazed, Patti opened a shutter and looked out. She saw a huge indoor pool, as the sounds had suggested, but not of the same shape and brightly chlorinated blue she expected. It was an awesome slime-black grotto that opened below her, bordered by rude sea-bearded rocks of cyclopean size. The sooty, viscous broth of its waters boiled with bulging elephantine shapes. . . .

From those shapes, when she had grasped them, she tore her eyes with desperate speed; long instants too late for her sanity. Nightmare ought not to be so simply *there* before her, so dizzyingly adjacent to Reality. That the shapes should be such seething plasms, such cunning titan maggots as she had dreamed of, this was just half the horror. The other half was the human head that decorated each of those boiling multimorphs, a comic excrescence from the nightmare mass—this and the rain of panicked beasts that fell from cagework above the pool and became in their frenzies both the toys and the food of the pulpy abominations.

She turned slack-mouthed to Fat Face. He stood by the great empty tub working at the system of buckles on his chest. "Do you understand, my dear? Please try! Your horror will improve your tang. *Your veil shall be the wash of blood that dims and drowns your dying eyes*. . . . You see, we find it easier to hold most of the shape with suits like these. We could mimic the entire body, but far more effort and concentration would be required."

He gave a last pull, and the row of buckles split crisply open. Ropy purple gelatin gushed from his suit front into the tub. Patti ran to the door, which had no knob. As she tore her nails against it and screamed, she remembered the fly at the window, and heard Fat Face continue behind her:

"So, we just imitate the head, and we never dissolve it, not to risk resuming it faultily and waking suspicions. Please struggle!"

She looked back and saw huge palps, like dreadful comic phalluses, spring from the tub of slime that now boiled with movement. She screamed.

"Oh yes!" fluted the Fat Face that now bobbed on the purple simmer. Patti's arms smoked where the palps took them. She was plucked from the floor as lightly as a struggling roach might be. "Oh yes, dear girl—*you'll have for bridesmaids Pain and Dread, for vows you'll jabber blasphemies*. . . ." As he brought her to hang above the cauldron of his acid body, she saw his eyes roll jet-black. He lowered her feet into himself. A last time before shock took her, Patti threw the feeble tool of her voice against the massive walls. She kicked as her feet sank into the scorching gelatin, kicked till her shoes dissolved, till her feet and ankles spread nebulae of liquefying flesh within the Shoggoth Lord's greedy substance. Then her kicking slowed, and she sank more deeply in. . . .

The Big Fish

KIM NEWMAN

The Bay City cops were rousting enemy aliens. As I drove through the nasty coast town, uniforms hauled an old couple out of a grocery store. The Taraki family's neighbours huddled in thin rain howling asthmatically for bloody revenge. Pearl Harbor had struck a lot of people that way. With the Tarakis on the bus for Manzanar, neighbours descended on the store like bedraggled vultures. Produce vanished instantly, then destruction started. Caught at a sleepy stoplight, I got a good look. The Tarakis had lived over the store; now, their furniture was thrown out of the second-storey window. Fine china shattered on the sidewalk, spilling white chips into the gutter like teeth. It was inspirational, the forces of democracy rallying round to protect the United States from vicious oriental grocers, fiendishly intent on selling eggplant to a hapless civilian population.

Meanwhile my appointment was with a gent who kept three pictures on his mantelpiece, grouped in a triangle around a statue of the Virgin Mary. At the apex was his white-haired mama, to the left Charles Luciano, and to the right, Benito Mussolini. The Tarakis, American-born and registered Democrats, were headed to a dustbowl concentration camp for the duration, while Gianni Pastore, Sicilianborn and highly unregistered capo of the Family business, would spend his war in a marble-fronted mansion paid for by nickels and dimes dropped on the numbers game, into slot machines, or exchanged for the favours of nice girls from the old country. I'd seen his mansion before and so far been able to resist the temptation to bean one of his twelve muse statues with a bourbon bottle.

Money can buy you love but can't even put down a deposit on good taste.

The palace was up in the hills, a little way down the boulevard from Tyrone Power. But now, Pastore was hanging his mink-banded fedora in a Bay City beachfront motel complex, which was a real-estate agent's term for a bunch of horrible shacks shoved together for the convenience of people who like sand on their carpets.

I always take a lungful of fresh air before entering a confined space with someone in Pastore's business, so I parked the Chrysler a few blocks from the Seaview Inn and walked the rest of the way, sucking on a Camel to keep warm in the wet. They say it doesn't rain in Southern California, but they also say the U.S. Navy could never be taken by surprise. This February, three months into a war the rest of the world had been fighting since 1936 or 1939 depending on whether you were Chinese or Polish, it was raining almost constantly, varying between a light fall of misty drizzle in the dreary daytimes to spectacular storms, complete with DeMille lighting effects, in our fear-filled nights. Those trusty Boy Scouts scanning the horizons for Jap subs and Nazi U-boats were filling up influenza wards, and manufacturers of raincoats and umbrellas who'd not yet converted their plants to defence production were making a killing. I didn't mind the rain. At least rainwater is clean, unlike most other things in Bay City.

A small boy with a wooden gun leaped out of a bush and sprayed me with sound effects, interrupting his onomatopoeic chirruping with a shout of "die you slant-eyed Jap!" I clutched my heart, staggered back, and he finished me off with a quick burst. I died for the Emperor and tipped the kid a dime to go away. If this went on long enough, maybe little Johnny would get a chance to march off and do real killing, then maybe come home in a box or with the shakes or a taste for blood. Meanwhile, especially since someone spotted a Jap submarine off Santa Barbara, California was gearing up for the War Effort. Aside from interning grocers, our best brains were writing songs like "To Be Specific, It's Our Pacific," "So Long Momma, I'm Off to Yokahama," "We're Gonna Slap the Jap Right Off the Map," and "When Those Little Yellow Bellies Meet the Cohens and the Kellys." Zanuck had donated his string of Argentine polo ponies to West Point and got himself measured for a comic-opera colonel's uniform so he could join the Signal Corps and defeat the Axis by posing for publicity photographs.

I'd tried to join up two days after Pearl Harbor, but they kicked me back onto the streets. Too many concussions. Apparently, I get hit on the head too often and have a tendency to black out. When they came to mention it, they were right.

The Seaview Inn was shuttered, one of the first casualties of war. It had its own jetty, and by it were a few canvas-covered motor launches shifting with the waves. In late afternoon gloom, I saw the silhouette of the *Montecito*, anchored strategically outside the three-mile limit. That was one good thing about the Japanese; on the downside, they might have sunk most of the U.S. fleet, but on the up, they'd put Laird Brunette's gambling ship out of business. Nobody was enthusiastic about losing their shirt-buttons on a rigged roulette wheel if they imagined they were going to be torpedoed any moment. I'd have thought that would add an extra thrill to the whole gay, delirious business of giving Brunette money, but I'm just a poor, twenty-five-dollars-a-day detective.

The Seaview Inn was supposed to be a stopping-off point on the way to the *Monty*, and now its trade was stopped off. The main building was sculpted out of dusty ice cream and looked like a three-storey radiogram with wave-scallop friezes. I pushed through double-doors and entered the lobby. The floor was decorated with a mosaic in which Neptune, looking like an angry Santa Claus in a swimsuit, was sticking it to a sea nymph who shared a hairdresser with Hedy Lamarr. The nymph was naked except for some strategic shells. It was very artistic.

There was nobody at the desk, and thumping the bell didn't improve matters. Water ran down the outside of the green-tinted windows. There were a few steady drips somewhere. I lit up another Camel and went exploring. The office was locked, and the desk register didn't have any entries after December 7, 1941. My raincoat dripped and began to dry out, sticking my jacket and shirt to my shoulders. I shrugged, trying to get some air into my clothes. I noticed Neptune's face quivering. A thin layer of water had pooled over the mosaic, and various anemonelike fronds attached to the sea god were apparently getting excited. Looking at the nymph, I could understand that. Actually, I realized, only the hair was from Hedy. The face and the body were strictly Janey Wilde.

I go to the movies a lot but I'd missed most of Janey's credits: *She-Strangler of Shanghai*, *Tarzan and the Tiger Girl*, *Perils of Jungle Jillian*. I'd seen her in the newspapers though, often in unnervingly close proximity to Pastore or Brunette. She'd started as an olympic swimmer, picking up medals in Berlin, then followed Weissmuller and Crabbe to Hollywood. She would never get an Academy Award, but her legs were in a lot of cheesecake stills publicizing no particular movie. Air-brushed and made-up like a good-looking corpse, she was a fine commercial for sex. In person she was as bubbly as domestic champagne, though now running to flat. Things were slow in the detecting business, since people were more worried about imminent invasion than missing daughters or misplaced love letters. So when Janey Wilde called on me in my office in the Cahuenga Building and asked me to look up one of her ill-chosen men friends, I checked the pile of old envelopes I use as a desk diary and informed her that I was available to make inquiries into the current whereabouts of a certain big fish.

Wherever Laird Brunette was, he wasn't here. I was beginning to figure Gianni Pastore, the gambler's partner, wasn't here either. Which meant I'd wasted an afternoon. Outside it rained harder, driving against the walls with a drumlike tattoo. Either there were hailstones mixed in with the water or the Jap air force was hurling fistfuls of pebbles at Bay City to demoralize the population. I don't know why they bothered. All Hirohito had to do was slip a thick envelope to the Bay City cops, and the city's finest would hand over the whole community to the Japanese Empire with a ribbon around it and a bow on top.

There were more puddles in the lobby, little streams running from one to the other. I was reminded of the episode of *The Perils of Jungle Jillian* I had seen while tailing a child molester to a Saturday matinee. At the end, Janey Wilde had been caught by the Panther Princess and trapped in a room which slowly filled with water. That room had been a lot smaller than the lobby of the Seaview Inn, and the water had come in a lot faster.

Behind the desk were framed photographs of pretty people in pretty clothes having a pretty time. Pastore was there, and Brunette, grinning like tiger cats, mingling with showfolk: Xavier Cugat, Janey Wilde, Charles Coburn. Janice Marsh, the pop-eyed beauty rumoured to have replaced Jungle Jillian in Brunette's affections, was well represented in artistic poses.

On the phone, Pastore had promised faithfully to be here. He hadn't wanted to bother with a small-timer like me, but Janey Wilde's name opened a door. I had a feeling Papa Pastore was relieved to be shaken down about Brunette, as if he wanted to talk about something. He must be busy, because there were several wars on. The big one overseas and a few little ones at home. Maxie Rothko, bar owner and junior partner in the *Monty*, had been found drifting in the seaweed around the Santa Monica pier without much of a head to speak of. And Phil Isinglass, man-about-town lawyer and Brunette frontman, had turned up in the storm drains, lungs full of sandy mud. Disappearing was the latest craze in Brunette's organization. That didn't sound good for Janey Wilde, though Pastore had talked about the Laird as if he knew Brunette was alive. But now Papa wasn't around. I was getting annoyed with someone it wasn't sensible to be annoyed with.

Pastore wouldn't be in any of the beach shacks, but there should be an apartment for his convenience in the main building. I decided to explore further. Jungle Jillian would expect no less. She'd hired me for five days in advance, a good thing, since I'm unduly reliant on eating and drinking and other expensive diversions of the monied and idle.

The corridor that led past the office ended in a walk-up staircase. As soon as I put my size nines on the first step, it squelched. I realized something was more than usually wrong. The steps were a quiet little waterfall, seeping rather than cascading. It wasn't just water, there was unpleasant slimy stuff mixed in. Someone had left the bath running. My first thought was that Pastore had been distracted by a bullet. I was wrong. In the long run, he might have been happier if I'd been right.

I climbed the soggy stairs and found the apartment door unlocked but shut. Bracing myself, I pushed the door in. It encountered resistance but then sliced open, allowing a gush of water to shoot around my ankles, soaking my dark blue socks. Along with water was a three-weeks-dead-in-the-water-with-sewage-and-rotten-fish smell that wrapped around me like a blanket. Holding my breath, I stepped into the room. The waterfall flowed faster now. I heard a faucet running. A radio played, with funny little gurgles mixed in. A crooner was doing his best with "Life Is Just a Bowl of Cherries," but he sounded as if he were drowned full fathom five. I followed the music and found the bathroom.

Pastore was facedown in the overflowing tub, the song coming from under him. He wore a silk lounging robe that had been pulled away from his back, his wrists tied behind him with the robe's cord. In the end he'd been drowned. But before that hands had been laid on him, either in anger or with cold professional skill. I'm not a coroner, so I couldn't tell how long the Family Man had been in the water. The radio still playing and the water still running suggested Gianni had met his end recently, but the stench felt older than sin.

I have a bad habit of finding bodies in Bay City, and the most profit-minded police force in the country have a bad habit of trying to make connections between me and a wide variety of deceased persons. The obvious solution in this case was to make a friendly phone call, absent-mindedly forgetting to mention my name while giving the flatfeet directions to the late Mr. Pastore. Who knows, I might accidentally talk to someone honest.

That is exactly what I would have done if, just then, the man with the gun hadn't come through the door. . . .

I had Janey Wilde to blame. She'd arrived without an appointment, having picked me on a recommendation. Oddly, Laird Brunette had once said something not entirely uncomplimentary about me. We'd met. We hadn't seriously tried to kill each other in a while. That was as good a basis for a relationship as any.

Out of her sarong, Jungle Jillian favoured sharp shoulders and a veiled pill-box. The kiddies at the matinee had liked her fine, especially when she was wrestling stuffed snakes, and dutiful daddies took no exception to her either, especially when she was tied down and her sarong rode up a few inches. Her lips were four red grapes plumped together. When she crossed her legs you saw swimmer's smooth muscle under her hose.

"He's very sweet, really," she explained, meaning Mr. Brunette never killed anyone within ten miles of her without apologizing afterwards, "not at all like they say in those dreadful scandal sheets."

The gambler had been strange recently, especially since the war shut him down. Actually the *Montecito* had been out of commission for nearly a year, supposedly for a refit, although as far as Janey Wilde knew no workmen had been sent out to the ship. At about the time Brunette suspended his crooked wheels, he came down with a common California complaint, a dose of crackpot religion. He'd been tangentially mixed up a few years ago with a psychic racket run by a bird named Amthor, but had apparently shifted from the mostly harmless bunco cults onto the hard stuff. Spiritualism, orgiastic rites, chanting, incense, the whole deal.

Janey blamed this sudden interest in matters occult on Janice Marsh, who had coincidentally made her name as the Panther Princess in *The Perils of Jungle Jillian*, a role which required her to torture Janey Wilde at least once every chapter. My employer didn't mention that her own career had hardly soared between *Jungle Jillian* and *She-Strangler of Shanghai*, while the erstwhile Panther Princess had gone from Republic to Metro and was being built up as an exotic in the Dietrich-Garbo vein. Say what you like about Janice Marsh's Nefertiti, she still looked like Peter Lorre to me. And according to Janey, the star had more peculiar tastes than a seafood buffet.

Brunette had apparently joined a series of fringe organizations and become quite involved, to the extent of neglecting his business and thereby irking his longtime partner, Gianni Pastore. Perhaps that was why person or persons unknown had decided the Laird wouldn't mind if his associates died one by one. I couldn't figure it out. The cults I'd come across mostly stayed in business by selling sex, drugs, power, or reassurance to rich, stupid people. The Laird hardly fell into the category. He was too big a fish for that particular bowl.

The man with the gun was English, with a Ronald Colman accent and a white aviator's scarf. He was not alone. The quiet truck-sized bruiser I made as a fed went through my wallet while the dapper foreigner kept his automatic pointed casually at my middle.

"Peeper," the fed snarled, showing the photostat of my licence and my supposedly impressive deputy's badge.

"Interesting," said the Britisher, slipping his gun into the pocket of his camel coat. Immaculate, he must have been umbrella-protected between car and building because there wasn't a spot of rain on him. "I'm Winthrop. Edwin Winthrop."

We shook hands. His other companion, the interesting one, was going through the deceased's papers. She looked up, smiled with sharp white teeth, and got back to work.

"This is Mademoiselle Dieudonné."

"Genevieve," she said. She pronounced it "Zhe-ne-vyev," suggesting Paris, France. She was wearing something white with silver in it and had quantities of pale blond hair.

"And the gentleman from your Federal Bureau of Investigation is Finlay."

The fed grunted. He looked as if he'd been brought to life by Willis H. O'Brien.

"You are interested in a Mr. Brunette," Winthrop said. It was not a question, so there was no point in answering him. "So are we."

"Call in a Russian and we could be the Allies," I said. Winthrop laughed. He was sharp. "True. I am here at the request of my government and working with the full cooperation of yours."

One of the small detective-type details I noticed was that no one even suggested informing the police about Gianni Pastore was a good idea.

"Have you ever heard of a place called Innsmouth, Massachusetts?"

It didn't mean anything to me and I said so.

"Count yourself lucky. Special Agent Finlay's associates were called upon to dynamite certain unsafe structures in the sea off Innsmouth back in the twenties. It was a bad business."

Genevieve said something sharp in French that sounded like swearing. She held up a photograph of Brunette dancing cheek to cheek with Janice Marsh.

"Do you know the lady?" Winthrop asked.

"Only in the movies. Some go for her in a big way, but I think she looks like Mr. Moto."

"Very true. Does the Esoteric Order of Dagon mean anything to you?"

"Sounds like a Church-of-the-Month alternate. Otherwise, no."

"Captain Obed Marsh?"

"Uh-huh."

"The Deep Ones?"

"Are they those coloured singers?"

"What about Cthulhu, Y'ha-nthlei, R'lyeh?"

"Gesundheit."

Winthrop grinned, sharp moustache pointing. "No, not easy to say at all. Hard to fit into human mouths, you know."

"He's just a bedroom creeper," Finlay said, "he don't know nothing."

"His grammar could be better. Doesn't J. Edgar pay for elocution lessons?"

Finlay's big hands opened and closed as if he were rather there were a throat in them.

"Gene?" Winthrop said.

The woman looked up, red tongue absently flicking across her red lips, and thought a moment. She said something in a foreign language that I did understand.

"There's no need to kill him," she said in French. Thank you very much, I thought.

Winthrop shrugged and said, "Fine by me." Finlay looked disappointed.

"You're free to go," the Britisher told me. "We shall take care of everything. I see no point in your continuing your current line of inquiry. Send in a chit to this address," he handed me a card, "and you'll be reimbursed for your expenses so far. Don't worry. We'll carry on until this is seen through. By the way, you might care not to discuss with anyone what you've seen here or anything I may have said. There's a War on, you know. Loose lips sink ships."

I had a few clever answers, but I swallowed them and left. Anyone who thought there was no need to kill me was all right in my book, and I wasn't using my razored tongue on them. As I walked to the Chrysler, several ostentatiously unofficial cars cruised past me, headed for the Seaview Inn.

It was getting dark and lightning was striking down out at sea. A flash lit up the *Montecito*, and I counted five seconds before the thunder boomed. I had the feeling there was something out there beyond the three-mile limit besides the floating former casino, and that it was angry.

I slipped into the Chrysler and drove away from Bay City, feeling better the farther inland I got.

I take *Black Mask*. It's a long time since Hammett and the fellow who wrote the Ted Carmady stories were in it, but you occasionally get a good Cornell Woolrich or Erle Stanley Gardner. Back at my office, I saw the newsboy had been by and dropped off the *Times* and next month's pulp. But there'd been a mix-up. Instead of the *Mask*, there was something inside the folded newspaper called *Weird Tales*. On the cover, a man was being attacked by two green demons and a stereotype vampire with a widow's peak. " 'Hell on Earth,' a Novelette of Satan in a Tuxedo by Robert Bloch" was blazed above the title. Also promised were "A New Lovecraft series, 'Herbert West—Re-Animator' " and " 'The Rat Master' by Greye la Spina." All for fifteen cents, kids. If I were a different type of detective, the brand who said *nom de* something and waxed a moustache whenever he found a mutilated corpse, I might have thought the substitution an omen.

In my office, I've always had five filing cabinets, three empty. I also had two bottles, only one empty. In a few hours, the situation would have changed by one bottle.

I found a glass without too much dust and wiped it with my clean handkerchief. I poured myself a generous slug and hit the back of my throat with it.

The radio didn't work, but I could hear Glenn Miller from somewhere. I found my glass empty and dealt with that. Sitting behind my desk, I looked at the patterns in rain on the window. If I craned I could see traffic on Hollywood Boulevard. People who didn't spend their working days finding bodies in bathtubs were going home not to spend their evenings emptying a bottle.

After a day, I'd had some excitement but I hadn't done much for Janey Wilde. I was no nearer being able to explain the absence of Mr. Brunette from his usual haunts than I had been when she left my office, leaving behind a tantalizing whiff of essence de chine.

She'd given me some literature pertaining to Brunette's cult involvement. Now, the third slug warming me up inside, I looked over it, waiting for inspiration to strike. Interesting echoes came up in relation to Winthrop's shopping list of subjects of peculiar interest. I had no luck with the alphabet-soup syllables he'd spat at me, mainly because "Cthulhu" sounds more like a cough than a word. But the Esoteric Order of Dagon was a group Brunette had joined, and Innsmouth, Massachusetts, was the East Coast town where the organization was registered. The Esoteric Order had a temple on the beachfront in Venice, and its mumbo-jumbo handouts promised "ancient and intriguing rites to probe the mysteries of the Deep." Slipped in with the recruitment bills was a studio biography of Janice Marsh, which helpfully revealed the movie star's place of birth as Innsmouth, Massachusetts, and that she could trace her family back to Captain Obed Marsh, the famous early-nineteenth-century explorer of whom I'd never heard. Obviously Winthrop, Genevieve, and the FBI were well ahead of me in making connections. And I didn't really know who the Englishman and the French girl were.

I wondered if I wouldn't have been better off reading *Weird Tales*. I liked the sound of Satan in a Tuxedo. It wasn't Ted Carmady with an automatic and a dame, but it would do. There was a lot more thunder and lightning and I finished the bottle. I suppose I could have gone home to sleep, but the chair was no more uncomfortable than my Murphy bed.

The empty bottle rolled and I settled down, tie loose, to forget the cares of the day.

Thanks to the War, Pastore only made page 3 of the *Times*. Apparently the noted gambler-entrepreneur had been shot to death. If that was true, it had happened after I'd left. Then, he'd only been tortured and drowned. Police Chief John Wax dished out his usual "over by Christmas" quote about the investigation. There was no mention of the FBI, or of our allies, John Bull in a tux and Mademoiselle la Guillotine. In prison, you get papers with neat oblongs cut out to remove articles the censor feels provocative. They don't make any difference: all newspapers have invisible oblongs. Pastore's sterling work with underprivileged kids was mentioned, but someone forgot to write about the junk he sold them when they grew into underprivileged adults. The obit photograph found him with Janey Wilde and Janice Marsh at the premiere of a George Raft movie. The phantom Jap sub off Santa Barbara got more column inches. General John L. DeWitt, head of the Western Defence Command, called for more troops to guard the coastline, prophesying "death and destruction are likely to come at any moment." Everyone in California was looking out to sea.

After my regular morning conference with Mr. Huggins and Mr. Young, I placed a call to Janey Wilde's Malibu residence. Most screen idols are either at the studio or asleep if you telephone before ten o'clock in the morning, but Janey, with weeks to go before shooting started on *Bowery to Bataan*, was at home and awake, having done her thirty lengths. Unlike almost everyone else in the industry, she thought a swimming pool was for swimming in rather than lounging beside.

She remembered instantly who I was and asked for news. I gave her a précis.

"I've been politely asked to refrain from further investigations," I explained. "By some heavy hitters."

"So you're quitting?"

I should have said yes, but "Miss Wilde, only you can require me to quit. I thought you should know how the federal government feels."

There was a pause.

"There's something I didn't tell you," she told me. It was an expression common among my clients. "Something important."

I let dead air hang on the line.

"It's not so much Laird that I'm concerned about. It's that he has Franklin."

"Franklin?"

"The baby," she said. "Our baby. My baby."

"Laird Brunette has disappeared, taking a baby with him?"

"Yes."

"Kidnapping is a crime. You might consider calling the cops."

"A lot of things are crimes. Laird has done many of them and never spent a day in prison."

That was true, which was why this development was strange. Kidnapping, whether personal or for profit, is the riskiest of crimes. As a rule, it's the province only of the stupidest criminals. Laird Brunette was not a stupid criminal.

"I can't afford bad publicity. Not when I'm so near to the roles I need."

Bowery to Bataan was going to put her among the screen immortals.

"Franklin is supposed to be Esther's boy. In a few years, I'll adopt him legally. Esther is my housekeeper. It'll work out. But I must have him back."

"Laird is the father. He will have some rights."

"He said he wasn't interested. He . . . um, moved on . . . to Janice Marsh while I was . . . before Franklin was born."

"He's had a sudden attack of fatherhood and you're not convinced?"

"I'm worried to distraction. It's not Laird, it's her. Janice Marsh wants my baby for something vile. I want you to get Franklin back."

"As I mentioned, kidnapping is a crime."

"If there's a danger to the child, surely . . ."

"Do you have any proof that there is danger?"

"Well, no."

"Have Laird Brunette or Janice Marsh ever given you reason to believe they have ill-will for the baby?"

"Not exactly."

I considered things.

"I'll continue with the job you hired me for, but you understand that's all I can do. If I find Brunette, I'll pass your worries on. Then it's between the two of you."

She thanked me in a flood, and I got off the phone feeling I'd taken a couple of strides farther into the La Brea tar pits and could feel sucking stickiness well above my knees.

I should have stayed out of the rain and concentrated on chess problems, but I had another four days' worth of Jungle Jillian's retainer in my pocket and an address for the Esoteric Order of Dagon in a clipping from a lunatic scientific journal. So I drove out to Venice, reminding myself all the way that my wipers needed fixing.

Venice, California, is a fascinating idea that didn't work. Someone named Abbott Kinney had the notion of artificially creating a city like Venice, Italy, with canals and architecture. The canals mostly ran dry and the architecture never really caught on in a town where, in the twenties, Gloria Swanson's bathroom was considered an aesthetic triumph. All that was left was the beach and piles of rotting fish. Venice, Italy, is the Plague Capital of Europe, so Venice, California, got one thing right.

The Esoteric Order was up the coast from Muscle Beach, housed in a discreet yacht-club building with its own small marina. From the exterior, I guessed the cult business had seen better days. Seaweed had tracked up the beach, swarmed around the jetty, and was licking the lower edges of the front wall. Everything had gone green: wood, plaster, copper ornaments. And it smelled like Pastore's bathroom, only worse. This kind of place made you wonder why the Japs were so keen on invading.

I looked at myself in the mirror and rolled my eyes. I tried to get that slap-happy, let-me-give-you-all-my-worldly-goods, gimme-some-mysteries-of-the-orient look I imagined typical of a communicant at one of these bughouse congregations. After I'd stopped laughing, I remembered the marks on Pastore and tried to take detecting seriously. Taking in my unshaven, slept-upright-in-his-clothes, two-bottles-a-day lost soul look, I congratulated myself on my foresight in spending fifteen years developing the ideal cover for a job like this.

To get in the building, I had to go down to the marina and come at it from the beach-side. There were green pillars of what looked like fungus-eaten cardboard either side of the impressive front door, which held a stained-glass picture in shades of green and blue of a man with the head of a squid in a natty monk's number, waving his eyes for the artist. Dagon, I happened to know, was half-man, half-fish, and God of the Philistines. In this town, I guess a Philistine God blended in well. It's a great country: if you're half-fish, pay most of your taxes, eat babies, and aren't Japanese, you have a wonderful future.

I rapped on the squid's head but nothing happened. I looked the squid in several of his eyes and felt squirmy inside. Somehow, up close, cephalopod-face didn't look that silly.

I pushed the door and found myself in a temple's waiting room. It was what I'd expected: subdued lighting, old but bad paintings, a few semi-pornographic statuettes, a strong smell of last night's incense to cover up the fish stink. It had as much religious atmosphere as a two-dollar bordello.

"Yoo-hoo," I said, "Dagon calling. . . ."

My voice sounded less funny echoed back at me.

I prowled, sniffing for clues. I tried saying *nom de* something and twiddling a nonexistent moustache, but nothing came to me. Perhaps I ought to switch to a meerschaum of cocaine and a deerstalker, or maybe a monocle and an interest in incunabula.

Where you'd expect a portrait of George Washington or Jean Harlow's mother, the Order had hung up an impressively ugly picture of "Our Founder," Captain Obed Marsh, dressed up like Admiral Butler, stood on the shore of a Polynesian paradise, his good ship painted with no sense of perspective on the horizon as if it were about three feet tall. The Captain, surrounded by adoring if funny-faced native tomatoes, looked about as unhappy as Errol Flynn at a Girl Scout meeting. The painter had taken a lot of trouble with the native nudes. One of the dusky lovelies had hips that would make Lombard green and a face that put me in mind of Janice Marsh. She was probably the Panther Princess's great-great-great-grandmother. In the background, just in front of the ship, was something like a squid emerging from the sea. Fumble-fingers with a brush had tripped up again. It looked as if the tentacle-waving creature were about twice the size of Obed's clipper. The most upsetting detail was a robed and masked figure standing on the deck with a baby's ankle in each fist. He had apparently just wrenched the child apart like a wishbone and was emptying blood into the squid's eyes.

"*Excuse* me," gargled a voice, "can I help you?"

I turned around and got a noseful of the stooped and ancient Guardian of the Cult. His robe matched the ones worn by squid-features on the door and baby-ripper in the portrait. He kept his face shadowed, his voice sounded about as good as the radio in Pastore's bath, and his breath smelled worse than Pastore after a week and a half of putrefaction.

"Good morning," I said, letting a bird flutter in the higher ranges of my voice, "my name is, er. . . ."

I put together the first things that came to mind.

"My name is Herbert West Lovecraft. Uh, H. W. Lovecraft the Third. I'm simply fascinated by matters Ancient and Esoteric, don't ch'know."

"Don't ch'know" I picked up from the fellow with the monocle and the old books.

"You wouldn't happen to have an entry blank, would you? Or any incunabula?"

"Incunabula?" He wheezed.

"Books. Old books. Print books, published before 1500 *anno Domini*, old sport." See, I have a dictionary too.

"Books . . ."

The man was a monotonous conversationalist. He also moved like Laughton in *The Hunchback of Notre Dame*, and the front of his robe, where the squid head was embroidered, was wet with what I was disgusted to deduce was drool.

"Old books. Arcane mysteries, don't ch'know. Anything cyclopaean and doom-haunted is just up my old alley."

"The *Necronomicon*?" He pronounced it with great respect, and great difficulty.

"Sounds just the ticket."

Quasimodo shook his head under his hood and it lolled. I glimpsed greenish skin and large, moist eyes.

"I was recommended to come here by an old pal," I said. "Spiffing fellow. Laird Brunette. Ever hear of him?"

I'd pushed the wrong button. Quasi straightened out and grew about two feet. Those moist eyes flashed like razors.

"You'll have to see the Captain's Daughter."

I didn't like the sound of that and stepped backwards, towards the door. Quasi laid a hand on my shoulder and held it fast. He was wearing mittens, and I felt he had too many fingers inside them. His grip was like a Gila monster's jaw.

"That will be fine," I said, dropping the flutter.

As if arranged, curtains parted, and I was shoved through a door. Cracking my head on the low lintel, I could see why Quasi spent most of his time hunched over. I had to bend at the neck and knees to go down the corridor. The exterior might be rotten old wood, but the heart of the place was solid stone. The walls were damp, bare, and covered in suggestive carvings that gave primitive art a bad name. You'd have thought I'd be getting used to the smell by now, but nothing doing. I nearly gagged.

Quasi pushed me through another door. I was in a meeting room no larger than Union Station, with a stage, rows of comfortable armchairs, and lots more squid-person statues. The centrepiece was very like the mosaic at the Seaview Inn, only the nymph had less shells and Neptune more tentacles.

Quasi vanished, slamming the door behind him. I strolled over to the stage and looked at a huge book perched on a straining lectern. The fellow with the monocle would have salivated, because this looked a lot older than 1500. It wasn't a Bible and didn't smell healthy. It was open to an illustration of something with tentacles and slime, facing a page written in several deservedly dead languages.

"The *Necronomicon*," said a throaty female voice, "of the mad Arab, Abdul Alhazred."

"Mad, huh?" I turned to the speaker. "Is he not getting his royalties?"

I recognized Janice Marsh straightaway. The Panther Princess wore a turban and green silk lounging pyjamas, with a floor-length housecoat that cost more than I make in a year. She had on jade earrings, a pearl cluster pendant, and a ruby-eyed silver squid brooch. The lighting made her face look green and her round eyes shone. She still looked like Peter Lorre, but maybe if Lorre put his face on a body like Janice Marsh's, he'd be up for sex-goddess roles too. Her silk thighs purred against each other as she walked down the temple aisle.

"Mr. Lovecraft, isn't it?"

"Call me H.W. Everyone does."

"Have I heard of you?"

"I doubt it."

She was close now. A tall girl, she could look me in the eye. I had the feeling the eye-jewel in her turban was looking me in the brain. She let her fingers fall on the tentacle picture for a moment, allowed them to play around like a fun-loving spider, then removed them to my upper arm, delicately tugging me away from the book. I wasn't unhappy about that. Maybe I'm allergic to incunabula or perhaps an undiscovered prejudice against tentacled creatures, but I didn't like being near the *Necronomicon* one bit. Certainly the experience didn't compare with being near Janice Marsh.

"You're the Captain's Daughter?" I said.

"It's an honorific title. Obed Marsh was my ancestor. In the Esoteric Order, there is always a Captain's Daughter. Right now, I am she."

"What exactly is this Dagon business about?"

She smiled, showing a row of little pearls. "It's an alternative form of worship. It's not a racket, honestly."

"I never said it was."

She shrugged. "Many people get the wrong idea."

Outside, the wind was rising, driving rain against the Temple. The sound effects were weird, like sickening whales calling out in the Bay.

"You were asking about Laird? Did Miss Wilde send you?"

It was my turn to shrug.

"Janey is what they call a sore loser, Mr. Lovecraft. It comes from taking all those bronze medals. Never the gold."

"I don't think she wants him back," I said, "just to know where he is. He seems to have disappeared."

"He's often out of town on business. He likes to be mysterious. I'm sure you understand."

My eyes kept going to the squid-face brooch. As Janice Marsh breathed, it rose and fell and rubies winked at me.

"It's Polynesian," she said, tapping the brooch. "The Captain brought it back with him to Innsmouth."

"Ah yes, your hometown."

"It's just a place by the sea. Like Los Angeles."

I decided to go fishing, and hooked up some of the bait Winthrop had given me. "Were you there when J. Edgar Hoover staged his fireworks display in the twenties?"

"Yes, I was a child. Something to do with rum-runners, I think. That was during Prohibition."

"Good years for the Laird."

"I suppose so. He's legitimate these days."

"Yes. Although if he were as Scotch as he likes to pretend he is, you can be sure he'd have been deported by now."

Janice Marsh's eyes were sea-green. Round or not, they were fascinating. "Let me put your mind at rest, Mr. Lovecraft, or whatever your name is," she said. "The Esoteric Order of Dagon was never a front for bootlegging. In fact it has never been a front for anything. It is not a racket for duping rich widows out of inheritances. It is not an excuse for motion-picture executives to gain carnal knowledge of teenage drug addicts. It is exactly what it claims to be, a church."

"Father, Son, and Holy Squid, eh?"

"I did not say we were a Christian church."

Janice Marsh had been creeping up on me and was close enough to bite. Her active hands went to the back of my neck and angled my head down like an adjustable lamp. She put her lips on mine and squashed her face into me. I tasted lipstick, salt, and caviar. Her fingers writhed up into my hair and pushed my hat off. She shut her eyes. After an hour or two of suffering in the line of duty, I put my hands on her hips and detached her body from mine. I had a fish taste in my mouth.

"That was interesting," I said.

"An experiment," she replied. "Your name has such a ring to it. Love . . . craft. It suggests expertise in a certain direction."

"Disappointed?"

She smiled. I wondered if she had several rows of teeth, like a shark.

"Anything but."

"So do I get an invite to the back row during your next Dagon hoedown?"

She was businesslike again. "I think you'd better report back to Janey. Tell her I'll have Laird call her when he's in town and put her mind at rest. She should pay you off. What with the War, it's a waste of manpower to have you spend your time looking for someone who isn't missing when you could be defending Lockheed from Fifth Columnists."

"What about Franklin?"

"Franklin the President?"

"Franklin the baby."

Her round eyes tried to widen. She was playing this scene innocent.

The Panther Princess had been the same when telling the white hunter that Jungle Jillian had left the Tomb of the Jaguar hours ago.

"Miss Wilde seems to think Laird has borrowed a child of hers that she carelessly left in his care. She'd like Franklin back."

"Janey hasn't got a baby. She can't have babies. It's why she's such a psychoneurotic case. Her analyst is getting rich on her bewildering fantasies. She can't tell reality from the movies. She once accused me of human sacrifice."

"Sounds like a square rap."

"That was in a film, Mr. Lovecraft. Cardboard knives and catsup blood."

Usually at this stage in an investigation, I call my friend Bernie at the District Attorney's office and put out a few fishing lines. This time, he phoned me. When I got into my office, I had the feeling my telephone had been ringing for a long time.

"Don't make waves," Bernie said.

"Pardon," I snapped back, with my usual lightning-fast wit.

"Just don't. It's too cold to go for a swim this time of year."

"Even in a bathtub."

"Especially in a bathtub."

"Does Mr. District Attorney send his regards?"

Bernie laughed. I had been an investigator with the DA's office a few years back, but we'd been forced to part company.

"Forget him. I have some more impressive names on my list."

"Let me guess. Howard Hughes?"

"Close."

"General Stilwell?"

"Getting warmer. Try Major Fletcher Bowron, Governor Culbert Olson, and State Attorney General Earl Warren. Oh, and Wax, of course."

I whistled. "All interested in little me. Who'd'a thunk it?"

"Look, I don't know much about this myself. They just gave me a message to pass on. In the building, they apparently think of me as your keeper."

"Do a British gentleman, a French lady, and a fed the size of Mount Rushmore have anything to do with this?"

"I'll take the money I've won so far, and you can pass that question on to the next sucker."

"Fine, Bernie. Tell me, just how popular am I?"

"Tojo rates worse than you, and maybe Judas Iscariot."

"Feels comfy. Any idea where Laird Brunette is these days?"

I heard a pause and some rumbling. Bernie was making sure his office was empty of all ears. I imagined him bringing the receiver up close and dropping his voice to a whisper.

"No one's seen him in three months. Confidentially, I don't miss him at all. But there are others. . . ." Bernie coughed, a door opened, and he started talking normally or louder. ". . . of course, honey, I'll be home in time for Jack Benny."

"See you later, Sweetheart," I said, "your dinner is in the sink and I'm off to Tijuana with a professional pool player."

"Love you," he said, and hung up.

I'd picked up a coating of green slime on the soles of my shoes. I tried scraping them off on the edge of the desk and then used yesterday's *Times* to get the stuff off the desk. The gloop looked damned esoteric to me.

I poured myself a shot from the bottle I had picked up across the street and washed the taste of Janice Marsh off my teeth.

I thought of Polynesia in the early nineteenth century and of those fish-eyed native girls clustering around Captain Marsh. Somehow, tentacles kept getting in the way of my thoughts. In theory, the Captain should have been an ideal subject for a Dorothy Lamour movie, perhaps with Janice Marsh in the role of her great-great-great and Jon Hall or Ray Milland as girl-chasing Obed. But I was picking up Bela Lugosi vibrations from the setup. I couldn't help but think of bisected babies.

So far none of this running around had got me any closer to the Laird and his heir. In my mind, I drew up a list of Brunette's known associates. Then, I mentally crossed off all the ones who were dead. That brought me up short. When people in Brunette's business die, nobody really takes much notice except maybe to join in a few drunken choruses of "Ding-Dong, the Wicked Witch Is Dead" before remembering there are plenty of other Wicked Witches in the sea. I'm just like everybody else: I don't keep a score of dead gambler-entrepreneurs. But, thinking of it, there'd been an awful lot recently, up to and including Gianni Pastore. Apart from Rothko and Isinglass, there'd been at least three other closed-casket funerals in the profession. Obviously you couldn't blame that on the Japs. I wondered how many of the casualties had met their ends in bathtubs. The whole thing kept coming back to water. I decided I hated the stuff and swore not to let my bourbon get polluted with it.

Back out in the rain, I started hitting the bars. Brunette had a lot of friends. Maybe someone would know something.

By early evening, I'd propped up a succession of bars and leaned on a succession of losers. The only thing I'd come up with was the blatantly obvious information that everyone in town was scared. Most were wet, but all were scared.

Everyone was scared of two or three things at once. The Japs were high on everyone's list. You'd be surprised to discover the number of shaky citizens who'd turned overnight from chisellers who'd barely recognize the flag into true red, white, and blue patriots prepared to shed their last drop of alcoholic blood for their country. Everywhere you went, someone sounded off against Hirohito, Tojo, the Mikado, kabuki, and origami. The current rash of accidental deaths in the Pastore-Brunette circle was a much less popular subject for discussion and tended to turn loudmouths into closemouths at the drop of a question.

"Something fishy," everyone said, before changing the subject.

I was beginning to wonder whether Janey Wilde wouldn't have done better spending her money on a radio commercial asking the Laird to give her a call. Then I found Curtis the Croupier in Maxie's. He usually wore the full soup and fish, as if borrowed from Astaire. Now he'd exchanged his carnation, starched shirtfront, and pop-up top hat for an outfit in olive drab with bars on the shoulder and a cap under one epaulette.

"Heard the bugle call, Curtis?" I asked, pushing through a crowd of patriotic admirers who had been buying the soldier boy drinks.

Curtis grinned before he recognized me, then produced a supercilious sneer. We'd met before, on the *Montecito*. There was a rumour going around that during Prohibition he'd once got involved in an honest card game, but if pressed he'd energetically refute it.

"Hey, cheapie," he said.

I bought myself a drink but didn't offer him one. He had three or four lined up.

"This racket must pay," I said. "How much did the uniform cost? You rent it from Paramount?"

The croupier was offended. "It's real," he said. "I've enlisted. I hope to be sent overseas."

"Yeah, we ought to parachute you into Tokyo to introduce loaded dice and rickety roulette wheels."

"You're cynical, cheapie." He tossed back a drink.

"No, just a realist. How come you quit the *Monty*?"

"Poking around in the Laird's business?"

I raised my shoulders and dropped them again.

"Gambling has fallen off recently, along with leading figures in the industry. The original owner of this place, for instance. I bet paying for wreaths has thinned your bankroll."

Curtis took two more drinks, quickly, and called for more. When I'd come in, there'd been a couple of chippies climbing into his hip pockets. Now he was on his own with me. He didn't appreciate the change of scenery, and I can't say I blamed him.

"Look, cheapie," he said, his voice suddenly low, "for your own good, just drop it. There are more important things now."

"Like democracy?"

"You can call it that."

"How far overseas do you want to be sent, Curtis?"

He looked at the door as if expecting five guys with tommy guns to come out of the rain for him. Then he gripped the bar to stop his hands shaking.

"As far as I can get, cheapie. The Philippines, Europe, Australia. I don't care."

"Going to war is a hell of a way to escape."

"Isn't it just? But wouldn't Papa Gianni have been safer on Wake Island than in the tub?"

"You heard the bathtime story, then?"

Curtis nodded and took another gulp. The jukebox played "Doodly-Acky-Sacky, Want Some Seafood, Mama" and it was scary. Nonsense, but scary.

"They all die in water. That's what I've heard. Sometimes, on the *Monty*, Laird would go up on deck and just look at the sea for hours. He was crazy, since he took up with that Marsh Popsicle."

"The Panther Princess?"

"You saw that one? Yeah, Janice Marsh. Pretty girl if you like clams. Laird claimed there was a sunken town in the bay. He used a lot of weird words, darkie bop or something. Jitterbug stuff. Cthul-whatever, Yog-Gimme-a-Break. He said things were going to come out of the water and sweep over the land, and he didn't mean U-boats."

Curtis was uncomfortable in his uniform. There were dark patches where the rain had soaked. He'd been drinking like W. C. Fields on a bender, but he wasn't getting tight. Whatever was troubling him was too much even for Jack Daniel's.

I thought of the Laird of the *Monty*. And I thought of the painting of Captain Marsh's clipper, with that out-of-proportion squid surfacing near it.

"He's on the boat, isn't he?"

Curtis didn't say anything.

"Alone," I thought aloud. "He's out there alone."

I pushed my hat to the back of my head and tried to shake booze out of my mind. It was crazy. Nobody bobs up and down in the water with a sign round their neck saying, "Hey Tojo, Torpedo Me!" The *Monty* was a floating target.

"No," Curtis said, grabbing my arm, jarring drink out of my glass. "He's not out there?"

He shook his head. "No, cheapie. He's not out there alone."

All the water taxis were in dock, securely moored and covered until the storms settled. I'd never find a boatman to take me out to the *Montecito* tonight. Why, everyone knew the waters were infested with Japanese subs. But I knew someone who wouldn't care anymore whether or not his boats were being treated properly. He was even past bothering if they were borrowed without his permission.

The Seaview Inn was still deserted, although there were police notices warning people away from the scene of the crime. It was dark, cold, and wet, and nobody bothered me as I broke into the boathouse to find a ring of keys.

I took my pick of the taxis moored to the Seaview's jetty and gassed her up for a short voyage. I also got my .38 Colt Super Match out from the glove compartment of the Chrysler and slung it under my armpit. During all this, I got a thorough soaking and picked up the beginnings of influenza. I hoped Jungle Jillian would appreciate the effort.

The sea was swelling under the launch and making a lot of noise. I was grateful for the noise when it came to shooting the padlock off the mooring chain, but the swell soon had my stomach sloshing about in my lower abdomen. I am not an especially competent seaman.

The *Monty* was out there on the horizon, still visible whenever the lightning lanced. It was hardly difficult to keep the small boat aimed at the bigger one.

Getting out on the water makes you feel small. Especially when the lights of Bay City are just a scatter in the dark behind you. I got the impression of large things moving just beyond my field of perception. The chill soaked through my clothes. My hat was a felt sponge, dripping down my neck. As the launch cut towards the *Monty*, rain and spray needled my face. I saw my hands white and bath-wrinkled on the wheel and wished I'd brought a bottle. Come to that, I wished I was at home in bed with a mug of cocoa and Claudette Colbert. Some things in life don't turn out the way you plan.

Three miles out, I felt the law change in my stomach. Gambling was legal, and I emptied my belly over the side into the water. I stared at the remains of my toasted cheese sandwich as they floated off. I thought I saw the moon reflected greenly in the depths, but there was no moon that night.

I killed the engine and let waves wash the taxi against the side of the *Monty*. The small boat scraped along the hull of the gambling ship, and I caught hold of a weed-furred rope ladder as it passed. I tethered the taxi and took a deep breath.

The ship sat low in the water, as if its lower cabins were flooded. Too much seaweed climbed up towards the decks. It'd never reopen for business, even if the War were over tomorrow.

I climbed the ladder, fighting the water-weight in my clothes, and heaved myself up on deck. It was good to have something more solid than a tiny boat under me, but the deck pitched like an airplane wing. I grabbed a rail and hoped my internal organs would arrange themselves back into their familiar grouping.

"Brunette," I shouted, my voice lost in the wind.

There was nothing. I'd have to go belowdecks.

A sheet flying flags of all nations had come loose and was whipped around with the storm. Japan, Italy, and Germany were still tactlessly represented, along with several European states that weren't really nations anymore. The deck was covered in familiar slime.

I made my way around towards the ballroom doors. They'd blown in and rain splattered against the polished wood floors. I got inside and pulled the .38. It felt better in my hand than digging into my ribs.

Lightning struck nearby and I got a flash image of the abandoned ballroom, orchestra stands at one end painted with the name of a disbanded combo.

The casino was one deck down. It should be dark, but I saw a glow under a walkway door. I pushed through and cautiously descended. It wasn't wet here but it was cold. The fish smell was strong.

"Brunette," I shouted again.

I imagined something heavy shuffling nearby and slipped a few steps, banging my hip and arm against a bolted-down table. I kept hold of my gun, but only through superhuman strength.

The ship wasn't deserted. That much was obvious.

I could hear music. It wasn't Cab Calloway or Benny Goodman. There was a Hawaiian guitar in there, but mainly it was a crazy choir of keening voices. I wasn't convinced the performers were human and wondered whether Brunette was working up some kind of act with singing seals. I couldn't make out the words, but the familiar hawk-and-spit syllables of "Cthulhu" cropped up a couple of times.

I wanted to get out and go back to nasty Bay City and forget all about this. But Jungle Jillian was counting on me.

I made my way along the passage, working towards the music. A hand fell on my shoulder, and my heart banged against the back sides of my eyeballs.

A twisted face stared at me out of the gloom, thickly bearded, crater-cheeked. Laird Brunette was made up as Ben Gunn, skin shrunk onto his skull, eyes large as hen's eggs.

His hand went over my mouth.

"Do Not Disturb," he said, voice high and cracked.

This wasn't the suave criminal I knew, the man with tartan cummerbunds and patent-leather hair. This was some other Brunette, in the grips of a tough bout with dope or madness.

"The Deep Ones," he said.

He let me go and I backed away.

"It is the time of the Surfacing."

My case was over. I knew where the Laird was. All I had to do was tell Janey Wilde and give her her refund.

"There's very little time."

The music was louder. I heard a great number of bodies shuffling around in the casino. They couldn't have been very agile, because they kept clumping into things and each other.

"They must be stopped. Dynamite, depth charges, torpedoes . . ."

"Who?" I asked. "The Japs?"

"The Deep Ones. The Dwellers in the Sister City."

He had lost me.

A nasty thought occurred to me. As a detective, I can't avoid making deductions. There were obviously a lot of people aboard the *Monty*, but mine was the only small boat in evidence. How had everyone else got out here? Surely they couldn't have swum?

"It's a war," Brunette ranted, "us and them. It's always been a war."

I made a decision. I'd get the Laird off his boat and turn him over to Jungle Jillian. She could sort things out with the Panther Princess and her Esoteric Order. In his current state, Brunette would hand over any baby if you gave him a blanket.

I took Brunette's thin wrist and tugged him towards the staircase. But a hatch clanged down and I knew we were stuck.

A door opened, and perfume drifted through the fish stink.

"Mr. Lovecraft, wasn't it?" a silk-scaled voice said.

Janice Marsh was wearing pendant squid earrings and a lady-sized gun. And nothing else.

That wasn't quite as nice as it sounds. The Panther Princess had no nipples, no navel, and no pubic hair. She was lightly scaled between the legs, and her wet skin shone like a shark's. I imagined that if you stroked her, your palm would come away bloody. She was wearing neither the turban she'd affected earlier nor the dark wig of her pictures. Her head was completely bald, skull swelling unnaturally. She didn't even have her eyebrows pencilled in.

"You evidently can't take good advice."

As mermaids go, she was scarier than cute. In the crook of her left arm, she held a bundle from which a white baby face peered with unblinking eyes. Franklin looked more like Janice Marsh than his parents.

"A pity, really," said a tiny ventriloquist voice through Franklin's mouth, "but there are always complications."

Brunette gibbered with fear, chewing his beard and huddling against me.

Janice Marsh set Franklin down and he sat up, an adult struggling with a baby's body.

"The Captain has come back," she explained.

"Every generation must have a Captain," said the thing in Franklin's mind. Dribble got in the way, and he wiped his angel-mouth with a fold of swaddle.

Janice Marsh clucked and pulled Laird away from me, stroking his face.

"Poor dear," she said, flicking his chin with a long tongue. "He got out of his depth."

She put her hands either side of Brunette's head, pressing the butt of her gun into his cheek.

"He was talking about a Sister City," I prompted.

She twisted the gambler's head around and dropped him on the floor. His tongue poked out and his eyes showed only white.

"Of course," the baby said. "The Captain founded two settlements. One beyond Devil Reef, off Massachusetts. And one here, under the sands of the Bay."

We both had guns. I'd let her kill Brunette without trying to shoot her. It was the detective's fatal flaw, curiosity. Besides, the Laird was dead inside his head long before Janice snapped his neck.

"You can still join us," she said, hips working like a snake in time to the chanting. "There are raptures in the deeps."

"Sister," I said, "you're not my type."

Her nostrils flared in anger and slits opened in her neck, flashing liverish red lines in her white skin.

Her gun was pointed at me, safety off. Her long nails were lacquered green.

I thought I could shoot her before she shot me. But I didn't. Something about a naked woman, no matter how strange, prevents you from killing them. Her whole body was moving with the music. I'd been wrong. Despite everything, she was beautiful.

I put my gun down and waited for her to murder me. It never happened.

I don't really know the order things worked out. But first there was lightning, then, an instant later, thunder.

Light filled the passageway, hurting my eyes. Then, a rumble of noise which grew in a crescendo. The chanting was drowned.

Through the thunder cut a screech. It was a baby's cry. Franklin's eyes were screwed up and he was shrieking. I had a sense of the Captain drowning in the baby's mind, his purchase on the purloined body relaxing as the child cried out.

The floor beneath me shook and buckled, and I heard a great straining of abused metal. A belch of hot wind surrounded me. A hole appeared. Janice Marsh moved fast and I think she fired her gun, but whether at me on purpose or at random in reflex I couldn't say. Her body sliced towards me, and I ducked.

There was another explosion, not of thunder, and thick smoke billowed through a rupture in the floor. I was on the floor, hugging the tilting deck. Franklin slid towards me and bumped, screaming, into my head. A half-ton of water fell on us, and I knew the ship was breached. My guess was that the Japs had just saved my life with a torpedo. I was waist-deep in saltwater. Janice Marsh darted away in a sinuous fish motion.

Then there were heavy bodies around me, pushing me against a bulkhead. In the darkness, I was scraped by something heavy, cold-skinned, and foul-smelling. There were barks and cries, some of which might have come from human throats.

Fires went out and hissed as the water rose. I had Franklin in my hands and tried to hold him above water. I remembered the peril of Jungle Jillian again and found my head floating against the hard ceiling.

The Captain cursed in vivid eighteenth-century language, Franklin's little body squirming in my grasp. A toothless mouth tried to get a biter's grip on my chin but slipped off. My feet slid and I was off-balance, pulling the baby briefly underwater. I saw his startled eyes through a wobbling film. When I pulled him out again, the Captain was gone and Franklin was screaming on his own. Taking a double gulp of air, I plunged under the water and struggled towards the nearest door, a hand closed over the baby's face to keep water out of his mouth and nose.

The *Montecito* was going down fast enough to suggest there were plenty of holes in it. I had to make it a priority to find one. I jammed my knee at a door and it flew open. I was poured, along with several hundred gallons of water, into a large room full of stored gambling equipment. Red-and-white chips floated like confetti.

I got my footing and waded towards a ladder. Something large reared out of the water and shambled at me, screeching like a seabird. I didn't get a good look at it. Which was a mercy. Heavy arms lashed me, flop-ping boneless against my face. With my free hand, I pushed back at the thing, fingers slipping against cold slime. Whatever it was was in a panic and squashed through the door.

There was another explosion and everything shook. Water splashed upwards and I fell over. I got upright and managed to get a one-handed grip on the ladder. Franklin was still struggling and bawling, which I took to be a good sign. Somewhere near, there was a lot of shouting.

I dragged us up rung by rung and slammed my head against a hatch. If it had been battened, I'd have smashed my skull and spilled my brains. It flipped upwards, and a push of water from below shoved us through the hole like a Ping-Pong ball in a fountain.

The *Monty* was on fire and there were things in the water around it. I heard the drone of airplane engines and glimpsed nearby launches. Gunfire fought with the wind. It was a full-scale attack. I made it to the deck-rail and saw a boat fifty feet away. Men in yellow slickers angled tommy guns down and sprayed the water with bullets.

The gunfire whipped up the sea into a foam. Kicking things died in the water. Someone brought up his gun and fired at me. I pushed myself aside, arching my body over Franklin, and bullets spanged against the deck.

My borrowed taxi must have been dragged under by the bulk of the ship.

There were definitely lights in the sea. And the sky. Over the city, in the distance, I saw firecracker bursts. Something exploded a hundred yards away and a tower of water rose, bursting like a puffball. A depth charge.

The deck was angled down and water was creeping up at us. I held on to a rope webbing, wondering whether the gambling ship still had any lifeboats. Franklin spluttered and bawled.

A white body slid by, heading for the water. I instinctively grabbed at it. Hands took hold of me, and I was looking into Janice Marsh's face. Her eyes blinked, membranes coming round from the sides, and she kissed me again. Her long tongue probed my mouth like an eel, then withdrew. She stood up, one leg bent so she was still vertical on the sloping deck. She drew air into her lungs—if she had lungs—and expelled it through her gills with a musical cry. She was slim and white in the darkness, water running off her body. Someone fired in her direction and she dived into the waves, knifing through the surface and disappearing towards the submarine lights. Bullets rippled the spot where she'd gone under.

I let go of the ropes and kicked at the deck, pushing myself away from the sinking ship. I held Franklin above the water and splashed with my legs and elbows. The *Monty* was dragging a lot of things under with it, and I fought against the pull so I wouldn't be one of them. My shoulders ached and my clothes got in the way, but I kicked against the current.

The ship went down screaming, a chorus of bending steel and dying creatures. I had to make for a launch and hope not to be shot. I was lucky. Someone got a polehook into my jacket and landed us like fish. I lay on the deck, water running out of my clothes, swallowing as much air as I could breathe.

I heard Franklin yelling. His lungs were still in working order.

Someone big in a voluminous slicker, a sou'wester tied to his head, knelt by me, and slapped me in the face.

"Peeper," he said.

"They're calling it the Great Los Angeles Air Raid," Winthrop told me as he poured a mug of British tea. "Sometime last night a panic started, and everyone in Bay City shot at the sky for hours."

"The Japs?" I said, taking a mouthful of welcome hot liquid.

"In theory. Actually, I doubt it. It'll be recorded as a fiasco, a lot of jumpy characters with guns. While it was all going on, we engaged the enemy and emerged victorious."

He was still dressed up for an embassy ball and didn't look as if he'd been on deck all evening. Genevieve Dieudonné wore a fisherman's sweater and fatigue pants, her hair up in a scarf. She was looking at a lot of sounding equipment and noting down readings.

"You're not fighting the Japs, are you?"

Winthrop pursed his lips. "An older war, my friend. We can't be distracted. After last night's action, our Deep Ones won't poke their scaly noses out for a while. Now I can do something to lick Hitler."

"What really happened?"

"There was something dangerous in the sea, under Mr. Brunette's boat. We have destroyed it and routed the . . . uh, the hostile forces. They wanted the boat as a surface station. That's why Mr. Brunette's associates were eliminated."

Genevieve gave a report in French, so fast that I couldn't follow.

"Total destruction," Winthrop explained, "a dreadful setback for them. It'll put them in their place for years. Forever would be too much to hope for, but a few years will help."

I lay back on the bunk, feeling my wounds. Already choking on phlegm, I would be lucky to escape pneumonia.

"And the little fellow is a decided dividend."

Finlay glumly poked around, suggesting another dose of depth charges. He was cradling a mercifully sleep-struck Franklin, but didn't look terribly maternal.

"He seems quite unaffected by it all."

"His name is Franklin," I told Winthrop. "On the boat, he was . . ."

"Not himself? I'm familiar with the condition. It's a filthy business, you understand."

"He'll be all right," Genevieve put in.

I wasn't sure whether the rest of the slicker crew were feds or servicemen, and I wasn't sure whether I wanted to know. I could tell a Clandestine Operation when I landed in the middle of one.

"Who knows about this?" I asked. "Hoover? Roosevelt?"

Winthrop didn't answer.

"Someone must know," I said.

"Yes," the Englishman said, "someone must. But this is a war the public would never believe exists. In the Bureau, Finlay's outfit are known as 'the Unnameables,' never mentioned by the press, never honoured or censured by the government, victories and defeats never recorded in the official history."

The launch shifted with the waves, and I hugged myself, hoping for some warmth to creep over me. Finlay had promised to break out a bottle later, but that made me resolve to stick to tea as a point of honour. I hated to fulfil his expectations.

"And America is a young country," Winthrop explained. "In Europe, we've known things a lot longer."

On shore, I'd have to tell Janey Wilde about Brunette and hand over Franklin. Some flack at Metro would be thinking of an excuse for the Panther Princess's disappearance. Everything else—the depth charges, the sea battle, the sinking ship—would be swallowed up by the War.

All that would be left would be tales. Weird tales.

"I Had Vacantly Crumpled It into My Pocket . . . But by God, Eliot, <u>It Was a Photograph from Life</u>!"

JOANNA RUSS

In an ancient rooming house in New York, where the dirt covered the molded plaster ceilings, where the creak of the stairs at night echoed like pistol shots in the dark, amid the rickety splendors of peeling red velvet wallpaper and indescribably varnished furniture, Irvin Rubin lived. He was a bookkeeper in a cheap publishing house: *Fantasy Press;* he worked there for the discounts. He told this story to a woman in the office, and she told it to me, one winter morning in a cafeteria with steam that covered the plate-glass windows running down in clear patches that displayed nothing at all, so distorted were they, but drops and streaks of the scene outside. Irvin Rubin, who never ate without a book propped up in front of his plate, his pale eyes fixed on it, his cheeks rhythmically bulging, and his fork blindly hunting in front of him, took all his meals in cafeterias. Then he read in his room. He had nothing in particular to do. He knew nobody. The woman who worked with him had tried to engage him in conversation, but fruitlessly, for Irv had nothing to say except shrill denunciations of the latest writers put out by Fantasy Press ("He called them a bunch of hacks," she said) or complaints about his desk, or his office-mates, or his salary, for on other topics he had no opinion at all, but one morning he came over to her desk and stood with his hands behind his back, red, sweating, and trying visibly to keep calm.

"Miss Kramer," he said to her, "where would you take a girl?"

"Goodness, do you have a girl?" she said lightly. He looked a little dazed.

"Where would you take a girl?" he repeated plaintively, apparently twisting his hands behind his back; then he said, "Where would you take *a real lady*, Miss Kramer?"

"I don't know," said she, "I don't know any," and Irvin—vastly relieved—dropped into the seat next to her desk. "Neither do I," he said simply. At this point (she told me) he smiled and June Kramer saw with something like dismay that for an instant his face became distinctly human, rather young (he was twenty-eight), and even genuinely sweet. He frowned and it vanished.

"I certainly wouldn't ask *anybody else*," he said significantly. "I wouldn't ask anybody else in this joint." He got up; shifted from foot to foot. He frowned again. "Do you think she'd like to read something?"

"Well—" said Miss Kramer, "I don't know—"

"Do you think she'd like to come to my place?" he burst out.

"Not right away," she said, alarmed. He looked at the floor.

"Perhaps you should go for a walk," said Miss Kramer cautiously, "or—or maybe she would like to go to the movies. Maybe you could see" (here Irv, looking at his feet, muttered, "it's all trash anyway") "well, maybe you could see—" but before she could finish her sentence, Irv started violently and then walked jerkily away—scuttled, rather. He had seen the supervisor coming.

"How's the nut?" said the supervisor in a whisper to June Kramer, who looked at him over her glasses, set her lips severely, and said nothing.

It turned out that Irv had met his girl near Central Park, walking two dachshunds on a leash, though neither June Kramer nor I could see what such a girl would want with him. Perhaps she was not a girl exactly, and perhaps not exactly a lady either, for although he always described her as a compound of a "real lady" and a "glamour girl" with "that husky sort of whisper, Miss Kramer" like you-know-who in the movies, Irv Rubin's girlfriend always seemed to me like the women drowned passively in mink or sable in the advertisement sketches— lost, lifeless, betrayed, undoubtedly kept by some rich sadist—at least that's how they strike me. He had caught glimpses of her many days before he actually met her, for Irv's furnished room was located in the decaying blocks near the rich section of Central Park West, and he had followed her pure profile down many side streets and even into the Park, catching glimpses of her black coat and bobbing, straining, double dogs in unlikely places—once, I believe, the supermarket.

Irv loved his girl. He dwelt on her obsessively with Miss Kramer, in a way that seemed new to him, as if he were awed, almost (said June Kramer) as if he were frightened by her superiority, by her elegance, by her fashion-model paleness, and most of all by the silence with which she tolerated him, by the way she listened to him as if he had a right to talk to her, to take her on walks, and to tell her (with spiritualized earnestness) that Howard Phillips Lovecraft was the greatest writer in the world.

He had met her, he told June Kramer, on Central Park West, on a cold, blue, brilliantly sunny Sunday afternoon, when every tree in the park was coated with ice and icicles hung from the eaves of the buildings along the street. Sundays were bad days for Irv; the bookstores were shut. (He gave Miss Kramer a recital of all the places he had been to on the last nine or ten Sundays; I forget most of them, but he went three times to the zoo and once rode up and down Fifth Avenue in a bus, though he said looking at expensive things in windows "was as nothing compared with the Imagination"; his own clothes were so old and in such bad repair that people noticed him in the street—at any rate, it was a pitiable catalogue.) He had seen the girl sitting on a park bench, reading a book, with her twin dachshunds nosing about in the snow in front of her, and he had crossed the street with his heart beating violently, knowing that he must speak to her. Luckily the book she was reading was by his favorite author. His voice cracking horribly, he had managed to excuse himself and inform her that the edition she was reading was not as complete as the one of 1939, and "pardon me, but it has everything; I got that book; it's much better; do you mind if I sit down next to you?"

No, she didn't mind. She listened to him, her thin, handsome face pale and composed, giving every now and then a little jerk to the leashes of the dachshunds who—thus caught up rather dryly in their explorations—whimpered a little. ("She's got real leather gloves," he told Miss Kramer, "black ones.") What she told him I do not know, for he couldn't remember it, but whatever it was (in her hoarse, husky whisper) it sounded to him like the assurance that he was the most intelligent man she had ever met, that she too thought the books of H. P. Lovecraft of the utmost importance ("He's a real writer," Irv used to say), and she thought she would like *very much* to take a walk with him. He told all this to Miss Kramer. He told of their walk through the park, amidst icicles falling to the ground with a *plink!* and everything shiveringly, blindingly bright under the sun—the mica in the rocks, the blue sky, the shriveled leaves hanging infrequently from the trees, the discolorations of the snow where mud, or dogs—or her dogs— stained the white. All the time his radiant companion (she was a little taller than he) walked beside him, with her black coat blossoming into a huge enveloping collar that half hid her face, with her black elegance, her black stockings, and crowning all a hat—but not a blue hat, a hat almost violet, a hat the color of twilight winter skies where the yellows and the greens and the hot, smoky pinks riot so gorgeously in the west while all the time you are freezing to death. He really made it come across. The hat she wore was made of that silky, iridescent, fashionable stuff, "and get this!" (he said) "get this, Miss Kramer, that hat is the *exact same color as her eyes*!"

Alas, poor Irvin Rubin! Miss Kramer thought, but his lady did not get tired of Irvin Rubin. They went to the movies. They went on walks. They went to bookstores. I saw them myself, once, from a distance. And every evening Irv's girl waved good-bye (though it is impossible to think of her doing anything even that vigorous) and walked into the park, into the blue with her blue eyes shining like stars. She lived on the fashionable East Side. Late one Saturday afternoon Irvin knocked on Miss Kramer's apartment door in the Stuyvesant Town project, and then stood there miserably with his hands balled in his jacket pockets while she fumbled with the latch. She had women friends in for bridge, who were playing cards in the living room.

"Miss Kramer!" said Irv breathlessly, "you just got to help me!"

"Well—well, come in," said she, sensing uneasily that her guests had stopped talking and were looking at Irvin in surprise. "Come into the kitchen. Just for a moment." He followed her like some ungainly creature in a fairy tale, only stopping to remark in surprise, "Gee, you're all dressed up" (her hair was newly set and she wore a suit), but otherwise taking no notice of his surroundings, not even the extreme tininess of the little kitchenette when the two of them had crowded into it.

"Now what is it, Irvin?" said Miss Kramer somewhat sharply, for she was thinking of her guests. She even made a mental note of the number of clean coffee cups left on top of the refrigerator. He looked vacantly round, his mouth open, his hands still in his pockets, one side of the ancient plush collar of his jacket turned up by mistake.

"Miss Kramer—" he faltered, "Miss Kramer—please—you got to help me!"

"Yes, what about, Irvin?" said she.

"Miss Kramer, she's coming up to my place tonight. She's coming up to see me." ("Really!" thought June Kramer, "what's so awful about that?") He dropped his gaze. "What I mean, Miss Kramer—I mean—" (he breathed heavily) "I don't want her to think—" and here he lifted his head suddenly and cried out, *Please, Miss Kramer, you come too!*"

"I?" said June, thinking of her guests.

"Yes, please!" cried Irv. "Please! I want—I mean—" and with a sort of shuddering sob, he burst out, "I told her there would be people there!" He turned his back on her and doggedly faced the refrigerator, rubbing his sleeve back and forth across his nose.

"Irvin, don't you think that was wrong?" said she. No answer. "Irvin," she said gently, "I think that if this girl likes you, you don't have to invent things that aren't true and if she doesn't really like you, well, she's going to find out what you're really like sooner or later. Now don't you think it would have been better to have told the truth? Don't you?"

"I don't know," muttered Irvin. He turned around. He looked at June Kramer silently, doggedly, the tears standing in his eyes, those pale-blue protuberant eyes that should have been nearsighted but were not, alas, too nearsighted to see silent, passive charmers sitting on park benches across Central Park West.

"Oh, all right," said June Kramer; "all right, Irvin," and she abandoned her friends, her cards, her little party, to make Irvin's girl think Irvin had friends.

"That'll look respectable, Miss Kramer, thank you," said he, and then he added—with a cunning so foreign to him that it was shocking—"She'll be impressed by you, Miss Kramer; you look so nice."

So Miss Kramer put on her coat with the rabbit's fur collar (to look nice) and they went to Irvin's boardinghouse, first on a bus that churned the slush in the roads, grinding and grinding; and then in a subway where the platform was puddled with melted snow—but no weather, bad or good, ever drew a comment from Irvin Rubin.

It was cold in the hallway of his boardinghouse, so deadly cold that you might fancy you saw the walls sweating, a kind of still, damp, petrified cold as of twenty winters back. The naked radiator in Irvin's room was cold. He took off his jacket and sat down on the ancient four-poster—the room held only that, an armchair, a dresser, and a green curtain across a sort of closet-alcove at the back—in nothing but his shirtsleeves. June Kramer shivered.

"Aren't you cold, Irvin?" she said. He said nothing. He was staring at the opposite wall. He roused himself, gave a sort of little shake, said, "She'll come soon, thank you Miss Kramer," and relapsed into a stupor. It had begun to snow outside, as June saw by pushing aside the plastic curtains. She let them fall. She walked past Irvin's bed—the bedspread was faded pink—past the dresser whose top held a brush, a comb, and a toothbrush, and whose mirror (set in romantic curlicues) was spotted and peeling, so that the room itself seemed to disappear behind clouds of ghostly shapes.

"This could be quite a nice room if you fixed it up, Irvin," she said brightly. He said nothing. She saw that he had gotten a book from somewhere and was reading; so she walked about the room again, glancing at the armchair, the bookshelf under the single window, and the bridge lamp under which Irvin sat. Shoes protruded from under the green curtain. Miss Kramer sat down in the armchair, beginning to feel the cold, and noticed that Irvin had pinned a snap-shot on the wall next to it, in the least accessible part of the room, a photograph apparently taken many years ago, of a boy standing with a dog under a tree. It was the only picture in the room.

"Is that you, Irvin?" said Miss Kramer, and Irvin (after a pause in which his eyes stopped moving over the pages of his book) nodded without looking up. Miss Kramer sat for a moment, then got up and walked over to the bookcase (it was full of Fantasy Press books), again parted the plastic curtains, again looked out into the snow (it was beginning to stick to the cleared sidewalk and the streetlight), again contemplated the photograph, whose faded sepia seemed to have reduced the tree to a piece of painted canvas, and finally said:

"Irvin Rubin, are you *sure* this girl is coming tonight?" This question had a surprising effect on him; hastily slamming down his book, he jumped to his feet with both mouth and eyes open, his face working.

"Oh, please—" he stammered, "oh, please—"

"Oh, I'm sure she's coming," said June, "but is she coming *tonight*? Are you sure you didn't get mixed up about the time? I don't mean to suggest—" but here he ran over to the alarm clock that stood on the floor by the other side of the bed and shook it; he listened to it; he tried to explain something to her, stuttering so that he frightened her.

"That's all right!" she cried; "that's all right!" and Irvin Rubin, his chest heaving, stood still, subsided, wiped his eyes with his hand, shuffled back to the near side of the bed where—oh, wonderful Rubin!—he recommended reading his book. She thought of asking him to put it away, but she was afraid of him, and afraid too of the silence of the room, which seemed to warn against being broken. I think she was afraid to move. It was not only the human desolation of that room, but the somehow terrifying vision it gave her of a soul that could live in such a room and not know it was desolate, the suggestion that this bleak prose might pass—by a kind of reaction—into an even more dreadful poetry. June Kramer began to wonder about Irv's girl. It occurred to her with agonizing vividness the number of evenings Irvin had come home to that awful room, had come home and pulled out a book and peopled that room with heaven knows what; and then gone to bed, and got up, and gone to work, and eaten and come home and pulled out a book again until it was time to lie in bed for eight long hours (Irvin was a punctual sleeper), dreaming dreams that however weird—and this was less disturbing—were at least more like the lives led by others in their dreams. But now he read. She almost fancied she saw a kind of cold mist rise from the page. At last (she was stiff with sitting tightly on the horsehair seat of the armchair) Miss Kramer struggled to her feet and said in a voice that sounded weak and feeble in her own ears:

"I'm afraid I have to go, Irvin, I really can't stay any longer." She saw that he had closed his book and was staring at her with his brow wrinkled. The light from the overhead fixture gave him an odd look.

"Don't go, Miss Kramer," he said in a low voice.

"I'm sure your young lady meant next week," said June desperately. "Or tomorrow. Yes, she'll come tomorrow—"

"Please! Please!" cried Irv. "Please!"

"I'm sorry, but I have to go," said June. "I have to," and quite unreasonably terrified, she turned and rattled open the latch of the door, letting in at once a draught of that cold, dead, still air from the hall. All at once she knew perfectly well what she had been comparing it to all this time, and as she dove downstairs, followed by a distraught Irvin Rubin, crying breathlessly about his girl and this the first social event of his life, she saw before her only the open grave into which she had stared some forty years before, when as a small child she had been forced to attend the funeral of her youngest sister. In the street she ran away from him, clutching her purse to her side, but as she reached the corner and slowed down, something—she never knew exactly what— made her stop and turn around.

Irv's girl had come. She was standing next to him on the steps. June Kramer saw clearly the coat and hat Irvin had described. She could even make out the black leather gloves and the black stockings. Although she could hardly see Irvin himself in the light from the streetlamp, she saw every feature of the girl's pale, powdered face as if it had been drawn: the thin eyebrows, the expressionless profile like a sketch on paper, and most clearly of all, those wonderful, wonderful violet eyes—"she's got such *pretty eyes*," Irvin used to say. "She's here, Miss Kramer, she's here!" Irvin was shouting cheerfully, beaming down, coatless, at his pale, real lady, when a gust of wind momently froze the street. Irvin's shirt flapped, Miss Kramer's coat performed a violent dance about her calves, but the strange lady's black envelope did not stir, nor did her black scarf, but hung down in carved folds as if it had been made of stone, as still as her hands, as cold as her face, and as dead as her expression, which seemed in its pale luminosity to be saying to June Kramer (with a spark of hatred) *I dare you. . . .*

But here Miss Kramer, although she knew she was imagining too much, gave way to cowardice and ran, ran, ran, gasping, until she had reached the subway station and could—burying her face in her handkerchief—give way to tears.

After that Irv was not well. He missed days. He came late to work. When she spoke to him he answered her shrilly, denouncing the office, the people, the books, the world, everyone. It was impossible to talk to him. Three days before he finally disappeared, he cornered June in the stockroom and cried out to her, with an air of pride mixed with defiance: "Miss Kramer, I'm going to get married! My girl is going to marry me!"

She said congratulations.

"We're going away, to stay at her folks' place," he said, "but don't you tell anybody, Miss Kramer; I wouldn't want any of those—those *shrimps* who work in this office to know about it! They're just cowards, they're stupid, they don't know anything. They don't know anything about literature! They don't know *anything*!"

"Irvin, please—" said Miss Kramer, alarmed and embarrassed.

"Go on!" he shouted; "go on, all of you!" and then he turned his back on her, rubbing his eyes, mumbling, looking at one title after another on the stockroom shelves—though all of them were the same, as June Kramer told me afterwards. She thought of touching him on the shoulder, then she thought better of it, she thought of saying "congratulations" again but was afraid it would set him off, so she backed off as quietly as she could. She paused unwillingly at the door (she said) and then Irvin Rubin turned round to look at her—the last time she ever saw him. His defiance and his pride were both gone, she said, and his face looked frightened. It was as if human knowledge had settled down on him at last; he was ill and terrified and his life was empty. It was like seeing a human face on an animal. June Kramer said, "I'm sure you'll be very happy, Irvin, congratulations," and hurried blindly back to her desk.

This is Irvin Rubin's story as Miss June Kramer told it to me one winter morning in the cafeteria with the windows weeping and the secretaries clattering their coffee and buns around us, but it is not his whole story. I know his whole story. I saw him enter the park early one winter evening with a young lady—it was probably the day he left work—and although I don't know for certain what happened, I can very well imagine their walk across the park, the young woman silent, Irvin slipping a little on the icy path, turning about perhaps to look at the apricot sky in the west—though, as June Kramer said, natural phenomena never got much notice from him. I can guess—although I did not actually know—how Irvin's true love opened her automatic arms to him in some secluded, snowy part of the park, perhaps between a stone wall and the leafless trees. I can see her fade away against the darkening air, that black coat that holds nothing, that black scarf that adorns nothing, her iridescent hat become an indistinguishable part of the evening sky, her legs confused with the tree trunks, and her eyes—those wild, lovely, violet eyes!—kindling brighter and brighter, radiant as twin planets, brilliant as twin pole-stars, out of a face now grown to the hue of paper. I can see them melting, flattening, and diffusing into a luminous freezing mist, a mist pouring out from sockets that are now sockets in nothing, doing God only knows what to poor Irv Rubin, who was found the next morning (as the janitor of my apartment building tells me) flat on his back in the snow and frozen to death.

A few days afterwards I saw Irv's ladylove across Central Park West, on a bright February afternoon, with the traffic plowing the snow into slushy furrows within ten feet of her and the dogs of twenty blocks around being walked up and down to leave their bright pats in the snow. She was reading a book, turning the pages effortlessly with her gloved fingertips. I was even able to make out the title of the book, though I rather wish I hadn't; it was Ovid's *Art of Love*, which seemed to degrade the whole affair into a very bad joke.

But of course by the time I managed to get across the street, she was gone.

H.P.L.

GAHAN WILSON

> I was far from home, and the spell of the eastern sea was upon me.
>
> —H.P. Lovecraft

And it was, it *was*!

Smelling deeply the rich, time-abiding scent of the coastal marshes, I greedily read juicily exotic names at random from the road map clutched in my hand—Westerly, Narragansett, Apponaug—and to the north, drawing nearer every minute as the bus trundled efficiently along the upward curve of the coastal road, was Providence!

There could be no doubting it at all—absolutely incontrovertible evidence was all about me in the form of swooping gulls and salty surf and bleached piers in varying states of Innsmouthian decay—I, Edward Haines Vernon, born and bred in and frustrated by the flat, flat flat-lands of the Midwest, having grown up by one shore of Lake Michigan with the sure and certain knowledge that its other, opposite shore was only a sunny day's excursion away, and that it would only be another boring Midwestern shore with more boring people talking about more boring things if I'd bothered to go there—that I, the aforementioned Edward Haines Vernon, was now actually on the coast of the great Atlantic, *the eastern sea* itself, on whose other coast would be nothing less magnificent than Europe, for God's sake!

I sat back, letting a bone-deep, noisy sigh of satisfaction escape simultaneously from my mouth and nostrils and shook my fist in the air before me with triumph; then I saw I'd alarmed the thin, grey lady sitting next to me. But after being irritated with her for the tenth part of a second, I realized that—of course—she was a fine, old *New England* lady and would be upset by the crude, uncultured ways of a clumsy, ill-bred Midwesterner such as myself, God bless her withered old heart, God bless her pale blue, disapproving eyes!

"Excuse me," I said, gently, "but I am new to your country and do not fully understand its ways. Please be kind enough to pardon my outburst."

She regarded me steadily for a long moment over the steel rims of her glasses, then sniffed and turned back to her perusal of *Prevention* magazine, God bless her again, as I, in turn, turned back to my wide-eyed gazing out of the window of the bus.

It had not—I realized that now—it had not really so far hit me that all of this was actually happening! I had dreamed of it and planned and schemed for it so many long years, for such a large part of my life, that I had grown entirely accustomed to thinking of it as lurking (I hoped) in the future. It was always going to happen later on, but suddenly it was happening now! Suddenly it was all here! And so was I!

Carefully, so as not to alarm my dear New England lady once more with any further *gaucherie*, I pulled my little overnight bag (though I planned to stay in these regions far longer than overnight—by God, I planned to *live* here!) from under my seat and zipped it open and carefully lifted out the neatly folded letter which rested inside it on top of everything else. Reverently, like a priest with some holy artifact, I opened the precious thing and scanned its tiny letters penned in that spidery, small hand, and the words swam in my eyes for a moment before I blinked the tears away and I could reread that golden first paragraph for the thousandth, perhaps the ten thousandth, time.

"Of course you must come and visit me, Edwardius—by all means. And please do stay in my house, a handsome structure which I am sure one gifted with your knowledge and admiration of the antique will be able to appreciate fully. In the past, because of painfully reduced circumstances, I was not able to play the host to favored correspondents in the style I would have wished. Perhaps the greatest pleasure attendant to my present state of prosperity is that now I can fully indulge myself in grandfatherly welcomings!"

This totally unanticipated invitation had come in response to a wistfully timid outburst in my preceding letter to him wherein I'd confessed I dreamed of one day walking the streets which he and Poe had walked, and told him how I indulged myself sometimes with fantasies of sitting on some tomb in St. John's Churchyard, during an appropriately Gothic night of fog or lightning flashes, and building poems and stories with him about the worms which crawled and fed in the mouldy ground beneath our feet.

After that first, dazzling paragraph, he made a little joke to the effect that the Churchyard was really a very pleasant place, not mouldy at all, and then went on to practical specifics as to my visit, even volunteering to pay for my transportation, if that should present a problem.

"Please do not take offense at this offer," he wrote. "You know, being familiar with my history, that I am only too well acquainted with the perils and varied embarrassments which poverty afflicts on those who, like yourself, affront the common herd by daring to value art above commerce."

I sent back a reply in the affirmative as soon as I could get a proper one on paper—it took me about a week and, I think, about a ream's worth of drafts!—and I was careful to explain that I had put aside sufficient funds to make the trip providing I employed economical means. His reply to that included a line or two of touchingly old-fashioned praise for my thrift and industry, and after a short exchange of correspondence, we had settled all the dates and details.

Suddenly my eyes widened and I shook myself from this reverie of past events, leaned forward in my seat, and found myself actually pressing my nose against the window (doubtless to the further horrification of my seatmate) because beyond the glass, before and above me, seeming to appear with the abruptness of a mystic's vision of a paradise long deferred, unexpectedly loomed the hoary spires and domes of College Hill—lost in dreams of anticipation, I had, all unknowing, been driven into Providence itself!

I stared out nervously as we pulled into the bus station. He'd said I would be met but had not, I suddenly realized, given me any clues to help me identify the person he planned to send to fetch me.

Then my heart stopped and I actually gasped aloud (earning another audible sniff of disapproval from my neighbor), for there, in the flesh, standing with a positively jaunty air on the platform, was Howard Phillips Lovecraft, H.P.L., himself!

I had thought that, because of his enormous age, he would have the gravest difficulties in moving about, that it was highly likely he was now permanently housebound, or possibly confined to some beloved antique wingback, or even permanently ensconced in a quaint canopied bed, but it was quite obvious I had severely underestimated his durability. Though he did seem just a tiny bit stooped, and there was some small trace of that cautious slowness in his movements usually associated with considerable age, he leaned only lightly on his cane and stood his ground easily against the push and press of the crowd as he peered up into the windows of the bus with a lively curiosity sparkling in his eyes.

Of course his long, gaunt, Easter Island face with its aquiline nose and hollow cheeks and overpowering jaw was as instantly recognizable to me as that of my father or mother, since I'd lovingly studied every photograph of Lovecraft I could get my hands on over the years, going from those black-and-white snaps taken in the twenties and thirties and bound into the old Arkham House collections, all the way on up to the underexposed—and therefore humorously greenish—Polaroid he'd enclosed with his letter of invitation: ". . . in order to prepare you for the shock of seeing Grandpa in his present corpselike condition."

I waved at him through the window with the eagerness of a child, and as his teeth flashed in a smile and he gave me exactly the sort of friendly little salute of recognition I had hoped for, I clumsily hauled my bag for the last time from its lair under the seat, and emerged from the bus directly behind my New England lady.

And then she stepped primly away from before me, leaving me exposed in full view, and I turned suddenly from the happiest of young men to one of the most miserable wretches in the world, for though he did his gentlemanly best to hide it, I caught the almost instantly extinguished, kindly amusement in Lovecraft's eyes as he took me in from head to toe, and, for the first time, standing before this man who had been my idol through the bulk of my formative years, the full extent of the incredible idiocy, the grotesque absurdity, the horrible *presumption* of my short, plump, silly self, affecting the mode of attire he'd taken up in his later years—the black cape and wide-brimmed hat—dawned on me with a fierce, merciless clarity which threatened to crush me to the ground, then and there, under its weight.

Frozen in my pose before the doorway of the bus, unable even to breathe, totally humiliated, I only barely managed to fight down a mad, desperate urge to turn and flee into the vehicle's dark interior and cower there until it should drive me back to my hated flatlands.

Then Lovecraft's face lit with that kindly radiance which one sees only rarely in his photos, and he moved toward me with his hand extended.

"I confess I am very touched, Edwardius," he said, speaking quickly and precisely in a high-pitched, gentle voice. "It truly is—as I am only now able to appreciate fully for the first time—the *sincerest* form of flattery. Please accept my gratitude."

He paused and gave my hand one brief, firm, friendly squeeze in what I realized must be a very Yankee form of handshake, then turned and waved his cane to indicate a large, black, very elegant old Rolls which, even under the gray, lowering sky, gleamed and glistened like a fine old British beetle in the parking lot by the side of the station.

"And now," he said, giving my shoulder a light, comradely pat, and studiously keeping his eyes from mine so that I might have sufficient privacy to put myself together, "let us saunter forth from this hub of public transport, you and I, and enjoy a form of locomotion more suitable to the gentry."

The driver's door of the Rolls opened as we approached and a tall, thin, bearded man emerged gracefully. He was wearing a very elegantly tailored blazer, and his perfect ascot evoked my idea of Saint-Tropez more than Providence. He watched the approach of Lovecraft and myself in our identical capes and hats with no visible sign of hilarity save for a slightly ironic tilt to his head, but I came to learn that cranial attitude was habitual with him.

"This, Edwardius, is my valued associate, Mr. Smith," said Lovecraft as we reached the thin man's side. "Mr. Smith, please allow me to present Mr. Vernon, the young fantasist whose work we have discussed so much of late."

Mr. Smith favored me with a shy, deeply wrinkled smile, and though his handshake was not particularly strong, he delivered it more along the lines of the heartier Midwestern style to which I was accustomed.

But then, from the unobtrusive alacrity with which he gently withdrew his hand and carefully placed it out of sight in the pocket of his blazer, I realized I had not managed altogether to cover my wince of distaste when I'd touched his flesh. It was singularly dry and oddly unyielding, and though he was so refined and physically delicate in every other aspect of his appearance that he put me instantly in mind of an Elizabethan dandy in some elegant portrait, the texture of his skin was shockingly coarse. It was obvious the poor man suffered from a hideously incongruous illness.

"I found myself particularly admiring your management of the worm king in 'The Enshrouding,'" he said, speaking softly in an accent obviously foreign to this region, and, to all appearances, completely unaware of the little pantomime which had just taken place between us. "But I must confess my special favorite so far has been your notion of a displeased god presenting its followers with a poisoned idol made in its own image."

As I thanked him for his gracious comments I found myself looking at him with an increasingly awed puzzlement because, even though I could not at this moment connect it with any specific association, I was now absolutely certain that I knew his face well and had seen its wise eyes looking out at me from their wrinkled settings many times.

By now Lovecraft had entered the back of the car—again with no visible sign that the burden of his great age was more than a trifling inconvenience—and he waved me in beside him as Mr. Smith arranged himself in the driver's seat in order to play the chauffeur while H.P.L. gave us a brief tour of his beloved Providence. He pointed out various landmarks significant in the old town's history and his own, spinning little stories about them all with numerous brilliant asides, and I did not even try to deny myself the gleeful delight of anticipating the envy my telling and retelling of this adventure would produce in my listeners' hearts down through the years to come. And so it has!

However, with each sidewise glance I stole at my host my astonishment at his remarkable preservation increased. Looking at him, one had no doubt that he was extraordinarily old, but there was also no doubt he was astoundingly—even eerily—fit and spry for a gentleman hovering around the century mark.

Also, the ravages of time seemed, in his case, to have followed some weird progression which differed significantly from the common patterns. He was not, for example, actually *wrinkled*, because instead of the deep fleshly canyons one is used to seeing, his face was covered with a sort of web of fine lines, thin as cobwebs and shallow as the cracklings in a quaint old doll. Also there were none of the standard grotesqueries associated with the very old, no enlargement of the ears, no wattling of the throat, and absolutely no thinning of the hair at all. The truth was that if you squinted your eyes, he looked very much as he had in those old photos taken back in the late thirties.

He finished his tour by pointing out the house he'd lived in during the last period of his "obscurity," as he called it.

"It was moved from its original location to Meeting Street," he said, "but, as you see, I managed to arrange to have it carefully brought back here to 66 College Street, where it belongs. And I saw to it that my aunts had the use of it, not just part of it, but the run of the whole building, until their deaths."

"That must have been very satisfying to you," I said.

"It was, Edwardius," he said with a smile that began a little grimly but then broadened. "However it was nothing next to the restoration, the re-creation, you might even fairly say the glorification, of my grandfather's place at 454 Angell Street, which is where Mr. Smith has now almost driven us. There it is, just ahead."

We paused briefly before a high, wrought-iron gate which opened smoothly when a button was pushed in the Rolls's dashboard, then rolled up the curve of a driveway and came to a gliding stop before a large, most imposing house.

"I admit to improving on its architecture," Lovecraft observed, exiting from the car with a light step and no use of his cane whatsoever. "Even to transforming it entirely. Whipple Van Buren Phillips's house was a simple clapboard affair, though of substantial size, and not at all the splendid Georgian manor which you see before you. I suppose I could be accused of being a trifle Williamsburgian in all this, but it's both aesthetically and emotionally authentic, and the material, garnered by my agents from all points in a quite Hearstian manner, is entirely period."

"It sounds just like the creation of the mansion in your story, 'The Rats in the Walls,' " I said, looking about at all this splendor more than a little wide-eyed.

"Of course it does," said Lovecraft, with a smile. "Of course it does. Good heavens, wasn't it painfully obvious my whole notion of that American millionaire creating an ideal ancestral home was the pathetic dream of an impoverished romantic? Ah, but I see from your expression that does not seem to have crossed your mind. Well then, perhaps that little tale of mine isn't quite as embarrassing as I'd feared all these years, after all."

By now Mr. Smith had opened and was standing by the many-paneled front door, tall and richly gleaming beneath its glorious fanlight. Lovecraft led the way inside, laid his cape and hat on a handsome Wedgwood table, and waited until I had done the same with mine.

"They look quite natural there, side by side, do they not?" he asked. "Perhaps, Edwardius, where I have failed to do so on my own, the two of us together may bring capes and broad-brimmed trilbies back in style!"

He walked to a handsome double door, paused with his hand on one of its brightly polished knobs, then turned back to me with a mildly vexed expression.

"Please do accept my apologies," he said. "I have grown thoughtless in my solitary, self-indulgent ways. I was about to drag you on through an extended tour of the house, as I know there is much you will want to see, particularly in the library—oh, just wait 'til you see the library!—but it completely slipped my mind that you've only just climbed off that obviously uncomfortable bus and would doubtless very much enjoy some freshening up."

He paused to snap open and consult a wonderfully quaint old watch which he'd extracted from a pocket in his vest.

"It's a little over an hour to four," he said. "If Mr. Smith will be kind enough to show you to your room, you'll have plenty of time for a wash-up and perhaps even a short nap before tea, which is a custom we have taken to observing in recent years. Also, quite frankly, it will give your grandpa a chance for a little nod as well!"

Mr. Smith led me to my quarters and introduced me to its quirks, most helpfully the involved controls on an imported shower in the bathroom. After he left I spent a few minutes gaping in wonder at the room's marvelous antique furnishings, including a dazed, indeterminate period of time standing before a huge, lovely, glowing landscape which I took to be a Turner until I bent to examine the small gold plate fixed to its bottom frame and read that it portrayed the fabled realm of Ooth-Nargai from Lovecraft's novel *Beyond the Wall of Sleep* and that its artist was "unknown."

Standing back from the painting I felt a slight dizziness and finally realized that Lovecraft had been quite right. I *was* exhausted (my prim New England lady would be shocked to learn how loudly she snored).

So I hung up my one spare suit, washed some of the grime of travel from my hands and face, and it seemed to me I had barely stretched out on the bed when I found myself suddenly being dragged out of a profound slumber by a gentle tapping and Mr. Smith's voice informing me from the other side of the door that tea would shortly be served.

I reared up on my elbows and lay there for a second or two trying to pull back the vanishing recollections of what must have been a spectacularly interesting nightmare. It had been quite Lovecraftian, which was, of course, appropriate. I'd been in a harsh landscape, cold, windy, and mountainous, and seen bits and pieces of something huge and grey with an appalling wingspan come flapping down toward me through the snowy air, clacking its teeth horribly and ever more eagerly with each lurching drop in its descent. Its small red eyes burned piercingly down at me with an intent interest which somehow struck me as hideously *personal*, and I heard it caw tremendously: "Perfect, ah, but you're *perfect*!" just before it reached out its claws and I felt the first taloned squeeze of its inescapable grip. "You're next!" it cawed. "You're next! You're next!"

Some important aspect of the dream seemed determined to evade me, but I pursued it determinedly until I felt my stomach contract with the peculiarly horrible recollection that I'd been looking up at the monster from the very stalks and bracken of the creature's nest.

I shook my head without clearing it all that much, did another quick wash, tightened my tie, and started down the softly carpeted steps, but my downward progress was slowed considerably by the wonderful discovery that the ancestor portraits which lined the wall of the landing and stairway and which I'd only dimly noticed on my way up were, in fact, quite marvelous oil paintings of some of the principal villains in Lovecraft's novels and stories, each one of their names and birth and death dates neatly engraved on little golden plaques mounted at the bottoms of their frames.

Along the wall of the landing was hung a triptych of portraits, the center one being the slim, subtly gruesome figure of Joseph Curwen, the resurrected necromancer from *The Case of Charles Dexter Ward*, and it was flanked by the likenesses of the two ghastly, grinning ancients who were his mentors and assistant magicians in the novel, Simon Orne, originally of Salem, and Edward Hutchinson, later known as Baron Ferenczy of Transylvania. Among the other wonderfully sinister villains depicted in paintings descending the handsome staircase, I came across the hunched and leering Keziah Mason from "Dreams in the Witch House," with her horrendous familiar, Brown Jenkin, curling nastily round her feet, and an enormous, towering oil of Wilbur Whateley, the hybrid sorcerer of "The Dunwich Horror," seemingly all unaware that his vest had come slightly open and the viewer had an appalling peek at the writhing monstrosity which was his chest.

The front part of the ground floor was deserted, but I heard a cozy clatter coming from the rear of the house and soon found my way to an exceptionally comfortable, sunny, and obviously well-equipped kitchen where I came across Mr. Smith leaning over a counter and humming to himself, serenely engaged in cutting tiny triangular sandwiches for tea.

"Ah, Mr. Vernon," he said, looking up at my entrance and smiling. "Did you have a pleasant rest?"

I smiled back at him and had actually opened my mouth to make some insignificant joke about my nightmare of being in the monster's nest, when the sunlight shone on his cheek in a certain way and I recognized him at last.

He stopped his cutting and began to observe me with some concern because my expression most certainly had abruptly turned very odd indeed, and I'm sure I must have gone pale as a corpse.

"Is there something wrong?" he asked. "Can I get you a glass of water, Mr. Vernon?"

"Edwardius," I said, then realized I had barely croaked the name, so I cleared my throat and swallowed before continuing. "I should be very honored if you would call me Edwardius, just as Lovecraft does. After all, he has always acknowledged you as his peer."

"His peer?" asked Mr. Smith.

"You," I said, "because you are Clark Ashton Smith, poet, author, artist, and honored friend of Lovecraft, of H.P.L. Please don't deny it because I'm sure of it."

I paused, and then, aware of my heart beating in my chest, I said the other part.

"Of course I know it's impossible because you are dead."

He stared at me for a moment, then he frowned slightly and went back thoughtfully to his cutting. He made about three more little sandwiches and stacked them carefully on a silver tray with the rest, then he lay the knife on the counter.

"I suppose it was bound to happen one day, sooner or later," he murmured to the sandwiches, and then he gave a tiny shrug and looked up directly into my eyes.

"Very well, you're right," he said. "About both those things. I *am* Clark Ashton Smith, and I *am* dead. As you see, it turned out not to be impossible."

I stared at him, then groped forward and took hold of the counter with both hands because, to my great embarrassment, I appeared to be on the verge of fainting.

"There's a stool there, by your side, to your left," said Smith gently. "From the look of you, it might be a good idea if you sat on it. Carefully and slowly. It was quite thoughtless of me to be so abrupt."

I sat, carefully and slowly as he had said, and the pounding in my ears and the dancing spots of light before my eyes began to fade and dim.

"I thought you'd spotted me back at the bus terminal, you know," he said, handing me a glass of water which he had somehow filled without my noticing. "Then I saw you hesitate and falter into indecision, and I figured we'd got away with it again."

I took a long drink of the water, then another, and after a deep breath or two I decided I would probably be able to talk.

"I couldn't place you until just now," I said, speaking a little clearer with each word. "Then I saw the sun shining through your beard, and I knew."

He glanced at the window behind him and nodded with the relieved air of one who has solved a minor puzzle.

"Ah, yes. That *would* weaken its effect," he said. "It's the square cut extending from the sides of the jaw that does the job, you see. I thought it up myself and must admit I'm quite proud of the way it effectively obscures the essential triangularity of my face. Unless, as I now learn, the sun shines through it from behind."

"Of course it's particularly difficult to recognize someone in disguise when you think they're in their grave," I said, taking another sip of water.

"Naturally. That was our basic working assumption," he said. Then, with a small, resigned sigh, he added: "Not that I'm all that well known. It isn't as though we've been trying to conceal someone really famous."

The kettle on the burner started to whistle and he reached up, took two canisters from a shelf, then turned to me.

"What tea would you care for, Mr.—ah—Edwardius? We've finally managed to wean Howard away from sugar with a little coffee to a simple English breakfast blend. I, always the exotic, am attached to an odd Japanese concoction brewed from twigs, but it's not, confessedly, for every taste."

"I've never ventured out farther than Lipton's in a bag," I admitted.

"None of that here, I'm afraid," Smith said. "Far too common for the likes of us. Let's start you out with a Darjeeling; the highest quality, but quite undemanding."

He lost himself for a moment or two in contentedly and efficiently assembling pots and cups and saucers, but then he stared at his hands, stopped still, and looked up at me from a neatly squared stack of napkins with an expression of concern on his face which was more than a little pathetic.

"I hope you're not apprehensive about these hands of mine spreading some contagion," he said, holding them up before himself like two foreign objects. "They look this way, *I* look this way, because of an essential crudeness in my construction. It's not a disease, you know. It's nothing you can catch."

"I'm sorry I pulled my hand away from yours back at the bus station," I said, after a pause.

"Oh, no, you had every right to. They're horrible," he said. *"Horrible!"*

He turned toward the window and rotated his hands on his wrists so that they caught the sunlight this way and that.

"I'm like this all over, you know," he said. "Every inch of me. And it's not just my skin, worse luck, it's the same with my insides. My bowels, my heart, no doubt my brain itself, must be made of this repellent, defective stuff."

He rubbed his hands as if he were trying to smooth them, to reduce their gaping pores, and then looked back at me over his shoulder.

"You must forgive him," he said. "He was lonely, you see. I know it's difficult for one as young as yourself to begin to imagine how impossibly isolating it is to have the world one was born in die off with the passage of the years. *Along* with all of its inhabitants, mind. People and things keep vanishing only to be replaced by other people and things which vanish in their turn until even the *memories* of everything and everybody you grew up with and held dear are reduced to tiresome, passé jokes."

He had turned back to the tea tray, busying and calming himself with a final supply and inventory of its contents as he talked.

"You said it yourself, Edwardius," he said, filling the creamer with a hand that betrayed only the tiniest tremble. "I was one of the very few people he considered his peer. I was also, very importantly, an inhabitant of his original world; a contemporary. Unfortunately for him, I was also dead. But H.P.L. had, some time ago, hit on a way past that. He'd purloined the basic notion from a book by none other than good old Cotton Mather—the idea of raising the dead from their 'essential salts'—attributed it to the French scholar Borellus, and used it as the basic modus operandi for his scurvy Frankensteins in *The Case of Charles Dexter Ward*. My present resurrection represents his second practical application of the technique."

"That's horrible!" I cried.

"Yes," he said. "I confess that now and then I find myself wishing he hadn't done it, as death was really quite a relief. But, as I say, he was lonely. And eventually I will die again. I need only be patient."

A faint sigh sounded from the back of the kitchen.

"Well, well, Klarkash-Ton," said Lovecraft softly, employing the eerie nickname he'd concocted for his friend during their famous correspondence in the thirties. He stood framed by the doorway, leaning forward slightly with both hands interlaced atop the handle of his cane. "Things seem to have moved along smartly during Grandpa's nap."

I jumped to my feet as clumsily as a startled calf, but Smith merely turned his head and nodded as Lovecraft advanced into the room, looking carefully first at one and then the other of us.

"The boy has so far exceeded our most hopeful expectations. He recognized me, Howard," Smith said. "He recognized me—thereby setting himself apart from all previous visitors—and being a meticulous scholar of our little literary circle, he knew of my generally unheralded demise."

"So you went ahead and told him the truth without overmuch preamble, as we planned," he said, then walked slowly over to my side. "And you, Edwardius? Have you believed him? From the look of you it would appear you have."

"My presence is difficult to refute," observed Smith. "As are my grisly looks. More importantly than all that, our friend appears to have taken the complete and sudden overturning of reality as he knew it with commendable equanimity. It seems our speculations based on the promise of his tales were quite correct, and that—unlike the common herd—Edwardius is blessed with an open mind."

Lovecraft rubbed his huge jaw thoughtfully, studied me silently for a long moment.

"Excellent," he said at length, and, after a moment more, he added: "The two of us have for some time felt the growing need for a knowledgeable assistant, Edwardius. Also, certain signs which have cropped up repeatedly in my studies and experiments indicate strongly that our establishment is on the brink of some important transformation and that new blood will very shortly be required. We have been studying your writings and been impressed by them, not only because of their obvious literary merit, but because they seem to tell us that there is something remarkably *right* about you for the sort of activities in which we are engaged. We have both, in short, come to the conclusion that you would fit nicely into our little association."

I was amazed, even dazzled, by this totally unexpected turn. For a space I could only gape at the two of them—with my mouth wide open I am sure—but eventually I managed to gather myself together enough to speak.

"I'm honored," I said, "more honored than I can say, that you would even consider such a thing!"

"Very well, then, let us see how things work out," said Lovecraft with a small nod as he studied me intently, eye to eye. "Your ability to accept Klarkash-Ton's resurrection was the passing of an important test. Perhaps after we've all enjoyed a little tea, Edwardius, you'll be up to accepting a few other things. But be warned, please *do* be warned, they'll be a lot harder to swallow than our ghostly Mr. Smith!"

The sandwiches tasted even better than they had looked, an almond cake which Smith had purchased from a Portuguese bakery was superb, and the Darjeeling demonstrated clearly that my accustomed bag of Lipton's, though perfectly serviceable, by no means exhausted the subject of tea.

"Delightful," said Lovecraft, leaning back comfortably into exactly the sort of leather wing chair I had hoped he'd have. "And now that we're sated, thanks to the efforts of Klarkash-Ton and his foreign baker friend, I think it's time we quit this lovely, sunny Georgian parlor and give Edwardius a little tour of the premises."

We rose and Lovecraft headed for one of the tall white doors with me in his wake, but Smith produced the silver tray and began collecting cups and saucers.

"I think I'll stay behind and tidy up," he said. "Am I to assume you won't be giving our young friend the usual restricted and misleading tour?"

"He shall see every trapdoor and secret panel," said Lovecraft, smiling. "Events have proceeded rather more quickly than I'd planned, thanks to Edwardius's astute perceptions and flexibility, so things are ahead of schedule. I believe the time has well and truly arrived to enlighten him as fully as possible about his present company. I'll begin the job in the library, rather than putting it off for a final treat, since I believe its atmosphere and impressive contents will go a long way toward lending credence to the admittedly implausible information I plan to impart."

Smith, nodding, said no more, and as he bent to sorting china with his usual mild but interested bemusement, I followed Lovecraft through the door and soon found myself being led down a handsome hallway which, like so much of the house, was lined with paintings associated with my host's works. These, however, were far more disturbing than the ones I'd seen heretofore, since they were all depictions of various fabulous monsters described in his tales.

"I'm quite pleased with myself for coming up with the idea of hanging these huge oils in such a constricted area," said Lovecraft, grinning at me over his shoulder and casually indicating a remarkably horrific visualization of what—from its fanged, vertical mouth and jutting pink eyes—could only be one of the gigantic, ever-ravenous Gugs which prowled the pages of his *Dream-Quest of Unknown Kadath*. "It renders them particularly overpowering, does it not? And forces one into a threatening intimacy with the creatures which the timid viewer could avoid in the space provided by a room."

I glanced—a little nervously, I'm not ashamed to admit—this side and that at the looming horrors that towered so very oppressively near to us as we passed, and I freely confess that I actually started and drew back when the sleeve of my jacket accidentally brushed against an almost fiendishly well-executed painting of that shifting conglomeration of iridescent globes which is Yog-Sothoth, one of the most puissant and awful gods in Lovecraft's mythos.

Eventually he paused before a large, elaborately paneled door made of almost ebon teak and, producing a heavy gold chain loaded with formidable-looking keys, operated no less than three locks before turning a huge brass knob sculpted to resemble an unwinking octopoid eye framed with undulating tentacles, and pushed the portal open.

"My library," he said simply, but with obvious pride, and led the way inside.

Of course I had realized some time ago that everything about this house far surpassed all aspects of that one owned by Whipple Van Buren Phillips, but I felt certain nothing about this dream version of Lovecraft's favorite childhood home would have awed his grandfather more than the library which I now found myself entering.

There were shelves upon shelves of books, two full stories of them. Outside of the space taken up by the three tall windows on the side of the room facing the entrance, absolutely every available inch of wall above and below the encircling balcony was filled with books, and there were piles more of them on the two long tables, and on the high-backed chairs, and stacks more yet were on the floor and heaped in the corners. It was a collector's wonder, a scholar's marvel, and I burned to feel the bindings and turn the pages and read the words.

"Impressive, isn't it?" said my host. "I fancy it is by far the best collection in the entire world of volumes dealing with the macabre and the fantastic. Over there, for instance, under that Grecian niche containing a pallid bust of Pallas, is the sort of marvelous accumulation of first editions and manuscripts—along with other, rather more exotic artifacts—of Poe which I had never dared even hope to see, let alone touch, let alone own, back in the days of my obscurity."

He walked slowly down the long room, pointing his cane toward this or that fabulous rarity and contentedly describing their queer particulars and complex histories, and I stumbled after him in a sort of daze, gaping with increasing astonishment at all these legendary treasures, astounded to see books by giants such as Arthur Machen and Ambrose Bierce and Arthur Conan Doyle which I, a specialist in the field, did not even know existed.

Eventually we reached the far wall of the room, and standing by one of the curling steel stairways leading to the balcony, Lovecraft placed his hand carefully on the head of a tiny gargoyle carved into the shelving beside him and regarded me with an extremely solemn and serious expression on his long, lean face.

"You must promise me, most earnestly," he said, speaking quite severely with all trace of banter gone from his voice, "that you will never reveal anything of what you are about to see next unless you have my clear permission to do so."

I studied him for some sign which would indicate that this sudden extreme sternness was some sort of amusing pose, but then I realized he really was, indeed, deadly serious and nodded my head affirmatively.

"I'm afraid I need more than a nod on this," he said, with no trace of humor in his voice.

"I promise I'll keep secret whatever you're going to show me," I said. "I do, really."

He searched my face for a long moment, then smiled, gave the little gargoyle a precise poke on its nose, and—without a whisper of sound—the shelving slid smoothly aside to reveal an even deeper layer of rows and rows of books hidden a yard or two behind. There was a smaller—and, I could tell it at once, far more sinister—second library hidden craftily within the first!

"These books, too, are related to the macabre fantastic," observed Lovecraft, entering into this mysteriously revealed little room with something of a saunter. He still preserved traces of that new solemnity, but with his much more familiar tone of underlying mockery once again apparent. "The essential event is that we have now passed beyond the fiction department of my little collection and have moved into that portion concerned with fact, and though a great many of its facts would be vehemently denied by this world's contemporary wisdom, there is much here which would be approved of by the staidest investigators."

He waved his fingers at the section of newer-looking books which nearly filled one side wall, and a quick scan of them revealed a multitude of names well known to anyone pretending to the slightest familiarity with modern physics.

"Of course even in this supposedly safer area I have a number of items which might very seriously disturb the present scientific community," he said. "The formulae scrawled in that little notebook of Einstein's just in front of your nose, for instance. But I think that a scholar of your particular tastes, Edwardius, will be more interested in having a look at those volumes over there."

I stared at the far side of the room which he had indicated and was puzzled because it seemed to me that there was something very strange and wrong about the sight of it. I could not quite pin down what it was save to say that the whole area seemed oddly dark, as if it were somehow veiled—a distasteful and highly disturbing image of horribly sticky spiderwebs out of focus floated into my mind—and it seemed, in some weird fashion, as if that corner of the little library was disproportionately far away. I had the most peculiar notion that I would never be able to walk the whole distance if I spent hours or even weeks at it, and that I would very likely die under hideous circumstances somewhere along the journey if I undertook to try it.

But obviously none of this made sense, so I pulled myself together and had taken a step toward the shelves Lovecraft had indicated when he laid a hand gently on my arm to stop me, then sidled past me and—with his back turned scrupulously in my direction so as to block my view—he appeared neatly and efficiently to execute a brief series of ritualistic gestures before standing aside, almost with a little bow, and indicating I should pass. I looked at the corner again and had to smile at all my previous imaginings because now there was no sign of any odd darkness there at all, and if there ever had been that strange spatial distortion and I hadn't fantasized it completely, it had entirely disappeared.

But as I approached those shelves and began to be able to read some of the titles of the books resting on them, I felt my smile vanishing rapidly. I reached out with a hand gone suddenly clammy, plucked a worm-eaten volume from the shelf before me, and nervously turned several of its pages—which were not paper, but something disgustingly thick, almost *flabby*, which seemed to flop mockingly from my fingertips with a life quite their own—before total revulsion overcame me completely and I hurriedly stuffed it back into its place with a violent shudder. I turned to Lovecraft and saw that he was leaning forward on his cane with both hands and smiling at me with the air of one who has pulled off a marvelous jest.

"It can't be," I gasped, and then I swallowed and seemed to understand. "I see . . . you're smiling because you've fooled me, because the thing's a wonderful forgery and you've frightened me with it!"

"No, not at all," he said, still grinning. "I smile because it's real, because your fear is well founded, because you remind me so much of myself and my horror when I first came across that book."

"But—*De Vermis Mysteriis*!" I cried. "There isn't any such book! It was made up by Robert Bloch in the mid-thirties for a story in *Weird Tales* when you and he and all those other authors were playing that wonderful literary game of making up a world of monsters and their cults. The book was just a black-magical prop for his fictitious magicians. You even helped Bloch create it when you wrote him a letter and told him how to Latinize the title!"

Lovecraft nodded solemnly, but the grin never left his face.

"True, all true," he said. "And in my letters I often addressed Robert as Ludvig, after Ludvig Prinn, the bizarre scholar who authored the *grimoire*, and Robert and I and all of us firmly believed he'd made the old boy up out of whole wool."

Lovecraft leaned back and laughed, and the echoes of his laughter whispered back, bounced off the spines of all those books.

"Oh, we were all taken in, Edwardius, it's really quite amusing. We all thought we knew so much, but we were only cocky, clever children toying with Yog-Sothothery—your old Grandpa included—and it turned out we didn't know a thing."

Then he paused and actually cackled.

"But we were right!" he said, looking up at me, twinkling. "Somehow, all along—we were *right*!"

Then he paused, took a deep breath, let it out slowly, and I saw him visibly gather himself before he continued.

"Edwardius, you are truly—as Klarkash-Ton observed—a formidable scholar of that small group of macabre writers with whom Smith and I are proud to be associated. You know much of all our histories, including my own particular, personal history, but I must tell you now that there are many turnings of considerable importance in that latter history which you do *not* know for the very good reason that I have gone to great lengths, and employed many ingenious stratagems, to keep them carefully hidden."

He made his way out of the small library, and we sat on opposite sides of the nearest table in the larger room. Lovecraft shoved aside a jumble of stuff including a battered metal box, some yellowed newspaper clippings, and a dusty slab of dried clay to clear the space between us, and then he leaned forward on his elbows, settled himself, and began to talk.

"You know of my severe illness in 1937. I had been pursued by an increasingly distressing digestive trouble for years which I had stoically and foolishly ignored, but by degrees I apprehended the seriousness of my condition, and in February of that year I had very little doubt that I was dying. My diagnosis was confirmed by a specialist in March, and I soon found myself full of morphine in Jane Brown Memorial Hospital with nothing to do but write up my symptoms in the faint hope it might be of help to my physician.

"Sometime during the dark hours of the thirteenth the pain woke me in spite of my medication, and as I lay there, staring up at the ceiling and trying to isolate myself from the agony in my gut, a part of my mind, which had been almost entirely repressed for my life's whole duration until that moment, suddenly loosened its bindings and began to speak to the rest of me with such eager intensity and desperate emphasis that it almost seemed I could actually hear it whispering in my ear, whispering so distinctly that I began to grow concerned that the nurses might hear it and somehow shush it, and I didn't want that to happen, as it was telling me some remarkably interesting things."

He paused and looked at me, and in the darkening shadows of the library he seemed to be positively glowing with an air of excitement which made him look even younger than he'd seemed before.

"What if those awesome entities I had spent my whole life conjuring up and writing about—all those terrifying ancient monsters who'd wandered in from other planets and dimensions and whose powers were so vast and overwhelming—what if they were *real*? Suppose my minutely detailed, precise visualizations of all their horrendous particulars down to their last tentacle and claw, had not been my creation at all, but a slow unveiling of actual, existing beings?

"It's a matter of record that I had toyed with such notions before, but only as teasing, intellectual diversions. However, I think I must have known even then—though I surely would have denied it most righteously if pressed—that they spoke to something very deep within me, for they never failed to give me a profound and highly satisfactory ghoulish *frisson*. Could it be that I had been using talents and abilities which this sly whispering part of my mind had been aware of all along, but which my poor, straitlaced conscious mind, so pleased with limitations, had studiously—no doubt affrightedly—ignored? Had I all unknowing groped through the barriers which separated Them from us and *made an opening in the time and space between our different worlds*?"

He leaned forward, rattling the clay slab slightly on the table, and stared at me intently as if judging whether or not I was ready for what he was about to tell me next.

"I undertook a little experiment, Edwardius," he said. "A rather gaudy one for a quiet, reclusive author fond of his aunts, I'll admit, but, after all, I *was* dying. I wouldn't have another chance.

"I located a thin, spidery crack running in the ceiling over my bed, and I stared and stared at that crack as hard as I could until I saw its central edges start to bulge. Then I found I was able to stare harder yet, and I saw those same central edges begin to separate, and then, incredibly, but with an odd feeling of relief which I cannot even possibly begin to describe, I observed two delicate black tentacles writhe out and pull the crack open just a little bit wider so that a small chunk of the ceiling dislodged and I felt it land with a soft little plunk on the coverlet over my chest.

"Now the whisperer within me employed my whole mind to speak to that Entity above, commanding it with the certain confidence of an experienced wizard, and I was aware of an enormous stirring behind the entire ceiling and extending down along the upper portions of the walls. Faint scratchings and brushings—something like the scurryings of a thousand furtive rats and something like the coilings of a vast multitude of swollen worms—seemed to sound from every point, and now the crack in the ceiling widened even farther, and oozing out from between those smaller tentacles emerged a long, serpentine appendage terminating in a complex swirl of undulating filaments. As I stared with bulging eyes, it swayed lower and I observed the filaments sink smoothly through my coverings and glide inside my flesh.

"I watched my cancer leave me, Edwardius, I saw it being taken away, sucked up through that living tube in a steady, bloody stream, and only when it was entirely gone, every last molecule of it—and I *knew* it was gone, Edwardius!—did that remarkable thing detach itself from my body and glide up again and vanish.

"As I stared up into the crack after it I saw, hovering in the darkness behind the ceiling, a glowing red eye with a slit pupil, and it winked at me, and I winked at it, and the small tentacles curled back in again, out of sight, exactly like inhaled smoke, and the crack closed almost as tight shut as it was before my little experiment, but not quite."

He paused a long moment, and then he grinned and chuckled softly.

"It was all such an exactly perfect, hilarious travesty of a fresco by Giotto—the bony, dying author on his staid Memorial Hospital bed staring up with glistening eyes at a vision of a portion of Shub-Niggurath emerging from on high—that I began to laugh, Edwardius. Quietly at first, then louder and louder, and soon the ward seemed full of puzzled nurses brushing plaster off of Mr. Lovecraft and wishing he would shut up, and I wouldn't or couldn't because ever since I'd been a child I'd burned to play with jinns and dryads and now, only barely in the nick of time, the whisperer had shown me how to do it!"

He sighed happily, let himself sag back into his chair, and gave an expansive wave with both arms at the library about us.

"It's helped me build and buy this house, too," he said, "since I could have in no way afforded it—could have afforded *none* of this— save for the great, the astounding success my small literary efforts have had, in themselves and in the films and the extraordinary variety of other enterprises, worthwhile and puerile, which have spun off from them. I think it's fair to say that that dreadful Saturday morning animated television program for children which the network has loathsomely entitled *Cthulhu Kiddies* alone covers our ordinary daily expenses. All of that success has occurred since my recovery on that most eventful night, and its origins trace back clearly to the contract I made on that occasion."

I stared at him, my mind in a whirl, and stuttered out the burning question.

"Then those monsters you and Smith and Bloch and the others wrote about were real all along!"

"Just so!" he said. "But they weren't real in *our* reality. They were cut off from it, helpless in limbo, just like poor old Cthulhu in my stories. Our writings and dreamings touched and wakened them, but it was only after I'd actually pulled one of them out of the ceiling in order to save my life—dragged the thing out into this world of ours by a force of will absurdly magnified by the threat of imminent death—that they could start to manifest. They have been busily and ceaselessly continuing to follow up that first breakthrough into this dimensional knot of space and time wherein we make our home ever since, Edwardius, and, I must say, they have gone about it in the drollest way imaginable!"

He turned over the slab of clay and then pushed it across the table so that its face looked up at me.

"Do you recognize that?" he asked.

I studied it with growing astonishment. It was a rough rectangle less than an inch thick and about five by six inches in area. On its upper surface, in a sort of cross between cubist and art deco styles, very obviously out of the twenties or thirties, someone had modeled a remarkably disturbing low bas-relief of a winged, octopoid monster squatting evilly before a multiangled, Picassoid building.

"It's the dream-inspired sculpture of the artist Wilcox from 'The Call of Cthulhu,' " I said, excitedly. "It's the first tangible clue given in your mythos stories that the old gods exist!"

"Precisely," said Lovecraft, nodding, "but not *quite* precisely. You'll notice the signature of the artist cut into the slab's back is Wilton, not Wilcox, and the date is 1938, not 1925, as it is in the story. And though the withered newspaper clippings you see here follow the same general pattern I created in 'Call,' they are all *variations* on that pattern; they all concern real people with names which vary—sometimes subtly, sometimes quite widely—from the names I gave my fictitious characters, and they all date from after my medical adventures in Jane Brown Memorial Hospital.

"It is the same with these tattered old notebooks. You will observe that they are not written by the dear old Professor George Gammell Angell whom I first dreamed up during the miseries of my Brooklyn exile in 1925, but that they are the desperate scrawlings of a flesh-and-blood gentleman who is also a professor—of Physics, not Semitic Languages, it is interesting to note—named Horace Parker Whipple. Both of these gentlemen, however, real and fictitious, *did* die after being mysteriously jostled by a sailor. The strange forces shaping this ongoing realization of my fictitious world always adhere quite closely to my stories' more sinister original details.

"Along those lines it is also interesting to observe that—like those of my entirely imaginary Professor Angell—Whipple's notebooks show that he had come across a cult whose god's name *is*, indeed, Cthulhu. Though everything else in this continuing process of materializing the creatures and basic notions of my imaginary mythos and incorporating them into our universe seems subject to sometimes even whimsical change when needed, the names of all the deities and their servitors never vary by a letter from my original suggestions."

"But the books," I said. "If this changing of reality is all your doing, then how about the books? *De Vermis Mysteriis* and the others—I glimpsed some of the rest!—all those ancient tomes of black magic which I'd thought you and the others'd all made up for your stories—*Cultes des Goules, Unaussprechlichen Kulten*—those books are old! They're ancient! They were here long before you were born!"

Lovecraft smiled.

"Yes, they were," he said. "And all the hoary dates which Smith and Bloch and I and the others ascribed to them have turned out to be accurate. Oh, it's true enough we were all only naive paupers, scribblers for the pulps with pathetic pretensions to scholarship, and none of us were near sophisticated enough to have a clue that what we were writing down might actually be the truth. But those books existed, all right, and they were very carefully hidden under lock and key by scholars, exactly as we thought; mainly, I think, to protect presumptuous upstarts such as ourselves in the old *Weird Tales* gang from getting our uncultured paws on 'em! It's been quite a joke on us, not to mention our little planet, that the whole library of them turned out to be just as we'd made it up!"

He indulged himself once more in that rather unpleasant, somewhat witchlike cackle and leaned forward in a confidential manner.

"The only problem with those books, Edwardius," he whispered with a wink, "was that until I and the others wrote about them, and that until I made contact with the forces behind them on my supposed deathbed—the problem was they didn't work!"

He paused and leaned back with his fingers spread out on the dark wood of the table before him, and that stern solemnity I'd observed before fell over him, momentarily, like a shroud. Then, in a wink, it had lifted, and he was grinning triumphantly ear to ear.

"But now they work," he whispered. *"Now they work!"*

I sat like something carved in stone, groping unsuccessfully in the confused whirl of my brain for something solid to cling to. Then I heard a gently discreet rapping at the library door and jumped as if someone had fired off a cannon by my ear.

"That will be Smith," murmured Lovecraft; then called out, "Come in, Klarkash-Ton."

The door opened and Smith glided in quietly. He studied me with an interested expression on his lean, wrinkled face and then turned to Lovecraft.

"I see by our young friend's stunned expression that his initiation continues apace," he said. Then he turned back to me, examining me further in a kindly but penetrating manner. "Do not be too hard on yourself, Edwardius, it is all very difficult to grasp. I certainly found it was when H.P.L. tried to explain the state of affairs to me after he'd chanted Borellus's formula of evocation over my essential salts and brought me back to this simulacrum of my living self. And you are fortunate in that—when you finally do manage to grasp the situation's colorful implications—you will be able to console yourself with the knowledge that you are not among those responsible for its coming about. At least you had no part, as did Howard and myself, in setting these monsters free."

Lovecraft straightened in his chair, snorted softly, and glanced up at Smith with quiet disapproval.

"*Monsters*, Klarkash-Ton?" he asked. "Surely that is more than a little judgmental?"

"Monsters," said Smith, clearly and firmly, smiling at Lovecraft a little grimly, then turning to me still smiling. "Howard is never slow with the implication that I am cosmically xenophobic."

"I am not making an implication," said Lovecraft firmly. "I am stating a simple fact. These beings are in no way malevolent regarding life on our planet—I have said it all along in my stories and it has turned out to be the simple truth—they are merely indifferent to it."

Smith gazed at his old friend and sighed.

"When are you going to face it, Howard?" he asked. "These creatures we have let loose *are* monsters. They were monsters in whatever hell they came from, they are monsters here on Earth, and they will be monsters wherever they happen to go next. My good fortune is that I happen to be unfond enough of my fellow men and women not to be that overly disturbed at what we have unleashed upon them. Please don't take my attitude to be one of moral disapproval. It is not the sure and certain domination and destruction of my dreadful species which troubles me, it's embarrassment that my contribution was merely the accidental result of personal ineptness and ignorance. I would much rather have doomed my miserable race on purpose."

Lovecraft grimaced with distaste, waved Smith's comments aside with a weary gesture indicating he had done so many times before, and then looked at me from across the table with the air of a man who has suddenly had a very good idea.

"Since things are moving along so well and you've shown such a remarkable aptitude for expansion, Edwardius," he said, "I believe I've thought of a simple, reasonable way of putting to rest any little fears or nagging doubts which Klarkash-Ton's dreary speechifying may have roused within you regarding these visitors in our midst. It is, quite simply, to allow me to introduce one of them to you, in person, so that you can see it, talk with it, and then judge for yourself whether or not you think that it is a monster. Also, if you are to become involved with our continuing activities, it is important to discover whether or not they find *you* are tolerable. It is an obvious risk. Are you willing to take it?"

I gaped at him, my head spinning with the escalation of this whole affair.

"You're suggesting that you'll call one of these beings up?" I gasped.

"I do it all the time," said Lovecraft casually. "There's nothing simpler, once you've got the hang of it."

Smith stirred, and I saw his expression had become even more ironic than usual.

"I think it only fair, H.P.L.," he said, "to explain to Edwardius the little reason *why* you have such frequent occasion to summon up your chums."

Lovecraft glanced up at him with a small frown, then shrugged and turned to me with a slight spreading of his hands.

"As an accomplished student of our literary efforts," said Lovecraft, coolly, "you are, of course, aware that Klarkash-Ton is ever a lover of irony. The fact is that in order to continue on here in the luxury to which we have become accustomed, it is necessary, now and then, to offer up a little sacrifice. A human sacrifice, to be exact. Mind you, we have always been meticulously careful to offer up individuals whose loss either will not be missed or will actually be gratefully received by the thoughtful and intelligent. Arrogant or obtuse book critics, for instance, or some of those responsible for the cruder pastiches of my writings."

"And of mine," said Smith, with a grim little smile. "But, our good intentions aside, you must understand that if you allow Howard to make this proposed introduction you will be running the risk of becoming such a sacrifice yourself through misadventure. I am not sure these creatures can differentiate a bad critic from a good writer."

Lovecraft stood.

"What Klarkash-Ton says is perfectly true, Edwardius," he said. "This encounter will not be devoid of risk. But, unlike him, I can and do enthusiastically presume to recommend that you run that risk and undertake this adventure. I really think there is nothing I would not have gladly given if someone had proffered me an invitation such as this when *I* was a young man! So, then, Edwardius, are you game? Shall we do it?"

I hesitated a moment longer, then I rose and nodded firmly.

"I would never forgive myself if I didn't," I said.

Lovecraft and I left the library with a dubious Smith and made our way through halls and down stairways, myself always conscious of a painted villain or monster looking down at us from some wall. Lovecraft and I paused at the entrance to retrieve our capes and hats, since a fine, gusting drizzle had begun to fall, then the two of us were outside walking through grass as Lovecraft led me into a wooded area. After we'd made our way between its trees for some time more than I thought was likely in a property as small as this corner of Providence had seemed to be—especially when I noticed that those trees had turned from relatively new growth to wide-trunked, wizened old giants which were totally improbable in such an area—I turned to my host in some puzzlement.

"You are quite correct, Edwardius." He smiled at me and nodded. "All this is much larger and older than it has any right to be, but then we've cheated a little with its time and space. On this excursion we shall only penetrate a little bit into the forest's western edge. There is much more here, believe me, much for you to savor and explore once you've settled in with us. There's an ancient ruined city, for example, and a wonderfully gloomy swamp, and caves and grottos beneath which I haven't begun to explore. In any case, we've reached our goal."

We'd entered a clearing, and I was thrilled to find myself standing dwarfed amidst the primitive spires of a small but impressive circle of monoliths. Lovecraft walked up to a grey standing stone which towered twice his height and stroked the damp undulations of its mossy side affectionately.

"These old rocks were carefully removed from a high, lonely mountaintop in the real world's very nearly exact equivalent of Dunwich, which was, of course, the locale of my fictitious Wizard Whateley and his dangerous, not altogether human, brood," he said. "I had them removed, then carefully arranged here in exactly the same sinister circular formation they originally enjoyed, and I'm pleased to say they've lost none of their awesome powers."

He pointed at a formidable flat slab of granite in the center of the formation.

"That is the stone of sacrifice," he said. "It was baptized long before the witches came from Europe to claim it for their own. The Indians used it in their rituals since ancient times, and recent contacts I have made assure me that older, much weirder entities gave it what it wanted during previous millennia. Walk up to it, Edwardius. Feel it. Not just its texture, but its mood. It has been involved in countless potent workings and sopped up much blood of many different kinds."

The drizzle had now turned to a steady, windswept rain, and the smooth runnels carved into the stone caught the fallen water so that it gurgled suggestively as it was guided and poured into an insatiable, sloping pit dug into the stone's center. I reached down with my hand, and at the instant my fingers made contact with the spreading, lichen-specked discoloration surrounding the opening, the ground itself was jarred by the impact of an ear-shattering clap of thunder overhead.

"Oh, that's excellent," said Lovecraft, peering up at the sky, totally unaware of the rain cascading down his face. "Oh, that's very good. Look at the clouds, Edwardius—how smoothly they circle in from all horizons so as to form a single, larger cloud at that point overhead. Amusingly like witches scuttling to form a coven, isn't it?"

The wind had furiously increased and was whipping our legs and the bases of the stones with the tall grass of the clearing, and snapping our capes about our bodies. Lightning angled everywhere across the sky, and soon each thunderclap overlapped the one before so that there was only a perpetual, steady roaring.

But I was only dimly aware of all that, for it was slowly coming clear to me that I was observing a phenomenon unparalleled by anything I'd seen or heard of in the natural world. I stared up at it, fully as intently as Lovecraft did beside me, and the more I watched of its unfoldments, the more my terrified awe turned unexpectedly into a kind of reverence.

The clouds had merged into one huge thing above us which, as I watched, swiftly took on a highly discomforting solidity while the lightning—flashing about it and in its depths—began revealing innumerable, increasingly clear details which I could easily see now were no longer mere gaseous swirlings, but the conscious movements of a vast multitude of living organs—first crudely formed, but soon swiftly sculpted and refined—each one born in frantic, greedy motion.

The insane range and variety of these members became clearer as their shapes clarified and their outlines grew more distinct. Some of them bore varying degrees of resemblance to the organs of creatures dwelling on our planet, but others were so totally alien to anything of Earth that they seemed to offer no possible relationship to any species or function I had ever seen or heard of.

Among those limbs and extensions at least somewhat identifiable I could make out claws and pincers of all possible descriptions snapping hungrily at the air; a seething mass of spidery legs groping with obscene curiosity in every direction, and innumerable wings—some webbed, some scaled, some raggedly and darkly feathered, but all of enormous span—which completely surrounded the thing's entire body in a huge, vast ring, each one flapping in perfect time with all the rest.

Dominating all of this was an enormous, staring eye surrounded by four huge, quivering lids made up of thousands of smaller eyes, each one peering in a different direction from its own twisting stalk, with the result that the momentous entity above us would be all-seeing.

I jumped as Lovecraft's hand suddenly grasped my shoulder.

"What do you think of it, Edwardius?" he shouted over the thunder. "Isn't it magnificent? Isn't it *beautiful*? Monster, indeed!"

I could think of no reply. I seemed momentarily beyond reply, and, besides, the overpoweringly steady roar of the thunder seemed to mock any little noises I might make.

Then I stiffened as I realized the sound of the thunder had begun to change and modulate. It was a while before I understood what I was hearing: the thunder was shaping itself, much as the cloud's form had done before. It was steadily progressing from the random to the organic; it was starting to develop, in effect, a kind of mouth.

"You've grasped what's happening, haven't you, Edwardius?" said Lovecraft.

I started and turned and stared at him. I felt my legs tremble and leaned against the sacrificial stone for support. He frowned when he saw the gesture, and took hold of me and pulled me back.

"No," he said. "That's a mistake the victims always make. You stand by me."

"It's forming words," I said. "It's speaking!"

He cocked his head and listened critically.

"Well, not *quite*, not yet," he said. "But any minute now!"

Keeping one hand on my shoulder, he stood a little ahead, peering upward.

"This is Edwardius," he called out loud and clear. "He is a friend. He is to work with us. He is not a sacrifice."

He repeated my name again, shouting out its syllables one by one and sounding them carefully.

"Ehd-ward-dee-uhs," he called out. "Ehd-ward-dee-uhs!"

I stared up at the thing and saw with a new thrill of horror that a sort of titanic convulsion had started taking place in the center of its underside, a spreading, writhing, and untangling of tentacles and jointed legs, not to mention pseudo-pods and spiny, telescopic horrors, and other, totally incomprehensible things—it was like watching a sea of knots untie itself!

And, at that moment, the creature found its voice.

"AAAAAAY!" it roared in thunder. "AAAAAY!"

I felt Lovecraft stiffen slightly and look up in some concern.

"Odd," he said, sounding mildly puzzled and, for the first time, just the tiniest bit unsure of himself. "That doesn't sound right at all."

Then, freed of their entanglement with one another, all those awful organs stretched farther and impossibly farther out, until they extended even beyond the confines of their gigantic body. The whole thing looked like a horrible parody of a rayed, glistening star floating over a saint in a Russian icon.

"AAAAAY–CHaaa!" roared the voice, and I saw Lovecraft squint thoughtfully upward. "AAAAAY–CHaaa!"

"*Ehd-ward-dee-uhs!*" he shouted up at it, then turned to me with a mildly irritated shrug. "It's got your name wrong. You can imagine how difficult our language is to manage for something with its vocal apparatus."

The stretched limbs extending from the creature began a slow, very ominous, downward curving, and I cringed in spite of myself. Then they came lower yet, all those different graspers and clutchers and suckers and biting things, thousands of them coming closer and closer in a thousand different ways, and as they smoothly and inevitably continued their lowering swoop, what was at first only a terrible guess on my part slowly and surely hardened into a certainty.

"It's reaching for me, isn't it?" First I said it calmly, then not quite so calmly. "*It's reaching for me, isn't it?*"

"Now don't panic, don't panic," Lovecraft whispered in my ear, and then he shouted upward once again: "Ehd-ward-dee-uhs, he is a friend—*Ehd-ward-dee-uhs!*"

"AAAAAAAY–CHaaa PEEEEEEEE!" roared the voice from overhead, and the mighty circle of stones seemed to quiver at the sound.

Lovecraft's face suddenly paled, then reddened, and then his eyes widened in absolute astonishment.

"My goodness, I think I understand what that stanza in Geoffrey's *People of the Monolith* means at last," he said to himself, and then he turned to me. "What is the date, Edwardius?"

"September the fifteenth."

"Aha," he said, "I thought so. Don't worry, my boy; you're quite safe."

Then he gazed gently up with a shy wistfulness which was totally incongruous on his bony Easter Island face, and extraordinarily moving. "It's really quite extraordinarily touching," he said.

Then he turned to me and pointed overhead.

"It *is* beautiful, is it not?" he asked me.

"Yes," I said, calmed by his calmness. "It is. Klarkash-Ton's wrong about them."

"He can't help it; there's a bitterness about him. You must forgive him."

"AAAAAAAAY–CHaaa PEEEEEEEEE EHLLLLLLLLLLLL!" boomed the voice, and the stones reeled and tottered in their sockets of earth.

He took his hand away from my shoulder and advanced a pace or two, then, with a little leap executed with the ease and unconscious gracefulness of a small boy, he hopped onto the center of the sacrificial stone.

"I'm here," he called up in his high, thin voice to the enormous roiling on high. "I'm here!"

"AAAAAAAAY–CHaaa PEEEEEEEEE EHLLLLLLLLLLLLL!" boomed the thing again, and then: "ff—ff—ff—FATHER! FATHER!"

Lovecraft stood quietly, looking up wide-eyed at the huge business looming above him, at the tentacles and claws and oddly jointed fingers reaching for him. One of the monoliths, uprooted by the omnipresent roaring, fell with a great crash behind him, missing him only by inches, but he did not so much as notice.

"Ff—FATHER!" the voice boomed again as all those strange, horrific limbs tenderly took hold of Lovecraft, each one gentle in its separate way, according to its own bizarre anatomy, and together they lifted him carefully from the ground as he lay unresistingly in their grasps, their coilings, their enfoldments, as he stared upward and above them at the great eye of the thing which was raising him higher and even higher, and the last I saw of H.P.L., the expression on his lean, long, solemn face had the strange, uncanny, loving peace of a babe in its crib.

The door of the house was open when I came back and Smith was standing just inside, holding two glasses of wine, and watching my solitary approach without a trace of any visible surprise.

"How strange," he said. "How very strange. I knew, I absolutely *knew* it would be you instead of Howard coming back. I don't know why. Certainly the possibility never occurred to me with any of the others. Perhaps it's those quotes from the *Pnakotic Manuscripts* he's been dropping lately."

"It's the anniversary of 'The Dunwich Horror,' " I said. "It's the day Wilbur Whateley's brother went home at last."

He stared at me thoughtfully.

"So it turned out to be a sacrifice, after all," he said. "And it worked. There's no doubt of that. You've changed."

And at that moment I realized for the first time that I *had* changed, that there was something very different in the way I felt from any way I'd ever felt before. It was a kind of glowing, a kind of power. A very deep kind of power which I liked very much.

"We always drink a toast after the sacrifices," said Smith, handing me one of the glasses. "It's become a tradition."

We touched the rims in a toast, and the crystal made a magic little ringing. Smith tossed his wine back with one long, smooth swallow, but I just took a first sip. It was Amontillado, of course.

"I've got dinner ready for us whenever you're hungry," he said.

And that's the way it's been ever since, without either one of us feeling the slightest need for any discussion or agreement. Klarkash-Ton continues to be the sexton, I have taken over the position of wizard, and we've carried on the sacrifices with very little difficulty; there seems to be no foreseeable shortage of victims. We'd have a sufficiency with the disparaging researchers alone. I will admit I was startled to learn that they are ordinarily very bloody affairs, full of rippings and tearings and meltings down which bear small resemblance to the reverential ascension accorded H.P.L.

That first evening, however, Smith disappeared discreetly in the direction of the kitchen, pouring himself another glassful on the way, and I found myself walking with a quiet purposefulness toward the library. I was soon standing in the secret alcove at its back, reaching out for the tall, dark spine of the *Necronomicon*, which I had seen before but not quite dared to mention. My hand was still inches from the shelf when the book stirred like a gently wakened cat and glided into my fingers all on its own, settling softly into them as a bird settles into its nest.

It's bound in some sort of black pelt with long, thick hair, and after I'd held it a moment or two, I noticed that some of the longer strands had twined affectionately about my fingers. They still do it to this day, whenever I take the *Necronomicon* up, and sometimes they hold them very tightly. Particularly when I'm chanting.

The Unthinkable

BRUCE STERLING

Since the Strategic Arms Talks of the early 1970s, it had been the policy of the Soviets to keep to their own quarters as much as the negotiations permitted—in fear, the Americans surmised, of novel forms of technical eavesdropping.

Dr. Tsyganov's Baba Yaga hut now crouched warily on the meticulously groomed Swiss lawn. Dr. Elwood Doughty assembled a hand of cards and glanced out the hut's window. Protruding just above the sill was the great scaly knee of one of the hut's six giant chicken legs, a monstrous knobby member as big around as an urban water main. As Doughty watched, the chicken knee flexed restlessly, and the hut stirred around them, rising with a seasick lurch, then settling with a squeak of timbers and a rustle of close-packed thatch.

Tsyganov discarded, drew two cards from the deck, and examined them, his wily blue eyes shrouded in greasy wisps of long graying hair. He plucked his shabby beard with professionally black-rimmed nails.

Doughty, to his pleased surprise, had been dealt a straight flush in the suit of Wands. With a deft pinch, he dropped two ten-dollar bills from the top of the stack at his elbow.

Tsyganov examined his dwindling supply of hard currency with a look of Slavic fatalism. He grunted, scratched, then threw his cards faceup on the table. Death. The tower. The deuce, trey, and five of Coins.

"Chess?" Tsyganov suggested, rising.

"Another time," said Doughty. Though, for security reasons, he lacked any official ranking in the chess world, Doughty was in fact quite an accomplished chess strategist, particularly strong in the endgame. Back in the marathon sessions of '83, he and Tsyganov had dazzled their fellow arms wizards with an impromptu tournament lasing almost four months, while the team awaited (fruitlessly) any movement on the stalled verification accords. Doughty could not outmatch the truly gifted Tsyganov, but he had come to know and recognize the flow of his opponent's thought.

Mostly, though, Doughty had conceived a vague loathing for Tsyganov's prized personal chess set, which had been designed on a Reds versus Whites Russian Civil War theme. The little animate pawns uttered tiny, but rather dreadful, squeaks of anguish, when set upon by the commissar bishops and cossack knights.

"Another time?" murmured Tsyganov, opening a tiny cabinet and extracting a bottle of Stolichnaya vodka. Inside the fridge, a small overworked frost demon glowered in its trap of coils and blew a spiteful gasp of cold fog. "There will not be many more such opportunities for us, Elwood."

"Don't I know it." Doughty noted that the Russian's vodka bottle bore an export label printed in English. There had been a time when Doughty would have hesitated to accept a drink in a Russian's quarters. Treason in the cup. Subversion potions. Those times already seemed quaint.

"I mean this will be over. History, grinding on. This entire business"—Tsyganov waved his sinewy hand, as if including not merely Geneva, but a whole state of mind—"will become a mere historical episode."

"I'm ready for that," Doughty said stoutly. Vodka splashed up the sides of his shot glass with a chill, oily threading. "I never much liked this life, Ivan."

"No?"

"I did it for duty."

"Ah." Tsyganov smiled. "Not for the travel privileges?"

"I'm going home," Doughty said. "Home for good. There's a place outside Fort Worth where I plan to raise cattle."

"Back to Texas?" Tsyganov seemed amused, touched. "The hardline weapons theorist become a *farmer*, Elwood? You are a second Roman Cincinnatus!"

Doughty sipped vodka and examined the gold-flake socialist-realist icons hung on Tsyganov's rough timber walls. He thought of his own office, in the basement of the Pentagon. Relatively commodious, by basement standards. Comfortably carpeted. Mere yards from the world's weightiest centers of military power. Secretary of Defense. Joint Chiefs of Staff. Secretaries of the Army, Navy, Air Force. Director of Defense Research and Necromancy. The Lagoon, the Potomac, the Jefferson Memorial. The sight of pink dawn on the Capitol Dome after pulling an all-nighter. Would he miss the place? No. "Washington, D.C., is no proper place to raise a kid."

"Ah." Tsyganov's peaked eyebrows twitched. "I heard you had

married at last." He had, of course, read Doughty's dossier. "And your child, Elwood, he is strong and well?"

Doughty said nothing. It would be hard to keep the tone of pride from his voice. Instead, he opened his wallet of tanned basilisk skin and showed the Russian a portrait of his wife and infant son. Tsyganov brushed hair from his eyes and examined the portrait closely. "Ah," he said. "The boy much resembles you."

"Could be," Doughty said.

"Your wife," Tsyganov said politely, "has a very striking face."

"The former Jeane Siegel. Staffer on the Senate Foreign Relations Committee."

"I see. The defense intelligentsia?"

"She edited *Korea and the Theory of Limited War*. Considered one of the premier works on the topic."

"She must make a fine little mother." Tsyganov gulped his vodka, ripped into a crust of black rye bread. "My son is quite grown now. He writes for *Literaturnaya Gazeta*. Did you see his article on the Iraqi arms question? Some very serious developments lately concerning the Islamic jinni."

"I should have read it," Doughty said. "But I'm getting out of the game, Ivan. Out while the getting's good." The cold vodka was biting into him. He laughed briefly. "They're going to shut us down in the States. Pull our funding. Pare us back to the bone, and past the bone. 'Peace dividend.' We'll all fade away. Like MacArthur. Like Robert Oppenheimer."

" 'I am become Death, the Destroyer of Worlds,' " Tsyganov quoted.

"Yeah," Doughty mused. "That was too bad about poor old Oppy having to become Death."

Tsyganov examined his nails. "Will there be purges, you think?"

"I beg your pardon?"

"I understand the citizens in Utah are suing your federal government. Over conduct of the arms tests, forty years ago . . ."

"Oh," Doughty said. "The two-headed sheep, and all that . . . There are still night gaunts and banshees downwind of the old test sites. Up in the Rockies . . . Not a place to go during the full moon." He shuddered. "But 'purges'? No. That's not how it works for us."

"You should have seen the sheep around Chernobyl."

" 'Bitter wormwood,' " Doughty quoted.

"No act of duty avoids its punishment." Tsyganov opened a can of dark fish that smelled like spiced kippered herring. "And what of the Unthinkable, eh? What price have you paid for *that* business?"

Doughty's voice was level, quite serious. "We bear any burden in defense of freedom."

"Not the best of your American notions, perhaps." Tsyganov

speared a chunk of fish from the can with a three-tined fork. "To deliberately contact an utterly alien entity from the abyss between universes ... an ultrademonic demigod whose very geometry is, as it were, an affront to sanity ... that Creature of nameless eons and inconceivable dimensions...." Tsyganov patted his bearded lips with a napkin. "That hideous Radiance that bubbles and blasphemes at the center of all infinity—"

"You're being sentimental," Doughty said. "We must recall the historical circumstances in which the decision was made to develop the Azathoth Bomb. Giant Japanese Majins and Gojiras crashing through Asia. Vast squadrons of Nazi juggernauts blitzkrieging Europe ... and their undersea leviathans, preying on shipping...."

"Have you ever seen a *modern* leviathan, Elwood?"

"Yes, I witnessed one ... feeding. At the base in San Diego." Doughty could recall it with an awful clarity—the great finned navy monster, the barnacled pockets in its vast ribbed belly holding a slumbering cargo of hideous batwinged gaunts. On order from Washington, the minor demons would waken, slash their way free of the monster's belly, launch, and fly to their appointed targets with pitiless accuracy and the speed of a tempest. In their talons, they clutched triple-sealed spells that could open, for a few hideous microseconds, the portal between universes. And for an instant, the Radiance of Azathoth would gush through. And whatever that Color touched—wherever its unthinkable beam contacted earthly substance—the Earth would blister and bubble in cosmic torment. The very dust of the explosion would carry an unearthly taint.

"And have you seen them test the bomb, Elwood?"

"Only underground. The atmospheric testing was rather before my time...."

"And what of the poisoned waste, Elwood? From beneath the cyclopean walls of our scores of power plants ..."

"We'll deal with that. Launch it into the abyss of space, if we must." Doughty hid his irritation with an effort. "What are you driving at?"

"I worry, my friend. I fear that we've gone too far. We have been responsible men, you and I. We have labored in the service of responsible leaders. Fifty long years have passed, and not once has the Unthinkable been unleashed in anger. But we have trifled with the Eternal in pursuit of mortal ends. What is our pitiful fifty years in the eons of the Great Old Ones? Now, it seems, we will rid ourselves of our foolish applications of this dreadful knowledge. But will we ever be clean?"

"That's a challenge for the next generation. I've done what I can. I'm only mortal. I accept that."

"I do not think we can put it away. It is too close to us. We have lived in its shadow too long, and it has touched our souls."

"I'm through with it," Doughty insisted. "My duty is done. And I'm tired of the burden. I'm tired of trying to grasp issues, and imagine horrors, and feel fears and temptations, that are beyond the normal bounds of sane human contemplation. I've earned my retirement, Ivan. I have a right to a human life."

"The Unthinkable has touched you. Can you truly put that aside?"

"I'm a professional," Doughty said. "I've always taken the proper precautions. The best military exorcists have looked me over. . . . I'm clean."

"Can you know that?"

"They're the best we have; I trust their professional judgment. . . . If I find the shadow in my life again, I'll put it aside. I'll cut it away. Believe me, I know the feel and smell of the Unthinkable—it'll never find a foothold in my life again. . . ." A merry chiming came from Doughty's right trouser pocket.

Tsyganov blinked, then went on. "But what if you find it is simply too close to you?"

Doughty's pocket rang again. He stood up absently. "You've known me for years, Ivan," he said, digging into his pocket. "We may be mortal men, but we were always prepared to take the necessary steps. We were prepared. No matter what the costs."

Doughty whipped a large square of pentagram-printed silk from his pocket, spread it with a flourish.

Tsyganov was startled. "What is that?"

"Portable telephone," Doughty said. "Newfangled gadget . . . I always carry one now."

Tsyganov was scandalized. "You brought a telephone into my private quarters?"

"Damn," Doughty said with genuine contrition. "Forgive me, Ivan. I truly forgot that I had this thing with me. Look, I won't take the call here. I'll leave." He opened the door, descended the wooden stair into grass and Swiss sunlight.

Behind him, Tsyganov's hut rose on its monster chicken legs, and stalked away—wobbling, it seemed to Doughty, with a kind of offended dignity. In the hut's retreating window, he glimpsed Tsyganov, peering out half-hidden, unable to restrain his curiosity. Portable telephones. Another technical breakthrough of the inventive West.

Doughty smoothed the ringing silk on the top of an iron lawn table and muttered a Word of power. An image rose sparkling above the woven pentagram—the head and shoulders of his wife.

He knew at once from her look that the news was bad. "Jeane?" he said.

"It's Tommy," she said.

"What happened?"

"Oh," she said with brittle clarity, "nothing. Nothing you'd see. But the lab tests are in. The exorcists—they say he's tainted."

The foundation blocks of Doughty's life cracked swiftly and soundlessly apart. "Tainted," he said blankly. "Yes . . . I hear you, dear. . . ."

"They came to the house and examined him. They say he's monstrous."

Now anger seized him. "Monstrous. How can they say that? He's only a four-month-old kid! How the hell could they know he's monstrous? What the hell do they really know, anyway? Some crowd of ivory-tower witch doctors . . ."

His wife was weeping openly now. "You know what they recommended, Elwood? You know what they want us to do?"

"We can't just . . . put him away," Doughty said. "He's our son." He paused, took a breath, looked about him. Smooth lawns, sunlight trees. The world. The future. A bird flickered past him.

"Let's think about this," he said. "Let's think this through. Just how monstrous is he, exactly?"

Black Man with a Horn

T.E.D. KLEIN

1.

The Black [words obscured by postmark] was fascinating—I
must get a snap shot of him.

—H. P. LOVECRAFT, POSTCARD TO
E. HOFFMANN PRICE, 7/23/1934

There is something inherently comforting about the first-person past
tense. It conjures up visions of some deskbound narrator puffing con-
templatively upon a pipe amid the safety of his study, lost in tranquil
recollection, seasoned but essentially unscathed by whatever experience he's about to relate. It's a tense that says, "I am here to tell the
tale. I lived through it."

The description, in my own case, is perfectly accurate—as far as it
goes. I am indeed seated in a kind of study: a small den, actually, but
lined with bookshelves on one side, below a view of Manhattan
painted many years ago, from memory, by my sister. My desk is a
folding bridge table that once belonged to her. Before me the electric
typewriter, though somewhat precariously supported, hums soothingly, and from the window behind me comes the familiar drone of the
old air conditioner, waging its lonely battle against the tropic night.
Beyond it, in the darkness outside, the small night-noises are doubtless
just as reassuring: wind in the palm trees, the mindless chant of
crickets, the muffled chatter of a neighbor's TV, an occasional car
bound for the highway, shifting gears as it speeds past the house. . . .

House, in truth, may be too grand a word; the place is a green stucco
bungalow just a single story tall, third in a row of nine set several hundred yards from the highway. Its only distinguishing features are the
sundial in the front yard, brought here from my sister's former home,
and the flimsy little picket fence, now rather overgrown with weeds,
which she erected despite the protests of neighbors.

It's hardly the most romantic of settings, but under normal circumstances it might make an adequate background for meditations in the past tense. "I'm still here," the writer says, adjusting to the tone. (I've even stuck the requisite pipe in my mouth, stuffed with a plug of latakia.) "It's over now," he says. "I've lived through it."

A comforting premise, perhaps. Only, in this case, it doesn't happen to be true. Whether the experience is really "over now" no one can say; and if, as I suspect, the final chapter has yet to be enacted, then the notion of my "living through it" will seem a pathetic conceit.

Yet I can't say I find the thought of my own death particularly disturbing. I get so tired, sometimes, of this little room, with its cheap wicker furniture, the dull outdated books, the night pressing in from outside. . . . And of that sundial out there in the yard, with its idiotic message. *Grow old along with me. . . .* "

I have done so, and my life seems hardly to have mattered in the scheme of things. Surely its end cannot matter much either.

Ah, Howard, you would have understood.

2.

> That, boy, was what I call a travel-experience!
> —LOVECRAFT, 3/12/1930

If, while I'm setting it down, this tale acquires an ending, it promises to be an unhappy one. But the beginning is nothing of the kind; you may find it rather humorous, in fact—full of comic pratfalls, wet trouser cuffs, and a dropped vomit-bag.

"I steeled myself to *endure* it," the old lady to my right was saying. "I don't mind telling you, I was exceedingly frightened. I held on to the arms of the seat and just *gritted my teeth*. And then, you know, right after the captain warned us about that *turbulence*, when the tail lifted and fell, flip-flop, flip-flop, *well*"—she flashed her dentures at me and patted my wrist—"I don't mind telling you, there was simply nothing for it but to *heave*."

Where had the old girl picked up such expressions? And was she trying to pick me up as well? Her hand clamped wetly round my wrist. "I *do* hope you'll let me pay for the dry cleaning."

"Madam," I said, "think nothing of it. The suit was already stained."

"Such a nice man!" She cocked her head coyly at me, still gripping my wrist. Though their whites had long since turned the color of old piano keys, her eyes were not unattractive. But her breath repelled me. Slipping my paperback into a pocket, I rang for the stewardess.

The earlier mishap had occurred several hours before. In clambering aboard the plane at Heathrow, surrounded by what appeared to be an aboriginal rugby club (all dressed alike, navy blazers with bone buttons), I'd been shoved from behind and had stumbled against a black cardboard hatbox in which some Chinaman was storing his dinner; it was jutting into the aisle near the first-class seats. Something inside sloshed over my ankles—duck sauce, soup perhaps—and left a sticky yellow puddle on the floor. I turned in time to see a tall, beefy Caucasian with an Air Malay bag and a beard so thick and black he looked like some heavy from the silent era. His manner was equally suited to the role, for after shouldering me aside (with shoulders broad as my valises), he pushed his way down the crowded passage, head bobbing near the ceiling like a gas balloon, and suddenly disappeared from sight at the rear of the plane. In his wake I caught the smell of treacle, and was instantly reminded of my childhood: birthday hats, Callard & Bowser gift packs, and afterdinner bellyaches.

"So very sorry." A bloated little Charlie Chan looked fearfully at this departing apparition, then doubled over to scoop his dinner beneath the seat, fiddling with the ribbon.

"Think nothing of it," I said.

I was feeling kindly toward everyone that day. Flying was still a novelty. My friend Howard, of course (as I'd reminded audiences earlier in the week), used to say he'd "hate to see aëroplanes come into common commercial use, since they merely add to the goddam useless speeding up of an already over-speeded life." He had dismissed them as "devices for the amusement of a gentleman"—but then, he'd only been up once, in the twenties, a brief $3.50 flight above Buzzard's Bay. What could he have known of whistling engines, the wicked joys of dining at thirty thousand feet, the chance to look out a window and find that the earth is, after all, quite round? All this he had missed; he was dead and therefore to be pitied.

Yet even in death he had triumphed over me. . . .

It gave me something to think about as the stewardess helped me to my feet, clucking in professional concern at the mess on my lap—though more likely she was thinking of the wiping up that awaited her once I'd vacated the seat. "Why do they make those bags so *slippery*?" my elderly neighbor asked plaintively. "And all over this nice man's suit. You really should do something about it." The plane dropped and settled; she rolled her yellowing eyes. "It could happen again."

The stewardess steered me down the aisle toward a restroom at the middle of the plane. To my left a cadaverous young woman wrinkled her nose and smiled at the man next to her. I attempted to disguise my defeat by looking bitter, as if to say, "Someone else has done this deed!"—but doubt I succeeded. The stewardess's arm supporting mine was superfluous but comfortable; I leaned on her more heavily with each step. There are, as I'd long suspected, precious few advantages in being seventy-six and looking it—yet among them is this: though one is excused from the frustration of flirting with a stewardess, one gets to lean on her arm. I turned toward her to say something funny, but paused; her face was blank as a clock's.

"I'll wait out here for you," she said, and pulled open the smooth white door.

"That will hardly be necessary." I straightened up. "But could you—do you think you might find me another seat? I have nothing against that lady, you understand, but I don't want to see any more of her lunch."

Inside the restroom the whine of the engines seemed louder, as if the pink plastic walls were all that separated me from the jet stream and its arctic winds. Occasionally the air we passed through must have grown choppy, for the plane rattled and heaved like a sled over rough ice. If I opened the john I half expected to see the earth miles below us, a frozen grey Atlantic fanged with icebergs. England was already a thousand miles away.

With one hand on the door handle for support, I wiped off my trousers with a perfumed paper towel from a foil envelope and stuffed several more into my pocket. My cuffs still bore a residue of Chinese goo. This, it seemed, was the source of the treacle smell; I dabbed ineffectually at it. Surveying myself in the mirror—a bald, harmless-looking old baggage with stooped shoulders and a damp suit (so different from the self-confident young fellow in the photo captioned "*HPL and disciple*")—I slid open the bolt and emerged, a medley of scents. The stewardess had found an empty seat for me near the back of the plane.

It was only as I made to sit down that I noticed who occupied the adjoining seat: he was leaning away from me, asleep with his head resting against the window, but I recognized the beard.

"Uh, stewardess—?" I turned, but saw only her uniformed back retreating up the aisle. After a moment's uncertainty I inched myself into the seat, making as little noise as possible. I had, I reminded myself, every right to be here.

Adjusting the recliner position (to the annoyance of the black behind me), I settled back and reached for the paperback in my pocket. They'd finally gotten around to reprinting one of my earlier tales, and already I'd found four typos. But then, what could one expect? The anthology's front cover, with its crude cartoon skull, said it all: *Goosepimples: Thirteen Cosmic Chillers in the Lovecraft Tradition*. On the back, listed among a dozen other writers whose names I barely recognized, I was described as "a disciple."

So this was what I'd been reduced to—a lifetime's work shrugged off by some blurb-writer as "worthy of the Master himself," the creations of my brain dismissed as mere pastiche. My meticulously wrought fiction, once singled out for such elaborate praise, was now simply—as if this were commendation enough—"Lovecraftian." Ah, Howard, your triumph was complete the moment your name became an adjective.

I'd suspected it for years, of course, but only with the past week's conference had I been forced to acknowledge the fact: that what mattered to the present generation was not my own body of work, but rather my association with Lovecraft. And even this was demeaned: after years of friendship and support, to be labeled—simply because I'd been younger—a mere disciple. It seemed too cruel a joke.

Every joke must have a punchline. This one's was still in my pocket, printed in italics on the folded yellow conference schedule. I didn't need to look at it again: there I was, characterized for all time as "a member of the Lovecraft circle, New York educator, and author of the celebrated collection *Beyond the Garve*."

That was it, the crowning indignity: to be immortalized by a misprint! You'd have appreciated this, Howard. I can almost hear you chuckling from—where else?—beyond the *garve*. . . .

Meanwhile, from the seat next to me came the rasping sounds of a constricted throat; my neighbor must have been caught in a dream. I put down my book and studied him. He looked older than he had at first—perhaps sixty or more. His hands were roughened, powerful looking; on one of them was a ring with a curious silver cross. The glistening black beard that covered the lower half of his face was so thick as to be nearly opaque; its very darkness seemed unnatural, for above it the hair was streaked with grey.

I looked more closely, to where beard joined face. Was that a bit of gauze I saw, below the hair? My heart gave a little jump. Leaning forward for a closer look, I peered at the skin to the side of his nose; though burned from long exposure to the sun, it had an odd pallor. My gaze continued upward, along the weathered cheeks toward the dark hollows of his eyes.

They opened.

For a moment they stared into mine without apparent comprehension, glassy and bloodshot. In the next instant they were bulging from his head and quivering like hooked fish. His lips opened, and a tiny voice croaked, "*Not here*."

We sat in silence, neither of us moving. I was too surprised, too embarrassed, to answer. In the window beyond his head the sky looked bright and clear, but I could feel the plane buffeted by unseen blasts, its wingtips bouncing furiously.

"Don't do it to me here," he whispered at last, shrinking back into his seat.

Was the man a lunatic? Dangerous, perhaps? Somewhere in my future I saw spinning headlines: JETLINER TERRORIZED . . . RETIRED NYC TEACHER VICTIM . . . My uncertainty must have shown, for I saw him lick his lips and glance past my head. Hope, and a trace of cunning, swept his face. He grinned up at me. "Sorry, nothing to worry about. Whew! Must have been having a nightmare." Like an athlete after a particularly tough race, he shook his massive head, already regaining command of the situation. His voice had a hint of Tennessee drawl. "Boy"—he gave what should have been a hearty laugh—"I'd better lay off the Kickapoo juice!"

I smiled to put him at ease, though there was nothing about him to suggest that he'd been drinking. "That's an expression I haven't heard in years."

"Oh, yeah?" he said, with little interest. "Well, I've been away." His fingers drummed nervously—impatiently?—on the arm of his chair.

"Malaya?"

He sat up, and the color left his face. "How did you know?"

I nodded toward the green flight-bag at his feet. "I saw you carrying that when you came aboard. You, uh—you seemed to be in a little bit of a hurry, to say the least. In fact, I'm afraid you almost knocked me down."

"Hey." His voice was controlled now, his gaze level and assured. "Hey, I'm really sorry about that, old fella. The fact is, I thought someone might be following me."

Oddly enough, I believed him; he looked sincere—or as sincere as anyone can be behind a phony black beard. "You're in disguise, aren't you?" I asked.

"You mean the whiskers? They're just something I picked up in Singapore. Shucks, I knew they wouldn't fool anyone for long, at least not a friend. But an enemy, well . . . maybe." He made no move to take them off.

"You're—let me guess—you're in the service, right?" The foreign service, I meant; frankly, I took him for an aging spy.

"In the service?" He looked significantly to the left and right, then dropped his voice. "Well, yeah, you might say that. In *His* service." He pointed toward the roof of the plane.

"You mean—?"

He nodded. "I'm a missionary. Or was until yesterday."

3.

Missionaries are infernal nuisances who ought to be kept at home.
                                          —LOVECRAFT, 9/12/1925

Have you ever seen a man in fear of his life? I had, though not since my early twenties. After a summer of idleness I'd at last found temporary employment in the office of what turned out to be a rather shady businessman—I suppose today you'd call him a small-time racketeer—who, having somehow offended "the mob," was convinced he'd be dead by Christmas. He had been wrong, though; he'd been able to enjoy that and many other Christmases with his family, and it wasn't till years later that he was found in his bathtub, facedown in six inches of water. I don't remember much about him, except how hard it had been to engage him in conversation; he never seemed to be listening.

Yet talking with the man who sat next to me on the plane was all too easy; he had nothing of the other's distracted air, the vague replies and preoccupied gaze. On the contrary, he was alert and highly interested in all that was said to him. Except for his initial panic, in fact, there was little to suggest he was a hunted man.

Yet so he claimed to be. Later events would, of course, settle all such questions, but at the time I had no way to judge if he was telling the truth, or if his story was as phony as his beard.

If I believed him, it was almost entirely due to his manner, not the substance of what he said. No, he didn't claim to have made off with the Eye of Klesh; he was more original than that. Nor had he violated some witch doctor's only daughter. But some of the things he told me about the region in which he'd worked—a state called Negri Sembilan, south of Kuala Lumpur—seemed frankly incredible: houses invaded by trees, government-built roads that simply disappeared, a nearby colleague returning from a ten-day vacation to find his lawn overgrown with ropy things they'd had to burn twice to destroy. He claimed there were tiny red spiders that jumped as high as a man's shoulder—"there was a girl in the village gone half-deaf because one of the nasty little things crawled in her ear and swelled so big it plugged up the hole"—and places where mosquitoes were so thick they suffocated cattle. He described a land of steaming mangrove swamps and rubber plantations as large as feudal kingdoms, a land so humid that wallpaper bubbled on the hot nights and Bibles sprouted mildew.

As we sat together on the plane, sealed within an air-cooled world of plastic and pastel, none of these things seemed possible; with the frozen blue of the sky just beyond my reach, the stewardesses walking briskly past me in their blue-and-gold uniforms, the passengers to my left sipping Cokes or sleeping or leafing through copies of *In-flite*, I found myself believing less than half of what he said, attributing the rest to sheer exaggeration and a Southern penchant for tall tales. Only when I'd been home a week and paid a visit to my niece in Brooklyn did I revise my estimate upward, for glancing through her son's geography text I came upon this passage: "Along the [Malayan] peninsula, insects swarm in abundance; probably more varieties exist here than anywhere else on earth. There is some good hardwood timber, and camphor and ebony trees are found in profusion. Many orchid varieties thrive, some of extraordinary size." The book alluded to the area's "rich mixture of races and languages," its "extreme humidity" and "colorful native fauna," and added: "Its jungles are so impenetrable that even the wild beasts must keep to well-worn paths."

But perhaps the strangest aspect of this region was that, despite its dangers and discomforts, my companion claimed to have loved it. "They've got a mountain in the center of the peninsula—" He mentioned an unpronounceable name and shook his head. "Most beautiful thing you ever saw. And there's some real pretty country down along the coast, you'd swear it was some kind of South Sea island. Comfortable, too. Oh, it's damp all right, especially in the interior where the new mission was supposed to be—but the temperature never even hits a hundred. Try saying that for New York City."

I nodded. "Remarkable."

"And the *people*," he went on, "why, I believe they're just the friendliest people on earth. You know, I'd heard a lot of bad things about the Moslems—that's what most of them are, part of the Sunni sect—but I'm telling you, they treated us with real neighborliness . . . just so long as we made the teachings *available*, so to speak, and didn't interfere with their affairs. And we didn't. We didn't have to. What we provided, you see, was a hospital—well, a clinic, at least, two RNs and a doctor who came through twice a month—and a small library with books and films. And not just theology, either. All subjects. We were right outside the village, they'd have to pass us on their way to the river, and when they thought none of the *lontoks* were looking, they'd just come in and look around."

"None of the what?"

"Priests, sort of. There were a lot of them. But they didn't interfere with us, we didn't interfere with them. I don't know as we made all that many converts, actually, but I've got nothing bad to say about those people."

He paused, rubbing his eyes; he suddenly looked his age. "Things were going fine," he said. "And then they told me to establish a second mission, further in the interior."

He stopped once more, as if weighing whether to continue. A squat little Chinese woman was plodding slowly up the aisle, holding on to the chairs on each side for balance. I felt her hand brush past my ear as she went by. My companion watched her with a certain unease, waiting till she'd passed. When he spoke again his voice had thickened noticeably.

"I've been all over the world—a lot of places Americans can't even go these days—and I've always felt that, wherever I was, God was surely watching. But once I started getting up into those hills, well. . . . " He shook his head. "I was pretty much on my own, you see. They were going to send most of the staff out later, after I'd got set up. All I had with me was one of our groundskeepers, two bearers, and a guide who doubled as interpreter. Locals, all of them." He frowned. "The groundskeeper, at least, was a Christian."

"You needed an interpreter?"

The question seemed to distract him. "For the new mission, yes. My Malay stood me well enough in the lowlands, but in the interior they used dozens of local dialects. I would have been lost up there. Where I was going they spoke something which our people back in the village called *agon di-gatuan*—'the Old Language.' I never really got to understand much of it." He stared down at his hands. "I wasn't there long enough."

"Trouble with the natives, I suppose."

He didn't answer right away. Finally he nodded. "I truly believe they must be the nastiest people who ever lived," he said with great deliberation. "I sometimes wonder how God could have created them." He stared out the window, at the hills of cloud below us. "They called themselves the Chauchas, near as I could make out. Some French colonial influence, maybe, but they looked Asiatic to me, with just a touch of black. Little people. Harmless looking." He gave a small shudder. "But they were nothing like what they seemed. You couldn't get to the bottom of them. They'd been living way up in those hills I don't know how many centuries, and whatever it is they were doing, they weren't going to let a stranger in on it. They called themselves Moslems, just like the lowlanders, but I'm sure there must have been a few bush-gods mixed in. I thought they were primitive, at first. I mean, some of their rituals—you wouldn't believe it. But now I think they weren't primitive at all. They just kept those rituals because they enjoyed them!" He tried to smile; it merely accentuated the lines in his face.

"Oh, they seemed friendly enough in the beginning," he went on. "You could approach them, do a bit of trading, watch them breed their animals; they were good at that. You could even talk to them about salvation. And they'd just keep smiling, smiling all the time. As if they really *liked* you."

I could hear the disappointment in his voice, and something else.

"You know," he confided, suddenly leaning closer, "down in the lowlands, in the pastures, there's an animal, a kind of snail the Malays kill on sight. A little yellow thing, but it scares them silly: they believe that if it passes over the shadow of their cattle, it'll suck out the cattle's life force. They used to call it a 'Chaucha snail.' Now I know why."

"Why?" I asked.

He looked around the plane, and seemed to sigh. "You understand, at this stage we were still living in tents. We had yet to build anything. Well, the weather got bad, the mosquitoes got worse, and after the groundskeeper disappeared the others took off. I think the guide persuaded them to go. Of course, this left me—"

"Wait. You say the man disappeared?"

"Yes, before the first week was out. It was late afternoon. We'd been pacing out one of the fields less than a hundred yards from the tents, and I was pushing through the long grass thinking he was behind me, and I turned around and he wasn't."

He was speaking all in a rush now. I had visions out of 1940s movies, frightened natives sneaking off with the supplies, and I wondered how much of this was true.

"So with the others gone, too," he said, "I had no way of communicating with the Chauchas, except through a kind of pidgin language, a mixture of Malay and their tongue. But I knew what was going on. All that week they kept laughing about something. Openly. And I got the impression that they were somehow responsible. I mean, for the man's disappearance. You understand? He'd been the one I trusted." His expression was pained. "A week later, when they showed him to me, he was still alive. But he couldn't speak. I think they wanted it that way. You see, they'd—they'd *grown* something in him." He shuddered.

Just at that moment, from directly behind us came an inhumanly high-pitched caterwauling that pierced the air like a siren, rising above the whine of the engines. It came with heart-stopping suddenness, and we both went rigid. I saw my companion's mouth gape as if to echo the scream. So much for the past; we'd become two old men gone all white and clutching at themselves. It was really quite comical. A full minute must have passed before I could bring myself to turn around.

By this time the stewardess had arrived and was dabbing at the place where the man behind me, dozing, had dropped his cigarette on his lap. The surrounding passengers, whites especially, were casting angry glances at him, and I thought I smelled burnt flesh. He was at last helped to his feet by the stewardess and one of his teammates, the latter chuckling uneasily.

Minor as it was, the accident had derailed our conversation and unnerved my companion; it was as if he'd retreated into his beard. He would talk no further, except to ask me ordinary and rather trivial questions about food prices and accommodations. He said he was bound for Florida, looking forward to a summer of, as he put it, "R and R," apparently financed by his sect. I asked him, a bit forlornly, what had happened in the end to the groundskeeper; he said that he had died. Drinks were served; the North American continent swung toward us from the south, first a finger of ice, soon a jagged line of green. I found myself giving the man my sister's address—Indian Creek was just outside Miami, where he'd be staying—and immediately regretted doing so. What did I know of him, after all? He told me his name was Ambrose Mortimer. "It means 'Dead Sea' " he said. "From the Crusades."

When I persisted in bringing up the subject of the mission, he waved me off. "I can't call myself a missionary anymore," he said. "Yesterday, when I left the country, I gave up that calling." He attempted a smile. "Honest, I'm just a civilian now."

"What makes you think they're after you?" I asked.

The smile vanished. "I'm not so sure they are," he said, not very convincingly. "I may just be spooking myself. But I could swear that in New Delhi, and again at Heathrow, I heard someone singing—singing a certain song. Once it was in the men's room, on the other side of a partition; once it was behind me on line. And it was a song I recognized. It's in the Old Language." He shrugged. "I don't even know what the words mean."

"Why would anyone be singing? I mean, if they were following you?"

"That's just it. I don't know." He shook his head. "But I think—I think it's part of the ritual."

"What sort of ritual?"

"I don't know," he said again. He looked quite pained, and I resolved to bring this inquisition to an end. The ventilators had not yet dissipated the smell of charred cloth and flesh.

"But you'd heard the song before," I said. "You told me you recognized it."

"Yeah." He turned away and stared at the approaching clouds. We had already passed over Maine. Suddenly the earth seemed a very small place. "I'd heard some of the Chaucha women singing it," he said at last. "It was a sort of farming song. It's supposed to make things grow."

Ahead of us loomed the saffron yellow smog that covers Manhattan like a dome. The NO SMOKING light winked silently on the console above us.

"I was hoping I wouldn't have to change planes," my companion said presently. "But the Miami flight doesn't leave for an hour and a half. I guess I'll get off and walk around a bit, stretch my legs. I wonder how long customs'll take." He seemed to be talking more to himself than to me. Once more I regretted my impulsiveness in giving him Maude's address. I was half tempted to make up some contagious disease for her, or a jealous husband. But then, quite likely he'd never call on her anyway; he hadn't even bothered to write down the name. And if he did pay a call—well, I told myself, perhaps he'd unwind when he realized he was safe among friends. He might even turn out to be good company; after all, he and my sister were practically the same age.

As the plane gave up the struggle and sank deeper into the warm encircling air, passengers shut books and magazines, organized their belongings, and made last hurried forays to the bathroom to pat cold water on their faces. I wiped my spectacles and smoothed back what remained of my hair. My companion was staring out the window, the green Air Malay bag in his lap, his hands folded on it as if in prayer. We were already becoming strangers.

"Please return seat backs to the upright position," ordered a disembodied voice. Out beyond the window, past the head now turned completely away from me, the ground rose to meet us and we bumped along the pavement, jets roaring in reverse. Already stewardesses were rushing up and down the aisles pulling coats and jackets from the overhead bins; executive types, ignoring instructions, were scrambling to their feet and thrashing into raincoats. Outside I could see uniformed figures moving back and forth in what promised to be a warm grey drizzle. "Well," I said lamely, "we made it." I got to my feet.

He turned and flashed me a sickly grin. "Good-bye," he said. "This really has been a pleasure." He reached for my hand.

"And do try to relax and enjoy yourself in Miami," I said, looking for a break in the crowd that shuffled past me down the aisle. "That's the important thing—just to relax."

"I know that." He nodded gravely. "I know that. God bless you."

"I found my slot and slipped into line. From behind me he added, "And I won't forget to look up your sister." My heart sank, but as I moved toward the door I turned to shout a last farewell. The old lady with the eyes was two people in front of me, but she didn't so much as smile.

One trouble with last farewells is that they occasionally prove redundant. Some forty minutes later, having passed like a morsel of food through a series of white plastic tubes, corridors, and customs lines, I found myself in one of the airport gift shops, whiling away the hour till my niece came to collect me; and there, once again, I saw the missionary.

He did not see me. He was standing before one of the racks of paperbacks—the so-called classics section, haunt of the public domain—and with a preoccupied air he was glancing up and down the rows, barely pausing long enough to read the titles. Like me, he was obviously just killing time.

For some reason—call it embarrassment, a certain reluctance to spoil what had been a successful good-bye—I refrained from hailing him. Instead, stepping back into the rear aisle, I took refuge behind a rack of gothics, which I pretended to study while in fact studying him.

Moments later he looked up from the books and ambled over to the bin of cellophane-wrapped records, idly pressing his beard back into place below his right sideburn. Without warning he turned and surveyed the store; I ducked my head toward the gothics and enjoyed a vision normally reserved for the multifaceted eyes of an insect: women, dozens of them, fleeing an equal number of tiny mansions.

At last, with a shrug of his huge shoulders, he began flipping through the albums in the bin, snapping each one forward in an impatient staccato. Soon, the assortment scanned, he moved to the bin on the left and started on that.

Suddenly he gave a little cry, and I saw him shrink back. He stood immobile for a moment, staring down at something in the bin; then he whirled and walked quickly from the store, pushing past a family about to enter.

"Late for his plane," I said to the astonished salesgirl, and strolled over to the albums. One of them lay faceup in the pile—a jazz record featuring John Coltrane on saxophone. Confused, I turned to look for my erstwhile companion, but he had vanished in the crowd hurrying past the doorway.

Something about the album had apparently set him off; I studied it more carefully. Coltrane stood silhouetted against a tropical sunset, his features obscured, head tilted back, saxophone blaring silently beneath the crimson sky. The pose was dramatic but trite, and I could see in it no special significance: it looked like any other black man with a horn.

4.

New York eclipses all other cities in the spontaneous cordiality and generosity of its inhabitants—at least, such inhabitants as I have encountered.

—LOVECRAFT, 9/29/1922

How quickly you changed your mind! You arrived to find a gold Dunsanian city of arches and domes and fantastic spires . . . or so you told us. Yet when you fled two years later you could see only "alien hordes."

What was it that so spoiled the dream? Was it that impossible marriage? Those foreign faces on the subway? Or was it merely the theft of your new summer suit? I believed then, Howard, and I believe it still, that the nightmare was of your own making; though you returned to New England like a man reemerging into sunlight, there was, I assure you, a very good life to be found amid the shade. I remained—and survived.

I almost wish I were back there now, instead of in this ugly little bungalow, with its air conditioner and its rotting wicker furniture and the humid night dripping down its windows.

I almost wish I were back on the steps of the Natural History Museum where, that momentous August afternoon, I stood perspiring in the shadow of Teddy Roosevelt's horse, watching matrons stroll past Central Park with dogs or children in tow and fanning myself ineffectually with the postcard I'd just received from Maude. I was waiting for my niece to drive by and leave off her son, whom I planned to take round the museum; he'd wanted to see the life-size mockup of the blue whale and, just upstairs, the dinosaurs.

I remember that Ellen and her boy were more than twenty minutes late. I remember too, Howard, that I was thinking of you that afternoon, and with some amusement: much as you disliked New York in the twenties, you'd have reeled in horror at what it's become today. Even from the steps of the museum I could see a curb piled high with refuse and a park whose length you might have walked without once hearing English spoken. Dark skins crowded out the white, and salsa music echoed from across the street.

I remember all these things because, as it turned out, this was a special day: the day I saw, for the second time, the black man and his baleful horn.

My niece arrived late, as usual, with the usual apologies about the crosstown traffic and, for me, the usual argument. "How can you still live over here?" she asked, depositing Terry on the sidewalk. "I mean, just look at those people." She nodded toward a rowdy group of half-naked teenagers who were loitering by the entrance to the park.

"Brooklyn is so much better?" I countered, as tradition dictated.

"Of course," she said. "In the Heights, anyway. I don't understand it—why this pathological hatred of moving? You might at least try the East Side. You can certainly afford it." Terry watched us impassively, lounging against the fender of their car. I think he sided with me over his mother, but he was too wise to show it.

"Believe me, Ellen," I said, "the West Side's changing. It's on the way up again."

She made a face. "Not up where *you* live."

"Sooner or later that'll change too," I said. "Besides, I'm just too old to start hanging around East Side singles bars. Over there they read nothing but best-sellers, and they hate anyone past sixty. I'm better off where I grew up—at least I know where the cheap restaurants are." It was, in fact, a thorny problem: forced to choose between whites whom I despised and blacks whom I feared, I somehow preferred the fear.

To mollify Ellen I read aloud her mother's postcard. It was the pre-stamped kind that bore no picture. "I'm still getting used to the cane," Maude had written, her penmanship as flawless as when she'd won the school medallion. "Livia has gone back to Vermont for the summer, so the card games are suspended & I'm hard into Pearl Buck. Your friend Rev. Mortimer dropped by & we had a nice chat. What amusing stories! Thanks again for the subscription to the *Geographic*; I'll send Ellen my old copies. Look forward to seeing you all after the hurricane season."

Terry was eager to confront the dinosaurs; he was, in fact, getting a little old for me to superintend, and was halfway up the steps before I'd arranged with Ellen where to meet us afterward. With school out the museum was almost as crowded as on weekends, the halls' echo turning shouts and laughter into animal cries. We oriented ourselves on the floor plan in the main lobby—YOU ARE HERE read a large green spot, below which someone had scrawled *"Too bad for you"*—and trooped toward the Hall of Reptiles, Terry impatiently leading the way. "I saw that in school." He pointed toward a redwood diorama. "That too"—the Grand Canyon. He was, I believe, about to enter seventh grade, and until now had been little given to talk; he looked younger than the other children.

We passed toucans and marmosets and the new Urban Ecology wing ("concrete and cockroaches," sneered Terry), and duly stood before the brontosaurus, something of a disappointment: "I forgot it was nothing but the skeleton," he said. Beside us a sleepy-looking black girl with a baby in her arms and two preschoolers in tow tried ineffectually to keep one of the children from climbing on the guard rail. The baby set up an angry howl. I hurried my nephew past the assembled bones and through the most crowded doorway, dedicated, ironically, to Man in Africa. "This is the boring part," said Terry, unmoved by masks and spears. The pace was beginning to tire me. We passed through another doorway—Man in Asia—and moved quickly past the Chinese statuary. "I saw that in school." He nodded at a stumpy figure in a glass case, wrapped in ceremonial robes. Something about it was familiar to me, too; I paused to stare at it. The outer robe, slightly tattered, was spun of some shiny green material and displayed tall, twisted-looking trees on one side, a kind of stylized river on the other. Across the front ran five yellow-brown figures in loincloth and headdress, presumably fleeing toward the robe's frayed edges; behind them stood a larger shape, all black. In its mouth was a pendulous horn. The image was crudely woven—little more than a stick figure, in fact—but it bore an unsettling resemblance, in both pose and proportion, to the one on the album cover.

Terry returned to my side, curious to see what I'd found. *"Tribal garment,"* he read, peering at the white plastic notice below the case. *"Malay Peninsula, Federation of Malaysia, early nineteenth century."* He fell silent.

"Is that all it says?"

"Yep. They don't even have which tribe it's from." He reflected a moment. "Not that I really care."

"Well, I do," I said. "I wonder who'd know."

Obviously I'd have to seek advice at the information counter in the main lobby downstairs. Terry ran on ahead while I followed, even more slowly than before; the thought of a mystery evidently appealed to him, even one so tenuous and unexciting as this.

A bored-looking young college girl listened to the beginning of my query and handed me a pamphlet from below the counter. "You can't see anyone till September," she said, already beginning to turn away. "They're all on vacation."

I squinted at the tiny print on the first page: "Asia, our largest continent, has justly been called the cradle of civilization, but it may also be a birthplace of man himself." Obviously the pamphlet had been written before the current campaigns against sexism. I checked the date on the back: "Winter 1958." This would be of no help. Yet on page four my eye fell on the reference I sought:

> . . . The model next to it wears a green silk ceremonial robe from Negri Sembilan, most rugged of the Malayan provinces. Note central motif of native man blowing ceremonial horn, and the graceful curve of his instrument; the figure is believed to be a representation of "Death's Herald," possibly warning villagers of approaching calamity. Gift of an anonymous donor, the robe is probably Tcho-tcho in origin and dates from the early 19th century.

"What's the matter, Uncle? Are you sick?" Terry gripped my shoulder and stared up at me, looking alarmed; my behavior had obviously confirmed his worst fears about old people. "What's it say in there?"

I gave him the pamphlet and staggered to a bench near the wall. I wanted time to think. The Tcho-Tcho People, I knew, had figured in a number of tales by Lovecraft and his disciples—Howard himself had referred to them as "the wholly abominable Tcho-Tchos"—but I couldn't remember much about them except that they were said to worship one of his imaginary deities. I had always assumed that he'd taken the name from Robert W. Chambers's novel *The Slayer of Souls*, which mentions an Asian tribe called "the Tchortchas" and their "ancient air, 'The Thirty Thousand Calamities.' "

But whatever their attributes, I'd been certain of one thing: the Tcho-Tchos were completely fictitious.

Obviously I'd been wrong. Barring the unlikely possibility that the pamphlet itself was a hoax, I was forced to conclude that the malign beings of the stories were in fact based upon an actual race inhabiting the Southeast Asian subcontinent—a race whose name my missionary friend had mistranslated as "the Chauchas."

It was a rather troublesome discovery. I had hoped to turn some of Mortimer's recollections, authentic or not, into fiction; he'd unwittingly given me the material for two or three good plots. Yet I'd now discovered that my friend Howard had beaten me to it, and that I'd been put in the uncomfortable position of living out another man's horror stories.

5.

> Epistolary expression is with me largely replacing conversation.
> —LOVECRAFT, 12/23/1917

I hadn't expected my second encounter with the black horn-player. A month later I got an even bigger surprise: I saw the missionary again.

Or at any rate, his picture. It was in a clipping my sister had sent me from the *Miami Herald*, over which she had written in ballpoint pen, *"Just saw this in the paper—how awful!!"*

I didn't recognize the face; the photo was obviously an old one, the reproduction poor, and the man was clean-shaven. But the words below it told me it was him.

CLERGYMAN MISSING IN STORM

(Wed.) The Rev. Ambrose B. Mortimer, 56, a lay pastor of the Church of Christ, Knoxville, Tenn., has been reported missing in the wake of Monday's hurricane. Spokesmen for the order say Mortimer had recently retired after serving 19 years as a missionary, most recently in Malaysia. After moving to Miami in July, he had been a resident of 311 Pompano Canal Road.

Here the piece ended, with an abruptness that seemed all too appropriate to its subject. Whether Ambrose Mortimer still lived I didn't know, but I felt certain now that, having fled one peninsula, he had strayed onto another just as dangerous, a finger thrust into the void. And the void had swallowed him up.

So, anyway, ran my thoughts. I have often been prey to depressions of a similar nature, and subscribe to a fatalistic philosophy I'd shared with my friend Howard: a philosophy one of his less sympathetic biographers has dubbed "futilitarianism."

Yet pessimistic as I was, I was not about to let the matter rest. Mortimer may well have been lost in the storm; he may even have set off somewhere on his own. But if, in fact, some lunatic religious sect had done away with him for having pried too closely into its affairs, there were things I could do about it. I wrote to the Miami police that very day.

"Gentlemen," I began. "Having learned of the recent disappearance of the Reverend Ambrose Mortimer, I think I can provide information which may prove of use to investigators."

There is no need to quote the rest of the letter here. Suffice it to say that I recounted my conversation with the missing man, emphasizing the fears he'd expressed for his life: pursuit and "ritual murder" at the hands of a Malayan tribe called the Tcho-Tcho. The letter was, in short, a rather elaborate way of crying "foul play." I sent it care of my sister, asking that she forward it to the correct address.

The police department's reply came with unexpected speed. As with all such correspondence, it was more curt than courteous. "Dear Sir," wrote a Detective Sergeant A. Linahan; "In the matter of Rev. Mortimer we had already been apprised of the threats on his life. To date a preliminary search of the Pompano Canal has produced no findings, but dredging operations are expected to continue as part of our routine investigation. Thanking you for your concern—"

Below his signature, however, the sergeant had added a short postscript in his own hand. Its tone was somewhat more personal; perhaps typewriters intimidated him. "You may be interested to know," it said, "that we've recently learned a man carrying a Malaysian passport occupied rooms at a North Miami hotel for most of the summer, but checked out two weeks before your friend disappeared. I'm not at liberty to say more, but please be assured we are tracking down several leads at the moment. Our investigators are working full-time on the matter, and we hope to bring it to a speedy conclusion."

Linahan's letter arrived on September twenty-first. Before the week was out I had one from my sister, along with another clipping from the *Herald*; and since, like some old Victorian novel, this chapter seems to have taken an epistolary form, I will end it with extracts from these two items.

The newspaper story was headed WANTED FOR QUESTIONING. Like the Mortimer piece, it was little more than a photo with an extended caption:

(Thurs.) A Malaysian citizen is being sought for questioning in connection with the disappearance of an American clergyman, Miami police say. Records indicate that the Malaysian, Mr. D. A. Djaktu-tchow, had occupied furnished rooms at the Barkleigh Hotella, 2401 Culebra Ave., possibly with an unnamed companion. He is believed still in the greater Miami area, but since August 22 his movements cannot be traced. State Dept. officials report Djaktu-tchow's visa expired August 31; charges are pending.

The clergyman, Rev. Ambrose B. Mortimer, has been missing since September 6.

The photo above the article was evidently a recent one, no doubt reproduced from the visa in question. I recognized the smiling moon-wide face, although it took me a moment to place him as the man whose dinner I'd stumbled over on the plane. Without the moustache, he looked less like Charlie Chan.

The accompanying letter filled in a few details. "I called up the *Herald*," my sister wrote, "but they couldn't tell me any more than was in the article. Just the same, finding that out took me half an hour, since the stupid woman at the switchboard kept putting me through to the wrong person. I guess you're right—anything that prints color pictures on page one shouldn't call itself a newspaper.

"This afternoon I called up the police department, but they weren't very helpful either. I suppose you just can't expect to find out much over the phone, though I still rely on it. Finally I got an Officer Linahan, who told me he's just replied to that letter of yours. Have you heard from him yet? The man was very evasive. He was trying to be nice, but I could tell he was impatient to get off. He did give me the full name of the man they're looking for—Djaktu Abdul Djaktu-tchow, isn't that marvelous?—and he told me they have some more material on him which they can't release right now. I argued and pleaded (you know how persuasive I can be!), and finally, because I claimed I'd been a close friend of Rev. Mortimer's, I wheedled something out of him which he swore he'd deny if I told anyone but you. Apparently the poor man must have been deathly ill, maybe even tubercular—I intended to get a patch test next week, just to play safe, and I recommend that you get one too—because it seems that, in the reverend's bedroom, they found something *very* odd. They said it was pieces of lung tissue."

6.

I, too, was a detective in youth.

—LOVECRAFT, 2/17/1931

Do amateur detectives still exist? I mean, outside of the pages of books? Who, after all, has the time for such games today? Not I, unfortunately; though for more than a decade I'd been nominally retired, my days were quite full with the unromantic activities that occupy people my age: letters, luncheon dates, visits to my niece and to my doctor; books (not enough) and television (too much) and perhaps a Golden Agers' matinee (though I have largely stopped going to films, finding myself increasingly out of sympathy with their heroes). I also spent Halloween week on the Jersey shore, and most of another attempting to interest a rather patronizing young publisher in reprinting some of my early work.

All this, of course, is intended as a sort of apologia for my having put off further inquiries into poor Mortimer's case till mid-November. The truth is, the matter almost slipped my mind; only in novels do people not have better things to do.

It was Maude who reawakened my interest. She had been avidly scanning the papers—in vain—for further reports on the man's disappearance; I believe she had even phoned Sergeant Linahan a second time, but had learned nothing new. Now she wrote me with a tiny fragment of information, heard at thirdhand: one of her bridge partners had had it on the authority of "a friend in the police force" that the search for Mr. Djaktu was being widened to include his presumed companion—"a Negro child," or so my sister reported. Although there was every possibility that this information was false, or that it concerned an entirely different case, I could tell she regarded it all as rather sinister.

Perhaps that was why the following afternoon found me struggling once more up the steps of the Natural History Museum—as much to satisfy Maude as myself. Her allusion to a Negro, coming after the curious discovery in Mortimer's bedroom, had recalled to mind the figure on the Malayan robe, and I had been troubled all night by the fantasy of a black man—a man much like the beggar I'd just seen huddled against Roosevelt's statue—coughing his lungs out into a sort of twisted horn.

I had encountered few other people on the streets that afternoon, as it was unseasonably chilly for a city that's often mild till January; I wore a muffler, and my grey tweed overcoat flapped round my heels. Inside, however, the place, like all American buildings, was overheated; I was soon the same as I made my way up the demoralizingly long staircase to the second floor.

The corridors were silent and empty but for the morose figure of a guard seated before one of the alcoves, head down as if in mourning, and, from above me, the hiss of the steam radiators near the marble ceiling. Slowly, and rather enjoying the sense of privilege that comes from having a museum to oneself, I retraced my earlier route past the immense skeletons of dinosaurs (*"These great creatures once trod the earth where you now walk"*) and down to the Hall of Primitive Man, where two Puerto Rican youths, obviously playing hooky, stood by the African wing gazing worshipfully at a Masai warrior in full battle gear. In the section devoted to Asia I paused to get my bearings, looking in vain for the squat figure in the robe. The glass case was empty. Over its plaque was taped a printed notice: "Temporarily removed for restoration."

This was no doubt the first time in forty years that the display had been taken down, and of course I'd picked just this occasion to look for it. So much for luck. I headed for the nearest staircase, at the far end of the wing. From behind me the clank of metal echoed down the hall, followed by the angry voice of the guard. Perhaps that Masai spear had proved too great a temptation.

In the main lobby I was issued a written pass to enter the north wing, where the staff offices were located. "You want the workrooms on basement level," said the woman at the information counter; the summer's bored coed had become a friendly old lady who eyed me with some interest. "Just ask the guard at the bottom of the stairs, past the cafeteria. I do hope you find what you're looking for."

Carefully keeping the pink slip she'd handed me visible for anyone who might demand it, I descended. As I turned onto the stairwell, I was confronted with a kind of vision: a blond Scandinavian-looking family were coming up the stairs toward me, the four upturned faces almost interchangeable, parents and two little girls with the pursed lips and timidly hopeful eyes of the tourist, while just behind them, like a shadow, apparently unheard, capered a grinning black youth, practically walking on the father's heels. In my present state of mind the scene appeared particularly disturbing—the boy's expression was certainly one of mockery—and I wondered if the guard who stood before the cafeteria had noticed. If he had, however, he gave no sign; he glanced without curiosity at my pass and pointed toward a fire door at the end of the hall.

The offices in the lower level were surprisingly shabby—the walls here were not marble but faded green plaster—and the entire corridor had a "buried" feeling to it, no doubt because the only outside light came from ground-level window gratings high overhead. I had been told to ask for one of the research associates, a Mr. Richmond; his office was part of a suite broken up by pegboard dividers. The door was open, and he got up from his desk as soon as I entered; I suspect that, in view of my age and grey tweed overcoat, he may have taken me for someone important.

A plump young man with sandy-colored beard, he looked like an out-of-shape surfer, but his sunniness dissolved when I mentioned my interest in the green silk robe. "And I suppose you're the man who complained about it upstairs, am I right?"

I assured him I was not.

"Well, someone sure did," he said, still eyeing me resentfully; on the wall behind him an Indian war-mask did the same. "Some damn tourist, maybe in town for a day and out to make trouble. Threatened to call the Malaysian Embassy. If you put up a fuss, those people upstairs get scared it'll wind up in the *Times*."

I understood his allusion; in previous years the museum had gained considerable notoriety for having conducted some really appalling— and, to my mind, quite pointless—experiments on cats. Most of the public had, until then, been unaware that the building housed several working laboratories.

"Anyway," he continued, "the robe's down in the shop, and we're stuck with patching up the damn thing. It'll probably be down there for the next six months before we get to it. We're so understaffed right now it isn't funny." He glanced at his watch. "Come on, I'll show you. Then I've got to go upstairs."

I followed him down a narrow corridor that branched off to either side. At one point he said, "On your right, the infamous zoology lab." I kept my eyes straight ahead. As we passed the next doorway I smelled a familiar odor.

"It makes me think of treacle," I said.

"You're not so far wrong." He spoke without looking back. "The stuff's mostly molasses. Pure nutrient. They use it for growing micro-organisms."

I hurried to keep up with him. "And for other things?"

He shrugged. "I don't know, Mister. It's not my field."

We came to a door barred by a black wire grille. "Here's one of the shops," he said, fitting a key into the lock. The door swung open on a long unlit room smelling of wood shavings and glue. "You sit down over here," he said, leading me to a small anteroom and switching on the light. "I'll be back in a second." I stared at the object closest to me, a large ebony chest, ornately carved. Its hinges had been removed. Richmond returned with the robe draped over his arm. "See?" he said, dangling it before me. "It's really not in such bad condition, is it?" I realized he still thought of me as the man who'd complained.

On the field of rippling green fled the small brown figures, still pursued by some unseen doom. In the center stood the black man, black horn to his lips, man and horn a single line of unbroken blackness.

"Are the Tcho-Tchos a superstitious people?" I asked.

"They *were*," he said pointedly. "Superstitious and not very pleasant. They're extinct as dinosaurs now. Supposedly wiped out by the Japanese or something."

"That's rather odd," I said. "A friend of mine claims to have met up with them earlier this year."

Richmond was smoothing out the robe; the branches of the snake-trees snapped futilely at the brown shapes. "I suppose it's possible," he said, after a pause. "But I haven't read anything about them since grad school. They're certainly not listed in the textbooks anymore. I've looked, and there's nothing on them. This robe's over a hundred years old."

I pointed to the figure in the center. "What can you tell me about this fellow?"

"Death's Herald," he said, as if it were a quiz. "At least that's what the literature says. Supposed to warn of some approaching calamity."

I nodded without looking up; he was merely repeating what I'd read in the pamphlet. "But isn't it strange," I said, "that these others are in such a panic? See? They aren't even waiting around to listen."

"Would you?" He snorted impatiently.

"But if the black one's just a messenger of some sort, why's he so much *bigger* than the others?"

Richmond began folding the cloth. "Look, Mister," he said, "I don't pretend to be an expert on every tribe in Asia. But if a character's important, they'd sometimes make him larger. Anyway, that's what the Mayans did. Listen, I've really got to get this put away now. I've got a meeting to go to."

While he was gone I sat thinking about what I'd just seen. The small brown figures, crude as they were, had expressed a terror no mere messenger could inspire. And that great black shape standing triumphant in the center, horn twisting from its mouth—that was no messenger either, I was sure of it. That was no Death's Herald. That was Death itself.

I returned to my apartment just in time to hear the telephone ringing, but by the time I'd let myself in it had stopped. I sat down in the living room with a mug of coffee and a book which had lain untouched on the shelf for the last thirty years: *Jungle Ways*, by that old humbug, William Seabrook. I'd met him back in the twenties and had found him likeable enough, if rather untrustworthy. His book described dozens of unlikely characters, including "a cannibal chief who had got himself jailed and famous because he had eaten his young wife, a handsome, lazy wench called Blito, along with a dozen of her girlfriends." But I discovered no mention of a black horn-player.

I had just finished my coffee when the phone rang again. It was my sister.

"I just wanted to let you know that there's another man missing," she said breathlessly. I couldn't tell if she was frightened or merely excited. "A busboy at the San Marino. Remember? I took you there."

The San Marino was an inexpensive little luncheonette on Indian Creek, several blocks from my sister's house. She and her friends ate there several times a week.

"It happened last night," she went on. "I just heard about it at my card game. They say he went outside with a bucket of fish heads to dump in the creek, and he never came back."

"That's very interesting, but ..." I thought for a moment; it was highly unusual for her to call me like this. "But really, Maude, couldn't he have simply run off? I mean, what makes you think there's any connection—"

"Because I took Ambrose there, too!" she cried. "Three or four times. That was where we used to meet."

Apparently Maude had been considerably better acquainted with the Reverend Mortimer than her letters would have led one to believe. But I wasn't interested in pursuing that line right now.

"This busboy," I asked, "was he someone you knew?"

"Of course," she said. "I know everyone in there. His name was Carlos. A quiet boy, very courteous. I'm sure he must have waited on us dozens of times."

I had seldom heard my sister so upset, but for the present there seemed no way of calming her fears. Before hanging up she made me promise to move up the month's visit I'd expected to pay her over Christmas; I assured her I would try to make it down for Thanksgiving, then only a week away, if I could find a flight that wasn't filled.

"Do try," she said—and, were this a tale from the old pulps, she would have added: "If anyone can get to the bottom of this, you can." In truth, however, both Maude and I were aware that I had just celebrated my seventy-seventh birthday and that, of the two of us, I was by far the more timid; so that what she actually said was, "Looking after you will help take my mind off things."

7.

I couldn't live a week without a private library.

—LOVECRAFT, 2/25/1929

That's what I thought, too, until recently. After a lifetime of collecting I'd acquired thousands upon thousands of volumes, never parting with a one; it was this cumbersome private library, in fact, that helped keep me anchored to the same West Side apartment for nearly half a century.

Yet here I sit, with no company save a few gardening manuals and a shelf of antiquated best-sellers—nothing to dream on, nothing I'd want to hold in my hand. Still, I've survived here a week, a month, almost a season. The truth is, Howard, you'd be surprised what you can live without. As for the books I've left in Manhattan, I just hope someone appreciates them when I'm gone.

But I was by no means so resigned that November when, having successfully reserved a seat on an earlier flight, I found myself with less than a week in New York. I spent all my remaining time in the library—the public one on Forty-second Street, with the lions in front and with no book of mine on its shelves. Its two reading rooms were the haunt of men my age and older, retired men with days to fill, poor men just warming their bones; some leafed through newspapers, others dozed in their seats. None of them, I'm sure, shared my sense of urgency: there were things I hoped to find out before I left, things for which Miami would be useless.

I was no stranger to this building. Long ago, during one of Howard's visits, I had undertaken some genealogical researches here in the hope of finding ancestors more impressive than his, and as a young man I had occasionally attempted to support myself, like the denizens of Gissing's *New Grub Street*, by writing articles compiled from the work of others. But by now I was out of practice: how, after all, does one find references to an obscure Southeast Asian tribal myth without reading everything published on that part of the world?

Initially that's exactly what I tried; I looked through every book I came across with "Malaya" in its title. I read about rainbow gods and phallic altars and something called "the *tatai*," a sort of unwanted companion; I came across wedding rites and the Death of Thorns and a certain cave inhabited by millions of snails. But I found no mention of the Tcho-Tcho, and nothing on their gods.

This in itself was surprising. We are living in a day when there are no more secrets, when my twelve-year-old nephew can buy his own grimoire, and books with titles like *The Encyclopaedia of Ancient and Forbidden Knowledge* are remaindered at every discount store.

Though my friends from the twenties would have hated to admit it, the notion of stumbling across some moldering old "black book" in the attic of a deserted house—some lexicon of spells and chants and hidden lore—is merely a quaint fantasy. If the *Necronomicon* actually existed, it would probably be out in paperback with a preface by Colin Wilson.

It's appropriate, then, that when I finally came upon a reference to what I sought, it was in that most unromantic of forms, a mimeographed film-script.

"Transcript" would perhaps be closer to the truth, for it was based upon a film shot in 1937 and that was now presumably crumbling in some forgotten storehouse. I discovered the item inside one of those brown cardboard packets, held together with ribbons, which libraries use to protect books whose bindings have worn away. The book itself, *Malay Memories*, by a Reverend Morton, had proved a disappointment despite the author's rather suggestive name. The transcript lay beneath it, apparently slipped there by mistake, but though it appeared unpromising—only sixty-six pages long, badly typed, and held together by a single rusty staple—it more than repaid the reading. There was no title page, nor do I think there'd ever been one; the first page simply identified the film as *Documentary—Malaya Today*, and noted that it had been financed, in part, by a U.S. government grant. The filmmaker or makers were not listed.

I soon saw why the government may have been willing to lend the venture some support, for there were a great many scenes in which the proprietors of rubber plantations expressed the sort of opinions Americans might want to hear. To an unidentified interviewer's query, "What other signs of prosperity do you see around you?" a planter named Mr. Pierce had obligingly replied, "Why, look at the living standard—better schools for the natives and a new lorry for me. It's from Detroit, you know. May even have my own rubber in it."

INT: And how about the Japanese? Are they one of today's better markets?

PIERCE: Oh, see, they buy our crop all right, but we don't really trust 'em, understand? (Smiles) We don't like 'em half so much as the Yanks.

The final section of the transcript was considerably more interesting, however. It recorded a number of brief scenes that must never have appeared in the finished film. I quote one of them in its entirety:

PLAYROOM, CHURCH SCHOOL—LATE AFTERNOON.
(DELETED)

INT: This Malay youth has sketched a picture of a demon he
calls Shoo Goron. (*To Boy*) I wonder if you can tell me
something about the instrument he's blowing out of. It
looks like the Jewish *shofar*, or ram's horn. (*Again to Boy*)
That's all right. No need to be frightened.

BOY: He no blow out. Blow in.

INT: I see—he draws air in through the horn, is that right?

BOY: No horn. Is no horn. (*Weeps*) Is *him*.

8.

Miami did not produce much of an impression. . . .
—LOVECRAFT, 7/19/1931

Waiting in the airport lounge with Ellen and her boy, my bags already
checked and my seat number assigned, I fell prey to the sort of anxiety
that had made me miserable in youth: it was a sense that time was
running out; and what caused it now, I think, was the hour that
remained before my flight was due to leave. It was too long a time to
sit making small talk with Terry, whose mind was patently on other
things; yet it was too short to accomplish the task which I'd suddenly
realized had been left undone.

But perhaps my nephew would serve. "Terry," I said, "How'd you
like to do me a favor?" He looked up eagerly; I suppose children his age
love to be of use. "Remember the building we passed on the way here?
The International Arrivals Building?"

"Sure," he said. "Right next door."

"Yes, but it's a lot farther away than it looks. Do you think you'd
be able to get there and back in the next hour and find something out
for me?"

"Sure." He was already out of his seat.

"It just occurs to me that there's an Air Malay reservations desk in
that building, and I wonder if you could ask someone there—"

My niece interrupted me. "Oh no, he won't," she said firmly. "First
of all, I won't have him running across that highway on some silly
errand"—she ignored her son's protests—"and secondly, I don't want
him involved in this game you've got going with Mother."

The upshot of it was that Ellen went herself, leaving Terry and me
to our small talk. She took with her a slip of paper upon which I'd

written *Shoo Goron*, a name she regarded with sour skepticism. I wasn't sure she would return before my departure (Terry, I could see, was growing increasingly uneasy), but she was back before the second boarding call.

"She says you spelled it wrong," Ellen announced.

"Who's she?"

"Just one of the flight attendants," said Ellen. "A young girl, in her early twenties. None of the others were Malayan. At first she didn't recognize the name, until she read it out loud a few times. Apparently it's some kind of fish, am I right? Like a suckerfish, only bigger. Anyway, that's what she said. Her mother used to scare her with it when she was bad."

Obviously Ellen—or, more likely, the other woman—had misunderstood. "Sort of a bogeyman figure?" I asked. "Well, I suppose that's possible. But a fish, you say?"

Ellen nodded. "I don't think she knew that much about it, though. She acted a little embarrassed, in fact. Like I'd asked her something dirty." From across the room a loudspeaker issued the final call for passengers. Ellen helped me to my feet, still talking. "She said she was just a Malay, from somewhere on the coast—Malacca? I forget— and that it's a shame I didn't drop by three or four months ago, because her summer replacement was part Chocha—Chocho?—something like that."

The line was growing shorter now. I wished the two of them a safe Thanksgiving and shuffled toward the plane.

Below me the clouds had formed a landscape of rolling hills. I could see every ridge, every washed-out shrub, and in the darker places, the eyes of animals.

Some of the valleys were split by jagged black lines that looked like rivers on a map. The water, at least, was real enough: here the cloud-bank had cracked and parted, revealing the dark sea beneath.

Throughout the ride I'd been conscious of lost opportunity, a sense that my destination offered a kind of final chance. With Howard gone these more than forty years I still lived out my life in his shadow; certainly his tales had overshadowed my own. Now I found myself trapped within one of them. Here, miles above the earth, I felt great gods warring; below, the war was already lost.

The very passengers around me seemed participants in a masque: the oily little steward who smelled of something odd; the child who stared and wouldn't look away; the man asleep beside me, mouth slack, who'd chuckled and handed me a page ripped from his inflight magazine: NOVEMBER PUZZLE PAGE, with an eye staring in astonishment from a swarm of dots. "Connect the dots and see what you'll be *least* thankful for this Thanksgiving!" Below it, half buried amid "*B'nai B'rith to Host Song Fest*" and advertisements for beach clubs, a bit of local color found me in a susceptible mood:

HAVE FINS, WILL TRAVEL

(Courtesy *Miami Herald*) If your hubby comes home and swears he's just seen a school of fish walk across the yard, don't sniff his breath for booze. He may be telling the truth! According to U. of Miami zoologists, catfish will be migrating in record numbers this fall and South Florida residents can expect to see hundreds of the whiskered critters crawling overland, miles from water. Though usually no bigger than your pussycat, most breeds can survive without. . . .

Here the piece came to a ragged end where my companion had torn it from the magazine. He stirred in his sleep, lips moving. I turned and put my head against the window, where the limb of Florida was swinging into view, veined with dozens of canals. The plane shuddered and slid toward it.

Maude was already at the gate, a black porter towering beside her with an empty cart. While we waited by a hatchway in the basement for my luggage to be disgorged, she told me the sequel to the San Marino incident: the boy's body found washed up on a distant beach, lungs in mouth and throat. "Inside out," she said. "Can you imagine? It's been on the radio all morning. With tapes of some ghastly doctor talking about smoker's cough and the way people drown. I couldn't even listen for a while." The porter heaved my bags onto the cart, and we followed him to the taxi stand, Maude using her cane to gesticulate. If I hadn't seen how aged she'd become, I'd have thought the excitement was agreeing with her.

We had the driver make a detour westward along Pompano Canal Road, where we paused at number 311, one of nine shabby green cabins that formed a court round a small and very dirty wading pool; in a cement pot beside the pool drooped a solitary half-dead palm, like some travesty of an oasis. This, then, had been Ambrose Mortimer's final home. My sister was very silent, and I believed her when she said she'd never been here before. Across the street glistened the oily waters of the canal.

The taxi turned east. We passed interminable rows of hotels, motels, condominiums, shopping centers as big as Central Park, souvenir shops with billboards bigger than themselves, baskets of seashells and wriggly plastic auto toys out front. Men and women our age and younger sat on canvas beach chairs in their yards, blinking at the traffic. Some of the older women were nearly as bald as I was; men, like women, wore clothes the color of coral, lime, and peach. They walked very slowly as they crossed the street or moved along the sidewalk. Cars moved almost as slowly, and it was forty minutes before we reached Maude's house, with its pastel orange shutters and the retired druggist and his wife living upstairs. Here, too, a kind of languor was upon the block, one into which I knew, with just a memory of regret, I would soon be settling. Life was slowing to a halt, and once the taxi had roared away the only things that stirred were the geraniums in Maude's window box, trembling slightly in a breeze I couldn't even feel.

A dry spell. Mornings in my sister's air-conditioned parlor, luncheons with her friends in air-conditioned coffee shops. Inadvertent afternoon naps, from which I'd awaken with headaches. Evening walks to watch the sunsets, the fireflies, the TV screens flashing behind neighbors' blinds. By night, a few faint cloudy stars; by day, tiny lizards skittering over the hot pavement, or boldly sunning themselves on the flagstones. The smell of oil paints in my sister's closet, and the insistent buzz of mosquitoes in her garden. Her sundial, a gift from Ellen, with Terry's message painted on the rim. Lunch at the San Marino and a brief, halfhearted look at the fatal dock in back, now something of a tourist attraction. An afternoon at a branch library in Hialeah, searching through its shelves of travel books, an old man dozing at the table across from me, a child laboriously copying her school report from the encyclopedia. Thanksgiving dinner, with its half-hour's phone call to Ellen and the boy, and the prospect of turkey for the rest of the week. More friends to visit, and another day at the library.

Later, driven by boredom and the ghost of an impulse, I phoned the Barkleigh Hotella in North Miami and booked a room there for two nights. I don't remember the dates I settled for, because that sort of thing no longer had much meaning, but I know it was for midweek; "we're deep in the season," the proprietress informed me, and the hotel would be filled each weekend till long past New Year's.

My sister refused to accompany me out to Culebra Avenue; she saw no attraction in visiting the place once occupied by a fugitive Malaysian, nor did she share my pulp-novel fantasy that, by actually living there myself, I might uncover some clue unknown to the police. ("Thanks to the celebrated author of *Beyond the Garve* . . .") I went alone, by cab, taking with me half a dozen volumes from the branch library. Beyond the reading, I had no other plans.

The Barkleigh was a pink adobe building two stories tall, surmounted by an ancient neon sign on which the dust lay thick in the early afternoon sunlight. Similar establishments lined the block on both sides, each more depressing than the last. There was no elevator here and, as I learned to my disappointment, no rooms available on the first floor. The staircase looked like it was going to be an effort.

In the office downstairs I inquired, as casually as I could, which room the notorious Mr. Djaktu had occupied; I'd hoped, in fact, to be assigned it, or one nearby. But I was doomed to disappointment. The preoccupied little Cuban behind the counter had been hired only six weeks before and claimed to know nothing of the matter; in halting English he explained that the proprietress, a Mrs. Zimmerman, had just left for New Jersey to visit relatives and would not be back till Christmas. Obviously I could forget about gossip.

By this point I was half tempted to cancel my visit, and I confess that what kept me there was not so much a sense of honor as the desire for two days' separation from Maude, who, having been on her own for nearly a decade, had grown somewhat difficult to live with.

I followed the Cuban upstairs, watching my suitcase bump rhythmically against his legs, and was led down the hall to a room facing the rear. The place smelled vaguely of salt air and hair oil; the sagging bed had served many a desperate holiday. A small cement terrace overlooked the yard and a vacant lot behind it, the latter so overgrown with weeds and the grass in the yard so long unmown that it was difficult to tell where one began and the other ended. A clump of palms rose somewhere in the middle of this no-man's-land, impossibly tall and thin, with only a few stiffened leaves to grace the tops. On the ground below them lay several rotting coconuts.

This was my view the first night when I returned after dining at a nearby restaurant. I felt unusually tired and soon went inside to sleep. The night being cool, there was no need for the air conditioner; as I lay in the huge bed I could hear people stirring in the adjoining room, the hiss of a bus moving down the avenue, and the rustle of palm leaves in the wind.

I spent part of the next morning composing a letter to Mrs. Zimmerman, to be held for her return. After the long walk to a coffee shop for lunch, I napped. After dinner I did the same. With the TV turned on for company, a garrulous blur at the other side of the room, I went through the pile of books on my night table, final cullings from the bottom of the travel shelf; most of them hadn't been taken out since the thirties. I found nothing of interest in any of them, at least upon first inspection, but before turning out the light I noticed that one, the reminiscences of a Colonel E. G. Paterson, was provided with an index. Though I looked in vain for the demon Shoo Goron, I found reference to it under a variant spelling.

The author, no doubt long deceased, had spent most of his life in the

Orient. His interest in Southeast Asia was slight, and the passage in question consequently brief:

> . . . Despite the richness and variety of their folklore, however, they have nothing akin to the Malay *shugoran*, a kind of bogey-man used to frighten naughty children. The traveller hears many conflicting descriptions of it, some bordering on the obscene. (*Oran*, of course, is Malay for 'man,' while *shug*, which here connotes 'sniffing' or 'questing,' means literally, 'elephant's trunk.') I well recall the hide which hung over the bar at the Traders' Club in Singapore, and which, according to tradition, represented the infant of this fabulous creature; its wings were black, like the skin of a Hottentot. Shortly after the War a regimental surgeon was passing through on his way back to Gibraltar and, after due examination, pronounced it the dried-out skin of a rather large catfish. He was never asked back.

I kept my light on until I was ready to fall asleep, listening to the wind rattle the palm leaves and whine up and down the row of terraces. As I switched off the light, I half expected to see a shadowy shape at the window; but I saw, as the poet says, nothing but the night.

The next morning I packed my bag and left, aware that my stay in the hotel had proved fruitless. I returned to my sister's house to find her in agitated conversation with the druggist from upstairs; she was in a terrible state and said she'd been trying to reach me all morning. She had awakened to find the flower box by her bedroom window overturned and the shrubbery beneath it trampled. Down the side of the house ran two immense slash marks several yards apart, starting at the roof and continuing straight to the ground.

9.

> My gawd, how the years fly. Stolidly middle-aged—when only yesterday I was young and eager and awed by the mystery of an unfolding world.
>
> —LOVECRAFT, 8/20/1926

There is little more to report. Here the tale degenerates into an unsifted collection of items which may or may not be related: pieces of a puzzle for those who fancy themselves puzzle fans, a random swarm of dots, and in the center, a wide unwinking eye.

Of course, my sister left the house on Indian Creek that very day and took rooms for herself in a downtown Miami hotel. Subsequently she moved inland to live with a friend in a green stucco bungalow several miles from the Everglades, third in a row of nine just off the main highway. I am seated in its den as I write this. After the friend died my sister lived on here alone, making the forty-mile bus trip to Miami only on special occasions: theater with a group of friends, one or two shopping trips a year. She had everything else she needed right here.

I returned to New York, caught a chill, and finished out the winter in a hospital bed, visited rather less often than I might have wished by my niece and her boy. Of course, the drive in from Brooklyn is nothing to scoff at.

One recovers far more slowly when one has reached my age; it's a painful truth we all learn if we live long enough. Howard's life was short, but in the end I think he understood. At thirty-five he could deride as madness a friend's "hankering after youth," yet ten years later he'd learned to mourn the loss of his own. "The years tell on one!" he'd written. "You young fellows don't know how lucky you are!"

Age is indeed the great mystery. How else could Terry have emblazoned his grandmother's sundial with that saccharine nonsense?

> Grow old along with me,
> The best is yet to be.

True, the motto is traditional to sundials—but that young fool hadn't even kept to the rhyme. With diabolical imprecision he had actually written, *"The best is yet to come"*—a line to make me gnash my teeth, if I had any left to gnash.

I spent most of the spring indoors, cooking myself wretched little meals and working ineffectually on a literary project that had occupied my thoughts. It was discouraging to find that I wrote so slowly now, and changed so much. My sister only reinforced the mood when, sending me a rather salacious story she'd found in the *Enquirer*—about the "thing like a vacuum cleaner" that snaked through a Swedish sailor's porthole and "made his face all purple"—she wrote at the top, *"See? Right out of Lovecraft."*

It was not long after this that I received, to my surprise, a letter from Mrs. Zimmerman, bearing profuse apologies for having misplaced my inquiry until it turned up again during "spring cleaning." (It is hard to imagine any sort of cleaning at the Barkleigh Hotella, spring or otherwise, but even this late reply was welcome.) "I am sorry that the minister who disappeared was a friend of yours," she wrote. "I'm sure he must have been a fine gentleman.

"You asked me for 'the particulars,' but from your note you seem to know the whole story. There is really nothing I can tell you that I did not tell the police, though I do not think they ever released all of it to the papers. Our records show that our guest Mr. Djaktu arrived here nearly a year ago, at the end of June, and left the last week of August owing me a week's rent plus various damages which I no longer have much hope of recovering, though I have written the Malaysian Embassy about it.

"In other respects he was a proper boarder, paid regularly, and in fact hardly ever left his room except to walk in the backyard from time to time or stop at the grocer's. (We have found it impossible to discourage eating in rooms.) My only complaint is that in the middle of the summer he may have had a small colored child living with him without our knowledge, until one of the maids heard him singing to it as she passed his room. She did not recognize the language, but said she thought it might be Hebrew. (The poor woman, now sadly taken from us, was barely able to read.) When she next made up the room, she told me that Mr. Djaktu claimed the child was 'his,' and that she left because she caught a glimpse of it watching her from the bathroom. She said it was naked. I did not speak of this at the time, as I do not feel it is my place to pass judgment on the morals of my guests. Anyway, we never saw the child again, and we made sure the room was completely sanitary for our next guests. Believe me, we have received nothing but good comments on our facilities. We think they are excellent and hope you agree, and I also hope you will be our guest again on your next visit to Florida."

Unfortunately, my next visit to Florida was for my sister's funeral late that winter. I know now, as I did not know then, that she had been in ill health for most of the previous year, but I cannot help thinking that the so-called incidents—the senseless acts of vandalism directed against lone women in the inland South Florida area, culminating in several reported attacks by an unidentified prowler—may have hastened her death.

When I arrived here with Ellen to take care of my sister's affairs and arrange for the funeral, I intended to remain a week or two at most, seeing to the transfer of the property. Yet somehow I lingered, long after Ellen had gone. Perhaps it was the thought of that New York winter, grown harsher with each passing year; I just couldn't find the strength to go back. Nor, in the end, could I bring myself to sell this house. If I am trapped here, it's a trap I'm resigned to. Besides, moving has never much agreed with me; when I grow tired of this little room— and I do—I can think of nowhere else to go. I've seen all the world I want to see. This simple place is now my home—and I feel certain it will be my last. The calendar on the wall tells me it's been almost three months since I moved in. Somewhere in its remaining pages you will find the date of my death.

The past week has seen a new outbreak of "incidents." Last night's was the most dramatic by far. I can recite it almost word for word from the morning news. Shortly before midnight Mrs. Florence Cavanaugh, a housewife living at 7 Alyssum Terrace, Cutter's Grove, was about to close the curtains in her front room when she saw, peering through the window at her, what she described as "a large Negro man wearing a gas mask or scuba outfit." Mrs. Cavanaugh, who was dressed only in her nightgown, fell back from the window and screamed for her husband, asleep in the next room, but by the time he arrived the Negro had made good his escape.

Local police favor the "scuba" theory, since near the window they've discovered footprints that may have been made by a heavy man in swim fins. But they haven't been able to explain why anyone would wear underwater gear so many miles from water.

The report usually concludes with the news that "Mr. and Mrs. Cavanaugh could not be reached for comment."

The reason I have taken such an interest in the case—sufficient, anyway, to memorize the above details—is that I know the Cavanaughs rather well. They are my next-door neighbors.

Call it an aging writer's ego, if you like, but somehow I can't help thinking that last evening's visit was meant for me. These little green bungalows all look alike in the dark.

Well, there's still a little night left outside—time enough to rectify the error. I'm not going anywhere.

I think, in fact, it will be a rather appropriate end for a man of my pursuits—to be absorbed into the denouement of another man's tale.

> Grow old along with me,
> The best is yet to come.

Tell me, Howard: how long before it's my turn to see the black face pressed to my window?

Love's Eldritch Ichor

ESTHER M. FRIESNER

From the Desk of Marybeth Conran, Editor-in-Chief, Columbine Press, Inc.

August 3, 1990

Dear Ms. Pickman,

Thank you *so* very much for your submission. While there will undoubtedly be one or two details which may need some editorial adjustment in your final draft, for the most part I find the outline and sample chapters from your proposed romance novel, *Fires on the Sea*, to be just the sort of thing Columbine Press wants to publish. We are prepared to offer you a $1200 advance against royalties, details as outlined in the enclosed contracts. Please sign all three copies and return them to me at your earliest possible convenience.

Much as I would *love* to edit your wonderful book myself, my duties as editor-in-chief here at Columbine Press will not allow me to give your work the time and attention it deserves. I am *devastated*, especially since I was the one to "discover" your manuscript on the recommendation of our mutual acquaintance, Mr. Charles Dexter Ward.

Within the week you will hear from Mr. Robin Pennyworth, the editor who will be working most closely with you in seeing *Fires on the Sea* into print. Like myself, Mr. Pennyworth *lives* for the discovery of exciting new talent in the romance field. I can't tell you how anxiously he is looking forward to working with you.

Very truly yours,
Marybeth Conran

P.S. Just a suggestion regarding the *nom de plume* under which you submitted the manuscript. Certainly we here at Columbine Press have no objections to pen names—most of our authors prefer to use them for whatever reason—but they must be appropriate to the genre. The last name you have chosen is utterly perfect—our readers would concur with you that love *is* a craft as well as an art. However, while the use of first- and middle-name initials is all very well for female science-fiction writers, romance readers prefer to know their favorite author's full name, and the more feminine-sounding the better.

Honoria Paige Lovecraft?

Heather Phyllis?

Hester Prynne?

I'm certain that you and Mr. Pennyworth will be able to come up with something.

Robin Pennyworth caught himself chewing the tip of his thumb again. Something about these weekly editorial meetings with Ms. Conran always aggravated his urge toward self-cannibalization.

Perhaps, he rationalized, *I'm trying to eradicate my own finger-prints so that when I finally do pick up something hefty and bash in Marybeth's skull, they'll never be able to pin the rap on me.* In his heart, he knew he had about as much chance of acting out these homicidally macho thoughts as of opening a Budweiser bottle with his teeth. Sooner would the Velveteen Rabbit go Rambo. Meetings with Ms. Conran only made him desperate to hide somewhere— anywhere!—even if only inside his own digestive tract.

What would the Lavender Ogress have in store for him this time? The mind boggled, then screamed and hid under the sofa. Waiting for the meeting to start was almost as bad as the torture session itself. Ms. Conran liked to play hardball with the psyches of her editorial under-lings. Her favorite method was to name a meeting time, then leave them to cool their heels for a half-hour minimum in the ghastly bread-mold-and-gristle-colored waiting area outside the conference room.

Robin did not handle tension well. He had been forced to quit his last editorial position at March or Die Books when reading too many espionage/suspense manuscripts gave him chronic vertigo and nose-bleeds. So far today Ms. Conran had kept everyone waiting nigh onto a full hour. This augured more than a few strychnine-laced surprises to be hand-fed to the editorial staff at the meeting proper. Ms. Conran always *did* have her little ways.

Robin gnawed faster, a cold sweat dampening his brow. Three hours spent that morning with blow-drier and mousse went to hell in a hand-basket as his carefully coiffed locks were infected by rampaging mole-cules of raw panic. In a brief, unequal struggle, his hair went limp as month-old lettuce. He brushed clammy blond bangs out of his eyes and stared at the closed conference-room door, willing it to go away.

Despite half a week's salary spent on self-actualization tapes, the unleashed powers of Robin's mind didn't change squat, except for giving him a baby migraine. The door stayed where it was, finally opening when Ms. Conran's secretary announced that the meeting was about to begin. There was a dovelike rustling of papers and a 'gatorish snapping of leather portfolios all around Robin as the other editors gathered up their things and filed in. They were actually *smiling*, the beasts! Why was he the only man among them who felt as if he were being marched aboard a Roman galley, chained at wrist, neck, and ankle?

Maybe because he was the only man among them.

Robin's coworkers jostled for the seats nearest Ms. Conran's throne of office while he hung back, content to shrivel into the most insignificant position available. People who knew him well often remarked that here was a man who made Yorkshire terriers seem emotionally stable. In saying so, they wronged the terriers. Robin Pennyworth might have nerves tauter than size 3 Spandex shorts on a size 10 rock star, but he also had a wonderful array of self-preservation devices.

He would need them.

The meeting went about as well as Robin's second-worst nightmares predicted. Ms. Conran used flip-charts the way a seasoned ninja used his *shurikens*. One by one the vapid smiles were sliced away as Robin's female colleagues received swift, cold shots to the heart in the form of sales reports, input on returns, bad reviews, and the arcane, occult, mystic, dread, and horripilating "Word from Upstairs." Not one man-jack (or woman-jill) among them but had championed a title that had failed to perform up to snuff. *Snuff* was now the operative word in Ms. Conran's gently upcurving mouth, referring to the fate of their several editorial futures.

Every time Ms. Conran mentioned "the numbers" on someone else's book, Robin cringed. It was a reflex, rather like the way Transylvanian peasants crossed themselves and cast a weather-eye on the garlic supply whenever someone took the name of the local neighborhood vampire in vain. Through all this terrifying litany of shortfalls, letdowns, and documented financial failures, he alone remained unscathed. For some reason, this was no comfort. Rather his continued immunity made him ever antsier as the meeting wore on and bodies toppled every which way around him. Only by crushing his favorite nibbling finger in a grip of steel did he manage to keep from chowing down on it up to the wrist in Ms. Conran's very presence. And then . . .

"Now Robin, dear—" *El momento de la verdad*, as Hemingway would say. Hemingway also would have disdained to use Robin Pennyworth as shark chum.

Robin gave a yip and a badly restrained jump in his seat as Ms. Conran swerved her beady gaze to rest upon him at last. Exquisitely applied makeup and three pairs of false eyelashes notwithstanding, Marybeth Conran's benign countenance still made Robin think of a king cobra with prickly heat.

"Yes, Ms. Conran?" he replied, controlling the instinct to cut and run all the way back to Des Moines (provided he survived his planned leap out the window nearest him). *They can smell fear,* he told himself, mentally clinging to his mantra like a drowning man.

"Robin, I'd like to take this chance to compliment you. Our sales force tells me that buyer response to *Silk Seduction*, *Satin Sins* and *Velvet Voluptuary* has been too utterly delicious. The way you handled Jasmine O'Hara's books is an example to us all. *Isn't* it?" She stared meaningly at the other editors.

They stared just as meaningly at Robin, who felt his veins fill with freon. Flawlessly lipsticked mouths that moments past had all been dutifully puckered, ready to kiss whatever Ms. Conran specified, were now drawn back into rigid little *ricti* baring wicked teeth. Long, sharp acrylic nails drummed Robin's funeral dirge on the tabletop. The autodefenestration plan was looking better by the nanosecond.

"And so"—Ms. Conran steepled her fingers daintily—"I have decided to put *you* in charge of Columbine Press's latest discovery, Ms. Sarah Pickman. I would like to see you privately after the meeting to discuss specific plans."

"Yes, Ms. Conran," Robin said dully.

"Good. Any new business?" Her voice gave it to be known that there had better not be. "Good. Now let's all see if we can't do better by next week, hm?" She rose, and the editors scattered before her like geese in a cyclone.

Shortly later, alone with Ms. Conran in her office, Robin listened fascinated as his boss briefed him on certain aspects of the Pickman file which were most emphatically *not* for dissemination.

"*No* publishing experience whatsoever. Precious little experience of any sort at all, truth to tell. I've never met the girl myself, but Chuckie Ward assures me that she's led a life that makes Emily Dickinson's look like the Playmate of the Year's by comparison."

Robin blushed. Ms. Conran was so wrapped up in dishing out the details of Sarah Pickman's bizarre background that she didn't notice.

"—raised in some godforsaken Yankee white trash town called Arkham, where I suppose the main industry is marrying your sister, and never went *anywhere* else. She even went to school right there: Miskatonic. Chuckie swears up and down that it's an actual *University*! I never heard of it, of course."

Robin could understand Ms. Conran's scorn for Miskatonic. She made damn sure that everyone who worked at Columbine Press knew that she herself had attended Vassar, completing the ever-popular interdisciplinary major, English Literature for the Hermetically Sealed Mind. It must have been difficult for her to imagine higher education existing anywhere outside the cosmopolitan whirl of Poughkeepsie.

"She came right straight home after graduation, and there she stayed. Went nowhere, saw nothing. Chuckie even claims she holed up in a shuttered room at the top of the old family pesthole for *ages*—but then, Chuckie can be *such* a tease." Her eyes sparkled avidly as she arched one playful brow at Robin "You *do* see what all this means to us, don't you, dear boy?"

Robin gulped down the truth, but it stuck in his throat. "Not—not as well as I'd like to, Ms. Conran."

Ms. Conran, triumphant, shoved a signed copy of the contract for *Fires on the Sea* across the desk. Robin read it, his eyes growing wider by the clause. Done, he looked up.

"*Twelve hundred dollars?*" His voice achieved orbit. "For a *whole* advance?"

"Payable on publication, no less. And *we* get to keep subsidiary rights!" Ms. Conran all but slurped and smacked her lips. "Every last one. *Plus* an airtight option clause. No other publisher can so much as look at one of Sarah Pickman's used Kleenex tissues before we do."

"I take it she has no agent."

"Amazing deduction, Robin. Where *do* you get such stupendous powers of insight?" Ms. Conran's talons wrung the neck of an invisible pigeon. "Yes, you are correct: Ms. Pickman has no agent. What agent with more than Tinkertoys for brains would negotiate a deal like that? One payment of twelve hundred dollars *on signing*, one *on submission of the complete manuscript, and one on our acceptance* of the book—well, *that* would still be niggardly, but at least it would make more sense."

"Like the deal Jasmine O'Hara's agent just proposed for her next book, *Damask Deception*," Robin commented. "Only he wants three payments of twelve *thousand*." The numbers on O'Hara books being what they were, he'd get it, too.

Ms. Conran's eyes got small. "Jasmine O'Hara's agent." The words were bile. "The agent little Miss *Rayon Rape* got herself when she stopped being so bloody grateful to have *anyone* look twice at *Denim Doo-Doo* and realized that we mean business. One day she's a dowdy little Kmart cashier from Grand Rapids, whose *real* name is Ethel Bukowski, and the next she's a shark; a shark with the smarts to hire one of the best lampreys in the business to represent her!"

Marybeth Conran plucked the gold Mark Cross pencil from her desk set and snapped it in half as if it were a toothpick. "If Jasmine O'Hara only had stayed just as sweet—and stupid—as she was, I can't begin to tell you how many yumsy deals we might have milked out of her before she woke up. Writers with the talent and exploitation potential of Ethel 'Flannel Flatulence' Bukowski are no common commodity. We lost our chance with her." She sighed. "You don't often get second chances in publishing, Robin."

The way she looked at him when she said that spoke volumes, with all sequels and book-club sale rights included. Suddenly Robin knew that he was a man with a mission, and he knew just what that mission was.

"I'm supposed to make sure that Sarah Pickman never does wake up," he stated.

"Bingo."

August 18, 1990

Dear Ms. Pickman,

I'm *so* glad to hear that our Mr. Pennyworth has expressed such immediate enthusiasm for your work-in-progress. I knew I was doing the right thing by entrusting your fabulous book to him. I do so hope that you will place as much trust in him as I do.

Please excuse my earlier assumptions with regard to your pen name. I had no idea that *Fires on the Sea* was not entirely your own creation, but based on the work of a deceased distant relative under whose actual name you chose to submit the book. How thrilling for you to have discovered all of those charming manuscripts in that quaint old trunk in your family's attic room! No wonder you were able to provide us with the complete text of *Fires* so quickly.

Mr. Pennyworth informs me that you have expressed some doubts about appropriating and adapting your ancestor's work for the romance market. Your scruples are admirable, if misdirected. If you had not used Ms. Lovecraft's text as the basis for our novel, *Fires on the Sea* would have languished as unknown as its first authoress. What a loss to us all that would have been!

Do let's keep the truth about your deceased relative our little secret. Once we have established Lovecraft as one of the leading names in Romance, the publicity resulting from eventual revelation of the authoress's true identity should generate scads of reader interest. I know that you will come to look upon this, as I do, as both tribute and homage to the too-long-neglected artistic gifts of the late Ms. Lovecraft.

There are a few questions Mr. Pennyworth has brought to my attention concerning *Fires*. He has already underscored many words which he feels are just too complex for our readers. This in no way implies that our audience is uneducated! For the most part they are bright, successful young careerwomen who turn to Columbine Press books for a brief respite from the demands of the workaday world.

I'm certain you understand that they just don't want to be bothered looking up words like "tesselated" and "batrachian." *Could* you see your way clear to meeting our Mr. Pennyworth in Boston so that the two of you could work out these little glitches together? He is awfully eager to make your acquaintance and establish the working arrangement of mutual trust, respect, honesty, and integrity that is the basis of every writer-editor relationship.

Best,
Marybeth Conran

P.S. You *are* quite sure that you are Ms. Lovecraft's only living relative? We wouldn't want any *contretemps* to fuss our Legal Department later on, would we?

By the bye, what *is* her full name? Here's hoping it's something divinely romantic! Hesper Pegeen? Henriette Patricia? Do tell!

For the twentieth time in as many minutes, Robin Pennyworth tried to make himself comfortable on the dented aluminum bench. The plastic dome overhead was supposed to shelter anyone unlucky enough to be caught waiting at the bus stop; it didn't. It had more holes in it than poor Ms. Pickman's contract. He pulled up the collar of his raincoat, shivering miserably in the oily drizzle. Although Labor Day was more than a week away, he felt as if he'd stepped into the bleak heart of November the instant he'd stepped off that bus and onto the main street of Arkham.

Main Street! There's a laugh! he thought, in no mood for laughter. It was Saturday afternoon, but not one of the stores was open. There was nowhere for him to take shelter from the rain, nowhere for him to go, and no way for him to escape until Monday, when the next bus back to Boston passed through this pig-piddle of a town.

Freely he cursed himself, Ms. Conran, and Ms. Pickman: Ms. Conran for insisting he meet with Ms. Pickman; Ms. Pickman for being just as insistent that she couldn't possibly deal with the fluster and expense of a trip to Boston; himself for gallantly offering to visit Ms. Pickman on her home turf instead. Her acceptance was so ecstatic it almost leaped off the page and licked his face. She gave detailed driving directions, but in case he would rather use public transportation she included train and plane schedules to Boston, bus schedules to Arkham, and the promise to pick him up promptly on arrival at the depot. Depot! There was another laugh for him, if he had the heart left to take it. Well, here he was at the so-called *depot*, but where was Ms. Pickman?

The rain wasn't heavy, but it was cold and determined to break his spirit. That would be easy: there were sea cucumbers born with more intestinal fortitude than Robin Pennyworth. He could feel the heebie-jeebies inching farther up his shins with every drop of rain that oozed down the back of his neck. In desperation for any kind of distraction, he stood and paced up and down the broken pavement, gazing morosely into the grimy shop windows.

Most of Arkham's merchants appeared to be in the cobweb trade. The only storefront holding anything of interest was the travel agency. That figured. Robin knew that if he had to live in a place like Arkham, his every ambition would be focused on getting the hell out. He stared at dusty brochures for exotic destinations: Fiji, Aruba, Club Med Leng, Sunken R'ly— *What* did that last folder say? Though he wiped the rain from his glasses, he still couldn't make it out and soon gave up.

Farther up the street he saw the white marquee of a movie theater, a kindled beacon against the gloomy weather. Now *that* made sense. If you couldn't escape Arkham one way, you could always fly out on Imagination Airlines. He hurried toward the lights, only to stop when he saw that the ticket seller's window was deserted, the first show not scheduled to start until eight that night. There were no posters to tell him what was playing, and when he tilted his head back to read the marquee he saw that most of the letters were missing:

THE   NECR   OMIC N!
W YNE NEWT N DE BY BOONE LYMPIA D KAK S
You L ved T e Bo k, Now Se   The Movie!

"Mr. Pennyworth?"

Robin felt his heart try for a new pole-vault record. He spun around so fast he got a return attack of his old March or Die Books vertigo. His vision swam, but still he managed to identify the speaker: a young woman behind the wheel of a car that was three parts rust to one part vehicle.

"Oh! Did I startle you? I'm so sorry." She was out of the car and at his side with a fluid grace Robin had only seen in his childhood collection of tropical fish, before his mother claimed that algae aggravated his allergies and flushed the lot of them.

Suddenly, the universe stood up on its hind legs and barked like a seal. The world slipped from its axis and executed a beerhouse polka across the cosmos. Shy and gentle hormones, long wrapped in the tender sleep of ages, opened their drowsy eyes within the secret places of Robin Pennyworth's body, put lampshades on their heads, turned on MTV, and ordered out for *dim sum*. The heavens opened up and glad-handed an indifferent earth with the joy-buzzer of Love.

Robin gasped. *Why . . . she's beautiful.* His lips were dry, his eyes moist, his palms damp, and his feet soaking wet. The relative humidity no longer concerned him. He could only gaze, enchanted, upon the face and form of Ms. Pickman.

No one could accuse Sarah Pickman of being a model of conventional beauty. Even the besotted young editor had to admit that her physical attractions were not cut from the standard mold. No, the mold from which she had sprung was of another sort altogether.

"Mr. Pennyworth? Are you—are you quite well?" Ms. Pickman laid a solicitous hand on Robin's sleeve. "I'm sorry to be so late, but I had another of those awful altercations with the terrible old man who lives next door to us. I came as soon as I could. Won't you—?" She indicated that he should get into the car.

All the way out to the Pickman house, Robin sat like one who dreams, and in dreams quests for something unknown, yet earnestly desired. In vain did Ms. Pickman mention the many points of local interest they passed on their drive. The brooding towers of Miskatonic University elicited as little response from her enamored swain as did the Black Goat of the Woods Dairy Farm.

At last the ancient car took a sharp turn off the main road and began to climb a badly potholed and rutted street. The rain had stopped, and a thick white mist clung to the windows. Higher and higher they climbed. Robin wondered how his fair conductress could see her hand in front of her face under such conditions. True, it was a hand rather . . . *wider* than the norm; longer as well as wider, with the most enchanting little webs of translucent skin between the fingers.

Ms. Pickman's eyes were equally extraordinary, albeit they protruded perhaps a *smidgen* more than the currently acceptable "look" for women. Robin gave a mental snort. What traitorous thoughts were these, to expect his newfound ladylove to truckle to hollow aesthetic trends? If Brooke Shields could set a new fashion for Sasquatch eyebrows, why couldn't Ms. Pickman do the same for eyes that were— *what* was the word he sought? And why did he keep thinking of Kermit the Frog?

Wonderful eyes! The thicker and more impenetrable the miasma surrounding the vehicle, the rounder they seemed to get. Indeed, they appeared to glow with an alien luminescence, although Robin shrugged this observation aside as the fanciful imaginings of his passion-pummeled heart. He took full advantage of her concentration on the road to pay her silent worship.

"*Here* we are!" Ms. Pickman's exclamation of victory and relief shattered Robin's tender dream of love. She leaped from the car with that same ichthyous grace which had first captivated him. He did his clumsy best to scramble after.

His first sight of the Pickman residence froze him in his tracks.

The strange high house in the mist loomed above them. Robin had never seen a gambrel roof before, especially not one with a Garfield wind sock hanging from the eaves. The clapboard walls were speckled with unwholesome fungoid growths whose very forms bespoke an age-less, dreaming evil from before the dawn of Time; especially the patch of phosphorescent mildew just under the front windows in the shape of Papa Smurf. The chill, malevolent eyes of the plastic flamingos on the lawn fixed upon his every move, and their sinister painted beaks whispered of the black and terrible voids between the stars where even now, Elvis might still be alive.

Every healthy instinct for survival screamed for Robin to flee. But there was Ms. Pickman, silhouetted in the open doorway, beckoning to him.

"I can't tell you how much I appreciate your coming all this way to help me with my book, Mr. Pennyworth," she breathed. "Now, you come right inside and take off those wet things." As she stepped from sight, he could just barely hear her add, "You can get a fantastic view of the Arkham Megamall from the attic, if I can manage to get those silly old shutters pried open."

He could do no more than follow where his heart led. The door slammed shut behind him with dreadful finality.

Somewhere a nameless horror gibbered.

August 30, 1990

Dear Ms. Pickman:

Your letter of the 20th was such a wonderful surprise. To think that our Mr. Pennyworth was instrumental in persuading you to visit New York! All of us here at Columbine Press are looking forward to welcoming you on your first trip to the "Big Apple."

You mention that you will be accompanied by some old family connections, in the capacity of chaperones. How perfectly charming and Old World-y of you! Their expressed concern for your safety here is laudable, if unnecessary. I trust that all of you will soon see that New York is not *quite* the hotbed of vice and crime that the more sensationalism-minded newspapers paint it to be.

When you do arrive, I hope we can settle the last few miniscule quibbles I have with the manuscript of *Fires on the Sea* which Mr. Pennyworth brought back from your first meeting. I am still enchanted by the book's setting. The sleepy little port of Innsmouth is *so* small-town America, and therefore so perfect for reader-identification. If torrid passions can blaze in Innsmouth, there may be hope for Buffalo.

I also *adore* your mysterious sea-captain hero. Who'd have thought a name like Uriah Whateley could be so sexy? But it is! I can just picture Richard Chamberlain in the part, come blockbuster mini-series time.

My quibble is with your heroine—or should I say the late Ms. Lovecraft's heroine? (I still think of *Fires* as *your* book.) As you can see from the enclosed Writers' Guidelines, strong reader-empathy with the heroine is a must. I just can't see enough of our readers identifying with Captain Whateley's exotic South Seas bride. Could you rewrite her into the role of the "other woman" and have him courting one of the local girls instead? Maybe Lavinia Gilman? And while you're making those little changes on the Polynesian lady, could you please do something about her *teeth*?

I am very surprised that our Mr. Pennyworth did not make a similar suggestion to you. He usually has a keen eye for such things. But then, he has not been in the best of health since his return from Arkham.

I am looking forward to meeting you soon.

                                                                Best,
                                                                Marybeth

Robin Pennyworth closed his eyes, gritted his teeth, and tried to think of Sarah. It didn't work any better than those hokey self-actualization tapes. Ms. Conran remained behind the desk, at the helm, and on his ass.

"—all the stupid ideas you've ever had—!" Gone was the smile, the insinuating charm, all mention of his previous successes with the O'Hara *Fabric and Flagrante Delicto* series. No sooner had the polished toe of his Italian wing tip crossed her threshold, but Marybeth Conran gave him to know that he had been demoted from *dear boy* to *dog meat*.

"—*and* her goddam chaperones for me to feed! *Chaperones!* No wonder the sex scenes in *Fires* suck dead seagulls."

Robin puffed out his chest, trying to look formidable. It didn't work. Even sitting down, Ms. Conran was a head taller than he. With all the dignity he could muster, Robin replied, "*I* thought she handled those scenes very well."

"If that's all she handled." Ms. Conran had a nasty chuckle, the sort of laugh capable of assuming an independent existence of pinching beachboys and stuffing sawbucks down the front of Chippendale's dancers' working togs.

"Ms. Conran, what are you implying?" Robin felt his blotchy complexion flame a uniform lobster-red.

The disreputable chuckle returned, accompanied by a vulgar snicker it had picked up in a dockside bar. "Oh, nothing, Robin. Not a thing; except that *someone* in this room called into the office from Arkham to take *five* vacation days all of a sudden. *Five*!"

Robin pursed his lips. "There were a number of questions I had to resolve with Ms. Pickman concerning her book. I thought that as long as I was there already—"

"Oh, no, darling; that won't wash. You're also the bright boy who convinced our Ms. Pickman to come to New York. *After* she summoned that precious coterie of *chaperones* from the nethermost pit of Hell!"

Robin startled. "How did you know where they came—?"

Ms. Conran ignored him, on a full-scale rant. "You can't fool me, Robin. *I* know what's what. The only creature more starved for passion than a Romance reader is a Romance writer. Clever Robin, to seize the opportunity. Heaven knows, you mustn't get too many of them. I could almost find it in me to pity the poor child. If everything Chuckie Ward tells me is true, she's led a life of such isolation that when *you* stumbled into her life, no wonder she mistook you for a man."

No spectrograph in the world could accurately chart the rapid ebb and flow of colors that washed over Robin Pennyworth's face. He went so far as to show his teeth to Ms. Conran in something other than a sycophantic smile. "That's—that's a l—a piece of disinformation! Ms. Pickman and I are in love!"

The moment he said it, he wished he had the power to retroactively cut out his tongue and feed it to the formless abominations that wallowed in the primordial ooze of some blue-litten abyss and were allergic to pizza.

Ms. Conran's lips tilted upward with the lazy grace of a python in a locked chicken coop. "Love? Is that it, dear boy? Is that why the shy and retiring Ms. Pickman agreed to come to New York after all, when the thought of *Boston* once scared her out of her miniscule mind? To be with the man of her dreams?" Ms. Conran's voice went sharply from molasses taffy to *A Night on Bald Mountain*. "To allow her to talk to *other writers*? To introduce her to *agents*? Even, dare I say, *to show that petticoated snip what a* real *book contract should look like!*"

Robin's tongue, still in place, was rendered useless by Ms. Conran's tirade. Finally he was able to regain control of it long enough to stammer, "I—I never—I—I guess this means I'm fired?"

Anger spent, Ms. Conran folded her hands and gave Robin a smile that peeled his neurons raw. "Hardly," she purred. She came from behind her desk, and as she spoke, she began to pace the dhurrie in gradually expanding helices that brought her subtly nearer to her prey.

"Really, Robin, if I fired everyone who made an itsy-bitsy *faux pas*, however would I explain to Ms. Smith why there was no one at the Christmas party?" Even Marybeth Conran's normally unassailable calm quivered to the roots at mention of Ms. Clarissa Ashley Smith, publisher and avatar of Columbine Press.

"Then you understand—?" Robin could scarcely believe it. Visions of his head on a cartoon chopping block faded.

By this, Ms. Conran was close enough to drape her arm around his shoulders. "Certainly. Provided that we clean up the little mess we've made. I just reread *Fires on the Sea* this morning. If the torchlight dance on the reef scene doesn't rope in the readers, I'll go back to editing *Elves with Really Big Swords* trilogies."

Robin could feel Destiny pressing down upon his shoulders with an even heavier hand than Ms. Conran's. His guts told him not to listen to another word from his diabolical mentor's mouth; rather to square his shoulders, stiffen his upper lip, and tell the lady just where she could stick her trilogies. Alas for the heroic gesture, he was a man in love, and as such had given bound and wriggling human sacrifices to Fortune. Suddenly job security had become intrinsically tied to dreams of the tastefully small wedding, the rose-covered condo, the pitter-patter and slap-slap-slap of little feet. He could not go through with it.

"What do you want me to do, Ms. Conran?" he asked.

She smiled.

Sarah Pickman sat primly on the edge of the hotel bed, reading a note that her Robin had left for her at the front desk. Her accommodations had been selected on the basis of economy alone, and would give Leona Helmsley a case of the screaming pips. Most of the decorative accessories had been bolted to the nearest convenient surface, although it was difficult to visualize anyone wanting to steal them. Perhaps the establishment's owner was anticipating the advent of the occasional guest with taste, who might try to remove the bulbous lamp, the sappy "art" print, or the mutant swan-and-potato-shaped ashtray in order to give them decent burial. The room's minimal charms were further diminished by the fact that the special New York godling in charge of Optimized Tourist Aggravation had caused the air-conditioning to die on the hottest Labor Day weekend in ages. The room was cramped, ugly, sweltering, suffocating, nearly lightless, and a miasma of nauseous smells.

"Ahhhh," Great Cthulhu sighed, stretching out in the bathtub. "All the comforts of home."

"Sshhh." Sarah laid a finger to her lips. "I'm trying to read."

"Read it out loud," came a voice from the closet. "And *good* and loud. These damned shoggoths are making so much noise I can hardly hear myself gibber."

"Why do you need to know what's in Sarah's mail?" Great Cthulhu shot back.

"Oh, *that's* right." The thing in the closet uttered a sarcastic snort. "Nobody has to know anything around here but Great Cthulhu. Nobody can take a little healthy interest in what Sarah's doing or who she's seeing but you, right, you bet, sure. Who am I to ask one little question about the things that matter to her? I'm just Nyarlathotep, that's all. You got a message for one of the Great Old Ones, then right away it's 'Yo, Nyarlathotep! Lookin' goo, homeboy! You wanna take this message to Azathoth at the center of all infinity and see if you can get him to stop bubbling and blaspheming long enough to give me a straight answer for a change?' Sure, when it's neither-snow-nor-rain-nor-fungi-from-Yuggoth time, *then* it's anything I want. But the minute I'm off-duty it's 'Shove him in the closet with the shoggoths!' You ever been stuck with a bunch of shoggoths any length of time? Do you know how damned many knock-knock jokes they tell? Do you?"

A squamous tentacle whipped out the bathroom door, flicked open the closet, and jabbed inside. A pained yelp responded, then silence.

Great Cthulhu made a world-weary sound midway between *tsk-tsk* and *n'ha'ghaa*. "Nobody likes a *kvetcher*, Nyarlathotep," he said.

"I don't mind reading this aloud," Sarah said, raising meek eyes toward the open bathroom door. "It does concern all of us."

Great Cthulhu waved one paw and a selection of tentacles at her in a gesture of regal munificence. "Proceed."

Sarah cleared her throat and did so: " 'September 2, 1990—

" 'My darling Sarah!

" 'Oh, my beloved girl, was it just minutes ago that you and I clasped hands above the brioches? Some call it brunch; I call it Heaven. Anyplace is Heaven, to my eyes, if you are there.' "

The closet gave a nasty titter. "Clearly a man who's never been to sunken R'lyeh for the I ♥ Dagon Festival."

Sarah shushed him and went on. " 'Our eyes sought each other with a hunger that could not be denied. My lips thirsted to drink love's rapturous bliss from those delicious lips of yours. My whole being longed to enfold your adorable form in an eternal embrace which—' "

"Are you sure you want to read this out loud?" Great Cthulhu came out of the bathroom, all the towels and a bedspread wrapped around his waist.

"No, no, let her read!" Nyarlathotep called from the closet. "This is getting good."

"This is getting *personal*." Very much on his dignity, the Great Old One flushed a rosy red to the tips of his tentacles.

"Yah! Cthulhu's a pru-ude, Cthulhu's a pru-ude!" Nyarlathotep's singsong taunt was taken up by a mixed shoggoth chorus, with a few dholes chiming in to chant bass.

"Now that will be enough of *that*." Sarah waggled an admonishing finger at the closet. "If I don't see some improvement in the general level of behavior around here, I'm not taking any of you with me to visit Red Hook tomorrow."

The threat worked on Nyarlathotep, who stopped teasing Great Cthulhu and commenced whining about how it wasn't *fair*, that *he* was being nice as pie, that *some* people he could mention ate the bellhop and tried to blame it on others.

Sarah confronted Cthulhu, shocked. "You *ate* the bellhop?"

The Great Old One looked shamefaced. "It seemed the easiest thing to do at the time. I never know how much to tip them, so—" Abruptly, he went on the offensive. "Anyhow, I don't need *you* to take me to Red Hook. *I* am privy to the secret passageways of sunken R'lyeh. *I* have flown between the cosmic gulfs of Eblis. *I* have inscribed arcane and eldritch graffiti upon the walls of Eryx. *I* have howled obscenities at alien moons and stalked the witch-haunted streets of—"

"*You* have never taken the subway to Brooklyn," Sarah said, putting paid to all the dread Ancient One's posturings. "Now would you *please* pay attention to what Robin writes? This concerns us all."

Having restored order and maintained authority, Sarah Pickman skipped over several further paragraphs of Robin's most empurpled prose and finally arrived at:

" '—it is therefore with the deepest sorrow that I must now urge you to return to Arkham, my darling. You must know how every moment out of sight of those delectably batrachian orbs of yours is like a dagger through my heart—' "

"He'd better be referring to your eyes," Great Cthulhu muttered. "Orbs indeed."

" '—and yet I will make the sacrifice because it is for your own good. New York is in truth a monstrous and chaotic wasteland of nighted monoliths, their insane angles answering only to a hideous and unwholesome geometry whose origins are not of this world. You know what I mean; you saw *Batman*. And can I, solely for the selfish gratification of my own desires, ask you to spend any more time than needful in this quagmire of hellish horror? No, for your welfare is infinitely more precious to me.

" 'Go then, my love, but go with the knowledge that our parting will be a brief one. Could I live were it not so? Ms. Conran has promised me a raise and a promotion in the near future, to coincide with the publication date of *Fires on the Sea*. When that happy event transpires, I will at last be able to ask you the question nearest my heart. Dare I hope your answer will be . . . "Yes"? Your Robin.' "

Sarah folded the letter and laid it in her lap. Her eyes filled with tears, her thin lips trembled. In a quaking voice she asked, "Well, what do you make of that?"

From the air shaft just outside the room's only window, an answer came: "If you want my opinion, the little bastard's giving you the old heave-ho. Breaking off the relationship. Looking for more 'personal space.' Initiating a cooling-off period. *El dumpo supremo.* Giving you the gate. Sending you pack—"

"Shut up, Hastur," Great Cthulhu directed. "For someone who's so damned proud of being called 'the Unspeakable,' you could do us all a favor and try to be 'the Unspeaking' too. Who devolved to primal ooze and made you the big expert on personal space?"

"You kidding? In the midnight abyss where the black stars hang we got nothing *but* personal space!"

Sore pressed, Sarah at last gave in to the urge to sob. Her grief immediately turned the Great Old Ones' attention from their petty squabbles. Great Cthulhu himself slid a paw and two tentacles around the girl's heaving shoulders.

"There, there, baby. Don't you waste another thought on that creep. You're too good for him. Want me to eat him?"

Sarah shook her head emphatically. "Don't you see? This letter isn't *right*! It doesn't sound like Robin at all. He loves me—I know he does—and he wouldn't ask me to go back to Arkham just like that. It was all his idea that we come to New York. He said there were lots of things I ought to learn about publishing firsthand. Why would he change so radically, so suddenly? Something's the matter. Something has forced him to write this letter; some influence of abhorred and acherontic evil."

"Hey! Don't look at me!" Nyarlathotep protested. "I was out walking the Hounds of Tindalos all morning."

"Give me the letter," Great Cthulhu said. He held the paper up to the light, inhaled its distinctive fragrance, and munched on one corner of the Columbine Press stationery before rendering his verdict. "Yes, Sarah, you are correct. There is great evil at work here, a horror of unspeakable proportions, an abomination of such grotesque depravity as to send the sane mind reeling madly down the nightmare corridors of—"

"Get *on* with it, blubber-breath!" Hastur heckled from the air shaft.

"Go kiss Tsathoggua, you refugee from a Carl Sagan special," Cthulhu responded. "You're just pissed because I got a double-column entry in *De Vermis Mysteriis* and the only reason you got that one lousy paragraph in the *Necronomicon* was because you sent Abbie Alhazred those five dancing girls and a fruit basket."

"Ghouls and dholes may drink our souls, but names will never hurt me!" Hastur shot back.

"Please, Great Old One," Sarah said, laying a hand on Cthulhu's scaly forearm. "This unhallowed menace that has enslaved my Robin—can you vanquish it? Will you help us?"

"I don't know," the Ancient One admitted. "I can only try. I've never dealt with an editor-in-chief before."

* * *

Marybeth Conran checked the time on her Rolex and scowled. "It's almost ten o'clock. This had better be good," she said between gritted teeth.

Robin Pennyworth took his thumb out of his mouth long enough to reply, "I'm sorry, Ms. Conran. I honestly don't know any more about this meeting than you do. Sarah sent me word to stay after work tonight and report to your office at nine. I guess she told you the same?"

"She *requested* the same of me." Ms. Conran spoke in clipped tones that instantly conveyed the message, *There is only one party around here who* tells *other people what to do.* Columbine Press's editor-in-chief shuffled a stack of fax flimsies irritably. "She gave me to understand that she wishes to amend her contract."

Robin gulped burning air. "Ms. Conran, I swear I had nothing to do with that! I did just what you told me: I didn't let her near anyone who knows anything about publishing. I kept her busy. I urged her to go back to Arkham. In the short time she's been in the city, she couldn't have met a soul who'd tell her what a miserable—uh—unique contract she's got with us. Even if she did, there's no way she could renegotiate it and—"

"You're babbling, dear boy." Ms. Conran's expression was inscrutable. "A pity you *can't* claim credit for Ms. Pickman's notion to change our working agreement. You see, she has asked to meet with me in order to insert a clause requesting *no* advance monies to be paid on publication of *Fires*; or at any time, for that matter. Straight royalties all the way."

Robin shuddered for his naive beloved. Columbine Press had a reputation in the trade for the highest *per capita* rate of authors reduced to slobbering conniptions while trying to get a cogent royalty statement out of their Accounting Department. And as for extracting an actual check—? Rumor had it that by the time you saw your money, you'd have to cash the draft at the First National Bank of Doomsday.

"At least now I know why you hung around here so late, you old bat," he muttered.

"Did you say something, Robin?" Ms. Conran's eyes glittered with a cold red light. He was quick to assure her of his absolute and obedient silence. "Good." Her fingernail began to carve little notches on the edge of her desk blotter.

Ms. Conran had reduced the blotter to fringe before Robin calculated it was safe to make a fresh inquiry. "Um . . . did Sarah happen to explain *why* she wants to make that contract change?"

The question was shrugged aside. "Some silly Yankee work-ethic qualms about taking money she had not yet properly earned. You know, the scruples thing. You know me, Robin: *anything* to set our authors' minds at rest." She checked the Rolex again. "However, if that precious clot-brain bimbette of yours doesn't show up soon, I'm going to—"

There was a knock at the door.

"That's odd," Ms. Conran mused. "No one's supposed to be able to get up here at this hour without Security ringing us first. Who's there?" she called.

"Cthul!" came the answer.

"Cthul who?" Ms. Conran's logical response was greeted by much raucous merriment from the far side of the closed door. Chittering laughter came to an abrupt halt with the sound of many healthy cuffs, slaps, buffets, and upside-the-heads being meted out to the deserving.

"Stupid shoggoths," someone snarled.

"Who-is-*there*?" Ms. Conran bellowed. The door opened by degrees, and Sarah Pickman crept meekly into the royal presence.

Robin flew to her side at once and clasped her to him, heart pulsating with love's wild surrender. Her eyes held all passion's tender fury as their gazes met, and only sweet, savage sensibleness kept them from devouring each other with an onslaught of rapture's fiery kisses right in front of the dumbstruck and visibly queasy Ms. Conran.

Robin's superior coughed up a whole symphony of hem-haw noises before she could crowbar their attention away from each other. "I believe you wished to see me, Ms. Pickman?" Treacle hardened into crackling shells over her every word.

Sarah separated herself from Robin with the greatest reluctance and approached the throne, hand extended in fellowship. "I'm so pleased to meet you at last, Ms. Conran," she said, beaming.

"Mutual." Ms. Conran yanked open a drawer and slapped a copy of the infamous contract onto her desktop. "Robin can go out to my secretary's workstation and whip us up a cup of cappuccino while we make those contract changes you requested. It's rather late, Ms. Pickman, and I think we'll all feel so much better once we get this little business done and we can all go home. Especially since I believe you *will* be heading back to Arkham tomorrow?"

"Oh, not tomorrow." A twinkle touched Sarah's eyes, making them resemble sequined Ping-Pong balls.

"The day after, then. Such a shame. I did so want to show you a little of New York." It would have required radical cardiac surgery to make the invitation any more halfhearted. "Since you'll be leaving us so soon, I suppose I must also forgo the pleasure of meeting your chaperones."

"No, you won't." She turned gracefully toward the door. "Ahem. Iä. Iä! Yoo-hoo? Iä, everybody!"

The door swung wide, revealing an impossible avenue of cyclopean megaliths whose gleaming basalt surfaces were carved with cryptic writings of hideous significance. Faceless, misshapen creatures shambled between the pylons, while farther off in the distance, leprous forms gyred and capered in savage, degraded revelry.

"Good God," Ms. Conran breathed.

"Anyone out there seen a cappuccino-maker?" Robin piped.

And then, half-creeping, half-shuffling down that monumental way, there came the ultimate vision of noisome horror, lashing tentacles still draped with the clammy seaweeds of his sunken kingdom. Inexorably on and on he came, his hellish minions cavorting in his wake. Their blasphemous litany accompanied his progress until, at last, his sinister bulk overshadowed office, desk, and trembling Marybeth Conran.

"Hi," he said. "I'm Cthuhu. I tried to call, but I kept getting your stupid answering machine."

Marybeth fainted.

From the Desk of Clarissa Ashley Smith, Publisher, Columbine Press, Inc.

November 2, 1990

Dear Mr. Pennyworth:

I would like to thank you personally for taking over the duties of our former editor-in-chief, Marybeth Conran, during what was a period of grievous trial for all of us here at Columbine Press. In addition to covering her regular duties, as well as your own, you are to be commended for taking the bold, independent, and innovative step of rushing *Fires on the Sea* into print. Our salespeople inform me that buyer response is of such unprecedented magnitude and enthusiasm that Steel, Krantz, Plain, and Barker had best look to their laurels. From this day forward, Lovecraft will be a name with which to reckon.

In recognition of your contributions to the market success of Columbine Press, it is my pleasure to offer you the recently vacated position of Editor-in-Chief. It is my most earnest desire that you utilize your new situation to vigorously pursue additional fresh talent in the Romance field, hopefully on a par with that of Ms. Lovecraft herself.

The enclosed check represents your adjusted salary, plus a small token of my goodwill and best wishes to you and your new bride on the occasion of your marriage.

Sincerely,
Clarissa Ashley

P.S. I regret I do not have better news to pass on to you regarding the state of Ms. Conran's mental health. Her attending physicians at

Dunwich Hills Sanatorium inform me that when she is not whispering in darkness she is lurking on thresholds.

From the Desk of Robin Pennyworth, Editor-in-Chief, Columbine Press, Inc.

November 3, 1990

Dear Ms. Cromwell:

Thank you for submitting your historical romance, *The Barbarian's Woman*, to Columbine Press. We are all very excited by it and think it will be a significant contribution to the field. We are prepared to offer you a $10,000 advance against royalties, full terms explained in the enclosed contracts. Please sign all three copies and return them to us as soon as possible.

Of course you realize you will have to make a few minor changes in the manuscript, to meet the demands of a changing Romance market. Your heroine is made-to-order for our readership—a strong woman who is not afraid to say "No" to the wrong man—but her name suggests a Russian setting. Czarist, perhaps, or do you intend the sobriquet "Red" in its political sense? You could then have your Sonja use a troika whip instead of a broadsword to defend her virtue in the first scene. Not only would this be a more romantic, exotic, and ladylike weapon, but we can avoid any possible allegations of sexism likely to crop up in response to the term *broad*sword.

I do wish it were feasible for me to edit your delightful book myself, but my administrative obligations will not permit this, alas. Our Mr. Alhazred will give it the care and attention it deserves, being himself a writer as well as one of our best editors. I promise you, he is just mad about *The Barbarian's Woman*.

Very truly yours,
Robin Pennyworth

P.S. One more preliminary question about a detail in your manuscript, if I may: while I looked and looked for mention of a place-name you use, consulting the *Britannica and* the geographical listings in the *Unabridged*, it only shows up as an adjective. It sounds *so* familiar. I *think* I may have heard of a Trump resort located there, but correct me if I'm wrong.

Where *is* Stygia?

The Last Feast of Harlequin

THOMAS LIGOTTI

1.

My interest in the town of Mirocaw was first aroused when I heard that an annual festival was held there which promised to include, to some extent, the participation of clowns among its other elements of pageantry. A former colleague of mine, who is now attached to the anthropology department of a distant university, had read one of my recent articles ("The Clown Figure in American Media," *Journal of Popular Culture*), and wrote to me that he vaguely remembered reading or being told of a town somewhere in the state that held a kind of "Fool's Feast" every year, thinking that this might be pertinent to my peculiar line of study. It was, of course, more pertinent than he had reason to think, both to my academic aims in this area and to my personal pursuits.

Aside from my teaching, I had for some years been engaged in various anthropological projects with the primary ambition of articulating the significance of the clown figure in diverse cultural contexts. Every year for the past twenty years I have attended the pre-Lenten festivals that are held in various places throughout the southern United States. Every year I learned something more concerning the esoterics of celebration. In these studies I was an earlier participant—along with playing my part as an anthropologist, I also took a place behind the clownish mask myself. And I cherished this role as I did nothing else in my life. To me the title of Clown has always carried connotations of a noble sort. I was an adroit jester, strangely enough, and had always taken pride in the skills I worked so diligently to develop.

I wrote to the State Department of Recreation, indicating what information I desired and exposing an enthusiastic urgency which came naturally to me on this topic. Many weeks later I received a tan envelope imprinted with a government logo. Inside was a pamphlet that catalogued all of the various seasonal festivities of which the state was officially aware, and I noted in passing that there were as many in late autumn and winter as in the warmer seasons. A letter inserted within the pamphlet explained to me that, according to their voluminous records, no festivals held in the town of Mirocaw had been officially registered. Their files, nonetheless, could be placed at my disposal if I should wish to research this or similar matters in connection with some definite project. At the time this offer was made I was already laboring under so many professional and personal burdens that, with a weary hand, I simply deposited the envelope and its contents in a drawer, never to be consulted again.

Some months later, however, I made an impulsive digression from my responsibilities and, rather haphazardly, took up the Mirocaw project. This happened as I was driving north one afternoon in late summer with the intention of examining some journals in the holdings of a library at another university. Once out of the city limits the scenery changed to sunny fields and farms, diverting my thoughts from the signs that I passed along the highway. Nevertheless, the subconscious scholar in me must have been regarding these with studious care. The name of a town loomed into my vision. Instantly the scholar retrieved certain records from some deep mental drawer, and I was faced with making a few hasty calculations as to whether there was enough time and motivation for an investigative side trip. But the exit sign was even hastier in making its appearance, and I soon found myself leaving the highway, recalling the road sign's promise that the town was no more than seven miles east.

These seven miles included several confusing turns, the forced taking of a temporarily alternate route, and a destination not even visible until a steep rise had been fully ascended. On the descent another helpful sign informed me that I was within the city limits of Mirocaw. Some scattered houses on the outskirts of the town were the first structures I encountered. Beyond them the numerical highway became Townshend Street, the main avenue of Mirocaw.

The town impressed me as being much larger once I was within its limits than it had appeared from the prominence just outside. I saw that the general hilliness of the surrounding countryside was also an internal feature of Mirocaw. Here, though, the effect was different. The parts of the town did not look as if they adhered very well to one another. This condition might be blamed on the irregular topography of the town. Behind some of the old stores in the business district, steeply roofed houses had been erected on a sudden incline, their peaks appearing at an extraordinary elevation above the lower buildings. And because the foundations of these houses could not be glimpsed, they conveyed the illusion of being either precariously suspended in air, threatening to topple down, or else constructed with an unnatural loftiness in relation to their width and mass. This situation also created a weird distortion of perspective. The two levels of structures overlapped each other without giving a sense of depth, so that the houses, because of their higher elevation and nearness to the foreground buildings, did not appear diminished in size as background objects should. Consequently, a look of flatness as in a photograph, predominated in this area. Indeed, Mirocaw could be compared to an album of old snapshots, particularly ones in which the camera had been upset in the process of photography, causing the pictures to develop on an angle: a cone-roofed turret, like a pointed hat jauntily askew, peeked over the houses on a neighboring street; a billboard displaying a group of grinning vegetables tipped its contents slightly westward; cars parked along steep curbs seemed to be flying skyward in the glare-distorted windows of a five-and-ten; people leaned lethargically as they trod up and down sidewalks; and on that sunny day the clock tower, which at first I mistook for a church steeple, cast a long shadow that seemed to extend an impossible distance and wander into unlikely places in its progress across the town. I should say that perhaps the disharmonies of Mirocaw are more acutely affecting my imagination in retrospect than they were on that first day, when I was primarily concerned with locating the city hall or some other center of information.

I pulled around a corner and parked. Sliding over to the other side of the seat, I rolled down the window and called to a passerby: "Excuse me, sir," I said. The man, who was shabbily dressed and very old, paused for a moment without approaching the car. Though he had apparently responded to my call, his vacant expression did not betray the least awareness of my presence, and for a moment I thought it just a coincidence that he halted on the sidewalk at the same time I addressed him. His eyes were focused somewhere beyond me with a weary and imbecilic gaze. After a few moments he continued on his way and I said nothing to call him back, even though at the last second his face began to appear dimly familiar. Someone else finally came along who was able to direct me to the Mirocaw City Hall and Community Center.

The city hall turned out to be the building with the clock tower. Inside I stood at a counter behind which some people were working at desks and walking up and down a back hallway. On one wall was a poster for the state lottery: a jack-in-the-box with both hands grasping green bills. After a few moments, a tall, middle-aged woman came over to the counter.

"Can I help you?" she asked in a neutral, bureaucratic voice.

I explained that I had heard about the festival—saying nothing about being a nosy academic—and asked if she could provide me with further information or direct me to someone who could.

"Do you mean the one held in the winter?" she asked.

"How many of them are there?"

"Just that one."

"I supposed, then, that that's the one I mean." I smiled as if sharing a joke with her.

Without another word, she walked off into the back hallway. While she was absent I exchanged glances with several of the people behind the counter who periodically looked up from their work.

"There you are," she said when she returned, handing me a piece of paper that looked like the product of a cheap copy machine. *Please Come to the Fun*, it said in large letters. *Parades*, it went on, *Street Masquerade, Bands, The Winter Raffle*, and *The Coronation of the Winter Queen*. The page continued with the mention of a number of miscellaneous festivities. I read the words again. There was something about that imploring little "please" at the top of the announcement that made the whole affair seem like a charity function.

"When is it held? It doesn't say when the festival takes place."

"Most people already know that." She abruptly snatched the page from my hands and wrote something at the bottom. When she gave it back to me, I saw "Dec. 19–21" written in blue-green ink. I was immediately struck by an odd sense of scheduling on the part of the festival committee. There was, of course, solid anthropological and historical precedent for holding festivities around the winter solstice, but the timing of this particular event did not seem entirely practical.

"If you don't mind my asking, don't these days somewhat conflict with the regular holiday season? I mean, most people have enough going on at that time."

"It's just tradition," she said, as if invoking some venerable ancestry behind her words.

"That's very interesting," I said as much to myself as to her.

"Is there anything else?" she asked.

"Yes. Could you tell me if this festival has anything to do with clowns? I see there's something about a masquerade."

"Yes, of course there are some people in . . . costumes. I've never been in that position myself . . . that is, yes, there are clowns of a sort."

At that point my interest was definitely aroused, but I was not sure how much further I wanted to pursue it. I thanked the woman for her help and asked the best means of access to the highway, not anxious to retrace the labyrinthine route by which I had entered the town. I walked back to my car with a whole flurry of half-formed questions, and as many vague and conflicting answers, cluttering my mind.

The directions the woman gave me necessitated passing through the south end of Mirocaw. There were not many people moving about in this section of town. Those that I did see, shuffling lethargically down a block of battered storefronts, exhibited the same sort of forlorn expression and manner as the old man from whom I had asked directions earlier. I must have been traversing a central artery of this area, for on either side stretched street after street of poorly tended yards and houses bowed with age and indifference. When I came to a stop at a street corner, one of the citizens of this slum passed in front of my car. This lean, morose, and epicene person turned my way and sneered outrageously with a taut little mouth, yet seemed to be looking at no one in particular. After progressing a few streets farther, I came to a road that led back to the highway. I felt detectably more comfortable as soon as I found myself traveling once again through the expanses of sun-drenched farmlands.

I reached the library with more than enough time for my research, and so I decided to make a scholarly detour to see what material I could find that might illuminate the winter festival held in Mirocaw. The library, one of the oldest in the state, included in its holdings the entire run of the Mirocaw *Courier*. I thought this would be an excellent place to start. I soon found, however, that there was no handy way to research information from this newspaper, and I did not want to engage in a blind search for articles concerning a specific subject.

I next turned to the more organized resources of the newspapers for the larger cities located in the same county, which incidentally shares its name with Mirocaw. I uncovered very little about the town, and almost nothing concerning its festival, except in one general article on annual events in the area that erroneously attributed to Mirocaw a "large Middle Eastern community" which every spring hosted a kind of ethnic jamboree. From what I had already observed, and from what I subsequently learned, the citizens of Mirocaw were solidly Midwestern-American, the probable descendants in a direct line from some enterprising pack of New Englanders of the last century. There was one brief item devoted to a Mirocavian event, but this merely turned out to be an obituary notice for an old woman who had quietly taken her life around Christmastime. Thus, I returned home that day all but empty-handed on the subject of Mirocaw.

However, it was not long afterward that I received another letter from the former colleague of mine who had first led me to seek out Mirocaw and its festival. As it happened, he rediscovered the article that caused him to stir my interest in a local "Fool's Feast." This article had its sole appearance in an obscure festschrift of anthropology studies published in Amsterdam twenty years ago. Most of these papers were in Dutch, a few in German, and only one was in English:

"The Last Feast of Harlequin: Preliminary Notes on a Local Festival." It was exciting, of course, finally to be able to read this study, but even more exciting was the name of its author: Dr. Raymond Thoss.

2.

Before proceeding any further, I should mention something about Thoss, and inevitably about myself. Over two decades ago, at my alma mater in Cambridge, Massachusetts, Thoss was a professor of mine. Long before playing a role in the events I am about to describe, he was already one of the most important figures in my life. A striking personality, he inevitably influenced everyone who came in contact with him. I remember his lectures on social anthropology, how he turned that dim room into a brilliant and profound circus of learning. He moved in an uncannily brisk manner. When he swept his arm around to indicate some common term on the blackboard behind him, one felt he was presenting nothing less than an item of fantastic qualities and secret value. When he replaced his hand in the pocket of his old jacket this fleeting magic was once again stored away in its well-worn pouch, to be retrieved at the sorcerer's discretion. We sensed he was teaching us more than we could possibly learn, and that he himself was in possession of greater and deeper knowledge than he could possibly impart. On one occasion I summoned up the audacity to offer an interpretation— which was somewhat opposed to his own—regarding the tribal clowns of the Hopi Indians. I implied that personal experience as an amateur clown and special devotion to this study provided me with an insight possibly more valuable than his own. It was then he disclosed, casually and very obiter dicta, that he had actually acted in the role of one of these masked tribal fools and had celebrated with them the dance of the *kachinas*. In revealing these facts, however, he somehow managed not to add to the humiliation I had already inflicted upon myself. And for this I was grateful to him.

Thoss's activities were such that he sometimes became the object of gossip or romanticized speculation. He was a fieldworker par excellence, and his ability to insinuate himself into exotic cultures and situations, thereby gaining insights where other anthropologists merely collected data, was renowned. At various times in his career there had been rumors of his having "gone native" à la the Frank Hamilton Cushing legend. There were hints, which were not always irresponsible or cheaply glamourized, that he was involved in projects of a freakish sort, many of which focused on New England. It is a fact that he spent six months posing as a mental patient at an institution in western Massachusetts, gathering information on the "culture" of the psychically disturbed. When his book *Winter Solstice: The Longest Night of a Society* was published, the general opinion was that it was disappointingly subjective and impressionistic, and that, aside from a few moving but "poetically obscure" observations, there was nothing at all to give it value. Those who defended Thoss claimed he was a kind of super-anthropologist: while much of his work emphasized his own mind and feelings, his experience had in fact penetrated to a rich core of hard data which he had yet to disclose in objective discourse. As a student of Thoss, I tended to support this latter estimation of him. For a variety of tenable and untenable reasons, I believed Thoss capable of unearthing hitherto inaccessible strata of human existence. So it was gratifying at first that this article entitled "The Last Feast of Harlequin" seemed to uphold the Thoss mystique, and in an area I personally found captivating.

Much of the content of the article I did not immediately comprehend, given its author's characteristic and often strategic obscurities. On first reading, the most interesting aspect of this brief study—the "notes" encompassed only twenty pages—was the general mood of the piece. Thoss's eccentricities were definitely present in these pages, but only as a struggling inner force which was definitely contained—incarcerated, I might say—by the somber rhythmic movements of his prose and by some gloomy references he occasionally called upon. Two references in particular shared a common theme. One was a quotation from Poe's "The Conqueror Worm," which Thoss employed as a rather sensational epigraph. The point of the epigraph, however, was nowhere echoed in the text of the article save in another passing reference. Thoss brought up the well-known genesis of the modern Christmas celebration, which of course descends from the Roman Saturnalia. Then, making it clear he had not yet observed the Mirocaw festival and had only gathered its nature from various informants, he established that it too contained many, even more overt, elements of the Saturnalia. Next he made what seemed to me a trivial and purely linguistic observation, one that had less to do with his main course of argument than it did with the equally peripheral Poe epigraph. He briefly mentioned that an early sect of the Syrian Gnostics called themselves "Saturnians" and believed, among other religious heresies, that mankind was created by angels who were in turn created by the Supreme Unknown. The angels, however, did not possess the power to make their creation an erect being, and for a time he crawled upon the earth like a worm. Eventually, the Creator remedied this grotesque state of affairs. At the time I supposed that the symbolic correspondences of mankind's origins and ultimate condition being associated with worms, combined with a year-end festival recognizing the winter death of the earth, was the gist of this Thossian "insight," a poetic but scientifically valueless observation.

Other observations he made on the Mirocaw festival were also strictly etic; in other words, they were based on secondhand sources, hearsay testimony. Even at that juncture, however, I felt Thoss knew more than he disclosed; and, as I later discovered, he had indeed included information on certain aspects of Mirocaw suggesting he was already in possession of several keys which for the moment he was keeping securely in his own pocket. By then I myself possessed a most revealing morsel of knowledge. A note to the "Harlequin" article apprised the reader that the piece was only a fragment in rude form of a more wide-ranging work in preparation. This work was never seen by the world. My former professor had not published anything since his withdrawal from academic circulation some twenty years ago. Now I suspected where he had gone.

For the man I had stopped on the streets of Mirocaw and from whom I tried to obtain directions, the man with the disconcertingly lethargic gaze, had very much resembled a superannuated version of Dr. Raymond Thoss.

3.

And now I have a confession to make. Despite my reasons for being enthusiastic about Mirocaw and its mysteries, especially its relationship to both Thoss and my own deepest concerns as a scholar—I contemplated the days ahead of me with no more than a feeling of frigid numbness and often with a sense of profound depression. Yet I had no reason to be surprised at this emotional state, which had little relevance to the outward events in my life but was determined by inward conditions that worked according to their own, quite enigmatic, seasons and cycles. For many years, at least since my university days, I have suffered from this dark malady, this recurrent despondency in which I would become buried when it came time for the earth to grow cold and bare and the skies heavy with shadows. Nevertheless, I pursued my plans, though somewhat mechanically, to visit Mirocaw during its festival days, for I superstitiously hoped that this activity might diminish the weight of my seasonal despair. In Mirocaw would be parades and parties and the opportunity to play the clown once again.

For weeks in advance I practiced my art, even perfecting a new feat of juggling magic, which was my special forte in foolery. I had my costumes cleaned, purchased fresh makeup, and was ready. I received permission from the university to cancel some of my classes prior to the holiday, explaining the nature of my project and the necessity of arriving in the town a few days before the festival began, in order to do some preliminary research, establish informants, and so on. Actually, my plan was to postpone any formal inquiry until after the festival and to involve myself beforehand as much as possible in its activities. I would, of course, keep a journal during this time.

There was one resource I did want to consult, however. Specifically, I returned to that outstate library to examine those issues of the Mirocaw *Courier* dating from December two decades ago. One story in particular confirmed a point Thoss made in the "Harlequin" article, though the event it chronicled must have taken place after Thoss had written his study.

The *Courier* story appeared two weeks after the festival had ended for that year and was concerned with the disappearance of a woman named Elizabeth Beadle, the wife of Samuel Beadle, a hotel owner in Mirocaw. The county authorities speculated that this was another instance of the "holiday suicides" which seemed to occur with inordinate seasonal regularity in the Mirocaw region. Thoss documented this phenomenon in his "Harlequin" article, though I suspect that today these deaths would be neatly categorized under the heading "seasonal affective disorder." In any case, the authorities searched a half-frozen lake near the outskirts of Mirocaw where they had found many successful suicides in years past. This year, however, no body was discovered. Alongside the article was a picture of Elizabeth Beadle. Even in the grainy microfilm reproduction one could detect a certain vibrancy and vitality in Mrs. Beadle's face. That a hypothesis of "holiday suicide" should be so readily posited to explain her disappearance seemed strange and in some way unjust.

Thoss, in his brief article, wrote that every year there occurred changes of a moral or spiritual cast which seemed to affect Mirocaw along with the usual winter metamorphosis. He was not precise about its origin or nature but stated, in typically mystifying fashion, that the effect of this "subseason" on the town was conspicuously negative. In addition to the number of suicides actually accomplished during this time, there was also a rise in treatment of "hypochondriacal" conditions, which was how the medical men of twenty years past characterized these cases in discussions with Thoss. This state of affairs would gradually worsen and finally reach a climax during the days scheduled for the Mirocaw festival. Thoss speculated that given the secretive nature of small towns, the situation was probably even more intensely pronounced than casual investigation could reveal.

The connection between the festival and this insidious subseasonal climate in Mirocaw was a point on which Thoss did not come to any rigid conclusions. He did write, nevertheless, that these two "climatic aspects" had had a parallel existence in the town's history as far back as available records could document. A late-nineteenth-century history of Mirocaw County speaks of the town by its original name of New Colstead, and castigates the townspeople for holding a "ribald and soulless feast" to the exclusion of normal Christmas observances. (Thoss comments that the historian had mistakenly fused two distinct aspects of the season, their actual relationship being essentially antagonistic.) The "Harlequin" article did not trace the festival to its earliest appearance (this may not have been possible), though Thoss emphasized the New England origins of Mirocaw's founders. The festival, therefore, was one imported from this region and could reasonably be extended at least a century; that is, if it had not been brought over from the Old World, in which case its roots would become indefinite until further research could be done. Surely Thoss's allusion to the Syrian Gnostics suggested the latter possibility could not entirely be ruled out.

But it seemed to be the festival's link to New England that nourished Thoss's speculations. He wrote of this patch of geography as if it were an acceptable place to end the search. For him, the very words "New England" seemed to be stripped of all traditional connotations and had come to imply nothing less than a gateway to all lands, both known and suspected, and even to ages beyond the civilized history of the region. Having been educated partly in New England, I could somewhat understand this sentimental exaggeration, for indeed there are places that seem archaic beyond chronological measure, appearing to transcend relative standards of time and achieving a kind of absolute antiquity which cannot be logically fathomed. But how this vague suggestion related to a small town in the Midwest I could not imagine. Thoss himself observed that the residents of Mirocaw did not betray any mysteriously primitive consciousness. On the contrary, they appeared superficially unaware of the genesis of their winter merrymaking. That such a tradition had endured through the years, however, even eclipsing the conventional Christmas holiday, revealed a profound awareness of the festival's meaning and function.

I cannot deny that what I had learned about the Mirocaw festival did inspire a trite sense of fate, especially given the involvement of such an important figure from my past as Thoss. It was the first time in my academic career that I knew myself to be better suited than anyone else to discern the true meaning of scattered data, even if I could only attribute this special authority to chance circumstances.

Nevertheless, as I sat in that library on a morning in mid-December I doubted for a moment the wisdom of setting out for Mirocaw rather than returning home, where the more familiar *rite de passage* of winter depression awaited me. My original scheme was to avoid the cyclical blues the season held for me, but it seemed this was also a part of the history of Mirocaw, only on a much larger scale. My emotional instability, however, was exactly what qualified me most for the particular fieldwork ahead, though I did not take pride or consolation in the fact. And to retreat would have been to deny myself an opportunity that might never offer itself again. In retrospect, there seems to have been no fortuitous resolution to the decision I had to make. As it happened, I went ahead to the town.

4.

Just past noon, on December 18, I started driving toward Mirocaw. A blur of dull, earthen-colored scenery extended in every direction. The snowfalls of late autumn had been sparse, and only a few white patches appeared in the harvested fields along the highway. The clouds were gray and abundant. Passing by a stretch of forest, I noticed the black, ragged clumps of abandoned nests clinging to the twisted mesh of bare branches. I thought I saw black birds skittering over the road ahead, but they were only dead leaves and they flew into the air as I drove by.

I approached Mirocaw from the south, entering the town from the direction I had left it on my visit the previous summer. This took me once again through that part of town which seemed to exist on the wrong side of some great invisible barrier dividing the desirable sections of Mirocaw from the undesirable. As lurid as this district had appeared to me under the summer sun, in the thin light of that winter afternoon it degenerated into a pale phantom of itself. The frail stores and starved-looking houses suggested a borderline region between the material and nonmaterial worlds, with one sardonically wearing the mask of the other. I saw a few gaunt pedestrians who turned as I passed by, though seemingly not *because* I passed by, making my way up to the main street of Mirocaw.

Driving up the steep rise of Townshend Street, I found the sights there comparatively welcoming. The rolling avenues of the town were in readiness for the festival. Streetlights had their poles raveled with evergreen, the fresh boughs proudly conspicuous in a barren season. On the doors of many of the businesses on Townshend were holly wreaths, equally green but observably plastic. However, although there was nothing unusual in this traditional greenery of the season, it soon became apparent to me that Mirocaw had quite abandoned itself to this particular symbol of Yuletide. It was garishly in evidence everywhere. The windows of stores and houses were framed in green lights, green streamers hung down from storefront awnings, and the beacons of the Red Rooster Bar were peacock green floodlights. I supposed the residents of Mirocaw desired these decorations, but the effect was one of excess. An eerie emerald haze permeated the town, and faces looked slightly reptilian.

At the time I assumed that the prodigious evergreen, holly wreaths, and colored lights (if only of a single color) demonstrated an emphasis on the vegetable symbols of the Nordic Yuletide, which would inevitably be muddled into the winter festival of any northern country just as they had been adopted for the Christmas season. In his "Harlequin" article Thoss wrote of the pagan aspect of Mirocaw's festival, likening it to the ritual of a fertility cult, with probable connections to chthonic divinities at some time in the past. But Thoss had mistaken, as I had, what was only part of the festival's significance for the whole.

The hotel at which I had made reservations was located on Townshend. It was an old building of brown brick, with an arched doorway and a pathetic coping intended to convey an impression of neoclassicism. I found a parking space in front and left my suitcases in the car.

When I first entered the hotel lobby it was empty. I thought perhaps the Mirocaw festival would have attracted enough visitors to at least bolster the business of its only hotel, but it seemed I was mistaken. Tapping a little bell, I leaned on the desk and turned to look at a small, traditionally decorated Christmas tree on a table near the entranceway. It was complete with shiny egg-fragile bulbs; miniature candy canes; flat, laughing Santas with arms wide; a star on top nodding awkwardly against the delicate shoulder of an upper branch; and colored lights that bloomed out of flower-shaped sockets. For some reason this seemed to me a sorry little piece.

"May I help you?" said a young woman arriving from a room adjacent to the lobby.

I must have been staring rather intently at her, for she looked away and seemed quite uneasy. I could hardly imagine what to say to her or how to explain what I was thinking. In person she immediately radiated a chilling brilliance of manner and expression. But if this woman had not committed suicide twenty years before, as the newspaper article had suggested, neither had she aged in that time.

"Sarah," called a masculine voice from the invisible heights of a stairway. A tall, middle-aged man came down the steps. "I thought you were in your room," said the man, whom I took to be Samuel Beadle. Sarah, not Elizabeth, Beadle glanced sideways in my direction to indicate to her father that she was conducting the business of the hotel. Beadle apologized to me, and then excused the two of them for a moment while they went off to one side to continue their exchange.

I smiled and pretended everything was normal, while trying to remain within earshot of their conversation. They spoke in tones that suggested their conflict was a familiar one: Beadle's overprotective concern with his daughter's whereabouts and Sarah's frustrated understanding of certain restrictions placed upon her. The conversation ended, and Sarah ascended the stairs, turning for a moment to give me a facial pantomime of apology for the unprofessional scene that had just taken place.

"Now, sir, what can I do for you?" Beadle asked, almost demanded.

"Yes, I have a reservation. Actually, I'm a day early, if that doesn't present a problem." I gave the hotel the benefit of the doubt that its business might have been secretly flourishing.

"No problem at all, sir," he said, presenting me with the registration form, and then a brass-colored key dangling from a plastic disk bearing the number 44.

"Luggage?"

"Yes, it's in my car."

"I'll give you a hand with that."

While Beadle was settling me in my fourth-floor room it seemed an opportune moment to broach the subject of the festival, the holiday suicides, and perhaps, depending upon his reaction, the fate of his wife. I needed a respondent who had lived in the town for a good many years and who could enlighten me about the attitude of Mirocavians toward their season of sea-green lights.

"This is just fine," I said about the clean but somber room. "Nice view. I can see the bright green lights of Mirocaw just fine from up here. Is the town usually all decked out like this? For the festival, I mean."

"Yes, sir, for the festival," he replied mechanically.

"I imagine you'll probably be getting quite a few of us out-of-towners in the next couple days."

"Could be. Is there anything else?"

"Yes, there is. I wonder if you could tell me something about the festivities."

"Such as . . ."

"Well, you know, the clowns and so forth."

"Only clowns here are the ones that're . . . well, picked out, I suppose you would say."

"I don't understand."

"Excuse me, sir. I'm very busy right now. Is there anything else?"

I could think of nothing at the moment to perpetuate our conversation. Beadle wished me a good stay and left.

I unpacked my suitcases. In addition to regular clothing I had also brought along some of the items from my clown's wardrobe. Beadle's comment that the clowns of Mirocaw were "picked out" left me wondering exactly what purpose these street masqueraders served in the festival. The clown figure has had so many meanings in different times and cultures. The jolly well-loved joker familiar to most people is actually but one aspect of this protean creature. Madmen, hunchbacks, amputees, and other abnormals were once considered natural clowns; they were elected to fulfill a comic role which could allow others to see them as ludicrous rather than as terrible reminders of the forces of disorder in the world. But sometimes a cheerless jester was required to draw attention to this same disorder, as in the case of King Lear's morbid and honest fool, who of course was eventually hanged, and so much for his clownish wisdom. Clowns have often had ambiguous and sometimes contradictory roles to play. Thus, I knew enough not to brashly jump into costume and cry out, "Here I am again!"

That first day in Mirocaw I did not stray far from the hotel. I read and rested for a few hours and then ate at a nearby diner. Through the window beside my table I watched the winter night turn the soft green glow of the town into a harsh and almost totally new color as it contrasted with the darkness. The streets of Mirocaw seemed to me unusually busy for a small town at evening. Yet it was not the kind of activity one normally sees before an approaching Christmas holiday. This was not a crowd of bustling shoppers loaded with bright bags of presents. Their arms were empty, their hands shoved deep in their pockets against the cold, which nevertheless had not driven them to the solitude of their presumably warm houses. I watched them enter and exit store after store without buying; many merchants remained open late, and even the places that were closed had left their neons illuminated. The faces that passed the window of the diner were possibly just stiffened by the cold, I thought; frozen into deep frowns and nothing else. In the same window I saw the reflection of my own face. It was not the face of an adept clown; it was slack and flabby and at that moment seemed the face of someone less than alive. Outside was the town of Mirocaw, its streets dipping and rising with a lunatic severity, its citizens packing the sidewalks, its heart bathed in green: as promising a field of professional and personal challenge as I had ever encountered—and I was bored to the point of dread. I hurried back to my hotel room.

"Mirocaw has another coldness within its cold," I wrote in my journal that night. "Another set of buildings and streets that exists behind the visible town's facade like a world of disgraceful back alleys." I went on like this for about a page, across which I finally engraved a big *X*. Then I went to bed.

* * *

In the morning I left my car at the hotel and walked toward the main business district a few blocks away. Mingling with the good people of Mirocaw seemed like the proper thing to do at that point in my scientific sojourn. But as I began laboriously walking up Townshend (the sidewalks were cramped with wandering pedestrians), a glimpse of someone suddenly replaced my haphazard plan with a more specific and immediate one. Through the crowd and about fifteen paces ahead was my goal.

"Dr. Thoss," I called.

His head almost seemed to turn and look back in response to my shout, but I could not be certain. I pushed past several warmly wrapped bodies and green-scarved necks, only to find that the object of my pursuit appeared to be maintaining the same distance from me, though I did not know if this was being done deliberately or not. At the next corner, the dark-coated Thoss abruptly turned right onto a steep street which led downward directly toward the dilapidated south end of Mirocaw. When I reached the corner I looked down the sidewalk and could see him very clearly from above. I also saw how he managed to stay so far ahead of me in a mob that had impeded my own progress. For some reason the people on the sidewalk made room so that he could move past them easily, without the usual jostling of bodies. It was not a dramatic physical avoidance, though it seemed nonetheless intentional. Fighting the tight fabric of the throng, I continued to follow Thoss, losing and regaining sight of him.

By the time I reached the bottom of the sloping street the crowd had thinned out considerably, and after walking a block or so farther I found myself practically a lone pedestrian pacing behind a distant figure that I hoped was still Thoss. He was now walking quite swiftly and in a way that seemed to acknowledge my pursuit of him, though really it felt as if he were leading me as much as I was chasing him. I called his name a few more times at a volume he could not have failed to hear, assuming that deafness was not one of the changes to have come over him; he was, after all, not a young man, nor even a middle-aged one any longer.

Thoss suddenly crossed in the middle of the street. He walked a few more steps and entered a signless brick building between a liquor store and a repair shop of some kind. In the "Harlequin" article Thoss had mentioned that the people living in this section of Mirocaw maintained their own businesses, and that these were patronized almost exclusively by residents of the area. I could well believe this statement when I looked at these little sheds of commerce, for they had the same badly weathered appearance as their clientele. The formidable shoddiness of these buildings notwithstanding, I followed Thoss into the plain brick shell of what had been, or possibly still was, a diner.

Inside it was unusually dark. Even before my eyes made the adjustment I sensed that this was not a thriving restaurant cozily cluttered with chairs and tables—as was the establishment where I had eaten the night before—but a place with only a few disarranged furnishings, and very cold. It seemed colder, in fact, than the winter streets outside.

"Dr. Thoss?" I called toward a lone table near the center of the long room. Perhaps four or five were sitting around the table, with some others blending into the dimness behind them. Scattered across the top of the table were some books and loose papers. Seated there was an old man indicating something in the pages before him, but it was not Thoss. Beside him were two youths whose wholesome features distinguished them from the grim weariness of the others. I approached the table and they all looked up at me. None of them showed a glimmer of emotion except the two boys, who exchanged worried and guilt-ridden glances with each other, as if they had just been discovered in some shameful act. They both suddenly burst from the table and ran into the dark background, where a light appeared briefly as they exited by a back door.

"I'm sorry," I said diffidently. "I thought I saw someone I knew come in here."

They said nothing. Out of a back room others began to emerge, no doubt interested in the source of the commotion. In a few moments the room was crowded with these tramplike figures, all of them gazing emptily in the dimness. I was not at this point frightened of them; at least I was not afraid they would do me any physical harm. Actually, I felt as if it was quite within my power to pummel them easily into submission, their mousy faces almost inviting a succession of firm blows. But there were so many of them.

They slid slowly toward me in a wormlike mass. Their eyes seemed empty and unfocused, and I wondered a moment if they were even aware of my presence. Nevertheless, I was the center upon which their lethargic shuffling converged, their shoes scuffing softly along the bare floor. I began to deliver a number of hasty inanities as they continued to press toward me, their weak and unexpectedly odorless bodies nudging against mine. (I understood now why the people along the sidewalks seemed instinctively to avoid Thoss.) Unseen legs became entangled with my own; I staggered and then regained my balance. This sudden movement aroused me from a kind of mesmeric daze into which I must have fallen without being aware of it. I had intended to leave that dreary place long before events had reached such a juncture, but for some reason I could not focus my intentions strongly enough to cause myself to act. My mind had been drifting farther away as these slavish things approached. In a sudden surge of panic I pushed through their soft ranks and was outside.

The open air revived me to my former alertness, and I immediately started pacing swiftly up the hill. I was no longer sure that I had not simply imagined what had seemed, and at the same time did not seem, like a perilous moment. Had their movements been directed toward a harmful assault, or were they trying merely to intimidate me? As I reached the green-glazed main street of Mirocaw I really could not determine what had just happened.

The sidewalks were still jammed with a multitude of pedestrians, who now seemed more lively than they had been only a short time before. There was a kind of vitality that could only be attributed to the imminent festivities. A group of young men had begun celebrating prematurely and strode noisily across the street at midpoint, obviously intoxicated. From the laughter and joking among the still sober citizens I gathered that, Mardi Gras style, public drunkenness was within the traditions of this winter festival. I looked for anything to indicate the beginnings of the Street Masquerade, but saw nothing: no brightly garbed harlequins or snow-white pierrots. Were the ceremonies even now in preparation for the coronation of the Winter Queen? "The Winter Queen," I wrote in my journal. "Figure of fertility invested with symbolic powers of revival and prosperity. Elected in the manner of a high-school prom queen. Check for possible consort figure in the form of a representative from the underworld."

In the predarkness hours of December 19 I sat in my hotel room and wrote and thought and organized. I did not feel too badly, all things considered. The holiday excitement which was steadily rising in the streets below my window was definitely infecting me. I forced myself to take a short nap in anticipation of a long night. When I awoke, Mirocaw's annual feast had begun.

5.

Shouting, commotion, carousing. Sleepily I went to the window and looked out over the town. It seemed all the lights of Mirocaw were shining, save in that section down the hill which became part of the black void of winter. And now the town's greenish tinge was even more pronounced, spreading everywhere like a great green rainbow that had melted from the sky and endured, phosphorescent, into the night. In the streets was the brightness of an artificial spring. The byways of Mirocaw vibrated with activity: on a nearby corner a brass band blared; marauding cars blew their horns and were sometimes mounted by laughing pedestrians; a man emerged from the Red

Rooster Bar, threw up his arms, and crowed. I looked closely at the individual celebrants, searching for the vestments of clowns. Soon, delightedly, I saw them. The costume was red and white, with matching cap, and the face painted a noble alabaster. It almost seemed to be a clownish incarnation of that white-bearded and black-booted Christmas fool.

This particular fool, however, was not receiving the affection and respect usually accorded to a Santa Claus. My poor fellow-clown was in the middle of a circle of revelers who were pushing him back and forth from one to the other. The object of this abuse seemed to accept it somewhat willingly, but this little game nevertheless appeared to have humiliation as its purpose. "Only clowns here are the ones that're picked out," echoed Beadle's voice in my memory. "Picked *on*" seemed closer to the truth.

Packing myself in some heavy clothes, I went out into the green gleaming streets. Not far from the hotel I was stumbled into by a character with a wide blue-and-red grin and bright baggy clothes. Actually he had been shoved into me by some youths outside a drugstore.

"See the freak," said an obese and drunken fellow. "See the freak fall."

My first response was anger, and then fear as I saw two others flanking the fat drunk. They walked toward me, and I tensed myself for a confrontation.

"This is a disgrace," one said, the neck of a wine bottle held loosely in his left hand.

But it was not to me they were speaking; it was to the clown, who had been pushed to the sidewalk. His three persecutors helped him up with a sudden jerk and then splashed wine in his face. They ignored me altogether.

"Let him loose," the fat one said. "Crawl away, freak. Oh, he flies!"

The clown trotted off, becoming lost in the throng.

"Wait a minute," I said to the rowdy trio, who had started lumbering away. I quickly decided that it would probably be futile to ask them to explain what I had just witnessed, especially amid the noise and confusion of the festivities. In my best jovial fashion I proposed we all go someplace where I could buy them each a drink. They had no objection, and in a short while we were all squeezed around a table in the Red Rooster.

Over several drinks I explained to them that I was from out of town, which pleased them no end for some reason. I told them there were things I did not understand about their festival.

"I don't think there's anything *to* understand," the fat one said. "It's just what you see."

I asked him about the people dressed as clowns.

"Them? They're the freaks. It's their turn this year. Everyone takes their turn. Next year it might be mine. Or *yours*," he said, pointing at one of his friends across the table. "And when we find out which one you are—"

"You're not smart enough," said the defiant potential freak.

This was an important point: the fact that individuals who played the clowns remained, or at least attempted to remain, anonymous. This arrangement would help remove inhibitions a resident of Mirocaw might have about abusing his own neighbor or even a family relation. From what I later observed, the extent of this abuse did not go beyond a kind of playful roughhousing. And even so, it was only the occasional group of rowdies who actually took advantage of this aspect of the festival, the majority of the citizens very much content to stay on the sidelines.

As far as being able to illuminate the meaning of this custom, my three young friends were quite useless. To them it was just amusement, as I imagine it was to the majority of Mirocavians. This was understandable. I suppose the average person would not be able to explain exactly how the profoundly familiar Christmas holiday came to be celebrated in its present form.

I left the bar alone and not unaffected by the drinks I had consumed there. Outside, the general merrymaking continued. Loud music emanated from several quarters. Mirocaw had fully transformed itself from a sedate small town to an enclave of Saturnalia within the dark immensity of a winter night. But Saturn is also the planetary symbol of melancholy and sterility, a clash of opposites contained within that single word. And as I wandered half-drunkenly down the street, I discovered that there was a conflict within the winter festival itself. This discovery indeed appeared to be that secret key which Thoss withheld in his study of the town. Oddly enough, it was through my unfamiliarity with the outward nature of the festival that I came to know its true nature.

I was mingling with the crowd on the street, warmly enjoying the confusion around me, when I saw a strangely designed creature lingering on the corner up ahead. It was one of the Mirocaw clowns. Its clothes were shabby and nondescript, almost in the style of a tramp-type clown, but not humorously exaggerated enough. The face, though, made up for the lackluster costume. I had never seen such a strange conception for a clown's countenance. The figure stood beneath a dim streetlight, and when it turned its head my way I realized why it seemed familiar. The thin, smooth, and pale head; the wide eyes; the oval-shaped features resembling nothing so much as the skull-faced, screaming creature in that famous painting (memory fails me). This clownish imitation rivaled the original in suggesting stricken realms of abject horror and despair: an inhuman likeness more proper to something under the earth than upon it.

From the first moment I saw this creature, I thought of those inhabitants of the ghetto down the hill. There was the same nauseating passivity and languor in its bearing. Perhaps if I had not been drinking earlier I would not have been bold enough to take the action I did. I decided to join in one of the upstanding traditions of the winter festival, for it annoyed me to see this morbid imposter of a clown standing up. When I reached the corner I laughingly pushed myself into the creature— "Whoops!"—who stumbled backward and ended up on the sidewalk. I laughed again and looked around for approval from the festivalers in the vicinity. No one, however, seemed to appreciate or even acknowledge what I had done. They did not laugh with me or point with amusement, but only passed by, perhaps walking a little faster until they were some distance from this street-corner incident. I realized instantly I had violated some tacit rule of behavior, though I had thought my action well within the common practice. The idea occurred to me that I might even be apprehended and prosecuted for what in any other circumstances was certainly a criminal act. I turned around to help the clown back to his feet, hoping somehow to redeem my offense, but the creature was gone. Solemnly I walked away from the scene of my inadvertent crime and sought other streets away from its witnesses.

Along the various back avenues of Mirocaw I wandered, pausing exhaustedly at one point to sit at the counter of a small sandwich shop that was packed with customers. I ordered a cup of coffee to revive my overly alcoholed system. Warming my hands around the cup and sipping slowly from it, I watched the people outside as they passed the front window. It was well after midnight, but the thick flow of passersby gave no indication that anyone was going home early. A carnival of profiles filed past the window and I was content simply to sit back and observe, until finally one of these faces made me start. It was that frightful little clown I had roughed up earlier. But although its face was familiar in its ghastly aspect, there was something different about it. And I wondered that there should be two such hideous freaks.

Quickly paying the man at the counter, I dashed out to get a second glimpse of the clown, who was now nowhere in sight. The dense crowd kept me from pursuing this figure with any speed, and I wondered how the clown could have made its way so easily ahead of me. Unless the crowd had instinctively allowed this creature to pass unhindered through its massive ranks, as it did for Thoss. In the process of searching for this particular freak, I discovered that inter-spersed among the celebrating populace of Mirocaw, which included the sanctioned festival clowns, there was not one or two, but a considerable number of these pale wraithlike creatures. And they all drifted along the streets unmolested by even the rowdiest of revelers. I now understood one of the taboos of the festival. These other clowns were not to be disturbed and should even be avoided, much as were the residents of the slum at the edge of town. Nevertheless, I felt instinctively that the two groups of clowns were somehow identified with each other, even if the ghetto clowns were not welcome at Mirocaw's winter festival. Indeed, they were not simply part of the community and celebrating the season in their own way. To all appearances, this group of melancholy mummers constituted nothing less than an entirely independent festival—a festival within a festival.

Returning to my room, I entered my suppositions into the journal I was keeping for this venture. The following are excerpts:

There is a superstitiousness displayed by the residents of Mirocaw with regard to these people from the slum section, particularly as they lately appear in those dreadful faces signifying their own festival. What is the relationship between these simultaneous celebrations? Did one precede the other? If so, which? My opinion at this point—and I claim no conclusiveness for it—is that Mirocaw's winter festival is the later manifestation, that it appeared after the festival of those depressingly pallid clowns, in order to cover it up or mitigate its effect. The holiday suicides come to mind, and the subclimate Thoss wrote about, the disappearance of Elizabeth Beadle twenty years ago, and my own experience with this pariah clan existing outside yet within the community. Of my own experience with this emotionally deleterious subseason I would rather not speak at this time. Still not able to say whether or not my usual winter melancholy is the cause. On the general subject of mental health, I must consider Thoss's book about his stay in a psychiatric hospital (in western Mass., almost sure of that. Check on this book & Mirocaw's New England roots). The winter solstice is tomorrow, albeit sometime past midnight (how blurry these days and nights are becoming!). It is, of course, the day of the year in which night hours surpass daylight hours by the greatest margin. Note what this has to do with the suicides and a rise in psychic disorder. Recalling Thoss's list of documented suicides in his article, there seemed to be a recurrence of specific family names, as there very likely might be for any kind of data collected in a small town. Among these names was a Beadle or two. Perhaps, then, there is a genealogical basis for the suicides which has nothing to do with Thoss's mystical subclimate, which is a colorful idea to be sure and one that seems fitting for this town of various outward and inward aspects, but is not a conception that can be substantiated.

One thing that seems certain, however, is the division of Mirocaw into two very distinct types of citizenry, resulting in two festivals and the appearance of similar clowns—a term now used in an extremely loose sense. But there is a connection, and I believe I have some idea of what it is. I said before that the normal residents of the town regard those from the ghetto, and especially their clown figures, with superstition. Yet it's more than that: there is fear, perhaps a kind of hatred—the particular kind of hatred resulting from some powerful and irrational memory. What threatens Mirocaw I think I can very well understand. I recall the incident earlier today in that vacant diner. "Vacant" is the appropriate word here, despite its contradiction of fact. The congregation of that half-lit room formed less a presence than an absence, even considering the oppressive number of them. Those eyes that did not or could not focus on anything, the pining lassitude of their faces, the lazy march of their feet. I was spiritually drained when I ran out of there. I then understood why these people and their activities are avoided.

I cannot question the wisdom of those ancestral Mirocavians who began the tradition of the winter festival and gave the town a pretext for celebration and social intercourse at a time when the consequences of brooding isolation are most severe, those longest and darkest days of the solstice. A mood of Christmas joviality obviously would not be sufficient to counter the menace of this season. But even so, there are still the suicides of individuals who are somehow cut off, I imagine, from the vitalizing activities of the festival.

It is the nature of this insidious subseason that seems to determine the outward forms of Mirocaw's winter festival: the optimistic greenery in a period of gray dormancy; the fertile promise of the Winter Queen; and, most interesting to my mind, the clowns. The bright clowns of Mirocaw who are treated so badly; they appear to serve as substitute figures for those dark-eyed mummers of the slums. Since the latter are feared for some power or influence they possess, they may still be symbolically confronted and conquered through their counterparts, who are elected for precisely this function. If I am right about this, I wonder to what extent there is a conscious awareness among the town's populace of this indirect show of aggression. Those three young men I spoke with tonight did not seem to possess much insight beyond seeing that there was a certain amount of robust fun in the festival's tradition. For that matter, how much awareness is there on the *other side* of these two antagonistic festivals? Too horrible to think of such a thing, but I must wonder if, for all their apparent aimlessness, those inhabitants of the ghetto are not the only ones who know what they are about. No denying that behind those inhumanly limp expressions there seems to lie a kind of obnoxious intelligence.

Now I realize the confusion of my present state, but as I wobbled from street to street tonight, watching those oval-mouthed clowns, I could not help feeling that all the merrymaking in Mirocaw was somehow allowed only by their sufferance. This I hope is no more than a fanciful Thossian intuition, the sort of idea that is curious and thought-provoking without ever seeming to gain the benefit of proof. I know my mind is not entirely lucid, but I feel that it may be possible to penetrate Mirocaw's many complexities and illuminate the hidden side of the festival season. In particular I must look for the significance of the other festival. Is it also some kind of fertility celebration? From what I have seen, the tenor of this "celebrating" subgroup is one of *anti*fertility, if anything. How have they managed to keep from dying out completely over the years? How do they maintain their numbers?

But I was too tired to formulate any more of my sodden speculations. Falling onto my bed, I soon became lost in dreams of streets and faces.

6.

I was, of course, slightly hung over when I woke up late the next morning. The festival was still going strong, and blaring music outside roused me from a nightmare. It was a parade. A number of floats proceeded down Townshend, a familiar color predominating. There were theme floats of pilgrims and Indians, cowboys and Indians, and clowns of an orthodox type. In the middle of it all was the Winter Queen herself, freezing atop an icy throne. She waved in all directions. I even imagined she waved up at my dark window.

In the first few groggy moments of wakefulness I had no sympathy with my excitation of the previous night. But I discovered that my former enthusiasm had merely lain dormant, and soon returned with an even greater intensity. Never before had my mind and senses been so active during this usually inert time of year. At home I would have been playing lugubrious old records and looking out the window quite a bit. I was terribly grateful in a completely abstract way for my commitment to a meaningful mania. And I was eager to get to work after I had had some breakfast at the coffee shop.

When I got back to my room I discovered the door was unlocked. And there was something written on the dresser mirror. The writing was red and greasy, as if done with a clown's makeup pencil—my own, I realized. I read the legend, or rather I should say *riddle*, several times: "What buries itself before it is dead?" I looked at it for quite a while, very shaken at how vulnerable my holiday fortifications were. Was this supposed to be a warning of some kind? A threat to the effect that if I persisted in a certain course I would end up prematurely interred? I would have to be careful, I told myself. My resolution was to let nothing deter me from the inspired strategy I had conceived for myself. I wiped the mirror clean, for it was now needed for other purposes.

I spent the rest of the day devising a very special costume and the appropriate face to go with it. I easily shabbied up my overcoat with a torn pocket or two and a complete set of stains. Combined with blue jeans and a pair of rather scuffed-up shoes, I had a passable costume for a derelict. The face, however, was more difficult, for I had to experiment from memory. Conjuring a mental image of the screaming pierrot in that painting (*The Scream*, I now recall), helped me quite a bit. At nightfall I exited the hotel by the back stairway.

It was strange to walk down the crowded street in this gruesome disguise. Though I thought I would feel conspicuous, the actual experience was very close, I imagined, to one of complete invisibility. No one looked at me as I strolled by, or as they strolled by, or as we strolled by each other. I was a phantom—perhaps the ghost of festivals past, or those yet to come.

I had no clear idea where my disguise would take me that night, only vague expectations of gaining the confidence of my fellow specters and possibly in some way coming to know their secrets. For a while I would simply wander around in that lackadaisical manner I had learned from them, following their lead in any way they might indicate. And for the most part this meant doing almost nothing and doing it silently. If I passed one of my kind on the sidewalk there was no speaking, no exchange of knowing looks, no recognition at all that I was aware of. We were there on the streets of Mirocaw to create a presence and nothing more. At least this is how I came to feel about it. As I drifted along with my bodiless invisibility, I felt myself more and more becoming an empty, floating shape, seeing without being seen and walking without the interference of those grosser creatures who shared my world. It was not an experience completely without interest or even pleasure. The clown's shibboleth of "here we are again" took on a new meaning for me as I felt myself a novitiate of a more rarefied order of harlequinry. And very soon the opportunity to make further progress along this path presented itself.

Going the opposite direction, down the street, a pickup truck slowly passed, gently parting a sea of zigging and zagging celebrants. The cargo in the back of this truck was curious, for it was made up entirely of my fellow sectarians. At the end of the block the truck stopped and another of them boarded it over the back gate. One block down I saw still another get on. Then the truck made a U-turn at an intersection and headed in my direction.

I stood at the curb as I had seen the others do. I was not sure the truck would pick me up, thinking that somehow they knew I was an imposter. The truck did, however, slow down, almost coming to a stop when it reached me. The others were crowded on the floor of the truck bed. Most of them were just staring into nothingness with the usual indifference I had come to expect from their kind. But a few actually glanced at me with some anticipation. For a second I hesitated, not sure I wanted to pursue this ruse any further. At the last moment, some impulse sent me climbing up the back of the truck and squeezing myself in among the others.

There were only a few more to pick up before the truck headed for the outskirts of Mirocaw and beyond. At first I tried to maintain a clear orientation with respect to the town. But as we took turn after turn through the darkness of narrow country roads, I found myself unable to preserve any sense of direction. The majority of the others in the back of the truck exhibited no apparent awareness of their fellow passengers. Guardedly, I looked from face to ghostly face. A few of them spoke in short whispered phrases to others close by. I could not make out what they were saying, but the tone of their voices was one of innocent normalcy, as if they were not of the hardened slum-herd of Mirocaw. Perhaps, I thought, these were thrill-seekers who had disguised themselves as I had done, or, more likely, initiates of some kind. Possibly they had received prior instructions at such meetings as I had stumbled onto the day before. It was also likely that among this crew were those very boys I had frightened into a precipitate exit from that old diner.

The truck was now speeding along a fairly open stretch of country, heading toward those higher hills that surrounded the now distant town of Mirocaw. The icy wind whipped around us, and I could not keep myself from trembling with cold. This definitely betrayed me as one of the newcomers among the group, for the two bodies that pressed against mine were rigidly still and even seemed to be radiating a frigidity of their own. I glanced ahead at the darkness into which we were rapidly progressing.

We had left all open country behind us now, and the road was enclosed by thick woods. The mass of bodies in the truck leaned into one another as we began traveling up a steep incline. Above us, at the top of the hill, were lights shining somewhere within the woods. When the road leveled off, the truck made an abrupt turn, steering into what looked like a great ditch. There was an unpaved path, however, upon which the truck proceeded toward the glowing in the near distance.

The glowing became brighter and sharper as we approached it, flickering upon the trees and revealing stark detail where there had formerly been only smooth darkness. As the truck pulled into a clearing and came to a stop, I saw a loose assembly of figures, many of which held lanterns that beamed with a dazzling and frosty light. I stood up in the back of the truck to unboard as the others were doing. Glancing around from that height, I saw approximately thirty more of those cadaverous clowns milling about. One of my fellow passengers spied me lingering in the truck and in a strangely high-pitched whisper told me to hurry, explaining something about the "apex of darkness." I thought again about this solstice night; it was technically the longest period of darkness of the year, even if not by a very significant margin from many other winter nights. Its true significance, though, was related to considerations having little to do with either statistics or the calendar.

I went over to the place where the others were forming into a tighter crowd, which betrayed a sense of expectancy in the subtle gestures and expressions of its individual members. Glances were now exchanged, the hand of one lightly touched the shoulder of another, and a pair of circled eyes gazed over to where two figures were setting their lanterns on the ground about six feet apart. The illumination of these lanterns revealed an opening in the earth. Eventually the awareness of everyone was focused on this roundish pit, and as if by prearranged signal we all began huddling around it. The only sounds were those of the wind and our own movements as we crushed frozen leaves and sticks underfoot.

Finally, when we had all surrounded this gaping hole, the first one jumped in, leaving our sight for a moment but then reappearing to take hold of a lantern which another handed him from above. The miniature abyss filled with light, and I could see it was no more than six feet deep. One of its walls opened into the mouth of a tunnel. The figure holding the lantern stooped a little and disappeared into the passage.

Each of us, in turn, dropped into the darkness of this pit, and every fifth one took a lantern. I kept to the back of the group, for whatever subterranean activities were going to take place, I was sure I wanted to be on their periphery. When only about ten of us remained on the ground above, I maneuvered to let four of them precede me so that as the fifth I might receive a lantern. This was exactly how it worked out, for after I had leaped to the bottom of the hole a light was ritually handed down to me. Turning about-face, I quickly entered the passageway. At that point I shook so with cold that I was neither curious nor afraid, but only grateful for the shelter.

I entered a long, gently sloping tunnel, just high enough for me to stand upright. It was considerably warmer down there than outside in the cold darkness of the woods. After a few moments I had sufficiently thawed out so that my concerns shifted from those of physical comfort to a sudden and justified preoccupation with my survival. As I walked, I held my lantern close to the sides of the tunnel. They were relatively smooth, as if the passage had not been made by manual digging but had been burrowed by something which left behind a clue to its dimensions in the tunnel's size and shape. This delirious idea came to me when I recalled the message that had been left on my hotel-room mirror: "What buries itself before it is dead?"

I had to hurry along to keep up with those uncanny spelunkers who preceded me. The lanterns ahead bobbed with every step of their bearers, the lumbering procession seeming less and less real the farther we marched into that snug little tunnel. At some point I noticed the line ahead of me growing shorter. The processioners were emptying out into a cavernous chamber where I, too, soon arrived. This area was about thirty feet in height, its other dimensions approximating those of a large ballroom. Gazing into the distance above made me uncomfortably aware of how far we had descended into the earth. Unlike the smooth sides of the tunnel, the walls of this cavern looked jagged and irregular, as though they had been gnawed at. The earth had been removed, I assumed, either through the tunnel from which we had emerged, or else by way of one of the many other black openings that I saw around the edges of the chamber, for possibly they too led back to the surface.

But the structure of this chamber occupied my mind a great deal less than did its occupants. There to meet us on the floor of the great cavern was what must have been the entire slum population of Mirocaw, and more, all with the same eerily wide-eyed and oval-mouthed faces. They formed a circle around an altarlike object which had some kind of dark, leathery covering draped over it. Upon the altar, another covering of the same material concealed a lumpy form beneath.

And behind this form, looking down upon the altar, was the only figure whose face was not greased with makeup.

He wore a long snowy robe that was the same color as the wispy hair berimming his head. His arms were calmly at his sides. He made no movement. The man I once believed would penetrate great secrets stood before us with the same professorial bearing that had impressed me so many years ago, yet now I felt nothing but dread at the thought of what revelations lay pocketed within the abysmal folds of his magisterial attire. Had I really come here to challenge such a formidable figure? The name by which I knew him seemed itself insufficient to designate one of his stature. Rather I should name him by his other incarnations: god of all wisdom, scribe of all sacred books, father of all magicians, thrice great and more—rather I should call him *Thoth*.

He raised his cupped hands to his congregation, and the ceremony was under way.

It was all very simple. The entire assembly, which had remained speechless until this moment, broke into the most horrendous high-pitched singing that can be imagined. It was a choir of sorrow, of shrieking delirium, and of shame. The cavern rang shrilly with the dissonant whining chorus. My voice, too, was added to the congregation's, trying to blend with their maimed music. But my singing could not imitate theirs, having a huskiness unlike their cacophonous keening wail. To keep from exposing myself as an intruder I continued to mouth their words without sound. These words were a revelation of the moody malignancy which until then I had no more than sensed whenever in the presence of these fixtures. They were singing to the "unborn in paradise," to the "pure unlived lives." They sang a dirge for existence, for all its vital forms and seasons. Their ideals were those of darkness, chaos, and a melancholy half-existence consecrated to all the many shapes of death. A sea of thin, bloodless faces trembled and screamed with perverted hopes. And the robed, guiding figure at the heart of all this—elevated over the course of twenty years to the status of high priest—was the man from whom I had taken so many of my own life's principles. It would be useless to describe what I felt at that moment, and a waste of the time I need to describe the events which followed.

The singing abruptly stopped, and the towering white-haired figure began to speak. He was welcoming those of the new generation—twenty winters had passed since the "Pure Ones" had expanded their ranks. The word *pure* in this setting was a violence to what sense and composure I still retained, for nothing could have been more foul than what was to come. Thoss—and I employ this defunct identity only as a convenience—closed his sermon and drew closer to the dark-skinned altar. Then, with all the flourish of his former life, he drew back the topmost covering. Beneath it was a limp-limbed effigy, a collapsed puppet sprawled upon the slab. I was standing toward the rear of the congregation and attempted to keep as close to the exit passage as I could. Thus, I did not see everything as clearly as I might have.

Thoss looked down upon the crooked, doll-like form and then out at the gathering. I even imagined that he made knowing eye-contact with myself. He spread his arms, and a stream of continuous and unintelligible words flowed from his moaning mouth. The congregation began to stir, not greatly but perceptibly. Until that moment there was a limit to what I believed was the evil of these people. They were, after all, only that. They were merely morbid, self-tortured souls with strange beliefs. If there was anything I had learned in all my years as an anthropologist, it was that the world is infinitely rich in strange ideas, even to the point where the concept of strangeness itself had little meaning for me. But with the scene I then witnessed, my conscience bounded into a realm from which it will never return.

For now was the transformation scene, the culmination of every harlequinade.

It began slowly. There was increasing movement among those on the far side of the chamber from where I stood. Someone had fallen to the floor, and the others in the area backed away. The voice at the altar continued its chanting. I tried to gain a better view, but there were too many of them around me. Through the mass of obstructing bodies I caught only glimpses of what was taking place.

The one who had swooned to the floor of the chamber seemed to be losing all former shape and proportion. I thought it was a clown's trick. They were clowns, were they not? I myself could make four white balls transform into four black balls as I juggled them. And this was not my most astonishing feat of clownish magic. And is there not always a sleight-of-hand inherent in all ceremonies, often dependent on the transported delusions of the celebrants? This was a good show, I thought, and giggled to myself. The transformation scene of Harlequin throwing off his fool's facade. O God, Harlequin, do not move like that! Harlequin, where are your arms? And your legs have melted together and begun squirming upon the floor. What horrible, mouthing umbilicus is that where your face should be? *What is it that buries itself before it is dead?* The almighty serpent of wisdom—the Conqueror Worm.

It now started happening all around the chamber. Individual members of the congregation would gaze emptily—caught for a moment in a frozen trance—and then collapse to the floor to begin the sickening metamorphosis. This happened with ever-increasing frequency the louder and more frantically Thoss chanted his insane prayer or curse. Then there began a writhing movement toward the altar, and Thoss welcomed the things as they curled their way to the altar-top. I knew now what lax figure lay upon it.

This was Kora and Persephone, the daughter of Ceres and the Winter Queen: the child abducted into the underworld of death. Except this child had no supernatural mother to save her, no living mother at all. For the sacrifice I witnessed was an echo of one that had occurred twenty years before, the carnival feast of the preceding generation— O *carne vale!* Now both mother and daughter had become victims of this subterranean sabbath. I finally realized this truth when the figure stirred upon the altar, lifted its head of icy beauty, and screamed at the sight of mute mouths closing around her.

I ran from the chamber into the tunnel. (There was nothing else that could be done, I have obsessively told myself.) Some of the others who had not yet changed began to pursue me. They would have caught up to me, I have no doubt, for I fell only a few yards into the passage. And for a moment I imagined that I too was about to undergo a transformation, but I had not been prepared as the others had been. When I heard the approaching footsteps of my pursuers, I was sure there was an even worse fate facing me upon the altar. But the footsteps ceased and retreated. They had received an order in the voice of their high priest. I too heard the order, though I wish I had not, for until then I had imagined that Thoss did not remember who I was. It was that voice which taught me otherwise.

For the moment I was free to leave. I struggled to my feet and, having broken my lantern in the fall, retraced my way back through cloacal blackness.

Everything seemed to happen very quickly once I emerged from the tunnel and climbed up from the pit. I wiped the reeking greasepaint from my face as I ran through the woods and back to the road. A passing car stopped, though I gave it no other choice except to run me down.

"Thank you for stopping."

"What the hell are you doing out here?" the driver asked.

I caught my breath. "It was a joke. The festival. Friends thought it would be funny. . . . Please drive on."

My ride let me off about a mile out of town, and from there I could find my way. It was the same way I had come into Mirocaw on my first visit the summer before. I stood for a while at the summit of that high hill just outside the city limits, looking down upon the busy little hamlet. The intensity of the festival had not abated, and would not until morning. I walked down toward the welcoming glow of green, slipped through the festivities unnoticed, and returned to the hotel. No one saw me go up to my room. Indeed, there was an atmosphere of absence and abandonment throughout that building, and the desk in the lobby was unattended.

I locked the door to my room and collapsed upon the bed.

7.

When I awoke the next morning I saw from my window that the town and surrounding countryside had been visited during the night by a snowstorm, one which was entirely unpredicted. The snow was still falling on the now-deserted streets of Mirocaw. The festival was over. Everyone had gone home.

And this was exactly my own intention. Any action on my part concerning what I had seen the night before would have to wait until I was away from the town. I am still not sure it will do the slightest good to speak up like this. Any accusations I could make against the slum populace of Mirocaw would be resisted, as well they should be, as unbelievable. Perhaps in a very short while none of this will be my concern.

With packed suitcases in both hands I walked up to the front desk to check out. The man behind the desk was not Samuel Beadle, and he had to fumble around to find my bill.

"Here we are. Everything all right?"

"Fine," I answered in a dead voice. "Is Mr. Beadle around?"

"No, I'm afraid he's not back yet. Been out all night looking for his daughter. She's a very popular girl, being the Winter Queen and all that nonsense. Probably find she was at a party somewhere."

A little noise came out of my throat.

I threw my suitcases in the backseat of my car and got behind the wheel. On that morning nothing I could recall seemed real to me. The snow was falling and I watched it through my windshield, slow and silent and entrancing. I started up my car, routinely glancing in my rearview mirror. What I saw there is now vividly framed in my mind, as it was framed in the back window of my car when I turned to verify its reality.

In the middle of the street behind me, standing ankle-deep in snow, was Thoss and another figure. When I looked closely at the other, I recognized him as one of the boys whom I surprised in that diner. But he had now taken on a corrupt and listless resemblance to his new family. Both he and Thoss stared at me, making no attempt to forestall my departure. Thoss knew that this was unnecessary.

I had to carry the image of those two dark figures in my mind as I drove back home. But only now has the full weight of my experience descended upon me. So far I have claimed illness in order to avoid my teaching schedule. To face the normal flow of life as I had formerly known it would be impossible. I am now very much under the influence of a season and a climate far colder and more barren than all the winters in human memory. And mentally retracing past events does not seem to have helped; I can feel myself sinking deeper into a velvety white abyss.

At certain times I could almost dissolve entirely into this inner realm of awful purity and emptiness. I remember those invisible moments when in disguise I drifted through the streets of Mirocaw, untouched by the drunken, noisy forms around me: untouchable. But instantly I recoil at this grotesque nostalgia, for I realize what is happening and what I do not want to be true, though Thoss proclaimed it was. I recall his command to those others as I lay helplessly prone in the tunnel. They could have apprehended me, but Thoss, my old master, called them back. His voice echoed throughout that cavern, and it now reverberates within my own psychic chambers of memory.

"He is one of us," it said. "He has *always* been one of us."

It is this voice which now fills my dreams and my days and my long winter nights. I have seen you, Dr. Thoss, through the snow outside my window. Soon I will celebrate, alone, that last feast which will kill your words, only to prove how well I have learned their truth.

The Shadow on the Doorstep

JAMES P. BLAYLOCK

It was several months after I had dismantled my aquaria that I heard a rustling in the darkness, a scraping of what sounded like footsteps on the front porch of my house. It startled me out of a literary lethargy built partly of three hours of Jules Verne, partly of a nodding acquaintance with a bottle of single malt scotch. In the yellow glow of the porch lamp, through the tiny distorting panes of the mullioned upper half of the oaken door, I saw only a shadow, a face perhaps, half turned away. The dark outline of it was lost in the shaded confusion of an unpruned hibiscus.

The porch itself was a rectangular island of hooded light, cut with drooping shadows of potted plants and the rectilinear darkness of a pair of weather-stained mission chairs. Encircling it was a tumult of shrubbery. Beyond lay the street and the feeble glow of globed lamps, all of it washed in pale moonlight that served only to darken that wall of shrubbery, so that the porch with its yellow bug light and foliage seemed a self-contained world of dwindling enchantment.

I couldn't say with any confidence as I sat staring in sudden, unexplained horror at the start this late visitor had given me, that the leafy appendages thrusting away on either side of him weren't arms or some strange mélange of limbs and fins. With the weak light at his back he was a fishy shadow suffused in the amber aura of porch light, something that had crawled dripping out of a late Devonian sea.

In the interests of objectivity, I'll say again that I had been reading Jules Verne. And it's altogether reasonable that a mixture of the book, the shadows, the embers aglow in the fireplace, the late hour, and a morbid suspicion that nothing but trouble travels in the suburbs after dark combined to enchant into existence this troublesome shade that was nothing, in fact, but the scraping of a branch of hibiscus against the windowpane. But you can understand that I wasn't anxious to open the door.

I set the book down silently, the afterimage of the interior of the

Nautilus slanting across my consciousness and then submerging, and I remember wondering at the appropriateness of the scene in the novel: the crystal panels bound in copper beyond which floated transparent sheets of water illuminated by sunlight; the lazy undulations of eels and fishes, of lampreys and Japanese salamanders and blue-and-silver clouds of schooling mackerel. Slipping into the shadows beyond the couch, I pressed myself against the wall and crept into the darkened study where a window would afford me a view of most of the porch.

My aquaria, as I've said, were dismantled some months earlier—six, I believe—the water siphoned out a window and into a flower bed, the waterweeds collapsed in a soggy heap, the fish astonished to find themselves imprisoned in a three-gallon bucket. These last I gave to a nearby tropical fish store; the empty aquaria with its gravel and lumps of petrified stone I stored beneath a bench in the shed under my avocado tree. It was a sad undertaking, all in all, like bundling up pieces of my boyhood and packing them away in a crate. I sometimes have the notion that opening the crate would restore them wholesale, that the re-creation of years gone by could be effected by dragging in a hose and filling the tanks with clear water, by banking the gravel around rocks heaped to form dark caverns, the entrances of which are shadowed by the reaching tendrils of waterweeds through which glow watery rays of reflected light. But the visitor on the porch that night dissuaded me.

Three aquarium shops sit neatly in my memory by day and are confused and shuffled by night, giddily trading fishes and facades, all of them alive with the hum and bubble of pumps and filters and the damp, musty smell of fish tanks drip-dripping tropical water onto concrete floors. One I discovered by bicycle when I was thirteen. It was a clapboard house on a frontage road along a freeway, the exhaust of countless roaring trucks and automobiles having dusted the peeling white paint with black grime. Inside sat dozens of ten-gallon tanks, poorly lit, the water within them half evaporated. There wasn't much to recommend it, even to a thirteen-year-old, aside from a door in the back—what used to be a kitchen door, I suppose—that led along a gravel path to what had been a garage.

These thirty years later I can recall the very day I discovered it— the gravel path, that is—easily a year after my first bicycle journey to the shop. I wandered around inside, shaking my head at the condition of the aquaria, despising the guppies and goldfish and tetras that swam sluggishly past their scattered dead companions. My father waited in a Studebaker at the curb outside, drumming his fingers along the top of the passenger seat. A sign in pencil scrawl attracted my eye, advertising another room of fish "outside." And so out I stepped along that gravel path, shoving into the darkened back half of the garage, which was unlit save for the incandescent bulbs in aquarium reflectors.

I shut the door behind me for no other reason than to keep out sunlight. Banks of aquaria lined three walls, all of them a deep greenish-black, the water within lit against a backdrop of elodea and Amazon swordplant and the waving lacy branches of ambulia and sagittaria. There was the faint bursting of fine bubbles that danced toward the surface from aerators trapped beneath mossy stones. On the sandy floor of one aquarium lay a half-dozen mottled freshwater rays from the Amazon, their poisonous tails almost indistinguishable from the gravel they rested on. A half-score of buffalo-head cichlids hovered in the shelter of an arched heap of waterfall rock, under which was coiled the long finny serpent's tail of a reedfish.

The aquarium seemed to me to be prodigiously deep, a trick, perhaps, of reflection and light and the clever arrangement of rocks and waterplants. But it suggested, just for a moment, that the shadowed water within was somehow vast as the sea bottom or was a sort of antechamber to the driftwood and pebble floor of a tropical river. Other aquaria flanked it. Gobies peered up at me from out of burrows in the sand. An enormous compressiceps, flat as a plate, blinked out from behind a tangle of cryptocoryne grasses. Leaf fish floated amid the lacy brown of decaying vegetation, and a hovering pair of golfball-sized puffers, red eyes blinking, tiny pectoral fins whirring like submarine propellers, peered suspiciously from beneath a ledge of dark stone. There was something utterly alien about that room full of fishes, existing in manufactured amber light, a thousand miles removed from the dusty gravel of the yard outside, from the roaring freeway traffic not sixty feet distant.

I stood staring, oblivious to the time, until the door swung open in a flood of sunlight and my father peeked in. In the sudden illumination the odd atmosphere of the room seemed to decay, to disperse, and it reminds me now of what must happen to a forest glade when the morning sun evaporates the damp enchanted pall that is summoned each night by moonlight from the roots and mulch and earth of the forest floor.

One dimmed tank was lit briefly by the sunlight, and in it, crouched behind a tumble of dark stone, was an almost hidden creature with an enormous head and eyes, the eyes of a squid or a spaniel, eyes that were lidded, that blinked slowly and sadly past the curious scattered decorations of its tank: a half-dozen agate marbles, a platoon of painted lead soldiers, a brass sheriff's star, and a little tin shovel angling from a bucket half full of tilted sand and painted in tints of azure and yellow, a scene of children playing along a sunset beach.

I was old enough and imaginative enough to be struck by the incongruity of the contents of that aquarium. I wasn't, though, well enough schooled in ichthyology to remark on the lidded eyes of the creature in the tank—which is just as well. I was given over to nightmares as it was. A year passed before I had occasion to visit the shop beside the freeway again, and I can recall bicycling along wet streets through intermittent showers, hunched over in a yellow, hooded slicker, my pant legs soaked from the knees down, rewarded finally with the sight of no shop at all, but of a vacant lot, already up in weeds, the concrete foundation of the clapboard house and garage brown with rainwater and mud.

Here it was nearly midnight, thirty years later, and something was stirring on my front porch. Wind out of the west shuffled the foliage, and I could hear the sighing of fronds in the queen palms along the curb. I stood in shadow, wafered against a tilted bookcase, peering past the edge of the casement at nothing. There was a rustling of bushes and swaying shadow. Something—what was it?—was skulking out there. I was certain. Hairs prickled along the back of my neck. A low mournful boom of distant thunder followed a windy clatter of rain-drops. The wet ozone smell of rain on concrete washed through the room, and I realized with a start that a window had blown open behind me. I turned and pushed it shut, crouching below the sill so as not to be seen, thinking without meaning to of wandering in the rain across the ruins of that tropical fish shop, searching in the weeds for nothing I could name and finding only shards of broken glass and a ceramic fish-bowl castle the color of an Easter egg.

I slipped tight the bolt on the window and crept across to my book-case, peering once again out into the seemingly empty night where the branches of hibiscus with their drooping pink flowers danced in the wind and rain.

In San Francisco, in Chinatown, in an alley off Washington, lies the second of the three aquarium shops. I was a student at the time. I'd eaten a remarkable dinner at a restaurant called Sam Wo and was wandering along the foggy evening street, looking for a set of those compressed origami flowers that bloom when dropped into water, when I saw a sign depicting Chinese ideographs and a lacy-looking tri-colored koi. I slouched down a narrow alley between canted buildings, the misty air smelling of garlic and fog, barbecued duck and spilled garbage. Through a slender doorway veiled with the scent of musty sand there sounded the familiar hum of aquaria.

The shop itself was vast and dark beneath low ceilings. Dim rooms, lost in shadow, stretched away beneath the street, scattered aquarium lights glowing like misty distant stars. Flat breeding tanks were stacked five deep on rusted steel stands below a row of darkened transom windows that fronted the alley. Exotic goldfish labored to stay afloat, staring through bubble eyes, their caudal fins so enormously overgrown that they seemed to drag the creatures backward. One of the fish, I remember, was the size and shape of a grapefruit, a stupendous freak bred for the sake of nothing more than curiosity. Illogically, perhaps because of my having stumbled years earlier upon that shed full of odd fish along the freeway, it occurred to me that the more distant rooms would contain even more curious fish, so I hesitantly wandered deeper, under Washington, I suppose, only to discover that yet farther rooms existed, that rooms seemed to open onto others through arched doors, the ancient plaster of which was so discolored and mossy from the constant humidity that it appeared as if the openings were chipped out of stone. Vast aquaria full of trailing waterweeds sat bank upon bank, and in them swam creatures that had, weeks earlier, lurked in driftwood grottoes in the Amazon and Orinoco.

There was something about the place that brought to mind the shovel and bucket, the promise of pending mystery, perhaps horror. Each aquarium with its shadowy corners and heaped stone and lacy plants seemed a tiny enclosed world, as did the shop itself, utterly adrift from the noisy Chinatown alleyways and streets above, which crisscrossed in a foggy tapestry of a world alien to the hilly sprawl of San Francisco, each successive layer full of wonder and threat. There was something in my reaction to it akin to the attraction Professor Aronnax felt to the interior of the *Nautilus* with its library of black-violet ebony and brass, its twelve thousand books, its luminous ceilings and pipe organ and jars of mollusks and sea stars and black pearls larger than pigeons' eggs and its glass walls through which, as if from within an aquarium, one had a night-and-day view of the depths of the sea.

I was confronted on the edge of the second chamber by a tiny Oriental man, his face lost in shadow. I hadn't heard him approach. He held in his hand a dripping net, large enough to snare a sea bass, and he wore rubber boots as if he were in the habit of clambering into aquaria to pursue fish. His sudden appearance startled me out of a peculiar frame of mind that accounted for, I'm certain, the curious idea that in the faint pearl-like luminosity of aquarium light, the arm and hand that held the net were scaled.

I found my way to the street. He hadn't said anything, but the slow shaking of his head had seemed to indicate that I wasn't entirely welcome there, that it was a hatchery, perhaps, a wholesale house in which casual strollers would find nothing that would interest them.

And it was nothing, years later, that I found on the front porch. The wind blew rain under the eaves and against the panes of the window. Water ran along them in rivulets, distorting even further the waving foliage on the porch, making it impossible to determine whether the dark places were mere shadow or were more than that. I returned to my couch and book and fireplace, piling split cedar logs atop burned-down fragments, and blowing on the embers until the wood popped and crackled and firelight danced on the walls of the living room. It must have been two o'clock in the morning by then, a morbid hour, it seems to me, but somehow I was disinclined toward bed and so I sat browsing in my book, idly sipping at my glass, and half listening to the shuffle and scrape of things in the night and the occasional rumble of faraway thunder.

I couldn't, somehow, keep my eyes off the door, although I pretended to continue to read. The result was that I focused on nothing at all, but must have fallen asleep, for I lurched awake at the sound of a clay flowerpot crashing to bits on the porch outside, the victim, possibly, of a rainy gust of wind. I sat up, tumbling Jules Verne to the rug, a half-formed dream of tilted pier pilings and dark stone pools of placid water dissolving into mist in my mind. A shadow loomed beyond the door. I snatched at the little pull-chain of the wall sconce overhead and pitched the room into darkness, thinking to hide my own movements as well as to illuminate those of the thing on the porch.

But almost as soon as the light evaporated, leaving only the orange glow of the settled fire, I switched the light back on. It was futile to think of hiding myself, and as for whatever it was that lurked on the threshold, I hadn't any monumental desire to confront it. So I sat trembling. The shadow remained, as if it watched and listened, satisfied to know that I knew it was there.

There had been another tropical fish store in San Pedro in a dockside street of thrift shops and bars and boarded-up windows. The harbor side of the street was built largely upon pilings, and below the slumping wooden buildings were shadowy broken remnants of abandoned wharfs and the shifting gray Pacific tide. The windows of the shop were obscured by heavy dust that had lain on the cracked panes for years, and there were only dim, scattered lights shining beyond to indicate that the building wasn't deserted. A painted sign on the door read TROPICAL RARITIES—FISH AND AMPHIBIA and below it, taped to the inside of the door and barely visible through the dust, was a yellowed price list, advertising, I recall, Colombian horned frogs and tiger salamanders, at prices twenty years out-of-date.

The door was locked. But from within, I was certain of it, came the humming of aquaria and the swish-splash of aerated water against a background of murmuring voices. Had I been ten years younger, I would have rapped on the glass, perhaps shouted. But my interest in aquaria had waned, and I had come to the neighborhood, actually, to purchase tickets for a boat ride to Catalina Island. So I turned to leave, only vaguely curious, noting for the first time a wooden stairway angling steeply away toward the docks, its stile gate left carelessly ajar. I hesitated before it, peering down along the warped banister, and saw hanging from the wooden siding of the building a simple wordless sign depicting ideographs and a tricolored koi. It was a shock of curious recognition as much as anything that impelled me down those stairs, grinning foolishly, rehearsing what it was I'd say to whomever I'd meet at the bottom.

But I met no one—only the lapping of dark water against the stones and a scattering of red crabs that scuttled away into the shadows of mossy rock. Overhanging buildings formed a sort of open-air cellar, dark and cool and smelling of mussels and barnacles and mudflats. At first the darkness within was impenetrable, but as I shaded my eyes and stepped into the shadows I made out a half-dozen dim rings of mottled stone—amphibian pools, I imagined, their sides draped with trailing water plants.

"Hello," I called, timorously, I suppose, and was met with silence except for a brief splashing in one of the pools. I stepped forward hesitantly. I had no business being there, but I was struck with curious wonder at what it was that dwelt within those circular pools.

The first appeared to be empty of life aside from great tendrils of tangled elodea and a floating carpet of broadleaf duckweed. I knelt on the wet stone and swept the duckweed aside with my hands, squinting into the depths. Some few bits of clouded daylight filtered in from above, but the feeble illumination was hardly enough to lighten the pool. Something, though, glistened for a moment below, as if beckoning, signifying, and I found myself glancing around me guiltily even as I rolled up my shirtsleeve. In for a penny . . . , I thought to myself, plunging my arm in up to the shoulder.

There was a movement then beneath the water, as if the pool were deeper than I'd thought and I'd disturbed the solitude of some submerged creature. I groped among plants and gravel, nearly dipping my ear into the water. There it was, lying on its side. My fingers closed over the half hoop of its handle just as a slow scuffling sounded from the far end of the twilit room.

I stood up, prepared for heaven knew what, holding in my hand, impossibly, a familiar tin pail, its side now dented in, its blue ocean bent over and half submerging the children still at play, these many years later, along its sandy beach. Before me crouched a small Oriental man, staring oddly, as if he half-recognized my face and was amazed to find me, it seemed, in the act of purloining that bent toy pail. I dropped it into the pool, began to speak, then turned and hurried away. The man who had confronted me wore no rubber boots, and he carried no enormous fishnet in his hand. In the dim half-light of that strange oceanside grotto his skin, at a hasty glance, was nothing more than skin. I could insist for the sake of cheap adventure that he was scaled, gilled, perhaps, with webbed hands and an ear-to-ear mouth. And he easily might have been. I left without a backward glance, focusing on the alligator blue paint of the ramshackle stairway, and on the shingled roof that rose into view on the opposite side of the street as I climbed, step by creaking step. I drove home, I recall, punching randomly at the buttons of my car radio, turning it on and off, aware of the incongruity, the superfluousness of the music and the newscasts and the foolish and alien radio chatter.

The incident rather took the wind out of the sails of my tropical fish collecting—sails that were half furled anyway. And certain odd, otherwise innocent, pictures began to haunt my dreams—random images of pale angular faces, of painted lead soldiers scattered in a weedy lot, of the furtive movement of fish in weed-shadowed aquaria, of a wooden signboard swinging and swinging in wind-driven rain.

Beyond the locked front door lies nothing more than the shadow of evening foliage, stirring in the rainy wind. Common sense would have it so; would say, in a smug and tiresome voice, that I've been confused by a dangerous combination of coincidence and happenstance. It would be an invitation to madness not to heed such a voice.

But it's not a night for heeding voices. The wind and rain lash at the dark shrubbery; the shadows waver and dance. Through the window glass nothing at all can be seen beyond the pallid light of the porch lamp. Two hours from now the sun will rise, and with it will come a manufactured disregard for the suggestion of connections, of odd patterns behind the seemingly random. The front porch—rainwater drying in patches, the mission chairs sitting solid and substantial, the oranges and pinks of hibiscus bloom grinning at the day—will be inhabited only by a hurrying square-jawed milkman in a white cap and by the solid clink of bottles in a galvanized wire basket.

Lord of the Land

GENE WOLFE

The Nebraskan smiled warmly, leaned forward, and made a sweeping gesture with his right hand, saying, "Yes indeed, that's exactly the sort of thing I'm most interested in. Tell me about it, Mr. Thacker, please."

All this was intended to keep old Hop Thacker's attention away from the Nebraskan's left hand, which had slipped into his left jacket pocket to turn on the miniature recorder there. Its microphone was pinned to the back of the Nebraskan's lapel, the fine brown wire almost invisible.

Perhaps old Hop would not have cared in any case; old Hop was hardly the shy type. "Waul," he began, "this was years an' years back, the way I hear'd it. Guess it'd have been in my great granpaw's time, Mr. Cooper, or mebbe before."

The Nebraskan nodded encouragingly.

"There's these three boys, an' they had an old mule, wasn't good fer nothin' 'cept crowbait. One was Colonel Lightfoot—course didn't nobody call him colonel then. One was Creech an' t'other 'un . . ." The old man paused, fingering his scant beard. "Guess I don't rightly know. I *did* know. It'll come to me when don't nobody want to hear it. He's the one had the mule."

The Nebraskan nodded again. "Three young men, you say, Mr. Thacker?"

"That's right, an' Colonel Lightfoot, he had him a new gun. An' this other 'un—he was a friend of my granpaw's or somebody—he had him one everybody said was jest about the best shooter in the county. So this here Laban Creech, he said *he* wasn't no bad shot hisself, an' he went an' fetched his'un. He was the 'un had that mule. I recollect now.

"So they led the ol' mule out into the medder, mebbe fifty straddles from the brake. You know how you do. Creech, he shot it smack in the ear, an' it jest laid down an' died, it was old, an' sick, too, didn't kick or nothin'. So Colonel Lightfoot, he fetched out his knife an' cut it up the belly, an' they went on back to the brake fer to wait out the crows."

299

"I see," the Nebraskan said.

"One'd shoot, an' then another, an' they'd keep score. An' it got to be near to dark, you know, an' Colonel Lightfoot with his new gun an' this other man that had the good 'un, they was even up, an' this Laban Creech was only one behind 'em. Reckon there was near to a hundred crows back behind in the gully. You can't jest shoot a crow an' leave him, you know, an' 'spect the rest to come. They look an' see that dead 'un, an' they say, Waul, jest look what become of *him*. I don't calc'late to come anywheres near *there*."

The Nebraskan smiled. "Wise birds."

"Oh, there's all kinds of stories 'bout 'em," the old man said. "Thankee, Sarah."

His granddaughter had brought two tall glasses of lemonade; she paused in the doorway to dry her hands on her red-and-white checkered apron, glancing at the Nebraskan with shy alarm before retreating into the house.

"Didn't have a lick, back then." The old man poked an ice cube with one bony, somewhat soiled finger. "Didn't have none when I was a little 'un, neither, till the TVA come. Nowadays you talk 'bout the TVA an' they think you mean them programs, you know." He waved his glass. "I watch 'em sometimes."

"Television," the Nebraskan supplied.

"That's it. Like, you take when Bud Bloodhat went to his reward, Mr. Cooper. Hot? You never seen the like. The birds all had their mouths open, wouldn't fly fer anything. Lost two hogs, I recollect, that same day. My paw, he wanted to save the meat, but 'twasn't a bit of good. He says he thought them hogs was rotten 'fore ever they dropped, an' he was 'fraid to give it to the dogs, it was that hot. They was all asleepin' under the porch anyhow. Wouldn't come out fer nothin'."

The Nebraskan was tempted to reintroduce the subject of the crow shoot, but an instinct born of thousands of hours of such listening prompted him to nod and smile instead.

"Waul, they knowed they had to git him under quick, didn't they? So they got him fixed, cleaned up an' his best clothes on an' all like that, an' they was all in there listenin', but it was terrible hot in there an' you could smell him pretty strong, so by an' by I jest snuck out. Wasn't nobody payin' attention to *me*, do you see? The women's all bawlin' an' carryin' on, an' the men thinkin' it was time to put him under an' have another."

The old man's cane fell with a sudden, dry rattle. For a moment as he picked it up, the Nebraskan glimpsed Sarah's pale face on the other side of the doorway.

"So I snuck out on the stoop. I bet it was a hundred easy, but it felt good to me after bein' inside there. That was when I seen it comin' down the hill t'other side of the road. Stayed in the shadow much as it could, an' looked like a shadow itself, only you could see it move, an' it was always blacker than what they was. I knowed it was the soul-sucker an' was afeered it'd git my ma. I took to cryin', an' she come outside an' fetched me down the spring fer a drink, an' that's the last time anybody ever did see it, far's I know."

"Why do you call it the soul-sucker?" the Nebraskan asked.

" 'Cause that's what it does, Mr. Cooper. Guess you know it ain't only folks that has ghosts. A man can see the ghost of another man, all right, but he can see the ghost of a dog or a mule or anythin' like that, too. Waul, you take a man's, 'cause that don't make so much argyment. It's his soul, ain't it? Why ain't it in Heaven or down in the bad place like it's s'possed to be? What's it doin' in the haint house, or walkin' down the road, or wherever 'twas you seen it? I had a dog that seen a ghost one time, an' that'n was another dog's, do you see? *I* never did see it, but he did, an' I knowed he did by how he acted. What was it doin' there?"

The Nebraskan shook his head. "I've no idea, Mr. Thacker."

"Waul, I'll tell you. When a man passes on, or a horse or a dog or whatever, it's s'pposed to git out an' git over to the Judgment. The Lord Jesus Christ's our judge, Mr. Cooper. Only sometimes it won't do it. Mebbe it's afeared to be judged, or mebbe it has this or that to tend to down here yet, or anyhow reckons it does, like showin' somebody some money what it knowed about. Some does that pretty often, an' I might tell you 'bout some of them times. But if it don't have business an' is jest feared to go, it'll stay where 'tis—that's the kind that haints their graves. They b'long to the soul-sucker, do you see, if it can git 'em. Only if it's hungered it'll suck on a live person, an' he's bound to fight or die." The old man paused to wet his lips with lemonade, staring across his family's little burial plot and fields of dry cornstalks to purple hills where he would never hunt again. "Don't win, not particular often. Guess the first 'un was a Indian, mebbe. Somethin' like that. I tell you how Creech shot it?"

"No you didn't, Mr. Thacker." The Nebraskan took a swallow of his own lemonade, which was refreshingly tart. "I'd like very much to hear it."

The old man rocked in silence for what seemed a long while. "Waul," he said at last, "they'd been shootin' all day. Reckon I said that. Fer a good long time anyhow. An' they was tied, Colonel Lightfoot an' this here Cooper was, an' Creech jest one behind 'em. 'Twas Creech's time next, an' he kept on sayin' to stay fer jest one more, then he'd go an' they'd all go, hit or miss. So they stayed, but wasn't no more crows 'cause they'd 'bout kilt every crow in many a mile. Started gittin' dark fer sure, an' this Cooper, he says, Come on, Lab, couldn't nobody hit nothin' now. You lost an' you got to face up.

"Creech, he says, waul, 'twas my mule. An' jest 'bout then here comes somethin' bigger'n any crow, an' black, hoppin' 'long the ground like a crow will sometimes, do you see? Over towards that dead mule. So Creech ups with his gun. Colonel Lightfoot, he allowed afterwards he couldn't have seed his sights in that dark. Reckon he jest sighted 'longside the barrel. 'Tis the ol' mountain way, do you see, an' there's lots what swore by it.

"Waul, he let go an' it fell over. You won, says Colonel Lightfoot, an' he claps Creech on his back, an' let's go. Only this Cooper, he knowed it wasn't no crow, bein' too big, an' he goes over to see what 'twas. Waul, sir, 'twas like to a man, only crooked-legged an' wry neck. 'Twasn't no man, but like to it, do you see? Who shot me? it says, an' the mouth was full of worms. Grave worms, do you see?

"Who shot me? An' Cooper, he said Creech, then he hollered fer Creech an' Colonel Lightfoot. Colonel Lightfoot says, boys, we got to bury this. An' Creech goes back to his home place an' fetches a spade an' a ol' shovel, them bein' all he's got. He's shakin' so bad they jest rattled together, do you see? Colonel Lightfoot an' this Cooper, they seed he couldn't dig, so they goes hard at it. Pretty soon they looked around, an' Creech was gone, an' the soul-sucker, too."

The old man paused dramatically. "Next time anybody seed the soul-sucker, 'twas Creech. So he's the one I seed, or one of his kin anyhow. Don't never shoot anythin' without you're dead sure what 'tis, young feller."

Cued by his closing words, Sarah appeared in the doorway. "Supper's ready. I set a place for you, Mr. Cooper. Pa said. You sure you want to stay? Won't be fancy."

The Nebraskan stood up. "Why, that was very kind of you, Miss Thacker."

His granddaughter helped the old man rise. Propped by the cane in his right hand and guided and supported by her on his left, he shuffled slowly into the house. The Nebraskan followed and held his chair.

"Pa's washin' up," Sarah said. "He was changin' the oil in the tractor. He'll say grace. You don't have to get my chair for me, Mr. Cooper, I'll put on till he comes. Just sit down."

"Thank you." The Nebraskan sat across from the old man.

"We got ham and sweet corn, biscuits, and potatoes. It's not no company dinner."

With perfect honesty the Nebraskan said, "Everything smells wonderful, Miss Thacker."

Her father entered, scrubbed to the elbows but bringing a tang of crankcase oil to the mingled aromas from the stove. "You hear all you wanted to, Mr. Cooper?"

"I heard some marvelous stories, Mr. Thacker," the Nebraskan said.

Sarah gave the ham the place of honor before her father. "I think it's truly fine, what you're doin', writin' up all these old stories 'fore they're lost."

Her father nodded reluctantly. "Wouldn't have thought you could make a livin' at it, though."

"He don't, Pa. He teaches. He's a teacher." The ham was followed by a mountainous platter of biscuits. Sarah dropped into a chair. "I'll fetch our sweet corn and potatoes in just a shake. Corn's not quite done yet."

"O Lord, bless this food and them that eats it. Make us thankful for farm, family, and friends. Welcome the stranger 'neath our roof as we do, O Lord. Now let's eat." The younger Mr. Thacker rose and applied an enormous butcher knife to the ham, and the Nebraskan remembered at last to switch off his tape recorder.

Two hours later, more than filled, the Nebraskan had agreed to stay the night. "It's not real fancy," Sarah said as she showed him to their vacant bedroom, "but it's clean. I just put those sheets and the comforter on while you were talkin' to Grandpa." The door creaked. She flipped the switch.

The Nebraskan nodded. "You anticipated that I'd accept your father's invitation."

"Well, he hoped you would." Careful not to meet his eye, Sarah added, "I never seen Grandpa so happy in years. You're goin' to talk to him some more in the mornin'? You can put the stuff from your suitcase right here in this dresser. I cleared out these top drawers, and I already turned your bed down for you. Bathroom's on past Pa's room. You know. I guess we seem awful country to you, out here."

"I grew up on a farm near Fremont, Nebraska," the Nebraskan told her. There was no reply. When he looked around, Sarah was blowing a kiss from the doorway; instantly she was gone.

With a philosophical shrug, he laid his suitcase on the bed and opened it. In addition to his notebooks, he had brought his well-thumbed copy of *The Types of the Folktale* and Schmit's *Gods before the Greeks*, which he had been planning to read. Soon the Thackers would assemble in their front room to watch television. Surely he might be excused for an hour or two? His unexpected arrival later in the evening might actually give them pleasure. He had a sudden premonition that Sarah, fair and willow-slender, would be sitting alone on the sagging sofa, and that there would be no unoccupied chair.

There was an unoccupied chair in the room, however; an old but sturdy-looking wooden one with a cane bottom. He carried it to the window and opened Schmit, determined to read as long as the light lasted. Dis, he knew, had come in his chariot for the souls of departed Greeks, and so had been called the Gatherer of Many by those too fearful to name him; but Hop Thacker's twisted and almost pitiable soul-sucker appeared to have nothing else in common with the dark and kingly Dis. Had there been some still earlier deity who clearly pre-figured the soul-sucker? Like most folklorists, the Nebraskan firmly believed that folklore's themes were, if not actually eternal, for the most part very ancient indeed. *Gods before the Greeks* seemed well indexed.

> **Dead,** their mummies visited by An-uat, 2.

The Nebraskan nodded to himself and turned to the front of the book.

> An-uat, Anuat, "Lord of the Land (the Necropolis)," "Opener to the North." Though frequently confused with Anubis, to whom he lent his form, it is clear that An-uat the jackal-god maintained a separate identity into the New Kingdom period. Souls that had refused to board Ra's boat (and thus to appear before the throne of the resurrected Osiris) were dragged by An-uat, who visited their mummies for this purpose, to Tuat, the lightless, demon-haunted valley stretching between the death of the old sun and the rising of the new. An-uat and the less threatening Anubis can seldom be distinguished in art, but where such distinction is possible, An-uat is the more powerfully muscled figure. Van Allen reports that An-uat is still invoked by the modern (Moslem or Coptic) magicians of Egypt, under the name Ju'gu.

The Nebraskan rose, laid the book on his chair, and strode to the dresser and back. Here was a five-thousand-year-old myth that paralleled the soul-sucker in function. Nor was it certain by any means that the similarity was merely coincidental. That the folklore of the Appalachians could have been influenced by the occult beliefs of modern Egypt was wildly improbable, but by no means impossible. After the Civil War the United States Army had imported not only camels but camel drivers from Egypt, the Nebraskan reminded himself; and the escape artist Harry Houdini had once described in lurid detail his imprisonment in the Great Pyramid. His account was undoubtedly highly colored—but had he, perhaps, actually visited Egypt as an extension of some European tour? Thousands of American servicemen must have passed through Egypt during the Second World

War, but the soul-sucker tale was clearly older than that, and probably older than Houdini.

There seemed to be a difference in appearance as well; but just how different were the soul-sucker and this Ju'gu, really? An-uat had been depicted as a muscular man with a jackal's head. The soul-sucker had been. . . .

The Nebraskan extracted the tape recorder from his pocket, rewound the tape, and inserted the earpiece.

Had been "like to a man, only crooked-legged an' wry neck." Yet it had not *been* a man, though the feature that separated it from humanity had not been specified. A doglike head seemed a possibility, surely, and An-uat might have changed a good deal in five thousand years.

The Nebraskan returned to his chair and reopened his book, but the sun was already nearly at the horizon. After flipping pages aimlessly for a minute or two, he joined the Thackers in their living room.

Never had the inanities of television seemed less real or less significant. Though his eyes followed the movements of the actors on the screen, he was in fact considerably more attentive to Sarah's warmth and rather too generously applied perfume, and still more to a scene that had never, perhaps, taken place: to the dead mule lying in the field long ago, and to the marksmen concealed where the woods began. Colonel Lightfoot had no doubt been a historical person, locally famous, who would be familiar to the majority of Mr. Thacker's hearers. Laban Creech might or might not have been an actual person as well. Mr. Thacker had—mysteriously, now that the Nebraskan came to consider it—given the Nebraskan's own last name, Cooper, to the third and somewhat inessential marksman.

Three marksmen had been introduced because numbers greater than unity were practically always three in folklore, of course; but the use of his own name seemed odd. No doubt it had been no more than a quirk of the old man's failing memory. Remembering *Cooper*, he had attributed the name incorrectly.

By imperceptible degrees, the Nebraskan grew conscious that the Thackers were giving no more attention to the screen than he himself was; they chuckled at no jokes, showed no irritation at even the most insistent commercials, and spoke about the dismal sitcom neither to him nor to one another.

Pretty Sarah sat primly beside him, her knees together, her long legs crossed at their slender ankles, and her dishwater-reddened hands folded on her apron. To his right, the old man rocked, the faint protests of his chair as regular, and as slow, as the ticking of the tall clock in the corner, his hands upon the crook of his cane, his expression a sightless frown.

To Sarah's left, the younger Mr. Thacker was almost hidden from the Nebraskan's view. He rose and went into the kitchen, cracking his knuckles as he walked, returned with neither food nor drink, and sat once more for less than half a minute before rising again.

Sarah ventured, "Maybe you'd like some cookies, or some more lemonade?"

The Nebraskan shook his head. "Thank you, Miss Thacker; but if I were to eat anything else, I wouldn't sleep."

Oddly, her hands clenched. "I could fetch you a piece of pie."

"No, thank you."

Mercifully, the sitcom was over, replaced by a many-colored sunrise on the plains of Africa. There sailed the boat of Ra, the Nebraskan reflected, issuing in splendor from the dark gorge called Tuat to give light to mankind. For a moment he pictured a far smaller and less radiant vessel, black-hulled and crowded with the recalcitrant dead, a vessel steered by a jackal-headed man: a minute fleck against the blazing disk of the African sun. What was that book of von Däniken's? *Ships*—no, *Chariots of the Gods*. Spaceships nonetheless—and that was folklore, too, or at any rate was quickly passing into folklore; the Nebraskan had encountered it twice already.

An animal, a zebra, lay still upon the plain. The camera panned in on it; when it was very near, the head of a huge hyena appeared, its jaws dripping carrion. The old man turned away, his abrupt movement drawing the Nebraskan's attention.

Fear. That was it, of course. He cursed himself for not having identified the emotion pervading the living room sooner. Sarah was frightened, and so was the old man—horribly afraid. Even Sarah's father appeared fearful and restless, leaning back in his chair, then forward, shifting his feet, wiping his palms on the thighs of his faded khaki trousers.

The Nebraskan rose and stretched. "You'll have to excuse me. It's been a long day."

When neither of the men spoke, Sarah said, "I'm 'bout to turn in myself, Mr. Cooper. You want to take a bath?"

He hesitated, trying to divine the desired reply. "If it's not going to be too much trouble. That would be very nice."

Sarah rose with alacrity. "I'll fetch you some towels and stuff."

He returned to his room, stripped, and put on pajamas and a robe. Sarah was waiting for him at the bathroom door with a bar of Zest and half a dozen towels at least. As he took the towels the Nebraskan murmured, "Can you tell me what's wrong? Perhaps I can help."

"We could go to town, Mr. Cooper." Hesitantly she touched his arm. "I'm kind of pretty, don't you think so? You wouldn't have to marry me or nothin', just go off in the mornin'."

"You are," the Nebraskan told her. "In fact, you're very pretty; but I couldn't do that to your family."

"You get dressed again." Her voice was scarcely audible, her eyes on the top of the stairs. "You say your old trouble's startin' up, you got to see the doctor. I'll slide out the back and 'round. Stop for me at the big elm."

"I really couldn't, Miss Thacker," the Nebraskan said.

In the tub he told himself that he had been a fool. What was it that girl in his last class had called him? A hopeless romantic. He could have enjoyed an attractive young woman that night (and it had been months since he had slept with a woman) and saved her from . . . what? A beating by her father? There had been no bruises on her bare arms, and he had noticed no missing teeth. That delicate nose had never been broken, surely.

He could have enjoyed the night with a very pretty young woman—for whom he would have felt responsible afterward, for the remainder of his life. He pictured the reference in *The Journal of American Folklore:* "Collected by Dr. Samuel Cooper, U. Neb., from Hopkin Thacker, 73, whose granddaughter Dr. Cooper seduced and abandoned."

With a snort of disgust, he stood, jerked the chain of the white rubber plug that had retained his bathwater, and snatched up one of Sarah's towels, at which a scrap of paper fluttered to the yellow bathroom rug. He picked it up, his fingers dampening lined notebook filler.

Do not tell him anything grandpa told you. A woman's hand, almost painfully legible.

Sarah had anticipated his refusal, clearly; anticipated it, and coppered her bets. *Him* meant her father, presumably, unless there was another male in the house or another was expected—her father almost certainly.

The Nebraskan tore the note into small pieces and flushed them down the toilet, dried himself with two towels, brushed his teeth and resumed his pajamas and robe, then stepped quietly out into the hall and stood listening.

The television was still on, not very loudly, in the front room. There were no other voices, no sound of footsteps or of blows. What had the Thackers been afraid of? The soul-sucker? Egypt's mouldering divinities?

The Nebraskan returned to his room and shut the door firmly behind him. Whatever it was, it was most certainly none of his business. In the morning he would eat breakfast, listen to a tale or two from the old man, and put the whole family out of his mind.

Something moved when he switched off the light. And for an instant he had glimpsed his own shadow on the window blind, with that of someone or something behind him, a man even taller than he, a broad-shouldered figure with horns or pointed ears.

Which was ridiculous on the face of it. The old-fashioned brass chandelier was suspended over the center of the room; the switch was by the door, as far as possible from the windows. In no conceivable fashion could his shadow—or any other—have been cast on that shade. He and whatever he thought he had glimpsed would have to have been standing on the other side of the room, between the light and the window.

It seemed that someone had moved the bed. He waited for his eyes to become accustomed to the darkness. What furniture? The bed, the chair in which he had read—that should be beside the window where he had left it—a dresser with a spotted mirror, and (he racked his brain) a nightstand, perhaps. That should be by the head of the bed, if it were there at all.

Whispers filled the room. That was the wind outside; the windows were open wide, the old house flanked by stately maples. Those windows were visible now, pale rectangles in the darkness. As carefully as he could he crossed to one and raised the blind. Moonlight filled the bedroom; there was his bed, here his chair, in front of the window to his left. No puff of air stirred the leaf-burdened limbs.

He took off his robe and hung it on the towering bedpost, pulled top sheet and comforter to the foot of the bed, and lay down. He had heard something—or nothing. Seen something—or nothing. He thought longingly of his apartment in Lincoln, of his sabbatical—almost a year ago now—in Greece. Of sunshine on the Saronic Gulf . . .

Circular and yellow-white, the moon floated upon stagnant water. Beyond the moon lay the city of the dead, street after narrow street of silent tombs, a daedal labyrinth of death and stone. Far away, a jackal yipped. For whole ages of the world, nothing moved; painted likenesses with limpid eyes appeared to mock the empty, tumbled skulls beyond their crumbling doors.

Far down one of the winding avenues of the dead, a second jackal appeared. Head high and ears erect, it contemplated the emptiness and listened to the silence before turning to sink its teeth once more in the tattered thing it had already dragged so far. Eyeless and desiccated, smeared with bitumen and trailing rotting wrappings, the Nebraskan recognized his own corpse.

And at once was there, lying helpless in the night-shrouded street. For a moment the jackal's glowing eyes loomed over him; its jaws closed, and his collarbone snapped. . . .

The jackal and the moonlit city vanished. Bolt upright, shaking and shaken, he did not know where. Sweat streamed into his eyes.

There had been a sound.

To dispel the jackal and the accursed sunless city, he rose and groped for the light switch. The bedroom was—or at least appeared to be—as he recalled it, save for the damp outline of his lanky body on the sheet. His suitcase stood beside the dresser; his shaving kit lay upon it; *Gods before the Greeks* waited his return on the cane seat of the old chair.

"*You must come to me.*"

He whirled. There was no one but himself in the room, no one (as far as he could see) in the branches of the maple or on the ground below. Yet the words had been distinct, the speaker—so it had seemed—almost at his ear. Feeling an utter fool, he looked under the bed. There was nobody there, and no one in the closet.

The doorknob would not turn in his hand. He was locked in. That, perhaps, had been the noise that woke him: the sharp click of the bolt. He squatted to squint through the old-fashioned keyhole. The dim hallway outside was empty, as far as he could see. He stood; a hard object gouged the sole of his right foot, and he bent to look.

It was the key. He picked it up. Somebody had locked his door, pushed the key under it, and (possibly) spoken through the keyhole.

Or perhaps it was only that some fragment of his dream had remained with him; that had been the jackal's voice, surely.

The key turned smoothly in the lock. Outside in the hall, he seemed to detect the fragrance of Sarah's perfume, though he could not be sure. If it had been Sarah, she had locked him in, providing the key so that he could free himself in the morning. Whom had she been locking out?

He returned to the bedroom, shut the door, and stood for a moment staring at it, the key in his hand. It seemed unlikely that the crude, outmoded lock would delay any intruder long, and of course it would obstruct him when he answered—

Answered whose summons?

And why should he?

Frightened again, frightened still, he searched for another light. There was none: no reading light on the bed, no lamp on the night-stand, no floor lamp, no fixture upon any of the walls. He turned the key in the lock, and after a few seconds' thought dropped it into the topmost drawer of the dresser and picked up his book.

Abaddon. The angel of destruction dispatched by God to turn the Nile and all its waters to blood, and to kill the first-born male child in every Egyptian family. Abaddon's hand was averted from the Children of Israel, who for this purpose smeared their doorposts with the blood of the paschal lamb. This substitution has frequently been considered a foreshadowing of the sacrifice of Christ.

Am-mit, Ammit, "Devourer of the Dead." This Egyptian goddess guarded the throne of Osiris in the underworld and feasted upon the

souls of those whom Osiris condemned. She had the head of a croco-
dile and the forelegs of a lion. The remainder of her form was that of a
hippopotamus, Figure 1. Am-mit's great temple at Henen-su (Herak-
leopolis) was destroyed by Octavian, who had its priests impaled.

An-uat, Anuat, "Lord of the Land (the Necropolis)," "Opener to
the North." Though frequently confused with Anubis—

The Nebraskan laid his book aside; the overhead light was not well
adapted to reading in any case. He switched it off and lay down.

Staring up into the darkness, he pondered An-uat's strange title,
Opener to the North. Devourer of the Dead and Lord of the Land
seemed clear enough. Or rather Lord of the Land seemed clear once
Schmit explained that it referred to the necropolis. (That explanation
was the source of his dream, obviously.) Why then had Schmit not
explained Opener to the North? Presumably because he didn't understand it either. Well, an opener was one who went before, the first to
pass in a certain direction. He (or she) made it easier for others to
follow, marking trails and so on. The Nile flowed north, so An-uat
might have been thought of as the god who went before the Egyptians
when they left their river to sail the Mediterranean. He himself had
pictured An-uat in a boat earlier, for that matter, because there was
supposed to be a celestial Nile. (Was it the Milky Way?) Because he
had known that the Egyptians had believed there was a divine analog
to the Nile along which Ra's sun-boat journeyed. And of course the
Milky Way actually was—really is in the most literal sense—the
branching star-pool where the sun floats. . . .

The jackal released the corpse it had dragged, coughed, and vomited,
spewing carrion alive with worms. The Nebraskan picked up a stone
fallen from one of the crumbling tombs, and flung it, striking the
jackal just below the ear.

It rose upon its hind legs, and though its face remained that of a
beast, its eyes were those of a man. "This is for you," it said, and
pointed toward the writhing mass. "Take it, and come to me."

The Nebraskan knelt and plucked one of the worms from the
reeking spew. It was pale, streaked, and splotched with scarlet, and
woke in him a longing never felt before. In his mouth, it brought
peace, health, love, and hunger for something he could not name.

Old Hop Thacker's voice floated across infinite distance: "Don't
never shoot anythin' without you're dead sure what 'tis, young feller."

Another worm and another, and each as good as the last.

"We will teach you," the worms said, speaking from his own
mouth. "Have we not come from the stars? Your own desire for them
has wakened, Man of Earth."

Hop Thacker's voice: "Grave worms, do you see?"

"Come to me."

The Nebraskan took the key from the drawer. It was only necessary to open the nearest tomb. The jackal pointed to the lock.

"If it's hungered, it'll suck on a live person, an' he's bound to fight or die."

The end of the key scraped across the door, seeking the keyhole.

"Come to me, Man of Earth. Come quickly."

Sarah's voice had joined the old man's, their words mingled and confused. She screamed, and the painted figures faded from the door of the tomb.

The key turned. Thacker stepped from the tomb. Behind him his father shouted, "Joe, boy! Joe!" And struck him with his cane. Blood streamed from Thacker's torn scalp, but he did not look around.

"Fight him, young feller! You got to fight him!"

Someone switched on the light. The Nebraskan backed toward the bed.

"Pa, DON'T!" Sarah had the huge butcher knife. She lifted it higher than her father's head and brought it down. He caught her wrist, revealing a long raking cut down his back as he spun about. The knife, and Sarah, fell to the floor.

The Nebraskan grabbed Thacker's arm. "What is this!"

"It is love," Thacker told him. "That is your word, Man of Earth. It is love." No tongue showed between his parted lips; worms writhed there instead, and among the worms gleamed stars.

With all his strength, the Nebraskan drove his right fist into those lips. Thacker's head was slammed back by the blow; pain shot along the Nebraskan's arm. He swung again, with his left this time, and his wrist was caught as Sarah's had been. He tried to back away; struggled to pull free. The high old-fashioned bed blocked his legs at the knees.

Thacker bent above him, his torn lips parted and bleeding, his eyes filled with such pain as the Nebraskan had never seen. The jackal spoke: *"Open to me."*

"Yes," the Nebraskan told it. "Yes, I will." He had never known before that he possessed a soul, but he felt it rush into his throat.

Thacker's eyes rolled upward. His mouth gaped, disclosing for an instant the slime-sheathed, tentacled thing within. Half falling, half rolling, he slumped upon the bed.

For a second that felt much longer, Thacker's father stood over him with trembling hands. A step backward, and the older Mr. Thacker fell as well—fell horribly and awkwardly, his head striking the floor with a distinct crack.

"Grandpa!" Sarah knelt beside him.

The Nebraskan rose. The worn brown handle of the butcher knife protruded from Thacker's back. A little blood, less than the Nebraskan would have expected, trickled down the smooth old wood to form a crimson pool on the sheet.

"Help me with him, Mr. Cooper. He's got to go to bed."

The Nebraskan nodded and lifted the only living Mr. Thacker onto his feet. "How do you feel?"

"Shaky," the old man admitted. "Real shaky."

The Nebraskan put the old man's right arm about his own neck and picked him up. "I can carry him," he said. "You'll have to show me his bedroom."

"Most times Joe was just like always." The old man's voice was a whisper, as faint and far as it had been in the dream-city of the dead. "That's what you got to understand. Near all the time, an' when— when he did, they was dead, do you see? Dead or near to it. Didn't do a lot of harm."

The Nebraskan nodded.

Sarah, in a threadbare white nightgown that might have been her mother's once, was already in the hall, stumbling and racked with sobs.

"Then you come. An' Joe, he made us. Said I had to keep on talkin' an' she had to ask you fer supper."

"You told me that story to warn me," the Nebraskan said.

The old man nodded feebly as they entered his bedroom. "I thought I was bein' slick. It was true, though, 'cept 'twasn't Cooper, nor Creech neither."

"I understand," the Nebraskan said. He laid the old man on his bed and pulled up a blanket.

"I kilt him didn't I? I kilt my boy Joe."

"It wasn't you, Grandpa." Sarah had found a man's bandana, no doubt in one of her grandfather's drawers; she blew her nose into it.

"That's what they'll say."

The Nebraskan turned on his heel. "We've got to find that thing and kill it. I should have done that first." Before he had completed the thought, he was hurrying back toward the room that had been his.

He rolled Thacker over as far as the knife handle permitted and lifted his legs onto the bed. Thacker's jaw hung slack; his tongue and palate were thinly coated with a clear glutinous gel that carried a faint smell of ammonia; otherwise his mouth was perfectly normal.

"It's a spirit," Sarah told the Nebraskan from the doorway. "It'll go into Grandpa now, 'cause he killed it. That's what he always said."

The Nebraskan straightened up, turning to face her. "It's a living creature, something like a cuttlefish, and it came here from—" He waved the thought aside. "It doesn't really matter. It landed in North Africa, or at least I think it must have, and if I'm right, it was eaten by a jackal. They'll eat just about anything, from what I've read. It survived inside the jackal as a sort of intestinal parasite. Long ago, it transmitted itself to a man, somehow."

Sarah was looking down at her father, no longer listening. "He's restin' now, Mr. Cooper. He shot the old soul-sucker in the woods one day. That's what Grandpa tells, and he hasn't had no rest since, but he's peaceful now. I was only eight or 'bout that, and for a long time Grandpa was 'fraid he'd get me, only he never did." With both her thumbs, she drew down the lids of the dead man's eyes.

"Either it's crawled away—" the Nebraskan began.

Abruptly, Sarah dropped to her knees beside her dead parent and kissed him.

When at last the Nebraskan backed out of the room, the dead man and the living woman remained locked in that kiss, her face ecstatic, her fingers tangled in the dead man's hair. Two full days later, after the Nebraskan had crossed the Mississippi, he still saw that kiss in shadows beside the road.

The Faces at Pine Dunes

RAMSEY CAMPBELL

1.

When his parents began arguing Michael went outside. He could still hear them through the thin wall of the caravan. "We needn't stop yet," his mother was pleading.

"We're stopping," his father said. "It's time to stop wandering."

But why should she want to leave here? Michael gazed about the Pine Dunes Caravanserai. The metal village of caravans surrounded him, cold and bright in the November afternoon. Beyond the dunes ahead he heard the dozing of the sea. On the three remaining sides a forest stood; remnants of autumn, ghosts of colour, were scattered over the trees; distant branches displayed a last golden mist of leaves. He inhaled the calm. Already he felt at home.

His mother was persisting. "You're still young," she told his father.

She's kidding! Michael thought. Perhaps she was trying flattery. "There are places we haven't seen," she said wistfully.

"We don't need to. We need to be here."

The slowness of the argument, the voices muffled by the metal wall, frustrated Michael; he wanted to be sure that he was staying here. He hurried into the caravan. "I want to stay here. Why do we have to keep moving all the time?"

"Don't come in here talking to your mother like that," his father shouted.

He should have stayed out. The argument seemed to cramp the already crowded space within the caravan; it made his father's presence yet more overwhelming. The man's enormous wheezing body sat plumped on the couch, which sagged beneath his weight; his small frail wife was perched on what little of the couch was unoccupied, as though she'd been squeezed tiny to fit. Gazing at them, Michael felt suffocated. "I'm going out," he said.

"Don't go out," his mother said anxiously; he couldn't see why. "We won't argue anymore. You stay in and do something. Study."

"Let him be. The sooner he meets people here, the better."

Michael resented the implication that by going out he was obeying his father. "I'm just going out for a walk," he said. The reassurance might help her; he knew how it felt to be overborne by the man.

At the door he glanced back. His mother had opened her mouth, but his father said, "We're staying. I've made my decision." And he'd lie in it, Michael thought, still resentful. All the man could do was lie there, he thought spitefully; that was all he was fat for. He went out, sniggering. The way his father had gained weight during the past year, his coming to rest in this caravan park reminded Michael of an elephant's arrival at its graveyard.

It was colder now. Michael turned up the hood of his anorak. Curtains were closing and glowing. Trees stood, intricately precise, against a sky like translucent papery jade. He began to climb the dunes towards the sea. But over there the sky was blackened; a sea dark as mud tossed nervously and flopped across the bleak beach. He turned towards the forest. Behind him sand hissed through grass.

The forest shifted in the wind. Shoals of leaves swam in the air, at the tips of webs of twigs. He followed a path which led from the Caravanserai's approach road. Shortly the diversity of trees gave way to thousands of pines. Pinecones lay like wattled eggs on beds of fallen needles. The spread of needles glowed deep orange in the early evening, an orange tapestry displaying rank upon rank of slender pines, dwindling into twilight.

The path led him on. The pines were shouldered out by stouter trees, which reached overhead, tangling. Beyond the tangle the blue of the sky grew deeper; a crescent moon slid from branch to branch. Bushes massed among the trunks; they grew higher and closer as he pushed through. The curve of the path would take him back towards the road.

The ground was turning softer underfoot. It sucked his feet in the dark. The shrubs had closed over him now; he could hardly see. He struggled between them, pursuing the curve. Leaves rubbed together rustling at his ear, like desiccated lips; their dry dead tongues rattled. All at once the roof of the wooden tunnel dropped sharply. To go further he would have to crawl.

He turned with difficulty. On both sides thorns caught his sleeves; his dark was hemmed in by two ranks of dim captors. It was as though midnight had already fallen here, beneath the tangled arches; but the dark was solid and clawed. Overhead, netted fragments of night sky illuminated the tunnel hardly at all.

He managed to extricate himself, and hurried back. But he had taken only a few steps when his way was blocked by hulking spiky darkness. He dodged to the left of the shrub, then to the right, trying irritably to calm his heart. But there was no path. He had lost his way in the dark. Around him dimness rustled, chattering.

He began to curse himself. What had possessed him to come in here? Why on earth had he chosen to explore so late in the day? How could the woods be so interminable? He groped for openings between masses of thorns. Sometimes he found them, though often they would not admit his body. The darkness was a maze of false paths.

Eventually he had to return to the mouth of the tunnel and crawl. Unseen moisture welled up from the ground, between his fingers. Shrubs leaned closer as he advanced, poking him with thorns. His skin felt fragile, and nervously unstable; he burned but his heat often seemed to break, flooding him with the chill of the night.

There was something even less pleasant. As he crawled, the leaning darkness—or part of it—seemed to move beside him. It was as though someone were pacing him, perhaps on all fours, outside the tunnel. When he halted, so did the pacing. It would reach the end of the tunnel just as he did.

Nothing but imagination, helped by the closely looming tree trunks beyond the shrubs. Apart from the creaking of wood and the rattling sway of leaves, there was no sound beyond the tunnel—certainly none of pacing. He crawled. The cumbersome moist sounds that accompanied the pacing were those of his own progress. But he crawled more slowly, and the darkness imitated him. Wasn't the thorny tunnel dwindling ahead? It would trap him. Suddenly panicking, he began to scrabble backwards.

The thorns hardly hindered his retreat. He must have broken them down. He emerged gasping, glad of the tiny gain in light. Around him shrubs pressed close as ever. He stamped his way back along what he'd thought was his original path. When he reached the hindrance he smashed his way between the shrubs, struggling and snarling, savage with panic, determined not to yield. His hands were torn; he heard cloth rip. Well, the thorns could have that.

When at last he reached an open space, his panic sighed loudly out of him. He began to walk as rapidly as seemed safe, towards where he remembered the road to be. Overhead black nets of branches turned, momentarily catching stars. Once, amid the enormous threshing of the woods, he thought he heard a heavy body shoving through the nearby bushes. Good luck to whoever it was. Ahead, in the barred dark, hung little lighted windows. He had found the caravan park, but only by losing his way.

He was home. He hurried into the light, smiling. In the metal alleys pegged shirts hung neck down, dripping; they flapped desperately on the wind. The caravan was dark. In the main room, lying on the couch like someone's abandoned reading, was a note: OUT, BACK LATER. His mother had added DON'T GO TO BED TOO LATE.

He'd been looking forward to companionship. Now the caravan seemed too brightly lit, and false: a furnished tin can. He made himself coffee, leafed desultorily through his floppy paperbacks, opened and closed a pocket chess set. He poked through his box of souvenirs: shells, smooth stones; a minute Bible; a globe of synthetic snow within which a huge vague figure, presumably meant to be a snowman, loomed outside a house; a dead flashlight fitted with a set of clip-on Halloween faces; a dull grey ring whose metal swelled into a bulge over which colours crawled slowly, changing. The cardboard box was full of memories: the Severn Valley, the Welsh hills, the garishly flittering mile of Blackpool; he couldn't remember where the ring had come from. But the memories were dim tonight, uninvolving.

He wandered into his parents' room. It looked to him like a second-hand store for clothes and toiletries. He found his father's large metal box, but it was locked as usual. Well, Michael didn't want to read his old books anyway. He searched for contraceptives, but as he'd expected, there were none. If he wasn't mistaken, his parents had no need for them. Poor buggers. He'd never been able to imagine how, out of proportion as they seemed to be, they had begot him.

Eventually he went out. The incessant rocking of the caravan, its hollow booming in the wind, had begun to infuriate him. He hurried along the road between the pines; wind sifted through needles. On the main road buses ran to Liverpool. But he'd already been there several times. He caught a bus to the opposite terminus.

The bus was almost empty. A few passengers rattled in their lighted pod over the bumpy country roads. Darkness streamed by, sometimes becoming dim hedges. The scoop of the headlamps set light to moths, and once to a squirrel. Ahead the sky glowed, as if with a localised dawn. Lights began to emerge from behind silhouetted houses; streets opened, brightening.

The bus halted in a square, beside a village cross. The passengers hurried away, snuggling into their collars. Almost at once the street was deserted, the bus extinguished. Folded awnings clattered, tugged by the wind. Perhaps after all he should have gone into the city. He was stranded here for—he read the timetable: God, two hours until the last bus.

He wandered among the grey stone houses. Streetlamps glared silver; the light coated shop windows, behind whose flowering of frost he could see faint ghosts of merchandise. Curtains shone warmly, chimneys smoked. His heels clanked mechanically on the cobbles. Streets, streets, empty streets. Then the streets became crowded, with gleaming parked cars. Ahead, on the wall of a building, was a plaque of coloured light. FOUR IN THE MORNING. A club.

He hesitated, then he descended the steps. Maybe he wouldn't fit in with the brand-new sports car set, but anything was better than wandering the icy streets. At the bottom of the stone flight, a desk stood beside a door to coloured dimness. A broken-nosed man wearing evening dress sat behind the desk. "Are you a member, sir?" he said in an accent that was almost as convincing as his suit.

Inside was worse than Michael had feared. On a dance-floor couples turned lethargically, glittering and changing colour like toy dancers. Clumps of people stood shouting at each other in country accents, swaying and laughing; some stared at him as they laughed. He heard their talk: motorboats, bloody bolshies, someone's third abortion. He didn't mind meeting new people—he'd had to learn not to mind—but he could tell these people preferred, now they'd stared, to ignore him.

His three pounds' membership fee included a free drink. I should think so too, he thought. He ordered a beer, to the barman's faint contempt. As he carried the tankard to one of the low bare tables he was conscious of his boots, tramping the floorboards. There was nothing wrong with them, he'd wiped them. He sipped, making the drink last, and gazed into the beer's dim glow.

When someone else sat at the table he didn't look at her. He had to glance up at last, because she was staring. What was the matter with her, was he on show? Often in groups he felt alien, but he'd never felt more of a freak than here. His large-boned arms huddled protectively around him, his gawky legs drew up.

But she was smiling. Her stare was wide-eyed, innocent, if somehow odd. "I haven't seen you before," she said. "What's your name?"

"Michael." It sounded like phlegm; he cleared his throat. "Michael. What's yours?"

"June." She made a face as though it tasted like medicine.

"Nothing wrong with that." Her hint of dissatisfaction with herself had emboldened him.

"You haven't moved here, have you? Are you visiting?"

There was something strange about her: about her eyes, about the way she seemed to search for questions. "My parents have a caravan," he said. "We're in the Pine Dunes Caravanserai. We docked just last week."

"Yeah." She drew the word out like a sigh. "Like a ship. That must be fantastic. I wish I had that. Just to be able to see new things all the time, new places. The only way you can see new things here is taking acid. I'm tripping now."

His eyebrows lifted slightly; his faint smile shrugged.

"That's what I mean," she said, smiling. "These people here would be really shocked. They're so provincial. You aren't."

In fact he hadn't been sure how to react. The pupils of her eyes were expanding and contracting rapidly, independently of each other. But her small face was attractive, her small body had large firm breasts.

"I saw the moon dancing before," she said. "I'm beginning to come down now. I thought I'd like to look at people. You wouldn't know I was tripping, would you? I can control it when I want to."

She wasn't really talking to him, he thought; she just wanted an audience to trip to. He'd heard things about LSD. "Aren't you afraid of starting to trip when you don't mean to?"

"Flashbacks, you mean. I never have them. I shouldn't like that." She gazed at his scepticism. "There's no need to be afraid of drugs," she said. "All sorts of people used to trip. Witches used to. Look, it tells you about it in here."

She fumbled a book out of her handbag; she seemed to have difficulty in wielding her fingers. *Witchcraft in England.* "You can have that," she said. "Have you got a job?"

It took him a moment to realise that she'd changed the subject. "No," he said. "I haven't left school long. I had to have extra school because of all the moving. I'm twenty. I expect I'll get a job soon. I think we're staying here."

"That could be a good job," she said, pointing at a notice behind the bar: TRAINEE BARMAN REQUIRED. "I think they want to get rid of that guy there. People don't like him. I know a lot of people would come here if they got someone friendly like you."

Was it just her trip talking? Two girls said good-bye to a group, and came over. "We're going now, June. See you shortly."

"Right. Hey, this is Michael."

"Nice to meet you, Michael."

"Hope we'll see you again."

Perhaps they might. These people didn't seem so bad after all. He drank his beer and bought another, wincing at the price and gazing at the job notice. June refused a drink: "It's a downer." They talked about his travels, her dissatisfactions, and her lack of cash to pay for moving. When he had to leave she said, "I'm glad I met you. I like you." And she called after him, "If you got that job I'd come here."

2.

Darkness blinded him. It was heavy on him, and moved. It was more than darkness: it was flesh. Beneath him and around him and above him, somnolent bodies crawled blindly. They were huge; so was he. As they shifted incessantly he heard sounds of mud or flesh.

He was shifting too. It was more than restlessness. His whole body felt unstable; he couldn't make out his own form—whenever he seemed to perceive it, it changed. And his mind; it felt too full, of alien chunks that ground harshly together. Memories of fantasies floated vaguely through him. Stone circles. Honeycombed mountains; glimmering faces like a cluster of bubbles in a cave mouth. Enormous dreaming eyes beneath stone and sea. A labyrinth of thorns. His own face. But why was his own face only a memory?

He woke. Dawn suffocated him like grey gas; he lay panting. It was all right. It hadn't been his own face that he'd seemed to remember in the dream. His body hadn't grown huge. His large bones were still lanky. But there was a huge figure, nonetheless. It loomed above him at the window, its spread of face staring down at him.

He woke, and had to grab the dark before he could find the light-switch. He twisted himself to sit on the edge of the couch, legs tangled in the blankets, so as not to fall asleep again. Around him the caravan was flat and bright, and empty. Beyond the ajar door of his parents' room he could see that their bed was smooth and deserted.

He was sure he'd had that dream before—the figure at the window. Somehow he associated it with a windmill, a childhood memory he couldn't locate. Had he been staying with his grandparents? The dream was fading in the light. He glanced at his clock: two in the morning. He didn't want to sleep again until the dream had gone.

He stood outside the caravan. A wind was rising; a loud whisper passed through the forest, unlit caravans rocked and creaked a little at their moorings; behind everything, vast and constant, the sea rushed vaguely. Scraps of cloud slid over the filling moon; light caught at them, but they slipped away. His parents hadn't taken the car. Where had they gone? Irrationally, he felt he knew, if only he could remember. Why did they go out at night so much?

A sound interrupted his musing. The wind carried it to him only to snatch it away. It seemed distant, and therefore must be loud. Did it contain words? Was someone being violently ill, and trying to shout? The moon's light flapped between a procession of dark clouds. A drunk, no doubt, shouting incoherently. Michael gazed at the edge of the forest and wondered about his parents. Light and wind shifted the foliage. Then he shrugged. He ought to be used to his parents' nocturnal behaviour by now.

He slammed the door. His dream was still clinging to him. There had been something odd about the head at the window, besides its size. Something about it had reminded him unpleasantly of a bubble. Hadn't that happened the first time he'd had the dream? But he was grinning at himself: never mind dreams, or his parents. Think of June.

She had been in the club almost every evening since he'd taken the job, a month ago. He had dithered for a week, then he'd returned and asked about the notice. Frowning, the barman had called the manager—to throw Michael out? But June had told them her parents knew Michael well. "All right. We'll give you six weeks and see how you do." The barman had trained him, always faintly snooty and quick to criticise. But the customers had begun to prefer Michael to serve them. They accepted him, and he found he could be friendly. He'd never felt less like an outsider.

So long as the manager didn't question June's parents. June had invited Michael to the cottage a couple of times. Her parents had been polite, cold, fascinated, contemptuous. He'd tried to fit his lanky legs beneath his chair, so that the flares of his trousers would cover up his boots—and all the while he'd felt superior to these people in some way, if only he could think of it. "They aren't my kind of people either," June had told him, walking to the club. "When can we go to your caravan?"

He didn't know. He hadn't yet told his parents about her; the reaction to the news of his job hadn't been what he'd hoped. His mother had gazed at him sadly, and he'd felt she was holding more of her feelings hidden, as they all had to in the cramped caravan. "Why don't you go to the city? They'll have better jobs there."

"But I feel at home here."

"That's right," his father had said. "That's right." He'd stared at Michael strangely, with a kind of uneasy joy. Michael had felt oppressed, engulfed by the stare. Of course there was nothing wrong, his father had become uneasy on hearing of his son's first job, his first step in the world, that was all.

"Can I borrow the car to get to the club?"

His father had become dogmatic at once; his shell had snapped tight. "Not yet. You'll get the key soon enough."

It hadn't seemed worth arguing. Though his parents rarely used the car at night, Michael was never given the key. Where *did* they go at night? "When you're older" had never seemed much of an explanation. But surely their nocturnal excursions were more frequent now they'd docked at Pine Dunes? And why was his mother so anxious to persuade him to leave?

It didn't matter. Sometimes he was glad that they went out; it gave him a chance to be alone, the caravan seemed less cramped, he could breathe freely. He could relax, safe from the threat of his father's overwhelming presence. And if they hadn't gone out that night he would never have met June.

Because of the wanderings of the caravan he had never had time for close friendships. He had felt more attached to this latest berth than to any person—until he'd met June. She was the first girl to arouse him. Her small slim body, her bright quick eyes, her handfuls of breast—he felt his body stirring as he thought of her.

For years he'd feared he was impotent. Once, in a village school, a boy had shown him an erotic novel. He'd read about the gasps of pleasure, the creaking of the bed. Gradually he'd realised why that troubled him. The walls of the caravan were thin; he could always hear his father snoring or wheezing, like a huge fish stranded on the shore of a dream. But he had never heard his parents copulating.

Their sexual impulse must have faded quickly, soon after he was born—as soon, he thought, as it had served its purpose. Would his own be as feeble? Would it work at all? Yes, he'd gasped over June, the first night his parents were out. "I think it'd be good to make love on acid," she'd said as they lay embraced. "That way you really become one, united together." But he thought he would be terrified to take LSD, even though what she'd said appealed deeply to him.

He wished she were here now. The caravan rocked; his parents' door swung creaking, imitated by the bathroom door, which often sprang open. He slammed them irritably. The dream of the bubbling head at the window—if that had been what was wrong with it—was drifting away. Soon he'd sleep. He picked up *Witchcraft in England*. It looked dull enough to help him sleep. And it was June's.

Naked witches danced about on the cover, and on many of the pages. They danced obscenely. They danced lewdly. They chanted obscenely. And so on. They used poisonous drugs, such as belladonna. No doubt that had interested June. He leafed idly onward; his gaze flickered impatiently.

Suddenly he halted, at a name: Severnford. Now that *was* interesting. We can imagine, the book insisted, the witches rowing out to the island in the middle of the dark river, and committing unspeakable acts before the pallid stone in the moonlight; but Michael couldn't imagine anything of the kind, nor did he intend to try. Witches are still reputed to visit the island, the book told him before he interrupted it and riffled on. But a few pages later his gaze was caught again.

He stared at this new name. Then reluctantly he turned to the index. At once words stood out from the columns, eager to be seen. They slipped into his mind as if their slots had been ready for years. Exham. Whitminster. The Old Horns. Holihaven. Dilham. Severnford. His father had halted the caravan at all of them, and his parents had gone out at night.

He was still staring numbly at the list when the door snapped open. His father glanced sharply at him, then went into the bedroom. "Come on," he told Michael's mother, and sat heavily on the bed, which squealed. To Michael's bewildered mind his father's body seemed to spread as he sat down, like a dropped jelly. His mother sat obediently; her gaze dodged timidly, she looked pale and shrunken—by fear, Michael knew at once. "Go to bed," his father told him, raising one foot effortlessly to kick the door shut. Almost until dawn Michael lay in the creaking unstable dark, thinking.

3.

"You must have seen all sorts of places," June said.

"We've seen a few," said Michael's mother. Her eyes moved uneasily. She seemed nervously resentful, perhaps at being reminded of something she wanted desperately to forget. At last, as if she'd struggled and found courage, she managed to say, "We may see a few more."

"Oh no, we won't," her husband said. He sat slumped on the couch, as though his body were a burden he'd had to drop there. Now that there were four people in the caravan he seemed to take up even more room; his presence overwhelmed all the spaces between them.

Michael refused to be overwhelmed. He stared at his father. "What made you choose the places we've lived?" he demanded.

"I had my reasons."

"What reasons?"

"I'll tell you sometime. Not now, son. You don't want us arguing in front of your girlfriend, do you?"

Into the embarrassed silence June said, "I really envy you, being able to go everywhere."

"You'd like to, would you?" Michael's mother said.

"Oh yes. I'd love to see the world."

His mother turned from the stove. "You ought to. You're the right age for it. It wouldn't do Michael any harm, either."

For a moment her eyes were less dull. Michael was glad: he'd thought she would approve of June's wanderlust—that was one reason why he'd given in to June's pleas to meet his parents. Then his father was speaking, and his mother dulled again.

"Best to stay where you're born," his father told June. "You won't find a better place than here. I know what I'm talking about."

"You should try living where I do. It'd kill your head in no time."

"Mike feels at home here. That's right, isn't it, son? You tell her."

"I like it here," Michael said. Words blocked his throat. "I mean, I met you," he hawked at June.

His mother chopped vegetables: chop, chop, chop—the sound was harsh, trapped within the metal walls.

"Can I do anything?" June said.

"No, thank you. It's all right," she said indifferently. She hadn't accepted June yet, after all.

"If you're so keen on seeing the world," his father demanded, "what's stopping you?"

"I can't afford it, not yet. I work in a boutique, I'm saving the money I'd have spent on clothes. And then I can't drive. I'd need to go with someone who can."

"Good luck to you. But I don't see Mikey going with you."

Well, ask *me*! Michael shouted at her, gagged (by unsureness: she mightn't have had him in mind at all). But she only said, "When I travel I'm going to have things from everywhere."

"I've got some," he said. "I've kept some things." He carried the cardboard box to her, and displayed his souvenirs. "You can have them if you like," he said impulsively; if she accepted he would be more sure of her. "The flashlight only needs batteries."

But she pushed the plastic faces aside, and picked up the ring. "I'd like that," she said, turning it so that its colours spilled slowly over one another, merging and separating. She whispered, "It's like tripping."

"There you are. I'm giving it to you."

His father stared at the ring, then a smile spread his mouth. "Yes, you give her that. It's as good as an engagement, that ring."

Michael slid the ring onto her finger before she could change her mind; she had begun to look embarrassed. "It's lovely," she said. "Have we time for Mike to take me for a walk before dinner?"

"You can stay out for an hour if you like," his mother said, then anxiously: "Go down to the beach. You might get lost in the woods, in the fog."

The fog was ambiguous: perhaps thinning, perhaps gathering again. Inside a caravan a radio sang Christmas carols. A sharp-edged bronze sun hung close to the sea. Sea and fog had merged, and might be advancing over the beach. June took Michael's hand as they climbed the slithering dunes. "I just wanted to come out to talk," she explained.

So had he. He wanted to tell her what he'd discovered. That was his main reason for inviting her: he needed her support in confronting his parents, he would be too disturbed to confront them alone—he'd needed it earlier when he'd tried to interrogate his father. But what could he tell her? I've found out my parents are witches? You know that book you lent me—

"No, I didn't really want to talk," she said. "There were just too many bad vibes in there. I'll be all right, we'll go back soon. But they're strange, your parents, aren't they? I didn't realise your father was so heavy."

"He used to be like me. He's been getting fatter for the last few months." After a pause he voiced his worst secret fear: "I hope I never get like him."

"You'll have to get lots of exercise. Let's walk as far as the point."

Ahead along the beach, the grey that lay stretched on the sea was land, not fog. They trudged towards it. Sand splashed from his boots; June slid, and gripped his hand. He strained to tell her what he'd found out, but each phrase he prepared sounded more absurd: his voice echoed hollowly, closed into his mind. He'd tell her—but not today. He relaxed, and felt enormously relieved; he enjoyed her hand small in his. "I like fog," she said. "There are always surprises in it."

The bronze sun paced them, sinking. The sea shifted restlessly, muffled. To their left, above the dunes, trees were a flat mass of prickly fog. They were nearly at the point now. It pulled free of the grey, darkening and sharpening. It looked safe enough for them to climb the path.

But when they reached the top it seemed hardly worth the effort. A drab patch of beach and dunes, an indistinct fragment of sea scattered with glitterings of dull brass, surrounded them in a soft unstable frame of fog. Otherwise the view was featureless, except for a tree growing beside the far dunes. Was it a tree? Its branches seemed too straight, its trunk too thick. Suddenly troubled, Michael picked his way over the point as far as he dared. The fog withdrew a little. It wasn't a tree. It was a windmill.

A windmill by the sea! "My grandparents lived there," he blurted.

"Oh, did they?"

"You don't understand. They lived near that windmill. It's the same one, I know it is."

He still wasn't sure whether she felt his confusion. Memories rushed him, as if all at once afloat: he'd been lying on the couch in his grandparents' decrepit caravan, the huge head had loomed at the window, vague with dawn. It must have been a dream then too.

He followed June down the path. Chill fog trailed them, lapping the point. His thoughts drifted, swirling. What did his discovery mean? He couldn't remember his grandparents at all, not even what they'd looked like. They had been his father's parents—why had the man never mentioned them? Why hadn't he remarked that they'd lived here? The sun slid along the rim of the sea, swollen as though with glowing blood. Had his grandparents also been witches?

"Did Mike's grandparents live here, then?" June said.

His mother stared at her. The spoon and saucepan she was holding chattered like nervous teeth, he was sure she was going to scream and throw everything away—the utensils, her self-control, the mask behind which she'd hidden to protect him: for how long? For the whole of his childhood? But she stammered, "How did you know that?"

"Mike told me. The windmill just reminded him."

"Is dinner ready?" Michael interrupted. He wanted to think everything out before questioning his father. But June was opening her mouth to continue. The caravan was crowded, suffocating. Shut up! he screamed at her. Get out! "Were they born here, then?" June said.

"No, I don't think so." His mother had turned away and was washing vegetables. June went to hold the dishes. "So why did they come here?" she said.

His mother frowned, turning back; within her frown she was searching. "To retire," she smiled abruptly.

His father nodded and smiled to himself, squeezing forward his ruff of chins. "You could retire from the human race here," June said sourly, and he wheezed like a punctured balloon.

As the four ate dinner, their constraint grew. Michael and June made most of the conversation; his parents replied shortly when at all, and watched. His mother observed June uneasily; he read dislike in her eyes, or pity. He felt irritably resentful, her uneasiness made his skin nervous. Night edged closer to the windows, blank-faced.

His father leaned back as if his weight had toppled the chair, which creaked loudly. He patted his quaking stomach. "Just storing it up for the winter," he said, winking at June.

His arms flopped around her shoulders and Michael's. "You two go well together. Don't they, eh?"

But his wife said only, "I'm going to bed now. I'm very tired. Perhaps we'll see you again," which sounded like dutiful politeness.

"I hope so," June said.

"I know we will," Michael's father said expansively.

Michael walked June to the bus stop. "I'll see you at the club," she said through a kiss. Smouldering cones of yellow light led the bus away, and were engulfed. As he walked back, twisted shapes of fog bulked between the trees. Nearby in the dark, something shifted moistly.

He halted. What had it been? Blurred trees creaked with a deadened sound, thin trails of fog reached out for him from branches. He'd heard a shifting, deep in the dark. A vague memory plucked at him. He shivered as if to shake it free, into the chill clinging night. A restless moist shifting. He felt as though the depths of the forest were reaching for his mind with ambiguous tatters of grey. He strode rapidly towards the invisible light. Again he heard the slow moist shifting. Only the sea, he told himself. Only the sea.

4.

As he emerged into the open, the clouds parted and the moon rolled free. The enormous shape in the open space glistened with moonlight. The unstable head turned its crawling face towards him.

The dream trailed him to Liverpool, to the central library, although the space and the head had faded before he could make them out—if indeed he had wanted to. A rush of rain, and the bright lights of the library, washed the dream away. He hurried up the wide green stairs to the Religion and Philosophy section.

He pulled books from the shelves. *Lancashire Witches. North-West Hauntings. Ghostly Lancashire.* The banality of their covers was reassuring; it seemed absurd that his parents could be mixed up in such things. Yet he couldn't quite laugh. Even if they were, what could he do? He slammed the books angrily on the table, startling echoes.

As he read he began to feel safer. Pine Dunes wasn't indexed in *North-West Hauntings.* His attention strayed, fascinated into irrelevances. The hanged man's ghost in Everton Library. The poltergeist of the Palace Hotel, Birkdale. Jokey ghost stories in Lancashire dialect, 'ee lad. Rain and wind shook the windows, fluorescent light lay flat on the tables. Beyond a glass partition people sat studying, library staff clattered up and down open staircases, carrying scraps of paper. Reassured, he turned to *Lancashire Witches.* Pine Dunes. It was there, on three pages.

When he made himself search the pages, they didn't say much. Over the centuries, witches had been rumoured to gather in the Pine Dunes forest. Was that surprising? Wouldn't they naturally have done so, for concealment? Besides, these were only rumours; few people would have bothered struggling through the undergrowth. He opened *Ghostly Lancashire,* expecting irrelevances. But the index showed that Pine Dunes covered several pages.

The author had interviewed a group the other books ignored; the travellers. Their stories were unreliable, he warned, but fascinating. Few travellers would walk the Pine Dunes road after dark; they kept their children out of the woods even by day. A superstitious people, the author pointed out. The book had been written thirty years ago, Michael reminded himself. And the travellers gave no reason for their nervousness except vague tales of something unpleasantly large glimpsed moving beyond the most distant trees. Surely distance must have formed the trees into a solid wall; how could anyone have seen beyond?

One traveller, senile and often incoherent, told a story. A long time ago he, or someone else—the author couldn't tell—had wandered back to the travellers' camp, very drunk. The author didn't believe the story, but included it because it was vivid and unusual. Straying from the road, the man had become lost in the forest. Blinded by angry panic, he'd fought his way towards an open space. But it wasn't the camp, as he'd thought. He had lost his footing on the slippery earth and had gone skidding into a pit.

Had it been a pit, or the mouth of a tunnel? As he'd scrabbled, bruised but otherwise unhurt, for a foothold on the mud at the bottom, he'd seen an opening that led deeper into darkness. The darkness had begun moving slowly and enormously towards him, with a sound like that of a huge shifting beneath mud—darkness which had parted loudly, resolving itself into several sluggish forms that glistened dimly as they advanced to surround him. Terror had hurled him in a leap halfway up the pit, his hands had clamped on rock, and he'd wrenched himself up the rest of the way. He'd run blindly. In the morning he'd found himself full of thorns on a sprung bed of undergrowth.

So what did all that prove? Michael argued with himself on the bus to Pine Dunes. The man had been drunk. All right, so there were other tales about Pine Dunes, but nothing very evil. Why shouldn't his parents go out at night? Maybe they were ghost-hunters, witch-hunters. Maybe they were going to write a book about their observations. How else could such books be written? His mind was becoming desperate as he kept remembering his mother's masked fear.

His parents were asleep. His father lay beached on the bed, snoring flabbily; beyond his stomach his wife could hardly be seen. Michael was glad, for he hadn't known what to say to them. He wheeled out the bicycle he'd bought from his first month's wages.

He cycled to the Four in the Morning. His knees protruded on either side of him, jerking up and down. Hedges sailed by slowly; their colours faded and dimmed into twilight. The whirr of his dynamo caught among the leaves. He struggled uphill, standing on the pedals. Dim countryside opened below him, the sea glinted dully. As he poised on the edge of the downhill rush, he knew how he could unburden himself, or begin to. Tonight he would tell June everything.

But she didn't come to the club. People crowded in; the lights painted them carelessly monochrome. Discotheque records snarled and thumped, swirls of tobacco-smoke glared red, pink, purple. Michael hurried about, serving. Dim wet discoloured faces jostled to reach him, shouting, "Mike! Mike!" Faces rose obsessively to the surface of the jostling: June's, who wasn't there; his mother's, her eyes trying to dodge fear. He was suffocating. His frustration gathered within him; he felt swollen, encumbered. He stared at the luridly pink smoke while voices called. "I've got to go home," he told the barman.

"Had enough, have you?"

"My parents aren't well. I'm worried."

"Strange you didn't say so when you came in. Well, I've managed by myself before." He turned away, dismissing Michael. "You'll have to make do with me tonight," he told the shouting.

The last of the lit streets faded behind Michael. The moon was full, but blurred by unkempt fields of cloud; it showed him only a faint windy swaying that surrounded him for miles. When he confronted his father, what would his mother do? Would she break down? If she admitted to witchcraft and said it was time Michael knew, the scene would be easier—if she did. The moon struggled among plump clouds, and was engulfed.

He cycled fast up the Pine Dunes road. Get there, don't delay to reconsider. Gravel ground together squeaking beneath his wheels; his yellow light wobbled, plucking at trees. The depths of the forest creaked, distant tree trunks were pushed apart to let a huge unstable face peer through. He was overtired—of course there was nothing among the far trees but dark. He sped into the Caravanserai; random patches of unlit caravans bobbed up and faded by. His caravan was unlit too.

Perhaps his parents weren't there. He realised furiously that he felt relieved. They were in there all right, they'd be asleep. He would wake his father, the man might betray himself while still half-asleep. He'd dazzle his father awake, like an interrogator. But his parents' bed was empty.

He punched the wall, which rang flatly. His father had outwitted him again. He stared around the room, enraged. His father's huge suits dangled emptily, like sloughed skin; his mother's clothes hid in drawers. His father's metal box of books sat on top of the wardrobe. Michael glanced resentfully at it, then stared. It was unlocked.

He lifted it down and made to sit on his parents' bed. That made him feel uneasy; he carried the box into the main room. Let his father come in and find him reading. Michael hoped he would. He tugged at the lid, which resisted, then sprang open with a loud clang.

He remembered that sound. He'd heard it when he was quite young, and his mother's voice, pleading: "Let him at least have a normal childhood." After a moment he'd heard the box close again. "All right. He'll find out when it's time," he'd heard his father say.

The box contained no printed books, but several notebooks. They had been written in by numerous people; the inks in the oldest notebook, whose spine had given way, were brown as old bloodstains. Some of the writing in the latest book was his mother's. Odd pages showed rough maps: The Old Horns, Exham, Whitminster, though none of Pine Dunes. These he recognised; but he couldn't understand a word of the text.

Most of it was in English, but might as well not have been. It consisted largely of quotations copied from books; sometimes the source was indicated—*Necro, Revelations Glaaki, Garimiaz, Vermis, Theobald*, whatever they were. The whole thing reminded him of pamphlets issued by cranky cults—like the people who gave all their worldly goods to a man in America, or the others who'd once lured Michael into a seedy hotel for a personality profile, which they'd lied would be fun. He read, baffled.

After a while he gave up. Even the entries his mother had written made no sense. Some of the words he couldn't even pronounce. Kuthullhoo? Kuthoolhew? And what was supposed to be so Great about it, whatever it was?

He shrugged, sniggering a little. He didn't feel so worried now. If this was all his parents were involved in, it seemed silly and harmless. The fact that they'd concealed it from him so successfully for so long seemed to prove as much. They were so convincingly normal, it couldn't be anything very bad. After all, many businessmen belonged to secret societies with jargon nobody else could understand. Maybe his father had been initiated into this society as part of one of the jobs he'd taken in his wanderings!

One thing still troubled Michael: his mother's fear. He couldn't see what there was to fear in the blurred language of the notebooks. He made a last effort, and let the books fall open where they would—at the pages that had been read most frequently.

What a waste of time! He strained his mind, but the pages became more bewildering still; he began to laugh. What on earth was "the millennial gestation"? Something to do with "the fosterling of the Great Old Ones"? "The hereditary rebirth"? "Each of Its rebirths comes closer to incarnation"? "When the mind opens to all the dimensions will come the incarnation. Upon the incarnation all minds will become one." Ah, that explains it! Michael sniggered wildly. But there was more: "the ingestion," "the mating beyond marriage," "the melting and merging"—

He threw the book angrily into the box. The skin of his eyes crawled hotly; he could hardly keep them open, yet he was wasting his time reading this. The caravan rocked as something huge tugged at it: the wind. The oldest, spineless, notebook began to disintegrate. As he knocked it square, an envelope slipped out.

It was addressed in his father's large handwriting; the last word had had to be cramped. TO MICHAEL: NOT TO BE OPENED UNTIL AFTER I AM GONE. He turned it over and began to tear, but his hand faltered. He'd been unreasonable enough to his father for one day. After a moment he put the envelope unopened in his pocket, feeling sly and ashamed. He replaced the box, then he prepared to sleep. In the dark he tried to arrange his limbs on the sagging couch. Rocking, the caravan sounded like a rusty cradle.

He slept. He wasn't sure whether he was asleep when he heard his mother's low voice. He must be awake, for he could feel her breath on his face. "Don't stay here." Her voice trembled. "Your girlfriend's got the right idea. Go away with her if that's what you want. Just get away from here."

His father's voice reached for her out of the dark. "That's enough. He's asleep. You come to bed."

Silence and darkness settled down for the night. But in the night, or in Michael's dream, there were noises: the stealthy departure of a car from the park; heavy footsteps trying not to disturb the caravan; the gingerly closing of his parents' door. Sleep seemed more important.

His father's voice woke him, shouting into the bedroom. "Wake up. The car's gone. It's been stolen."

Daylight blazed through Michael's eyelids. He was sure at once what had happened. His father had hidden the car, so that nobody could get away. Michael lay paralysed, waiting for his mother's cry of panic. Her silence held time immobile. He squeezed his eyelids tighter, filling his eyes with red.

"Oh," his mother said at last, dully. "Oh dear."

There was more in her voice than resignation: she sounded lethargic, indifferent. Suddenly Michael remembered what he'd read in June's book. Witches used drugs. His eyes sprang wide. He was sure that his father was drugging his mother.

5.

It didn't take the police long to find the car, abandoned and burnt out, near the windmill. "Kids, probably," one of the policemen said. "We may be in touch with you again." Michael's father shook his head sadly, and they left.

"I must have dropped the car keys while we were out." Michael thought his father hardly bothered to sound convincing. Why couldn't he tell the man so, confront him? Because he wasn't sure; he might have dreamed the sounds last night— He raged at his own cowardice, staring at his mother. If only he could be certain of her support! She wandered desultorily, determinedly cleaning the caravan, as though she were ill but expecting company.

When his gagged rage found words at last it weakened immediately. "Are you all right?" he demanded of her, but then could only stammer, "Do you think you'd better see a doctor?"

Neither of his parents responded. His unsureness grew, and fed his frustration. He felt lethargic, unable to act, engulfed by his father's presence. Surely June would be at the club tonight. He had to talk to someone, to hear another interpretation; perhaps she would prove that he'd imagined everything.

He washed and shaved. He was glad to retreat, even into the cramped bathroom; he and his parents had been edging uneasily around one another all day—the caravan made him think unpleasantly of a tin can full of squirming. As he shaved, the bathroom door sprang open, as it often did. His father appeared behind him in the mirror, staring at him.

Steam coated the mirror again. Beneath the steam, his father's face seemed to writhe like a plastic mask on fire. Michael reached to clear the mirror, but already his father and the man's emotions were upon him. Before Michael could turn, his father was hugging him violently, his flesh quivering as though it would burst. Michael held himself stiff, refusing to be engulfed. What are you doing? Get away! In a moment his father turned clumsily and plodded out. The caravan rumbled, shaking.

Michael sighed loudly. God, he was glad that was over. He finished shaving and hurried out. Neither of his parents looked at him; his father pretended to read a book, and whistled tunelessly; his mother turned vaguely as he passed. He cycled to the club.

"Parents all right?" the barman said indifferently.

"I'm not sure."

"Good of you to come." Perhaps that was sarcasm. "There's some things for you to wash."

Michael could still feel his father's clinging embrace; he kept trying to wriggle it away. He welcomed the press of bodies at the bar, shouting "Mike!"—even though June wasn't among them. He welcomed the companionship of ordinary people. He strode expertly about, serving, as the crowd grew, as smoke gathered. He could still feel swollen flesh pressed hotly against his back. He won't do that to me again, he thought furiously. He'll never— A tankard dropped from his hand, beneath a beer tap. "Oh my God," he said.

"What's up with you now?" the barman demanded.

When his father had embraced him, Michael had thought of nothing but escape. Now at last he realised how final his father's gesture had been. "My parents," he said. "They're, they're worse."

"Just sent you a message, did they? Off home again now, I suppose? You'd better see the manager, or I will— Will you watch that bloody beer you're spilling!"

Michael slammed shut the tap and struggled through the crowd. People grimaced sympathetically at him, or stared. It didn't matter, his job didn't matter. He must hurry back to head off whatever was going to happen. Someone bumped into him in the doorway, and hindered him when he tried to push them aside. "What's the matter with you?" he shouted. "Get out of the way!" It was June.

"I'm really sorry I didn't come last night," she said. "My parents dragged me out to dinner."

"All right. Okay. Don't worry."

"You're angry. I really am sorry, I wanted to see you— You're not going, are you?"

"Yes, I've got to. Look, my parents aren't well."

"I'll come back with you. We can talk on the way. I'll help you look after them." She caught at his shoulder as he tried to run upstairs. "Please, Mike. I'll feel bad if you just leave me. We can catch the last bus in five minutes if we run. It'll be quicker than your bike."

God! She was worse than his father! "Listen," he snarled, having clambered to street level. "It isn't ill, they aren't ill," he said, letting words tumble wildly as he tried to flee. "I've found out what they do at night. They're witches."

"Oh no!" She sounded shocked but delighted.

"My mother's terrified. My father's been drugging her." Now that he was able to say so, his urgency diminished a little; he wanted to release all he knew. "Something's going to happen tonight," he said.

"Are you going to try and stop it? Let me come too. I know about it. I showed you my book." When he looked doubtful she said: "They'll have to stop when they see me."

Perhaps she could look after his mother while he confronted his father. They ran to the bus, which sat unlit in the square for minutes, then dawdled along the country roads, hoping for passengers who never appeared. Michael's frustration coiled tighter again. He explained to June what he'd discovered: "Yeah," she kept saying, excited and fascinated. Once she began giggling uncontrollably. "Wouldn't it be weird if we saw your father dancing naked?" He stared at her until she said, "Sorry." Her pupils were expanding and contracting slightly, randomly.

As they ran along the Pine Dunes road the trees leaned closer, creaking and nodding. Suppose his parents hadn't left the caravan yet?

What could he say? He'd be tongue-tied again by his unsureness, and June would probably make things worse. He gasped with relief when he saw that the windows were dark, but went inside to make sure. "I know where they've gone," he told June.

Moonlight and unbroken cloud spread the sky with dim milk; dark smoky breaths drifted across the glow. He heard the incessant restlessness of the sea. Bare black silhouettes crowded beside the road, thinly intricate against the sky. He hurried June towards the path.

Why should his parents have gone that way? Something told him they had—perhaps the maze he remembered, the tunnel of undergrowth: that was a secret place. The path wound deeper into the woods, glinting faintly; trees rapidly shuttered the glow of the moon. "Isn't this fantastic," June said, hurrying behind him.

The pines gave out, but other trees meshed thickly overhead. The glimpses of flat whitish sky, smouldering with darker cloud, dwindled. In the forest everything was black or blanched, and looked chill, although the night was unseasonably mild. Webs of shadow lay on the path, tangling Michael's feet; tough grass seized him. Bushes massed around him, towering, choking the gaps between trees. The glimpses of sky were fewer and smaller. "What's that?" June said uneasily.

For a moment he thought it was the sound of someone's foot, unplugging itself from the soft ground: it sounded like a loud slow gulp of mud. But no, it wasn't that. Someone coughing? It didn't sound much like a human cough. Moreover, it sounded as though it were straining to produce a sound, a single sound; and he felt inexplicably that he ought to know what that was.

The bushes stirred, rattling. The muddy sound faded, somewhere ahead. There was no point in telling June his vague thoughts. "It'll be an animal," he said. "Probably something's caught it."

Soon they reached the tunnel. He knelt at once and began to crawl. Twigs scraped beside his ears, a clawed dry chorus. He found the experience less disturbing now, less oppressive; the tunnel seemed wider, as though someone stout had recently pushed his way through. But behind him June was breathing heavily, and her voice fluttered in the dark. "There's something following us outside the tunnel," she said tightly, nervously.

He crawled quickly to the end and stood up. "There's nothing here now. It must have been an animal."

He felt odd: calm, safe, yet slyly and elusively excited. His eyes had grown equal to the dark. The trees were stouter, and even closer; they squeezed out masses of shrub between them. Overhead, a few pale scraps of sky were caught in branches. The ground squelched underfoot, and he heard another sound ahead: similar, but not the same.

June emerged panting. "I thought I'd finished tripping. Where are we going?" she said unevenly. "I can't see."

"This way." He headed at once for a low opening in the tangled growth. As he'd somehow expected, the passage twisted several times, closing almost impenetrably, then widened. Perhaps he'd noticed that someone before him had thrust the bushes apart.

"Don't go so fast," June said in the dark, almost weeping. "Wait for me."

Her slowness annoyed him. His indefinable excitement seemed to affect his skin, which crawled with nervousness like interference on the surface of a bubble. Yet he felt strangely powerful, ready for anything. Wait until he saw his father! He stood impatiently, stamping the mushy ground, while June caught up with him. She gripped his arm. "There it is again," she gasped.

"What?" The sound? It was only his feet, squelching. But there was another sound, ahead in the tangled creaking dark. It was the gurgling of mud, perhaps of a muddy stream gargling ceaselessly into the earth. No: it was growing louder, more violent, as though the mud were straining to spew out an obstruction. The sound was repeated, again and again, becoming gradually clearer: a single syllable. All at once he knew what it was. Somewhere ahead in the close dark maze, a thick muddy voice was struggling to shout his name.

June had recognised the sound too, and was tugging at his arm. "Let's go back," she pleaded. "I don't like it. Please."

"God," he scoffed. "I thought you were going to help me." The muddy sounds blurred into a mumble, and were gone. Twigs shook in the oppressive dark, squeaking hollowly together. Suddenly, ahead of him, he heard his father's voice; then, after a long silence, his mother's. Both were oddly strained and muffled. As though this were a game of hide-and-seek, each had called his name.

"There," he said to June. "I haven't got time to take you back now." His excitement was mounting, his nervous skin felt light as a dream. "Don't you want to look after my mother?" he blurted.

He shouldered onward. After a while he heard June following him timidly. A wind blundered through the forest, dragging at the bushes. Thorns struggled overhead, clawing at the air; the ground gulped his feet, sounding to his strained ears almost like words. Twice the walls of the passage tried to close, but someone had broken them apart. Ahead the passage broadened. He was approaching an open space.

He began to run. Bushes applauded like joyful bones. The thick smoky sky rushed on, fighting the moonlight. The vociferous ground was slippery; he stumbled as he ran, and almost tripped over a dark huddle. It was his parents' clothes. Some of them, as he glanced back impatiently, looked torn. He heard June fall slithering against bushes. "Don't!" she cried. But he had reached the space.

It was enclosed by trees. Ivy thickened the trunks and had climbed to mat the tangle overhead; bushes crowded the cramped gaps between the trees. In the interstices of the tangle, dark sky smouldered.

Slowly his eyes found the meagre light; outlines gathered in the clearing, dimmer than mist. Bared wooden limbs groped into the space, creaking. The dimness sketched them. He could see now that the clearing was about thirty feet wide, and roughly circular. Dimness crawled on it, as though it were an infested pond. At the far side, a dark bulk stood between him and the trees.

He squinted painfully, but its shape persisted in eluding him. Was it very large, or was the dark lying? Across the clearing mud coughed and gurgled thickly, or something did. Dimness massed on the glistening shape. Suddenly he saw the shape was moving lethargically, and alive.

June had hung back; now she ran forward, only to slip at the edge of the clearing. She clutched his arm to steady herself, then she gazed beyond him, trembling. "What is it?" she cried.

"Shut up," he said savagely.

Apart from her interruption, he felt more calm than he had ever felt before. He knew he was gazing at the source of his dreams. The dreams returned peacefully to his mind and waited to be understood. For a moment he wondered whether this was like June's LSD. Something had been added to his mind, which seemed to be expanding awesomely. Memories floated free, as though they had been coded deep in him: wombs of stone and submarine depths; hovering in a medium that wasn't space, somehow linked to a stone circle on a hill, being drawn closer to the circle, towards terrified faces that stared up through the night; a pregnant woman held writhing at the centre of the circle, screaming as he hovered closer and reached for her. He felt primed with centuries of memories. Inherited memories, or shared; but whose?

He waited. All was about to be clarified. The huge bulk shifted, glistening. Its voice, uncontrollably loud and uneven, struggled muddily to speak. The trees creaked ponderously, the squashed bushes writhed, the sky fled incessantly. Suddenly, touched by an instinct he couldn't define, Michael realised how he and June must look from the far side of the clearing. He took her arm, though she struggled briefly, and they stood waiting: bride and bridegroom of the dark.

After a long muddy convulsion in the dimness, words coughed free. The voice seemed unable to speak more than a phrase at a time; then it would blur, gurgling. Sometimes his father's voice, and occasionally his mother's—high-pitched, trembling—seemed to help. Yet the effect was disturbing, for it sounded as though the muddy voice were attempting muffled imitations of his parents. He held himself calm, trusting that this too would be clarified in due course.

The Great Old Ones still lived, the halting voice gurgled loudly. Their dreams could reach out. When the human race was young and strayed near the Old Ones, the dreams could reach into the womb and make the unborn in their image. Something like his mother's voice spoke the last words, wavering fearfully. June struggled, but he gripped her arm.

Though the words were veiled and allusive, he understood instinctively what was being said. His new memories were ready to explain. When he read the notebooks again he would understand consciously. He listened and gazed, fascinated. He was in awe of the size of the speaking bulk. And what was strange about the head? Something moved there, rapid as the whirl of colours on a bubble. In the dark the face seemed to strain epileptically, perhaps to form words.

The Old Ones could wait, the voice or voices told him. The stars would come right. The people the Old Ones touched before birth did not take on their image all at once but gradually, down the centuries. Instead of dying, they took on the form that the Old Ones had placed in the womb of an ancestor. Each generation came closer to the perfect image.

The bulk glistened as though flayed; in the dimness it looked pale pink, and oddly unstable. Michael stared uneasily at the head. Swift clouds dragged darknesses over the clearing and snatched them away. The face looked so huge, and seemed to spread. Wasn't it like his father's face? But the eyes were swimming apart, the features slid uncontrollably across the head. All this was nothing but the antics of shadows. A tear in the clouds crept towards the dimmed moon. June was trying to pull away. "Keep still," he snarled, tightening his grip.

They would serve the Old Ones, the voice shouted thickly, faltering. That was why they had been made: to be ready when the time came. They shared the memories of the Old Ones, and at the change their bodies were transformed into the stuff of the Old Ones. They mated with ordinary people in the human way, and later in the way the Old Ones had decreed. That way was. . . .

June screamed. The tear in the clouds had unveiled the moon. Her cry seemed harsh enough to tear her throat. He turned furiously to silence her; but she dragged herself free, eyes gaping, and fled down the path. The shadow of a cloud rushed towards the clearing. About to pursue June, he turned to see what the moon had revealed.

The shadow reached the clearing as he turned. For a moment he saw the huge head, a swollen bulb which, though blanched by moonlight, reminded him of a mass dug from within a body. The glistening lumpy forehead was almost bare, except for a few strands that groped restlessly over it—strands of hair, surely, though they looked like strings of livid flesh.

On the head, seeming even smaller amid the width of flesh, he saw his mother's face. It was appallingly dwarfed, and terrified. The strands flickered over it, faster, faster. Her mouth strained wordlessly, gurgling.

Before he could see the rest of the figure, a vague gigantic squatting sack, the shadow flooded the clearing. As it did so, he thought he saw his mother's face sucked into the head, as though by a whirlpool of flesh. Did her features float up again, newly arranged? Were there other, plumper, features jostling among them? He could be sure of nothing in the dark.

June cried out. She'd stumbled; he heard her fall, and the thud of her head against something; then silence. The figure was lumbering towards him, its bulk quaking. For a moment he was sure that it intended to embrace him. But it had reached a pit, almost concealed by undergrowth. It slid into the earth, like slow jelly. The undergrowth sprang back rustling.

He stood gazing at June, who was still unconscious. He knew what he would tell her; she had had a bad LSD experience, that had been what she'd seen. LSD reminded him of something. Slowly he began to smile.

He went to the pit and peered down. Faint sluggish muddy sounds retreated deep into the earth. He knew he wouldn't see his parents for a long time. He touched his pocket, where the envelope waited. That would contain his father's explanation of their disappearance, which he could show to people, to June.

Moonlight and shadows raced nervously over the pit. As he stared at the dark mouth he felt full of awe, yet calm. Now he must wait until it was time to come back here, to go into the earth and join the others. He remembered that now; he had always known, deep in himself, that this was home. One day he and June would return. He gazed at her unconscious body, smiling. Perhaps she had been right; they might take LSD together, when it was time. It might help them to become one.

On the Slab

HARLAN ELLISON

Lightning was drawn to the spot. Season after season, August to November, but most heavily in September, the jagged killing bolts sought out George Gibree's orchard.

Gibree, a farmer with four acres of scabrous apple trees whose steadily diminishing production of fruit would drive him, one year later, to cut his throat with a rabbit-skinning knife and to bleed to death in the loft of his barn in Chepachet, near Providence, Rhode Island, *that* George Gibree found the dismal creature at the northeast corner of his property late in September. In the season of killing bolts.

The obscenely crippled trees—scarred black as if by fireblight—had withstood one attack after another; splintering a little more each year; withering a little more each year; dying a little more each year. The McIntoshes they produced, hideous and wrinkled as thalidomide babies. Night after night the lightning, drawn to the spot, cracked and thrashed, until one night, as though weary of the cosmic game, a monstrous forked bolt, sizzling with power, uncovered the creature's graveplace.

When he went out to inspect the orchard the next morning, holding back the tears till he was well out of sight of Emma and the house, George Gibree looked down into the crater and saw it stretched out on its back, its single green eye with the two pupils glowing terribly in the morning sunlight, its left forearm—bent up at the elbow—seeming to clutch with spread fingers at the morning air. It was as if the thing had been struck by the sky's fury as it was trying to dig itself out.

For just a moment as he stared down into the pit, George Gibree felt as if the ganglia mooring his brain were being ripped loose. His head began to tremble on his neck . . . and he wrenched his gaze from the impossible titan, stretched out, filling the thirty-foot-long pit.

In the orchard there could be heard the sounds of insects, a few birds, and the whimpering of George Gibree.

* * *

Children, trespassing to play in the orchard, saw it; and the word spread through town, and by stringer to a free-lance writer who did occasional human-interest pieces for the Providence *Journal*. She drove out to the Gibree farm and, finding it impossible to speak to George Gibree, who sat in a straight-back chair, staring out the window without speaking or even acknowledging her presence, managed to cajole Emma Gibree into letting her wander out to the orchard alone.

The item was small when published, but it was the beginning of October and the world was quiet. The item received interested attention.

By the time a team of graduate students in anthropology arrived with their professor, pieces of the enormous being had been torn away by beasts of the field and by curious visitors. They sent one of their group back to the University of Rhode Island, in Kingston, advising him to contact the University's legal representatives, readying them for the eventual purchase of this terrifying, miraculous discovery. Clearly, it was not a hoax; this was no P. T. Barnum "Cardiff Giant," but a creature never before seen on the Earth.

And when night fell, the professor was forced to badger the most amenable of the students into staying with the thing. Coleman lanterns, down jackets, and a ministove were brought in. But by morning all three of the students had fled.

Three days later, a mere six hours before the attorneys for the University could present their offer to Emma Gibree, a rock concert entrepreneur from Providence contracted for full rights to, and ownership of, the dead giant for three thousand dollars. Emma Gibree had been unable to get her husband to speak since the morning he had stood on the lip of the grave and stared down at the one-eyed being; she was in a panic; there were doctors and hospitals in her future.

Frank Kneller, who had brought every major rock group of the past decade to the city, rented exposition space in the Providence Civic Center at a ridiculously low rate because it was only the second week in October . . . and the world was quiet. Then he assigned his public relations firm the task of making the giant a national curiosity. It was not a difficult task.

It was displayed via minicam footage on the evening news of all three major networks. Frank Kneller's flair for the dramatically staged was not wasted.

The thirty-foot humanoid, pink-skinned and with staring eye malevolently directed at the cameraman's lens, was held in loving close-up on the marble slab Kneller had had hewn by a local monument contractor.

Pilbeam of Yale came, and Johanson of the Cleveland Museum of Natural History, and both the Leakeys, and Taylor of Riverside came with Hans Suess from the University of California at La Jolla. They all said it was genuine. But they could not say where the thing had come from. It was, however, native to the planet: thirty feet in height, Cyclopean, as hard as rhinoceros horn . . . but human. And they all noticed one more thing.

The chest, just over the place where the heart lay, was hideously scarred. As though centurions had jammed their pikes again and again into the flesh when this abomination had been crucified. Terrible weals, puckered skin still angrily crimson against the gentle pink of the otherwise unmarred body.

Unmarred, that is, but for the places where the curious had used their nail files and penknives to gouge out souvenirs.

And then Frank Kneller made them go away, shaking their heads in wonder, mad to take the creature back to their laboratories for private study, but thwarted by Kneller's clear and unshakable ownership. And when the last of them had departed, and the view of the Cyclops on its slab could be found in magazines and newspapers and even on posters, *then* Frank Kneller set up his exposition at the Civic Center.

There, within sight of the Rhode Island State House, atop whose dome stands the twelve-foot high, gold-leafed statue of the Independent Man.

The curious came by the thousands to line up and pay their three dollars a head, so they could file past the dead colossus, blazoned on life-sized thirty-foot-high posters festooning the outer walls of the Civic Center as *The 9th Wonder of the World!* (Ninth, reasoned Frank Kneller with a flash of wit and a sense of history uncommon to popularizers and entrepreneurs, because King Kong had been the Eighth.) It was a gracious *hommage* that did not go unnoticed by fans of the cinematically horrific; and the gesture garnered for Kneller an acceptance he might not have otherwise known from the cognoscenti.

And there was an almost symphonic correctness to the titan's having been unearthed in Providence, in Rhode Island, in that Yankee state so uncharacteristic of New England; that situs founded by Roger Williams for "those distressed for cause of conscience" and historically identified with independence of thought and freedom of religion; that locale where the odd and the bizarre melded with the mundane: Poe had lived there, and Lovecraft; and they had had strange visions, terrible dreams that had been recorded, that had influenced the course of literature; the moral ownership of the city by the modern coven known as the Mafia; these, and uncountable reports of bizarre happenings, sightings, gatherings, beliefs that made it seem the Providence *Journal* was an appendix to the writings of Charles Fort . . . provided a free-floating ambience of the peculiar.

The lines never seemed to grow shorter. The crowds came by the busloads, renting cassette players with background information spoken by a man who had played the lead in a television series dealing with the occult. Schoolchildren were herded past the staring green eye in gaggles; teenagers whose senses had been dulled by horror movies came in knots of five and ten; young lovers needing to share stopped and wondered; elderly citizens from whose lives had been leached all wonder smiled and pointed and clucked their tongues; skeptics and cynics and professional debunkers stood frozen in disbelief and came away bewildered.

Frank Kneller found himself involved in a way he had never experienced before, not even with the most artistically rewarding groups he had booked. He went to bed each night exhausted, but uplifted. And he awoke each day feeling his time was being well-spent. When he spoke of the feeling to his oldest friend, his accountant, with whom he had shared lodgings during college days, he was rewarded with the word *ennobled*. When he dwelled on the word, he came to agree.

Showing the monstrosity was *important*.

He wished with all his heart to know the reason. The single sound that echoed most often through the verdant glade of his thoughts was *why?*

"I understand you've taken to sleeping in the rotunda where the giant is on display?" The host of the late-night television talk show was leaning forward. The ash on his cigarette was growing to the point where it would drop on his sharply creased slacks. He didn't notice.

Kneller nodded. "Yes, that's true."

"Why?"

"*Why* is a question I've been asking myself ever since I bought the great man and started letting people see him. . . ."

"Well, let's be honest about it," the interviewer said. "You don't *let* people see the giant . . . you charge them for the privilege. You're showing an attraction, after all. It's not purely an humanitarian act."

Kneller pursed his lips and acceded. "That's right, that's very true. But I'll tell you, if I had the wherewithal, I'd do it free of charge. I don't, of course, so I charge what it costs me to rent space at the Civic Center. That much; no more."

The interviewer gave him a sly smile. "Come *on* . . ."

"No, really, honest to God, I mean it," Frank said quickly. "It's been eleven months, and I can't begin to tell you how many hundreds of thousands of people have come to see the great man; maybe a million or more; I don't know. And everybody who comes goes away feeling a little bit better, a little more important. . . ."

"A religious experience?" The interviewer did not smile.

Frank shrugged. "No, what I'm saying is that people feel *ennobled* in the presence of the great man."

"You keep calling the giant 'the great man.' Strange phrase. Why?"

"Seems right, that's all."

"But you still haven't told me why you sleep there in the place where he's on display every day."

Frank Kneller looked straight into the eyes of the interviewer, who had to live in New York City every day and so might not understand what peace of mind was all about, and he said, "I like the feeling. I feel as if I'm worth the trouble it took to create me. And I don't want to be away from it too long. So I set up a bed in there. It may sound freaky to you, but . . ."

But if he had not been compelled to center his life around the immobile figure on the marble slab, then Frank Kneller would not have been there the night the destroyer came.

Moonlight flooded the rotunda through the enormous skylights of the central display areas.

Kneller lay on his back, hands behind his head, as usual finding sleep a long way off, yet at peace with himself, in the presence of the great man.

The titan lay on his marble slab, tilted against the far wall, thirty feet high, his face now cloaked in shadows. Kneller needed no light. He knew the single great eye was open, the twin pupils staring straight ahead. They had become companions, the man and the giant. And, as usual, Frank saw something that none of the thousands who had passed before the colossus had ever seen. In the darkness up there near the ceiling, the scars covering the chest of the giant glowed faintly, like amber plankton or the minuscule creatures that cling to limestone walls in the deepest caverns of the earth. When night fell, Frank was overcome with an unbearable sadness. Wherever and however this astounding being had lived . . . in whatever way he had passed through the days and nights that had been his life . . . he had suffered something more terrible than anyone merely human could conceive. What had done such awesome damage to his flesh, and how he had regenerated even as imperfectly as this, Kneller could not begin to fathom.

But he knew the pain had been interminable, and terrible.

He lay there on his back, thinking again, as he did every night, of the life the giant had known, and what it must have been for him on this Earth.

The questions were too potent, too complex, and beyond Frank Kneller's ability even to pose properly. The titan defied the laws of nature and reason.

And the shadow of the destroyer covered the skylight of the

rotunda, and the sound of a great wind rose around the Civic Center, and Frank Kneller felt a terror that was impossible to contain. Something was coming from the sky, and he knew without looking up that it was coming for the great man on the slab.

The hurricane wind shrieked past the point of audibility, vibrating in the roots of his teeth. The darkness outside seemed to fall toward the skylight, and with the final sound of enormous wings beating against the night, the destroyer splintered the shatterproof glass.

Razor-edged stalactites struck the bed, the floor, the walls; one long spear imbedded itself through the pillow where Frank's head had lain a moment before, penetrating the mattress and missing him by inches where he cowered in the darkness.

Something enormous was moving beyond the foot of the bed.

Glass lay in a scintillant carpet across the rotunda. Moonlight still shone down and illuminated the display area.

Frank Kneller looked up and saw a nightmare.

The force that had collapsed the skylight was a bird. A bird so enormous he could not catalog it in the same genus with the robin he had found outside his bedroom window when he was a child . . . the robin that had flown against the pane when sunlight had turned it to a mirror . . . the robin that had struck and fallen and lain there till he came out of the house and picked it up. Its blood had been watery, and he could feel its heart beating against his palm. It had been defenseless and weak and dying in fear, he could feel that it was dying in fear. And Frank had rushed in to his mother, crying, and had begged her to help restore the creature to the sky. And his mother had gotten the old eyedropper that had been used to put cod-liver oil in Frank's milk when he was younger, and she had tried to get the robin to take some sugar-water.

But it had died.

Tiny, it had died in fear.

The thing in the rotunda was of that genus, but it was neither tiny nor fearful.

Like no other bird he had ever seen, like no other bird that had ever *been* seen, like no other bird that had ever existed. Sinbad had known such a bird, perhaps, but no other human eyes had ever beheld such a destroyer. It was gigantic. Frank Kneller could not estimate its size, because it was almost as tall as the great man, and when it made the hideous watery cawing sound and puffed out its bellows chest and jerked its wings into a billowing canopy, the pinfeathers scraped the walls of the rotunda on either side. The walls were seventy-five feet apart.

The vulture gave a hellish scream and sank its scimitar talons in the petrified flesh of the great man, its vicious beak in the chest, in the puckered area of scars that had glowed softly in the shadows.

It ripped away the flesh as hard as rhinoceros horn.

Its head came away with the beak locked around a chunk of horny flesh. Then, as Kneller watched, the flesh seemed to lose its rigidity, it softened, and blood ran off the carrion crow's killer beak. And the great man groaned.

The eye blinked.

The bird struck again, tossing gobbets of meat across the rotunda.

Frank felt his brain exploding. He could not bear to see this.

But the vulture worked at its task, ripping out the area of chest where the heart of the great man lay under the scar tissue. Frank Kneller crawled out of the shadows and stood helpless. The creature was immense. *He* was the robin: pitiful and tiny.

Then he saw the fire extinguisher in its brackets on the wall, and he grabbed the pillow from the bed and rushed to the compartment holding the extinguisher and he smashed the glass with the pillow protecting his hand. He wrenched the extinguisher off its moorings and rushed the black bird, yanking the handle on the extinguisher so hard the wire broke without effort. He aimed it up at the vulture just as it threw back its head to rid itself of its carrion load, and the virulent Halon 1301 mixture sprayed in a white stream over the bird's head. The mixture of fluorine, bromine, iodine, and chlorine washed the vulture, spurted into its eyes, filled its mouth. The vulture gave one last violent scream, tore its claws loose, and arced up into the darkness with a spastic beating of wings that caught Frank Kneller across the face and threw him thirty feet into a corner. He struck the wall; everything slid toward gray.

When he was able to get to his knees, he felt an excruciating pain in his side and knew at once several ribs had been broken. All he could think of was the great man.

He crawled across the floor of the rotunda to the base of the slab, and looked up. There, in the shadows . . .

The great man, in terrible pain, was staring down at him.

A moan escaped the huge lips.

What can I do? Kneller thought, desperately.

And the words were in his head. *Nothing. It will come again.*

Kneller looked up. Where the scar tissue had glowed faintly, the chest was ripped open, and the great man's heart lay there in pulsing blood, part of it torn away.

Now I know who you are, Kneller said. *Now I know your name.*

The great man smiled a strange, shy smile. The one great green eye made the expression somehow winsome. *Yes,* he said, *yes, you know who I am.*

Your tears mingled with the earth to create us.
Yes.
You gave us fire.
Yes; and wisdom.
And you've suffered for it ever since.
Yes.

"I have to know," Frank Kneller said, "I have to know if *you* were what *we* were before we became what we are now."

The sound of the great wind was rising again. The destroyer was in the night, on its way back. The chemicals of man could not drive it away from the task it had to perform, could not drive it away for long.

It comes again, the great man said in Kneller's mind. *And I will not come again.*

"Tell me! Were you what we were . . . ?"

The shadow fell across the rotunda and darkness came down upon them as the great man said, in that final moment, *No, I am what you would have become . . .*

And the carrion crow sent by the gods struck him as he said one more thing . . .

When Frank Kneller regained consciousness, hours later, there on the floor where the scissoring pain of his broken ribs had dropped him, he heard those last words reverberating in his mind. And heard them endlessly all the days of his life.

No, I am what you would *have become . . . if you had been worthy.*

And the silence was deeper that night across the face of the world, from pole to pole, deeper than it had ever been before in the life of the creatures that called themselves human.

But not as deep as it would soon become.

24 Views of Mt. Fuji, by Hokusai

ROGER ZELAZNY

1. MT. FUJI FROM OWARI

Kit lives, though he is buried not far from here; and I am dead, though I watch the days-end light pinking cloud-streaks above the mountain in the distance, a tree in the foreground for suitable contrast. The old barrel-man is dust; his cask, too, I daresay. Kit said that he loved me and I said I loved him. We were both telling the truth. But love can mean many things. It can be an instrument of aggression or a function of disease.

My name is Mari. I do not know whether my life will fit the forms I move to meet on this pilgrimage. Nor death. Not that tidiness becomes me. So begin anywhere. Either arcing of the circle, like that vanished barrel's hoop, should lead to the same place. I have come to kill. I bear the hidden death, to cast against the secret life. Both are intolerable. I have weighed them. If I were an outsider I do not know which I would choose. But I am here, me, Mari, following the magic footsteps. Each moment is entire, though each requires its past. I do not understand causes, only sequences. And I am long weary of reality-reversal games. Things will have to grow clearer with each successive layer of my journey, and like the delicate play of light upon my magic mountain they must change. I must die a little and live a little each moment.

I begin here because we lived near here. I visited the place earlier. It is, of course, changed. I recall his hand upon my arm, his sometime smiling face, his stacks of books, the cold, flat eye of his computer terminal, his hands again, positioned in meditation, his smile different then. Distant and near. His hands, upon me. The power of his programs, to crack codes, to build them. His hands. Deadly. Who would have thought he would surrender those rapid-striking weapons, delicate instruments, twisters of bodies? Or myself? Paths . . . Hands . . .

I have come back. It is all. I do not know whether it is enough.

The old barrel-maker within the hoop of his labor . . . Half-full, half-empty, half-active, half-passive . . . Shall I make a yin-yang of that famous print? Shall I let it stand for Kit and myself? Shall I view it as the great Zero? Or as infinity? Or is all of this too obvious? One of those observations best left unstated? I am not always subtle. Let it stand. Fuji stands within it. And is it not Fuji one must climb to give an accounting of one's life before God or the gods?

I have no intention of climbing Fuji and accounting for myself, to God or to anything else. Only the insecure and the uncertain require justification. I do what I must. If the deities have any questions they can come down from Fuji and ask me. Otherwise, this is the closest commerce between us. That which transcends should only be admired from afar.

Indeed. I of all people should know this. I, who have tasted transcendence. I know, too, that death is the only god who comes when you call.

Traditionally, the *henro*—the pilgrim—would dress all in white. I do not. White does not become me, and my pilgrimage is a private thing, a secret thing, for so long as I can keep it so. I wear a red blouse today and a light khaki jacket and slacks, tough leather hiking shoes; I have bound my hair; a pack on my back holds my belongings. I do carry a stick, however, partly for the purpose of support, which I require upon occasion; partly, too, as a weapon should the need arise. I am adept at its use in both these functions. A staff is also said to symbolize one's faith in a pilgrimage. Faith is beyond me. I will settle for hope.

In the pocket of my jacket is a small book containing reproductions of twenty-four of Hokusai's forty-six prints of Mt. Fuji. It was a gift, long ago. Tradition also stands against a pilgrim's traveling alone, for practical purposes of safety as well as for companionship. The spirit of Hokusai, then, is my companion, for surely it resides in the places I would visit if it resides anywhere. There is no other companion I would desire at the moment, and what is a Japanese drama without a ghost?

Having viewed this scene and thought my thoughts and felt my feelings, I have begun. I have lived a little, I have died a little. My way will not be entirely on foot. But much of it will be. There are certain things I must avoid in this journey of greetings and farewells. Simplicity is my cloak of darkness, and perhaps the walking will be good for me.

I must watch my health.

2. MT. FUJI FROM A TEAHOUSE AT YOSHIDA

I study the print: A soft blueness to the dawn sky, Fuji to the left, seen through the teahouse window by two women; other bowed, drowsing figures like puppets on a shelf. . . .

It is not this way here, now. They are gone, like the barrel-maker—the people, the teahouse, that dawn. Only the mountain and the print remain of the moment. But that is enough.

I sit in the dining room of the hostel where I spent the night, my breakfast eaten, a pot of tea before me. There are other diners present, but none near me. I chose this table because of the window's view, which approximates that of the print. Hokusai, my silent companion, may be smiling. The weather was sufficiently clement for me to have camped again last night, but I am deadly serious in my pilgrimage to vanished scenes in this life-death journey I have undertaken. It is partly a matter of seeking and partly a matter of waiting. It is quite possible that it may be cut short at any time. I hope not, but the patterns of life have seldom corresponded to my hopes—or, for that matter, to logic, desire, emptiness, or any patterns of my own against which I have measured them.

All of this is not the proper attitude and occupation for a fresh day. I will drink my tea and regard the mountain. The sky changes even as I watch. . . .

Changes . . . I must be careful on departing this place. There are precincts to be avoided, precautions to be taken. I have worked out all of my movements—from putting down the cup, rising, turning, recovering my gear, walking—until I am back in the country again. I must still make patterns, for the world is a number-line, everywhere dense. I am taking a small chance in being here.

I am not so tired as I had thought I would be from all yesterday's walking, and I take this as a good sign. I have tried to keep in decent shape, despite everything. A scroll hangs on the wall to my right depicting a tiger, and I want this too, for a good omen. I was born in the Year of the Tiger, and the strength and silent movements of the big striped cat are what I most need. I drink to you, Shere Khan, cat who walks by himself. We must be hard at the right time, soft at the proper moment. Timing . . .

We'd an almost telepathic bond to begin with, Kit and I. It drew us to each other, grew stronger in our years together. Empathy, proximity, meditation . . . Love? Then love can be a weapon. Spin its coin and it comes up yang.

Burn bright, Shere Khan, in the jungle of the heart. This time we are the hunter. Timing is all—and *suki*, the opening. . . .

I watch the changes of the sky until a uniform brightness is achieved, holds steady. I finish my tea. I rise and fetch my gear, don my backpack, take up my staff. I head for the short hall which leads to a side door.

"Madam! Madam!"

It is one of the place's employees, a small man with a startled expression.

"Yes?"

He nods at my pack.

"You are leaving us?"

"I am."

"You have not checked out."

"I have left payment for my room in an envelope on the dresser. It says 'cashier' on it. I learned the proper amount last night."

"You must check out at the desk."

"I did not check in at the desk. I am not checking out at the desk. If you wish, I will accompany you back to the room, to show you where I left the payment."

"I am sorry, but it must be done with the cashier."

"I am sorry also, but I have left payment and I will not go to the desk."

"It is irregular. I will have to call the manager."

I sigh.

"No," I say. "I do not want that. I will go to the lobby and handle the checking out as I did the checking in."

I retrace my steps. I turn left toward the lobby.

"Your money," he says. "If you left it in the room you must get it and bring it."

I shake my head.

"I left the key, also."

I enter the lobby. I go to the chair in the corner, the one farthest from the work area. I seat myself.

The small man has followed me.

"Would you tell them at the desk that I wish to check out?" I ask him.

"Your room number . . . ?"

"Seventeen."

He bows slightly and crosses to the counter. He speaks with a woman, who glances at me several times. I cannot hear their words. Finally, he takes a key from her and departs. The woman smiles at me.

"He will bring the key and the money from your room," she says. "Have you enjoyed your stay?"

"Yes," I answer. "If it is being taken care of, I will leave now."

I begin to rise.

"Please wait," she says, "until the paperwork is done and I have given you your receipt."

"I do not want the receipt."

"I am required to give it to you."

I sit back down. I hold my staff between my knees. I clasp it with both hands. If I try to leave now she will probably call the manager. I do not wish to attract even more attention to myself. I wait. I control my breathing. I empty my mind.

After a time the man returns. He hands her the key and the envelope. She shuffles papers. She inserts a form into a machine. There is a brief stutter of keys. She withdraws the form and regards it. She counts the money in my envelope.

"You have the exact amount, Mrs. Smith. Here is your receipt."

She peels the top sheet from the bill.

There comes a peculiar feeling in the air, as if a lightning stroke had fallen here but a second ago. I rise quickly to my feet.

"Tell me," I say, "is this place a private business or part of a chain?"

I am moving forward by then, for I know the answer before she says it. The feeling is intensified, localized.

"We are a chain," she replies, looking about uneasily.

"With central bookkeeping?"

"Yes."

Behind the special place where the senses come together to describe reality I see the form of a batlike epigon taking shape beside her. She already feels its presence but does not understand. My way is *mo chih ch'u*, as the Chinese say—immediate action, without thought or hesitation—as I reach the desk, place my staff upon it at the proper angle, lean forward as if to take my receipt and nudge the staff so that it slides and falls, passing over the countertop, its small metal tip coming to rest against the housing of the computer terminal. Immediately, the overhead lights go out. The epigon collapses and dissipates.

"Power failure," I observe, raising my staff and turning away. "Good day."

I hear her calling for a boy to check the circuit box.

I make my way out of the lobby and visit a rest room, where I take a pill, just in case. Then I return to the short hall, traverse it, and depart the building. I had assumed it would happen sooner or later, so I was not unprepared. The microminiature circuitry within my staff was sufficient to the occasion, and while I would rather it had occurred later, perhaps it was good for me that it happened when it did. I feel more alive, more alert from this demonstration of danger. This feeling, this knowledge, will be of use to me.

And it did not reach me. It accomplished nothing. The basic situation is unchanged. I am happy to have benefited at so small a price.

Still, I wish to be away and into the countryside, where I am strong and the other is weak.

I walk into the fresh day, a piece of my life upon the breakfast moment's mountain.

3. MT. FUJI FROM HODOGAYA

I find a place of twisted pines along the Tokaido, and I halt to view Fuji through them. The travelers who pass in the first hour or so of my vigil do not look like Hokusai's, but no matter. The horse, the sedan chair, the blue garments, the big hats—faded into the past, traveling forever on the print now. Merchant or nobleman, thief or servant—I choose to look upon them as pilgrims of one sort or another, if only into, through, and out of life. My morbidity, I hasten to add, is excusable, in that I have required additional medication. I am stable now, however, and do not know whether medication or meditation is responsible for my heightened perception of the subtleties of the light. Fuji seems almost to move within my gazing.

Pilgrims . . . I am minded of the wanderings of Matsuo Bashō, who said that all of us are travelers every minute of our lives. I recall also his reflections upon the lagoons of Matsushima and Kisagata—the former possessed of a cheerful beauty, the latter the beauty of a weeping countenance. I think upon the complexion and expressions of Fuji and I am baffled. Sorrow? Penance? Joy? Exaltation? They merge and shift. I lack the genius of Bashō to capture them all in a single character. And even he . . . I do not know. Like speaks to like, but speech must cross a gulf. Fascination always includes some lack of understanding. It is enough for this moment, to view.

Pilgrims . . . I think, too, of Chaucer as I regard the print. His travelers had a good time. They told each other dirty stories and romances and tales with morals attached. They ate and they drank and they kidded each other. Canterbury was their Fuji. They had a party along the way. The book ends before they arrive. Fitting.

I am not a humorless bitch. It may be that Fuji is really laughing at me. If so, I would like very much to join in. I really do not enjoy moods such as this, and a bit of meditation interruptus would be welcome if only the proper object would present itself. Life's soberer mysteries cannot be working at top-speed all the time. If they can take a break, I want one, too. Tomorrow, perhaps . . .

Damn! My presence must at least be suspected, or the epigon would not have come. Still, I have been very careful. A suspicion is not a certainty, and I am sure that my action was sufficiently prompt to preclude confirmation. My present location is beyond reach as well as knowledge. I have retreated into Hokusai's art.

I could have lived out the rest of my days upon Oregon's quiet coast. The place was not without its satisfactions. But I believe it was Rilke who said that life is a game we must begin playing before we have learned the rules. Do we ever? Are there really rules?

Perhaps I read too many poets.

But something that seems a rule to me requires I make this effort. Justice, duty, vengeance, defense—must I weigh each of these and assign it a percentage of that which moves me? I am here because I am here, because I am following rules—whatever they may be. My understanding is limited to sequences.

His is not. He could always make the intuitive leap. Kit was a scholar, a scientist, a poet. Such riches. I am smaller in all ways.

Kokuzo, guardian of those born in the Year of the Tiger, break this mood. I do not want it. It is not me. Let it be an irritation of old lesions, even a renewal of the demyelination. But do not let it be me. And end it soon. I am sick in my heart and my reasons are good ones. Give me strength to detach myself from them, Catcher in the Bamboo, lord of those who wear the stripes. Take away the bleakness, gather me together, inform me with strength. Balance me.

I watch the play of light. From somewhere I hear the singing of children. After a time of gentle rain begins to fall. I don my poncho and continue to watch. I am very weary, but I want to see Fuji emerge from the fog which has risen. I sip water and a bit of brandy. Only the barest outline remains. Fuji is become a ghost mountain within a Taoist painting. I wait until the sky begins to darken. I know that the mountain will not come to me again this day, and I must find a dry place to sleep. These must be my lessons from Hodogaya: Tend to the present. Do not try to polish ideals. Have sense enough to get in out of the rain.

I stumble off through a small wood. A shed, a barn, a garage . . . Anything that stands between me and the sky will do.

After a time I find such a place. No god addresses my dreaming.

4. MT. FUJI FROM THE TAMAGAWA

I compare the print with the reality. Not bad this time. The horse and the man are absent from the shore, but there is a small boat out on the water. Not the same sort of boat, to be sure, and I cannot tell whether it bears firewood, but it will suffice. I would be surprised to find perfect congruence. The boat is moving away from me. The pink of the dawn sky is reflected upon the water's farther reaches and from the snow-streaks on Fuji's dark shoulder. The boatman in the print is poling his way outward. Charon? No, I am more cheerful today than I was at Hodogaya. Too small a vessel for the *Narrenschiff*, too slow for the Flying Dutchman. "La navicella." Yes. "La navicella del mio ingegno"—"the little bark of my wit" on which Dante hoisted sail for that second realm, Purgatory. Fuji then . . . Perhaps so. The hells beneath, the heavens above, Fuji between—way station, stopover, terminal. A decent metaphor for a pilgrim who could use a purge. Appropriate. For it contains the fire and the earth as well as the air, as I gaze across the water. Transition, change. I am passing.

The serenity is broken and my reverie ended as a light airplane, yellow in color, swoops out over the water from someplace to my left. Moments later the insectlike buzzing of its single engine reaches me. It loses altitude quickly, skimming low over the water, then turns and traces its way back, this time swinging in above the shoreline. As it nears the point where it will pass closest to me, I detect a flash of reflected light within the cockpit. A lens? If it is, it is too late to cover myself against its questing eye. My hand dips into my breast pocket and withdraws a small gray cylinder of my own. I flick off its endcaps with my thumbnail as I raise it to peer through the eyepiece. A moment to locate the target, another to focus . . .

The pilot is a man, and as the plane banks away I catch only his unfamiliar profile. Was that a gold earring upon his left earlobe?

The plane is gone, in the direction from which it had come. Nor does it return.

I am shaken. Someone had flown by for the sole purpose of taking a look at me. How had he found me? And what did he want? If he represents what I fear most, then this is a completely different angle of attack than any I had anticipated.

I clench my hand into a fist and I curse softly. Unprepared. Is that to be the story of my entire life? Always ready for the wrong thing at the right time? Always neglecting the thing that matters most?

Like Kendra?

She is under my protection, is one of the reasons I am here. If I succeed in this enterprise, I will have fulfilled at least a part of my obligation to her. Even if she never knows, even if she never understands . . .

I push all thoughts of my daughter from my mind. If he even suspected. . . .

The present. Return to the present. Do not spill energy into the past. I stand at the fourth station of my pilgrimage and someone takes my measure. At the second station an epigon tried to take form. I took extreme care in my return to Japan. I am here on false papers, traveling under an assumed name. The years have altered my appearance somewhat and I have assisted them to the extent of darkening my hair and

my complexion, defying my customary preferences in clothing, alter-
ing my speech patterns, my gait, my eating habits—all of these things
easier for me than most others because of the practice I've had in the
past. The past . . . Again, damn it! Could it have worked against me
even in this matter? Damn the past! An epigon and a possible human
observer this close together. Yes, I am normally paranoid and have
been for many years, for good reason. I cannot allow my knowledge of
the fact to influence my judgment now, however. I must think clearly.

I see three possibilities. The first is that the flyby means nothing,
that it would have occurred had anyone else been standing here—or no
one. A joyride, or a search for something else.

It may be so, but my survival instinct will not permit me to accept
it. I must assume that this is not the case. Therefore, someone is
looking for me. This is either connected with the manifestation of
the epigon or it is not. If it is not, a large bag of live bait has just been
opened at my feet and I have no idea how to begin sorting through the
intertwined twistings. There are so many possibilities from my former profession, though I had considered all of these long closed off.
Perhaps I should not have. Seeking there for causes seems an impossible undertaking.

The third possibility is the most frightening: that there is a connection between the epigon and the flight. If things have reached the point
where both epigons and human agents can be employed, then I may
well be doomed to failure. But even more than this, it will mean that
the game has taken on another, awesome dimension, an aspect which I
had never considered. It will mean that everyone on Earth is in far
greater peril than I had assumed, that I am the only one aware of it and
that my personal duel has been elevated to a struggle of global proportions. I cannot take the risk of assigning it to my paranoia now. I must
assume the worst.

My eyes overflow. I know how to die. I once knew how to lose with
grace and detachment. I can no longer afford this luxury. If I bore any
hidden notion of yielding, I banish it now. My weapon is a frail one,
but I must wield it. If the gods come down from Fuji and tell me,
"Daughter, it is our will that you desist," I must still continue in this
to the end, though I suffer in the hells of the *Yü Li Ch'ao Chuan* forever. Never before have I realized the force of fate.

I sink slowly to my knees. For it is a god that I must vanquish.

My tears are no longer for myself.

5. MT. FUJI FROM FUKAGAWA IN EDO

Tokyo. Ginza and confusion. Traffic and pollution. Noise, color and faces, faces, faces. I once loved scenes such as this, but I have been away from cities for too long. And to return to a city such as this is overpowering, almost paralyzing.

Neither is it the old Edo of the print, and I take yet another chance in coming here, though caution rides my every move.

It is difficult to locate a bridge approachable from an angle proper to simulate the view of Fuji beneath it, in the print. The water is of the wrong color, and I wrinkle my nose at the smell; this bridge is not that bridge; there are no peaceful fisher-folk here; and gone the greenery. Hokusai exhales sharply and stares as I do at Fuji-san beneath the metal span. His bridge was a graceful rainbow of wood, product of gone days.

Yet there is something to the thrust and dream of any bridge. Hart Crane could find poetry in those of this sort. "Harp and altar, of the fury fused . . . "

And Nietzsche's bridge that is humanity, stretching on toward the superhuman . . .

No. I do not like that one. Better had I never become involved with that which transcends. Let it be my *pons asinorum*.

With but a slight movement of my head I adjust the perspective. Now it seems as if Fuji supports the bridge and without his presence it will be broken like Bifrost, preventing the demons of the past from attacking our present Asgard—or perhaps the demons of the future from storming our ancient Asgard.

I move my head again. Fuji drops. The bridge remains intact. Shadow and substance.

The backfire of a truck causes me to tremble. I am only just arrived and I feel I have been here too long. Fuji seems too distant and I too exposed. I must retreat.

Is there a lesson in this or only a farewell?

A lesson, for the soul of the conflict hangs before my eyes: I will not be dragged across Nietzsche's bridge.

Come, Hokusai, *ukiyo-e* Ghost of Christmas Past, show me another scene.

6. MT. FUJI FROM KAJIKAZAWA

Misted, mystic Fuji over water. Air that comes clean to my nostrils. There is even a fisherman almost where he should be, his pose less dramatic than the original, his garments more modern, above the infinite Fourier series of waves advancing upon the shore.

On my way to this point I visited a small chapel surrounded by a stone wall. It was dedicated to Kwannon, goddess of compassion and mercy, comforter in times of danger and sorrow. I entered. I loved her when I was a girl, until I learned that she was really a man. Then I felt cheated, almost betrayed. She was Kwan Yin in China, and just as merciful, but she came there from India, where she had been a bod-hisattva named Avalokitesvara, a man—"the Lord Who Looks Down with Compassion." In Tibet he is Chen-re-zi—"He of the Compassionate Eyes"—who gets incarnated regularly as the Dalai Lama. I did not trust all of this fancy footwork on his/her part, and Kwannon lost something of her enchantment for me with this smattering of history and anthropology. Yet I entered. We revisit the mental landscape of childhood in times of trouble. I stayed for a time and the child within me danced for a moment, then fell still.

I watch the fisherman above those waves, smaller versions of Hokusai's big one, which has always symbolized death for me. The little deaths rolling about him, the man hauls in a silver-sided catch. I recall a tale from the Arabian Nights, another of American Indian origin. I might also see Christian symbolism, or a Jungian archetype. But I remember that Ernest Hemingway told Bernhard Berenson that the secret of his greatest book was that there was no symbolism. The sea was the sea, the old man an old man, the boy a boy, the marlin a marlin, and the sharks the same as other sharks. People empower these things themselves, groping beneath the surface, always looking for more. With me it is at least understandable. I spent my earliest years in Japan, my later childhood in the United States. There is a part of me which likes to see things through allusions and touched with mystery. And the American part never trusts anything and is always looking for the real story behind the front one.

As a whole, I would say that it is better not to trust, though lines of interpretation must be drawn at some point before the permutations of causes in which I indulge overflow my mind. I am so, nor will I abandon this quality of character which has served me well in the past. This does not invalidate Hemingway's viewpoint any more than his does mine, for no one holds a monopoly on wisdom. In my present situation, however, I believe that mine has a higher survival potential, for I am not dealing only with *things*, but of something closer to the time-honored Powers and Principalities. I wish that it were not so and that an epigon were only an artifact akin to the ball lightning Tesla studied. But there is something behind it, surely as that yellow airplane had its pilot.

The fisherman sees me and waves. It is a peculiar feeling, this sudden commerce with a point of philosophical departure. I wave back with a feeling of pleasure.

I am surprised at the readiness with which I accept this emotion. I feel it has to do with the general state of my health. All of this fresh air and hiking seems to have strengthened me. My senses are sharper, my appetite better. I have lost some weight and gained some muscle. I have not required medication for several days.

I wonder . . . ?

Is this entirely a good thing? True, I must keep up my strength. I must be ready for many things. But too much strength . . . Could that be self-defeating in terms of my overall plan? A balance, perhaps I should seek a balance—

I laugh, for the first time since I do not remember when. It is ridiculous to dwell on life and death, sickness and health this way, like a character of Thomas Mann's, when I am barely a quarter of the way into my journey. I will need all of my strength—and possibly more—along the way. Sooner or later the bill will be presented. If the timing is off, I must make my own *suki*. In the meantime, I resolve to enjoy what I have.

When I strike, it will be with my final exhalation. I know that. It is a phenomenon familiar to martial artists of many persuasions. I recall the story Eugen Herrigel told, of studying with the *kyudo* master, of drawing the bow and waiting, waiting till something signaled the release of the string. For two years he did this before his *sensei* gave him an arrow. I forget for how long it was after that that he repeated the act with the arrow. Then it all began to come together, the timeless moment of rightness would occur and the arrow would have to fly, would have to fly for the target. It was a long while before he realized that this moment would always occur at the end of an exhalation.

In art, so in life. It seems that many important things, from death to orgasm, occur at the moment of emptiness, at the point of the breath's hesitation. Perhaps all of them are but reflections of death. This is a profound realization for one such as myself, for my strength must ultimately be drawn from my weakness. It is the control, the ability to find that special moment, that troubles me most. But like walking, talking, or bearing a child, I trust that something within me knows where it lies. It is too late now to attempt to build it a bridge to my consciousness. I have made my small plans. I have placed them upon a shelf in the back of my mind. I should leave them and turn to other matters.

In the meantime I drink this moment with deep draught of salty air, telling myself that the ocean is the ocean, the fisherman is a fisherman, and Fuji is only a mountain. Slowly then, I exhale it. . . .

7. MT. FUJI FROM THE FOOT

Fire in your guts, winter tracks above like strands of ancient hair. The print is somewhat more baleful than the reality this evening. That awful red tinge does not glow above me against a horde of wild clouds. Still, I am not unmoved. It is difficult, before the ancient powers of the Ring of Fire, not to stand with some trepidation, sliding back through geological eons to times of creation and destruction when new lands were formed. The great outpourings, the bomblike flash and dazzle, the dance of the lightnings like a crown . . .

I meditate on fire and change.

Last night I slept in the precincts of a small Shingon temple, among shrubs trimmed in the shapes of dragons, pagodas, ships, and umbrellas. There were a number of pilgrims of the more conventional sort present at the temple, and the priest performed a fire service—a *goma*—for us. The fires of Fuji remind me, as it reminded me of Fuji.

The priest, a young man, sat at the altar which held the fire basin. He intoned the prayer and built the fire and I watched, completely fascinated by the ritual, as he began to feed the fire with the hundred and eight sticks of wood. These, I have been told, represent the hundred and eight illusions of the soul. While I am not familiar with the full list, I felt it possible that I could come up with a couple of new ones. No matter. He chanted, ringing bells, striking gongs and drums. I glanced at the other *henros*. I saw total absorption upon all of their faces. All but one.

Another figure had joined us, entering with total silence, and he stood in the shadows off to my right. He was dressed all in black, and the wing of a wide upturned collar masked the lower portion of his face. He was staring at me. When our eyes met, he looked away, focusing his gaze upon the fire. After several moments I did the same.

The priest added incense, leaves, oils. The fire sizzled and spit, the flames leaped, the shadows danced. I began to tremble. There was something familiar about the man. I could not place him, but I wanted a closer look.

I edged slowly to my right during the next ten minutes, as if angling for better views of the ceremony. Suddenly then, I turned and regarded the man again.

I caught him studying me once more, and again he looked away quickly. But the dance of the flames caught him full in the face with light this time, and the jerking of his head withdrew it from the shelter of his collar.

I was certain, in that instant's viewing, that he was the man who had piloted the small yellow plane past me last week at Tamagawa.

Though he wore no gold earring, there was a shadow-filled indentation in the lobe of his left ear.

But it went beyond that. Having seen him full-face I was certain that I had seen him somewhere before, years ago. I have an unusually good memory for faces, but for some reason I could not place his within its prior context. He frightened me, though, and I felt there was good reason for it.

The ceremony continued until the final stick of wood was placed in the fire and the priest completed his liturgy as it burned and died down. He turned then, silhouetted by the light, and said that it was time for any who were ailing to rub the healing smoke upon themselves if they wished.

Two of the pilgrims moved forward. Slowly, another joined them. I glanced to my right once more. The man was gone, as silently as he had come. I cast my gaze all about the temple. He was nowhere in sight. I felt a touch upon my left shoulder.

Turning, I beheld the priest, who had just struck me lightly with the three-pronged brass ritual instrument which he had used in the ceremony.

"Come," he said, "and take the smoke. You need healing of the left arm and shoulder, the left hip and foot."

"How do you know this?" I asked him.

"It was given to me to see this tonight. Come."

He indicated a place to the left of the altar and I moved to it, startled at his insight, for the places he had named had been growing progressively more numb throughout the day. I had refrained from taking my medicine, hoping that the attack would remit of its own accord.

He massaged me, rubbing the smoke from the dying fire into the places he had named, then instructing me to continue on my own. I did so, and some on my head at the end, as is traditional.

I searched the grounds later, but my strange observer was nowhere to be found. I located a hiding place between the feet of a dragon and cast my bedroll there. My sleep was not disturbed.

I awoke before dawn to discover that full sensation had returned to all of my previously numbed areas. I was pleased that the attack had remitted without medication.

The rest of the day, as I journeyed here, to the foot of Fuji, I felt surprisingly well. Even now I am filled with unusual strength and energy, and it frightens me. What if the smoke of the fire ceremony has somehow effected a cure? I am afraid of what it could do to my plans, my resolve. I am not sure that I would know how to deal with it.

Thus, Fuji, Lord of the Hidden Fire, I have come, fit and afraid. I will camp near here tonight. In the morning I will move on. Your presence overwhelms me at this range. I will withdraw for a different, more distant, perspective. If I were ever to climb you, would I cast one hundred and eight sticks into your holy furnace, I wonder? I think not. There are some illusions I do not wish to destroy.

8. MT. FUJI FROM TAGONOURA

I came out in a boat to look back upon the beach, the slopes, and Fuji. I am still in glowing remission. I have resigned myself to it, for now. In the meantime, the day is bright, the sea breeze cool. The boat is rocked by the small deaths, as the fisherman and his sons whom I have paid to bring me out steer it at my request to provide me with the view most approximating that of the print. So much of the domestic architecture in this land recommends to my eye the prows of ships. A convergence of cultural evolution where the message is the medium? The sea is life? Drawing sustenance from beneath the waves we are always at sea? Or, the sea is death, it may rise to blight our lands and claim our lives at any moment? Therefore, we bear this *memento mori* even in the roofs above our heads and the walls which sustain them? Or, this is the sign of our power, over life and death?

Or none of the above. It my seem that I harbor a strong deathwish. This is incorrect. My desires are just the opposite. It may indeed be that I am using Hokusai's prints as a kind of Rorschach for self-discovery, but it is death-fascination rather than death-wish that informs my mind. I believe that this is understandable in one suffering a terminal condition with a very short term to it.

Enough of that for now. It was meant only as a drawing of my blade to examine its edge for keenness. I find that my weapon is still in order and I resheathe it.

Blue-gray Fuji, salted with snow, long angle of repose to my left . . . I never seem to look upon the same mountain twice. You change as much as I myself, yet you remain what you are. Which means that there is hope for me.

I lower my eyes to where we share this quality with the sea, vast living data-net. Like yet unlike, you have fought that sea as I—

Birds. Let me listen and watch them for a time, the air-riders who dip and feed.

I watch the men work with the nets. It is relaxing to behold their nimble movements. After a time, I doze.

Sleeping, I dream, and dreaming I behold the god Kokuzo. It can be no other, for when he draws his blade which flashes like the sun and points it at me, he speaks his name. He repeats it over and over as I tremble before him, but something is wrong. I know that he is telling me something other than his identity. I reach for but cannot grasp the meaning. Then he moves the point of his blade, indicating something beyond me. I turn my head. I behold the man in black—the pilot, the watcher at the *goma*. He is studying me, just as he was that night. What does he seek in my face?

I am awakened by a violent rocking of the boat as we strike a rougher sea. I catch hold of the gunwale beside which I sit. A quick survey of my surroundings shows me that we are in no danger, and I turn my eyes to Fuji. Is he laughing at me? Or is it the chuckle of Hokusai, who squats on his hams beside me tracing naughty pictures in the moisture of the boat's bottom with a long, withered finger?

If a mystery cannot be solved, it must be saved. Later, then. I will return to the message when my mind has moved into a new position.

Soon, another load of fish is being hauled aboard to add to the pungency of this voyage. Wriggle howsoever they will, they do not escape the net. I think of Kendra and wonder how she is holding up. I hope that her anger with me has abated. I trust that she has not escaped her imprisonment. I left her in the care of acquaintances at a primitive, isolated commune in the Southwest. I do not like the place, nor am I overfond of its residents. Yet they owe me several large favors—intentionally bestowed against these times—and they will keep her there until certain things come to pass. I see her delicate features, fawn eyes, and silken hair. A bright, graceful girl, used to some luxuries, fond of long soaks and frequent showers, crisp garments. She is probably mud-spattered or dusty at the moment, from slopping hogs, weeding, planting vegetables or harvesting them, or any of a number of basic chores. Perhaps it will be good for her character. She ought to get something from the experience other than preservation from a possibly terrible fate.

Time passes. I take my lunch.

Later, I muse upon Fuji, Kokuzo, and my fears. Are dreams but the tranced mind's theater of fears and desires, or do they sometimes truly reflect unconsidered aspects of reality, perhaps to give warning? To reflect . . . It is said that the perfect mind reflects. The *shintai* in its ark in its shrine is the thing truly sacred to the god—a small mirror—not the images. The sea reflects the sky, in fullness of cloud or blue emptiness. Hamlet-like, one can work many interpretations of the odd, but only one should have a clear outline. I hold the dream in my mind once more, absent all querying. Something is moving. . . .

No. I almost had it. But I reached too soon. My mirror is shattered.

As I stare shoreward, the matter of synchronicity occurs. There is a new grouping of people. I withdraw my small spy-scope and take its measure, already knowing what I will regard.

Again, he wears black. He is speaking with two men upon the beach. One of the men gestures out across the water, toward us. The distance is too great to make out features clearly, but I know that it is the same man. But now it is not fear that I know. A slow anger begins to burn within my *hara*. I would return to shore and confront him. He is only one man. I will deal with him now. I cannot afford any more of the unknown than that for which I have already provided. He must be met properly, dismissed or accounted for.

I call to the captain to take me ashore immediately. He grumbles. The fishing is good, the day still young. I offer him more money. Reluctantly, he agrees. He calls orders to his sons to put the boat about and head in.

I stand in the bow. Let him have a good look. I send my anger on ahead. The sword is as sacred an object as the mirror.

As Fuji grows before me the man glances in our direction, hands something to the others, then turns and ambles away. No! There is no way to hasten our progress, and at this rate he will be gone before I reach land. I curse. I want immediate satisfaction, not extension of mystery.

And the men with whom he was speaking. . . . Their hands go to their pockets, they laugh, then walk off in another direction. Drifters. Did he pay them for whatever information they gave him? So it would seem. And are they heading now for some tavern to drink up the price of my peace of mind? I call out after them, but the wind whips my words away. They, too, will be gone by the time I arrive.

And this is true. When I finally stand upon the beach, the only familiar face is that of my mountain, gleaming like a carbuncle in the sun's slanting rays.

I dig my nails into my palms, but my arms do not become wings.

9. MT. FUJI FROM NABORITO

I am fond of this print: the torii of a Shinto shrine are visible above the sea at low tide, and people dig clams amid the sunken ruins. Fuji of course is visible through the torii. Were it a Christian church beneath the waves, puns involving the Clam of God would be running through my mind. Geography saves, however.

And reality differs entirely. I cannot locate the place. I am in the area and Fuji properly situated, but the torii must be long gone and I have no way of knowing whether there is a sunken temple out there.

I am seated on a hillside looking across the water, and I am suddenly not just tired but exhausted. I have come far and fast these past several days, and it seems that my exertions have all caught up with me. I will sit here and watch the sea and the sky. At least my shadow, the man in black, has been nowhere visible since the beach at

Tagonoura. A young cat chases a moth at the foot of my hill, leaping into the air, white-gloved paws flashing. The moth gains altitude, escapes in a gust of wind. The cat sits for several moments, big eyes staring after it.

I make my way to a declivity I had spotted earlier, where I might be free of the wind. There I lay my pack and cast my bedroll, my poncho beneath it. After removing my shoes I get inside quickly. I seem to have taken a bit of a chill, and my limbs are very heavy. I would have been willing to pay to sleep indoors tonight, but I am too tired to seek shelter.

I lie here and watch the lights come on in the darkening sky. As usual in cases of extreme fatigue, sleep does not come to me easily. Is this legitimate tiredness or a symptom of something else? I do not wish to take medication merely as a precaution, though, so I try thinking of nothing for a time. This does not work. I am overcome with the desire for a cup of hot tea. In its absence I swallow a jigger of brandy, which warms my insides for a time.

Still, sleep eludes me and I decide to tell myself a story as I did when I was very young and wanted to make the world turn into dream.

So . . . Upon a time during the troubles following the death of the Retired Emperor Sutoku a number of itinerant monks of various persuasions came this way, having met upon the road, traveling to seek respite from the wars, earthquakes, and whirlwinds which so disturbed the land. They hoped to found a religious community and pursue the meditative life in quiet and tranquillity. They came upon what appeared to be a deserted Shinto shrine near the seaside, and there they camped for the night, wondering what plague or misfortune might have carried off its attendants. The place was in good repair and no evidence of violence was to be seen. They discussed then the possibility of making this their retreat, of themselves becoming the shrine's attendants. They grew enthusiastic with the idea and spent much of the night talking over these plans. In the morning, however, an ancient priest appeared from within the shrine, as if to commence a day's duties. The monks asked him the story of the place, and he informed them that once there had been others to assist him in his duties but that they had long ago been taken by the sea during a storm, while about their peculiar devotions one night upon the shore. And no, it was not really a Shinto shrine, though in outward appearance it seemed such. It was actually the temple of a far older religion of which he could well be the last devotee. They were welcome, however, to join him here and learn of it if they so wished. The monks discussed it quickly among themselves and decided that since it was a pleasant-seeming place, it might be well to stay and hear whatever teaching the old man possessed. So they became residents at the strange shrine. The place troubled several of them considerably at first, for at night they seemed to hear the calling of musical voices in the waves and upon the sea wind. And on occasion it seemed as if they could hear the old priest's voice responding to these calls. One night one of them followed the sounds and saw the old man standing on the beach, his arms upraised. The monk hid himself and later fell asleep in a crevice in the rocks. When he awoke, a full moon stood high in the heavens and the old man was gone. The monk went down to the place where he had stood and there saw many marks in the sand, all of them the prints of webbed feet. Shaken, the monk returned and recited his experience to his fellows. They spent weeks thereafter trying to catch a glimpse of the old man's feet, which were always wrapped and bound. They did not succeed, but after a time it seemed to matter less and less. His teachings influenced them slowly but steadily. They began to assist him in his rituals to the Old Ones, and they learned the name of this promontory and its shrine. It was the last above-sea remnant of a large sunken island, which he assured them rose on certain wonderous occasions to reveal a lost city inhabited by the servants of his masters. The name of the place was R'lyeh, and they would be happy to go there one day. By then it seemed a good idea, for they had noticed a certain thickening and extension of the skin between their fingers and toes, the digits themselves becoming sturdier and more elongated. By then, too, they were participating in all of the rites, which grew progressively abominable. At length, after a particularly gory ritual, the old priest's promise was fulfilled in reverse. Instead of the island rising, the promontory sank to join it, bearing the shrine and all of the monks along with it. So their abominations are primarily aquatic now. But once every century or so the whole island does indeed rise up for a night, and troops of them make their way ashore seeking victims. And of course, tonight is the night. . . .

A delicious feeling of drowsiness has finally come over me with this telling, based upon some of my favorite bedtime stories. My eyes are closed. I float on a cotton-filled raft . . . I—

A sound! Above me! Toward the sea. Something moving my way. Slowly, then quickly.

Adrenaline sends a circuit of fire through my limbs. I extend my hand carefully, quietly, and take hold of my staff.

Waiting. Why now, when I am weakened? Must danger always approach at the worst moment?

There is a thump as it strikes the ground beside me, and I let out the breath I have been holding.

It is the cat, little more than a kitten, which I had observed earlier. Purring, it approaches. I reach out and stroke it. It rubs against me. After a time I take it into the bag. It curls up at my side, still purring, warm.

It is good to have something that trusts you and wants to be near you. I call the cat R'lyeh. Just for one night.

10. MT. FUJI FROM EJIRI

I took the bus back this way. I was too tired to hike. I have taken my medicine as I probably should have been doing all along. Still, it could be several days before it brings me some relief, and this frightens me. I cannot really afford such a condition. I am not certain what I will do, save that I must go on.

The print is deceptive, for a part of its force lies in the effects of a heavy wind. Its skies are gray, Fuji is dim in the background, the people on the road and the two trees beside it all suffer from the wind's buffeting. The trees bend, the people clutch at their garments, there is a hat high in the air, and some poor scribe or author has had his manuscript snatched skyward to flee from him across the land (reminding me of an old cartoon—Editor to Author: "A funny thing happened to your manuscript during the St. Patrick's Day Parade"). The scene which confronts me is less active at a meteorological level. The sky is indeed overcast but there is no wind, Fuji is darker, more clearly delineated than in the print, there are no struggling pedestrians in sight. There are many more trees near at hand. I stand near a small grove, in fact. There are some structures in the distance which are not present in the picture.

I lean heavily upon my staff. Live a little, die a little. I have reached my tenth station, and I still do not know whether Fuji is giving me strength or taking it from me. Both, perhaps.

I head off into the wood, my face touched by a few raindrops as I go. There are no signs posted and no one seems to be about. I work my way back from the road, coming at last to a small clear area containing a few rocks and boulders. It will do as a campsite. I want nothing more than to spend the day resting.

I soon have a small fire going, my tiny teapot poised on rocks above it. A distant roll of thunder adds variety to my discomfort, but so far the rain has held off. The ground is damp, however. I spread my poncho and sit upon it while I wait. I hone a knife and put it away. I eat some biscuits and study a map. I suppose I should feel some satisfaction, in that things are proceeding somewhat as I intended. I wish that I could, but I do not.

An unspecified insect which has been making buzzing noises somewhere behind me ceases its buzzing. I hear a twig snap a moment later. My hand snakes out to fall upon my staff.

"Don't," says a voice at my back.

I turn my head. He is standing eight or ten feet from me, the man in black, earring in place, his right hand in his jacket pocket. And it looks as if there is more than his hand in there, pointed at me.

I remove my hand from my staff and he advances. With the side of his foot he sends the staff partway across the clearing, out of my reach. Then he removes his hand from his pocket, leaving behind whatever it held. He circles slowly to the other side of the fire, staring at me the while.

He seats himself upon a boulder, lets his hands rest upon his knees.

"Mari?" he asks then.

I do not respond to my name, but stare back. The light of Kokuzo's dream-sword flashes in my mind, pointing at him, and I hear the god speaking his name only not quite.

"Kotuzov!" I say then.

The man in black smiles, showing that the teeth I had broken once long ago are now neatly capped.

"I was not so certain of you at first either," he says.

Plastic surgery has removed at least a decade from his face, along with a lot of weathering and several scars. He is different about the eyes and cheeks, also. And his nose is smaller. It is a considerable improvement over the last time we met.

"Your water is boiling," he says then. "Are you going to offer me a cup of tea?"

"Of course," I reply, reaching for my pack, where I keep an extra cup.

"Slowly."

"Certainly."

I locate the cup, I rinse them both lightly with hot water, I prepare the tea.

"No, don't pass it to me," he says, and reaches forward and takes the cup from where I had filled it.

I suppress a desire to smile.

"Would you have a lump of sugar?" he asks.

"Sorry."

He sighs and reaches into his other pocket, from which he withdraws a small flask.

"Vodka? In tea?"

"Don't be silly. My tastes have changed. Its Wild Turkey liqueur, a wonderful sweetener. Would you care for some?"

"Let me smell it."

There is a certain sweetness to the aroma.

"All right," I say, and he laces our tea with it.

We taste the tea. Not bad.

"How long has it been?" he asks.

"Fourteen years—almost fifteen," I tell him. "Back in the eighties."

"Yes."

He rubs his jaw. "I'd heard you'd retired."

"You heard right. It was about a year after our last—encounter."

"Turkey—yes. You married a man from your Code Section."

I nod.

"You were widowed three or four years later. Daughter born after your husband's death. Returned to the States. Settled in the country. That's all I know."

"That's all there is."

He takes another drink of tea.

"Why did you come back here?"

"Personal reasons. Partly sentimental."

"Under a false identity?"

"Yes. It involves my husband's family. I don't want them to know I'm here."

"Interesting. You mean that they would watch arrivals as closely as we have?"

"I didn't know you watched arrivals here."

"Right now we do."

"You've lost me. I don't know what's going on."

There is another roll of thunder. A few more drops spatter about us.

"I would like to believe that you are really retired," he says. "I'm getting near that point myself, you know."

"I have no reason to be back in business. I inherited a decent amount, enough to take care of me and my daughter."

He nods.

"If I had such an inducement I would not be in the field," he says. "I would rather sit home and read, play chess, eat and drink regularly. But you must admit it is quite a coincidence your being here when the future success of several nations is being decided."

I shake my head.

"I've been out of touch with a lot of things."

"The Osaka Oil Conference. It begins two weeks from Wednesday. You were planning perhaps to visit Osaka at about that time?"

"I will not be going to Osaka."

"A courier then. Someone from there will meet you, a simple tourist, at some point in your travels, to convey—"

"My God! Do you think everything's a conspiracy, Boris? I am just taking care of some personal problems and visiting some places that mean something to me. The conference doesn't."

"All right." He finishes his tea and puts the cup aside. "You know that we know you are here. A word to the Japanese authorities that you are traveling under false papers, and they will kick you out. That would be simplest. No real harm done and one agent nullified. Only it would be a shame to spoil your trip if you are indeed only a tourist . . . "

A rotten thought passes through my mind as I see where this is leading, and I know that my thought is far rottener than his. It is something I learned from a strange old woman I once worked with who did not look like an old woman.

I finish my tea and raise my eyes. He is smiling.

"I will make us some more tea," I say.

I see that the top button of my shirt comes undone while I am bent partly away from him. Then I lean forward with his cup and take a deep breath.

"You would consider not reporting me to the authorities?"

"I might," he says. "I think your story is probably true. And even if it is not, you would not take the risk of transporting anything now that I know about you."

"I really want to finish this trip," I say, blinking a few extra times. "I would do anything not to be sent back now."

He takes hold of my hand.

"I am glad you said that, Maryushka," he replies. "I am lonely, and you are still a fine-looking woman."

"You think so?"

"I always thought so, even that day you bashed in my teeth."

"Sorry about that. It was strictly business, you know."

His hand moves to my shoulder.

"Of course. They looked better when they were fixed than they had before, anyway."

He moves over and sits beside me.

"I have dreamed of doing this many times," he tells me, as he unfastens the rest of the buttons on my shirt and unbuckles my belt.

He rubs my belly softly. It is not an unpleasant feeling. It has been a long time.

Soon we are fully undressed. He takes his time, and when he is ready I welcome him between my legs. All right, Boris. I give the ride, you take the fall. I could almost feel a little guilty about it. You are gentler than I'd thought you would be. I commence the proper breathing pattern, deep and slow. I focus my attention on my *hara* and his, only inches away. I feel our energies, dreamlike and warm, moving. Soon, I direct their flow. He feels it only as pleasure, perhaps more draining than usual. When he has done, though. . . .

"You said you had some problem?" he inquires in that masculine coital magnanimity generally forgotten a few minutes afterward. "If it is something I could help you with, I have a few days off, here and there. I like you, Maryushka."

"It's something I have to do myself. Thanks anyway."

I continue the process.

Later, as I dress myself, he lies there looking up at me.

"I must be getting old, Maryushka," he reflects. "You have tired me. I feel I could sleep for a week."

"That sounds about right," I say. "A week and you should be feeling fine again."

"I do not understand. . . . "

"You've been working too hard, I'm sure. That conference . . . "

He nods.

"You are probably right. You are not really involved . . . ?"

"I am really not involved."

"Good."

I clean the pot and my cups. I restore them to my pack.

"Would you be so kind as to move, Boris dear? I'll be needing the poncho very soon, I think."

"Of course."

He rises slowly and passes it to me. He begins dressing. His breathing is heavy.

"Where are you going from here?"

"Mishima-goe," I say, "for another view of my mountain."

He shakes his head. He finishes dressing and seats himself on the ground, his back against a tree trunk. He finds his flask and takes a swallow. He extends it then.

"Would you care for some?"

"Thank you, no. I must be on my way."

I retrieve my staff. When I look at him again, he smiles faintly, ruefully.

"You take a lot out of a man, Maryushka."

"I had to," I say.

I move off. I will hike twenty miles today, I am certain. The rain begins to descend before I am out of the grove; leaves rustle like the wings of bats.

11. MT. FUJI FROM MISHIMA-GOE

Sunlight. Clean air. The print shows a big cryptomeria tree, Fuji looming behind it, crowned with smoke. There is no smoke today, but I have located a big cryptomeria and positioned myself so that it cuts Fuji's shoulder to the left of the cone. There are a few clouds, no so popcorny as Hokusai's smoke (he shrugs at this), and they will have to do.

My stolen *ki* still sustains me, though the medication is working now beneath it. Like a transplanted organ, my body will soon reject the borrowed energy. By then, though, the drugs should be covering for me.

In the meantime, the scene and the print are close to each other. It is a lovely spring day. Birds are singing, butterflies stitch the air in zigzag patterns; I can almost hear the growth of plants beneath the soil. The world smells fresh and new. I am no longer being followed. Hello to life again.

I regard the huge old tree and listen for its echoes down the ages: Yggdrasil, the Golden Bough, the Yule tree, the Tree of the Knowledge of Good and Evil, the Bo beneath which Lord Gautama found his soul and lost it. . . .

I move forward to run my hand along its rough bark.

From that position I am suddenly given a new view of the valley below. The fields look like raked sand, the hills like rocks, Fuji a boulder. It is a garden, perfectly laid out. . . .

Later I notice that the sun has moved. I have been standing here for hours. My small illumination beneath a great tree. Older than my humanity, I do not know what I can do for it in return.

Stooping suddenly, I pick up one of its cones. A tiny thing, for such a giant. It is barely the size of my little fingernail. Delicately incised, as if sculpted by fairies.

I put it in my pocket. I will plant it somewhere along my way.

I retreat then, for I hear the sound of approaching bells and I am not yet ready for humanity to break my mood. But there was a small inn down the road which does not look to be part of a chain. I will bathe and eat there and sleep in a bed tonight.

I will still be strong tomorrow.

12. MT. FUJI FROM LAKE KAWAGUCHI

Reflections.

This is one of my favorite prints in the series: Fuji as seen from across the lake and reflected within it. There are green hills at either hand, a small village upon the far shore, a single small boat in sight upon the water. The most fascinating feature of the print is that the reflection of Fuji is not the same as the original; its position is wrong, its slope is wrong, it is snow-capped and the surface view of Fuji itself is not.

I sit in the small boat I have rented, looking back. The sky is slightly hazy, which is good. No glare to spoil the reflection. The town is no longer as quaint as in the print, as it has grown. But I am not concerned with details of this sort. Fuji is reflected more perfectly in my viewing, but the doubling is still a fascinating phenomenon for me.

Interesting, too . . . In the print the village is not reflected, nor is there an image of the boat in the water. The only reflection is Fuji's. There is no sign of humanity.

I see the reflected buildings near the water's edge. And my mind is stirred by other images than those Hokusai would have known. Of course drowned R'lyeh occurs to me, but the place and the day are too idyllic. It fades from mind almost immediately, to be replaced by sunken Ys, whose bells still toll the hours beneath the sea. And Selma Lagerlöf's *Nils Holgersson*, the tale of the shipwrecked sailor who finds himself in a sunken city at the bottom of the sea—a place drowned to punish its greedy, arrogant inhabitants, who still go about their business of cheating each other, though they are all of them dead. They wear rich, old-fashioned clothes and conduct their business as they once did above in this strange land beneath the waves. The sailor is drawn to them, but he knows that he must not be discovered or he will be turned into one of them, never to return to the earth, to see the sun. I suppose I think of this old children's story because I understand now how the sailor must have felt. My discovery, too, could result in a transformation I do not desire.

And of course, as I lean forward and view my own features mirrored in the water, there is the world of Lewis Carroll beneath its looking-glass surface. To be an Ama diving girl and descend . . . To spin downward, and for a few minutes to know the inhabitants of a land of paradox and great charm . . .

Mirror, mirror, why does the real world so seldom cooperate with our aesthetic enthusiasms?

Halfway finished. I reach the midpoint of my pilgrimage to confront myself in a lake. It is a good time and place to look upon my own countenance, to reflect upon all of the things which have brought me here, to consider what the rest of the journey may hold. Though images may sometimes lie. The woman who looks back at me seems composed, strong, and better-looking than I had thought she would. I like you, Kawaguchi, lake with a human personality. I flatter you with literary compliments, and you return the favor.

Meeting Boris lifted a burden of fear from my mind. No human agents of my nemesis have risen to trouble my passage. So the odds have not yet tipped so enormously against me as they might.

Fuji and image. Mountain and soul. Would an evil thing cast no reflection down here—some dark mountain where terrible deeds were performed throughout history? I am reminded that Kit no longer casts a shadow, has no reflection.

Is he truly evil, though? By my lights he is. Especially if he is doing the things I think he is doing.

He said that he loved me, and I did love him, once. What will he say to me when we meet again, as meet we must?

It will not matter. Say what he will, I am going to try to kill him. He believes that he is invincible, indestructible. I do not, though I do believe that I am the only person on Earth capable of destroying him. It took a long time for me to figure the means, an even longer time before the decision to try it was made for me. I must do it for Kendra as well as for myself. The rest of the world's population comes third.

I let my fingers trail in the water. Softly, I begin to sing an old song, a love song. I am loath to leave this place. Will the second half of my journey be a mirror-image of the first? Or will I move beyond the looking-glass, to pass into that strange realm where he makes his home?

I planted the cryptomeria's seed in a lonesome valley yesterday afternoon. Such a tree will look elegant there one day, outliving nations and armies, madmen and sages.

I wonder where R'lyeh is? She ran off in the morning after breakfast, perhaps to pursue a butterfly. Not that I could have brought her with me.

I hope that Kendra is well. I have written her a long letter explaining many things. I left it in the care of an attorney friend, who will be sending it to her one day in the not-too-distant future.

The prints of Hokusai . . . They could outlast the cryptomeria. I will not be remembered for any works.

Drifting between the worlds I formulate our encounter for the thousandth time. He will have to be able to duplicate an old trick to get what he wants. I will have to perform an even older one to see that he doesn't get it. We are both out of practice.

It has been long since I read *The Anatomy of Melancholy*. It is not the sort of thing I've sought to divert me in recent years. But I recall a line or two as I see fish dart by: "Polycrates Samius, that flung his ring into the sea, because he would participate in the discontent of others, and had it miraculously restored to him again shortly after, by a fish taken as he angled, was not free from melancholy dispositions. No man can cure himself. . . . " Kit threw away his life and gained it. I kept mine and lost it. Are rings ever really returned to the proper people? And what about a woman curing herself? The cure I seek is a very special one.

Hokusai, you have shown me many things. Can you show me an answer?

Slowly, the old man raises his arm and points to his mountain. Then he lowers it and points to the mountain's image.

I shake my head. It is an answer that is no answer. He shakes his head back at me and points again.

The clouds are massing high above Fuji, but that is no answer. I study them for a long while but can trace no interesting images within.

Then I drop my eyes. Below me, inverted, they take a different form. It is as if they depict the clash of two armed hosts. I watch in fascination as they flow together, the forces from my right gradually rolling over and submerging those to my left. Yet in so doing, those from my right are diminished.

Conflict? That is the message? And both sides lose things they do not wish to lose? Tell me something I do not already know, old man.

He continues to stare. I follow his gaze again, upward. Now I see a dragon, diving into Fuji's cone.

I look below once again. No armies remain, only carnage; and here the dragon's tail becomes a dying warrior's arm holding a sword.

I close my eyes and reach for it. A sword of smoke for a man of fire.

13. MT. FUJI FROM KOISHIKAWA IN EDO

Snow, on the roofs of houses, on evergreens, on Fuji—just beginning to melt in places, it seems. A windowful of women—geishas, I would say—looking out at it, one of them pointing at three dark birds high in the pale sky. My closest view of Fuji to that in the print is unfortunately snowless, geishaless, and sunny.

Details . . .

Both are interesting, and superimposition is one of the major forces of aesthetics. I cannot help but think of the hot-spring geisha Komako in *Snow Country*—Yasunari Kawabata's novel of loneliness and wasted, fading beauty—which I have always felt to be the great antilove story of Japan. This print brings the entire tale to mind for me. The denial of love. Kit was no Shimamura, for he did want me, but only on his own highly specialized terms, terms that must remain unacceptable to me. Selfishness or selflessness? It is not important. . . .

And the birds at which the geisha points . . . ? "Thirteen Ways of Looking at a Blackbird"? To the point. We could never agree on values.

The Twa Corbies? And throw in Ted Hughes's pugnacious Crow? Perhaps so, but I won't draw straws— An illusion for every allusion, and where's yesterday's snow?

I lean upon my staff and study my mountain. I wish to make it to as many of my stations as possible before ordering the confrontation. Is that not fair? Twenty-four ways of looking at Mt. Fuji. It struck me that it would be good to take one thing in life and regard it from many viewpoints, as a focus for my being, and perhaps as a penance for alternatives missed.

Kit, I am coming, as you once asked of me, but by my own route and for my own reasons. I wish that I did not have to, but you have deprived me of a real choice in this matter. Therefore, my action is not truly my own, but yours. I am become then your own hand turned against you, representative of a kind of cosmic aikido.

I make my way through town after dark, choosing only dark streets where the businesses are shut down. That way I am safe. When I must enter town I always find a protected spot for the day and do my traveling on these streets at night.

I find a small restaurant on the corner of such a one, and I take my dinner there. It is a noisy place, but the food is good. I also take my medicine, and a little saké.

Afterward, I indulge in the luxury of walking rather than take a taxi. I've a long way to go, but the night is clear and star-filled and the air is pleasant.

I walk for the better part of ten minutes, listening to the sounds of traffic, music from some distant radio or tape deck, a cry from another street, the wind passing high above me and rubbing its rough fur upon the sides of buildings.

Then I feel a sudden ionization in the air.

Nothing ahead. I turn, spinning my staff into a guard position.

An epigon with a six-legged canine body and a head like a giant fiery flower emerges from a doorway and sidles along the building's front in my direction.

I follow its progress with my staff, feinting as soon as it is near enough. I strike, unfortunately with the wrong tip, as it comes on. My hair begins to rise as I spin out of its way, cutting, retreating, turning, then striking again. This time the metal tip passes into that floral head.

I had turned on the batteries before I commenced my attack. The charge creates an imbalance. The epigon retreats, head ballooning. I follow and strike again, this time midbody. It swells even larger, then collapses in a shower of sparks. But I am already turning away and striking again, for I had become aware of the approach of another even as I was dealing with the first.

This one advances in kangaroolike bounds. I brush it by with my staff, but its long bulbous tail strikes me as it passes. I recoil involuntarily from the shock I receive, my reflexes spinning the staff before me as I retreat. It turns quickly and rears then. This one is a quadruped, and its raised forelimbs are fountains of fire. Its faceful of eyes blazes and hurts to look upon.

It drops back onto its haunches then springs again.

I roll beneath it and attack as it descends. But I miss, and it turns to attack again even as I continue thrusting. It springs and I turn aside, striking upward. It seems that I connect, but I cannot be certain.

It lands quite near me, raising its forelimbs. But this time it does not spring. It simply falls forward, hind feet making a rapid shuffling movement the while, the legs seeming to adjust their lengths to accommodate a more perfect flow.

As it comes on, I catch it square in the midsection with the proper end of my staff. It keeps coming, or falling, even as it flares and begins to disintegrate. Its touch stiffens me for a moment, and I feel the flow of its charge down my shoulder and across my breast. I watch it come apart in a final photoflash instant and be gone.

I turn quickly again, but there is no third emerging from the doorway. None overhear either. There is a car coming up the street, slowing, however. No matter. The terminal's potential must be exhausted for the moment, though I am puzzled by the consideration of how long it must have been building to produce the two I just dispatched. It is best that I be away quickly now.

As I resume my progress, though, a voice calls to me from the car, which has now drawn up beside me:

"Madam, a moment please."

It is a police car, and the young man who has addressed me wears a uniform and a very strange expression.

"Yes, Officer?" I reply.

"I saw you just a few moments ago," he says. "What were you doing?"

I laugh.

"It is such a fine evening," I say then, "and the street was deserted. I thought I would do a *kata* with my *bo*."

"I thought at first that something was attacking you, that I saw something. . . . "

"I am alone," I say, "as you can see."

He opens the door and climbs out. He flicks on a flashlight and shines its beam across the sidewalk, into the doorway.

"Were you setting off fireworks?"

"No."

"There were some sparkles and flashes."

"You must be mistaken."

He sniffs the air. He inspects the sidewalk very closely, even the gutter.

"Strange," he says. "Have you far to go?"

"Not too far."

"Have a good evening."

He gets back into the car. Moments later it is headed up the street.

I continue quickly on my way. I wish to be out of the vicinity before another charge can be built. I also wish to be out of the vicinity simply because being here makes me uneasy.

I am puzzled at the ease with which I was located. What did I do wrong?

"My prints," Hokusai seems to say, after I have reached my destination and drunk too much brandy. "Think, daughter, or they will trap you."

I try, but Fuji is crushing my head, squeezing off thoughts. Epigons dance on his slopes. I pass into a fitful slumber.

In tomorrow's light perhaps I shall see. . . .

14. MT. FUJI FROM MEGURO IN EDO

Again, the print is not the reality for me. It shows peasants amid a rustic village, terraced hillsides, a lone tree jutting from the slope of the hill to the right, a snowcapped Fuji partly eclipsed by the base of the rise.

I could not locate anything approximating it, though I do have a partly blocked view of Fuji—blocked in a similar manner, by a slope— from this bench I occupy in a small park. It will do.

Partly blocked, like my thinking. There is something I should be seeing, but it is hidden from me. I felt it the moment the epigons appeared, like the devils sent to claim Faust's soul. But I never made a pact with the Devil . . . just Kit, and it was called marriage. I had no way of knowing how similar it would be.

Now . . . What puzzles me most is how my location was determined despite my precautions. My head-on encounter must be on my terms, not anyone else's. The reason for this transcends the personal, though I will not deny the involvement of the latter.

In *Hagakure*, Yamamoto Tsunetomo advised that the Way of the Samurai is the Way of Death, that one must live as though one's body were already dead in order to gain full freedom. For me, this attitude is not so difficult to maintain. The freedom part is more complicated, however; when one no longer understands the full nature of the enemy, one's actions are at least partly conditioned by uncertainty.

My occulted Fuji is still there in his entirety, I know, despite my lack of full visual data. By the same token I ought to be able to extend the lines I have seen thus far with respect to the power which now devils me. Let us return to death. There seems to be something there, though it also seems that there is only so much you can say about it and I already have.

Death . . . Come gentle . . . We used to play a parlor game, filling in bizarre causes on imaginary death certificates: "Eaten by the Loch Ness monster." "Stepped on by Godzilla." "Poisoned by a ninja." "Translated."

Kit had stared at me, brow knitting, when I'd offered that last one.

"What do you mean 'translated'?" he asked.

"Okay, you can get me on a technicality," I said, "but I still think the effect would be the same. 'Enoch was translated that he should not see death'—Paul's Epistle to the Hebrews, 11:5."

"I don't understand."

"It means to convey directly to heaven without messing around with the customary termination here on earth. Some Moslems believe that the Mahdi was translated."

"An interesting concept," he said. "I'll have to think about it."

Obviously, he did.

I've always thought that Kurosawa could have done a hell of a job with *Don Quixote*. Say there is this old gentleman living in modern times, a scholar, a man who is fascinated by the early days of the samurai and the Code of Bushido. Say that he identifies so strongly with these ideals that one day he loses his senses and comes to believe that he *is* the old-time samurai. He dons some ill-fitting armor he had collected, takes up his *katana*, goes forth to change the world. Ultimately, he is destroyed by it, but he holds to the Code. That quality of dedication sets him apart and ennobles him, for all of his ludicrousness. I have never felt that *Don Quixote* was merely a parody of chivalry, especially not after I'd learned that Cervantes has served under Don John of Austria at the battle of Lepanto. For it might be argued that Don John was the last European to be guided by the medieval code of chivalry. Brought up on medieval romances, he had conducted his life along these lines. What did it matter if the medieval knights themselves had not? He believed and he acted on his belief. In anyone else it might simply have been amusing, save that time and circumstance granted him the opportunity to act on several large occasions, and he won. Cervantes could not but have been impressed by his old commander, and who knows how this might have influenced his later literary endeavor? Ortega y Gasset referred to Quixote as a Gothic Christ. Dostoevsky felt the same way about him, and in his attempt to portray a Christ-figure in Prince Myshkin he, too, felt that madness was a necessary precondition for this state in modern times.

All of which is preamble to stating my belief that Kit was at least partly mad. But he was no Gothic Christ. An Electronic Buddha would be much closer.

"Does the data-net have the Buddha-nature?" he asked me one day.

"Sure," I said. "Doesn't everything?" Then I saw the look in his eyes and added, "How the hell should I know?"

He grunted then and reclined his resonance couch, lowered the induction helmet, and continued his computer-augmented analysis of a Lucifer cipher with a 128-bit key. Theoretically, it would take thousands of years to crack it by brute force, but the answer was needed within two weeks. His nervous system coupled with the data-net, he was able to deliver.

I did not notice his breathing patterns for some time. It was not until later that I came to realize that after he had finished his work, he would meditate for increasingly long periods of time while still joined with the system.

When I realized this, I chided him for being too lazy to turn the thing off.

He smiled.

"The flow," he said. "You do not fixate at one point. You go with the flow."

"You could throw the switch before you go with the flow and cut down on our electric bill."

He shook his head, still smiling.

"But it is that particular flow that I am going with. I am getting farther and farther into it. You should try it sometime. There have been moments when I felt I could translate myself into it."

"Linguistically or theologically?"

"Both," he replied.

And one night he did indeed go with the flow. I found him in the morning—sleeping, I thought—in his resonance couch, the helmet still in place. This time, at least, he had shut down our terminal. I let him rest. I had no idea how late he might have been working. By evening, though, I was beginning to grow concerned and I tried to rouse him. I could not. He was in a coma.

Later, in the hospital, he showed a flat EEG. His breathing had grown extremely shallow, his blood pressure was very low, his pulse feeble. He continued to decline during the next two days. The doctors gave him every test they could think of but could determine no cause for his condition. In that he had once signed a document requesting that no heroic measures be taken to prolong his existence should something irreversible take him, he was not hooked up to respirators and pumps and IVs after his heart had stopped beating for the fourth time. The autopsy was unsatisfactory. The death certificate merely showed: "Heart stoppage. Possible cerebro-vascular accident." The latter was pure speculation. They found no sign of it. His organs were not distributed to the needy as he had once requested, for fear of some strange new virus which might be transmitted.

Kit, like Marley, was dead to begin with.

15. MT. FUJI FROM TSUKUDAJIMA IN EDO

Blue sky, a few low clouds, Fuji across the bay's bright water, a few boats and an islet between us. Again, dismissing time's changes, I find considerable congruence with reality. Again, I sit within a small boat. Here, however, I've no desire to dive beneath the waves in search of sunken splendor or to sample the bacteria-count with my person.

My passage to this place was direct and without incident. Preoccupied I came. Preoccupied I remain. My vitality remains high. My health is no worse. My concerns also remain the same, which means that my major question is still unanswered.

At least I feel safe out here on the water. "Safe," though, is a relative term. "Safer" then, than I felt ashore and passing among possible places of ambush. I have not really felt safe since that day after my return from the hospital. . . .

I was tired when I got back home, following several sleepless nights. I went directly to bed. I did not even bother to note the hour, so I have no idea how long I slept.

I was awakened in the dark by what seemed to be the ringing of the telephone. Sleepily, I reached for the instrument, then realized that it was not actually ringing. Had I been dreaming? I sat up in bed. I rubbed my eyes. I stretched. Slowly, the recent past filled my mind and I knew that I would not sleep again for a time. A cup of tea, I decided, might serve me well now. I rose, to go to the kitchen and heat some water.

As I passed through the work area, I saw that one of the CRT's for our terminal was lit. I could not recall its having been on, but I moved to turn it off.

I saw then that its switch was not turned on. Puzzled, I looked again at the screen and for the first time realized that there was a display present:

MARI.

ALL IS WELL.

I AM TRANSLATED.

USE THE COUCH AND THE HELMET.

KIT

I felt my fingers digging into my cheeks, and my chest was tight from breath retained. Who had done this? How? Was it perhaps some final delirious message left by Kit himself before he went under?

I reached out and flipped on the ON-OFF switch back and forth several times, leaving it finally in the OFF position.

The display faded but the light remained on. Shortly, a new display was flashed upon the screen:

YOU READ ME. GOOD.

IT IS ALL RIGHT. I LIVE.

I HAVE ENTERED THE DATA-NET.

SIT ON THE COUCH AND USE THE HELMET.

I WILL EXPLAIN EVERYTHING.

I ran from the room. In the bathroom I threw up, several times. Then I sat upon the toilet, shaking. Who would play such a horrible joke on me? I drank several glasses of water and waited for my trembling to subside.

When it had, I went directly to the kitchen, made the tea, and drank some. My thoughts settled slowly into the channels of analysis. I considered possibilities. The one that seemed more likely than most was that Kit had left a message for me and that my use of the induction interface gear would trigger its delivery. I wanted that message, whatever it might be, but I did not know whether I possessed sufficient emotional fortitude to receive it at the moment.

I must have sat there for the better part of an hour. I looked out the window once and saw the sky was growing light. I put down my cup. I returned to the work area.

The screen was still lit. The message, though, had changed:

DO NOT BE AFRAID.

SIT ON THE COUCH AND USE THE HELMET.

THEN YOU WILL UNDERSTAND.

I crossed to the couch. I sat on it and reclined it. I lowered the helmet. At first there was nothing but field noise.

Then I felt his presence, a thing difficult to describe in a world customarily filled only with data flows. I waited. I tried to be receptive to whatever he had somehow left imprinted for me.

"I am not a recording, Mari," he seemed to say to me then. "I am really here."

I resisted the impulse to flee. I had worked hard for this composure, and I meant to maintain it.

"I made it over," he seemed to say. "I have entered the net. I am spread out through many places. It is pure kundalini. I am nothing but flow. It is wonderful. I will be forever here. It is nirvana."

"It really is you," I said.

"Yes. I have translated myself. I want to show you what it means."

"Very well."

"I am gathered here now. Open the legs of your mind and let me in fully."

I relaxed and he flowed into me. Then I was borne away and I understood.

16. MT. FUJI FROM UMEZAWA

Fuji across lava fields and wisps of fog, drifting clouds; birds on the wing and birds on the ground. This one at least is close. I lean on my staff and stare at his peaceful reaches across the chaos. The lesson is like that of a piece of music: I am strengthened in some fashion I cannot describe.

And I had seen blossoming cherry trees on the way over here, and fields purple with clover, cultivated fields yellow with rape-blossoms, grown for its oil, a few winter camellias still holding forth their reds and pinks, the green shoots of rice beds, here and there a tulip tree dashed with white, blue mountains in the distance, foggy river valleys. I had passed villages where colored sheet metal now covers the roofs' thatching—blue and yellow, green, black, red—and yards filled with the slate-blue rocks so fine for landscape gardening; an occasional cow, munching, lowing softly; scarlike rows of plastic-covered mulberry bushes where the silkworms are bred. My heart jogged at the sights— the tiles, the little bridges, the color. . . . It was like entering a tale by Lafcadio Hearn, to have come back.

My mind was drawn along the path I had followed, to the points of its intersection with my electronic bane. Hokusai's warning that night I drank too much—that his prints may trap me—could well be correct. Kit had anticipated my passage a number of times. How could he have?

Then it struck me. My little book of Hokusai's prints—a small clothbound volume by the Charles E. Tuttle Company—had been a present from Kit.

It is possible that he was expecting me in Japan at about this time, because of Osaka. Once his epigons has spotted me a couple of times, probably in a massive scanning of terminals, could he have correlated my movements with the sequence of the prints in *Hokusai's Views of Mt. Fuji*, for which he knew my great fondness, and simply extrapolated and waited? I've a strong feeling that the answer is in the affirmative.

Entering the data-net with Kit was an overwhelming experience. That my consciousness spread and flowed I do not deny. That I was many places simultaneously, that I rode currents I did not at first understand, that knowledge and transcendence and a kind of glory were all about me and within me, was also a fact of peculiar perception. The speed with which I was borne seemed instantaneous, and this was a taste of eternity. The access to multitudes of terminals and enormous memory banks seemed a measure of omniscience. The possibility of the manipulation of whatever I would change within this realm and its consequences at that place where I still felt my distant body seemed a version of omnipotence. And the feeling . . . I tasted the sweetness, Kit with me and within me. It was self-surrendered and recovered in a new incarnation, it was freedom from mundane desire, liberation . . .

"Stay with me here forever," Kit seemed to say.

"No," I seemed to answer, dreamlike, finding myself changing even further. "I cannot surrender myself so willingly."

"Not for this? For unity and the flow of connecting energy?"

"And this wonderful lack of responsibility?"

"Responsibility? For what? This is pure existence. There is no past."

"Then conscience vanishes."

"What do you need it for? There is no future either."

"Then all actions lose their meaning."

"True. Action is an illusion. Consequence is an illusion."

"And paradox triumphs over reason."

"There is no paradox. All is reconciled."

"Then meaning dies."

"Being is the only meaning."

"Are you certain?"

"Feel it!"

"I do. But it is not enough. Send me back before I am changed into something I do not wish to be."

"What more could you desire than this?"

"My imagination will die, also. I can feel it."

"And what is imagination?"

"A thing born of feeling and reason."

"Does this not feel right?"

"Yes, it feels right. But I do not want that feeling unaccompanied. When I touch feeling with reason, I see that it is sometimes but an excuse for failing to close with complexity."

"You can deal with any complexity here. Behold the data! Does reason not show you that this condition is far superior to that you knew but moments ago?"

"Nor can I trust reason unaccompanied. Reason without feeling has led humanity to enact monstrosities. Do not attempt to disassemble my imagination this way."

"You retain your reason and your feelings!"

"But they are coming unplugged—with this storm of bliss, this shower of data. I need them conjoined, else my imagination is lost."

"Let it be lost, then. It has served its purpose. Be done with it now. What can you imagine that you do not already have here?"

"I cannot yet know, and that is its power. If there be a will with a spark of divinity to it, I know it only through my imagination. I can give you anything else, but that I will not surrender."

"And that is all? A wisp of possibility?"

"No. But it alone is too much to deny."

"And my love for you?"

"You no longer love in the human way. Let me go back."

"Of course. You will think about it. You will return."

"Back! Now!"

I pushed the helmet from my head and rose quickly. I returned to the bathroom, then to my bed. I slept as if drugged, for a long while.

Would I have felt differently about possibilities, the future, imagination, had I not been pregnant—a thing I had suspected but not yet mentioned to him, and which he had missed learning with his attention focused upon our argument? I like to think that my answers would have been the same, but I will never know. My condition was confirmed by a local doctor the following day. I made the visit I had been putting off because my life required a certainty of something then—a certainty of anything. The screen in the work area remained blank for three days.

I read and I meditated. Then of an evening the light came on again:

ARE YOU READY?

I activated the keyboard. I typed one word:

NO.

I disconnected the induction couch and its helmet then. I unplugged the unit itself, also.

The telephone rang.

"Hello?" I said.

"Why not?" he asked me.

I screamed and hung up. He had penetrated the phone circuits, appropriated a voice.

It rang again. I answered again.

"You will never know rest until you come to me," he said.

"I will if you will leave me alone," I told him.

"I cannot. You are special to me. I want you with me. I love you."

I hung up. It rang again. I tore the phone from the wall.

I had known that I would have to leave soon. I was overwhelmed and depressed by all the reminders of our life together. I packed quickly and I departed. I took a room at a hotel. As soon as I was settled into it, the telephone rang and it was Kit again. My registration had gone into a computer and. . . .

I had them disconnect my phone at the switchboard. I put out a DO NOT DISTURB sign. In the morning I saw a telegram protruding from beneath the door. From Kit. He wanted to talk to me.

I determined to go far away. To leave the country, to return to the States.

It was easy for him to follow me. We leave electronic tracks almost everywhere. By cable, satellite, optic fiber he could be wherever he chose. Like an unwanted suitor now he pestered me with calls, interrupted television shows to flash messages upon the screen, broke in on my own calls, to friends, lawyers, realtors, stores. Several times, horribly, he even sent me flowers. My electric bodhisattva, my hound of heaven, would give me no rest. It is a terrible thing to be married to a persistent data-net.

So I settled in the country. I would have nothing in my home whereby he could reach me. I studied ways of avoiding the system, of slipping past his many senses.

On those few occasions when I was careless, he reached for me again immediately. Only he had learned a new trick, and I became convinced that he had developed it for the purpose of taking me into his world by force. He could build up a charge at a terminal, mold it into something like ball lightning and animal-like, and send that short-lived artifact a little distance to do his will. I learned its weakness, though, in a friend's home when one came for me, shocked me, and attempted to propel me into the vicinity of the terminal, presumably for purposes of translation. I struck at the epigon—as Kit later referred to it in a telegram of explanation and apology—with the nearest object to hand—a lighted table lamp, which entered its field and blew a circuit immediately. The epigon was destroyed, which is how I discovered that slight electrical disruption created an instability within the things.

I stayed in the country and raised my daughter. I read and I practiced my martial arts and I walked in the woods and climbed mountains and sailed and camped: rural occupations all, and very satisfying to me after a life of intrigue, conflict, plot and counterplot, violence, and then that small, temporary island of security with Kit. I was happy with my choice.

Fuji across the lava beds . . . Springtime . . . Now I am returned. This was not my choice.

17. MT. FUJI FROM LAKE SUWA

And so I come to Lake Suwa, Fuji resting small in the evening distance. It is no Kamaguchi of powerful reflections for me. But it is serene, which joins my mood in a kind of peace. I have taken the life of the spring into me now, and it has spread through my being. Who would disrupt this world, laying unwanted forms upon it? Seal your lips.

Was it not in a quiet province where Bōtchan found his maturity? I've a theory concerning books like that one of Natsume Soseki's. Someone once told me that this is the one book you can be sure that every educated Japanese has read. So I read it. In the States I was told that *Huckleberry Finn* was the one book you could be sure that every educated Yankee had read. So I read it. In Canada it was Stephen Leacock's *Sunshine Sketches of a Little Town*. In France it was *Le Grand Meaulnes*. Other countries have their books of this sort. They are all of them pastorals, having in common a closeness to the countryside and the forces of nature in days just before heavy urbanization and mechanization. These things are on the horizon and advancing, but they only serve to add the spice of poignancy to the taste of simpler values. They are youthful books, of national heart and character, and they deal with the passing of innocence. I have given many of them to Kendra.

I lied to Boris. Of course I know all about the Osaka Conference. I was even approached by one of my former employers to do something along the lines Boris had guessed at. I declined. My plans are my own. There would have been a conflict.

Hokusai, ghost and mentor, you understand chance and purpose better than Kit. You know that human order must color our transactions with the universe, and that this is not only necessary but good, and that the light still comes through.

Upon this rise above the water's side I withdraw my hidden blade and hone it once again. The sun falls away from my piece of the world, but the darkness, too, is here my friend.

18. MT. FUJI FROM THE OFFING IN KANAGAWA

And so the image of death. The Big Wave, curling above, toppling upon, about to engulf the fragile vessels. The one print of Hokusai's that everyone knows.

I am no surfer. I do not seek the perfect wave. I will simply remain here upon the shore and watch the water. It is enough of a reminder. My pilgrimage winds down, though the end is not yet in sight.

Well . . . I see Fuji. Call Fuji the end. As with the barrel's hoop of the first print, the circle closes about him.

On my way to this place I halted in a small glade I came upon and bathed myself in a stream which ran through it. There I used the local wood to construct a low altar. Cleansing my hands each step of the way, I set before it incense made from camphorwood and from white sandalwood; I also placed there a bunch of fresh violets, a cup of vegetables, and a cup of fresh water from the stream. Then I lit a lamp I had purchased and filled with rapeseed oil. Upon the altar I set my image of the god Kokuzo, which I had brought with me from home, facing to the west where I stood. I washed again, then extended my right hand, middle finger bent to touch my thumb as I spoke the mantra for invoking Kokuzo. I drank some of the water. I lustrated myself with sprinklings of it and continued repetition of the mantra. Thereafter, I made the gesture of Kokuzo three times, hand to the crown of my head, to my right shoulder, left shoulder, heart and throat. I removed the white cloth in which Kokuzo's picture had been wrapped. When I had sealed the area with the proper repetitions, I meditated in the same position as Kokuzo in the picture and invoked him. After a time the mantra ran by itself, over and over.

Finally, there was a vision, and I spoke, telling all that had happened, all that I intended to do, and asking for strength and guidance. Suddenly, I saw his sword descending, descending like slow lightning, to sever a limb from a tree, which began to bleed. And then it was raining, both within the vision and upon me, and I knew that that was all to be had on the matter.

I wound things up, cleaned up, donned my poncho, and headed on my way.

The rain was heavy, my boots grew muddy, and the temperature dropped. I trudged on for a long while, and the cold crept into my bones. My toes and fingers became numb.

I kept constant lookout for a shelter, but did not spot any place where I could take refuge from the storm. Later, it changed from a downpour to a drizzle to a weak mistlike fall when I saw what could be a temple or shrine in the distance. I headed for it, hoping for some hot tea, a fire, and a chance to change my socks and clean my boots.

A priest stopped me at the gate. I told him my situation, and he looked uncomfortable.

"It is our custom to give shelter to anyone," he said. "But there is a problem."

"I will be happy to make a cash donation," I said, "if too many others have passed this way and reduced your stores. I really just wanted to get warm."

"Oh no, it is not a matter of supplies," he told me, "and for that matter very few have been by here recently. The problem is of a different sort, and it embarrasses me to state it. It makes us sound old-fashioned and superstitious, when actually this is a very modern temple. But recently we have been—ah—haunted."

"Oh?"

"Yes. Bestial apparitions have been coming and going from the library and record room beside the head priest's quarters. They stalk the shrine, pass through our rooms, pace the grounds, then return to the library or else fade away."

He studied my face, as if seeking derision, belief, disbelief—anything. I merely nodded.

"It is most awkward," he added. "A few simple exorcisms have been attempted but to no avail."

"For how long has this been going on?" I asked.

"For about three days," he replied.

"Has anyone been harmed by them?"

"No. They are very intimidating, but no one has been injured. They are distracting, too, when one is trying to sleep—that is, to meditate—for they produce a tingling feeling and sometimes cause the hair to rise up."

"Interesting," I said. "Are there many of them?"

"It varies. Usually just one. Sometimes two. Occasionally three."

"Does your library by any chance contain a computer terminal?"

"Yes, it does," he answered. "As I said, we are very modern. We keep our records with it, and we can obtain printouts of sacred texts we do not have on hand—and other things."

"If you will shut the terminal down for a day, they will probably go away," I told him, "and I do not believe they will return."

"I would have to check with my superior before doing a thing like that. You know something of these matters?"

"Yes, and in the meantime I would still like to warm myself, if I may."

"Very well. Come this way."

I followed him, cleaning my boots and removing them before entering. He led me around to the rear and into an attractive room which looked upon the temple's garden.

"I will go and see that a meal is prepared for you, and a brazier of charcoal that you may warm yourself," he said as he excused himself.

Left by myself I admired the golden carp drifting in a pond only a few feet away, its surface occasionally punctuated by raindrops, and a little stone bridge which crossed the pond, a stone pagoda, paths wandering among stones and shrubs. I wanted to cross that bridge—how unlike that metal span, thrusting, cold, and dark!—and lose myself there for an age or two. Instead, I sat down and gratefully gulped the tea which arrived moments later, and I warmed my feet and dried my socks in the heat of the brazier which came a little while after that.

Later, I was halfway through a meal and enjoying a conversation with the young priest, who had been asked to keep me company until the head priest could come by and personally welcome me, when I saw my first epigon of the day.

It resembled a very small, triple-trunked elephant walking upright along one of the twisting garden paths, sweeping the air to either side of the trail with those snakelike appendages. It had not yet spotted me.

I called it to the attention of the priest, who was not faced in that direction.

"Oh my!" he said, fingering his prayer beads.

While he was looking that way, I shifted my staff into a readily available position beside me.

As it drifted nearer, I hurried to finish my rice and vegetables. I was afraid my bowl might be upset in the skirmish soon to come.

The priest glanced back when he heard the movement of the staff along the flagstones.

"You will not need that," he said. "As I explained, these demons are not aggressive."

I shook my head as I swallowed another mouthful.

"This one will attack," I said, "when it becomes aware of my presence. You see, I am the one it is seeking."

"Oh my!" he repeated.

I stood then as its trunks swayed in my direction and it approached the bridge.

"This one is more solid than usual," I commented. "Three days, eh?"

"Yes."

I moved about the tray and took a step forward. Suddenly, it was over the bridge and rushing toward me. I met it with a straight thrust, which it avoided. I spun the staff twice and struck again as it was turning. My blow landed, and I was hit by two of the trunks simultaneously—once on the breast, once on the cheek. The epigon went out like a burned hydrogen balloon and I stood there rubbing my face, looking about me the while.

Another slithered into our room from within the temple. I lunged suddenly and caught it on the first stroke.

"I think perhaps I should be leaving now," I stated. "Thank you for your hospitality. Convey my regrets to the head priest that I did not get to meet him. I am warm and fed and I have learned what I wanted to know about your demons. Do not even bother about the terminal. They will probably cease to visit you shortly, and they should not return."

"You are certain?"

"I know them."

"I did not know the terminals were haunted. The salesman did not tell us."

"Yours should be all right now."

He saw me to the gate.

"Thank you for the exorcism," he said.

"Thanks for the meal. Good-bye."

I traveled for several hours before I found a place to camp in a shallow cave, using my poncho as a rain-screen.

And today I came here to watch for the wave of death. Not yet, though. No truly big ones in this sea. Mine is still out there, somewhere.

19. MT. FUJI FROM SHICHIRIGAHAMA

Fuji past pine trees, through shadow, clouds rising beside him . . . It is getting on into the evening of things. The weather was good today, my health stable.

I met two monks upon the road yesterday, and I traveled with them for a time. I was certain that I had seen them somewhere else along the way, so I greeted them and asked if this were possible. They said that they were on a pilgrimage of their own, to a distant shrine, and they admitted that I looked familiar, also. We took our lunch together at the side of the road. Our conversation was restricted to generalities, though they did ask me whether I had heard of the haunted shrine in Kanagawa. How quickly such news travels. I said that I had, and we reflected upon its strangeness.

After a time I became annoyed. Every turning of the way that I took seemed a part of their route, also. While I'd welcomed a little company, I'd no desire for long-term companions, and it seemed their choices of ways approximated mine too closely. Finally, when we came to a split in the road I asked them which fork they were taking. They hesitated, then said that they were going right. I took the left-hand path. A little later they caught up with me. They had changed their minds, they said.

When we reached the next town, I offered a man in a car a good sum of money to drive me to the next village. He accepted, and we drove away and left them standing there.

I got out before we reached the next town, paid him, and watched him drive off. Then I struck out upon a footpath I had seen, going in the general direction I desired. At one point I left the trail and cut through the woods until I struck another path.

I camped far off the trail when I finally bedded down, and the following morning I took pains to erase all sign of my presence there. The monks did not reappear. They may have been quite harmless, or their designs quite different, but I must be true to my carefully cultivated paranoia.

Which leads me to note that man in the distance—a Westerner, I'd judge, by his garments. . . . He has been hanging around taking pictures for some time. I will lose him shortly, of course, if he is following me—or even if he isn't.

It is terrible to have to be this way for too long a period of time. Next I will be suspecting schoolchildren.

I watch Fuji as the shadows lengthen. I will continue to watch until the first star appears. Then I will slip away.

And so I see the sky darken. The photographer finally stows his gear and departs.

I remain alert, but when I see the first star, I join the shadows and fade like the day.

20. MT. FUJI FROM INUME PASS

Through fog and above it. It rained a bit earlier. And there is Fuji, storm clouds above his brow. In many ways I am surprised to have made it this far. This view, though, makes everything worthwhile.

I sit upon a mossy rock and record in my mind the changing complexion of Fuji as a quick rain veils his countenance, ceases, begins again.

The winds are strong here. The fogbank raises ghostly limbs and lowers them. There is a kind of numb silence beneath the wind's monotone mantra.

I make myself comfortable, eating, drinking, viewing, as I go over my final plans once again. Things wind down. Soon the circle will be closed.

I had thought of throwing away my medicine here as an act of bravado, as a sign of full commitment. I see this now as a foolishly romantic gesture. I am going to need all of my strength, all of the help I can get, if I am to have a chance at succeeding. Instead of discarding the medicine here I take some.

The winds feel good upon me. They come on like waves, but they are bracing.

A few travelers pass below. I draw back, out of their line of sight. Harmless, they go by like ghosts, their words carried off by the wind, not even reaching this far. I feel a small desire to sing, but I restrain myself.

I sit for a long while, lost in a reverie of the elements. It has been good, this journey into the past, living at the edge once again. . . .

Below me. Another vaguely familiar figure comes into view, lugging equipment. I cannot distinguish features from here, nor need I. As he halts and begins to set up his gear, I know that it is the photographer of Shichirigahama, out to capture another view of Fuji more permanent than any I desire.

I watch him for a time, and he does not even glance my way. Soon I will be gone again, without his knowledge. I will allow this one as a coincidence. Provisionally, of course. If I see him again, I may have to kill him. I will be too near my goal to permit even the possibility of interference to exist.

I had better depart now, for I would rather travel before than behind him.

Fuji-from-on-high, this was a good resting place. We will see you again soon.

Come, Hokusai, let us be gone.

21. MT. FUJI FROM THE TŌTŌMI MOUNTAINS

Gone the old sawyers, splitting boards from a beam, shaping them. Only Fuji, of snow and clouds, remains. The men in the print work in the old way, like the Owari barrel-maker. Yet, apart from those of the fishermen who merely draw their needs from nature, these are the only two prints in my book depicting people actively shaping something in their world. Their labors are too traditional for me to see the image of the Virgin and the Dynamo within them. They could have been performing the same work a thousand years before Hokusai.

Yet it is a scene of humanity shaping the world, and so it leads me down trails of years to this time, this day of sophisticated tools and large-scale changes. I see within it the image of what was later wrought, of the metal skin and pulsing flows the world would come to wear. And Kit is there, too, godlike, riding electronic waves.

Troubling. Yet bespeaking an ancient resilience, as if this, too, is but an eyeblink glimpse of humanity's movement in time, and whether I win or lose, the raw stuff remains and will triumph ultimately over any obstacle. I would really like to believe this, but I must leave certainty to politicians and preachers. My way is laid out and invested with my vision of what must be done.

I have not seen the photographer again, though I caught sight of the monks yesterday, camped on the side of a distant hill. I inspected them with my telescope, and they were the same ones with whom I had traveled briefly. They had not noticed me, and I passed them by way of a covering detour. Our trails have not crossed since.

Fuji, I have taken twenty-one of your aspects within me now. Live a little, die a little. Tell the gods, if you think of it, that a world is about to die.

I hike on, camping early in a field close to a monastery. I do not wish to enter there after my last experience in a modern holy place. I bed down in a concealed spot nearby, amid rocks and pine tree shoots. Sleep comes easily, lasts till some odd hour.

I am awake suddenly and trembling, in darkness and stillness. I cannot recall a sound from without or a troubling dream from within. Yet I am afraid, even to move. I breathe carefully and wait.

Drifting, like a lotus on a pond, it has come up beside me, towers above me, wears stars like a crown, glows with its own milky supernal light. It is a delicate-featured image of a bodhisattva, not unlike Kwannon, in garments woven of moonbeams.

"Mari."

Its voice is soft and caressing.

"Yes?" I answer.

"You have returned to travel in Japan. You are coming to me, are you not?"

The illusion is broken. It is Kit. He has carefully sculpted this epigon-form and wears it himself to visit me. There must be a terminal in the monastery. Will he try to force me?

"I was on my way to see you, yes," I manage.

"You may join me now, if you would."

He extends a wonderfully formed hand, as in benediction.

"I've a few small matters I must clear up before we are reunited."

"What could be more important? I have seen the medical reports. I know the condition of your body. It would be tragic if you were to die upon the road, this close to your exaltation. Come now."

"You have waited this long, and time means little to you."

"It is you that I am concerned with."

"I assure you I shall take every precaution. In the meantime, there is something which has been troubling me."

"Tell me."

"Last year there was a revolution in Saudi Arabia. It seemed to promise well for the Saudis, but it also threatened Japan's oil supply. Suddenly the new government began to look very bad on paper, and a new counterrevolutionary group looked stronger and better-tempered than it actually was. Major powers intervened successfully on the side of the counterrevolutionaries. Now they are in power and they seem even worse than the first government which had been overthrown. It seems possible, though incomprehensible to most, that computer read-outs all over the world were somehow made to be misleading. And now the Osaka Conference is to be held to work out new oil agreements with the latest regime. It looks as if Japan will get a very good deal out of it. You once told me that you are above such mundane matters, but I wonder? You are Japanese, you loved your country. Could you have intervened in this?"

"What if I did? It is such a small matter in the light of eternal values. If there is a touch of sentiment for such things remaining within me, it is not dishonorable that I favor my country and my people."

"And if you did it in this, might you not be moved to intervene again one day, on some other matter where habit or sentiment tell you you should?"

"What of it?" he replies. "I but extend my finger and stir the dust of illusion a bit. If anything, it frees me even further."

"I see," I answer.

"I doubt that you do, but you will when you have joined me. Why not do it now?"

"Soon," I say. "Let me settle my affairs."

"I will give you a few more days," he says, "and then you must be with me forever."

I bow my head.

"I will see you again soon," I tell him.

"Good night, my love."

"Good night."

He drifts away then, his feet not touching the ground, and he passes through the wall of the monastery.

I reach for my medicine and my brandy. A double dose of each . . .

22. MT. FUJI FROM THE SUMIDA RIVER IN EDO

And so I come to the place of crossing. The print shows a ferryman bearing a number of people across the river into the city and evening. Fuji lies dark and brooding in the farthest distance. Here I do think of Charon, but the thought is not so unwelcome as it once might have been. I take the bridge myself, though.

As Kit has promised me a little grace, I walk freely the bright streets, to smell the smells and hear the noises and watch the people going their ways. I wonder what Hokusai would have done in contemporary times? He is silent on the matter.

I drink a little, I smile occasionally, I even eat a good meal. I am tired of reliving my life. I seek no consolations of philosophy or literature. Let me merely walk in the city tonight, running my shadow over faces and storefronts, bars and theaters, temples and offices. Anything which approaches is welcome tonight. I eat *sushi*, I gamble, I dance. There is no yesterday, there is no tomorrow for me now. When a man places his hand upon my shoulder and smiles, I move it to my breast and laugh. He is good for an hour's exercise and laughter in a small room he finds us. I make him cry out several times before I leave him, though he pleads with me to stay. Too much to do and see, love. A greeting and a farewell.

Walking . . . Through parks, alleys, gardens, plazas. Crossing . . . Small bridges and larger ones, streets and walkways. Bark, dog. Shout, child. Weep, woman. I come and go among you. I feel you with a dispassionate passion. I take all of you inside me that I may hold the world here, for a night.

I walk in a light rain and in its cool aftermath. My garments are damp, then dry again. I visit a temple. I pay a taximan to drive me about the town. I eat a late meal. I visit another bar. I come upon a deserted playground, where I swing and watch the stars.

And I stand before a fountain splaying its waters into the lightening sky, until the stars are gone and only their lost sparkling falls about me.

Then breakfast and a long sleep, another breakfast and a longer one . . .

And you, my father, there on the sad height? I must leave you soon, Hokusai.

23. MT. FUJI FROM EDO

Walking again, within a cloudy evening. How long has it been since I spoke with Kit? Too long, I am sure. An epigon could come bounding my way at any moment.

I have narrowed my search to three temples—none of them the one in the print, to be sure, only that uppermost portion of it viewed from that impossible angle, Fuji back past its peak, smoke, clouds, fog between—but I've a feeling one of these three will do in the blue of evening.

I have passed all of them many times, like a circling bird. I am loath to do more than this, for I feel the right choice will soon be made for me. I became aware sometime back that I was being followed, really followed this time, on my rounds. It seems that my worst fear was not ungrounded; Kit is employing human agents as well as epigons. How he sought them and how he bound them to his service, I do not care to guess. Who else would be following me at this point, to see that I keep my promise, to force me to it if necessary?

I slow my pace. But whoever is behind me does the same. Not yet. Very well.

Fog rolls in. The echoes of my footfalls are muffled. Also those at my back. Unfortunate.

I head for the other temple. I slow again when I come into its vicinity, all of my senses extended, alert.

Nothing. No one. It is all right. Time is no problem. I move on.

After a long while I approach the precincts of the third temple. This must be it, but I require some move from my pursuer to give me the sign. Then, of course, I must deal with that person before I make my own move. I hope that it will not be too difficult, for everything will turn upon that small conflict.

I slow yet again, and nothing appears but the moisture of the fog upon my face and the knuckles of my hand wrapped about my staff. I halt. I seek in my pocket after a box of cigarettes I had purchased several days ago in my festive mood. I had doubted they would shorten my life.

As I raise one to my lips, I hear the words, "You desire a light, madam?"

I nod my head as I turn.

It is one of the two monks who extends a lighter to me and flicks forth its flame. I noticed for the first time the heavy ridge of callous along the edge of his hand. He had kept it carefully out of sight before, as we sojourned together. The other monk appears to his rear, to his left.

"Thank you."

I inhale and send smoke to join the fog.

"You have come a long way," the man states.

"Yes."

"And your pilgrimage has come to an end."

"Oh? Here?"

He smiles and nods. He turns his head toward the temple.

"This is our temple," he says, "where we worship the new bodhisattva. He awaits you within."

"He can continue to wait, till I finish my cigarette," I say.

"Of course."

With a casual glance, I study the man. He is probably a very good *karateka*. I am very good with the *bo*. If it were only him, I would bet on myself. But two of them, and the other probably just as good as this one? Kokuzo, where is your sword? I am suddenly afraid.

I turn away, I drop the cigarette, I spin into my attack. He is ready, of course. No matter. I land the first blow.

By then, however, the other man is circling and I must wheel and move defensively, turning, turning. If this goes on for too long, they will be able to wear me down.

I hear a grunt as I connect with a shoulder. Something, anyway . . .

Slowly, I am forced to give way, to retreat toward the temple wall. If I am driven too near it, it will interfere with my strokes. I try again to hold my ground, to land a decisive blow. . . .

Suddenly, the man to my right collapses, a dark figure on his back. No time to speculate. I turn my attention to the first monk, and moments later I land another blow, then another.

My rescuer is not doing so well, however. The second monk has shaken him off and begins striking at him with bone-crushing blows. My ally knows something of unarmed combat, though, for he gets into a defensive stance and blocks many of these, even landing a few of his own. Still, he is clearly overmatched.

Finally I sweep a leg and deliver another shoulder blow. I try three strikes at my man while he is down, but he rolls away from all of them and comes up again. I hear a sharp cry from my right, but I cannot look away from my adversary.

He comes in again, and this time I catch him with a sudden reversal and crush his temple with a follow-up. I spin then, barely in time, for my ally lies on the ground and the second monk is upon me.

Either I am lucky or he has been injured. I catch the man quickly and follow up with a rapid series of strikes which take him down, out, and out for good.

I rush to the side of the third man and kneel beside him, panting. I had seen his gold earring as I moved about the second monk.

"Boris." I take his hand. "Why are you here?"

"I told you—I could take a few days—to help you," he says, blood trickling from the corner of his mouth. "Found you. Was taking pictures . . . And see . . . You needed me."

"I'm sorry," I say. "Grateful, but sorry. You're a better man than I thought."

He squeezes my hand, "I told you I liked you—Maryushka. Too bad . . . we didn't have—more time. . . ."

I lean and kiss him, getting blood on my mouth. His hand relaxes within my own. I've never been a good judge of people, except after the fact.

And so I rise. I leave him there on the wet pavement. There is nothing I can do for him. I go into the temple.

It is dark near the entrance, but there are many votive lights to the rear. I do not see anyone about. I did not think that I would. It was just to have been the two monks, ushering me to the terminal. I head toward the lights. It must be somewhere back there.

I hear rain on the rooftop as I search. There are little rooms, off to either side, behind the lights.

It is there, in the second one. And even as I cross the threshold, I feel that familiar ionization which tells me that Kit is doing something here.

I rest my staff against the wall and go nearer. I place my hand upon the humming terminal.

"Kit," I say, "I have come."

No epigon grows before me, but I feel his presence and he seems to speak to me as he did on that night so long ago when I lay back upon the couch and donned the helmet:

"I knew that you would be here tonight."

"So did I," I reply.

"All of your business is finished?"

"Most of it."

"And you are ready now to be joined with me?"

"Yes."

Again I feel that movement, almost sexual in nature, as he flows into me. In a moment he would bear me away into his kingdom.

Tatemae is what you show to others. *Honne* is your real intention. As Musashi cautioned in the *Book of Waters*, I try not to reveal my *honne* even at this moment. I simply reach out with my free hand and topple my staff so that its metal tip, batteries engaged, falls against the terminal.

"Mari! What have you done?" he asks, within me now, as the humming ceases.

"I have cut off your line of retreat, Kit."

"Why?"

The blade is already in my hand.

"It is the only way for us. I give you this *jigai*, my husband."

"No!"

I feel him reaching for control of my arm as I exhale. But it is too late. It is already moving. I feel the blade enter my throat, well-placed.

"Fool!" he cries. "You do not know what you have done! I cannot return!"

"I know."

As I slump against the terminal I seem to hear a roaring sound, growing, at my back. It is the Big Wave, finally come for me. My only regret is that I did not make it to the final station, unless, of course, that is what Hokusai is trying to show me, there beside the tiny window, beyond the fog and the rain and the night.

24. MT. FUJI IN A SUMMER STORM